THE CHILD FROM THE SEA

Lucy Walter, secretly married to Charles the
Second, his wife as an exile in Holland and
Paris, and mother of the Duke of Monmouth—
had she other attributes than beauty? Has her
character been misrepresented down the years?
Elizabeth Goudge, with good reason to believe
so, presents her life-story in a fresh and
fascinating light. It begins with her childhood
at Roch Castle, Pembrokeshire, and ends when
Charles is restored to the throne of England.

For
FREDA GREEN

Acknowledgements

The extracts from *Medieval Welsh Lyrics* by
J. P. Clancy are reproduced by permission of
Macmillan and Company Limited, London; The
Macmillan Company of Canada Limited; and
St Martin's Press, Inc., Macmillan and Company
Limited, New York.

Contents

From The Diary of
Samuel Pepys

He told me what great faction there is at Court; and above all, what is whispered, that young Crofts[1] is lawful son to the King, the King being married to his mother. How true this is, God knows; but I believe the Duke of York will not be fooled in this of three crowns ...

The Duke of Monmouth is in so great splendour at Court, and so dandled by the King, that some doubt, that, if the King should have no child by the Queene (which there is yet no appearance of), whether he would not be acknowledged for a lawful son; and that there will be difference follow between the Duke of York and him; which God prevent! ...

This day the little Duke of Monmouth was marryed at White Hall, in the King's chamber; and to night is a great supper and dancing at his lodging, near Charing-Cross. I observed his coate at the tail of his coach: he gives the arms of England, Scotland, and France, quartered upon some other fields, but what it is that speaks of his being a bastard I know not ...[2]

The Queene (which I did not know,) it seems was at Windsor, at the late St. George's feast there: and the Duke of Monmouth dancing with his hat in his hand, the King came in and kissed him, and made him put on his hat, which everybody took notice of ...[3]

There was a French book in verse, the other day, translated and presented to the Duke of Monmouth in such a high style, that the Duke of York, he tells me, was mightily offended at it.

[1] The Duke of Monmouth was called James Crofts when as a young boy he came to England after the Restoration.

[2] The bar sinister had been omitted from the coat of arms.

[3] Only a Prince of the blood royal might dance with the Queen with his hat on.

The Duke of Monmouth's mother's brother hath a place at court; and being a Welchman, (I think he told me,) will talk very broad of the King's being married to his sister . . .

Foreword

This book began ten years ago with a visit to St. Davids in
Pembrokeshire. Sitting on the cliffs above St. Bride's Bay, overwhelmed by the magic of the place and above all by the Cathedral, I saw in the distance a castle appearing through the
mist, high up against the sky. Perhaps the reason why it made
such an impact was that it appeared as though veiled in mystery. On a clear day it would probably have made a lesser
impression and I might not have become obsessed by the idea
that I had to write a book about someone who had lived there.
These obsessions probably only afflict romantic novelists, and
are a mistake, for they are likely to land an ill-equipped writer
with a task better left to a competent historian. A Welsh
friend told me I had seen Roch Castle, which had belonged to
the Walter family, and that Lucy Walter, the mother of the
Duke of Monmouth, had probably been born there. My heart
sank for the only thing I knew about Lucy was that very little
is know about her, and that little not to her credit. Then I
was lent a book written by Lord George Scott, one of her descendants, and the whole picture changed. Her biographer
had examined all the evidence and had come to the conclusion, for reasons that he makes clear in his book, that her
character has been misrepresented. Now a storyteller who is
told that a historical character may have been entirely
different from what we had previously supposed, is lost. A
carrot of that sort has to be pursued, and so Lord George
Scott's book is the basis of my story.

One knows nothing of Lucy's childhood except the bare fact
of removal from one place to another, and so the first half of
this book is largely fiction. I must apologize however for
making her childhood coincide with "Vicar Pritchard's" term
of office as Chancellor of St. David's Cathedral. He is such a
delightful character that he could hardly be left out. The

mystery of Lucy's possible marriage to Charles is not likely to be cleared up now. The most likely explanation would seem to be that a marriage ceremony took place but was proved later not to have been legal. The question of its place has given rise to several legends. There is a tradition that Charles and Lucy were married in Pembrokeshire. I do not see how that could have been possible, for how did he get so far in the middle of a civil war? But I have adopted it simply because it *is* a Pembrokeshire tradition. According to the legend of the stolen marriage register it took place at Haverfordwest, but after spending some while in the little church at Roch, sheltering from Pembrokeshire rain, and looking at the wonderful old font where the Walter children were perhaps baptized, for me it could only have been in that church.

When the story moves to Holland and France then Lucy comes on to the stage of history. Her movements are roughly known but the truth behind the facts remains confused and mysterious. Especially is this so with regard to the extraordinary journey to London with her son, and their imprisonment in the Tower. It happened, but why is a mystery. Even her portraits are mysterious because they do not seem to be of the same girl. None is certainly authentic, which is a relief, since only one suggests the beauty and charm she undoubtedly possessed.

I would like to express my gratitude for a talk I heard years ago on the B.B.C. It was for Welsh schools and was given by Madean Stewart. She described how she played her flute to the seals. I have described something similar in this book, but without her talk I should not have known such a thing was possible.

BOOK I

The Child

One

The child awoke with the sun, as was her custom, and shot up instantly out of the nest of blankets, her brown feet reaching for the uneven floor almost before she had rubbed the sleep out of her eyes. She was one of the vital, quicksilver children, born beneath a star. Even when her father roared at her, "For God's sake child stand still!" she was tense as springy heather beneath his hand on the top of her head, and the moment he lifted it to aim a clumsy blow at her backside she was gone and his language, once more, was the cross that her gentle mother bore with such patience.

William Walter was not a very effective father but he was warm-hearted and Lucy adored him. Father! Suddenly she was afraid he might have died in the night and she ran to the curtain that shut off her turret room from her parents' bed-chamber. She lifted it and peeped round, her heart beating hard with anxiety, but behind the curtains of the great four-poster his cheerful snoring was reassuring as a humming kettle. There was no sound from her mother's side of the bed for her mother was a very great lady, with the blood of the Plantagenets showing blue in her delicate veins, and people with blue veins do not snore. Her father too was of royal blood, for he was descended from Welsh princes, but he was always a man to hide his light under a bushel. Lucy did not worry about her mother dying in the night as much as she worried about her father. She did worry, because she loved her mother, but not as much. It grieved her that she could not love every-one equally but she had accepted that as one of the facts of life that are inescapable.

For a moment or two she lingered, her vivid triangular face floating like that of a disembodied cherub above the darkness of the velvet curtain that she had gathered beneath her chin,

15

to hide from a possibly wakeful mother, looking through the
chink where the curtains did not quite meet at the foot of the
bed, the fact that she had once more taken off her nightshift
and was naked. Skirts bothered her in bed just as they did by
day. She wished she had been born a boy. She lingered because
the sunlight lay so warmly on the carved oak of the great bed,
and the scarlet rug that lay on the floor. The walls were the
rough hewn stone walls of the castle tower but the sunlight
brought out in them faint gleams of lilac and blue, for the
rocks of Pembrokeshire of which this castle had been built
were rainbow-tinted. Her eyes went from the walls to the curtain that hid the other turret room where the boys slept, Richard who was ten years old and Justus her special brother,
seven years old and a year younger than herself. The two-
year-old twins Dewi and Betsi slept with Nan-Nan and were
kept safe by her. The older children were protected from the
dangerous night world of storm and darkness, thieves and
warlocks by the interposition of their parents' bedchamber
and their father's sword standing ready to his hand beside the
great bed. Nothing could get at them and they could not get
out. Or so their parents thought.

Lucy dropped the curtain and began pulling on the old pair
of breeches and the jerkin which had once belonged to Richard, which she wore for her more adventurous outings but
wore in defiance of her mother's orders. She did not bother
with washing or with trying to comb out her thick brown hair.
It was coarse rebellious hair and not even Nan-Nan could
bring any sort of ladylike order to it. She ran barefoot to the
narrow window, flung it open and leaned over the iron bar
that had been fixed across the window to keep her, in her
younger days, from falling out.

Her breath caught as the loveliness rose like a wave and
broke over her. It was half past five on a May morning, cool,
with a tang in the air, and though the sky was deep blue overhead the high white clouds sailing in from the sea were still
bright with the gold of the dayspring. She blinked at the
brightness and looked down to the sea of new green leaves
below her, but that was dazzling too for the dew sparkled on

every leaf. Roch Castle, in this year of grace 1638 three centuries old, was built on an outcrop of volcanic rock and upon this, the landward side, it crowned a precipice. The rocks thrust out just under Lucy's window and the leaves of the trees in the wood below ruffled against them like water. Looking down she could see the sunbeams caught in the leaves, the birds' nests, and even gleams of azure where the first bluebells had appeared on the floor of the wood. To her right she could see the steep lane that wound up from the valley, and upon the other side of it the tower of the church thrusting up through green leaves. A small village lay at the feet of church and castle, a thatched roof visible here and there, and beyond a stream ran under an old arched bridge. Lucy could not see it but she could hear its voice, a clear and constant rill of sound threading in and out of the singing of the birds and the bleating of lambs. Beyond the stream the trees thinned out and green hills rose towards the distant mountains.

Lucy removed the iron bar from the window. Richard, who was clever with his hands, had loosened it for her; though not for her only, because an entirely selfless action was not Richard's métier. This window was a useful escape route for himself at times, because on his side of the tower the castle's rock foundation thrust out at a much lower level and there was no way down. Lucy climbed backwards out of the window, lowered her feet to the rock, clung with her strong brown hands and felt with her bare toes for the familiar footholds. It was not an easy climb; if she had slipped she might have been killed and either of her parents, seeing her, would not have been the same again; but Lucy was fearless because she trusted the world. How should this glory of which she was a part do her any harm?

She reached the sea of leaves and went down through it into the branches of the old oak tree that was her friend. The wood was oak and ash and sycamore and here in the sheltered valley behind the castle the trees were not stunted like so many in this windswept land. She climbed down to the floor of the wood and stood for a few moments among the bluebells, listening to the birds whose song was rising up now from all the mysterious places in the folds of the hills where there was shade and water and the springs of being. She sang too, word-lessly, her voice running up and down that small scale of notes that is one of the ladders to heaven.

Then she ran out of the wood and up the steep lane to the place where four ways met and the castle stood foursquare to all the winds. Here the breath of the sea met her. Almost every day it met her when she ran abroad, because the wind was from the sea more often than not, yet each time it was some-thing new and miraculous. She picked her way along the rutted lane. The soles of her feet were hardened by always running barefoot but she knew she had to avoid the sharp points of stones and hardened mud. The lane was deeply sunken in the earth, the steep banks wet and green with spark-ling ferns, the flowering thorn trees bent over so far by the prevailing wind that they looked like white polled dwarfs all running as hard as they could away from the sea towards the sunrise. In the fields on either side, where ribs of rock thrust through the heather and gorse and tussocks of rough grass, her father's sheep and black and white cows were feeding. He possessed many acres of rough grazing ground, and inland fields of oats and barley and golden mustard. His kingdom was wide and Lucy owned it.

Presently the lane took a leap and plunged headlong into a deep green gully. A stream ran down one side of it now and it was so wet that the mud squelched between Lucy's toes. It was soft like silk and she sang for joy of the mud. The green walls on either side lifted and spread back like wings, there was sand mixed with the mud under foot and the smell of seaweed. The stream ran faster and Lucy with it. They reached the bay together and raced each other to the sea.

The small waves lapping about her ankles were very cold and she thrilled to their touch as they gently washed away the mud from her feet. The water was green and clear and looking down she could see the bright pebbles lying on the rippled sand and her own toes among them. Her feet had a strange beauty under the water and she gazed at them entranced, for they did not seem to belong to her any more but to the sea that

had bewitched them. She had a sudden longing to give herself
to the water, to pull off Richard's jerkin and breeches and run
naked into the waves and swim away to the uttermost parts of
the sea. It was the same sort of longing that came when she
watched the larks leaping up the stairways of the sky. She
wanted to leap with them and go up and up, but not to come
back as they did as soon as their wings began to sizzle in the
blazing sun. She would fly right on into the sun and get burnt
or not, just as the sun pleased. Something or someone, some
day, would pull her as moon and sun pull the tides and the
larks and she would go.

She pulled her feet away from the gentle hands about her
ankles, ran to the rock that was one of her special places and
climbed up it. Sitting cross-legged on its flat top, she had
the whole bay under her eagle eye. Except for that
one deep cleft where the lane and the stream came down
it was entirely surrounded by the cliffs. There were three caves
hidden in the rocks and Lucy knew them as she knew the
rooms of her home. One of them was above high water mark,
green ferns grew inside it and there was driftwood on its floor,
but the other two were washed by the high tides and the rock-
pools in them were full of sea anemones and frail seaweeds like
grasses, so light and airy that the slightest disturbance of a
scurrying crab would send them swaying in protest, and the
silver sand between the pools was strewn with shells. These
caves were small, as the bay itself was small, a safe place for
children, but there was another bay not far from this one that
could only be reached by boat or by a climb down a sheer cliff
face almost too dangerous to be attempted. In this bay there
was hardly any sand, only a shelving beach of pebbles and low
flat rocks, and its caves went so deep under the cliff that the sea
boomed in them like thunder. This was the seals' bay, and one
of their breeding places. The caves were their nurseries and
when the sun shone the gentle cows lay on the flat rocks with
their ivory pups lying beside them. Lucy had seen them from
above, standing on the edge of the cliff, holding her father's
hand and looking down and careful to make no sound, for the
slightest noise would send them all sliding off their rocks into

the sea. She often saw them from her own bay too, lying a little out to sea beyond the rocks and looking like rocks themselves. And she had heard their wild and dreadful singing and it had not frightened her as it did some people. Why should it frighten her? Seals had been human beings once and because of something they had done they had been banished to the sea, but they loved human beings even while they feared them, and through their music they tried to reach out and make contact with the life they had lost.

There were no seals in sight today but there were gulls everywhere, wheeling over the cliffs and the sea, and on the sandbank opposite her the busy oystercatchers were gossiping and strutting around and getting ready for the day. She got down from her throne and ran down to the sea again to make a sea posy for Nan-Nan. She gathered seaweeds, and samphire from the rocks, and tied them together with a bit of seaweed bright as a crimson ribbon. Nan-Nan liked sea posies. Elizabeth Walter thought them messy but she liked posies of wild flowers and Lucy never took anything home to Nan-Nan without taking something for her mother too. This was because she felt so guilty in loving Nan-Nan more than her mother. Elizabeth had reproached her for this once, saying bitterly, "You love everyone more than your mother." And Lucy had flung herself on her in a passion of tears and cried out, "Oh, madam mother, I love you! But I love Nan-Nan terribly much." And with tears rolling down crimson cheeks she had clutched at the bodice of her dress until she tore it. What, Elizabeth had wondered, could be done with such a tempestuous child? And from whom did she inherit these passions? Not from her mother, most certainly. And not from her father, who though uninhibited was placidly so. Was it, Elizabeth often wondered, anything to do with having been born upon volcanic rock?

With the posy in her hand Lucy ran up the lane till she was nearly at the top, scrambled up the bank to her left, forced her way through the thorn trees, ripping a triangular piece out of the seat of Richard's breeches, and came out upon the cliff top among the sheep. She ran to where the wild flowers grew, deep blue squills and pink and white campion, thrift and cowslips making a ribbon of clear colour along the cliff edge, with little isolated gardens down below wherever the crumbling cliff gave foothold. The sun was fully up now, light poured from the sky and land and sea reflected it back in singing colour. It seemed unkind to pick the flowers because indoors their bells were silent, and Lucy told them she was sorry but that she wanted them for her mother.

"Sun up, little madam, and the castle's stirring."

It was John Shepherd trudging slowly along with buckets of mash for the lambs. He was greybearded, mild and weather-worn, and advanced as though with each step he dragged up a load of mud from the earth, but Lucy did not know if he was old or not. She never thought of age in connection with the men who cared for her father's beasts and tilled his land. With their faces roughened like the barks of trees, their sweaty country smell and heavy deliberate movements they seemed as ageless as the land itself, and as trustworthy and inevitable, and she loved them as she loved the cliffs and the blue squills and the wild birds singing. And they in their turn kept a place in their hearts for the strange little creature who raced about barefoot in her boy's garments, wild and furious at times but openhanded as the spring.

"John Shepherd, John Shepherd," she cried, and ran to him, impetuously pulling her mother's posy apart so that she might make up a little one for him. He knew better than to say no for to refuse one of her offerings was to invite a passion of disap-pointed tears. He patiently put down the buckets and allowed her to tuck the posy into the buttonhole of his old coat. The squills were no bluer than her eyes. All that she was now in her vital springtime joy, all her woman's promise, shone in her eyes. Whether she was pretty or not it was hard to say, for she was never still or clean long enough for anyone to form a con-sidered opinion, but her eyes were unforgettable.

"Duwch, duwch! There's kind you are," said John Shep-herd, dragging his words up to the surface with the same patient effort with which he pulled his feet from the soil. "Cariad," he whispered half to himself, for he adored her.

John Shepherd, like Lucy, was bi-lingual, for this was the Little England beyond Wales where English adventurers had settled in William Rufus's days. Later the Flemish immigrants had come, dumped on the coast by Henry the Second who had not known what to do with them, and protected by a chain of castles South Pembrokeshire had become a replica of an English community. But its people had to talk Welsh as well as English for they had only to cross the brook at Newgale bridge, between Roch and St Davids, to find themselves in the 'Welshery' of Pembrokeshire, where English was an alien tongue.

"It's running home you should be," John Shepherd continued, a little anxiously because he always wanted to protect Lucy from the results of her impetuous actions. "Yes, yes. The castle's stirring."

In her joy Lucy had been oblivious of the passing of time but now she cast a glance of panic at the sky, observed the sun's position with alarm, subjected John Shepherd to a passionate embrace and fled. He watched her running like a hare, leaping over the stones and tussocks of heather in her path, and his face creaked slowly into a toothless smile. Then the smile faded. She must have made her exit from the castle long before the doors were open and she'd get into trouble Shaking his head with foreboding he plodded slowly on to his sheep.

2

Lucy, running, decided that she would not sneak in by any back entrances. She had been playing truant for a long while and had a feeling that it was about time she was brought to justice. She had a deep sense of justice and sometimes this made her feel as uncomfortable in her spirit if she deserved a whipping and did not get it as she felt in her body if she did get it, and of the two she preferred to suffer in body. Also with her love of drama she was not averse to occupying the centre of the stage.

"I shall go round to the front door and knock," she said to

herself. "And I shall say I am a princess. Shall I be Olwen or Nest?"

The Princess Nest, daughter of Rhys ap Tudor the great prince of South Wales, had been a lady of surpassing beauty and her loveliness was still spoken of with bated breath though she had died six centuries ago. Not Helen of Troy, or Deirdre or Fair Rosamund had been more beautiful than Nest. Perhaps not even Olwen of the Mabinogion, "Olwen of slender eyebrow, pure of heart," another great Welsh princess of whom the bards had delighted to sing. And Lucy was descended from Nest; at least so her father said though he seemed not able quite to prove it, as he was able to prove his descent from Rhys ap Thomas, an even greater man than Rhys ap Tudor, his forefinger tracing the lines down the parchment of the family tree. Nevertheless the Walter family, in company with all the great families of south Pembrokeshire, had no doubt at all that Nest was in their blood and the knowledge enormously increased their pride.

Lucy loved being Nest. She liked being her in the great hall, pacing up and down with the end of a dirty towel fastened to the belt of her dress and trailing on the floor like Nest's train of crimson velvet. And she liked being Olwen, waiting in the castle of the nine porters and the nine watchdogs for the glorious Prince Kilhwch to come and fetch her. She was never tired of hearing the story of Prince Kilhwch. He would come for her one day, she was quite sure, and lift her up in front of him on his horse of dappled grey, and they would go away together to fairyland.

"I think I'll be Kilhwch," she decided as she ran. "I'll be Kilhwch knocking at the castle door, come for Olwen. My father shall be Olwen's father, who propped his eyebrows up with forks, and madam my mother shall be Olwen."

At this point she tripped and fell flat in a patch of cow dung but it was dry and she was immediately up and running on again.

The length of the castle faced west towards the sea, battered by the great gales but indestructible. The entrance was to the north and Lucy ran diagonally across the field, scrambled up a bank and through another hedge of thorn trees and was on the rough road that ran northward along the battlemented walls of the inner bailey. To the west the outer bailey had disappeared now, in these comparatively peaceful days, though fallen stones in the fields showed where it had been, but to the east on the landward side it still stood in places, surrounding the farm buildings, granaries and workshops. Lucy ran across the road and along a grass-bordered lane that had the wall of the castle courtyard on the right and the stables on the left. She pushed open the stout oak door in the wall and was in the courtyard, which at great expenditure of gold and labour William Walter had transformed into a flower garden for his wife. Here within the shelter of the high walls she did not feel the winds she hated and could grow the roses and lilies she loved, with fruit trees against the walls. She had a knot garden of herbs here, a sundial and an arbour where the family could sit and make music on Sunday afternoons. Lucy ran up the path to the stone steps that led to the door of the great hall. Beside them there grew a very old rosemary tree, planted here years ago for the protection of the family, for rosemary is a holy herb. The living rooms were all on the first floor. Below there was a great kitchen, with the servant's quarters over it, and a maze of cellars and store rooms where in days past the men-at-arms of the castle had slept on a floor composed simply of lumpy and volcanic rock. Lucy banged on the door with her brown fists and cried, "Open in the name of Prince Kilhwch, cousin of King Arthur."

3

The door was opened by Richard. "If you think you are being funny," he said coldly, "you will not think so long."

At ten years he was old for his age, and the young heir. If he had not been her brother Lucy doubted if she would have liked him, and even though he was her brother her affection was not as deep as she would have wished. But she liked looking at him for he had his mother's smooth fair hair, falling gracefully to his shoulders, her cool grey eyes and perfect oval

face. Lucy swept past him, acknowledging with a princely inclination of the head the low bow which he had not given her,
and slipped through the screens that divided the main part of
the hall from the space under the musicians' gallery, out of
which opened the front door and the door to the kitchen. "I
am Prince Kilhwch, come to fetch the Lady Olwen," she cried
aloud as she strode up the hall. But her parents, who had just
finished their morning meal of ale and barley bread and
honey at the long table on the dais, did not seem to see a
prince. Their faces, turned towards her, showed them not sensible of the honour done them and the prince fell away from
Lucy, leaving her with a desolate numbness striking at her
loving heart. But she marched on without hesitation, facing
the issue.

A rough brown object, rising just clear of the table between
William and Elizabeth Walter, and looking like that beloved
dormouse in *Alice in Wonderland* of which children at that
date were so cruelly deprived, shot up and revealed itself as the
head of a small boy. Justus dived beneath the table and ran
down the steps of the dais towards Lucy. He had been
breeched but his hair was still cut short and stood straight up
on end, his cheeks were round and red as apples and his velvet-
brown eyes loyal and affectionate as those of the dogs who
followed at his heels, Elizabeth's black and white spaniel Jano
and William's favourite hounds Shôn and Twm. Justus flung
himself into Lucy's arms in welcome and the dogs leaped and
barked about her. Richard strolled slowly behind, hands in
breeches pockets, disassociating himself from the whole
affair.

"Come here, Justus," roared William. "Shôn. Twm. To heel,
Jano!"

They came, but at their own time, and accompanying Lucy.
William was obeyed by his dogs and children in reverse ratio
to the noise he made, for his family knew about his noise;
behind it he sheltered from the necessity for action, his over-
mastering desire in life being to be left in peace. Lucy climbed
the steps to the dais and stood before her parents. She curtseyed, the little bob comically at variance with her boy's

clothes, and then stood with her hands behind her back while William roared. When he had finished she turned her eyes to her mother and awaited her sentence. Standing just behind her Justus and the dogs shared her trouble with the loyalty of their kind.

Elizabeth was looking very beautiful in her rose-pink morning gown, her hair gathered under her mob cap. At thirty she thought of herself as already middle-aged, but there were no lines on her lovely face and her figure was slender and straight as when she had been a girl. But some of her grace had been lost now in too stiff a backbone and the stillness of her face was not that of peace. Now and then she betrayed herself by a nervous twitching of the eyebrows and often her hands were restless. She had been married to William Walter at the age of sixteen when he had been twenty-one, an arranged marriage between two great Pembrokeshire families.

"Lucy," she said quietly, "you have many times been forbidden to wear boy's attire."

"Yes, madam," said Lucy.

"Then why are you wearing it?"

"Madam, it is difficult to climb in skirts."

"Where have you been climbing?"

"Among the rocks in the bay, madam."

"Lucy, when your father and I awoke this morning you were not in your bed. And when we came to the hall we could not find you. Did you bribe one of the servants to let you out?"

"No, madam."

"Then how did you get out?"

"I got out of my window, madam."

"You what?" gasped Elizabeth, her control momentarily slipping as she visualized those rocks and the tree branches below. "But that is dangerous! You are never to do that again. Nor you, Richard. Do you hear, Richard?" White-faced she looked round at her elder son, but apparently he had not heard for he was sitting on the windowseat in the oriel window with his head bent studiously over a book. She turned her eyes back to her daughter. "I do not like you to be whipped, Lucy, but what else can be done? It seems that you will not learn any other way." She turned towards her husband, sitting with his legs thrust out before him and his chin sunk on his chest. He mumbled into his beard, something to the effect that Bud, his name for Lucy, had better sit down and have something to eat. He could not thrash a child on an empty stomach.

"I do not want to eat, sir," said Lucy. "If you please, sir, I would prefer to be whipped at once."

Elizabeth rose. "It is time I went to the kitchen," she said. "Come with me, Justus. Richard, take Shôn and Twm into the garden and groom them. If your father insists on bringing the hounds into the house at least someone should see that they are not coated in mud."

She went down the steps of the dais and down the hall towards the kitchen, her keys jangling at her waist, for she was a notable housewife. She looked like a tall pink tulip as she swayed down the hall and her husband watched her with a hungry wretchedness in his eyes. In his fashion he loved her. He knew that in comparison with her he was no more than a worm at her feet but he thought sometimes that if she had not known it too they might have been happier. She bore with him patiently at all times, and when he made love to her she bore it with exemplary wifely endurance, but held herself always at a distance. They seldom argued, her aristocratic training disliking the vulgarity of it, but he thought sometimes that a good flaming row might have done them a world of good. She disappeared through the screens, Justus and Jano trotting behind her. Richard followed with the hounds.

Silence fell in the great old hall that during three centuries had held so many miseries and witnessed so many cruelties. They were all present again as William rose heavily and held out his hand to Lucy. She took it and they walked together to the oriel window. They were as close together at this moment as two human beings can be. It is said that some mystical bond is formed between the tortured and the torturer and with them it was strengthened by the knowledge that the whipping of disobedient children is a religious duty, by the love they had for each other and by the fact <u>that</u> in their case the torturer always suffered more than the victim.

A little cane was kept in an oak chest near the oriel window. William stooped for it, then sat down on the windowseat. Lucy carefully laid down the two wilting posies she had picked for her mother and Nan-Nan and placed herself face downwards across his knees. The few swift cuts were light ones but heard in the attentive silence of the hall.

It was so quickly over, this thing that hurt them so much because it was so strange that it should have to be between them, yet it had seemed to take an eternity and a sob broke in William's throat. Lucy scrambled up on his knee and put her arms tightly round his neck. His beard was scratchy against her cheek and he smelt of ale and his farmyard, to both of which he was much attached, but she was none too clean herself and her love was not fastidious. She murmured soft endearments, and the nameless dreadful things that had brooded like bats up above them in the shadows of the vaulted roof vanished and in their place came all the joys of love and triumph that this hall had seen, and they gleamed and fluttered there like doves with the sun upon their wings.

"Damn it!" muttered William. "Why can I so seldom whip Richard? I do not mind whipping Richard."

"Better for people to whip those they love than those they do not love," said Lucy.

"Run off to Nan-Nan, Bud," he said, "and get her to salve the sore places."

She picked up the wilting posies and did as he bade her and he noticed what care she took to hold herself straight and run up the steps to the dais and away to the rooms beyond as though she had no soreness at all. She had guts, he thought, wisdom too, for that had been a sensible thing she had said about whipping. How cruel men could be without love to restrain them. From whom did she get her wisdom? Not from him. Not from her mother. Elizabeth had judgment but not wisdom, which must have its roots in love. His little daughter had reached far back in time for her qualities, he believed, back almost to the fresh beginnings of time, so vital was she in these days when the world was growing old and weary because, men said, the end of all things was at hand. He was not able to look forward for her as he did for his other children, for she seemed to go out into the light of legend and to vanish there, going down with the sun over the edge of the sea.

Two

I

The child gone, William was alone with Roch Castle, after Lucy and his land the great love of his life. It had not been long in the Walter family. William's father Rowland Walter of Trewerne had bought it from the de Longueville family and William himself had been its lord only since his father's death seven years ago. But he had been born and brought up here and loved it as deeply as though his family had owned it for generations. The mystery of love of place was something he had never considered, he only knew that away from Roch he was a lost man. And he was a farmer at heart. He loved the land itself, its very soil, as well as his sheep and cattle. To the dismay and disgust of his wife he liked to work with his men, ploughing, sowing and reaping, and shearing the sheep. Exiled from his land he became ill and miserable and his spirit withered. If only Elizabeth could have learned to love Roch he believed they might have been happy together.

She had been born inland in a sheltered valley in the home of John Protheroe of Hawksbrook, her father, but the place that she adored was her mother's birthplace of Golden Grove where she had visited so often in her childhood. Her uncle Lord Carbery had always been fond of her and his gracious house in the valley of the Towy, with the steep sheltering woods rising behind, and in front across the valley the great purple hill of Grongar, was her spiritual home. She fled to it whenever she could, taking the children with her, but William had been there only once, and had found himself stifled to death by the elegance and culture of that aristocratic, royalist and deeply religious family. Their voices were as gentle as the whisper of their silken garments. Nobody swore. Nobody drank too much. Such dogs as were allowed indoors smelled inexplicably of violets. But worst of all was the fact that here his Elizabeth was a different creature. The nervous tenseness and irritation went out of her and the colour bloomed in her cheeks. She was happy and no longer afraid.

She was always afraid at Roch, though she tried to hide her fear. William was not a wealthy man and there was no protecting veneer of fine living at Roch to create an illusion of safety in a dangerous world. The castle had been altered very little through the centuries, was cold and draughty and exposed to every wind that blew. The great storms from the sea that screamed round the tower where she and William slept terrified her so much that she sometimes thought her heart would stop for fear. And the castle, she believed, was haunted. The de Longuevilles had been a tragic family with a curse upon them. Doors burst open inexplicably and things like knives and spoons and her embroidery scissors were always turning up in unexpected places, moved, she was sure, by no human agency.

She was always fancying that she heard footsteps and the sighs of unseen presences. But the only time she had seen anything she had heard nothing. She had been sitting alone beside the fire in the hall one winter evening and feeling depressed because that afternoon one of the servants had died. Something made her turn her head and creeping up towards her through the shadows of the darkening hall she saw him, half naked and almost fleshless, a few wisps of hair clinging to a blackened skull. Death himself. Death threatening her and hers in this dreadful place. She had been too paralysed with terror even to scream and for a moment or two her sight had failed her. When she could see again he was gone. She had never spoken to anyone of what she had seen. It would have hurt her own proud image of herself to have been soothed as a child or laughed at as a hysterical woman.

But sometimes the bursting open of a door let in very concrete terrors, news of shipwreck which would take every able-bodied man down to the shore leaving the women and children unprotected, unknown travellers demanding food and shelter, and once a band of thieves whom William had had to fight back down the hall step by step with his naked sword.

And at any time the hall door might open very softly and the black figure of the queer old priest who lived at Brandy Mill would drift through lifeless as a shadow, looking for William or the children. Mercifully he was as frightened of her as she was of him and if she was alone his dazed blue eyes would fill with alarm, he would bow deeply and drift away again; but not before he had cast a blight upon her day.

Of these terrors William was aware because he loved her, but as she did not speak of them he did not know how cruelly they shadowed her mind or how deep was her suppressed resentment against himself. She had lost her first two children, one because William's favourite hound had jumped on her bed in the night and frightened her, causing a miscarriage, and the second because on a bitter evening he had gone into their bedchamber, where the baby was sleeping, to fetch something he wanted, and opening the window to investigate some sound outside had forgotten to close it again. The rising wind had blown the snow right on to the cradle and the baby had caught a chill and died. A careless man, he was not usually so where his children were concerned, but his friend George Wogan from Haverfordwest had been visiting him that afternoon and had brewed some Cardiganshire punch which he made to a miracle. The grief of the baby's death had turned William from a moderate drinker to a heavy one and brought Elizabeth's resentment one step nearer to hatred.

And now there was this business of the twins Dewi and Betsi. Elizabeth had gone to Golden Grove, taking the children with her, and stayed too long. William had grown lonely and depressed without them and Marged, one of the maid-servants, a pretty girl from the mountains, had a very sweet smile. At the time the affair had seemed to William comforting, inevitable and entirely harmless; but he had not meant it to happen and was astonished and slightly disturbed afterwards to find that it had happened. But he quickly forgot it and welcomed Elizabeth and the children home again with a face of blameless joy and innocence.

He had not been able to understand Elizabeth's cold misery and fury when a short time later she had to deal with the result of a momentary lapse which to his way of thinking had in no way affected his essential loyalty to her. He was very sorry and he said so, but she would not meet his sorrow with forgiveness; reconcilement between them had come only slowly and she had never allowed it to be the true reconcilement of the heart. Her attitude had angered him and for the first time in his life stiffened him into real resolution. Marged had been sent back to her mountain farm in floods of tears, that was inevitable, but he had refused to make her take the. twins with her. She did not want them and they were his responsibility, he told his wife. Equally with Richard, Lucy and Justus they were his children and must have the same love and care. Elizabeth rebelled but he insisted and went on insisting, and Dewi and Betsi stayed on at the castle adored by everyone except Elizabeth. She did her best for them but their presence, as though thrust by William into the place of the two babies for whose death she held him responsible, was bitter to her.

William, thinking of Dewi and Betsi, sighed and wondered what was to become of his children, for as things were going with him at present he would be able to make little provision for them. He had spent more than he could afford on Elizabeth, trying pathetically to buy her love with a coach, a flower garden, jewels and fine clothes; all of which she took entirely for granted because they had such things at Golden Grove as a matter of course. So now he was in debt, and efforts to improve matters by playing for high stakes at baccarat parties at Haverfordwest had been remarkably unsuccessful. He was no good at anything, he told himself wretchedly, not even at caring for what he so deeply loved, his children and his land.

The castle, he thanked God, was strong enough to take care of itself. He looked up at the timbered roof where the sunbeams were woven in and out of the smoky shadows that hung there, like the gold threads in Elizabeth's blue silk gown. Not all the sunshine was entangled in the roof. Pools of it lay on the oaken floor, polished and worn with age. The lower part of the walls of the hall were panelled with the same oak, and the musicians' gallery and the ancient table and chairs on the dais were oak too, but the stone of the castle walls showed rough and strong above the panelling and formed the hood of the vast fireplace opposite William. On the hearth a few tongues of flame licked the logs that were always burning there, resting in their own warm silver ash. A small stone figure stood in front of the hood and above the hearth, between the candle sconces. It was really the figure of a stork, the Walter family crest, but William and Lucy called it a heron, one of the herons of Brandy Brook.

He sighed again but this time with a sense of comfort. Nothing, he thought again, could destroy this great castle. Individual men and women were tossed up on the surface of life like waves and sank away again into the deep and were forgotten, but houses such as this were like the eternal caves within the rock, where the waves surged and fretted for a while without disturbing their peace. And on the sands of time the waves left their pretty playthings of shells and coloured stones, and these too could live longer than the restless creatures who had tossed them down. It was odd, William thought. The signet ring with the heron on it that he was now twisting backwards and forwards on his finger would last longer in this world than he, and the little figure of the heron across the hall, looking so alive in the firelight, was immutable. It pleased William at this moment to think of him as the family spirit. The men and women died but the heron had the courage to live on. He was courageous as eternity itself. A queer gust of joy came unexpectedly, brought him to his feet and sent him striding down the hall with lightness and eagerness.

He came through the screens and encountered his wife, Justus and Jano trotting behind her, coming from the kitchen. Richard had left the door into the garden open and he came lightly into brightness. Elizabeth stared at him and for an instant saw again the young man she had married, dark-eyed, alert and merry, a man with whom she could so easily have fallen in love had it not been that she had wanted another one. She had a sudden extraordinary awareness of superiority in him, a sense of herself falling, falling, that longest fall in the world that brings one to the feet of another in hearty loathing of oneself. It was as though the archangel Michael had come through the screens or, and her mind reeled, God himself. For one extraordinary moment she was nearly in his arms, that he flung out to her impulsively, but she managed to refuse them, clutching at her familiar supports, her sense of superiority and martyrdom, of injury and endurance, and the moment passed. She had, she thought, saved herself, and saw again the man she was accustomed to, his skin coarse and reddened with weather and ale, a man with a hang-dog deprecating air who looked much older than his thirty-five years. His arms dropped, he turned away and went down the steps to the garden, heavily and with a smothered oath. Elizabeth rounded on Justus.

"Justus, what are you doing here? Go and find Richard and go to your lessons. And where is Lucy? It is time she came to me for instruction. You children! You are all just like your father. I must always be goading you to your duty. How it wearies me! Oh, how it wearies me!"

2

Justus trotted off obediently to find Richard and go with him to school and Elizabeth went to her bower. When William had brought her to see the castle on their betrothal day she had not been able to hide her dismay at its lack of modern comforts. He had thought it perfect himself but to please her he had built out three rooms to the east, opening off the dais, the bower, the nursery and the washing place where there was actually a bath tub. This latter innovation William viewed with suspicion. It was not out of place to have a bath in the spring, for the grime of winter did tend to linger in nooks and crannies of the skin, and of course when the body was encrusted with mud or blood, after hunting or fighting, a bath was a convenience, but at other times he did not hold with it for the hot water removed the natural oils from the body to its detriment. His father had removed his only upon necessity, and William followed his example, and much disliked seeing these invaluable lubricants being removed weekly from the bodies of his children. But Elizabeth insisted. And certainly it would have been difficult to keep Lucy looking even moderately presentable without continual washing.

With her hand on the door of her bower Elizabeth called through the half-open nursery door, "Nan-Nan, it is time Lucy came to me for her lessons."

"Be patient just a minute, madam my love," said Nan-Nan with respectful firmness. "Not yet finished with the child I am. Stand still, cariad! I have laid out your paper and standish in your bower, madam fach. Writing today to your mother you should be."

Elizabeth went obediently to her bower and shut the door. Nan-Nan was privileged for she had come from Golden Grove. She had been in the nursery there and Elizabeth had always loved her and upon her marriage had begged that Nan-Nan should come to her, and Lady Carbery had given leave. She and Nan-Nan understood each other and Nan-Nan thoroughly agreed with Elizabeth that this draughty castle compared very unfavourably with Golden Grove, but she refused to say so. Nor would she permit any criticism of William. After the deaths of the babies two terrible outbursts of grief and anger had been wrung from her, but afterwards she had obeyed him with the same kindly tolerance as before, and she cared for him in any physical misfortune with the same brisk tenderness that she bestowed on his children. He was the master and she did not allow either herself or Elizabeth to forget it. When a woman was married she was married, poor soul. No good crying over spilt milk and least said soonest mended. Nan-Nan was fond of clichés. She found them strengthening.

Elizabeth's bower matched its old-fashioned name for she had made it as a bird makes its nest, to her taste and almost to her form. If she had not actually leaned her breast against the walls to round and soften them she had hung tapestries there and she had her special treasures in this room, a couch with rose-coloured cushions, a walnut cupboard and a writing-table in the window that looked on the garden. A second window looked east to the distant mountains. It was a window of yearning for beyond the mountains was England and the city of London that she had never seen. Her mother had lived there since her second marriage and she would have lived there too had she been able to marry the man she had wanted, the Englishman she had met at Golden Grove. He was at court now, at that enchanted court of Charles the First and his French queen. He had not been unwilling, though not as much in love as she, but he had been in need of wealth and her dowry, as one of nine children and several daughters, had been microscopic. So she had been married to William and out beyond those mountains was all she still dreamed of in mad, weakening daydreams and visions of the night.

She sat down at the table in the window and pulled her standish towards her, a lovely silver thing complete with inkpot, a perforated pot for sand and a small handbell. She shaped a quill pen and began to write to her mother but soon there was a slight movement and looking round she saw her daughter standing beside her, fresh from the hands of Nan-Nan, momentarily clean and tidy in a full ankle-length blue linen gown the colour of her eyes, her hornbook hanging demurely from her waist and her hair gathered back beneath a little white cap. She was holding out the bunch of wilting wild flowers that she had gathered on the cliff but Elizabeth did not see the flowers because her eyes were riveted on Lucy's small brown upturned face. A pang went through her, familiar to every mother who realizes for the first time that she is going to have a beautiful daughter, a pang of mingled apprehension, fear, exultation and, sometimes, jealousy. Elizabeth was suddenly violently jealous. Those very direct blue eyes were startling in contrast to the brown skin and dark hair and lashes and even in a moment such as this one, a moment of sore buttocks and sore heart, the child's vitality seemed to glow under the skin and to brim her eyes with light. Elizabeth had failed to get the man she wanted but Lucy would not fail because she was not empowered by her beauty only; her vitality and determination were as remarkable as her eyes.

"For you, madam. I picked them for you."

Lucy was too honest to ask forgiveness for actions she intended to commit again at the first opportunity, but she could offer consolatory gifts with a sweetness that was hard to withstand. Her lips that could set so hard when she was wilful were parted now and trembled slightly in her eagerness to make amends. She had a mouth that demanded kisses and her mother stooped to kiss it before she knew what she was doing. The touch banished her jealousy and in its place came a determination that Lucy should have what her mother had missed. She should not stay and eat her heart out in this storm-battered place. With her arm round Lucy she said, "London is behind those mountains. Shall we go there one day, you and I, and stay with your grandmother, and see the King and Queen and the lords and ladies going by in their coaches, and hear the bells ringing in the church towers?"

"We have a bell in our own church tower," said Lucy. "Have you ever been to London, madam?"

"Not yet," said Elizabeth. "But I am always begging your father to take us there for a winter."

"No, madam," said Lucy firmly. "I would like to see lords and ladies in their coaches but not if it means leaving Roch."

Elizabeth shrugged her shoulders, for it was exactly the answer William would have given. "Lessons, Lucy," she said irritably. "Pick up your hornbook."

Lucy laid aside the flowers her mother had forgotten, to be rescued later, and the light went out of her eyes, partly because of the flowers but also because she was not of the stuff of which scholars are made. She had a quick mind but not a scholarly one and found lessons a dreary business. If she could have joined Richard and Justus in their studies with Parson Peregrine she might have done better, for masculine company always stimulated her. She did not find women stimulating and sadly she picked up the hornbook which had been her mother's and grandmother's before her. Eight years old though she was she could still read and write only with difficulty but she did know her hornbook, alphabet and numerals, ave and paternoster and all. She said the Latin prayers parrot-wise to her mother, who knew no more Latin than she did, but the hornbook was a ritual and they could attend to nothing else until it was accomplished. The ritual over they turned to what Elizabeth considered really important, the sewing of the sampler which Lucy now took from the cupboard. At present she excelled in no feminine accomplishments whatever, except those of laughter and beguilement, and her sampler was a pitiful thing, grubby and bloodstained, and Elizabeth sighed afresh at sight of it. William, surprisingly clever at such things, had designed the sampler and drawn it out on the canvas. It had a simple all-over pattern, but was embellished with what Elizabeth's pattern book called "Sundry sorts of spots, as flowers, Birds and Fishes", and one of these birds was the family heron. Below, a space had been left for Lucy's initials, when the sampler should be finished; an outcome that was at present despaired of.

She stood now beside her mother, for in her sore state it was easier to stand than to sit on the wooden stool, tangling her thread and pricking her finger but doing her best. Elizabeth meanwhile went on with her letter, looking up now and then to inspect progress, but not looking at her daughter's face until the breath of a strangled sigh tickled her ear. Then she looked round and saw Lucy with her face drained of colour and dark smudges beneath her eyes.

"Are you tired, Lucy?"

"No, madam," said Lucy. But Elizabeth perceived that the child was very tired and putting her arm round her she guided her to the settle and made her lie down on her side on the cushions. She was full of compunction. Absorbed in her letter to her mother she had forgotten about Lucy's whipping.

"Did Nan-Nan give you breakfast, cariad?"

"She wished to, madam, but I did not want to eat."

Now that she was delivered from standing the colour was beginning to come back to Lucy's face and she realized that for once in a way she had her mother at her mercy. A small dimple that she had in her left cheek showed itself. "Could we have a reading lesson now, madam? Not me reading to you. You reading to me."

"What shall I read to you?"

"About Prince Kilhwch in the Mabinogion."

"Always the same story, cariad," said Elizabeth, as she took the old calfbound book from the cupboard. "Would you not like something different?"

Lying in state on the couch with her lady-in-waiting attending upon her Lucy was the Princess Nest. "I prefer the one I have mentioned," she said with hauteur.

Annihilated, Elizabeth sat on the floor beside her daughter and opened the book. It was a family heirloom. The pages were edged with gold and the capital letters beautified by delicate tracings in scarlet ink. The Mabinogion told the stories of the kings and queens and heroes of ancient Wales. It wove a web of mystery and glamour over the beginnings of the race, the same sort of splendour as had been woven for the English by *Le Morte d'Arthur*. It was a proud thing to belong to a people whose dawn had broken with such glory and if sceptics suggested exaggeration they could bring no proof to the support of their doubts.

Lucy and Elizabeth did not bother with doubts. The Mabinogion took them over the border to the other country and all that happened there was true for them because the country was true. Elizabeth had a beautiful voice and she read well, though slowly, for she was no more of a scholar than Lucy. She could do her household accounts and write a passable letter in a fine spidery hand, but when she read aloud it was with a difficulty which she disguised with this lovely carefulness that turned everything into poetry even if it were not poetry already. Though Lucy considered that the description of Prince Kilhwch was poetry already. "And the youth pricked forth upon a steed with head dappled grey, of four winters old, firm of limb, with shell-formed hoofs, having a bridle of linked gold on his head, and upon him a saddle of costly gold. And in the youth's hand were two spears of silver, sharp, well-tempered, headed with steel three ells in length, of an edge to wound the wind, and cause blood to flow, and swifter than the fall of the dewdrop from the blade of reed-grass upon the earth when the dew of June is at the heaviest. A gold-hilted sword was upon his thigh, the blade of which was of gold, bearing a cross of inlaid gold of the hue of the lightning of heaven: his war-horn was of ivory. Before him were two brindled white-breasted greyhounds, having strong collars of rubies about their necks, reaching from the shoulder to the ear. And the one that was on the left side bounded across to the right side, and the one on the right to the left, and like two sea-swallows sported around him. And his courser cast up four sods with his four hoofs, like four swallows in the air, about his head, now above, now below. About him was a four-cornered cloth of purple, and an apple of gold was at each corner, and every one of the apples was of the value of an hundred kine. And there was precious gold of the value of three hundred kine upon his shoes, and upon his stirrups, from his knee to the tip of his toe. And the blade of grass bent not beneath him, so light was his courser's tread."

And no less poetical was the description of Olwen. "More yellow was her head than the flower of the broom, and her skin was whiter than the foam of the wave, and fairer were her hands and her fingers than the blossoms of the wood anemone amidst the spray of the meadow fountain. The eye of the trained hawk, the glance of the three-mewed falcon was not brighter than hers. Her bosom was more snowy than the breast of the white swan, her cheek was redder than the reddest roses. Whoso beheld her was filled with her love. Four white trefoils sprung up wherever she trod. And therefore was she called Olwen."

"Pity it is her hair was gold," Lucy murmured. She was getting very sleepy and there came to her that double awareness that can draw the far into the near and see the near enclosed in the far and rest in their one-ness. The prince and princess of the story were not separated from the morning sunshine sparkling on the gold edged pages of the book, or her mother's rose-pink skirt spread out upon the floor. She took these things to herself as one thing and as the story progressed curled up inside it and went to sleep.

Three

Parson Peregrine was an excellent if eccentric instructor of the young. Richard was coming on well with his Latin and Justus could already read and write far better than Lucy. On the whole they liked their lessons, though Richard did not like Parson Peregrine, and they ran willingly to school on a warm rose-scented day a month later.

Richard ran the faster because of his slender lightness but Justus followed after at a good pace, his fat legs pounding gallantly. The boys were taught with the other village chil dren in the church, as was often the custom, but they had to go to the parsonage first to fetch their tutor, who would have forgotten all about them had he not been reminded of their existence. The parsonage was no more than a large cottage separated from the church by a grassy lane, its round chimney nearly disappearing in the deep thatch of the roof, with white-washed cob walls. It stood in an untidy little garden with a pig-sty at one side of it and the hen-run at the back. But Ptolemy the pig, and the hens who were named after the twelve tribes of Israel, went where they pleased. Ptolemy this morning was lying across the open front door and the boys had to scramble over his placid bulk to gain entrance, and the living room contained several Israelites pecking about on the floor of beaten earth. Parson Peregrine sat among them in his chair, his feet on the table among his pens and papers, lost in a book he was reading. There were many books in the room, in shelves and piled on the floor, but not much else, only the hearthplace and the old priest's cloak, green with age, hanging on a peg. The kitchen, where Parson Peregrine prepared the pig-wash and the chicken-food and his own scanty meals, led out of the living room, and the open door between the two rooms showed a scene of indescribable confusion. For Parson

42

Peregrine had no housekeeper and did not want one, or any female assistance whatever. A bachelor, and a scholar to the marrow of his bones, he was inimical to interruption of any sort except that demanded by his priestly work, and even to that he had to be recalled by the church bell or a hand on his shoulder. But though books were the love of his life he was not without affection for living creatures, especially if they were susceptible to instruction.

"Sir!" shouted Richard, his hand gripping his tutor's shoulder.

Parson Peregrine turned a page.

"Sir!" shouted Richard again and shook the old man with all his strength.

Parson Peregrine turned his head and transfixed Richard with a piercing glare. "Miserable boy!" he said with cold fury, and returned to his book. Richard took it forcibly from him and Justus removed his feet from the table. With the roar of a wounded bull he lurched to his feet, seized each boy by the scruff of his neck and knocked their heads together. But not too hard. They saw stars but not too many. "Wretched infants!" he groaned. "Deio! Deio! what troubles there are in the world!" Grasping the boys by their jerkins, one in each vast brown hand, he shook them like rats, kicking out meanwhile at the poultry squawking about his feet. "Benjamin. Judah. Dan. Detestable birds! Get you away out of my sight. That I should be so tormented in my old age! The devil take the lot of you!"

Suddenly it was all over. The hysterical hens scurried up and over the imperturbable form of Ptolemy and away into the garden, Parson Peregrine let go of the boys and thrust his feet into the clogs that stood beside his chair, staring at his pupils as though he had never set eyes on them before. In the deep silence that followed it was as though his mind, like a great gun, swung slowly into a fresh position. Then he got the new target into focus. Two small boys grinning at him and not at all afraid. His grim brown seamed face softened slightly. "Abominable children!" he growled with affection. "How long, O God, how long?"

He was an impressive if extraordinary figure when he stood upright. He was massive and strong and gave the impression of being rough-hewn from a piece of oak. His beard was red, streaked with grey, his eyes a fiery blue. His rough country clothes were strangely surmounted by the square scholar's cap he always wore on his bald head. He was fastidious in his person if not in his household, his beard carefully trimmed to a Vandycke point and his linen clean. He was well born and but for his intolerance and eccentricity he might have gone far in the world. As it was he remained a country parson with a stipend of twenty pounds a year, which he increased slightly by his teaching.

"Wretched child, fetch me my cloak," he said peremptorily to Justus.

Justus took the shabby cloak from its peg and the old man put it on. He always wore it, whatever the weather, when he took upon him his tutorial or priestly work, and with it a certain increase of dignity. Whatever he wore he could still command respect from others but only in his cloak could he still respect himself.

"Come on now, boys," he thundered. "Are we to be here all the morning? Out from under my feet, thou son of Belial."

The last remark was addressed to Ptolemy. The boys could climb over the pig's great bulk, but Parson Peregrine was rheumatic and could not. Ptolemy removed himself with a protesting grunt to a shady patch in the garden and the boys and their tutor progressed with dignity, in single file, down the garden path and across the lane to the churchyard. The trees drenched it in deep shade but here and there a shaft of sunlight pierced through and touched the moondaisies that grew among the graves. The wind from the sea stirred the tops of the trees, but the faint surge of sound could scarcely be heard above the singing of the birds. The path was mossgrown and dulled their footsteps so that they came with great quietness to the dark porch that was cold and dark as a cave. Parson Peregrine unlocked the door and they went in.

Inside the church the light was clear and cool for there was no stained glass in the windows, the colour in them being only the shimmering green of the leaves outside. Parson Peregrine, a disciple of Archbishop Laud whom he had known well when he was Bishop of St. Davids, now had all things in his church as the Archbishop would have wished. It had not been so when he had come here six years ago. He had found the church dirty and untidy and his parishioners slack about their religious duties, since they had found no help in their vicar, an old man who had despaired in his poverty and hanged himself from a tree in the churchyard. William had deplored his own youthful carelessness that had allowed such a thing to happen, and though he was a merely nominal churchman he had allowed himself to be elected as churchwarden and done what he could to help Parson Peregrine. Elizabeth's rigid piety had done the same and now the church had paving stones instead of the previous earth floor, a table under the east window with a rail in front and the ten commandments inscribed on the east wall to right and left. Parson Peregrine hankered after box pews instead of the old-fashioned benches but William had turned testy after the ten commandments. Parson Peregrine had painted them on the wall himself two years ago and entirely by accident had begun a fresh pot of paint at number seven so that it stood out very black. William was not a man to bear malice for long but his good humour was laced with obstinacy and Parson Peregrine knew that he would never now win his box pews. The church was the lovelier without them, had he but known, for they would have dwarfed the low beautiful font in which all the Walter children had been baptized and in which they took a personal pride.

The village children sat on benches under the tower but Richard and Justus, being the squire's sons, were taught in the vestry, among the old-fashioned suits of armour and the powder barrels and firearms stored there against invasion, but during instruction the curtains between vestry and church, gentry and proletariat, were looped back so that Parson Peregrine could pass backwards and forwards between the two. "Ring the bell, Richard," he commanded and Richard pulled at the bell-rope that hung beneath the tower and the single bell that summoned the village children rang out. They had been playing in the lane and soon there was a starling sound of wing rush and piping chatter, then the rattle of clogs in the flagged porch and they trooped in, the children of the men who cared for William Walter's land and beasts, a few yeomen's sons and the handful of children who lived in the fishermen's cottages at the bay below the mill. They were most of them poor children, bunchily clad in poor clothes, but sturdy and strong, for William saw to it that none of his people ever went hungry. They bobbed their curtseys and pulled at the ragged hair that fell over their eyes and scurried grinning to their places, while Parson Peregrine roared at the stragglers and reminded them of the rod for bad boys that he kept in the belfry. They had taken Parson Peregrine's measure long ago. He was as good as a cock fight and he never used that mythical rod.

Parson Peregrine opened precedings by instructing the castle and the village alike in the catechism and teaching them to repeat simple hymns by rote. Later, with the help of a blackboard, he taught the village a little simple arithmetic and as much reading and writing as he considered necessary for their station in life. Meanwhile Richard and Justus in the vestry were labouring at their Latin. Parson Peregrine passed backwards and forwards between the two and somehow, like a juggler tossing up coloured balls and catching them again, he kept them all hard at it.

This hour and a half of combined instruction ended with Parson Peregrine reading the children a chapter from the bible. Starting at the vestry, with his bible in his left hand and his right hand raised and moving in time to the magic of the verses, he would pace up the church to the chancel steps, turn and then come back again, and so till the chapter was finished. Though he raised his voice till it sounded like the sea booming in a cave it was not always possible for the children to hear what he said when his back was turned to them, but the very rhythm of the thing kept them spellbound and they never took their eyes off the erect pacing figure in the tattered cloak, his big head thrown back as he declaimed and sunlight, some-. times, glinting on his red beard. He chose the more dramatic of the old testament stories for declamation and the passage of the Red Sea, the falling of the walls of Jericho and the adventures of Elijah and of David became for the children marvellous experiences. The new testament chapters came in a different category for when he read these Parson Peregrine was different, less of a virtuoso and more of a priest, administering rather than entertaining. But he was no less dramatic. The Passion sequences made the more sensitive of the children tremble and the memory of Parson Peregrine crying out at the chancel steps, "In the beginning was the Word," was something that remained with Justus till the hour of his death. The reading over, the village children repeated the Lord's Prayer, were blessed and made for the door in an orderly manner. But outside pandemonium was heard to break forth. No more starling music. It was more like Ptolemy and his kind demanding their dinner. There was a quirk of amusement on their schoolmaster's grim mouth as he drew the vestry curtains, shutting himself in with his more advanced pupils. Then it vanished, his terrible red eyebrows drew together and Richard and Justus involuntarily tightened their muscles in apprehension.

For the next hour they were educated without mercy. They were intelligent boys and physically Richard was equal to the strain, but Justus was a little young for it, and when the church clock boomed out the hour of liberation he was a little white under his sunburn, and when they came out into the churchyard he was so happy to be free that he went leaping away through the wild flowers in the long grass, jumping over the low gravestones, cavorting like a pony that has been put out to grass.

"Leave him be," said Parson Peregrine to his more sober pupil, who walked beside him carrying his books. "But as for you, young jackanapes, you could have done better and you'll come home with me to give another hour to your Latin."

"Sir!" gasped poor Richard, for it was a long time since breakfast and his belly ached for a bit of bara ceich and a drink of buttermilk to bridge the void between now and dinner. But he knew it was no good for his tutor's hand was on his shoulder, hard and inexorable. He yielded but with an arrogant lift of his fair head. Parson Peregrine smiled grimly. He was not so fond of this boy as of the other. There was a coldness in him and the sort of ambition that might twist learning into a means of personal advantage, a defamation of the Word that to Parson Peregrine was sacrilege. But for this very reason he took infinite trouble with Richard, trying to set him alight so that his devious mind would know the warmth of dedication. He was the heir and what he thought and did would have importance in the days to come.

Parson Peregrine was extremely anxious about the future. These new men, these detestable Puritans, were setting themselves up against law and order in Church and State, refusing to use the prayer book or to venerate the tradition of the Church, preaching and praying as they pleased. True, they venerated the bible, Parson Peregrine would say that for them, but not so much as they venerated hearing themselves preach, and praying as they pleased. Inflating themselves up, that was all they cared about, inflating themselves against their God and King, whose direct appointment by God himself they were now daring to call in question. Resistance to the lawful prince and to the Church of the land as by God established was no longer called sin but liberty of conscience. Parson Peregrine growled in his red beard and propelled Richard up the weedgrown path into his cottage. A Latin lesson gave him plenty of opportunity for speaking of these things to Richard. What he did not know, for he was a man who neither considered nor cared what others thought of him, was that Richard was growing to hate him; consciously for this merciless instruction and unconsciously for the selfless enthusiasm that was a reproach to Richard's own cold and introverted mind and heart. Parson Peregrine was unable to realize, as he looked at the beautiful boy with his cavalier curls lying on his shoulders, that he was giving to Richard's mind the very bias that he was trying to avoid. He would have done better to concentrate on Justus who loved more easily than he hated.

At the moment Justus loved his morning bara ceich and

buttermilk with passion and was making for it at the double. He caught up with it on fine mornings in the arbour. The garden door crashed behind him, he raced round the sundial and bounded into the cool greenness of the arbour and the arms of Nan-Nan, who was sitting there with Lucy and the twins, the buttermilk and the bara ceich.

Nan-Nan was tiny as an elf-woman, one of the Tylwyth Teg, the fairy people whose stories she delighted to tell the children. She never raised her voice, and had a step as light as a falling leaf, yet her power was such that the life of Roch Castle radiated from her like spokes from the hub of a wheel. She never left the castle, unless it was with the children, and if she had any living relatives she never spoke of them. She lived her life in entire dedication to those she worked for but at the same time had every one of them completely under her thumb. In after years Lucy used to try and think what Nan-Nan had looked like and found it difficult to get a clear memory of anything except a voluminous grey gown, snowy-white apron and big mob cap invisibly animated by a bright-eyed spirit of love who comforted not so much with arms and a smile, though there was a smile somewhere in the memory, as by an envelopment of warmth that sent a glow of healing through the whole being of the afflicted child. So Justus now, though he scarcely felt the physical touch of her thin arms, and sitting on her knee was like sitting on a bodiless grey cloud, felt a glow in his empty stomach even before the nourishment had reached it, and his whole person, sorely wearied by education, relaxed in the comfort and was at rest.

"There, there now, bachgeni," she comforted, for she privately had a low opinion of intensive education for the very young. "Here's your buttermilk. Sit up now, cariad, and do not trouble your head with anything more at all. Lucy, pass the bara ceich."

Lucy passed the oat cake. She too, sitting close to Nan-Nan on the bench, was feeling warm and comfortable after an exhausting time with her sampler. The twins, Dewi and Betsi, were sitting on the grass just outside the arbour, towels round their necks, absorbing buttermilk loudly out of their mazers.

All the children had these little wooden bowls, graduating in size according to their age. Each had a silver lip-band and was decorated at the bottom with the family crest. The fun was to get down to the bottom of the mazer and find the silver heron, who would come flying to them through the milk or gruel, as though winging his way up through the white mists that hang sometimes over the low waters where the herons nest.

The twins emerged from their mazers breathless, milk-be-spattered and jubilant, Nan-Nan coaxed Justus down on to the bench beside Lucy and going to them wiped their faces with the towels, which she then removed and placed in the large basket which was her inseparable companion. The twins, two years old, were dressed in ankle-length dresses, with little aprons and close-fitting caps that covered their cropped hair. They were very alike and only those who loved them best, their father, Nan-Nan and Lucy, could tell at first sight which was the boy and which the girl. One told, Lucy thought, by the fact that Dewi's face was squarer and slightly more determined. Also he had more physical strength than his twin and his attitude towards her was already protective. Nan-Nan loved these two, with their black hair and eyes, no less than the other children, a love deepened by her compassion; though indeed she felt compassion for all five for where all is not well between the father and the mother the children cannot fail to suffer. She denied even to herself that she could have a favourite among her nurselings, but if she had it was Lucy.

"Look at the bees!" cried Lucy and in a moment she and Justus were out of the arbour and watching the bees in the flowers. This balmy warmth had come after a spell of cold wet weather and they were out in full force today, apparelled in velvet and gossamer, their humming harp music a glory and wonder after the silence of the winter. Unhurried but unresting they mined for their wealth, thrusting to the heart of the honeysuckle trumpets and the foxglove bells, and coming out gold-dusted with the pollen and with their treasure sacs growing heavier and heavier. They went away when they could carry no more but others took their places, citizens of many cities but with no hatred of each other, no envy and no greed.

"Old Parson will be happy now," said Lucy. "He'll be alive again now he's got his bees."

She did not mean Parson Peregrine but the queer old priest who lived at Brandy Mill. Everyone called him Old Parson because they did not know his name. Neither did he, though he sometimes called himself Jonah because he said he had been cast out of the boat, and at other times Saul because he was sorely troubled by a devil of misery. Many of the bees that came to the castle garden were his. He had four hives in the mill house garden and they were his life. He was not without intelligence and knew exactly what to do for his bees, but he could no longer manage the practical affairs of life and he could not remember what had happened to him before the winter day when William, riding home, had found him kneeling in the snow outside the castle, soaking wet and with the wound of a great blow on his head, dressed like a seaman but with the torn remnants of a priest's cloak hanging about his shoulders. William had brought him in and taken care of him for a while, and then had arranged comfortable lodging for him with Howel Perrot and Damaris his wife at Brandy Mill. He loved the old man and often went to see him. So did Lucy and Justus, but always when they were thought to be doing something else because their mother disliked and feared Old Parson and had forbidden them to visit him, and Nan-Nan always upheld their mother on principle. They looked at each other now, one of those quick glances by which, because of their love, they could communicate without words. This afternoon, now that he was alive again, they would go and see Old Parson.

2

After dinner Richard went riding with his father, and Lucy and Justus, who had been sent out to play in the garden, were seen by Nan-Nan, watching from the nursery window, to enter the arbour. Lucy was carrying a chap-book, a story with

pictures bought from a travelling pedlar the week before, and
Nan-Nan gave a sigh of relief. They would sit there now for
hours and she would be able to watch over the sleeping twins
and get on with her pillow lace. Lucy could scarcely be said to
read aloud, being no scholar, but with the help of the pictures
and a word here and there she was able to spin marvellous
tales out of the chap-book for the delight of Justus. He, actually, could read a good deal better than she could but refused
to do so out of school hours. But today they did no more than
turn over the pictures for ten minutes or so and then, knowing
that by this time Nan-Nan would no longer be watching, ran to
the door in the wall, opened it noiselessly in that special way
they knew and escaped up the lane to the road.

Here they turned right and ran fast until the road suddenly
plunged down hill, towards the hidden cwm where the mill
was built beside the Brandy Brook. Then they walked, hand
in hand, for this steep narrow lane was too precipitous for
running. It had very high banks, buried now in foxgloves and
honeysuckle.

The coast of Pembrokeshire was full of hidden places.
The gaunt windswept cliffs would suddenly open, like two
hands parting to show the treasure they hold, and there
inside would be a secret world, sometimes a narrow cwm, at
others a broader valley, but always a world to itself with its
own beauty and its own atmosphere. One of the loveliest of
these hidden worlds was the Valley of Roses, where the parting
hands held the cathedral of St. Davids. Brandy Cwm was a
small place compared with the Valley of Roses but in its own
way it was as beautiful.

As the children went deeper its special music came up to
meet them, the murmur of water and the ringing of birdsong,
for the trees that grew down there were wonderful nesting-
places for the birds. The lane took a final precipitous plunge
and they were there, standing on the old stone bridge, looking
down into the clear water of the brook below, and upstream to
the mill with its slowly turning wheel on the left bank.
Another bridge connected the mill with the mill house on the
right bank, with its farm buildings and garden. The mill was

old and so was the house. They seemed to rise up from the irises and lush green grass of this watered place as though they had always been here.

When the children turned their backs on the mill and leaned upon the opposite parapet they looked down into the steep little wood through which Brandy Brook tumbled to the sea, running out across the sands of Brandy Bay where the fishermen's cottages were. A cuckoo was calling not far away and when the children turned back again to the other parapet they saw a solitary heron standing in meditation by the mill pond. For fear of disturbing him they climbed very quietly down the steps that led to the mill house garden and went gently up the path that led to the house door. But quiet though they were he sensed their presence and rose up in clumsy flight. They watched him fade away up the cwm with great wings spread and long legs trailing behind him. He was returning to his nesting-place below the other old bridge, among the reeds down below the castle.

They knocked at the house door and Damaris opened it to them, a dark-eyed smiling woman, her hands floury because it was a baking day. Damaris was friendly, for her husband Howel was the second churchwarden and his bachelor brother Owen, who lived with them, was William's bailiff, but being much occupied today she was not inclined for much conversation. Old Parson, she said, was with his bees.

They ran round the corner of the house to the part of the garden where, well out of sight of the lane and the bridge and the watching eyes that scared him, Old Parson had his hives among the flowers that he tended himself for his bees. The little room that he inhabited led straight out into his garden and was like a hermitage with its whitewashed wall. It was not untidy like Parson Peregrine's living room for Old Parson possessed nothing at all except his bed, a table and chair and a small chest which held his few garments. Damaris brought him his food from her kitchen so he needed no cooking utensils. Parson Peregrine sometimes brought him a book or two and he courteously accepted the loan, but it was doubtful if he read them for he never spoke of them. Parson Peregrine thought that he shunned any aptitude that connected him with his past. Yet he did keep two links with it. He insisted on wearing a cassock and priest's cloak procured for him by Parson Peregrine out of money supplied by William, and he possessed a worn silver crucifix which hung round his neck, under his cassock, on a piece of knotted string. It appeared to Parson Peregrine, the only person who ever thought about him deeply, that perhaps a sub-consciously self-induced forget-fulness embraced not the fact of his priesthood but the manner of it. The fact of it, Parson Peregrine thought, was his life, for although he would not receive the sacrament he attended the services, hidden in a corner, and he prayed for hours alone in the church, and occasionally he cried when he prayed. Yet he looked a good old man and Parson Peregrine gave him the benefit of the doubt.

Lucy and Justus had no doubts. They never tried to separate sheep from goats. The vile platform in the heart which accommodates the self-conscious judge, separating himself in judgment, was empty in their hearts, as it was in William's. That was why Old Parson loved them.

He was sitting just inside his open doorway, and lost in shadow he saw them before they saw him. His eyes, today, were without their usual vacancy. He had occasional days when he could think and even, in disconnected flashes of anguish, remember. They were, he supposed, his good days but he did not welcome them for they brought a sense of hopeless dilemma. Without the lightning flashes he did not know of what he was repenting, but while they lasted he was too transfixed with horror, too paralysed, to be able to repent, and so he could never believe himself forgiven. But he tried not to despair for all summer long he had his bees and by some miracle of God's mercy he was always, whatever his state, aware of their wants and able to supply them.

"Lucy," he called from the shadows. "Justus."

They had been running down towards the bee hives but they turned and came back. Old Parson with his pink face and blue eyes, nodding and smiling at them from his dark doorway, had something of the look of an overgrown baby smiling from the shadows of the cradle, or a pink sea anemone peering from a hidden rock pool, something very innocent and gentle and withdrawn. It was only when one came nearer and saw his long wispy white hair and poignant mouth that one realized he was old. The hands that he held always clasped in front of him, as though in supplication to God to have mercy and to the world to leave him alone, were knotted with rheumatism. His feet hurt him when he walked and so did his knees, so that his gait was crab-like. It was his intention to walk now and the children pulled him up from his seat.

"I will show you my bees," he said.

It was what he always said to those of whom he felt no fear, a mark of his especial favour and he had said it to the children many times. But they were never bored by bees for like the white seal pups and the kingfisher they were one of the wonders of the world. The four round hives stood just where the garden ended and the ash and sycamore trees started to climb up the cwm. There was a wooden fence behind the hives with a gate in it so that Damaris could get up into the wood and gather firewood. For a little while the three of them watched the traffic of the brown multitudes, weaving their lines of communication between the flowers in a score of gardens and the fragrance of the cliff tops and the hidden woods. Lucy thought of them as a honey-scented web of gold threads too fine to see and she asked Old Parson if one broke the web as one ran about the world. He gravely inclined his head, as a wise baby does when his understanding has out-stripped his power of speech. "But they repair it again as a spider does," she said, and he smiled. Justus never understood these one-sided conversations that Lucy and Old Parson had together. "There's a honey pot and a bit of barley bread by the gate," he said, pointing with the index and little finger of his right hand, the thumb and the two middle fingers tucked down, so that his fat brown hand looked like a horned enquiring snail. "What for?"

"I have a few pots left," Old Parson said, "and I thought my friend would like some honey with his bread. When I have a gift for him I hide it in a place up in the wood."

Old Parson spoke with great deliberation, feeling for each word and testing it carefully like a man crossing a stream on wobbly stepping stones. Impatience in the hearer, even politely suppressed impatience, plunged him into instant confusion, but with the children who took no account of time he was able to reach the other side of his stream of thought with considerable success.

"By the gate is not up in the wood," Justus said with gentle kindness, and raising the horned snail he indicated a rock which showed among the trees above them. "Up there is up in the wood."

"It is my knees and my feet," Old Parson said.

"We will take it for you," said Lucy. "Where is the place?"

"Behind the rock," said Old Parson.

"Who is he?" asked Lucy.

"A noble man," said Old Parson. "A scapegoat."

They did not understand this but as asking Old Parson to explain himself only worried him they let it pass. But Justus, burning with curiosity, asked, "When does your friend come to fetch the gifts from behind the rock?"

"Most days," said Old Parson vaguely. "He is always hungry. A scapegoat."

Old Parson's eyes clouded and his chin began to wobble in a way it had when he was distressed. "Look at that bee!" cried Lucy. "He is the biggest bee I ever saw in my life."

Old Parson cheered up instantly. "My dear, it is not a he, it is a she," he said in shocked tones, for nothing shocked him more than ignorance about bees. "It is a worker bee. I have told you before that workers are lady bees. The gentlemen, the drones, are inside the hives." And he was off on a long slow dissertation on bees and had forgotten all about the pot of honey and the barley bread.

But Lucy had not forgotten and after they had taken him back to his room and settled him again in his chair, and had run down to the brook to watch the mill wheel turning, she said to Justus, "The scapegoat."

They opened the gates and climbed up the steep wooded

slope, carrying the honey and bread carefully. It was lovely in
the wood with the cuckoo calling and Brandy Brook singing
and chuckling down over the mossgrown stones, the ferns
pushing up all along its banks. They reached the grey rock and
went round behind it and saw a smaller stone, half-hidden by
brambles, leaning against it. Between the two stones was a
cavity and someone had hollowed out the earth inside it. This
must be the place. Lucy knelt down and put the honey and
bread carefully inside. Then running down to the brook they
scrambled on beside it, the slopes of the cwm growing wilder
and more brambly as they climbed. Presently they stopped,
for Lucy had got herself entangled with brambles, and while
she tugged impatiently at the thorny sprays Justus pulled off
his shoes, scrambled down into the brook and stood looking
down at the marvel of his feet magically changed by the water.
Could they be his feet? It was very eerie and strange, and the
queer feeling grew with the sparkle of thrusting sunlight on
the water and the sound of the brook in his ears, banishing
other sounds and enclosing him in a lonely watery world. He
began to feel very odd and looked round for Lucy, but in his
confusion he looked upstream, not towards the bank, and was
transfixed with terror.

It couldn't be a man. He had never seen a man like that, yet
it couldn't be any other creature than a man. Then he knew
what it was, a corpse that had been buried by mistake while it
was still alive and had fought its way out of the grave, choking
with dust and gasping for air, and had come to drink at the
stream. It was drinking in choking gulps, crouched down on
the bank and spooning the water up in skeleton hands. Rags
clothed its nakedness and the wrinkled skin was nearly black.
Justus's mouth was open, trying to scream, for the thought of
men buried alive was his special nightmare. But he could not.
No sound would come. And he could not move either. Somewhere inside him he began to call, Lucy, Lucy, but she did not
hear and she did not come. Then she did hear, though still he
made no sound, and was beside him in the stream, her hand
gripping his reassuringly. Her face was white but she was not
as terrified as he was.

"Crouch down," she whispered. "Then he will not see us. He is the scapegoat."

They crouched down and the ferns hid them. Justus let out a shuddering sigh of relief. The scapegoat. Not a man who had been buried alive but Old Parson's friend. But even so he was sufficiently terrible, and now he was standing up and perhaps he might see them, for they could see him quite plainly through the ferns. His grey beard was long and straggly and the brook water dripped from it, but only a few wisps of hair clung to his skull. There was no evil in the face but with the open gaping mouth, eyes swivelling from side to side as though he had heard something that had scared him, it was somehow dreadful. Neither child had as yet seen a prisoner being led to the gallows; if they had they might have recognized a man without hope whom terror and exhaustion had reduced to something scarcely human. They trembled, and though she did not know it Lucy had tears running down her cheeks. Then suddenly the man saw them and leaped aside and ran away through the wood. In a moment he had vanished, as though the earth in its pity had opened and swallowed him. Lucy pulled Justus up out of the water and hand in hand they plodded on, and now Justus as well as Lucy was crying. If the sun still shone they no longer noticed it, and they hardly knew where they were until they found themselves in the shallow valley behind the castle. Then Justus spoke. "I hope he will find the bread and honey."

"He ran that way," said Lucy, and they began to cheer up, for they were in green meadows where their father's cattle were feeding and in the distance was the bridge and the stream that Lucy saw from her bedroom window. They were nearly home now and their natural high spirits began to come back again.

They reached the bridge at about the same time as the trotting horsemen but there was nowhere to hide, and in any case Lucy would not have hidden for she knew how to manage her father.

"What are you two doing there?" demanded William, drawing rein on the bridge with Richard on his white pony just behind him. "This is not where you should be, I'll be bound." Where they should be he did not know but it was always safe to conclude that Lucy was where she should not be. And Justus went where Lucy led.

"They should be with Nan-Nan in the garden," said Richard haughtily. He was looking very beautiful, one gloved hand on his hip, the reins held nonchalantly in the other, his back very straight. Lucy, her hair dishevelled, the hem of her dress and her shoes and stockings soaking wet, knew that this was one of the times when she wished she could love Richard more than she did. Why should he give himself such insufferable airs just because he was naturally tidy and had been born first? But she could not quarrel with him for he had taken moderately well the fixing of three strong iron bars across her turret window, that had now put an end to his exits as well as hers. Pushing back her hair. she smiled up at her father and brother, and her eyes were so intensely blue that it was as though a kingfisher flashed across the stream. William was undone. Groaning he stretched out his arms to her and she jumped up and was enthroned-before him on his saddle.

"Come on, you abominable little tadpole," said Richard, and with Justus enthroned on the white pony with his brother the cavalcade paced slowly up the hill towards the castle. It towered up above them on its precipice of rock looking far taller and more impressive than it actually was, the tower seeming almost to touch the sky. It looked an impregnable fortress and Lucy had a sudden longing to be safely inside it. She had not known before what could happen to people who strayed homeless and alone in a world that looked so beautiful but could not be as lovely as it appeared, or the scapegoat would not look as he did.

3

The next day the Wogan boys, Rupert and John, rode over from Haverfordwest with their father and mother to spend the day at the castle; William and George Wogan, both justices of the peace, to discuss their mutual affairs together, the two ladies to gossip over their embroidery, the boys to spend the time with Richard. John was the same age as Richard and Rupert a little older. When evening came they were all to have supper together in the great hall and Lucy had been told she might sit up for it.

It was warm and fine and all went well at first. The boys bathed down in the castle bay and then adjourned to the churchyard to play their special game of throwing a ball against the church wall and bouncing it back with their rackets, a fast and furious game they had devised themselves to improve their tennis. Parson Peregrine had no objection, indeed he allowed such games even on Sundays, and he frequently read aloud from James the First's *Book of Sports* in church, as a counterblast against Puritanism. Lucy and Justus had both been allowed to sit on a tombstone and watch their elders, but were not permitted to take part in their sport. Justus, a born hero worshipper, was content to worship but Lucy was furious. With her skirt off she could play ball better than any of them and it maddened her to be relegated to a tombstone. Justus watched her a little nervously for her eyes were dangerously bright and she had a scarlet spot on each cheekbone. Though she sat so still, her hands linked round her knees, he knew very well that one of her rages was coming to the boil.

The older boys grew hot and tired and flung themselves down among the moondaisies in the long grass, and scraps of their conversation floated to the two children on the tombstone.

"My father says these damn Puritans should all have their ears cropped," said Rupert. "They turn the whole country into a moaning muckheap of snivelling devils who would abolish Sunday sports and music in the churches and even the wakes. They've no respect for holy things. If they had their way they'd drag the cross from the altar and the King from his throne."

"No!" said Richard hotly. "Stop him from being a tyrant; that is all. Stop him from levying unjust taxes without consent of parliament. He thinks he is God. He is not."

Rupert, a boy of choleric temper, was on his feet at once, as red in the face as Lucy. "Monarchy is divine," he shouted at Richard, "and resistance to one's lawful prince is an act of rebellion. I thought the Walters were loyal men."

"We are."

"Not you, you goddam traitor."

"Liar!" gasped Richard, as white with fury as Rupert was scarlet. "It's no treason, if your prince steals your liberties, to resist him."

"I tell you it is," retorted Rupert. "And who taught you your politics? Not your father, I'll be bound. Nor Parson Peregrine."

"I think for myself," said Richard. "Why should I believe what old Peregrine tells me? He's an old fool. As for my father he does not care for politics one way or the other. He only cares for his horses and his ale."

Lucy's breath was for a moment caught in a tight knot in her breast. How Richard dare speak like that about their father! She gasped and the knot released itself in a spring that sent her catapulting from the tombstone to land on Richard like an avenging fury. He rolled over on the grass, pummelled by her fists, but only for a moment for he heard Rupert's laughter and flinging her away from him he jumped up and went for Rupert, who hit back with far greater skill and strength. Lucy, too mad with rage to be capable of any proper family feeling, and aided by Justus according to his lesser capabilities, continued to go for Richard. John Wogan, an agile boy whose political feelings were no stronger than those attributed to William Walter, leapt to the aid of Richard simply because he was outnumbered. The affair had passed through the first glorious stage of shouts and thuds and battle cries and had sunk to the sobbing of exhausted breath and the bubbling of bleeding noses, when two fathers stepped over the wall and Parson Peregrine strolled along from the lychgate, his fingers still marking the place in the book he had been reading. He had come not so much to separate the combatants, which messy business he now left to the begetters of the abominable children, but to express his own sense of personal outrage. "Am I to have no peace?" he demanded. "Morning by morning I am forced to instruct these sons of Belial; must my afternoons also be rendered hideous by their brawls?"

He was not heard in the hubbub of parental pacification, and returned the way he had come. By the time he reached the lych-gate he was deep in his book again and by the time he was once more with Ptolemy and his armchair he had forgotten he had been out. Meanwhile, the combatants having been disentangled, questioned and cursed, a gloomy procession made its way back to the castle. That this scrimmage was a matter for gloom they all knew, for it threatened the evening's entertainment; that it was one of many such sparks all over the country, that would presently run together in a bitter conflagration, they refused to recognize, for the beginnings of tragedy, like the first warnings of pain, are always thrust out of sight; man's hope that what is pushed down into the dark will die there being as perennial as it is doomed.

Back in the castle cuts and bruises were attended to and punishment meted out. John and Rupert were sent home in disgrace in the care of a groom, to be dealt with by their father later, Richard was whipped and sent to his turret room and Lucy and Justus banished to the nursery. No child was to partake of supper. It was the parents only who feasted at the high table on capon and a leg of mutton, with a fine tart to follow, all washed down with claret and home brewed wine made from the wild raspberries that grew in the Prescelly mountains.

When the aroma of roasted meat stole through the nursery door Lucy, sitting on the floor with her head leaning against Nan-Nan's knees, could not forbear to weep a little. It was not for the food that she wept but because she was not sharing in the beauty of the occasion. She could not see the wax candles burning in the silver-branched candlesticks, and the best porcelain wine jugs patterned with flowers. And presently they would put fresh logs on the fire, as the evening chill came in from the sea with the rising tide, and her father would play the lute and Madam Wogan would sing in her deep contralto voice, and the other two would listen, the dogs lying at their feet.

"Cariad," murmured Nan-Nan. "Pity it is that you are not there, but with Nan-Nan you are, who loves you. And these two children love you. Specially that Dewi. Look at him, gazing at you with those great eyes of his. Dewi, asleep you should be. And you too, Betsi my fairy girl."

Dewi and Betsi could still manage to get into the two large wooden cradles that had been made for Walter twins a hundred years ago, and were placed near the fourposter in the corner of the nursery where Nan-Nan slept. They were sitting up in their frilled nightgowns, peeping out from within the wooden hoods that had wreaths of little birds carved about them, pink-cheeked and bright-eyed, with no desire whatever to go to sleep. Justus was not present for he had elected to keep Richard company. His noble name of Justus was one that he tried to live up to and as he had taken Lucy's side in the great fight he had to be with Richard now. Lucy missed him, even with Nan-Nan's hand on her hair, and with that scent of baked meat creeping under the door her stomach as well as her heart ached with emptiness. "Did not the servants bring you any supper, Nan-Nan?" she asked.

"Fetched it myself I did while you were in the washplace," said Nan-Nan. "I shall eat it later. Dewi and Betsi, pity it is you will not do as Nan-Nan tells you and close your eyes and go to sleep."

"Sing to them, Nan-Nan," said Lucy and nestled closer.

"Wishing for a song yourself you are," said Nan-Nan, but she fell in with the suggestion since she could see that the twins' wakefulness was purposeful. They adored being sung to. She moved herself and Lucy and her low nursing chair nearer to the cradles, so that she could rock them, and in a voice that was still sweet and true sang one of the old songs of Wales, one that the harpers sang in the mountains of Plynlimon, the enchanting country called by the ancients Eelineth, where the great rivers of Wales arise in their beauty and where she had been born. Peace rose up in Lucy, deep down as though the quietness inside her and Eelineth were one place.

The beauty she could not see in the hall became a part of Eelineth, and so did the garden outside the open window. The castle thrush was singing on top of the hawthorn tree behind the arbour and his song rang through Eelineth. The twins were soon asleep. Betsi, the more timid child, lay on her side with her thumb in her mouth, cuddled into her pillow as though she sought a refuge there, but Dewi lay spread-eagled on his back, one arm flung out in a lordly manner. Their eyelashes looked very long and dark on their flushed cheeks. The singing finished, Nan-Nan and Lucy knelt down at the side of the cradles and worshipped. Nan-Nan's grey skirt made a silver cloud about her as she knelt, and her face was grave and attentive, for she was one of those to whom the hour of Eelineth brings knowledge of the future.

"Dewi will stand by you and yours till the end of your days," she told Lucy. "Happy he'll be, for a king will love him."

"And Betsi?" asked Lucy.

"Belonging to the falling dew and the song of the thrush she is," said Nan-Nan and as though to forestall questioning arose and moved away from the cradles, drawing Lucy with her. "Those poor boys, pity it is for them with their bruises. Taking Richard and Justus a bit of comfort we should be. Come now."

She picked up a covered basket from the floor and opened the door quietly, for in crossing behind the screen at the back of the dais to the great bedchamber they must be careful not to disturb the ladies and gentlemen at their supper. No one saw them and Lucy caught just a glimpse of the beauty of candlelight and gleaming silver, and her mother in her best crimson gown and wedding pearls, before she and Nan-Nan vanished into the bedchamber and shut the door behind them. In the boys' turret room Richard was lying on his front, Justus on his back, and they were very sorry for themselves, especially Justus, not so much because he had been trampled on in the fight as because Richard had not wanted his company.

"See now, boys bach," said Nan-Nan briskly, "see what Nan-Nan has brought you." She took the napkin from the basket and inside was the most ravishing supper, cold capon, bara

ceich and a small tart, all in little dishes, and a bottle of raspberry wine and a cup of horn to drink it from. "Eat slowly
now," said Nan-Nan, "there's not much there for three. Take
turns with the cup for the wine."

Both boys now felt very much better and Justus rolled out of
his own bed and sat on Richard's with Lucy beside him.

"But it's *your* supper, Nan-Nan," protested Lucy.

"Old people do not feel hungry, cariad," explained Nan-
Nan. "A drink of buttermilk before I go to my bed is more to
my taste than pastry which I cannot digest at all. Now, boys,
you must understand that I do not approve of your wicked
ways. Ashamed of you I am, and of you too, Lucy. Setting an
example of politeness you should be instead of scratching and
spitting like a wild cat among the mountains. But you've
suffered, poor children, and I cannot find it in my heart that
you should go hungry to your beds. No more, Justus, no more
of the wine. That's enough now. There's my good children."

Never before had their nurselings heard her make such a
long speech. She was sitting on Justus's bed, her hands folded
in her lap, and her gentle words that touched them softly as
moths' wings, yet touched them unforgettably. The little
room, facing west, was filled with golden light and when Nan-
Nan was silent they could hear through the open window the
wash of the sea. All along the coast now the tide was coming
in, moving with smooth and gentle power over the rocks, cast-
ing half-moons of water higher and higher up the sands, swirling in and out of the caves. The stranded seaweed floated free
upon the green tide and the pools brimmed, and there was a
great fulfilment. Nan-Nan tucked the boys up in bed and
kissed them, and for once Richard did not mind being kissed
but flung his arms round her neck as he had been wont to do
when he was small. They were half asleep almost before she
and Lucy had left the room, and Nan-Nan thought Lucy was,
too, as she tucked the covers in about her, but suddenly the
child began to cry.

"What now, cariad?" asked Nan-Nan.

"Our lovely supper," said Lucy, "and perhaps he didn't even
find the bread and honey."

"Who, merchi?" demanded Nan-Nan.

"A scapegoat in the mill wood."

"There are no goats in the woods," said Nan-Nan. "Up in the mountains, plenty, but not in the woods. It's dreaming you are."

"He is not really a goat, Nan-Nan, he is a man and he is all bones and he wears rags."

"Some travelling vagabond," said Nan-Nan. "If you and Justus were running wild in the mill wood when you should have been playing in the garden, and he frightened you, a fright is what you deserved." Then she was suddenly alarmed. "This man, burnt near black by the sun was he?" she demanded. "And the hair of his head hanging to his scalp like sheeps' wool to brambles?" Lucy nodded and Nan-Nan clacked her tongue and was increasingly distressed. "It was the sin-eater you saw," she said. "Madam your mother would not like you to be having anything to do with him. Do you hear me, cariad? You and Justus must not go into the mill wood again."

Lucy was now sitting bolt upright, her tears dried by a burning compassionate curiosity. "What is a sin-eater, Nan-Nan? How can you eat sin? Sin is not a food. Is it eating sin that makes him so thin and bony?"

Nan-Nan was now coming round and blamed herself that shock and horror had made her question Lucy. But having done so she thought it best now to be explicit with the child. "Country folk are very ignorant, cariad," she said. "Still holding to heathen superstitions, things that should have vanished from a Christian country. They think that if food is placed on the breast of a corpse, and a man eats it, then the dead man is free from his sin, and the sin-eater suffers its punishment." Nan-Nan found it difficult to speak calmly: The sin-eaters were outcasts, living alone in deserted places, and even those who believed in their power and made use of them regarded them with loathing, and when their work was done would drive them out with blows and curses. Nan-Nan herself, the bravest of women, was terrified by them. The thought that a sin-eater's glance had fallen upon Lucy and Justus made her feel physically ill, so that she hid her hands under her apron to hide their trembling from Lucy. "Never must you go to the mill wood again," she said sternly. "Do you hear me, cariad?"

"He would not hurt us, Nan-Nan. He was frightened of us and ran away."

"That is as may be," said Nan-Nan. "But sin-eater or no sin-eater, madam your mother does not like you running wild in the woods and you must not do it."

"He must be a kind man," said Lucy thoughtfully. "Eating other people's sins and being punished for them when he has not done them himself. I would not like to do that."

Her eyelashes were slowly descending to her flushed cheeks and she appeared to be sinking into sleep. Nan-Nan shook her shoulder, "Never must you go to the mill wood alone, Lucy, do you hear me?"

Lucy's eyelids fluttered upwards for a moment. "I hear you," she murmured and appeared immediately to be asleep.

Nan-Nan struggled to her feet, her knees trembling so greatly that she had to sit on the stool a little while, rocking herself and keening under her breath. The evil eye had fallen upon her children. Now it would take every charm she knew, every spell and incantation taught her by old Rhys the Harper to shield them from disaster. She groped her way across the bedchamber and the dais, hardly seeing the two lovely ladies and their husbands laughing and talking before the fire. She gained the nursery and she went to bed, but all night long she lay awake. The weather was on the change and by midnight the chill of approaching rain had invaded the castle. A small wind moaned under the door and the drag of the waves along the shore grew louder and more melancholy. Nan-Nan had not until now shared Elizabeth's fear of the castle, for all places were alike to her if the nursery was satisfactory, but that night she too was afraid, and when the sky lightened again, and the singing of the birds sounded through the pattering of summer rain, she was not able to forget her fear.

Four

The Sunday of the pilgrimage started like any other Sunday except that Lucy did not want to go to church. She did not object to church in itself but it was August, and hot, and she did not want to wear her best blue silk gown with its voluminous skirt and petticoats. Sitting on the stool in the big bed-chamber, swinging her legs rebelliously inside the hot skirts while Nan-Nan endeavoured to bring order to her wild hair, she said she wished she was a mermaid.

"Why, cariad?" asked Nan-Nan.

"They do not wear clothes," said Lucy.

Elizabeth, seated before her mirror adjusting her black curly-brimmed hat, looked round in dismay. "That is a very unmaidenly remark," she chided gently.

"But I do not want to be a maiden," said Lucy. "I want to be a mermaid."

Though rebellious she was not cross, merely making a few truthful statements, but Nan-Nan misunderstood her mental state and gave her a sharp tap on the hand with the comb. Then she really was cross, for she thought Nan-Nan was being unfair and injustice always infuriated her. She jumped up, seized the comb and flung it into a far corner of the room. Then Nan-Nan was cross. Her serene temper failed her on an average only about once every three years, and this was the triennial failure. In the twinkling of an eye she herself was on the stool with Lucy laid across her knees, Lucy's petticoats were flung over her head and Nan-Nan's tiny hand was giving her a good hard slapping. She came right way up crimson-faced, her mouth open to yell, but was too astonished to do so, and before she knew where she was Nan-Nan had smacked her hat on top of her still unruly hair and had marshalled her and her equally astonished mother out of the bedchamber and down into the hall.

William and his two sons, marvellously attired in their best doublets and bucket-topped boots, their swords at their sides and their plumed hats in their hands, were waiting for them. Even Justus, now that he was breeched, had his little sword and it had transformed Sunday churchgoing from a weariness to an exultation of the spirit. The church bell was already ringing. William offered his arm to his wife and the procession set forth, joined at the screens by the servants and dogs who fell in two and two behind them, all except Nan-Nan, who had to stay behind to look after the twins, and the scullions who must get the dinner going.

Lucy's mouth slowly closed but her colour remained high. Nan-Nan had been unjust and her outraged feelings, denied expression, were seething inside her. They would explode soon, she knew they would, and it would not be her fault.

In dignity and beauty the Walter family and their household progressed to church, through the garden, along the road, under the lych-gate and through the church-yard. Many of the villagers were on their way too. They bowed and curtseyed to the squire and his wife and William and Elizabeth acknowledged the salutation as though they were the king and queen. They walked up the aisle with their beautiful children, the hounds Shôn and Twm and Jano the spaniel behind them, and settled themselves in the two leather-backed chairs that had been placed for them like thrones to the right of the aisle, before the chancel steps. It was Parson Peregrine's opinion that men should remove their hats in church but William would not do this. His obstinacy had perhaps something to do with the seventh commandment, facing him black and large upon the wall. He would sit glaring at it, very upright, the plume in his huge hat seeming to grow taller and taller as he glared. The children sat beside their parents on a backless bench while Shôn, Twm and Jano lay in the aisle, noses on paws, slumbered and had the best of it.

Just behind the Walter family were Howel and Damaris

THE CHILD FROM THE SEA

and Owen Perrot, and Rhys, Owen's dog, lay in the aisle just
behind the castle dogs. The bell quickened its pace, for James
Jones the Clerk who was ringing it was indicating to stragglers
that there were only three minutes left. The other two parish
servants, Bowen the Beadle and Price the Sexton, were in their
places under the tower. Bowen Beadle had his whip and dog
tongs ready to his hand and would forcibly remove anyone
who became disorderly during divine service. He was experienced in this kind of work for on weekdays he was assistant to
the village constable, impounded strange cattle and drove
vagabonds out of the parish. Price Sexton looked after the
church and dug graves for twopence a grave in the nave, six-
pence in the chancel, a ha'enny outside in the churchyard
and was entitled to beer and ale at Christmas. Also at the back
of the church, hidden in a corner behind a large tomb, was
Old Parson.

The bell stopped, Parson Peregrine entered in his surplice,
Jones Clerk walking behind him, the service began and the
explosive ball of hurt feelings inside Lucy, that had felt as big
as an apple, shrank to a little glowing thing the size of a
walnut. For until her back began to ache she liked listening to
Parson Peregrine's fine voice declaiming the ancient prayers
and reading the psalms, verse and verse about with Jones
Clerk, and she liked to hear and feel the hymn singing rolling
up the church behind her and smiting her in the small of the
back. They sang the hymns that had been composed for the
musical Welsh people by Chancellor Pritchard of St. David's
Cathedral, and though they had no hymnbooks they sang
from memory and by ear with great beauty. When they sat
down for the sermon it was with a sigh of pleasure in the
dying fall of the music that still echoed in their hearts.

Sermon time was not easy for the children. They had to sit
upright on the backless benches, feet together, hands folded in
their laps, and they were not allowed to fidget or whisper.
Their parents set them a good example, William stiff and staring as a painted figure on a monument, Elizabeth in her dove-
grey gown equally motionless but gracefully so, her delicate
oval face, faintly violet-shadowed by the sweep of her great

70

hat, turned attentively towards the preacher. But Parson Peregrine doubted if she was attending; or anyone else for that matter. It was not easy for him to preach simply to these simple people and he fancied sadly that they had long ago abandoned efforts to understand him. But they worked hard in the week and were glad of a rest and so for the children only did he feel compunction. Lucy's toes barely touched the ground and Justus's feet still dangled far above it. But today he only pitied them for ten minutes for at the end of that period Owen Perrot's dog Rhys suddenly arose and attacked Shôn in the rear.

Rhys, a comical mongrel, had always hated Shôn, a hound of impeccable breeding, and hated Sundays when he must keep his humble station behind Shôn in church, with the great hound's satin-smooth haunches rising so close to his twitching nose that he was choked with the hot, well-fed, blue-blooded smell of the great conceited beast. For three years he had suffered Shôn in silence, and if it had not been so hot today he might have continued to do so, for he knew his place even as his master did, sitting bareheaded behind William with his vision blinded by the squire's vast hat and nodding plume. But it was hot, good breeding weather for fleas, and Rhys itched, exploded and leapt. He was not a large dog but he was brave and even with the two hounds on top of him, and a roaring tumult like the end of the world filling his ears, he felt no fear, only relief and exultation in the liberation of the pent-up hatred. Shôn's left hind leg was gripped between his teeth, the taste of his enemy's blood was in his mouth and not to save his life would he have let go; indeed death would have been welcome in this glorious hour of his revenge.

Parson Peregrine's sermon came to a dead stop. "Bowen!" he roared.

But Bowen Beadle was already advancing at the double with the dog tongs and the whip and the congregation was rocked with delicious tumult. All the other dogs in church, forcibly restrained by their masters, were struggling and choking to rush up the aisle and join in, and William and Owen, entirely forgetting themselves, were on their feet swearing at their dogs and beating them with their hats. Jano, a delicate little dog, had leaped to Elizabeth's lap for safety and was having a nerve storm among her silks and laces, and all the children were bobbing up and down in excitement. But not Lucy, who loved Rhys dearly; far more than her father's arrogant hounds. With quiet resolve she flung herself into the mêlée to rescue him, and got her arms round Twm's neck in a throttling clutch just as William succeeded in getting hold of Shôn's collar. Bowen Beadle, with the skill and precision of long practice, gripped Rhys in the dog thongs and propelled him down the aisle. Parson Peregrine, erect in the pulpit with his arms folded and the light of battle in his eyes, thundered directions.

"Perrot, you may leave divine service to care for your dog. Children sit down. I beg that all the adult members of the congregation may also now be seated. Silence please. I will now continue my sermon."

He was a man who could impose silence when he wished. William returned to his seat, the feather in his hat much the worse for wear, and resumed his wooden rigidity. Twm and Shôn sank once more to the paving stones, to lick their minor wounds with loud noises, and Elizabeth, depositing the trembling Jano on the floor, was not surprised to find she was trembling herself. All these storms! The children and the dogs fighting, and soon now the autumn gales would be raging down the coast and then the darkness of winter would close in on her again, with the castle cold and clammy as a grave; and at the turn of the year, when the great rains were drowning the world, she would bear another child to this stranger beside her, this man so alien to her heart and spirit. Alien. It was all utterly alien. She could not be her true self in this savage place, she was too delicately nurtured. If only they could all spend the coming winter in London with her mother, and her child be born there in comfort, safety and peace! But William always refused her pleas for a winter in London. He could not leave his land, he said. It was nonsense. He had a good bailiff. Several times she had told Nan-Nan she would go without him, taking the children with her, but Nan-Nan had always put a stop to that with stern reminders of wifely duty.

"Strangers and pilgrims," declared Parson Peregrine, "we seek a country."

Since the dog fight he had abandoned his carefully prepared sermon and was telling simple stories about pilgrimages, journeys through desolate lands to holy places. Seeing the delight of the dog fight slowly fading from the faces of the children below him, wiped off by the return of their habitual puzzled boredom, he had addressed himself to winning back their pleasure. Was the divine task of awakening joy in the hearts of God's children in God's house to be left to a mongrel cur like Rhys? Gloom and boredom were the henchmen of the devil and the Puritans and he suddenly saw his duty as a preacher in a light so new and dazzling that it was like a sudden conversion. A romantic narrative style, long ago suppressed as undisciplined and unscholarly, welled up in him again and not only the children but the whole congregation listened to him spellbound. He might have been telling stories from the Mabinogion.

From the pilgrimage of the Magi through the desert to the cave of Bethlehem, and the desperate journeys of the pilgrims to Jerusalem, tossing in their small boats through the waste of foreign seas, he passed to the journeys nearer at hand, to the shrines of Saint Thomas at Canterbury, Our Lady at Walsingham or their own Saint David in Wales. In the great days of pilgrimages two to St. Davids had been considered the equivalent of one to Rome itself, so blessed was the shrine. But the journey had been hard, with the pilgrims often lost in the mists, hungry and footsore, guided along the pilgrim way by penitential crosses cut in the rocks, where they would stop and pray for forgiveness and for strength, but coming at last to the hidden paradise of the Valley of Roses. Though many of them knew it well he described it for them with its trees and green fields beside the stream, its sheltered peace, and the Cathedral rainbow-coloured like the breast of a rock dove, that bird of peace whose voice is heard all along the coast of Pembrokeshire. And he described the shrine itself, within the Cathedral, where in the pilgrim days men had prayed for and received forgiveness, the holiest place in all Wales, one of the holy places of the world. In such places, he said, men become aware of the reality of the light that burns at the ending of every journey that is begun, and struggles on, and so must end, in love.

He stopped abruptly, a patch of high colour on each cheek bone, half ashamed of himself, but glancing down as he turned to leave the pulpit he saw Lucy and paused. She was sitting on the extreme edge of the bench, tense as an arrow ready to leap through the air at a given signal. Her eyes glinted blue fire and her shining face dazzled him. What had he done to the child? A more urgent question, what because of him was she about to do? It alarmed him that she should be so instantly responsive to a momentary flash of emotion and he wished he had the training of her. Richard and Justus were ordinary enough children, the obvious offspring of their dull and moderately worthy parents, but that shining elf had alighted in the Walters' nest like a peacock butterfly in the midst of a handful of bawling young sparrows. These things were among the mysteries and he earnestly hoped that Nan-Nan, the only member of the household for whom he had the slightest respect, would contrive to live long.

The service ended and William offered his arm to his wife that they might lead the congregation out of church. His conviction that his children could be relied upon to follow behind in good order was usually justified, but today Lucy detached herself and scurried around the tomb into Old Parson's hidden corner and found him, as she had expected, on his knees and weeping. She did not know why it was that the things that made her happy made him weep, things like the first primroses or the twins in babyhood, fragrant and warm in a nest of shawls. But there it was, one of those grown-up things not to be understood but to be comforted if possible, and kneeling down beside him she flung her hat on top of the tomb and leaned her tousled head against his arm. Through the shaming tears he dimly saw the blue of her spreading skirts upon the paving stones, and thought confusedly that the pool of his

74

grief was reflecting the colour of the over-arching sky, the colour that for other men he associated always with the mercy of God. But for him there could be no mercy. Weep though he might his sins were never washed away. Whenever those flashes of remembrance came they were still there, unconfessed and unforgiven, yet when he struggled to ask for pardon he had again forgotten what they were. Yet today the blue of the sky was reflected in his grief and he could distinctly feel a compassionate touch upon his arm. Then, coming to himself a little, he looked down and saw the child's tousled head against his sleeve.

"We will go this afternoon," she said in matter of fact tones.

"Go where, child?" he asked her.

"On pilgrimage to St. Davids," she said. "To the Cathedral and the shrine."

Old Parson began to shake for he remembered now what it was that had flung him headlong into sorrow; the mention of that shrine where men received forgiveness. He had known about it for a long time but he had never dared to go there. He had always been afraid that as soon as he came anywhere near the holy place lightning would strike him down for his presumption.

"Would it be possible?" he whispered to Lucy. She thought he was referring to the long walk and his physical weakness. "Yes," she said. "We will ride there. I will bring the ponies and fetch you after dinner." Then suddenly she broke into a peal of laughter. "Oh look!" she cried, pointing. Her Sunday hat that she had tossed upon the tomb had landed upon the head of the dog who lay there recumbent at his master's feet, an amiable mongrel dog who bore a strong resemblance to Rhys. He looked very comical in a hat. Old Parson, who could still laugh with the children at what made them laugh, laughed with her. He had a small almost soundless laugh, like the creaking of the last two autumn leaves left on a wintry twig. Seeing him happier Lucy retrieved her hat and led him from the church. They went hand in hand along the sun-dappled path through the now deserted graveyard, the trees a grateful coolness over their heads.

2

When the formal, dignified Sunday dinner was over fate played into Lucy's hands. She had not known how she would manage to evade the Sunday afternoon gathering of the family to make music in the arbour, but as they rose from table Elizabeth complained of a headache and said she must lie down. "Madam, I will get you mint leaves to take away the pain," cried her daughter, and all in a loving flurry she seized Justus by the wrist and raced with him down the hall and out into the garden. The mint grew obligingly near the door into the lane. She grabbed a bunch of leaves and pushed it into Justus's fat hand. "Stay here for ten minutes and then take it to our mother," she commanded. "Tell them you've left me in the arbour and later, if they worry, tell them I shall be coming back."

"Where are you going?" demanded Justus, his cheeks already crimsoning with the anger he would feel if she was going on an adventure without him.

"I cannot tell you now but I will tell you afterwards," she said, and gave him a great hug. "You will do what I say because you love me," she whispered against his hot cheek, where already tears of fury were beginning to trickle. Then she closed the door in his face and ran like the wind to the stable. She heard him beginning to roar but she knew he would do what she said because for him obedience, even furious obedience, was the way of love. She knew just what he would do; sit on the grass and bellow for the stipulated time and then wipe his face on his sleeve and trot indoors with the mint. As she ran she grieved that she had told that lie about waiting in the arbour. It had popped up out of the repressed resentment of the morning, like a pea out of a pod. Sins did pop out one from the other in that way. It was a habit they had. Well, her hurt feelings had exploded now and apart from the lie her virtue was not in question, for Parson Peregrine had said it was a good and holy thing to go on pilgrimage.

She took the ponies' harness from the harness room and ran

out to the field beyond where they were grazing. There was a joyous whinnying when she appeared but she could not stop for conversation. "Prince," she called. "Jeremiah." Richard's white pony Prince was his private property and he would not allow the younger children to ride him. They had to make do with Jeremiah the kitchen pony who pulled the faggot cart and carried panniers full of apples in the autumn. Richard's selfishness over Prince was something Lucy resisted whenever possible, and she and Prince were mutually attached, but it was Jeremiah whom she most deeply loved and he came to her now as fast as he was able. He was old and stout but could still do a hard day's work because he was a mountain pony, wiry and strong, and at one time had been very wild. The wildness had been trained out of him but independence of character was still a marked characteristic. He was of comical appearance, piebald with the black patches very oddly placed, one across his face like a mask and the other across his broad back like a saddle. His eyes were surrounded by stubbly white lashes and were always very bright. Prince followed him closely, his long tail drifting out on the mild air like silver spume, his neck arched like a sea horse. Lucy harnessed them quickly and jumped on Prince's back and they were off. She did not have to lead Jeremiah for he followed like an old dog.

Old Parson, with Rhys beside him, was standing on the bridge but not waiting for them. He scarcely seemed aware of their arrival, though when Lucy slipped off Prince and took his hand his long cold fingers enclosed hers gratefully. He was watching for something, or rather the return of something, the expression of his face like that of a baby who has seen the gold watch swing one way and waits for the return of the miracle with awe and ecstasy. It came, the blue flash of a kingfisher from bank to bank below the mill, so rapid that the colour seemed still in the air, like a rainbow over the stream. Old Parson had forgotten all about the pilgrimage but now, with Lucy's hand in his, he remembered it, and the blue bow seemed almost like a promise that the arc of God's mercy might not always be only for other men. 'We will go now," he said to Lucy. She had her arms round Rhys, who was standing on his hind legs, his fore paws on her shoulders and his tail whirling around in circles almost as rapid as that of the kingfisher's flight. He wanted to come with them but they had to leave him behind, for his wounds were too sore for a long journey on a hot day.

They rode off at a good pace. Old Parson must at one time have been accustomed to the saddle for he seemed quite at home there, and although Lucy's Sunday dress was not very suitable for riding she was such a natural horsewoman that she could have ridden anything, anywhere, anyhow. It was ten miles to St. Davids and though Lucy had been there before it had been only in the coach with her mother, to a service at the Cathedral and to some party at a house in the village and she was always restless and irritated in the slow lumbering coach. But this journey was so entirely different that it seemed a journey through a strange land to an unknown city, as unknown to her as to Old Parson.

Yet she had one vivid memory of a previous visit, something that floated free of the spreading skirts and large hats that had hemmed her in. It was a small clear picture of tall pillars that went up into blue shadows, and lifted up among them a little man, black and white like a magpie in a nest. He stood up in the nest, lifting his arms like wings, and spoke, and when he spoke the rustlings and whispers fell silent, for he was a famous preacher. She could remember the silence, and his voice that was clear and loud. She had not understood what he said but she had sat gazing at him, hugging herself with glee as she remembered the story of his conversion, that she loved as well as any among the sagas of Wales. For the instrument of Chancellor Pritchard's conversion had been a mountain goat. Lucy loved the wild mountain goats of Wales, big as donkeys, and she was sure God loved them too or else why use a goat to convert Chancellor Pritchard? As they trotted along she told the story to Old Parson, enriching it with a wealth of detail accumulated by her lively mind over many tellings.

When Chancellor Pritchard had been Vicar Pritchard of Llandovey he had been a very merry man. Parsons were forbidden to enter a public house, or to touch cards or dice, but

Vicar Pritchard had done all these things and had enjoyed them enormously. So very merry had been his nightly car- ousels at the village inn that a special wheelbarrow had been kept for wheeling the parson back to bed at night. He had been travelling home one evening, pushed by other merry- makers, his legs stretched out in front of him, his voice up- raised in song and the wheelbarrow zigzagging from side to side, when he beheld in front of him, blocking the narrow lane, a large inebriated goat, blue-grey in colour and terrifying in appearance. Though it was not so much the great horns and hoofs and the long yellow teeth that horrified Vicar Pritchard as the spectacle of its inebriation. Its drunken bearded face seemed to him a reflection of his own and as he and the wheel- barrow rocked from side to side so the goat reeled from side to side, the hairy countenance coming always nearer and nearer to his own. It was when the creature's hot breath was actually in his face that he screamed with terror, leaped out of the wheelbarrow, raced up the lane to the vicarage and was not seen again for a fortnight. When he emerged he was a changed man, a man of penitence and prayer, and now he was Chancellor of St. David's Cathedral and the greatest preacher in the principality. Yet he still had a merry heart and still he liked to sing. They sang his hymns all over Wales.

"Was he forgiven?" asked Old Parson anxiously. "Did the scapegoat take away his sin?"

This was an aspect of the affair that Lucy had not thought of before. "I don't know," she said slowly. "I had not thought of that goat being a scapegoat, like the sin-eater."

And they began to talk about their friend up in the mill wood. For he was Lucy's friend too now. Old Parson could not always climb as far as the hiding place by the big stone and so now Lucy did the climbing for them both, carrying up the scraps of food that Old Parson collected or that she herself begged from the cook at the castle. Nan-Nan's eye upon her was very vigilant these days but she and Richard had organ- ized another escape route. He and the young fisherman with whom he sometimes went for early morning fishing ex- peditions had made a rope ladder which could be let down from the window in the boys' turret room, as far as the old fig tree which grew up the castle wall below. The descent was long and perilous and the manner in which the ladder was fixed to the crumbling stone upright in the centre of the window none too secure, and Richard did sometimes wonder if the fishing was worth it.

Lucy never doubted that the sin-eater was worth it. He was not always in the wood when she climbed up with his food, whistling the special bird call that was her signal to him, but when he was there he no longer ran from her. When she spoke to him he would utter strange sounds and then look at her with anguish, as though he longed to speak but could not recapture the words that had been long forgotten. Though he had taken upon himself so many sins he was not evil, and his helplessness broke her heart. When she left the sin-eater she went home weeping not only for him but for herself too because she did not understand.

But she and Old Parson forgot sadness in the delight of the journey. Their pilgrim way led them first downhill to New-gale, where the sands fell away from the great pebble ridge that protected the cottages and the old inn from the Atlantic storms. Newgale could be a drear and terrible place in stormy weather but today the fishermen sat on the pebble ridge mending their nets, their brown backs gleaming like bronze in the sun. Then uphill again to a great sweep of open country, thyme-scented in the heat, the turf cropped short by the grazing sheep. From here they could see Roch Castle on its rock, the Prescelly mountains remote and cloudlike to the east, and to the west the blue sweep of St. Bride's Bay. The off-shire islands looked unearthly today, half-veiled in the heat mist, bird haunted and mysterious. Inland the fields of oats and barley were ripe already and the light wind ran over them like the invisible feet of a multitude of elves. Here and there one-story whitewashed cottages crouched behind thick ramparts of oaks and thorns blown almost horizontal, and then the way plunged downhill again into a deep valley, to the little port of Solva. Then up again and along the top, and almost before they knew it they were in the little city of St. Davids, and the

way had become a lane winding between cottage gardens
where lilies, tansy and bergamot grew, and the tassels of tam-
arisks hung over the low stone walls.

The lane brought them to the cobbled square where stone
steps led to a high stone cross, and there was a drinking trough
beside the inn door. They dismounted and the ponies, hot and
tired now, drank gratefully while Lucy knocked on the inn
door and demanded of the sleepy old man who opened it buttermilk and bara ceich, and stabling for the ponies while she
and her friend went to the Cathedral. She asked politely but
imperiously, drawn up to her full height, every inch a very
great lady; all the more imperious because she had no money
in her pocket. He did her bidding instantly and she and Old
Parson ate and drank sitting on the bench at the door. It was
much cooler now, as though the movement of the tide was
once more towards them, and the blue shadow that stained the
cobbles beneath the inn wall was deep as the note of the bell
that tolled from somewhere near, yet sounded as far below
them as the caverns at the bottom of the sea. Lucy did not
count the notes of the bell for she never bothered about the
passing of time when she was happy. Old Parson was not
bothering either for this pilgrimage was like a causeway that
lifted him above time, and above the confused and troubled
self that belonged to time, and like Lucy he was happy.

Lucy jumped up and took his hand. They went down a
cobbled lane to a massive arched gateway, and passed under
the arch and stood upon the edge of another country; but they
looked down upon it, not up at it, as though it were not paradise itself but a reflection of it mirrored on the earth. There was
a wall here and they leaned upon it. This was the Valley of
Roses, one of the places of power of which there are not many
upon earth, and its living strength could smite even its familiar lovers with a perpetual shock of surprise. So ancient it was
always new. The walls and pinnacles and square tower of the
Cathedral, honey-coloured in the sun and violet after rain,
seemed always to live and breathe with the movement of
clouds and running shadows. The ruins of the bishop's palace
beyond, delicate with long arcadings of empty arches against

the sky, could look in some lights like festoons of shifting mist. There were tall green trees down there, and emerald turf where sheep were feeding, and the flash of a stream going down to the sea. The quietness held the sound of the water and the murmur of sleepy birds. The nature of the land that held this hidden place was forgotten until one looked across the valley and saw a harsh rim of rock brooding black and jagged against the sky. Yet that harsh reality was no more real than this. It was more apparent, but not more real, for all mirrors, by their very nature, must reflect truth.

"We will go in," said Lucy. She did not say go down, though that was what they would do, for a flight of steps descended towards the Cathedral, but go in, as of favour and invitation. An invisible door had opened for them. Hand in hand they went down the steps cut in the hillside to the green graveyard. They did not go at once to the Cathedral but walked to the stream, and stood on the old bridge that spanned it looking down into water so clear that they could see the pebbles on the bottom. The services of the day were over and there was no one about, only the dragonflies who pierced the sunshine with their jewelled dartings. They were close now to the roofless fourteenth-century palace and Lucy told Old Parson that it had been built by Bishop Gower, bishop of St. Davids and Chancellor of England, and stripped of its roof by Bishop Barlow, who had sold the lead to provide dowries for his five daughters who married five bishops. It was the achievement of Bishop Barlow rather than Bishop Gower that awed Lucy. Such fatherly affection seemed to her remarkable, but it was a pity it had destroyed the palace. "Yet it could not be more lovely," she said to Old Parson. "In June the wild roses grow all over the ruins and the banqueting hall has a floor of grass and moss, and there are dark crypts down below. Richard and Justus and I played there once and we thought we heard other children calling to us, calling and calling, but they weren't there at all, it was our voices echoing. And now we'll go in."

They went through the west door into cool peace and Lucy guided them to a bench. The first impression was of the muted silver and gold of a winter beech wood on a day of quiet sunshine. The gold slanted down through the upper traceries of the trees and lay in pools on the flagstones, and far overhead glowed in the old roof. The sense of a wood was increased by the tilt of the pillars, disturbed long ago, men said, by an earthquake, and the floor too was uneven, sloping upwards to where steps rose to the dark oak screen, pierced by an archway that led to the holy places beyond. Above the arch the rood hung from the ceiling but so far away that the outstretched arms of mercy could be seen only dimly. But they could be seen, especially at this moment, for sunbeams were gathered there. Old Parson knelt down and prayed while Lucy took off her shoes and paddled her hot bare feet in the coolness of the stone floor. Once more a bell tolled, far above her now, up in heaven and not down below in the sea, and once more the passage of time was not important. Old Parson ceased to pray but continued to kneel, his childlike blue eyes following the play of the sunbeams about the rood.

"May God bless you."

The quietly spoken words created no disturbance in the mind and Lucy and Old Parson turned their eyes only slowly towards the direction of a voice so musical that Lucy expected to find an angel there. But the grey-bearded man in a shabby cloak who stood beside her was too homely in appearance to be angelic, though he had an air of angelic authority, so much so that Old Parson got up from his knees and bowed and Lucy slid to her feet and curtseyed.

"We are pilgrims," she said bravely.

"Have you come from far?" asked the man, and his bright eyes darted with amusement from her tousled head to her bare feet.

Lucy opened her mouth to say they had come from Roch but before she could speak Old Parson replied for them both. "From a great distance," he said, and his voice had an unusual depth in it. Lucy saw that he was not afraid of this man, in spite of the authority, for he went on with a steadiness and clarity unusual with him, "I have come from the place of the husks and swine, and the child who brought me here, who knows where she came from? Is it true, sir, that if after long journeying pardon is asked at the shrine of St. David it is granted by the Most High God?"

"My dear sir," said the man, almost with irritation, "the journey of penitence is short. You do not need to travel from the other end of nowhere with peas in your shoes to reach that mercy," and he jerked his head up towards the rood. "It is in your heart."

"Then we need not have bothered to come," said the practical Lucy.

"Pilgrimages have their uses," explained the man. "They are sacraments and symbols, like the rood up there, and the bread and wine. They bring conviction." He turned back to Old Parson. "And if you, sir, have become so far desperate as to doubt the mercy of God you had best follow me now along the pilgrim way. No, not up the nave. They did not enter up the nave. We must go out and in again. Come, child."

He led the way back through the west door and round through the cloister quadrangle towards the door that led into the north transept. He went first, his hands placed palm to palm, pilgrim fashion, and Old Parson followed him, his head bent low over his prayerful hands, and Lucy came after, her shoes tucked under one arm and her brown palms pressed together very devoutly; her eyes twinkling with the sudden discovery that religion could be fun. The man's eyes had been twinkling too, she had noticed, when he had led them from the Cathedral, but there had been also a gravity that seemed vaguely familiar as though she had seen him before somewhere. Gravity came to her also as her bare feet in the green cloister grass became aware of the hidden path of the pilgrims. It was grass-grown now but her bare feet knew about it.

They went up the north transept and came to the holiest part of this Cathedral, the place of the altar, the shrines and chapels and the tombs of the great dead. Lucy had not been here before and she was too awed to be conscious of much more than sunbeams and pillars and fine carving that was like sea spray frozen into stillness. The way beneath her feet still held her and even if she had not been guided she would have followed it up the north choir aisle, to kneel where the pilgrims

84

had once knelt before a raised platform where the shrine containing the saint's relics had been placed at times of pilgrimage. They knelt there while the man told them this, and then they followed him to the sanctuary and saw the peep-hole in what had once been an outer wall, through which people outside could see the shrine, and here once more they knelt. The relics of St. David had been hidden at the time of the Reformation, no one quite knew where, and had not been found yet, but it was as their guide had hoped and the imaginations of the child and the child-like old man supplied what was wanting. For them, kneeling here so close to the high altar, St. David the great saint of Wales was truly present to aid them with his prayers. They knelt one on each side of the man facing towards the altar and to both of them the fancy came that he was himself the saint, for his authoritative presence held them with a sense of absolute security. If he said anything was so, it was so.

"If I ask St. David to make someone I love happy, will he do it?" asked Lucy.

"Certainly," said the man.

"The pardon is sure," pleaded Old Parson, plucking at his cloak.

"Perfectly," said the man.

"But I cannot remember my sins, you see," cried Old Parson in anguish. "How can I obtain pardon when I do not know what they are?"

"God knows what they are," said the man. "The only requisite on your part is penitence. Now, my dear sir, pray for forgiveness once and for all and know once and for all that you have received it. I meanwhile will show this child the tomb of the great Lord Rhys."

He spoke with such absolute conviction that he seemed to grow in stature as he spoke, and Lucy was quite sure that Old Parson would be happy now. For the next half-hour she and the man walked through the sunbeams, backwards and forwards through history. They saw the tomb of Rhys ap Tudor the father of the Princess Nest, and the tomb of Edward Earl of Richmond, father of King Henry the Seventh, and other great men whose stories the man told her, and then sitting in Bishop Vaughan's chapel behind the High Altar they talked of St. David himself.

They were still talking when they heard a step and looking up saw that Old Parson had joined them. His face was shining and rested, like the sand when the sea has washed over it and withdrawn again, leaving it renewed and clean beneath the sun. His eyes were bright like blue-washed stones.

"It broke over me," he said simply.

"I knew it would," said the man.

"Warm and gold," said Old Parson.

"Yes," said the man.

"Which way did the pilgrims go out?" asked Old Parson.

"Through the south door," said the man. "Shall we go now?"

They re-formed and with their hands palm to palm upon their breasts they walked with great rejoicing down the length of the Cathedral and out through the south door, and were met by more gold, as though this paradisal day had turned towards its ending.

"There is only one sin that you need now to remember," said the man to Old Parson, "and that is the one you must never commit. It is the sin of doubting if you are forgiven."

He bowed to them both, lifted his hand in a gesture of blessing and moved away. At the angle of the Cathedral wall he turned round and lifted both his arms in farewell. He looked like a winged bird. Then he disappeared into the western gold.

"He was no mortal man but St. David himself," said Old Parson with conviction.

But Lucy knew now who he was for she had recognized the same bird that she had seen in the pulpit. He was Chancellor Pritchard. But she left Old Parson thinking he was St. David because she thought it would be good for him to think that. She took his hand and they climbed back up the long flight of steps and stood for a while at the top looking back. The ruined palace dreamed in shadow but the tower of the Cathedral was alight with flame and all the stones of it glowed with gold.

They stood gazing for a long time and then went through the archway and climbed up the cobbled lane back to the inn.

Lucy offered the old landlord the little gold brooch she wore, in payment for their meal and the stabling of the ponies. He did not want to take it but she loved giving away her possessions and he could not withstand her pleading. But he gave them, for love's sake, more bara ceich and some home-cured ham and a couple of apples to eat on the way. As they left the village they found that the women were already bringing in their cows. In their dresses of homespun grey flannel, the cows tethered to their arms, they knitted as they walked but looked up to smile at the old man and the little girl as they passed. The last thing Old Parson and Lucy heard, as they gained the wild again, was the musical cow-call of the peasants. It rose and fell with unearthly beauty, dying away behind them as they rode off into the twilight.

3

It was a magic ride home. The ponies were fresh after their rest and they trotted sure-footed as conies. Something of the enchantment of twilight seemed to run like wine through their bodies and to lift and toss their manes as though with invisible fingers. Lucy had noticed before how animals in the wild at night suffer a change and are clothed with princeliness. The night is theirs, not man's. They take their true place. The dew fell and Lucy's wild rough hair was wet with it while upon Old Parson it alighted like a benediction; baptismal dew bringing newness of life. The stars pricked out and an eye of the harvest moon glimmered beyond the mountain. There was mist in the valleys and the sea breathed deeply. The rhythm of its breath seemed the heartbeat of the world, the pulse of life in the veins of men and ponies.

They did not stop to eat for they had decided that the food the landlord had given them was for the scapegoat, but their hunger gave them no pain, only a sharpening of the sense of joy and a deepening of their peace. They came to Newgale almost before they were aware of it and saw the lights in the fishermen's cottages, and then they were home, on the bridge where they had seen the kingfisher, and it was as though they had been away for a hundred years. The moon was up now and the Brandy Brook was like liquid silver flowing below the bridge. Everything was very clear in its light, most finely etched, more delicate than by day because unclouded by colour. They tethered the ponies and walked through the wet grass by the stream and climbed up through the wood.

"I wish he could have come too," said Lucy sadly. Yet she knew he could not have come for in the nature of things scape-goats were always outside the warm hut circle that men built about the fire. But there were other circles and other fires and perhaps he knew of them.

They came to the great rock and she gave her bird call. Was he here tonight? They waited, and then she called again, and he came from the trees above and stood peering down at them. For a few moments, as though he had been a shy wild animal, she took no notice of him, but busied herself putting the food in the hiding-place. Then leaving Old Parson beside the rock she climbed up to him, and he let her come nearer to him than ever before. Perhaps he would have fled before she could stretch out her hand, but she slipped on a stone and he shot out a long arm to keep her from falling, and she clung to his hand with both hers, smiling up at him. What can I do? she thought wildly. What can I give? But it seemed she could do and give nothing because he pulled his hand away and ran.

But there had been an exchange between them. She was left with the wound he had dealt her, from which compassion flowed, but he, hiding far up in the woods, wrapped his spirit about a new warmth. The darkness within him, which his groping awareness had always pictured as an emptiness falling to the abyss, had now a glow within it. The sins fell and fell through the darkness, yet he was never free of them because they came again thick and fast as bats on the wing, but this warm glow did not fall. Later, when he had fetched his food and eaten it in the turf hut he had made in the valley behind the wood, and laid himself down to sleep, he crossed his arms upon his breast as though to assist his spirit to keep it in place.

Then he contemplated it within himself, armed himself at it, and began to know that he need not fear its loss. Stars, he had discovered, could be obscured but did not fall. Only evil fell. The thought of his own eventual fall into damnation, dragged down headlong in the wake of the sins, that had drenched him with fear every time it confronted him, now lost something of its terror. Whatever in him could cling about the warmth and light would not fall. Whatever did fall would be a good riddance. He turned over and went to sleep.

Lucy returned to Old Parson and they climbed down again to the cwm. She kissed the old man goodbye at the door of his room, then fetched the ponies from the bridge and rode home up the hill. She knew she ought to take them to the stable, not to the meadow, to be rubbed down after the long ride home, but she was afraid the door might be locked. However, it was open and the stable empty, and the bridles of the riding horses were gone from their place. Then she realized what had happened. It was much later than she had realized and her father and the men servants were out looking for her, and her mother and Nan-Nan were perhaps very anxious. She felt a pang of compunction, but she unharnessed the two ponies and rubbed them down unhurriedly and fed and watered them. And then she thanked them for their great goodness. The moonlight and starlight shone through the stable window and they were spun about with silver. Prince might have been made of moonlight and even stout little Jeremiah had a radiance. She was loth to leave them and tired though she was she lingered, leaning her head against Jeremiah's neck. In spite of the happiness of the pilgrimage, and of Old Parson's joy and relief, she felt intensely sad. She was not afraid of punishment, for she was always ready to face the music, but now there was this wound at the centre of her joy, and she was changed. When she left the stable, crossed the lane to the garden and saw the castle blocked so strongly against the stars, the fancy came that it was receding. What had happened to her? As a child she had possessed her world. It was her first intimation that she might not always do so. In her panic she raced down the garden and up the steps to the hall door, sobbing, "Nan-Nan!" The door opened as she reached it, for her footsteps had been heard, and she was in Nan-Nan's arms, and then her mother's, and then Nan-Nan's again, and the queer new sadness was forgotten.

Five

Lucy was punished, but not severely, so thankful was the household to have her safely home. "Do you call that a whipping?" she enquired sarcastically of her father the next morning, for she had scarcely felt it. But she found that he had dropped the cane to blow his nose and she had to turn her attention to comforting him. "I just went to St. Davids," she said patiently. "On pilgrimage."

"Fool's rubbish," said William. "And let this teach you, Bud, never to listen to sermons. Parsons are all very well for marryings and buryings but once you start putting into practice the damn silly nonsense they preach you never know where it will lead you. I thought I'd lost you, Bud. I thought you'd fallen over the cliff."

"I've more sense than to fall over the cliff. Sir! Listen! You must let me go where I like, and do what I like or I will not be able to bear it!"

Then she in turn burst into tears and flung herself into his arms. What could she do? Here was her mother ill from the anxiety and her father crying and Nan-Nan strangely distant with her, and all because she had been away for a few hours on pilgrimage. She must be free. Couldn't they understand? She bellowed with grief and William picked her up and carried her, penitent as he believed, to her mother's bed, and the escapade was forgiven and dropped into the past.

But Nan-Nan, though loving, remained remote. Damaris Perrot had been awakened out of her first sleep that Sunday night by the sound of trotting ponies, had looked out of her window and seen Lucy and Old Parson climbing up into the wood, and had thought it her duty to tell Nan-Nan what she had seen. The top of the wood was one of the habitual haunts of the sin-eater and Nan-Nan had known then that Lucy had disobeyed her. Lucy, she now remembered, had made no promise of obedience, but all the same Nan-Nan was grieved at her heart, as well as deeply anxious for the safety of this unmanageable child. She began to think more favourably of Elizabeth's wish of spending a winter in London. Nan-Nan had never been outside Wales, or set eyes on any sizeable town, and her mental picture of London was a mixture of Golden Grove and the new Jerusalem of the Apocalypse. There was hope that such a place might have a civilizing influence on Lucy. But, and here Nan-Nan did not waver, William must not be left behind. Not again. Nor would it be wise for him to live with his mother-in-law for though they were mutually attached that was an arrangement that seldom succeeded. If they went at all they must hire their own little house for the winter and keep together. Nan-Nan was not yet certain of the wisdom of the step but whenever Elizabeth discussed it with her she was progressively more in sympathy with her mistress.

The fine weather broke in the first of the autumn gales. The rain drove horizontally from the sea before the wind, and it was so dark at midday that Elizabeth had to light the candle in her bower when she wanted to stitch at embroidered caps for the new baby. She felt ill and depressed and William, harassed by crops in danger, was not sympathetic. Only the children enjoyed themselves, splashing like ducks in the wet.

Then the gale blew itself out and it was summer again. The early mornings were cool, bespangled with silver spiders' webs, the days warm and still, scented by the first windfall apples and the first blackberries, and the harvest was saved after all. The weeks slipped by. The song of the robins was sharp and sweet and the starlings chattered like a lot of old wives outside an ale house. But the swallows were gathering to go away to the moon for the winter and Lucy felt uneasy. She was not going to the moon for the winter, she kept reminding herself, and her thoughts turned to Christmas in the great hall, the yule log leaping into golden flame, the kissing ring gay with ribbons and gleaming berries and the wassail bowl smelling of raisins and honey.

"Not much longer to Christmas," she said one evening to Gwladys the cook as she stood beside her in the kitchen watching her make suckets. With a long two-pronged fork she was packing fruit into earthenware jars. Presently she would fill up the jars with thick syrup, seal them and put them away. They would reappear at Christmas and the plums and ginger and blackberries would have become sucket sweetmeats such as the children loved.

" 'Tis greedy you are, Lucy fach," said Gwladys, but she laughed and gave her a handful of blackberries. Lucy crunched them with pleasure for though she had had her supper she was a child who always had room for more. She was wearing her nightshift stuffed into Richard's breeches, for Nan-Nan had put her to bed and left her apparently sleeping a quarter of an hour ago.

"Only young ones want winter," said John Shepherd. He was sitting on the seat inside the chimney by the fire and Lucy went to him and laid a hand upon his knee, for he had spoken sadly. There was no one in the kitchen except herself and John Shepherd and old Gwladys, for the young servants had gone to a merrymaking at the inn. The kitchen, so empty, seemed vast, like a cavern inside a mountain as she looked at it from the inside of the chimney, that was as big as a little room. The firelight was reflected in the pewter plates on the great dresser, and the rows of jugs on the hooks. In the centre of the stone floor was the castle well, a deep dark place where sometimes there were rumblings as of thunder. Lucy adored the kitchen. Here, where hummocks of rock showed among the uneven stone flags, one was down among the tree roots. From these rocks, the fire and the dark depth of water, the castle and its life had grown. She herself had grown from this, she thought, from the fire and the water and the rock. And from John Shepherd. Standing beside him, her hand still on his knee, she felt suddenly that he was as much a part of her beginning as her father and mother and Nan-Nan. Gwladys too. Such men and women had held it all up for generation after generation and when they did not do so the tree would fall. Yet no one considered them down here among the roots. They

93

were not remembered. She turned and put her arm round John Shepherd's neck and stood for a moment with her face pressed against his cheek. Then she ran to Gwladys and flung her arms as far round the old woman's vast waist as they would go. Then she burst into tears and vanished up the stone steps to the hall, so quickly that they scarcely saw her go. Gwladys turned to John Shepherd, her eyebrows raised in concern.

"Once in a generation they come," he said. "One of the Ty-lwyth Teg, born to an 'ooman."

"Silly old man," said Gwladys good-humouredly, but she remained disturbed. "It was as though she bade us farewell," she added.

"There's change coming," said John Shepherd.

"What sort of change?" asked Gwladys sharply, for John Shepherd was known to have the two sights.

But he hedged and said less than he knew. "A storm there'll be by morning," he said.

"Not a cloud in the sky," said Gwladys, looking out of the window. "So still it is out there you can hear the fish in the sea jumping."

"It's coming down the birds are," said John Shepherd.

"Coming down?" said Gwladys gravely. As a countrywoman she knew the meaning of this. The migrating birds, reaching the coast, knew it was not safe to go on over the sea.

The hall door was still open and Lucy ran down the steps and through the garden, across the road and through the hedge. She was still crying as she ran barefoot through the tuffety grass and heather, and was unaware that birds were dropping silently about her, but by the time she reached the edge of the cliff the sadness that pressed upon her had become too heavy for tears. It came partly from the new sorrow of the sin-eater, that had opened the door within her to the sorrow of the world, but also from something that she knew without knowing what it was that she knew. John Shepherd must know it too, she had felt it in him when she put her arms round his neck.

She stood knee-deep in tawny bracken and the vast sky above her was the dim gold of very old beaten metal, thunder gold. Yet there was no haze or oppression of thunder. The only hint of storm was the deep eerie boom of the tide in the caves below the cliff. The sea was calm gold, yet below the surface Lucy knew it must be stirring around the tree trunks of Cantre'r Gwaelod, the lost land under the waves. The orange sun was low over the sea, the path of its reflection trembling a little on the surface of the gold, but Lucy tonight would not see the green flash as it disappeared into the sea, for above the horizon was a bank of cloud the colour of the fading heather. The sun reached it and sank slowly, and then all the cloud bank was edged with fire. It grew colder and the land darkened and it seemed to Lucy that the sky reflected the darkness. Then from somewhere far down below her, from some hidden cave, came a great and tragic cry, like some heartbroken prophet crying out in despair at what he had seen. Coming at such a moment the seal's cry seemed dreadful to Lucy and she turned and fled inland.

It was then she became aware of the birds. They were coming down from the sky like drifting autumn leaves, martins, chaffinches, goldfinches and linnets, finding their way to the bracken-sheltered hollows and the warm dry hedges and the safe crannies of the rocks. Lucy had watched the bird migrations before but she had never seen one halted like this, halted as the warning sounded along the shore. She stood still, scarcely breathing, her arms out and her face turned up to the darkening sky, and they had no fear of her. A wing brushed her cheek and just for a moment some tired little being alighted on her hand, putting on one finger for ever the memory of a tiny claw that clung like a wedding ring. It was for her a moment of ecstasy, of marriage with all living creatures, of unity with life itself, and she whispered in Welsh, "Dear God, this happiness is too great for me!" Then she began to cry again and she no longer saw the birds, only heard them and felt them, drifting and rustling, their colours muted in the twilight, glad to drift upon the tides of the air, to fall and sleep.

The sheep and the cows were standing bunched together when she at last came to herself and ran across the fields.

2

The sea was loud all night though the wind came at first only in sudden flurries that brought no rain, only the mutter of thunder and the flicker of lightning against the darkness of the clouds that came up out of the west, putting out the stars one by one. There was no stopping them. There was nothing one could do. The coming storm was like blood welling from a deep wound. It was raining by morning, the thunder heat had vanished and the wind was fresher. By the early afternoon it was half a gale, the cloud mass had broken up and the clouds were racing across the sky like hounds let loose. They were the Cwn Annwn, Lucy told Justus, as they knelt in the window-seat of the oriel window in the hall, their faces pressed against the streaming pane, the dogs of storm that hunt lost souls across the sky.

They played games for the rest of the afternoon but with diminishing enthusiasm, for the gale increased with a steadiness that was alarming even to children who had grown up to take the storms beyond the window as much for granted as town children take the traffic rumbling by. They were disturbed too by their mother's white face and their father's restlessness. Even Nan-Nan did not appear quite herself. She told them stories as she put them to bed, and she sang the fretful twins to sleep, but her voice had weariness in it. Lucy did not sleep much that night. She remembered how she had heard the seal crying. Storms like this could dash seals to their death upon the rocks.

By the next morning both land and sea were drowned in rain and the waves crashed along the coast, mile after mile of continuous thunder. There was no question now of the children going down to the shore, they could not have stood against the wind, but William went out continually, his men with him, even John Shepherd, who always refused to be counted among the women when any danger threatened men or beasts. The women went about their tasks hardly knowing what they were doing, their faces taut with the strain of listening.

In the afternoon the rain stopped and an hour before sunset, when the tide turned, the wind gradually slackened. Great gusts still flung themselves at the castle with the booming of cannon, but between whiles came islands of peace when there was no sound of wind or rain, only the continual roar of the waves. It was in one of these moments of respite that they heard the gun they had been listening for, and knew that a ship was on the rocks. Richard, kept within doors until now only by the command of his father, was suddenly away like the wind before anyone could stop him. Elizabeth, who had been sitting embroidering by the fire, suddenly cried out and dropped her work in the ashes and Lucy ran to her. But she was not ill, it seemed, only suddenly brought to the end of her tether by Richard's danger. She allowed Lucy and Nan-Nan to put her to bed, give her a hot brick at her feet and pull the curtains round her, and took refuge within them from all that the night might bring.

Richard, soaked to the skin with spray, soon came dashing back, sent by William, to report that the wreck was just outside their own bay on their own rocks, and was gone again at once leaving the women in the castle in a flurry of preparation in case there should be survivors to be cared for. The flurry made it easy for Lucy and Justus to follow Richard.

He had not waited for them and they had not expected that he would. Lucy was hindered by her skirt, Justus by his weight and tender years, but even so they made good speed down the lane. For a moment, as she ran, Lucy remembered that the hedges were hiding a host of little birds sheltering warm and snug.

When they reached the bay it seemed already full of people, fishermen from hamlets along the coast, William and his men and a few women with shawls over their heads; they were wailing and the men shouting, for the drama was at its height and Welsh emotion at fever pitch. The wind had dropped now but sea and sky were still as dramatic as the men and women in the bay. The clouds were lit with the sunset and the waves came in like charge after charge of cavalry, their spume flung to a great height. In all the movement and turmoil the eye

could find only two centres of calm on which to rest, the
wrecked ship itself, wedged between two rocks, sometimes seen
for a moment then hidden again as the waves leaped at it, and
all along the horizon, where two nights ago there had been
that ominous bank of cloud, a long streak of tranquil lemon-
coloured sky. It would lift and lift all night, Lucy knew, until it
had imposed its tranquillity over the land and sea, and then all
the little birds hidden in the hedges would fly away.

Then she forgot the birds in the knowledge that men were
on that motionless ship and that they too were quiet; unable to
do anything more to help themselves. It was the people on
shore who were in a turmoil, for they did not know what to do.
It seemed impossible to launch small boats in this sea and
though the tide was going out it had nearly reached its limit
and would not bring the ship much nearer to them. But someone had brought ropes and a brawny fisherman climbed to the
top of Lucy's special rock holding one of them, gathering his
strength for the throw. William followed with another rope
and Lucy scrambled up to be with her father. He exclaimed
angrily, but let her stay. The moments of waiting were tense
with the expectation that at any moment the battered ship
might go to pieces. Then, with a shout from the bay, the rope
was flung. It fell short but was flung again, and again, and now
there was no more tumult, only shouts of command, and
finally a yell of triumph when the rope was caught and secured and the first man was seen coming down it to the sea. A
second rope was flung and men from the shore went out along
it to meet the exhausted men from the wreck. They went
out with the waves over their heads and seemed to disappear,
so that the women cried out. William leapt down from the
rock with Lucy, whom he then pulled from him and flung
away like a burr, and went out through the waves. And so did
John Shepherd.

They passed through the wall of water and Lucy did not see
them any more. It was as though a door had slammed in her
face, and was her first experience of terror. She stood still, her
mouth vacantly open, her hands twisted up in the stuff of
her dress. Men shouted at her to get out of the way and the

water washed round her ankles but she did not move. She did not see anything but the wall of water where the door was that might not open again. They had gone. From the rock beside her father she had seen the men on the wreck and her mind had known that they were in danger of death, but death then had seemed distant, something she did not know about, dreadful perhaps but exciting and mysterious like all unknown things. But it was not like that now. It was very simple. It meant that at one moment the person you loved best in the world was alive and warm beside you and the next there was no one there. She was stunned by the terror of this reversal. The fight to get the men in was going on all about her but she was too deeply shocked to know about it. She simply watched the wall of water that fell, and rose again immediately, but did not return her father and John Shepherd to her.

Justus pulling at her skirts brought her back, for she loved Justus best after Nan-Nan and William. "Our father said to go home at once," said Justus.

She swung round and at the same moment a beam of sunset light shone through a breaking cloud like a long finger of brightness and touched William. She saw him kneeling with his back to her, bending over a man who lay on his back on the sand, and suddenly the dreadful reversal was the other way round, from death to life. She flew to him, hitting out with her clenched fists at men in her path, and flung her arms round his neck. She could not speak but the stranglehold of her arms was the last straw for William at that moment. "S'truth! Lucy, get away," he swore at her. "Take Justus and go home, for God's sake." The face he turned up to her was a mask of exhaustion and anger but she did not mind being sworn at if he was alive. Then looking over his shoulder she saw the man who lay on the sand with his eyes shut. It was John Shepherd, but John so different that he no longer looked like himself. The shock came back. "John Shepherd is dead," she said.

"Not yet, the old fool!" said William, and pulling her arms from his neck he pushed her away from him. "Take her home, Justus," he said. "And where's Richard? Richard!"

His voice had risen to a roar, so like the roar of a wild beast

in grief and rage that it brought Richard running to him.
"Take these children home. What the devil were you doing
letting them come here at all? Take them home."

Richard marched them along in fury, driving them before
him like a herd of cattle. The ignominy of being rent from the
excitement on the beach to take the young ones home stuck in
his gizzard, but not sufficiently to impede speech. His opinion
of them buzzed and spat about their ears so nastily that half
way home Lucy swung round, twisted her hands in his wet
hair, braced herself with her knee in his stomach and pulled.
He stamped on her feet and she hit him on the nose and made
it bleed. Justus sat down on the wet bank to wait. He was tired
and very miserable because of John Shepherd. He cried
softly.

The affair ended as quickly as it had begun because Lucy
heard his weeping. She pulled him up out of the hedge and
they stumbled on together.

3

Of the evening of confusion that followed Lucy afterwards
recalled very little, though she remembered that Nan-Nan put
them to bed and that she got up again, crept past their
mother's fourposter to the dais and looked down on the scene
in the hall, dark now and lit by candles and firelight. The
shipwrecked men were being cared for there, the servants were
going backwards and forwards and Parson Peregrine and her
father were helping to look after them. The scene was wild
and strange for the candles flickered in the draught, the flames
of the hearth leaped and died and shadows rose and fell like
waves, revealing the men's faces then drowning them again in
darkness. It was as though the storm still broke over them all,
but silently. The noise of it was gone but the suffering ebbed
slowly. And she could not see John Shepherd.

She was caught by Nan-Nan and taken back to bed again.
"Where is John Shepherd?" she asked.

"In the kitchen," said Nan-Nan cheerfully. "It's warm there
by the fire. Better for him than in his own cottage with none to

care for him. He's tired and cold but not injured at all. Don't fret now, cariad. Tell me, am I to lock you into the nursery or will you stay in your bed near your mother?"

"I will stay," promised Lucy, for being locked in made her want to swear. Indeed in her younger days she had done so, beating her fists black and blue on the locked nursery door, and she felt she would have done the same thing tonight, as she lay in the darkness thinking about the storm and John Shepherd. She did not sleep well and with the first light she got up and dressed and went barefoot across the bedchamber and down through the hall.

The rescued sailors, wrapped in blankets, were lying about the fire asleep, safe and warm. It made her heart glow to think that Roch had saved them and now sheltered them. She went through the screens and down the stone steps to the kitchen. There was no one there except John Shepherd lying on a truckle bed by the fire, but someone must have been there on and off through the night, she thought, because the fire had not died down to ash but was burning well. She knelt by the old man and looked at him. His face was grey and his closed eyes seemed to have fallen back inside his head, and his cheeks had fallen in too. His mouth was open and his breath came in shallow gasps. The sour smell of old age came from him and the smell of death. But Lucy was not shocked or frightened, only furiously angry. Why should this happen to John Shepherd? He was a good old man and he had been trying to help save life down in the bay. Why should this happen? Why was not someone doing something? Why was he alone like this? She fumbled among the blankets and found his hand and held it, but he did not seem to know. She talked to him, telling him how much she loved him, but he did not seem to hear what she said. Then she began to cry and her tears dripped down on his hand, but he did not move. Then Gwladys came in, looking very puffy about the eyes as though it was she who had been up all night with John Shepherd, and told Lucy to go back to bed. "There's nothing you can do, cariad," she said. "The doctor came last night, and the parson, and could do nothing. John Shepherd is an old man, with his heart not strong at all, and he had no business to go down to the bay. Silly old fool!" And then she began to cry too. "He will not speak again," she sobbed.

And then John Shepherd suddenly surprised her, for he opened his eyes and spoke. "With all my sins upon me," he whispered in despair, and then he closed his eyes and his head upon the pillow began slowly turning from side to side. Lucy took his hand again and nothing that Gwladys could say to her would make her let go. Gwladys in despair fetched Nan-Nan, and then William, but she would not go. "Let her alone," said William at last. "We cannot have her screaming. Poor Bud, she has got to know one day."

John Shepherd lived until nearly midday. Screens were placed round the chimney corner where he lay, and though the work and traffic in the kitchen were heavy that morning men and women came and went silently, and Lucy scarcely heard them. But she knew just when John Shepherd died. A flame leaped in the fire and she turned her head towards the sudden explosion of light. When she looked back again John Shepherd had ceased to breathe. She could not believe it at first and she knelt on, still holding his hand. Then she knew. John Shepherd had gone through the door and this time he would not come back. She would never talk to him again. Some disasters could be righted but not this one. Yesterday she had feared without knowledge, as men fear pain who have never felt it burn into their own flesh, but now knowledge struck into her soul, not like burning but like the frost of winter. She no longer cried but shivered from head to foot. If this could happen at any moment to those one loved then all peace of mind was gone for ever, as John Shepherd was gone for ever. There was no foothold anywhere and she was appalled. Yet still she knelt on holding his hand. To do so was a sort of loyalty. She would not forsake the dead.

Someone came round the screens and cried out, and then they once more fetched William. He picked her up and this time she could not resist because she had no more strength. She was put to bed with a hot brick at her feet and given a hot posset and for most of the day she dozed exhaustedly, and

Nan-Nan sat by her darning the boys' stockings, and now and then her mother came. But whenever she woke she heard John Shepherd saying, "With all my sins upon me," and by the time the evening came she knew what he had meant. Busy with the sheep he had had no time to repent of his sins as Old Parson did, weeping and praying and going on pilgrimage. Death had come suddenly while he was still wearing them all like a dirty old coat. He would, she knew, be washed and wrapped in a shroud and go clean into his coffin. But not entirely clean if he still had those dirty sins. She must fetch the sin-eater.

When Nan-Nan was putting the twins to bed and Elizabeth had gone to her bower Lucy got up and dressed. The rescued seamen, none of whom had been seriously injured, had gone now to Solva and quietness had fallen on the castle. The day was turning westard as she ran through the garden and out to the lane, with an almost transparent veil of silver cloud spread thin as cobwebs over the golden sky. The mist lay like lamb's-wool in the hollows and there was no wind any more, only the boom of the waves along the coast, because the sea was not yet as quiet as the land. But the little birds would all have gone away, she thought. If she had been out on the cliffs she might have seen them coming out from the sheltered places, spreading their wings and spiring up to the unseen roads of the sky that went she knew not where. If any of them could look down upon her they would not know where her road went either, as she ran down the hill and was lost in the white lamb's-wool that filled the hollows of Brandy cwm.

The mist hid her from the eyes of the mill as she climbed up through the trees. It was almost dark under their branches and she found her way more by instinct than by sight. She did not doubt that she would find the scapegoat and just beyond the big rock she saw his dim figure, sitting with his hands dropped between his knees and his head upon his breast. She gave her clear bird call and he lifted his head but he did not move. It was as though he knew her purpose and was not now trying to escape from her. She came and knelt down beside him almost as though he were John Shepherd himself, and she said carefully in Welsh, "John Shepherd is dead," and she laid her clasped hands upon her breast and then upon his breast, to tell him of the load that must be lifted from one to another, and he sighed and got slowly to his feet. At the sound of the sigh she would have cried if she could, for its weariness was so great, but she had no tears left. She took his hand and they went together down through the wood and up the hill. They went slowly as though they were trying to make each moment together last as long as possible. All the burden of human parting was upon them, of human longing for complete understanding, and the failure of it, of shared sorrow in the sorrow of a bent world, of grief for impermanence and death. They understood none of it; only that this was the last time they would be together. He could not know how deeply he had touched the springs of compassion in her, for the benefit of other men rather than himself, nor did she know the value to him of her brief kindness. In the mystery of things it had been necessary that they should have been together. They only knew that to cease to do so was hard.

There was a door leading directly into the kitchen and they did not need to climb the steps to the hall. Gwladys was busy by the fire and several of the servants were there too, preparing the evening meal. Shadows and firelight chased each other over the high ceiling and there was laughter and talk, which dropped to instant horrified silence as Lucy and the sin-eater came in. The servants shrank back in loathing and the sin-eater in fear. Lucy, holding his hand firmly, kept close to him in protection.

"Where is John Shepherd?" she asked in a clear high voice. "This man has come to take away his sins."

Gwladys, whitefaced, came forward. "Thinking myself I was we should have the sin-eater," she said. "Come this way, cariad."

She took up a lump of barley bread and a piece of cold meat from the table and led the way to the archway at the corner of the kitchen. Beyond it was a little round room from which a stone staircase led to the servants' sleeping-quarters above the kitchen. John Shepherd lay here on a trestle-table with a sheet over him, waiting for his coffin. Gwladys turned down the sheet and laid the bread and meat upon his breast and then stood at his feet. The sin-eater stood on one side of John Shepherd and Lucy on the other, her back to the archway, looking down on John Shepherd's face that had become unrecognizable, frozen and profoundly quiet, but nothing to do with John Shepherd. The servants, huddled together, watched from beyond the archway. The sin-eater opened his slack mouth and strange sounds began to come out of it, rasping sounds at first, then words half-choked in his throat, as though he had no control over his voice. He spoke in an unknown tongue, Welsh perhaps, but a Welsh older than anything Lucy knew, an incantation that had come from so long ago that it brought the stench of old evil with it, a whiff of vileness more horrible than the smell of the man's unwashed body and rags of clothes. The sin-eater beat his breast as he spoke and his whole body trembled, and his eyes were as bright as though he had a fever. The incantation ceased as it had begun and he began to wolf the food, stuffing it into his mouth and choking it down in a manner so horrible that Lucy felt sick. She also felt extremely frightened, for this creature was no more her scapegoat than the corpse on the table was John Shepherd. It seemed as though there were two sorts of death and they had taken her two friends.

Then one of them was alive again, for there was no more evil. As Gwladys pulled up the sheet the sin-eater looked at Lucy and gave her what he had never given her before, the ghost of a wintry smile, as though he was glad he had done her will. His eyes were no longer bright but the trembling continued, and after he had smiled at her he shrank back against the wall, looking towards the archway with terror. Lucy turned round and saw the servants. They had come nearer to the archway and already they were beginning to mutter angrily. Lucy had a sudden panicky feeling that they had got the sin-eater cornered as though he were a badger or fox. If he tried to leave the little room they would do him some harm. Gwladys seemed to feel the same for she cried out sharply, "Now then! Now then! Let the poor man go."

Rage fell upon Lucy. She ran out of the archway like an

angry swan whose cygnet has been threatened and fell upon them. "Get back!" she cried, striking at them with her fists. "If you hurt him I will tell my father."

Then she darted back to the scapegoat, seized his hand and ran with him across the kitchen, and the servants drew back and let them go. They came out into the garden and to safety, but a few moments before William and Elizabeth had come down from the hall to walk a little in the quiet garden before supper. Seeing them the scapegoat wrenched his hand from Lucy and ran as though for his life, brushing against Elizabeth's skirt as he fled past her. Lucy never forgot her mother's scream.

4

In the days that followed Lucy felt like a small distracted furious toad living at the bottom of a turgid pond. For one thing the bad weather came back again, no more storms but ceaseless rain or drifting mist, cold, dark and clammy. And inside the castle things were not much better, with Elizabeth alternately crying on her bed or arguing with William behind the locked door of her bower. The servants were morose and insolent, left too much to themselves by a mistress who no longer cared what they did, and the twins caught colds in the head and were irritable and grizzly. Only Nan-Nan was herself, loving and gentle with them all, but she had aged, and Lucy was haunted by a remark of hers that she had overheard. "Yes, madam love," Nan-Nan had said, "I think as you do now." What did Nan-Nan think? Lucy's intuition told her that Nan-Nan had somehow turned against her and was not protecting her from some threatening danger. It was this that made her feel like the toad, flapping around in blinding mud with a weight of dark water over his head and no friend to help him out.

Richard, Lucy and Justus drew together. This was to Lucy the one ray of light that came down to the mud; that Richard was now close to her and Justus. One day the three of them ran out together through the rain and sat in the arbour and he told them what he had discovered. Their parents now spent much of each night talking within the curtains of the four-poster, and sometimes, forgetting the children, they raised their voices. Lucy wriggled down under the blankets when she began to hear what they were saying but Richard had no compunction in getting out of bed and listening behind the curtain. In this way he had pieced it together. "Our mother says she will not have the new baby here. The sin-eater has overlooked it and if she has it here it will die like the other two. She says the castle is haunted and full of evil. She says we must all go to London for a year and live close to her mother and she will have the baby there. Our father says she can have it at Haverfordwest or Golden Grove or anywhere near at hand that she likes, or she can go to London without him, but *he* won't go to London."

"What does Nan-Nan say?" asked Lucy under her breath.

"Nan-Nan is on our mother's side. I think she is frightened of the sin-eater too. I heard our mother tell our father that Nan-Nan thought a year in London would be good for you. Stop your running wild. Turn you into a young lady." He kicked her good-humouredly but for once she did not kick back. Nan-Nan to try to take them from Roch! The hurt was so great she could not speak.

A few days later, just before they went to bed, William called them to come and talk to him in the hall. Elizabeth was in the nursery with Nan-Nan and William and his three eldest were alone. He sat with Justus on his knees and Lucy and Richard beside him on the settle that he had pulled in front of the fire. It was raining as usual and the sad drops hissed in the flames. He told them what they knew already, but other things too. They would be leaving in a few weeks. They would go first to Golden Grove, and the children and their mother and Nan-Nan would stay there while he went on to London to find a house that he could rent for the winter. When he had found it they would follow him to London. He said heavily that they would like it in London. Richard and Justus would be able to go to a good school. Lucy would learn many feminine accomplishments from her dear grandmother, and others, and would become a little lady. They would see the sights of London, the King and Queen and the lions at the Tower, and so on. Above all it would be good for their dear mother's health, and that was the chief consideration just at present. The castle would not be left empty and the servants without work for their other grandmother, his mother, who after his father's death had married again, would come with her husband Nicholas Chappell and live here until they all came back again. The work of the farm and estate would go on as usual with Howel Perrot in charge. Yes, it would be a nice change for them all, William concluded wretchedly, and the time would pass, and now they had better go to bed. The boys, feeling already a pleasurable excitement, were kissed and blessed and went to bed, but Lucy refused to budge. She took Justus's place on her father's knee.

"Let them all go to London," she said. "You and I will stay here."

"But your mother tells me that you told her, some months ago, that you would enjoy a visit to London," said William.

"I said I would not mind seeing the King and Queen and lions," said Lucy. "But I would just like to see them and then come home again."

"It's only for the winter," said William.

"If we once go to London will my mother ever want to come home again?" asked Lucy.

Her intuition matched his own. They had the same fear. There was a silence and then Lucy flung her arms round his neck. "Do not go!" she pleaded. "Stay here with me!"

"Lucy," he whispered, "I am in debt. I owe a lot of money. Nicholas Chappell, God bless him, will shoulder the expenses of Roch while he is here. In London we can live very cheaply."

"That's not why you are going to London," she whispered back. "You are going to please madam my mother."

"She's a sick woman," he said, "and she is frightened here. More frightened than ever since the sin-eater. That was your fault, Bud."

"Yes," Lucy agreed. "It was a pity, and my mother should go away, but not you and me."

"She will not go without me, Bud. Nan-Nan says we must all keep together."

"Nan-Nan is wrong," she said. "You and I should stay here."

"We all stick together, Bud," he said with finality and she accepted the decision. They clung together in silence until the fire died down, and then he carried her to her little room, helped her to bed with clumsy tenderness, kissed her and blessed her. She lay awake for a long time listening to the rain sighing and rustling round the castle tower. Beyond their sorrow she could just hear the boom of the sea. How did one live away from the sound of the sea?

5

Elizabeth was not herself. The storm and then the sight of the sin-eater in the garden had caused deep shock and she could scarcely wait to get away from Roch. William's temper was continually cracking beneath the strain and one wet afternoon, when the children were roasting nuts before the fire, the door of the bower burst open and he came storming down the hall in a flaming temper, his face scarlet and tears on his cheeks. He strode past the three children without even seeing them and they heard the hall door crash behind him as he went out into the rain with neither cloak nor hat. Lucy would have flown after him but for Richard's restraining hand. "Let him go," said Richard. "He's drunk."

"He's not!" said Lucy.

"He has been drunk for three days,' said Richard. "Ever since our mother told him."

"Told him what?" demanded Lucy.

"Never you mind," said Richard in his maddening way. "I heard them talking. I know but I'm not going to tell you. Ask Nan-Nan."

Lucy leapt to her feet and ran to Nan-Nan, who was packing gowns and linen in the big bedchamber. She had not been well for three days and she had not been able to eat. Absorbed in her packing she did not hear Lucy come in and the child stood for a moment watching her in dismay. She looked smaller than ever and she was weeping. Never before had Lucy seen Nan-Nan cry. "Nan-Nan!" she gasped.

The old woman looked round and tried to smile but her control broke. She struggled to a stool and sitting down she rocked herself, crying out her grief in the Welsh tongue, lamenting as her forbears had lamented in centuries gone by when a sorrow had been too fearful to be borne. Lucy shut the door of the bedchamber and ran to Nan-Nan, flinging her arms round her and begging her to stop. "What is it, Nan-Nan?" she cried. "What is it?"

"Dewi and Betsi," sobbed Nan-Nan. "My lambs, my lambs!"

"But their colds are well now," said Lucy.

Nan-Nan shook her head helplessly. She was still rocking herself but no longer lamenting and presently she could speak coherently. "When I heard your father go down the hall I knew your mother had won her way," she said at last. "My lambs will be taken from me." Now that she had put it into words she was quiet and composed again and wiped her eyes on her apron.

"Taken from you?" gasped Lucy. "But we are all going to London together. My father said so."

"No," said Nan-Nan. "Not Dewi and Betsi."

Lucy could not understand it. "Not Dewi and Betsi?" she repeated stupidly.

Nan-Nan looked anxiously at Lucy. From her earliest childhood the adventurous little girl had been running away from the nursery whenever possible, making friends with the servants in the kitchen and the men and animals on the farm, and that she had painlessly absorbed the facts of life at an early age Nan-Nan was well aware, from a few carelessly dropped remarks of Lucy's which at the time had caused her acute dismay. But now she was glad. It was possible now to speak openly to a child too honest to be deceived by lies.

"Lucy fach, your mother will not take Dewi and Betsi to London, nor will she ever have them with us again. She does not love them at all. Have you noticed that?"

Lucy went white. Two years ago she and Richard and Justus had been sent to stay with their grandmother Madam Chappell and when they came back the babies had been in their cradles. She had wondered sometimes that her mother never took them in her arms or rocked the cradles. William often played with them, but not Elizabeth. But then her mother was never as openly affectionate as her father and it had not bothered her. "Why does my mother not love them?" she asked.

"Because they are not her children, Lucy fach."

"They are my father's children?"

"Yes, cariad."

Lucy was silent for a long time and Nan-Nan wondered anxiously just how far the child's comprehension went. Then Lucy said, "Dewi and Betsi are bastards."

"Yes, cariad. But none the less my sweet lambs for that," and she began to cry again, but quietly now.

Lucy shook Nan-Nan, her cheeks flaming. She was over the shock now and more angry than she had ever been. "What is to happen to Dewi and Betsi?" she demanded.

"They are to go to their mother," Nan-Nan sobbed. "She did not want them at the time, but now she is married to a man who has a farm at the foot of the mountains and he is willing to have them if your father pays well for their keep. But it is a rough life they will have there. Oh my lambs, my lambs!" and she began to rock herself again.

"Stop wailing, Nan-Nan!" said Lucy angrily. "What use to wail? I hate my mother."

Dismay seized Nan-Nan. In her weakness and sorrow she had been talking to Lucy as though she were adult. Now what had she done? "Do not say that, cariad," she implored. "Your poor mother has had more to try her than you know. When you are older you will understand her better. And she is a sick woman now. Oh duwch, duwch! What have I done, setting you against your mother? There now, I should never have told you."

Her distress was so great that Lucy's compassion, that was now the strongest thing in her, broke out through her anger.

They were both sitting on the floor now and she put her arms round the old woman and pressed her cheek against hers. "Do you remember your 'seeing', Nan-Nan? You said that Dewi would be a happy man and that a king would love him. And you said Betsi belonged with the thrush and the falling dew, and that sounded nice too. So do not cry, Nan-Nan."

Nan-Nan was a little happier. For a moment or two she clung to Lucy, then turned again to the comfort of work. She knelt upright and continued with her packing, and Lucy helped her. Presently she was so far recovered as to find this an occasion for improving the shining hour, a thing she delighted to do.

"Lucy fach," she said, "let this be a warning to you. You see the trouble that comes of children born out of wedlock. Never lie with a man, cariad, without your marriage lines."

It was Lucy's turn to burst suddenly into a storm of tears. "Never!" she sobbed. "Oh, poor Dewi and Betsi! Poor babies!"

Six

The departure of Dewi and Betsi left a scar on Lucy, or something more than a scar, for the wound never quite healed. That good people like her father and mother could throw two babies out of their nest as though they were of no more worth than a couple of sparrows shocked her deeply, and frightened her too. For the first time she was aware of sin as something that tangled up all human life, even the life of her father and mother and their children. She was never entirely a child again after Dewi and Betsi went away.

They did not understand and they laughed with delight when out in the lane Nan-Nan settled them in the panniers one on each side of Jeremiah's broad back, for they loved riding in the panniers. Jeremiah was going away too for he was to be the twins' pony at the farm and he seemed to know that he would never come back to Roch. He looked round once, turning his comical face towards Lucy, and his eyes met hers with a sadness deep as his love. Then William swung himself on to his horse and Jeremiah's bridle was handed up to him by his groom, for he was himself taking the twins to the farm at the foot of the mountain. He did not look at anyone either and his face was tight and hard with grief, but Lucy could not just now be sorry for him. The little cavalcade moved off, the groom riding behind. They turned the corner by the church and Betsi and Jeremiah went out of Lucy's life for ever. She and Nan-Nan turned and went back to the nursery where Lucy flung herself on the floor and burst into a flood of tears so wild that even Nan-Nan, used to her passions, was taken aback. It was a long while before she could be calmed and when at last she stopped crying she was so exhausted that she had to be put to bed.

The worst being past, Nan-Nan now became outwardly very

cheerful and busy. But for her they would never have got away
at all, but with infinite tact she persuaded and gently bullied
the family and household through the earthquake of packing
and leave-taking and then upheld them through the final pulling up of roots. "Only for six months," they had been saying to
everyone else, but when it came to the end they did not believe
what they said.

It was a still, grey October day. Lucy, dressed in her travelling clothes, was alone in the garden. The rest of the family
were still in the castle with William's mother and stepfather
and outside in the lane the coach and horses waited. The
silence seemed the deeper because up in the hall there had
been two final disagreements. William had said his wife must
travel on horseback, not in the coach, for the jolting of the
coach was more likely to bring on a miscarriage than riding.
Elizabeth had declared herself far too exhausted to ride. If the
events of the last few weeks had not caused her to drop this
child, nothing would, and she was going in the coach with
Nan-Nan, Lucy, Justus and Jano. Lucy on the other hand
had said that whoever was going in the coach she was not.
She was going to ride pillion with her father. Elizabeth had
said she was to do no such thing. The two allied arguments had raged with fury for ten minutes and then ceased
abruptly with victory for Elizabeth on both counts, because
Nan-Nan appeared upon the scene and said she was not to
be worried.

The quietness in the garden, after the arguments, was deep
as the quietness of John Shepherd's dying. It was a warm day
but Lucy was cold from head to foot. The family came down
the castle steps, the servants following at a respectful distance,
and they all moved silently out to the coach and horses.
Gwilym Thomas the coachman, Madog the postilion and the
man who drove the luggage cart were going with them to
Golden Grove. William was to ride Eve his chestnut mare and
Richard was to ride Prince. It was a confusing business getting
Elizabeth, Nan-Nan, the children, Jano and the bundles and
baskets settled inside the coach, but it broke the spell of silence
and when they moved off at last it was to a chorus of goodbyes

and good wishes, crunching wheels and the cracking of
Gwilym Coachman's whip.

As they rounded the corner they saw Howel Perrot, who
with his wife and brother and Parson Peregrine had come to
wave goodbye. Howel had Shôn and Twm on leash, for they
were to stay behind. Lucy saw their eyes and knew that they
understood as Betsi and Dewi had not been able to understand. And the last thing she saw, as they rounded the corner,
was Old Parson standing on a gravestone in the churchyard to
wave to them. He waved cheerfully, serene in his new-found
peace, confident that the departure was not for long. The
coach swayed and rumbled down the road to the bridge and
there was a heron standing by the brook. He turned his head
and looked at them and Lucy saw in his glance contemptuous
reproach, and soon after that she made a dive for the coach
window and was sick, and afterwards so faint that the cavalcade was halted; but seeing her father's anxious face looking
in at the window she was immediately much better. "The
coach sways too much for my stomach," she said in a voice
surprisingly strong for one so stricken. "I must ride with my
father."

Riding pillion behind William, the easy motion of the
horse beneath her and the air blowing about her, Lucy sighed
with relief and her spirits rose. The road to Golden Grove by
way of Haverfordwest and Carmarthen was one she had
travelled before, but she did not remember it clearly. Once
their cavalcade had creaked and clattered through the little
town of Haverfordwest she was no longer in familiar territory
and a sense of adventure came to her. She began to sing a little
song to herself and William smiled as the fountain of clear
notes sprang up in the small of his back. With Bud turning
cheerful once more things seemed not so bad.

Travelling so slowly they took three days to reach Carmarthen, an uneventful journey through misty rain with two
stops along the way at uncomfortable inns, coming to the little
town just as a lemon-coloured sun shone through the mist.
Carmarthen stood at the head of the tide water of the river
Towy and was the capital of South Wales and a stronghold of

the ancient Welsh blood, especially dear to William because his ancestor, and Elizabeth's too, Rhys ap Thomas, the greatest Welshman since the days of Owen Glendower, was buried here.

When the exhausted Elizabeth had been deposited in the best inn, with Nan-Nan to look after her, William took his three children swaggering through the streets of the capital to do homage at the great man's tomb in St. Peter's Church. Rhys ap Thomas and his lady lay carved in stone at the south end of the chancel, and the four of them stood in a row looking down at their ancestors with awe and pride. "Your great-great-great-great-greatgrandfather on my side, your great-great-great-greatgrandfather on your mother's side," William told his offspring and they counted on their fingers carefully; five greats on one side and four on the other made the great man very great indeed. "The Welshman Henry the Seventh would never have got to the throne of England without the help of Rhys ap Thomas," said William impressively. "He struck down the Yorkist king with his own hand and was knighted on the field of Bosworth by Henry himself. He became a Knight of the Garter and governor of South Wales, owning twenty castles."

"Why don't we own twenty castles now?" asked Justus.

William sighed gustily. "Great families are beset by many troubles. Financial troubles especially afflict men of noble minds, openhanded, generous men." He cheered up again. "But do not forget, children, that you have not only your mother's Plantagenet blood in your veins but also the blood of the Welsh princes. These Stuarts who are now on the throne of England, their blood is nothing to yours. As the years go on you may be poor, you may be despised, but the blood in your veins is royal and you must not forget it."

They promised him they never would and Lucy in particular never did. They bowed to Rhys ap Thomas and his lady and swaggered back to the inn.

The rest of the journey to Golden Grove was less fortunate. The first morning began well in brilliant sunshine and they travelled along the northern slope of the valley with the river below them running fast over stony shallows, sparkling from pool to pool, turning in great silver loops about green meadows which were a little flooded now after the rain, the flood water reflecting the brilliant blue of the sky and the white clouds that scudded before the wind. William eyed these clouds a little anxiously, for they travelled fast, but down in the valley it was warm and quiet as midsummer. That was a happy day, but it grew colder towards evening and the blue sky was lost in a tumbled darkness of flying clouds. The inn where they stopped that night was not a comfortable one. The mattresses were lumpy and smelled of mice, the rising wind whined in the chimneys and when the rain began it leaked through the thatch and pattered down on top of the fourposters. Elizabeth did not sleep at all and had a sore throat in the morning. So had Nan-Nan but she did not mention it.

William hurried them out and away very early for he did not like the weather at all and said they must reach Golden Grove before dark. He was irritable and would not let Lucy ride with him and Richard. He did not want a drowned little toad clinging round his waist, he said, catching a sore throat and complaining like her mother. She must go in the coach.

"I shall be sick," she said.

"The world will not end if you are, Bud," he said heartlessly.

So she went in the coach and did not mind too much for there was nothing to be seen outside now but the driving rain. She and Justus played cat's-cradle together, Elizabeth lay back with her eyes shut, and Nan-Nan, opposite them with her back to the horses, sat among the bundles wrapped up in her black cloak, with her black hood over her head, and looked like a small black beetle. Her tiny wrinkled face was grey with fatigue, but when either of the children looked at her she smiled her habitual smile of tender loving delight in them and her eyes in the gloom sparkled like diamonds.

The islands of pastureland they had seen yesterday, held in the loops of the river, disappeared as the hours passed and flood-water and river became one continuous lake slowly rising in the valley. The mud of the road grew deeper and stickier and clung like glue to the coach wheels and the hoofs of the horses. William allowed them only the shortest pause to eat the midday meal of cold meat and bread with which the inn had provided them. Nan-Nan handed supplies out to the men on their dripping horses and Lucy and Justus laughed to see the rivulets of water running off their hats and the ends of their noses, but their amusement was not reciprocated. Now that the creaking of the coach was still they could hear a continuous sound of water, the swollen river rushing over its stones and all the brimming streams coming down from the hills to swell the rising lake in the valley. The running water made almost more noise than the sound of the rain drumming on the coach roof and the soughing of the wind in the trees.

The last crumb swallowed, William hurried them on again but the coach went more and more slowly in the mud. The horses had a tough time dragging it uphill, and when they went downhill the whole outfit slithered so alarmingly that Elizabeth was nervous; and more than nervous when at the bottom of one hill they stuck fast with water swirling about the axles of the wheels. They had come to a dip in the road where water crossed it, no more than a quiet stream in normal weather but a swirling torrent now. To guard against flooding there was a raised plank bridge for pedestrians but it was no good for the coach.

"Drive on, Gwilym," roared William.

"That I cannot, sir," Gwilym Coachman called back. "The wheels are stuck fast."

"Whip up the horses," William commanded angrily.

Gwilym Coachman did so, the horses struggled desperately and with a rending sound the coach heeled over sideways. One of the back wheels, caught between two stones beneath the water, collapsed. Elizabeth gave one sharp cry and then was very quiet, Lucy and Justus rolled to the floor and lay giggling with delight, with Nan-Nan and her bags and bundles on top of them. The coach had not heeled over very far and no water was coming in. "There now," said Nan-Nan, placidly picking herself up. "Do not be afraid, madam my love, for 'tis steady we are now. We shall be righted in a moment."

But William and the servants, wading thigh-deep in water, could not get them righted. The coach was too firmly wedged. With great difficulty they got Elizabeth, Nan-Nan and the children out of it and on to the plank bridge and so across to the road, but the coach had to be abandoned.

"How far are we from Golden Grove?" asked Elizabeth, clinging to her husband, white-faced but fairly calm now, for seventeenth-century ladies were fairly accustomed to these mishaps.

"Four miles," said William. "Bess, girl, shall I leave you here and fetch a coach from Golden Grove or will you ride?"

"I will ride with you," said Elizabeth. "It would be quicker."

For a moment, before they mounted, he held her closely, looking down into her face with loving and questioning concern, and she clung to him as though she drew strength from his sturdy figure, and then looked up at him with the ghost of a reassuring smile. Lucy had never seen them like this before, needing each other, for a moment oblivious of everything except each other. She stared at them, bewildered and too young to understand that because they had made a new life between them, and the third life was in danger, they were shocked into the primeval unity. The picture of them locked together in the rain was one that she carried with her until she died.

The coach horses were unharnessed, William mounted his horse and Elizabeth was lifted up to ride behind him. Justus joined Richard on Prince and Lucy and Nan-Nan rode pillion behind Gwilym and Madog. The most vital of Nan-Nan's bundles were rescued and put in the luggage cart, the rest left in the coach, and the jingling cavalcade of riders started forward again.

They reached Golden Grove without further mishap, rode in through the great gates and saw the green stretches of the park swathed in the light rain that had now succeeded the downpour. Strange beauties were seen, vast tree trunks, a sudden fire of autumn leaves, the lifted head of a deer, a small

Greek temple white as ivory. And then at the end of the tree-lined avenue came the far-away vision of a creeper-covered house, and behind it a steep wooded hill, its summit hidden in the clouds.

Then they were at the foot of a flight of steps, getting off the horses, stiff and wet and tired. Somewhere above them doors were flung open and within the doors there was warmth and light. At the top of the steps Lucy lingered for a moment, trying to find the small child who had come here before in spring sunshine. She felt the roughness of the balustrade under her hand, and heard doves cooing in the rain. Suddenly that spring and this autumn ran together, and the child and the girl she now was became one. She looked round and saw the autumn damask rose tree growing at the end of the terrace, and the marble seat below it, and remembered that that was her special place where she had played her secret games. This was Golden Grove. She was back again. She turned and ran into the house.

2

Tired out, Lucy slept well that night in her small truckle bed beside Nan-Nan, but her dreams were not happy. Something, at some deep level, was troubling her. When she woke in the golden dawn she felt uneasy, and at first it was confusing to find herself not in her turret room at home. Then she became aware of unaccustomed luxury, panelled walls instead of cold stone, a soft goose-feathered mattress, curtains of embroidered linen drawn all round the fourposter beside her, and the awareness grew to a sleepy memory of last night; the big hall downstairs and gentle Lady Carbery bending down to kiss the children, and the Earl pinching their cheeks and asking them how they did. She was lapped about by the security and graciousness that were the atmosphere of this house, and yet at the same time she felt a pang of homesickness for the hardness of Roch.

"Nan-Nan!" she cried, but there was no answer. Nan-Nan must be still asleep. She jumped out of bed, parted the curtains and scrambled up to be with her. But the fourposter, big as a small room within the curtains, was empty. The counterpane stretched smooth and unruffled as a green lawn all about her, for Nan-Nan was not there. Through all the hours of the night Lucy, unknowing, had slept alone in this room with the empty bed beside her. Was Nan-Nan dead? Had she died of falling off the coach seat with the bundles? Her mouth was so dry that she kept having to swallow. The only sounds in the room were her swallows. Betsi and Dewi were gone, and Jeremiah the pony, and Roch was gone, and now Nan-Nan was dead.

The door opened softly and there was the faint rustle of a starched apron. Some maidservant had come to tell her that Nan-Nan was dead but she could neither move nor speak.

"Lucy!" cried Nan-Nan in alarm. "Lucy, cariad, merchi, where are you?"

Bellowing with relief Lucy tore aside the curtains and precipitated herself upon Nan-Nan, with such violence that the old woman staggered backward to a chair and collapsed into it with Lucy on top of her.

"You are not dead, Nan-Nan, you are not dead!" gasped Lucy when her storm of tears had subsided to a mere backwash of hiccups.

"I am not," said Nan-Nan. "And you should be ashamed to cry so at your age. You are a young lady now, not a baby, a young lady going to London for her education. There now, Lucy fach, time is passing. Getting you dressed I should be. Do not give me trouble, cariad, for it is tired I am."

Her voice, coming from a sore throat, was a mere hoarse thread of sound. It was the first complaint Lucy had ever heard from her and she gazed at her in astonishment. "Have not you been to bed all night, Nan-Nan?" she asked.

"No, cariad. Your mother has been ill all night. She is better now but I have something sorrowful to tell you."

"I know," said Lucy. "My mother has dropped a dead baby. I do not mind. You are not dead."

Her practical tone shocked Nan-Nan. "Lucy!" she expostulated. "You should be grieving for your poor mother."

"My father told her not to ride in the coach," said Lucy. "Soon I shall grieve for my mother, and for my father, for it is sad to lose a baby. But I cannot grieve overmuch just now because you are alive."

Nan-Nan clacked her tongue, dislodged Lucy from her lap and propelled her towards the ewer and basin that stood on a little chest. She said something about too many eggs in one basket leading to a broken heart, but Lucy could not hear it properly through the splashing of water.

3

William waited only until his wife had revived before setting out for London, for on this visit he had found himself even more uncomfortable than usual at Golden Grove. Those few moments on the bridge above the stream, when he had held Elizabeth in his arms and she had been glad to be there, had vanished like all the other moments when he had hoped he might even yet win her, no more than a sudden leap of flame from a dead fire, an intuition of what might have been instantly lost in the greyness of actuality. Lying against her lace-trimmed pillows, serene in the luxury that so befitted her, she allowed him to kiss her cool cheek in goodbye but she gave him no answering kiss, and her eyes, meeting his for a moment, answered his appeal with aloof reproach. Her eyes told him that she was in no way to blame for the loss of the child. Someone was, naturally, but not Elizabeth. This attitude was shared by the Earl and Lady Carbery. Their exquisite courtesy never failed them throughout William's visit, but Elizabeth belonged to Golden Grove through the double ties of relationship and compatibility and they were not able to take an objective view of her. Upon William it was possible to sit in silent judgment, and he was glad to say goodbye.

But not to Lucy, as she stood on the mounting block embracing his left leg. "No, you cannot come too, Bud," he said. "And you like being here."

She merely wept. His sons were close to them, his host and hostess still stood courteously at the top of the steps where they had bade him goodbye. There was nothing he could say. He put his hand for a moment on her rough dark head, lifted his hat in farewell and rode away. They watched him disappear down the avenue, through the drifting leaves and the thin autumn sunshine, getting smaller and smaller until he disappeared in the blue mist that spread beneath the trees. Then Lucy pushed her brothers, even Justus, fiercely out of the way and ran to her special place, the marble bench by the damask rose tree.

The moment she knew she was alone she felt better, for William would soon be sending for them and it was true that she liked being at Golden Grove. Though the wildness of Roch, and all it stood for in the way of freedom and adventure, was the true home of her buccaneering spirit, there was something in her that could rise to the royalty of Golden Grove. When occasion demanded she could play the great lady very well indeed; and quite instinctively, for the golden thread of the Princess Nest was interwoven with the buccaneer, and for a short while she could enjoy the calm of gracious living.

The peace of Golden Grove was not the quiet of the woods or the mountains, for staying here she was intuitively aware of the immensity of labour that had this quietness as its focal point. At home their old Gwladys and the others had seemed down among the stony roots of Roch, but here the toil seemed to stretch out and away like the spokes of a turning humming wheel. She could hear the faint humming, like distant music, here where she sat at the unmoving silent heart of it all, the music that others made for her, giving their peace for hers.

The marble seat was white as the last rose blossom, opening unexpectedly in this late glow of warmth. She felt the cool petals against her cheek and turning her head she saw the leaves like lifted hands holding it out to her. She lifted her hands too and then dropped them, afraid to touch the flower lest she bruise it. Instead she looked deep into its heart, that glowed golden at the centre of the exquisite whiteness. The very faint perfume came to her. She looked and time ceased. The world went away too, even Golden Grove. Only she and the flower existed. Then she too stole away from herself, though sight remained that could look upon the flower, and song remained, for she was singing to it. When she first began to hear the song she did not know it was herself that was singing, she thought it was a seraph behind her in the tree; or the tree itself. Yes, the tree was certainly singing. They sang together for a while, and the trees in the park sang; looking up she saw the gold and crimson leaves like tongues of singing fire drifting through the air. The terrace was carpeted with fallen leaves and when she stretched her toes down and touched them gently they sang too. The sharp sweetness of a robin's song chimed in and the world was full of praise.

A tall figure stood before her. She came back to herself and looking up saw Lord Carbery. She smiled at him. "Did you hear the singing?" she asked.

He had heard her soft piping, and the robin's song, a duet that had enchanted him, and he returned the smile with tenderness. He was an impressive figure in his mulberry-coloured coat with snowy collar and cuffs edged with lace. His greying hair fell curling to his shoulders, his beard was cut to a point and hid his alarming chin. But his aristocratic nose could alarm, and his penetrating glance. Lucy however was not afraid of him. Women frightened her sometimes, with their critical eyes and sharp tongues, but not men. She slid off the seat and curtseyed. When he had seen her last she had been a small child whom he had held on his knee and fed with comfits, but now she seemed almost a maiden. The two years that had passed for him as a mere flash of a bird's wing had been for her a long journey packed with new experience and astonishing growth. He was about to take a stroll around the nearer portions of his dominion and he desired her company. He held out his hand and she slipped hers into it. She suited her steps to his walk, lifting her skirts with her free hand. She chatted beside him as they went, knowing that gentlemen must be entertained. Being a little deaf and so far above her, he did not hear all she said, but the music of her voice was delightful to him.

They visited the stable, where the doves strutted on the cobbles and the great bell tolled out the hour over their heads.

They fed Prince with windfall apples and Lucy said sadly but with careful distinctness, for she had now realized the slight deafness, that though Richard had this pony of his own, she and Justus had no ponies. For the period of their visit that could be rectified, said the Earl. There were two gentle silver ponies who pulled his wife's chariot. They were found, inspected, approved and fed. Lucy was always very much at home in stables. She liked the smell of hay and horses, the stamping of hoofs on the cobbles, the sunlight slanting through dusty windows and the great coaches looming in the shadows of the coach houses. The humble stables at Roch could not compare with these but Lucy was loyal to them and remembered Jeremiah with a pain at her heart.

They inspected the walled kitchen garden, where the mellow sun was so trapped that it was as warm as summer, and paced slowly through the clipped yews to the pool where the fish swam, and then they threaded the maze of Lady Carbery's knot garden, fragrant with herbs. The Earl picked a sprig of rosemary for Lucy and presented it with a bow, as though she had been a great lady; there was no mockery in the bow for it was a heartfelt tribute to female charm. Lucy felt herself grow several inches during the period of this promenade, a faint pink flush came to her brown cheeks and she flashed her blue glance upwards as often as she dared, watching for the Earl's smile in response. She had already bewitched her father, John Shepherd, Old Parson and the sin-eater without being conscious of the fact, but the Earl was different, so different that she knew now what she could do.

The knot garden could be observed from the window of the small parlour where Elizabeth lay convalescing on the sofa, with Lady Carbery sitting beside her working at her embroidery.

"I think you may have difficulty in the upbringing of that child, Elizabeth," said Lady Carbery gently. "I have seldom seen my husband so infatuated."

Elizabeth sighed. The miscarriage had been an unhappy experience and she was not just now taking a very favourable view of motherhood. She groped for comfort. "It struck me the other day," she said, "that when she is grown Lucy may have beauty to commend her. I hope so, for our financial affairs are so disordered that we shall have very little to give her in the way of dowry, and I want her to marry well."

"Naturally," said Lady Carbery. "We will put our heads together, my dear, when she is a little older."

"What do you think of my boys?" asked Elizabeth.

"Nice boys," said Lady Carbery. "Richard is especially attractive. He has beautiful manners and takes after your side of the family."

There was a little pleasant conversation about the excellence of Elizabeth's family and then the Earl and Lucy entered with a request for the loan of Lady Carbery's two silver ponies.

4

And so, as the quiet days of St. Luke's summer slipped gently and peacefully away, the three children rode through the park and along the lanes of the beautiful countryside on two silver ponies and one white one, in the care of one of the grooms, and sometimes with Lord Carbery himself. The scarlet of rose hips in the hedges, and the glory of the golden bracken that clothed the high sheep walks, became for the children interwoven with the stories that he told them.

On the last day of their rides together he took them to Ogor Dinas and told them his last story. In these hills, he said, in hidden caves, the heroes of old Wales lie sleeping by their arms, awaiting the time when the trumpet calls them to awake and crush the enemies of their country. Owen Lawgoch, Owen of the Red Hand, one of the greatest of Welshmen, was buried in one of the caves. He had fought for the independence of Wales against the English, and he had fought at Poitiers, but at the height of his power he had been murdered. Once upon a time, said the Earl, a young man called Dafydd Bettws had found his way down to the underworld of the caves. In one of them, illumined by mysterious light, he found a giant seated in a great chair, asleep with his head upon his hand. His right hand, that was the colour of blood, grasped a sword and at his feet lay a large dog. Armour and weapons were stacked round the walls of the cave and on a stone near the chair were gold coins. Dafydd was afraid to take more than one coin but next day, feeling brave, he thought he would go back for more. But he could not find the entrance to the cave, and since his day no one else had found it. And the trumpet had not yet sounded. The heroes of Wales slept on.

They were sitting under the branches of a tawny oak tree on the hillside when the Earl told them this story, and he told it well, for he delighted in telling fairy tales to receptive children; and Lucy was the most instantly responsive child he had ever encountered. Their mounts were cropping the grass near them and the story finished he walked over to his horse to adjust a dragging rein. Lucy leapt to her feet, gave each brother a blow of her fist in the small of the back as a signal to stay where he was, and disappeared. The boys stayed where they were, Richard out of courtesy to his host and Justus because he was considerably winded. Lucy ran back along the bridle path they had been following, for she had seen the entrance to a cave up the hill under a rowan tree. She was inside it before Lord Carbery had finished with his horse.

It might be the very one, she thought, for it narrowed to a passage that sloped into the earth like a rabbit's burrow. Though the events of the past few weeks had brought her a considerable distance along the road to womanhood, the Earl's story had flung her right back into childhood again, and her mind was alight with the thought of those sleeping heroes. The rock tunnel darkened as she crept along it but she was never afraid of the dark.

And then the rock floor suddenly ended and she fell. It was a short fall, and then she landed on a flat rock, but one foot was twisted under her, and she was very bruised. She lay still for a few moments and then sat up. The pain in her leg made her gasp but she did not cry. She sat for some while too shocked and bewildered to think or remember, aware of nothing but the pain and a longing for Nan-Nan. It had been like this years ago when she had fallen out of bed, but then Nan-Nan had come at once. Now there was no Nan-Nan, though there was a gleam of a nightlight behind gold curtains. She looked at the glimmer, high up to her left, and slowly it became daylight shining through a curtain of golden bracken. Then she remembered where she was. This must be Dafydd's cave. She looked round with a tremor of fear, half expecting to see the old hero asleep with his head on his hand. But there was nothing to be seen in the dimness except a small empty cave with ferns growing here and there. The entrance was where gold bracken shone but it would mean a climb up the rocks to get to the light and she could not move for the pain. The enchantment that had brought her tumbling in here so crazily had vanished and fear came, cold and clammy, and it was difficult to breathe and impossible to think. She was lost in the depths of the earth and no one would ever find her.

Then suddenly courage and obstinacy revived and she knew she was not going to stay inside this horrible mountain with a long-dead hero, waiting for a trumpet that would never sound. She must get out. With her resolve the cave seemed not so terrible and reminded her of somewhere else, somewhere good. It was like the chapel in St. David's Cathedral where she and Old Parson had knelt with Chancellor Pritchard, a stony place where the light shone through golden bracken just as it had glowed through the window in the chapel. She had prayed then that Old Parson might be happy and God had answered her prayer. God had been in his Cathedral but she could not in her pain and fright feel that he was here. Nothing seemed here except herself and her pain and fright. Chancellor Pritchard had told Old Parson that the mercy of God was in his heart. She put her hand over her heart and it was jumping about more like a frightened bird than God. Yet she could not think of anywhere else inside her where God could be; unless he was inside this agitation. She put both hands now over her bumping heart and shut her eyes, trying to see him there. She could not. She saw instead the damask rose at Golden Grove, and it glowed at its heart and was still. She was exceedingly surprised. "God?" she asked. Then she spoke again, but a little afraid to hear her own voice saying the tremendous word out loud in this stony place. "God." After that she knew it was not true that she could not get to the light, and she began to drag herself over the stones.

The pain was so horrible that the journey seemed to go on for a lifetime, so bad at times that she seemed to go blind and could no longer see the light behind the bracken. At these times, with nothing there to give her a sense of direction, she would have liked not to go on. But she was hounded on by the strength that was beating in her blood and pulsing in her heart, always a little stronger than the pounding pain. Then her hands were parting the bracken stems and sunlight was on her face.

She could not remember afterwards how she got out of the hole. The next thing she remembered was lying in the bracken on the hillside. She heard the sheep crying up on the mountain and down below in the wood voices were calling her, Lord Carbery's deep voice, and Richard's treble and Justus's shrill little pipe. "Lucy, Lucy, Lucy," they called, and the sheep called back in answer, seeming to tell them where she was. And with the last of her strength she called too. "Richard! Justus!" And they came and found her.

5

She was a princess in good earnest after that, spending her luxurious days enthroned in Nan-Nan's bed with the green curtains, holding her court, Nan-Nan in constant attendance. She had never been so admired, so petted. The blame of her escapade was placed entirely upon Lord Carbery. It would, his wife hoped in the privacy of their fourposter, be a lesson to him. There had been trouble before with the innocent young believing every word of the ridiculous tales he told them. And it was scarcely dignified for a man in his position to be running round the countryside with a pack of children as though he were their tutor. He took her criticism peacefully, having learned the technique of using the rhythmical rise and fall of wifely remonstrance as a soporific, and the adventure did not lessen his infatuation for Lucy. He murmured sleepily that she had been courageous under the hands of the surgeon when he attended to that fracture; mercifully a simple one, but never-theless a painful business for a child. A gallant little maid. Not in the least like either of her parents.

"I see a strong likeness to her father," said Lady Carbery. "And do you realize that owing to this adventure we shall have the family with us for longer than we had feared?" She was a good woman, only very occasionally irritable, and then only to her husband, and it was actually the deep desire of her soul that Golden Grove should be a refuge for all lonely and homeless persons; but she was not strong and her fatigued mind and body were sometimes at outraged loggerheads with what her soul had done. But she loved children and was very tender to Lucy. She would come quietly into the room, her grey silk skirts rustling, and sit beside the child and read the bible to her. Lucy did not take much notice of the reading, for Lady Carbery did not read very well, but she liked to watch her gentle face and rest in her peacefulness, that was like that of the damask rose, and she would have grown to love her as much as she did the Earl if they had stayed longer at Golden Grove.

But the fracture mended quickly. William wrote to say he had found a house and it was time to leave Golden Grove. Their host and hostess planned an easy journey for them. Their own coach and servants would go back to Roch and they would travel to England with Lord and Lady Carbery, who were to visit friends near Hereford. The coach would then take them on to London, returning to pick up Lord and Lady Carbery for the return journey. The Carbery wealth spread such an aura of ease and safety over the prospect that Elizabeth looked forward to the journey without dread, her content spreading to Nan-Nan and the children.

But Lucy was sad on the last night, for saying goodbye to their own coach and servants had seemed to break the last link with Roch. But she had the wedding ring that the little bird had set upon her finger at the time of the great migration, and she had the damask rose. Out in the garden its petals had fallen but it still glowed within her busy heart.

She was sitting up in bed drinking her hot posset when she

heard the music. "Listen, Nan-Nan," she commanded. Nan-Nan, who was folding up Lucy's clothes, paused, and her small face was transfigured. "It's Geraint the Harper," she exclaimed in delight. "Come down from the mountains. Dulch! Dulch! That I should live to hear Geraint again. It's playing down in the hall he is."

She and Lucy listened intently. The music was like the first shuddering of a gale in the trees, so that Lucy trembled, but so beautiful that pictures started running through her mind. Swans flying low over a grey sea, their necks outstretched and their great wings beating out the exciting rhythm of their flight. The daffodils at Roch bending all one way in the wind, the sunlight running over them. The bright-eyed twins peeping out of their carved cradles and laughing. But when she thought of the twins she began to cry.

"Now now, cariad," said Nan-Nan, and wrapping Lucy in a blanket she took her along the corridor to the top of the great staircase, where they could peep through the balustrade unseen by the company below. Justus, who had also been put to bed, came trotting from the boys' room in his nightshirt, and he too was wrapped in a blanket. The three of them sat on the floor, the children cuddled close to Nan-Nan. Down below were Lord and Lady Carbery, Elizabeth and Richard seated in stately chairs, with the senior servants standing behind them. The small fry of scullions and chambermaids came and went in the doorway that led to the kitchen regions, like fish or mice looking in at human beings from the mystery of their own shadowed places. Geraint the Harper sat by the fire, his white beard flowing over his chest, his long brown fingers plucking the strings. His voice, that Nan-Nan remembered from her younger days as deep and thunderous, was not so strong now in his old age, yet still able to give a terrible power to Guto'r Glyn's lament for Siôn ap Medog Pilstwn, that he was singing when she and the children sat down behind the balustrade.

> *My tears flow like a river.*
> *I have wept blood on Siôn's bed.*
> *And thousands weep in Maelor*

Harder than a heavy rain ...
For his sake many fasted.
God paid no heed to wailing,
And would take no gold but him.
Right to fear, face of passion,
A Man who will not be bribed.

Though she understood little of the words the pictures that
came to Lucy with the wild music terrified her. A bloodstained bed and faces disfigured with weeping, and vast
against the night, blotting out the stars, dark and hard as iron,
the dreadful face of the God who would not be bribed. What
God was this? Who was he? Not the God of the cave. She
forced her eyes open, to get rid of him, and turned to Nan-Nan
for comfort, but Nan-Nan still had her eyes closed and her
tiny face looked curtained, like the outside of a house whose
owner has gone away. She seemed to have gone so far, to past
or future, that Lucy feared to drag her back.

Yesterday at home, proudly;
And today, under the shroud ...
Men who are youthful and brave
Go early up to heaven ...
Young he was, Owain's kinsman,
To be amidst oak and stone.
Why not bear off a miser,
God, not a bountiful man?

There was a moment's deep silence and the old Harper's chin
fell upon his breast. Then suddenly he looked up with a smile,
his eyes going from Lord and Lady Carbery, Elizabeth and
Richard, to the two children and Nan-Nan behind the balustrade, and he began to sing Guto'r Glyn's gay song of London
Town. The blood and darkness vanished and Lucy's mind was
full of wine-cups and apples, steepled churches and lovely
ladies in head-dresses tall and pointed like the steeples.

A kind, attractive city,
Most blest in its citizens,
Curtain-walled is the castle,

> *Best of cities, far as Rome! ...*
> *The London of Owain's land,*
> *Wine-filled homes, lands of orchards,*
> *It's a bright and blessed school,*
> *It's a city of preachers;*
> *Men wise in verse and grammar*
> *Touch God in the fair temple.*
> *The best church, splendid chalice,*
> *Its organ and its bells;*
> *The best choir, and skilful men,*
> *As far as Canterbury;*
> *The best band, delightful men,*
> *The men of the white abbey;*
> *The best of wives, fair their hair*
> *And their gowns, are of Oswallt.*
> *In it there's Cheapside's trading,*
> *And concord, and loyalty ...*
> *Grace to the town and townsmen,*
> *And God let this refuge last ...*
> *Forever their man am I.*

The music vanished in a final sweep of the strings that was like a chime of bells, and looking round at Nan-Nan Lucy saw that she was back again, bright-eyed and merry as she looked from one to the other of her children. But unfortunately she had returned to remembrance of their bedtime and she took them away. But it did not really matter for lying in their beds with the doors open they could still hear the harp music winging through the house.

6

The journey to London in the warm grey November weather was serenely uneventful. The Walter coach had rattled and jolted its way over stones and ruts like a child's toy jerked along at the end of a piece of string but the beautiful Golden Grove coach rose and fell and swayed like a ship at sea cresting the waves, and once you got used to the motion it was not so bad. Lady Carbery and Elizabeth, with Lucy between them,

133

sat facing the way they were going, with Justus and Nan-Nan and Lady Carbery's maid facing them with the bags and bundles. Lord Carbery rode his great black horse and Richard rode Prince. There was a train of servants with the luggage cart, so many that they need fear no sudden onslaught of thieves. They travelled at their leisure with a horseman going on ahead to prepare their noble way, so that when they came to an inn at nightfall they found blazing fires, warm beds and everyone rushing in all directions to satisfy their every need. The Princess Nest revelled in it all but the buccaneer found it a bit dull, and that strange third person of whom Lucy was occasionally aware of in herself, the one with the eyes from whom she had drawn back that the eyes might look at the damask rose, shut them and went to sleep.

Occasionally on this journey Lord Carbery allowed Lucy or Justus to ride with him, and the days when it was her turn were to Lucy the great days, for he continued his storytelling, though with a certain caution now, confining himself to matters of factual history. He told her about the drovers' road, down which were driven the cattle and sheep exported to England. The drovers would band together for security and King Charles's ship money tax, collected by the Welsh high sheriffs all in silver because there was no gold in South Wales at this time, travelled to England in their care. And there was the honey road that passed through the Vale of Usk upon the other side of the heather-covered Black Mountains. Down this road the eight loads of honey exacted by the Saxon kings as tribute had been carried on poles, two men to a pole. Lucy thrilled at the story of the honey, and to all that she saw, the mountains and the falling streams, the forests and the castles perched upon the hilltops. One of them, the Marcher castle of Clifford, drew from Lord Carbery the story of Fair Rosamund, the Welsh girl beloved of King Henry the Second, whose home it had been. He could not forbear to tell the story of Henry's Rose of the World, but he told it with a certain amount of misgiving. Lucy accepted it with calm pleasure and stored it away in her mind with Olwen and the Princess Nest.

At Hereford they said goodbye to Lord and Lady Carbery. Lucy clung passionately to the Earl and Elizabeth wept in Lady Carbery's arms. Elizabeth and Nan-Nan and the children stayed for a few days at the old coaching inn near the Cathedral, and a letter was sent post haste to William to tell him the day they hoped to arrive at High Wycombe, the last stopping place before London. Hereford was the first English town they had seen. The busy streets awed them and Nan-Nan thought that if London was noisier than this she would die of the racket, and the harshness of English voices positively hurt their ears.

They took coach again and rolled away into the English November countryside, where the meadows were green and wet and the last sad leaves fell through the rain. As they neared High Wycombe one of the servants rode on to make ready for them through a rainy twilight that seemed to Lucy, suffering from an acute attack of homesickness, the greyest sundown she had ever seen. When they reached High Wycombe it was difficult to see it, for the coach lights shining upon wet cobbles dazzled her eyes and the slanting rain seemed as thick as standing corn. They drove into an inn yard and light streamed from an open door. A man stood there, arms akimbo, watching the coaches as they came in, his sturdy figure outlined against the light behind him.

"Let me out!" yelled Lucy, struggling madly with the door handle. An ostler leapt to open it for her and she jumped out, in danger of breaking her leg all over again, and ran through the rain to William.

Seven

I

It was May sixteen hundred and forty and Elenor Gwinne sat in the parlour of her little house in the village of St. Giles. Her armchair was by the window and she sat looking out on the garden, her hands folded in her lap. Her peaceful face was set in lines of deep gravity, a sign that she was profoundly grieved. She was a woman who had attained to a serenity that lifted her well above fuss and worry, but not above grieving; she was the least selfish of women. She grieved now for so much; the state of the country, torn by strife, for the unhappiness of her daughter and son-in-law, Elizabeth and William Walter, and the effect it was having upon their children, and she grieved too that her own hard won peace was something she seemed unable to share with those she loved.

Peace, she supposed, was contingent upon a certain disposition of the soul, a disposition to receive the gift that only detachment from self made possible. Some had the inner strength to wrestle for that detachment, others had not, and the strength too was a gift. Why to one and not the other? This was a question that had for long puzzled her. Now, growing old, she could only say that it was a part of the perpetually growing mystery of things that once she had worried at like a dog with a bone. Now she let it alone, finding some comfort in the mere growth of the mystery, as though its vast shadow thrown across human life, like the shadow of some great iron head among the stars, promised some tremendous answer. But how she wished that these bestowals were not so deeply personal.

Her wrestling years had been the years of her first marriage. A delicate woman, difficult child-bearing had nearly broken her, but she had not died of the twelfth child. That way of escape, grasped at by so many women, she had refused. She had looked the possibility of a thirteenth steadily in the face and got well to find that her years of child-bearing were unbelievably over. After her husband's death her eldest son had inherited Trewerne and she had escaped to Golden Grove like a bird escaped from the net of the fowler.

Only to fall into the net of John Gwinne, the son of a family whose estates adjoined those of Lord Carbery. But this was a different matter. John Gwinne was a bibliophile who had caught sight of her peaceful face in the brief instant of shutting one book and opening another. The face had seemed consonant with his way of life and he had transported her to London that she might protect him from domestic disturbance. They had neither of them regretted their marriage and loved each other in a placid fashion that disturbed the peace of neither. John Gwinne's peace was of a different quality from that of his wife and had been more easily come by. It was that of a man shut up in his own fortress and utterly indifferent to what went on outside it. But he was so charming in his selfishness that everyone loved him.

Provided it made no breach in the wall of books he had built about him the state of the country did not and would not disturb John Gwinne. When, after eleven years of disastrous royal government parliament had once more assembled in pure Puritanical force and temper he had been a little alarmed to learn that his bibliophile friend Dr. Cosin, Master of Peterhouse and Vice-Chancellor of Cambridge, was likely to be impeached. That bibliophiles could be impeached was a slight crack in the wall. But then Dr. Cosin, the more fool he, had never built himself in with his books. His loyalties extended beyond them. He was a Royalist and high churchman who had defended his beliefs with more valour than prudence. He had introduced ornate ceremonial at Peterhouse chapel and with Archbishop Laud he had been the ruling spirit in the revision of the *Book of Common Prayer,* and was hated only a little less than the Archbishop and the Earl of Strafford. But after sitting for only three weeks Parliament had been dissolved, Dr. Cosin was for the moment safe and this very Sunday, being in town for Convocation, would dine with them. John Gwinne had gone back happily to his books, leaving anxiety for Dr. Cosin's future to his wife. What would it be, she wondered? Archbishop Laud had fortified his house and Puritan mobs were parading the streets, maddened at the rumour that Strafford was bringing over an army from Ireland to be used not only against rebellious Scots but against rebellious English too. It was not wise of John Cosin to have come to town.

She found to her surprise that she was crying, not now for John Cosin's danger but for that of Elizabeth and Walter. Elizabeth wanted her marriage to be legally ended. She could bring a good case before the courts, she said. She could plead William's infidelity and his cruelty; for had it not been cruel of him to force her to take care of Dewi and Betsi with her own children? And she could plead the fact that he was doing nothing for the support of his family, refusing to tie himself down to any work that would make eventual return to Roch more difficult. And he had become quite impossible to live with.

Elenor Gwinne, pleading with her for patience, had not spared her daugher her criticism, for she was a just woman and her sympathies during the last two years had been increasingly with her son-in-law. Elizabeth, delighting in the gaieties of the town and in her charming little house in the most fashionable square in London, had been extravagant that first winter and then at the end of it had refused to go back to Wales; for a host of reasons but primarily for one not mentioned and equally intolerable to William and her mother. She had met again the man she had fallen in love with in Wales as a girl and her friendship with him was now her chief delight. She kept it on the right side of safety and decorum, for she truly desired to be a virtuous woman, but in her power to do so there was an element of cold calculation that shocked Mrs. Gwinne. Compared with her daughter's loveless respectability she preferred her son-in-law's heartbroken lack of it. But she had now said all she could, and knew that it had slid off her daughter's bitterness like water off a duck's back. All she could do now was to pay what she could towards the children's edu-

cation and keep Lucy with her as much as possible, away from
the unhappy house in Covent Garden. The boys were by day
at St. Paul's School, and busy with their homework when they
came home in the evening, but Lucy was taught at home and
torn in pieces between conflicting loyalties. As was poor Nan-
Nan. When Lucy came to stay Mrs. Gwinne insisted that Nan-
Nan should come too, for her heart ached for Nan-Nan almost
more than for Lucy.

She remembered that they were coming today to spend a
few weeks with her and suddenly spring leaped through the
open window. St. Giles in the Fields was one of the loveliest
villages about London, lovelier even than Kensington or Pad-
dington. The little houses gathered about the old church were
charming, their gardens just now full of flowers, the meadows
beyond the village golden with buttercups. The scent of the
apple blossom in her own garden came to her on the south
wind, and the scent of pinks. The fashionable tulips, standing
very upright in their ranks of gold and scarlet, did not give
their faint scent to the wind, but now and then they bowed to
her slightly. She knew no more courteous or stiff-necked
flowers; they often reminded her of the royal family. But not
Prince Charles. There was nothing stiff-necked about that enchanting boy, who had every heart in England, even Puritan
hearts, in the hollow of his hand.

There was a sound of wheels in the lane behind the holly
hedge that protected the garden, the crack of a whip exploding in the blue air like a firework, the winding of a horn,
and then the clatter of horses' hoofs slithering to a lurching
standstill, and the high birdlike cries of excited children. The
clamour leaped through the open window as the spring had
done, and the blood pulsed in Mrs. Gwinne's veins as though
she were young again. Then it quieted with the sobering
thought, "Poor Nan-Nan."

She rose from her chair and moved with her slow, peaceful,
ageing step across the garden, through the tulips to the gate.
Outside in the lane was riotous confusion. Two wheels of a
hired hackney coach were half-way up the low bank below the
holly hedge and the rightful driver was trussed up in the boot,

his place on the box usurped by Richard and Justus in a state of inextinguishable laughter. An extremely handsome boy, Richard's friend Tom Howard, slid off one of the horses and bowed to Mrs. Gwinne. Within the coach Nan-Nan's face was that of a woman who commends her soul to God, but Lucy's glowed within her hood. Somewhere a lark was singing madly. Mrs. Gwinne saw it all in a brief kaleidoscope of colour, and felt the freshness of it on her skin, as though a rainbow had broken into fragments before her eyes and then fallen upon her in a spring shower. Then Lucy came tumbling from the rainbow and was in her arms, the hood fallen back from her face. So endearing was the whole affair that it took Mrs. Gwinne a few moments to realize that the behaviour of her grandchildren was increasingly outrageous. Their parents were now careless as to discipline, but the influence of Tom Howard was also to blame. A wild youth, she feared. Looking at him over Lucy's head she received his bright glance and another exquisite bow.

"Tom," she commanded, "get that unfortunate man out of the boot. Who tied him up there? Richard, help Nan-Nan from the coach. Justus, put that horn down. There has been enough noise for one day."

She did not need to raise her voice for they obeyed her instantly. The coachman was liberated and despatched to the kitchen for ale and comfort, the little boy who was weeding the garden appearing to hold the horses, Nan-Nan and her bundles were taken upstairs by Phoebe the cook and the children followed Mrs. Gwinne into the parlour, where Tabitha, the second handmaiden, brought them watered wine in crystal glasses and thin slices of saffron cake. Tom Howard, who considered himself old enough to take his wine neat, made a slight grimace as he tasted it, a mere wrinkling of the nose that might have been an incipient sneeze. But Mrs. Gwinne noticed it. "You would prefer your water plain, Tom?" she asked sweetly.

He smiled at her cheekily over the rim of his glass. He was dressed in jaffingale colours, green and scarlet, and his curly dark hair, disordered by the struggle with the coachman, lay long and tangled on his shoulders, proclaiming him a King's man. All committed males tended nowadays to be extreme in dress, proud of their allegiance to one side or the other. Richard proclaimed no committal. He wore sober dark blue with smooth shining fair hair that barely touched his shoulders. He was in looks extremely like his mother, too mature for his age, his cool eyes watchful. He was courteous and much liked, but not truly loved by anyone except his mother.

Justus had changed little during the last two years. His brown dormouse head reached a little higher up the door when his father measured him but otherwise he was the same, loyal and sweet-tempered as ever, a comforting and comfortable small boy. He was slowly developing a good steady brain and a strong sense of purpose. Richard, if he had any plans for his future, never divulged them, but Justus said he was going to be a barrister who would plead for poor men and stop their being hanged. This was the way that London had affected him. Too many poor men, he thought, and too many of them hanged.

Lucy at ten years old was also too old for her age, but her maturity was different from Richard's. The unhappiness of their home had closed his heart, that did not wish to feel, and turned his mind inward to his own affairs. But Lucy's mind had been turned outward, probing too early the world's tragedy and sin, that at times nearly broke her heart, and unable to be comfortable in her compassion as was Justus. Yet she was still a child in her vivid delight in the variety and beauty of the world, and in the vehemence of her loving, and the contrast of her childishness and maturity made up much of her fascination. Tom Howard's eyes kindled on her sparkling face and he lifted his glass to her. "To my little wife," he said.

It meant nothing for in the parlance of the day wife was merely another word for sweetheart, but Mrs. Gwinne glanced gravely from one to the other. Suitable alliances between families were arranged very early and she had already given thought to Lucy's future. Tom Howard, brother of the Duke of Suffolk, would be a fine match for her granddaughter. Yet she was not entirely sure that she liked him.

"You are not at your studies today?" she asked.

"It is a holiday, madam."

"A happy chance for all but the coachman, poor fellow."

"A pestilential Puritan, madam. He needed to be taught a lesson."

"He was insulting to you?"

"Yes, madam."

"No, Tom," said Lucy, flying hotly to the man's defence. "That is not true. He only called you a popinjay and said you needed a haircut. And you said he was a lousy rebel. How do you know he is a rebel? And you cannot know if he is lousy either, not without looking. You did not look. You jumped on him and tied him up. And I'm not your little wife. Call me that again and I will jump on you like you did on the coachman and pull your hair out."

A wave of despair passed over Mrs. Gwinne. For a year now she had been trying to turn Lucy into a lady, but the process had not been markedly successful. There were times when Lucy was the very pattern of a little princess, but at other times, no.

"Lucy!" she said sternly. "Tom Howard is your guest."

"No, madam," said Lucy. "We did not ask him to come with us. When we were setting off he was lounging about outside my Lord of Bedford's house and joined us without invitation."

"Then he did you honour," said Mrs. Gwinne. "And I beg that you will apologize to him for your rudeness."

"No, madam," said Lucy. "That was not rudeness, that was telling Tom what he ought to know."

Tom had been twirling his wineglass, his eyes as full of sparkle as the wine, but whether amusement or anger predominated Mrs. Gwinne could not tell. He had a crooked smile that at all times appeared mocking, whether mockery was in his heart or no. What was not in doubt was his exasperated delight in Lucy, and his pleasure in teasing her.

"You are my sweetheart whether you will or not," he told her.

Lucy became crimson to the roots of her hair. She would

have flown at Tom but for her grandmother's restraining hand on her shoulder.

"It is a fair morning," said Richard.

"There were larks in Seven Dials meadow," piped up Justus.

Richard's coolness rolled over the golden sparkles of Tom and Lucy and Mrs. Gwinne marvelled briefly at the strange power of a cold heart. It was as though sluice-gates had annihilated the buttercups in the meadow. But over the serene cold flood sang Justus's larks, and they had the last word. Justus, so his grandmother believed, was pure goodness and he so often had the last word. He did now. The little party simmered down into a state of decorum and presently the coach drove away through Long Acre field towards London with the boys inside and the coachman on the box.

Lucy and her grandmother, who had stood under the honeysuckle porch to see them go, turned back into the house hand in hand. "I have nearly finished my sampler, madam," said Lucy quietly, "I have only one rosebud left." The rest of the day passed peacefully, sitting under one of the apple trees in the garden, Lucy finishing her sampler while Mrs. Gwinne read aloud to her. Lucy loved her grandmother dearly and she was sorry that the necessity for plain speaking to Tom had grieved her. Lucy liked Tom and it was because she liked him that she kept having to face him with his lies. She could not explain this to her grandmother when Mrs. Gwinne gently scolded her for her rudeness, for she was like her father in that she was never able to explain herself.

"Ladies must always be gentle and courteous to gentlemen," said Mrs. Gwinne, closing her book and laying her clasped hands upon it. "And you must remember, Lucy, that a certain freedom of behaviour which is allowed to gentlemen is not permitted to ladies."

Now here was a thing which infuriated Lucy. Why one rule for gentlemen and another for ladies? But she swallowed the sudden spurt of anger and said gently, "Please, I have finished my sampler."

Mrs. Gwinne took it from her and admired the needlework.

Lucy sewed much better now, could dance lightly and grace-fully, play the spinet and sing like a robin, but though her mind was quick as her intuition she was still a poor scholar, able to read and write but not much more. Nor unfortunately was she much of a housewife. The house for her was still a place that she liked to run away from, and she still wished she was a boy.

Her grandmother looked at her. Would she be beautiful? In the last two years she had grown fast and was tall for ten years old, but she was thin and at that date a rounded cushioned figure was the ideal of feminine beauty. Her brown face, wide across the cheekbones, tapered to an obstinate chin and her lips met firmly. Her eyes, framed in short thick dark lashes, were still the most remarkable thing about her, brilliantly blue and disconcertingly direct. Passionate and volatile as she was she could sometimes be completely still, held in a deep atten-tion that to the beholder might have an apparent object or might not. Or, as now, she could be still for love's sake, sitting under an apple tree beside an old lady. She was now beginning to enjoy peacocking in gay clothes but her enjoyment was that of a gipsy's child; she liked the bright colours and the swish and rustle but seemed unaware of a torn petticoat or a skirt put on the wrong way round. She was fastidious but at the same time deplorably untidy.

The shadows were lengthening in the garden and Mr. Gwinne's bald head was thrust forth from the window of his library. Twice daily the rising tide of hunger washed him ashore from his books, and the hunger was so punctual that the maids could set the kitchen clock by it. The head was withdrawn and presently Mr. Gwinne came slowly across the lawn, his watch held open in the palm of his left hand. He was tall, with the stooped shoulders of a scholar and the uncertain walk of a man whose mind and body are seldom in the same century at the same time. His face was pale and leathery, his faded blue eyes remote. Brought up short by his wife's spread-ing skirts he carefully closed his watch, raised his head, regis-tered her whereabouts and bent to kiss her hand. Straight-ening again he became aware of Lucy's curtsey.

"Dear child!" he ejaculated, for he was very fond of her. "Why was I not told of your arrival?"

"Lucy had her dinner with us," his wife reminded him.

"Did she?" he asked, and laid his hand on her hair. People liked to feel Lucy's hair, springy as heather and warm and comforting as a dog's fur. "Will she be here long?"

"I had your thrice-given permission to invite her for several weeks," said Mrs. Gwinne. She felt it necessary sometimes to insist on these things, lest her husband's mind should lose touch altogether with its material surroundings. "Shall we go in to supper? We have a capon this evening."

His eyes brightened and he held out his hand to help her from her chair. She thanked heaven for his good digestion. While it lasted he was still hers.

2

"Madam my dearest," said Nan-Nan to Mrs. Gwinne the next day, "she grows so fast and destroys her clothes so quickly that I cannot keep her respectable. See, madam my dearest."

Mrs. Gwinne had been a child in Nan-Nan's first nursery and she was madam my dearest, while Elizabeth was merely madam my love. "Turn round, cariad," said Nan-Nan and Lucy turned obediently, so that her grandmother might see how she had shot up out of her second best gown. Her best gown, which she had worn to church this morning, had met with an accident on the way home, for they had encountered a village dog fight, with a small mongrel dog getting the worst of it, and her best gown was now ruined.

"Never mind, Nan-Nan," consoled Mrs. Gwinne. "Dr. Cosin will not notice that the second best dress is a little short. There is plenty of fullness for her to make her curtsey and the colour suits her."

The dress had the hue of pale wood violets and invested Lucy with an unusual air of gentle goodness, and when she put it on she more often than not put on behaviour to match. Her histrionic sense, though unconscious, was strong.

There was a sound of coach wheels in the lane. "I must go,"

said Mrs. Gwinne. "Send her down, Nan-Nan, when she is ready." Half-way to the door she came back again to kiss Nan-Nan, then left the room with her eyes full of sorrow.

Lucy too knew that Nan-Nan was not happy in London. She had the air of a bird whose nest has been torn to shreds in a storm, and who sits among the ruins shrunken and bewildered. But not leaving them. Lucy knew she could be relied on not to leave them while any nestlings remained among the twigs. Nor was she leaving Nan-Nan. With sudden passion she seized the comb with which Nan-Nan was tidying her hair, as she had done on another Sunday at Roch, and flung it across the room.

"I am not going down," she stormed. "I am staying here with you!"

"Pick up that comb, love," said Nan-Nan sternly. "Go down to Dr. Cosin, you must, and behave prettily to match your dress. He is the one who will always help you, God willing."

Nan-Nan's gentle voice had taken on the depth that it had when she was having one of her seeings, and she was forcing the comb through Lucy's tangled hair with great determination. "How do you know?" Lucy demanded.

"Who is to say how I know, cariad?" asked Nan-Nan. "I knew when I heard his step in the hall." A silver bell sounded from below. "There child! Go now and mind your curtsey and your manners."

Nan-Nan's extraordinary urgency communicated itself to Lucy and she ran down the stairs, opened the parlour door and came into the room as though a wind from the sea was behind her. Then she recollected herself and dropped the best curtsey of her life until now. Rising from it she lifted her chin and looked at Dr. Cosin in a way that might have seemed impudent but for its gravity.

John Cosin was a tall erect man with a large black beard and eyes that could kindle very suddenly into anger or laughter. His nose jutted from his face with a fearless aggressiveness that made him look much older than his forty-five years. His big mouth was grim but amused. "I've not seen a great man before," thought Lucy. "But he's not as good as my grandmother. He could be very angry." Then thoughts left her and she became only eyes, for this was one of her looking times.

Mrs. Gwinne was alarmed by the apparent rudeness of what she was afterwards to call "Lucy's dreadful blue stare", and thanked heaven that Dr. Cosin had small daughters of his own; though she was quite sure they were none of them so unpredictable in behaviour as Lucy. Mrs. Cosin was a wonderful mother and the manners of her offspring were invariably excellent.

But the great man was not offended. He laughed his great laugh and outlooked Lucy's looking, his eyes kindling with sudden affection. "She is much the same age as my daughter Mary," he said to Mrs. Gwinne. Then he abruptly turned from Lucy to his host, who for the last few minutes had been standing with an open book in his hand, discoursing on it with no idea at all that no one was listening to him.

They went into the dining parlour, where Lucy sat opposite Dr. Cosin, but to Mrs. Gwinne's relief her behaviour was now exemplary. When in the intervals of talk he smiled at her she returned the smile, and when his laugh rang out her face sparkled for a moment as though a small mirror had reflected a sunburst, but for the rest she spoke only if she was spoken to, and behaved in a manner entirely in keeping with the wood-violet dress. And she listened very intently to all that was said.

Though Dr. Cosin was as ardent a bibliophile as Mr. Gwinne he had not the one-track mind of his host and had much to say upon other topics, chief among them the sorrows of the times.

"These last few days have been critical," he said, "and I have been glad to share them with the Archbishop. But apart from an abusive mob outside his palace in the evening, there has been no serious disturbance. Things are quiet now and I hope to return to Cambridge on Tuesday."

"They say the Queen's mother has been most alarmed," said Mrs. Gwinne.

"Poor old lady, well she might be," said Dr. Cosin. "The King received a letter threatening to chase the Pope and the

devil from St. James's 'where is lodged the Queen, mother of
the Queen!' She refused to go to bed for fear of being murdered and the Prince of Wales, they say, wept for five days and
was much troubled by bad dreams."

Lucy looked up and for the first time spoke without being
spoken to. "Was he afraid?" she asked, her eyes intent and
anxious.

"Lucy!" chided Mrs. Gwinne, but Dr. Cosin answered the
child with consideration for her obvious concern. "I do not
think our Prince is ever afraid of physical danger, for he is an
exceptionally courageous boy, but he appears to have a strong
sense of personal property." Dr. Cosin threw back his head and
his laugh rang out again. "The Archbishop told me that when
his father asked the cause of his grief the Prince replied, 'My
grandfather left you four kingdoms and I am afraid Your
Majesty will leave me never one.' "

Lucy considered this reply with gravity but not amusement.
Though she had not yet seen the Prince she had an intensely
personal feeling for him because he was just her age. That
marvellous unknown planet that had swung into the daylight
sky at his birth, bringing the astonished people out into the
London streets to gaze at it, must have looked down on her
cradle too. They were born under the same star. But there was
no sentimentality in her feelings about him, though she saw
him always in the guise of Prince Kilhwch of the Mabinogion,
with his spears that could wound the wind, only a sense of
unity and a desire that he should be in all things perfect. Was
it right that he should be so concerned about his inheritance?
She was not sure, and she felt uneasy. Her eyes dropped to her
plate and the talk flowed to other matters; very quickly to that
overwhelming matter of these days, the King's belief in his
right to govern without Parliament and to impose taxes as he
wished without its consent.

"His father was of the same mind," said Dr. Cosin. "I remember King Jamie talking on the subject to two of the
bishops, my Lord of Durham and that good old man Bishop
Andrews of Ely. He asked my Lord of Durham, 'Cannot I take
my subjects' money when I want it without all this formality

of Parliament?' Neile, the wily old diplomat, said to him, 'God forbid, sir, but you should; you are the very breath of our nostrils.' Andrews would not reply at first, then he said with that sweet gentleness of his, 'Sir, I think it is lawful for you to take my brother Neile's money, because he offers it.' " When the reverberations of Dr. Cosin's laugh had died away Mrs. Gwinne asked him, "Had this saintly Bishop Andrews been alive today which side in this unhappy struggle would have engaged his loyalty?"

Dr. Cosin's mood could change very quickly. Amusement vanished and his face looked dark with tragedy as he answered. "Madam, he would have been loyal to Church and King. But in all these questions that today threaten our country's peace the issues are tangled and confused. There are honest men among our enemies, and would that it were possible to look at the darkening scene out of their eyes, not with an effort of imagination but in very truth. If it were possible wars would cease. How could you kill a man who had lent you his eyes? But it is not possible and all we can do is to try these matters with our own eyes, that see as heart and mind dictate. We can, we must, endeavour to purify our hearts and clarify our minds, but inborn loyalty has a fearful strength and can cloud our thinking more than any other emotion."

"Why do you say a fearful strength?" asked Mrs. Gwinne. "Is loyalty not admirable?"

"Certainly. Do we not suspect turncoats? and rightly. They are not usually good men. But very occasionally they may be. The threads of the web are tangled, madam. That is the tragedy of a world riddled by sin."

"And you?" asked Mrs. Gwinne.

A smile softened Dr. Cosin's rugged face. "Madam, I have thought deeply about these things, but I am a hot-tempered man and like all such men deeply committed. I love the King, whose chaplain I am, and the Church of England is my firstborn. That last sentence, madam, is one that could be written on my tombstone."

It had been a dialogue between the two of them, for Mr. Gwinne's thoughts had wandered to the book beside his plate, and Lucy could not understand all they said. But she knew about the tangled threads for she had discovered them at home in Wales, and she understood what loyalty was. There was disagreement in her home, forcing her to decision, and day by day for months past her heart had been like a ball tossed backwards and forwards between father and mother. Now, looking at Dr. Cosin's sternly resolved face, it seemed that her heart was at rest as she thought of her father. "He is my firstborn," she said to herself.

After dinner she went back to Nan-Nan, but she was called down later to say goodbye to Dr. Cosin. "When is your birthday, Lucy?" he asked her.

"April, sir."

"I am a month later with my good wishes," he said, and taking her hand put a silver piece into her palm and folded her fingers over it. "Buy a gift for Lucy," he commanded her.

A silver piece! No one had ever given her a silver piece before. She was speechless with joy as she made her curtsey, but her face was irradiated. He laughed and blessed her and went away.

3

The next few days were spent by Lucy and her grandmother sewing or reading in the garden, or strolling through the country lanes. A visit to London to shop or visit friends, something they both enjoyed when they were together, must wait until the disturbances had quieted down. Lucy waited with some impatience, for the city of noisy streets and quiet gardens, towers and pealing bells, squalor and splendour all mixed up together like one of those tumbling dreams that come to the over-active mind, had gone to her head like wine. Country child though she was she loved London. It was alive, a person not a place, and she loved it good and bad together because both were an integral part of the personality. Mrs. Gwinne and William both understood her excitement over London and now and then would take her on sight-seeing trips, but she was forbidden to go out alone and she at least tried to be obedient these days, though her efforts were not always successful.

The waiting was made easier for Lucy because she was endeavouring to read a book that Dr. Cosin had written. He was a distinguished writer and preacher, her grandmother had told her, but when Lucy had enquired, "Could I read anything he has written?" Mrs. Gwinne had looked doubtful. Then her face had brightened. "I think you could understand the book of prayers he compiled for the Queen's English maids of honour. Her Majesty's French ladies taunted the English ladies because having no breviaries they merely gossiped in their leisure moments, and His Majesty asked Dr. Cosin to prepare a book of prayers for them. He did so and for a time Her Majesty's entire entourage, French and English alike, looked very devout indeed." Mrs. Gwinne's eyes twinkled. "How much the ladies actually read of their books I cannot tell you, but I am sure your understanding is equal to theirs. Go to the library and ask your grandfather for Doctor Cosin's *Book of Devotions.*"

Lucy knocked on the library door and receiving no answer lifted the latch and walked in. Mr. Gwinne's library resembled a clearing in a forest, but the open space was by no means uncluttered, having a minor undergrowth of books piled on the floor, like the stumps of felled trees. Around the clearing great bookcases loomed from floor to ceiling, dark but yet alive with a glint of gold or crimson here and there, as though light shone faintly through massed leaves, and ominous with a motionless power. The light in the room was dim and green because of a creeper outside the window. It softly illumined Mr. Gwinne's bald head, bent over a writing table stacked with books and papers. He would have nothing touched on his table and a pleasing silver lichen of dust grew all over it. His bald head, Lucy thought, looked like a mushroom. She picked her way cautiously towards him, careful not to knock against the tree stumps of books, for some of them were very perilously balanced.

She placed herself at her relative's left elbow and spoke.

"Grandfather," she said in a clear voice, but there was no answer. She spoke several times to no avail, then leaned over and closed his book. He sighed, removed his spectacles and saw her beside him. He was a good-tempered man and uttered no reproach, merely consulted his interior clock and murmured vaguely, "It is not dinner time."

"No sir," said Lucy loudly. "But I want to read Doctor Cosin's *Book of Devotions*, that he wrote for the English court ladies. Will you lend it to me please?"

Mr. Gwinne rose instantly to his feet for his heart being in his books it could always be reached and touched by any appreciation of them. He approached one of the felled tree trunks and removed the first six volumes. Though the state of his library seemed to others chaotic he himself always knew exactly where to find any given volume. He took up the seventh and gave it to Lucy.

"Our friend's writings should be read with caution, my dear," he told her. "The admonitions of the learned doctor are excellent, and the prayers, both those derived from ancient sources and those composed by himself, leave nothing to be desired. His rendering of the *Veni Creator* is most distinguished. But beware his original poems. He is not a poet and it is to be regretted that he should have endeavoured to emulate the poetical works of Doctor Donne, of whose genius he has no spark. Doctor Cosin is a great man of letters but, I repeat, no poet. Do not base any efforts of your own on his verse." He had forgotten he was speaking to a child, and now he turned from her and went back to his table and in half a second had forgotten her existence. She picked her way carefully to the door and went out to the garden to sit beside her grandmother, the *Book of Devotions* open upon her lap. But it was very heavy going for a maiden who read with so much difficulty and Mrs. Gwinne took pity on her.

"Let me read to you, my love," she said, laying down her needlework and holding out her hand. "I will read you some of Doctor's Cosin's own delightful verses, and perhaps you could learn some of them by heart and repeat them to him when you see him again."

Lucy refrained from repeating Mr. Gwinne's disparaging remarks and handed over the book with gratitude. She could enjoy the melody of spoken words but her eyes could gather no music from black marks hurrying along white paper, and she was sure they never would. It made her feel quite ill to think of her grandfather, and men like him, shut up for a lifetime among billions of black marks. No wonder her grandfather was bald before his time.

"This is a prayer in verse for His Majesty," said Mrs. Gwinne. "And one we might pray daily in this time of trouble.

> Great God of Kings,
>   Whose gracious hand hath led
>   Our sacred Sovereign's head
> Unto the throne
>   From whence our bliss is bred;
> Oh, send Thine Angels
> To his blest side,
>   And bid them there abide,
> To be at once
>   His guardian and his guide.
> Dear be his life;
>   And glorious be his days;
>   And prospering all his ways,
> Late add Thy crown
>   To his peace and praise.
> And when he hath
>   Outlived the world's long date,
>   Let Thy last charge translate
> His earthly throne
>   To Thy celestial state."

"I will learn that," Lucy promised her. "I will learn two, but I would like the second one to be very short."

Mrs. Gwinne turned the pages and found a short evening admonition which Lucy approved for its brevity and learned on the spot, for she could learn by heart very quickly, and repeated to her grandmother.

Permit not sluggish sleep
  To close your waking eye,
Till that with judgment deep
  Your daily deeds you try.
He that his sins in conscience keeps,
  When he to quiet goes,
More desperate is than he that sleeps
  Amidst his mortal foes.

Then Mrs. Gwinne read her the *Veni Creator* and this time. the words filled her with a delight so keen that the tears stood on her eyelashes, and she sprang to the defence of her friend with a passion that surprised Mrs. Gwinne.

"Doctor Donne could not have written that!" she said. "My grandfather said Doctor Cosin has not Doctor Donne's genius, but Doctor Donne could not have written that."

"Doctor Cosin did not write the *Veni Creator*," Mrs. Gwinne explained gently. "It is his translation of a Latin hymn."

"Doctor Donne could not have translated it," said Lucy hotly. "And who," she asked with contempt, "is Doctor Donne?"

Mrs. Gwinne laughed. "He was dean of St. Paul's, Lucy. He has been dead for some years, alas."

"Why do you say alas?" asked Lucy. She was delighted to hear the man was dead for it gave Dr. Cosin the ascendancy. He at least was alive.

"Because he was a great man, a great poet and a great preacher. I was in London once or twice during his lifetime and I heard him preach. I heard his last sermon in St. Paul's. It was Easter Day sixteen-thirty, the spring that you were born. The experience was unforgettable."

Lucy's quick mind flew off at a fresh tangent. "I have seen St. Paul's outside," she said, "but I have not been inside. Will you take me, madam? And oh, madam, afterwards will you take me shopping on the bridge?" She was jumping up and down in her eagerness and Mrs. Gwinne could only yield. "When it is safe we will go," she said.

A few days later it was considered safe for gentlewomen properly attended to venture through the London streets. The old coach came out of the coach house, the horses were brought in from the field and the old coachman cum gardener climbed slowly to the box, Abel the garden boy, an added masculine protection, leaping joyously up beside him. Nan-Nan did not come for London so terrified her that she left Covent Garden only to visit Mrs. Gwinne.

It was a perfect day in June and the scent of the first wild roses came to the lowered coach window as they drove through the meadows, and left them only as the coach bumped over the cobbles of Drury Lane. The Lane was lined with houses now and Mrs. Gwinne deplored it. The pace at which London was spreading was causing a good deal of anxiety at this time. The walled city of London and the city of Westminster were now the body of a growing octopus, with tentacles reaching out to the villages of Stepney, Wapping and Kensington, and even to the fishing village of Putney, and not all the proclamations of King James and King Charles against new buildings had been able to halt the growth. "These foreigners who are here now are to blame for the over-crowding," lamented Mrs. Gwinne. "The new industries bring them, and of course the sea port and the new docks. They must live somewhere, poor things, one understands that, but where will it all end? How ugly these new houses are! Drury Lane was charming in the old days."

They drove on to London Wall and passed through the great gate into the old city that had always been here. The streets were very narrow and the traffic dense, carts and coaches jostling each other with great noise and confusion, for these streets had been made for men on horseback and for street barrows, not for the modern wheeled traffic.

At Paul's Cross they got out of the coach, and the old coachman was told to do some errands for Mrs. Gwinne and to fetch them later. Then they walked up the steps to the Cathedral. It was in a bad way just now for the spire had fallen and not been rebuilt, and much of the nave was in a ruinous state, but it was still a fine building. It surprised Lucy to find ladies and gentlemen using the nave as they used the piazza at Covent Garden, as a place for walking about together, and laughing and talking. There were plenty of children there too, playing games in corners, and one or two dog fights were in progress and no sexton came with the tongs to remove the fighters.

"It is not noisy like this in St. David's Cathedral," Lucy said to her grandmother.

"St. David's Cathedral is in Wales," replied Mrs. Gwinne. She needed to say no more. She and her grandchild, two exiles from a better country who lived their lives upon a higher plane, withdrew from the crowd and paced together down a quiet aisle, a place where sunlight touched the tombs of the dead, and their memorials upon the wall were silvery with the same soft dust that had drifted like sand into unswept corners, and like sand took the imprint as they passed of the slender feet of the lady and the child. Behind them the distant sound of the people was a sea surge. In front of them the sea caves of the holy places held only echo.

"This is like St. Davids," said Lucy. "Only there is no Chancellor Pritchard here."

Her grandmother, searching for something, was not attending. "There is the effigy of Doctor Donne," she said, and halted.

Dust could not soften the harsh outlines of the carved face at which they were gazing. It was the face of a dead man seen through the parted folds of the winding sheet, grim and frightening, retaining in death the hard living stamp of the power and passion of a lifetime.

Lucy's hand trembled in her grandmother's. "He is not like Chancellor Pritchard," she said, "but he looks a little like Doctor Cosin. Do all great men have big noses?"

"Not invariably," said Mrs. Gwinne. Then she considered the carving. "You are quite right, Lucy. They are a little alike. Both have fighters' faces. But the Dean, I think, fought his greatest battles within himself. Most of Doctor Cosin's enemies are without, and so his face is less tragic."

"Is it better to have your enemies outside?" asked Lucy

"Not necessarily better but certainly happier, for in exterior warfare you can more easily forget yourself."

"Is that good?"

"It is the only good, my dear."

There was a sound of mingled pattering and piping, as though a lot of small birds were singing through a spring shower beating on broad leaves. They looked round and saw a crocodile of little boys walking briskly up the nave two by two, weaving in and out of the promenade of ladies and gentlemen as expertly as a lizard through grass. They had bright shining faces, and their piping voices, as they chattered together, were sharp and clear. Black gowns lifted back from their shoulders and their thick shoes on the worn paving stones went clackety-clack with a heartening cheerfulness. They disappeared into the shadows and the sound of rain and birdsong died away.

"The choristers of St. Paul's," said Mrs. Gwinne. "When we see them again they will have their surplices on and the service will begin."

Already the organ was playing and quietness was falling upon the nave. Some of the ladies and gentlemen were going away and others were finding seats and talking to each other only quietly. Two men in black gowns, whom Lucy took to be a sexton and beadle such as they had at Roch, were shooing out children and dogs. Mrs. Gwinne and Lucy found seats in the nave and sat down and waited.

Presently they saw the little boys again, coming out of the shadows and filing up to the choir two by two, silent and decorous. The gentlemen singers and the cathedral dignitaries followed them and the service began.

Lucy had never heard music like this. It rose and fell, sometimes a mere thread of sound, sometimes a swell of glory. Now and then the music ceased altogether and a voice could be heard reading from the word of God, or praying. No words could be distinguished from where they sat, but the voice had a strange far-off beauty as though someone was speaking of glory from beyond the confines of the world. A line of poetry came to Lucy. "Touch God in the Fair Temple." The Harper had sung that in the Song of London Town. At the end of the service the boys alone sang a hymn. Until now the choir had been singing the music of William Byrd and the voices had sounded like musical instruments weaving their separate threads of sound in and out in a complicated pattern, but this hymn was sad and simple and touched Lucy to uncomprehending pity. She did not hear the final blessing, or see the choir filing out again, but sat with her eyes fixed unseeingly upon her clasped hands, and compassion flowed from her as she remembered the sin-eater. Where was he now, her poor scapegoat? She had not remembered him in a long while but now she saw again his frightened face as he ran away into the night, bearing with him the sins of John Shepherd. Her grandmother was speaking to her and she lifted her head.

"It is strange, Lucy, that they should have sung the Dean's own hymn today. He wrote it towards the end of his life and it was set to music. I was told that when the boys were to sing it, ill though he was he would come in wrapped in his cloak and sit in his stall and listen."

"Is it about sin?" asked Lucy.

Her grandmother looked at her, startled. "It is a hymn of penitence," she said.

"What did the Dean do?" asked Lucy.

Mrs. Gwinne was getting up and shaking out her skirts, and she had about her now the remoteness of a grown-up who wishes to change the conversation.

"There is no need to know about adult sin at your age, my dear," was her answer.

"I do know about it," said Lucy. "It is a tangle and we are all caught up in it, squirming like flies in a spider's web. I knew a sin-eater once and he was a very nice man. I could not hear all the words of the hymn. Will you say it to me, please?"

Mrs. Gwinne capitulated and sat down again, for she knew her granddaughter's tenacity. She repeated the poem as well as she could.

> *Wilt Thou forgive that sin where I begun,*
> *Which was my sin, though it was done before?*

158

Wilt Thou forgive that sin, through which I run,
And do run still: though still I do deplore?
When thou hast done, Thou hast not done,
   For I have more.

Wilt Thou forgive that sin which I have won
Others to sin? and made my sin their door?
Wilt Thou forgive that sin which I did shun
A year, or two, but wallowed in a score?
When Thou hast done, Thou hast not done,
   For I havè more.

I have a sin of fear, that when I have spun
My last thread, I shall perish on the shore;
But swear by Thyself, that at my death Thy Son
Shall shine as He shines now, and heretofore:
And having done that, Thou hast done,
   I fear no more.

"Was his last thread his last sin?" Lucy asked. "How nice to be dead and not have to sin any more."

"Poor old coachman must be tired of waiting for us," said Mrs. Gwinne. Rising now with finality she took her grandchild by the hand and led her firmly from the building.

Lucy's mood changed instantly. "Now for the bridge," she said joyously, and leaving her grandmother she ran on ahead to find the coach.

The southern boundary of the city was the river and they drove through the south gate on to London Bridge itself. Though there were thirty landing places on the Thames there was only this one bridge, and to Lucy it seemed one of the glories of the world. Eighteen great arches carried the famous shopping centre right across the river. The buildings were tall and some of the houses above the shops were carried by arches across the street. Between the blocks of buildings there were open bays and here one could lean over the wall and see the river and watch the shipping. The shops on the bridge held everything the heart could desire, silks and velvets, jewels and silverware, perfumes and spices from the East, fine china and delicate glassware. Everything that the ships brought up the river found its way to London Bridge. There was even a shop that sold parrots and lapdogs, and little monkeys and marmosets such as the Queen loved. Being so small herself Henrietta Maria liked diminutive creatures and people said that when she travelled she was followed by a whole coach full of monkeys and dwarfs. Lucy had visited this shop once before but it had broken her heart to see these little creatures. Their eyes were so sad as they sat shivering in their cages. There had been one especially, silver in colour with a black face, who had looked at her as though imploring her to buy him. But she had had no money then, and Mrs. Gwinne had told her this morning that a marmoset would cost more than one silver piece. Yet she could not forget him. "If we go past the shop today," she told herself. "I will shut my eyes."

They moved slowly along the bridge, stopping here and there for Mrs. Gwinne to make a few purchases. She was not a wealthy woman, least of all now with her grandchildren needing so much help, and she bought only a few things and these only after careful consideration. Lucy was not bored for everything she saw fascinated her, and today, for the first time in her life, she had money to spend. If Dr. Cosin's silver piece would not buy a marmoset it might buy the red shoes she saw in the window of the third shop they entered. She had always wanted red shoes. While Mrs. Gwinne was rubbing a piece of green cloth between finger and thumb, testing its worthiness to be made into a winter cloak and hood for her granddaughter, Lucy ran out of the shop to look at the shoes from outside. Running away from her grandmother was the last thing she intended, and she would have been back beside her again in a moment had it not been for the sudden excitement that broke out on the bridge.

"The Prince! The Prince! Coming up the river!" First one voice cried it out and then another, and there was a stampede of the passers-by to the open bays between the shops upon the east side of the bridge. There was one not far from the shop and Lucy was off like the wind. She would get to the front against the parapet or she would die. Diving this way and that wherever she saw an opening, thrusting with her sharp elbows and kicking hard, with her pink hood lost and her rose-coloured gown torn, she reached the parapet. But she could not get to the front for a solid line of bodies was leaning over it. Almost weeping with frustration she attacked the three backs nearest to her; slim backs clad in well-cut doublets, emerald green, silver grey and periwinkle blue. The emerald back had a familiar look and upon that she beat the hardest; then as its owner swung round with an oath she wriggled in between him and the taller figure in blue and hooked herself over the parapet of the bridge, clinging like a limpet with hands and feet and the whole of her defiant body. Let them unhook her if they dare!

"Lucy, you little devil!" ejaculated Tom Howard. He began to explain who she was and they all three burst out laughing, and the young man in blue put his arm round her to protect her from the pressure of the crowd behind them. She glanced up briefly, smiling, then turned back towards the river, for the barge was coming towards them.

He was coming up the river to Whitehall. The busy traffic on the water had come to a standstill, the boats and barges drawing in to the banks with the men pulling off their hats and cheering and the women waving their handkerchiefs. Were the King and Queen there? asked the gossips on the bridge. No, only the Prince and the Earl of Newcastle, his tutor, and his gentlemen, said a man behind Lucy. They wouldn't be cheering like that if the King and Queen were there. But everyone loved the Prince. Even the Puritans. It was said the Puritans wanted to depose the King and put the Prince on the throne. "Traitor devils!" murmured Tom Howard hotly, but the young man in blue who held Lucy replied under his breath, "It might be the answer."

Then Lucy heard no more for the barge was coming nearer and the people on the bridge were beginning to cheer too. The golden summer day was turning towards evening and a cool breeze came over the water, lifting the folds of the Royal Standard flying from the stern of the barge. It came strongly forward, two white-crested waves rippling back from the prow, the banks of oars rising and falling in perfect time. The level sunlight gleamed on the flashing blades of the oars and glinted back in points of light from the gilded carving of the barge. All was a swift movement of colour and light held in the blue of water and sky like a gliding star, the mysterious planet that had shone when the Prince was born.

He stood bareheaded in the prow, waving his hat to the cheering people. He was a tall boy for his age and stood very erect, with dignity and grace. His hair fell to his shoulders, black and shining. His doublet was of golden satin with a big white lace collar that contrasted startlingly with the darkness of his skin. The barge had come almost to the bridge and he looked up at the cheering people crowded against the balustrade, lifting his hat and smiling at them in the way he had been taught, but holding the smile with difficulty, licking his lips now and then when they grew stiff and dry with the effort. Lucy saw his face more clearly than she had ever seen anything in her life, a square face dominated by the big nose and the large dark eyes. The Prince, looking up, saw the little girl leaning over the parapet and knew with the instinct that all children have that here was someone of his own age. His difficult smile changed to a grin so merry and infectious that Lucy's intentness broke up and with the whole of her self she smiled back at him, her eyes sparkling. He tipped his head far back and they laughed and waved to each other until the last second. Then the barge shot forward under the bridge and he was gone.

She was so tired, she found, that when the young man in blue lifted her down from the wall she could scarcely stand and was glad to hold to his sleeve.

"You have lost your hood, Lucy," said Tom Howard. "And torn your gown. What a gipsy you are."

"Has she run away from her mother?" asked the other young man. Lucy, coming to herself again, looked up into the face above the blue sleeve to which she was clinging. She considered both the strange young men, flashing her glance from one to the other so piercingly that they laughed. They were brothers, she thought, for they were alike, tall and good to look at, with the easy manner of those who have never made contact with the necessity for earning a living. If they did not look as though they owned the earth that was because they had never given a thought to the fact that they did. It was a fact of nature that had not yet been called in question.

Tom told her their names, Algernon and Robert Sidney. It was Algernon who was dressed in dove grey and Robert who wore periwinkle blue. Though she had not heard their illustrious name before Lucy sensed that these were young men upon whom the Princess Nest would have looked with a favourable eye, and she walked away between them with an air of such delicate yet comical dignity that they laughed again. Then her mood changed, as the buccaneer suddenly became aware of grave financial loss. "My silver piece!" she cried, and pulling her hand from Algernon's she ran back towards the river wall, thrusting the people aside that she might search among the cobbles for her lost treasure. Tom Howard blushed for shame, disassociating himself from this dishevelled little bantam hen scrabbling for corn, but both the Sidneys followed her and endeavoured to be helpful.

"It was a large silver piece?" asked Algernon.

Lucy lifted a flushed face. "It was not large but Doctor Cosin gave it to me. When the Prince came I must have dropped it."

"We will not find it now," said Robert gently. "Do not grieve, Lucy. I will give you another silver piece. What do you long for? A marmoset?"

Lucy looked up at him, as transfigured as though she had lifted the edge of a curtain and looked into heaven. Then the curtain dropped again. "No," she said. "A pair of shoes. A silver piece would not buy a marmoset."

"But you want a marmoset," said Robert. "And I have several silver pieces and I want to give you a marmoset. Shall we choose one?"

The words were hardly out of his mouth before she was running across the bridge, in and out of the traffic, making for the pet shop upon the other side. Horrified, he leaped after her, afraid she would be run over. Laughing, Algernon returned to Tom.

Lucy's face was pressed against the shop window when Robert caught up with her, her eyes searching anxiously among the little creatures within. "There was a special one," she said, in desperate anxiety lest it should be gone. "Silver and small. There it is!"

"That one in the corner?" he asked dubiously, for the poor little creature looked very fragile. But Lucy was no longer with him. She was in the shop and had the marmoset in her arms. He followed her and looked into the great dark eyes so tragically set in a tiny velvet mask of a face. The eyes were too sorrowful to reflect light, and the silver body had become tarnished with misery, but the promise of beauty was there in the whiskers that fringed the little face; they shone in the sun like threads of fine spun glass. And it knew how to cling to what it wanted. It had its forearms round Lucy's neck, its tail was endeavouring to encircle her waist and it was giving little frantic cries of pleading. Lucy too knew what she wanted. Her eyes pierced straight through the doubtful Robert, transfixing him to her will.

Nevertheless he made enquiries of the salesman as to the marmoset's age and health. It was a young one, he was told, and valuable, but it had been difficult to keep alive because its mother had died; but with a good home it should not now be difficult to rear. With his back to Lucy Robert took out his purse and paid for the creature. When he turned to her again she was holding the marmoset in the crook of one arm as she had seen so many mothers holding an ailing child, and her face was grave. The child who had rushed across the road to find the marmoset had vanished now in someone much older. "I believe he cost too much," she said in a low voice. "But I cannot give him back for if I do not have him he will die. Can you afford it?"

He respected her feelings, and he did not laugh as he assured her that he could afford the marmoset.

"Thank you," said Lucy. "Thank you for my marmoset. His name is Jacob."

They crossed the bridge again and found Algernon Sidney and Tom with a very shaken Mrs. Gwinne. The face that she turned on her granddaughter was sterner than Lucy had ever seen it. "Madam, I did not mean to run away," she said.

Mrs. Gwinne, believing her, gravely inclined her head and by intuitive mutual consent the thrashing out of this matter was postponed until later. But the stern glance was not relaxed. It passed on to the marmoset and remained there.

"His name is Jacob," said Lucy with rock-like firmness.

Robert explained, recalling Mrs. Gwinne to the remembrance of a former brief meeting. His mother, he believed, had the honour to number Mrs. Gwinne among her friends. Mrs. Gwinne's face softened and she smiled. She was too good a woman to be a snob but nevertheless she was not averse to having her acquaintance with Lady Sidney expanded into friendship. Doing violence to a natural distaste for monkeys, and a prophetic foreboding as to this one, she forced herself to caress Jacob's velvet head and to express her gratitude, on her granddaughter's behalf, for so valuable a gift. Then the coach was found and the ladies handed into it.

"Have you seen the lions at the Tower of London, Lucy?" asked Robert. She shook her head. "Then with your grandmother's permission I will take you there one day."

"It is a bargain?" asked Lucy.

"It is a bargain," he said.

Eight

It was a month later, when she was back again in King Street,
Covent Garden, that Lucy's world collapsed about her. The
pattern of her childhood, the father and mother, the children
and Nan-Nan, had always seemed immutable to her. When
the family unit had been moved from Roch she had been disturbed, but it had been set up again in Covent Garden and she
could adjust herself to change of place if the family itself remained intact. The quarrels that broke out so often now between her father and mother made her feel as though pulled
two ways by a branching tree, but it had never occurred to her
that the tree could split in half and crash to the ground, bringing its nesting birds down with it in its fall.

The day began happily. She woke soon after dawn and
dressed quietly, because she shared this room at the top of the
house with Nan-Nan and she must not wake her. When she
was dressed she tiptoed across the room to the big bed. Ever
since the fright at Gold Grove, when she had woken up and
found the fourposter empty, she had needed constantly to
check that Nan-Nan was there. Being so small she tended to
get lost in the billows of her feather bed but she was more
visible than usual this morning, lying on her back as though
she had not moved all night. Yet Lucy doubted if she had
been sleeping during the hours when she had not moved.
Though oblivion had come to her now she lay like someone on
the rack. Lucy pushed the horrid idea away from her and
turned to pluck Jacob from the padded box beside her bed
where he slept. He protested, screwing his tiny hands in his
sleepy eyes, but when she tucked him in the crook of her left
arm and he felt the warmth of her body his whimper turned to
mutterings of pleasure. With her thin shoes hung round her
neck by their ribbons she crept out of the room and ran lightly

down the stairs, unbarred the door and came out into the fresh and dewy sparkle of Covent Garden; the loveliest square in London, and never lovelier than at five o'clock on a summer morning when there was no one there but Lucy and Jacob.

She put him down and he ran after her to where the stalls of the country people, who were allowed to come daily to sell fruit and flowers and fresh vegetables, stood empty and wait-ing. Here, for a few moments, they played together. Jacob was still a very small and thin monkey, but his coat was no longer tarnished and whenever he was with Lucy his great dark eyes reflected her love. For Lucy was his joy and his life. With her he was a charming and delightful little animal but apart from her he was cantankerous, mischievous and a perfect nuisance. With her this morning he leaped and played as though he had been the first monkey in Eden, and the growing light shone on his silver coat.

William, who had a grudging affection for this London square that he had chosen out of all others to be Lucy's home, had told her its history. The square had once been the convent garden of the monks of Westminster, the men of the White Abbey of whom the Harper had sung at Golden Grove. It adjoined their graveyard and had been called Frère Pye's garden, but William had not been able to tell Lucy anything about Frère Pye. What had happened to him, she often won-dered, when Henry the Eighth had turned out the monks? She hoped that loving this patch of earth so much he had become a shepherd when he could not be a monk any more, one of the King's shepherds whose sheep had grazed under the apple trees and among the gravestones of the monks.

This royal sheepfold had remained at peace for a long while, bounded to east and south by two great houses, Drury House and my Lord of Bedford's mansion, and to north and west by green fields, but a few years ago my Lord of Bedford, who owned the land, had had the idea of building a fine square north of the walled terrace of his own garden. He had asked Inigo Jones to design it for him and now it was finished, a church and fine houses surrounding the site of the old garden. The stones of the buildings, untarnished yet by London

smoke, sparkled in the sun and the portico of St. Paul's
Church, that formed one side of the square, glimmered like an
Athenian temple. At dawn the square might almost have been
that city of the Apocalypse that Nan-Nan had expected to see
when she came to London.

A seagull swept down low over the garden, turning and
swooping over the child and the monkey as though delighting
in their play. Looking up Lucy could see the great wings outlined against the sky, that was unfolding like a flower, and the
tips of the feathers were points of fire. Then the gull wheeled
up and away, back to the river, and with Jacob on her back
clinging round her neck, she ran after him.

In Southampton Street she had to stop and put her shoes on
and the bird escaped her. She saw him flash once at the end of
the street and then he was gone. She ran across the Strand
and down a narrow lane between the garden walls of two great
houses, and came out to where a flight of steps led down to a
narrow jetty thrust out into the water. This was a public landing place and later in the day would be crowded and noisy, but
in the quietness of dawn it was one of Lucy's two special
places, the other being inside St. Paul's Church. With Jacob
still clinging round her neck she climbed up the angle of a
garden wall to her left, where an old mulberry tree had placed
two branches like arms along the river wall and leaned there
to survey the scene. Settled comfortably within the arms of the
tree Lucy and Jacob did the same. Behind them in the garden
the thrushes and robins and blackbirds were singing their
hearts out for joy of the new day.

Whenever she was here Lucy could feel herself on her
special rock in the bay at Roch, for almost from the base of the
wall the sparkling flood of the Thames stretched like the sea.
and there was often a tang of salt in the air, if the wind blew
from the estuary. And there were multitudes of birds to be
seen, gulls and cormorants, swans and ducks, and their voices
kept Lucy stretched midway between ecstasy and grief. Across
the water, half seen in golden mist that had not yet been caught
up by the sun, the south bank was embowered in green, with
here and there a church tower soaring up, or the octagonal

block of a theatre. The Globe Theatre was there, not far from London Bridge, where she had seen Prince Charles. She had not seen him again but she could not forget him. His square brown face lived in her memory as did the damask rose, and the dark bearded face of Dr. Cosin, equally unforgettable and real.

A few ferrymen were on the water now, plying up and down on the look-out for early customers, and one or two of them saw the little girl and the monkey sitting in the arms of the mulberry tree and laughed and waved. The Thames ferrymen were a rough crowd, but Lucy was never scared of them and travelling on the river was for her one of the greatest joys that London had to offer.

She was watching now for the boats that would come presently from the golden mist across the river, bringing fruit and flowers and vegetables from the gardens of the south bank to the city shops and the stalls of Covent Garden. Many of these craft used sails when the wind was fair and presently she could pick out the small speeding boats that were bound for the landing place below her, and could hear singing coming clearly across the water. People who passed their lives among flowers and growing things always seemed happy, she had noticed. But then the ferrymen seemed happy too. Perhaps that had to do with the sea birds and the rhythmical plunge of oars in the river.

The boats were coming in one by one to the jetty, letting down their sails as a bird folds its wings, and she could smell the flowers. Laughing and talking the men and girls came up the steps carrying the piled baskets. Leaning out of the tree Lucy could see inside the baskets. The strawberries were over but they had raspberries and currants, picked in the dew and still glistening with it, and peas and beans as well as all the flowers. She called out to them and they laughed and waved to her as the ferrymen had done, for they knew her well by sight, and told her to send her nanny to the Garden presently to buy their wares. When they had gone she stayed on for a while listening to the lap of the water and the crying of the gulls, the music of the wind in the mulberry leaves and the singing of the birds in the garden. This was something that her rock in the bay at Roch had not been able to give her, the sound of water and leaves singing in unison and the gulls and the thrushes speaking together.

This morning she was able to listen, as on rare occasions she could look, in a manner that caused time to cease. Had the music continued in the silence she could have grown old listening, but London was stirring. The number of ferrymen was increasing and there was a distant rattle of carts on cobbles and the first street cries. The flower of the sky had now opened to the full and dropped its petals, leaving only its golden heart blazing in the unclouded blue, and the river was so brilliant, every ripple crested with fire, that it hurt the eyes to look at it. With Jacob on her back she climbed out of the tree and down the wall and ran up the lane to the Strand.

Southampton Street, that had been deserted when they ran down it, was now awake. Chimneys were sending up spirals of smoke, the sound of voices came from windows that had been flung wide to the sun and air, and Lucy and Jacob went warily past open doors lest a bucket full of slops, flung in the direction of the open kennel, should catch them. When they reached the Garden it was full of activity. The flower girls and fruit and vegetable men were at their stalls, spreading out their wares. Lucy, Jacob in her arms now, went to her favourite but one stall, where Nan Cookson, a freckled girl with a fascinating squint, was making up her posies. Lucy still had the habit of returning from her truancies with propitiatory offerings and she wanted one now for her mother.

"I have tuppence, Nan," she said, getting from her hanging pocket the two bright new pennies that Mr. Gwinne had given her on parting.

"What will you have, dearie?" asked Nan. "Rosebuds, stocks, heart's-ease or pinks?"

"Pinks, please, Nan," said Lucy.

Nan's big red hands moved so quickly in posy-making, bunching the flowers together and twisting long grasses round their stalks, that the posies fell from her fingers to her lap almost as though she were shelling pease, but she allowed a few extra seconds to Lucy's, choosing the flowers with care so that Lucy had a variety of pinks, frilled white ones, white ones stitched with scarlet round the edges, pale pink, a couple of sops-in-wine and one deep red clove carnation in the centre. It was a generous tuppence-worth and Nan was within her rights when she demanded, "Give us a kiss, dearie." Lucy leaned forward and kissed Nan's rough cheek, that smelt of carnations. Nan was steeped in her flowers and smelled of them from head to foot, as did Old Sage of his herbs.

Old Sage had his stall as close as possible to St. Paul's Church because he kept his main supply of herbs in the church loft. He was nicknamed Old Sage because no one knew his real name and he could not tell it because he was dumb. His stall was Lucy's favourite. There were trees at this end of the Garden and it was sheltered from the sun by a great yew tree which must have been growing here in the days of the monks, and being the last in the row of stalls it was the quietest. Old Sage sold herbs of every sort, bunches and packets of dried herbs, fresh bunches of mint, lavender, rosemary and marjoram, and also cloves and peppercorns and oranges stuck with cloves to keep away infection. He had stooped shoulders, a broad squashed nose and a great domed and wrinkled forehead. He would have been very ugly but for the expression of his face. Every wrinkle was full of humour and overlying the humour was the most extraordinary peace; which was strange because it was rumoured in the Garden that he was dumb because his tongue had been cut out by Portuguese pirates. His clothes were as ancient as he was himself, and when he moved herb dust sprayed from his person like pepper from a pot.

When he was not selling herbs Old Sage was reading a book, holding it close against his squashed nose because he was shortsighted. It was always the same book, brown and worn and dusty, and Lucy thought he must know it by heart by this time. She had asked him once what it was, and he had held it out for her to see, but as it was all written in a foreign language it had remained a mystery. But then this whole quiet corner was a mystery, something apart from the rest of the

Garden. The scent of herbs that came with the drift of every
warm breeze seemed to belong to some country that was not
England, as did the beautiful portico of the church, with its
simple columns. The shade of the trees lay gently over the stall
and patterned the white pillars with blue shadows. The tranquillity of this corner imposed quietness on all who came; but
not many did come, only those who wanted herbs, and tired
people who liked to rest in the portico.

A curious mistake made by Mr. Inigo Jones was one reason
for the quietness, for there was no entrance to the church from
the portico. My Lord of Bedford, planning his square, had
desired fine houses for the nobility and gentry, but as Almighty God unfortunately would not pay rent for his house
my Lord told his architect, "I will not have it much better
than a barn." So Mr. Inigo Jones had made it with the beautiful proportions of a tithe barn, the side walls being of rose-
brown brick; but the pillared portico caught the rising sun
upon a face that did not belong to the English countryside but
to the isles of Greece. That perhaps was the reason why Mr.
Inigo Jones did not remember until too late that the entrance
to a Christian church cannot be through the east wall, the
place of the altar. My Lord of Bedford had not remembered
this either, but after a short period of consternation they
lifted up their spirits and made the entrance in the plain west
wall, at the back of the church. It was a blessing in disguise for
churchgoers and sightseers entered from Bedford Street, walking along a path arched with trees that led through the monks'
churchyard, and the portico was undisturbed.

The only shopping Nan-Nan ever did in this terrible
London was at the herb stall. She felt at home in the quiet
corner, and very much at home with Old Sage. He kept her
generously supplied with all the herbs she wanted; especially
with the precious rosemary. Lucy never went to the stall without asking if there was some rosemary stowed away for Nan-
Nan, and as soon as he saw her Old Sage bent to a basket
behind his stall and handed her a bunch. Then he made a
gesture with his hands, disdaining payment. He did not like to
be paid for rosemary. For other household herbs he would ask

payment, holding up his fingers to indicate the number of pence he wanted, but not for rosemary; at least not for Nan-Nan's rosemary. The gesture ended, and his gestures were always very articulate and graceful, he took another bunch from the basket and bending forward tucked it into Lucy's hanging pocket. She looked into his dark eyes and remembered Old Parson. They were not alike, but for some unknown reason they came together in her mind, and remained so. Then he indicated that she should go home. She had meant to go to her other special place, the inside of the church, but she obeyed him and as she ran home all the clocks of London began to strike seven.

Nan-Nan was up and in the kitchen, for Polly the little maid who helped her with the cooking was flighty and needed a constant eye upon her. "Where have you been, Lucy?" she asked severely.

"Down to the river," said Lucy, "and then to the Garden."

Nan-Nan, passing her days in a maze of grief, was inclined to let her sorrow magnify the children's peccadillos out of all proportion, and she wrung her hands over Lucy's disobedience as though it were the worst crime in the calendar. "Dulch! Dulch! alone in this wicked city you were! It is murdered you could have been. Break my heart, you will."

Lucy refrained from argument and presented the rosemary. "Old Sage sent it to you," she said. "And he gave me some too."

Nan-Nan was holding the rosemary in her cupped hands as though it were a purse full of gold. "We shall need it this day," she said. Then Polly let the milk boil over and she turned to chide her.

Later, Lucy sat sewing with her mother in the window of the upstairs parlour. Elizabeth was teaching her household needlework, hemming and featherstitching, and the mending of fine linen and lace. Sewing together they could sometimes recapture the affection they had enjoyed during lesson times in the bower at Roch, but today this was difficult because William was slumped in a big chair by the hearth, a news sheet held open before his unseeing eyes. Elizabeth had brought the ignoring of her husband to a fine art and chatted to her daughter as though he were not there. But Lucy could not ignore him, for his unhappiness seemed pressing down on top of her head like a physical weight. "He is my first born," kept chiming in her weary head, and she was so dull and stupid over her work that her mother had to keep chiding her.

"Let the child alone!" said William suddenly. "She is doing her best."

Elizabeth did not even glance at him but next time she scolded her daughter her voice had so sharp an edge that the tears came into Lucy's eyes; but she was saved from weeping by the sudden winding of the postboy's horn in the square outside. The post, bringing William news of his crops and beasts, was his one link with sanity. He jumped up eagerly, flinging his news sheet untidily into the corner.

"Stay where you are, William!" said Elizabeth sharply. "We have servants, have we not? Sit down. Your letters will be brought to you."

He sat down again, drumming with his fingers on the arms of his chair in the way that drove his wife almost distracted, and presently Polly came in with the letters and handed them to her mistress. There was the usual pile of bills or dunning letters, and a packet from Roch folded in linen and tied with thread. With maddening deliberation Elizabeth cut the thread, unfolded the stained linen and sorted the enclosures. A letter from a sister in Wales was kept for herself, the rest she handed to Lucy to give to her father. One, addressed in the handwriting of Mrs. Chappell, William's mother, and sealed with a large black wafer, seemed unusually thick and heavy, and when she was back in her seat Lucy kept looking at it and wishing her father would open it, and not be so engrossed in the one from his bailiff, and then wishing that he would not open it.

"Lucy!" said her mother sharply, and she bent her head over her work. She did not look up again but she knew when her father took up his mother's letter. The room seemed very quiet, for Elizabeth was reading her sister's letter and she herself had ceased to sew because her hands were clammy.

William's cry was something between a sob and a roar of fury, all the more horrible because it did not issue properly but broke off strangled in his throat. When his wife and daughter looked round he was on his feet, trying to keep a hold of the paper with his shaking hand, his red face blotched with queer white patches.

"What in the world is the matter, William?" demanded Elizabeth, white-faced, her hand to her heart as was the mode now with fashionable ladies when agitation threatened.

"Betsi is dead," muttered William, and the letter fell from his fingers to the floor. He bent down, groping for it.

"Is that so?" asked Elizabeth. "Of what did she die? Some childish ailment? One of a twin is often weak."

Her hand dropped from her side. With their finances in such a delicate state she had feared to hear that the bailiffs would be in the house tomorrow. The colour came back to her face. Her relief was so apparent that it roused William to sudden deadly anger. He strode over to her and put his hands on her shoulders, forcing her to look at him. "My child is dead," he said, "and as much by your hand as though you yourself had killed her. No, Betsi was not strong. Not hardy enough for the life off a mountain farm. I told you so. You would not listen. Yes, she died of a childish ailment, one that would not have killed her had she been in Nan-Nan's care. I tell you that you killed her."

The thing that her mother said now haunted Lucy for the rest of her life; even though she realized later that Elizabeth, in her grief that William should love these children, not hers, so deeply, had hardly known what she was saying. "There is now one bastard the less in the world," she said.

William took his hands from her shoulders and stepped back. Lucy had been sitting motionless, paralysed by shock, but now the stricken look on her father's face woke up all her passionate maternal love and she ran to him, stretching her arms as far round him as they would go, her face pressed against his doublet. She could feel his shaking hand caressing her hair, and did not know that but for her body interposed between them it was a moment when he might have struck his wife.

Elizabeth meanwhile saw only her daughter's back turned upon her and felt herself forsaken. William had beguiled Lucy's love from her to himself. His carelessness had destroyed her first two babies and now he was taking Lucy from her too. She got to her feet, believing herself to be very composed and steady, and tried to tell William gently and calmly that if she had been indirectly responsible for the death of this child he had been responsible for the death of those other, infinitely more precious children; but the unhealed grieving for these two babies, and all her bitterness against William that she had kept hidden for so many years, betrayed her and the words poured out in a coroding flood that horrified her as much as it did William. She tried to check the flood but could not, and a moment later found herself, tears pouring down her face, trying to drag Lucy from her father.

"Madam!"

Nan-Nan was standing in the open doorway, her eyes blazing in her white face. Her controlled anger instantly dominated the distraught man and woman, but she took no further notice of them. "Lucy, come here to me," she said. But Lucy's legs had no strength left and William picked her up and carried her to Nan-Nan, then shut the door on them both and went back to his wife.

Lucy and Nan-Nan got as far as the adjoining room, Elizabeth's bedchamber, and collapsed there in each other's arms, as they had done at Roch when Nan-Nan had told Lucy that the twins were to go away. Only now Nan-Nan was as calmly collected as though nothing untoward had happened while Lucy, released now from the tension, was crying like a cataract.

"Betsi is dead," she sobbed.

"I know my little lamb is dead," said Nan-Nan quietly. "Many days ago I knew it. I have always known that she would die."

"But you are not crying, Nan-Nan."

"I wept for her at Roch but I cannot weep in this dreadful city, this Babylon. The wickedness of men and women dries up the fount of tears and a desert it leaves in the heart. But you, cariad, remember Betsi in her cradle with the bright eyes of her peeping from the hood and weep you. And then dry your eyes and rejoice for the children who die young and uncorrupted."

The words came from her in a slow lamentation and they brought comfort. Lucy's sobs began to hurt less and presently they ceased. She could smell the crushed rosemary in her pocket and almost thought herself back in Roch, hearing the sea, and the wind about the castle tower.

"Nan-Nan, will we ever go home?" she whispered.

"You will go home one day, cariad," Nan-Nan promised her. "And now we will go to the kitchen and make pastan for the boys' supper tonight. Grief or no grief, hungry boys must be fed."

Half an hour later, busy in the kitchen, they heard William go out and then came Elizabeth's voice calling for Nan-Nan. For the rest of that day Nan-Nan was busy with her, for she went sick and shaken to her bed and William did not return. Lucy employed herself as best she could, every now and then bursting into fresh tears as she thought of Betsi, and Dewi left by himself at the farm where perhaps they were not kind to him. And added to her grief was dread of she knew not what, and when the hours had dragged round to late afternoon she could bear it no longer. She took Jacob from the inside of the soup tureen on the kitchen dresser, where he liked to hide in times of domestic crisis, put him on her shoulder, opened the front door and slipped out into the Garden. It astonished her to find the sun still shining for she had thought the day had darkened. She ran quickly across King Street and turned left into the churchyard. It was quiet here under the trees and there was no one about. She opened the west door of the church and went to her favourite seat, where she sat down and took Jacob into her arms. He was very good, not restless and chattering but content to let her chin rest on his velvet head. He was sensitive to her moods, and provided his meals were punctual always anxious to please her.

The church was as dignified inside as it was outside but a little more ornate, for it had a side gallery and a painted roof and the candlesticks and cross on the altar had not yet been taken away by the puritans. It was cool and still and smelt of the herbs stored in the roof. The coolness flowed over Lucy like water, healing her tear-scorched cheeks and burning eyelids. The church did not feel unhappy, as the house had done all day, and after sitting quietly for a while her lonely grief began to have a faint bright edge, like a cloud that has the sun behind it. She and Jacob sat still as mice and as the brightness grew her sense of loneliness vanished. A presence was beside her, but she was reluctant to move or look up.

When she did she found Old Sage standing there. He had come softly because he always climbed with bare feet the ladder to the loft where his herbs were stored. She looked at his feet, large, ugly and strong, then up at his lined brown face, and then she said with complete simplicity, "I thought it was God there." A quirk of amusement, but no surprise, lined his face more deeply. He sat down beside her and placed his hands one on each knee. A cloud of herbal dust rose up about them both and then settled. Cuddled in Lucy's arms Jacob went to sleep. The breathing stillness of Old Sage, his living silence, became one thing with the quietness of the church and that too became for Lucy something alive. The livingness rose about her with such a brightness of compassion that there seemed to be no more grief. And yet her eyes saw nothing but the strong brown feet of Old Sage planted side by side on the floor. She did not know how long it was that they sat there, or when it was that the light sank back again behind her grief. But it was not as bad as it had been before because Old Sage was there, an old man who loved her and knew she was unhappy but could speak no words to comfort her. She looked up into his face wondering if he was grieved that he could not speak to her. But there was no sorrow in his face, it wore only his habitual look of strength and quietness. He placed one of his powerful hands upon her knee, left it there for a moment, then rose and went away.

Presently Lucy went away too, back into the bright sunshine of the Garden. A young man and girl were walking along King Street, her skirts billowing as he bore her along in his swift stride, her arm tucked tightly into his. She seemed almost floating in her joy, though her laughter was breathless, and he grinned as he looked down into her flushed face. They did not even see Lucy as she ran across the cobbles to her door. They were alone in their world. Had her father and mother ever walked together like that? No! she thought, repudiating the question. The one thing could not turn into the other. It could not possibly turn into this other, that she must face again upon the other side of the door.

2

William did not go to bed that night. Elizabeth lying wakeful, heard him go to the dining parlour where his desk was. He stayed there for an hour, then went to the small room where his clothes were kept and locked the door. She heard him moving about for some while but at daylight, exhausted, she slept. Later that morning she was with Lucy, Richard and Justus in the parlour when the door opened and he came in dressed for a journey. The violence and anger were now past but his face had a new hardness and he seemed to have aged ten years. It was a Sunday morning and the Garden outside was very quiet.

"Where are you going, William?" Elizabeth asked sharply.

"To my son," said William.

"Your son?" she gasped, and her eyes went to Richard and Justus.

"Dewi," said William. "I am not leaving him at that farm to die like his sister. I am returning to Roch to make some other arrangement for him. You and the children can follow me in the coach, if you wish, and we will start life together again in Wales. Not in the castle. We cannot afford that now. But somewhere. Or you can remain here and arrange for that separation between us for which you have been wishing for so long. Which will you do?"

Elizabeth and the three children stood without movement, as though they had suddenly died standing upright, for now that it had happened it suddenly did not seem possible or true. Richard stood stiffly beside his mother, Lucy by herself, and she had wrapped her hands up in her apron as though they were wounded. Justus also stood by himself. His mouth was open and tears rolled slowly down over the bulges of his rosy cheeks. William was stabbed by the sight of the two children who stood by themselves. Richard was so entirely his mother's that the breaking of the family bond would probably affect him very little; but the other two might never entirely recover from the lonely bewilderment of this moment. He waited for his wife's reply.

"I will never live with you again," said Elizabeth bitterly.

"Then get rid of this house, sell the furniture to pay our debts and go and live with your mother," said William.

"I will do that," said Elizabeth, "and bring my suit before the House of Lords as soon as possible. I hope never to see you again."

"You will see me when I return to contest the suit," said William grimly. "Do you suppose I will allow you to have the custody of my children without putting up a fight?"

"You will never have the custody of me, sir," said Richard contemptuously.

"I know that," said William, beating down his son's level look with one of sadness. "You have always been your mother's. I was referring to Lucy and Justus." He held out his hand. "Come, you two, come and say goodbye to me in the dining parlour."

They were at least now in movement again, with Lucy and Justus running to their father and Richard solicitous for his mother. She would not say goodbye to her husband or even look at him. He took the two younger children to the dining parlour and sat down, put Justus on his knee and held Lucy in the curve of his arm. "Have you hurt your hands, Lucy?" he asked gently. She unwrapped them and looked to see. "I do not think so," she said, bewildered. Why had she wrapped up her hands in that moment of agony? "I have engraved thee upon the palms of my hands." She had read or heard that some-where as an expression of profound love. Hands were alive as birds, they loved and prayed. Had hers been wounded, know-ing that they would not caress her father's face for years and years? But they would. "I am coming with you," she said. "And so is Justus. We are coming now. We will ride pillion." Justus, whose grief had now reached the backwash of hiccups, chirped and nodded.

William tried to explain. A journey on horseback would be too hard for children and would certainly be the death of Jacob. He did not know where he was going to live when he got to Roch, for he doubted if his mother and step-father would stay on at the castle. Conditions would be harsh. And it was very important that they should continue their education. And they would be happy with their grand-mother. And it would not be for long. He would return. His stumbling explanations reminded Lucy of the time at Roch when he had tried to make the leaving of it a happy thing, and she put no trust in them at all.

"I want only to be at Roch with you," she whispered.

"One day you will be," he said. "I promise."

Into the heart-broken silence came the sound of the Sunday bells and the clattering of hoofs outside. William's servant was bringing the horses to the door. William gasped and found himself with both children in his arms together, clinging to him like limpets. He had to half-carry them with him to the hall where he remembered that he had not blessed them. The stumbling parental blessing brought them to their knees, with Justus detached. But when he got outside Lucy was still there and when he was on his horse she was clinging to his leg. He bent down to her. "Lucy, can you understand this? I am a farmer with my life rooted in the earth of Roch. Here my life withers and I am little better than a captive beast. Can you understand?"

He straightened and sat his horse staring ahead of him, not daring again to touch her rough head or even look at her. The silence lengthened and he was aware in his own being of the tearing in half of hers with the splitting and falling of the tree.

She let go and he heard the light sound of her feet, running back to the house to Justus. She had Justus. Thinking of them together he was able to ride away to the sound of the bells. Down in the Strand the wind met him, he heard the gulls crying and turned westward with a lifting of the heart.

Nine

I

Lucy and Justus were not together for long; only for the short time it took to dispose of the house and furniture and remove Elizabeth, Nan-Nan and the children to the house at St. Giles, where Mrs. Gwinne received her daughter with love and sorrow but no reproach. What she had dreaded had happened and could not be undone and her task now was to comfort her beloved daughter and endeavour to soften her bitterness; while safeguarding her husband's quietness as far as possible, doing her best for the children and Nan-Nan and enduring Jacob. But it soon became clear that Mr. Gwinne's quietness was not compatible with boys in the house and after a tennis ball had in error entered his study window, struck his bald head and caused a slight concussion, it was decided that Richard and Justus must now become boarders, not day-boys, at St. Paul's school. The parting with Justus reopened for Lucy the wound of her father's going, and for a while she could not recover the health and sleep that had left her when he went. She was too vital a child to ail for long but as she grew strong again she became wild and unmanageable and, echoing her mood, so did Jacob.

Mrs. Gwinne and Nan-Nan might have loved her out of her wild state had not misfortune fallen upon the household in the shape of Aunt Margaret Gosfright, who according to her custom arrived upon the doorstep without warning and said she had quarrelled with Peter. Of Mrs. Gwinne's four married daughters, Mrs. Walter of Roch Castle, Mrs. Barlow of Slebeck, Mrs. Byshfield of the city of London and Mrs. Gosfright of Amsterdam, Margaret Gosfright was the least like her mother. The other three had grace and beauty but Margaret was dumpy and plain. Nevertheless the very bright eyes in her homely face had attracted a well-to-do Dutch merchant, often in London on business, and he had married her and carried her off to his comfortable house in Amsterdam. She was happy with him as a rule but there were exceptions to the rule, and times when Holland and the Dutch could no longer be endured. Then she came home to her mother until Peter, growing tired of a bachelor existence, came over and fetched her back again.

Mrs. Gwinne never felt there was any danger of Margaret's marriage breaking up, childless though it was. She liked her creature comforts, which Peter was well able to provide, and in her heart of hearts she liked Peter. And he liked her cooking and they always came together again with mutual appreciation. But just now her coming could only be regarded as a misfortune, for she and Elizabeth had never loved each other. Elizabeth as the most beautiful of the daughters had in the past patronized Margaret none too kindly, and if the plain daughter felt now a secret satisfaction in Elizabeth's discomfort it was not surprising. She said no more about having quarrelled with Peter. On the contrary her talk was incessantly of their married bliss.

On a golden October afternoon Mrs. Gwinne sat in her parlour with her daughters Elizabeth, Margaret and Anne, for pretty Mrs. Byshfield had come over to spend the day. Each lady had her needlework and Lucy, sitting in a corner with Jacob, was making him a jacket for the winter out of remnants of the material her grandmother had bought on London bridge for her cloak and hood. Mrs. Gwinne was stitching at Lucy's cloak now, as Lucy stitched at Jacob's jacket, and sometimes they smiled at each other. There was little opportunity nowadays for their shopping expeditions, for Mrs. Gwinne was too busy and too tired, but her grandmother's love and Nan-Nan's were the mooring ropes that kept Lucy where she was. But for them, she told herself, she would have run away long ago, back to Wales. If she had died on the journey it would have been better than living in this hot stuffy house shut up with a lot of gossiping women.

Her head was bent demurely over her sewing but her grandmother was aware of her mood. Like Justus, Mrs. Gwinne always knew when Lucy was on the boil. Her feet were swinging inside her skirts, swish, swish, in time to her jabbing needle, and every hair on her head appeared to be standing on end with irritation. Outside the garden glowed in autumn sunlight, yet here they were indoors with a fire because Elizabeth said she felt shivery all over, and Margaret, not to be outdone, said she was feeling her rheumatism. "Would you like to run out in the garden, Lucy?" asked Mrs. Gwinne.

Lucy jumped gratefully to her feet but Elizabeth said, "No, mother. Sit down, Lucy. The wind is in the east and I do not wish you to catch another cold."

The angry crimson flushed Lucy's face. Whatever her grandmother suggested for her was nowadays always refused by her mother. Her mother was jealous of her love for her grandmother. Her chin in the air she would have spoken naughtily to Elizabeth but Mrs. Gwinne's calm voice checked her. "Lucy, do what your mother tells you."

She obeyed, but the anger now was beating in her temples and tingling in her hands and feet and her needle went in and out of the green jacket with loud pops. The conversation of the four ladies continued where it had left off, the subject the interminable one of Elizabeth's petition for separation from her husband. It was making slow progress. In these days of national anxiety the House of Lords thought it a trivial matter. Her husband's past infidelity seemed to them not impressive, and his insistence on making her look after his bastards with her own children not the cruelty that she declared it to be. Occasional drinking and cockfighting, and the accumulation of a few gambling debts, were not unusual among gentlemen of spirit, and the only thing their lordships could find truly reprehensible was the fact that William had returned to Wales leaving his wife and family without any means of subsistence. An action had been brought against him for maintenance and he had been commanded to pay his wife sixty pounds a year from his estate.

And there the matter had been left. But not by Elizabeth. Legal separation and custody of the children she must have, she said, otherwise her life would be intolerable to her. The talk washed backwards and forwards in the hot little room until Elizabeth, criticized by one of her sisters, burst into tears and dropped her delicate embroidery on the floor. Jacob secretively stretched out a skinny hand, pulled it to himself and took it into a corner. Lucy did not see what he did, for the moment all attention was on her mother she had run from the room.

She fled down the passage to the library, crept quietly in and turned the key. For once Mr. Gwinne heard her, looked up from his book and exchanged with her the smile of a conspirator. Their opinion of chattering women was identical and during these last weeks the library had been a refuge that had never been denied to Lucy.

"Sit down, child," he murmured kindly, "take your book of comic horrors and hold your tongue."

But Lucy did not want to look at Foxe's *Book of Martyrs*. "Grandfather, give me paper and pen and one of your wafers," she commanded.

He waved his hand towards his writing table and she sat down in front of his big silver standish, and chose a quill pen with care. Apart from a couple of ill-spelt ink-blotted letters to her father this was the first letter she had ever written, and she found the big sheet of paper in front of her rather daunting. It was clean as a field covered with snow and it seemed to her wrong to put footsteps on it. And written words were footsteps, feet running hard to another person. Then she dipped the pen in the ink and smiled, for she wanted to write to this person, even though at the same time she was very angry with him.

"Sir," she wrote slowly and laboriously, "You promist to take me to see the lions at the Tower of Lundun but you hav not dun so. You sed it was a bargin but you hav not kept your bargin." She paused, searching in her mind for a long and impressive word whose meaning she had learned lately. "I think you are a perfidyus man but I am not happy at presunt and I wood like to see the lions at the Tower of Lundun. I am Sir your obedient servunt Lucy Walter."

As she picked up the silver castor and sprinkled the fine sand on the ink a breath of fresh air seemed to come to her, the breath of a man's outdoor world, of cheery laughter, horses and dogs, sowing and reaping, the world she had known at Roch. She must get back to it, away from the chattering ailing women, or she would explode and die. She folded her letter, sealed it with a wafer from the silver box, wrote Robert Sidney's name and then realized that she did not know where he lived and could write no address. She feared to ask her grandfather in case he should disapprove of her forwardness. Tom Howard would know but she saw Tom so seldom now. She was wondering what to do when she heard the parlour door open, letting out a shrill outcry of female distress, and then came the swish of skirts in the passage and onslaught upon the locked library door.

This was the one thing that roused Mr. Gwinne to mild anger, especially if perpetrated by one of his step-daughters, for whom his affection was not strong. He straightened himself and his voice rang out with all the vigour of his youth. "I am engaged in study and beg that I may remain undisturbed."

"Is Lucy with you, sir?" cried out Margaret Gosfright, and she dared to rattle the latch of the door.

He cleared his throat and was prepared to perjure himself but Lucy thrust the letter inside the bodice of her dress and went to the door and unlocked it. She was not going to let one of Aunt Margaret's scenes loose upon her grandfather, and besides, her own blood was up. She launched herself through the door and very nearly succeeded in knocking her aunt over. There was no love lost between herself and Aunt Margaret. Pretty Aunt Anne, amused and affectionate, she was fond of but not Aunt Margaret. "Come here at once, you naughty girl," said Mrs. Gosfright, and with her hand gripped tightly round Lucy's wrist she raced her back to the parlour.

It was a scene of varied emotion. Elizabeth was in a flood of desperate tears, Aunt Anne in fits of laughter, Mrs. Gwinne pale and shaken with the stress of divided sympathies, her arm round Elizabeth and her eyes twinkling at Anne. Elizabeth's beautiful embroidery lay in ribbons on the floor and Jacob was chattering with fury on top of the cupboard, and as he chattered he plucked the flowers from the beau-pot beside him and flung them on the carpet one by one. So great was the sympathy between them that he had reached breaking point at exactly the same moment as Lucy herself. Their eyes met in a passion of mutual affection, and flinging a chrysanthemum high in the air, to descend upon Aunt Margaret's head, he leaped from the cupboard into Lucy's arms.

Then all the Welshness of the Welsh ladies present soared up to bring a marvellous dramatic climax to the emotional scene. Their blood demanded of them that the thing must be finished off in style. Elizabeth cried out that the work of years was ruined, that Lucy loved a hateful little monkey more than her own mother, that Jacob must be got rid of somehow, anyhow, she did not care how, but he must go. Margaret's voice, sometimes rising with dramatic power above her sister's outcry, sometimes sinking below it as though two violins strove together for mastery, told Elizabeth what she thought of spoilt children in general, and Lucy in particular, passing on to denunciation of the whole monkey tribe and, with a falling cadence, to a moving description of the irritation she was this moment suffering in consequence of insect bites upon her person. Aunt Anne's musical laughter ran up and down like a peal of bells and Mrs. Gwinne, though seen to be speaking, was not heard. Nan-Nan appeared, wringing her hands and exclaiming over she knew not what, her celtic lament sounding among the bells and violins like the music of the double harp.

Lucy, the tears pouring down her face, cried out in passionate repudiation of the only two remarks she had been able to comprehend in the hubbub, that Jacob had fleas, and that he was in danger of being taken from her and done away with. Her eyes sought Mrs. Gwinne's and she believed that her grandmother was speaking to her, but she could not hear what she said, and she remembered how unsmiling she had been when confronted with Jacob on London bridge. Her grandmother, she intuitively knew, did not like monkeys. With Jacob gripped to her chest she left the room so quickly that she was scarcely seen to go. Flying down the passage she passed the open library door and was aware of her grandfather standing

there, listening with enormous enjoyment, but with his hand
upon the latch, ready to retreat as instantly as a hermit crab
should the disturbance approach nearer. Lucy had no time to
exchange glances with him. She wrenched open the door at
the end of the passage and sped out into the rose garden
behind the house, then through the vegetable patch and out
through the wicket-gate into the fields beyond.

2

She was running through amber sunshine, and the leaves from
the elm trees were drifting past her as once the birds had done
on the cliffs at Roch, and she remembered the little bird whose
tiny claw had encircled her finger like a wedding ring. She had
been espoused then to the world of woods and fields and water.
At the far end of the first field there was a coppice and she ran
into it and sat down on leaves and grasses that were warm
and dry, for it had been a dry season. All about her the nut
trees and maple trees were pale gold and amethyst, like royal
tapestry, festooned here and there with the pink and orange of
spindle-berries. It was like a bower and suddenly she felt supremely safe. The apparent security of a loved world can be an
illusion, as Lucy had discovered when the family nest fell to
pieces, but every time the badger returns to his holt he believes
himself to be safe.

Her breathing steadied and presently she was crooning to
Jacob as though she had not a trouble in the world, and she
had still not considered what she was to do when the sound of
the horn came to her, slanting down a beam of sunlight that
was turning the spindle-berries to jewels on the branch. She
listened at first in sleepy delight, and then with a thrill of
excitement, for there was enchantment about her. She was
back in the bower at Roch, with her mother sitting on the floor
beside her reading from the Mabinogion. The memory of that
closeness with her mother, gone now for ever, was a stab of
sudden pain. In this bower she was alone. Mother, Mother, she
cried within herself, but Elizabeth was changed and did not
hear, and the horn was calling again and she must go.

With Jacob in her arms she came to the farther end of the copse and ran under arching boughs into fairyland, where the very air was golden and the green grass spangled with gold. The gold trees reached to heaven and all the birds of paradise were singing in them. There was a bird singing over her head and she stopped under a branch to listen to him, craning her head back to see the speckled breast and throbbing throat and wild bright eyes of the golden thrush. "Look, look, look!" he said. "Look where the green and the blue are one."

She saw then how the green grass at her feet sloped down to an azure blue that lapped the meadow's end like water, and above made a smoky mystery of the fairy wood where the horn was sounding, now near, now far. She went a little forward and then stopped, for she could hear laughter in the wood and she was in awe as well as ecstasy. Who were they, laughing? They were riders, certainly, for she heard twigs cracking beneath horses' hoofs, and she saw, or thought she saw, a white unicorn appear through the haze and vanish again. But it was all muted by the blueness and distant like a dream.

Then, with a clear call, a boy in a green coat, on a black horse, came riding out of the dream, calling her name. "Lucy, Lucy, Lucy!" And behind her the thrush cried, "Look, look, look!" and it was her dear Tom Howard whom she had not seen since Richard and Justus went to boarding school. Then she saw that this was not fairyland after all, just one of the fields she knew, dandelion-spangled, the tall elms golden in the autumn sunlight. Tom jumped from his horse and clinging to him she did not mind that the dream had vanished. Indeed it seemed more wonderful, not less, to have been so enchanted by the commonplace, for it meant that the fields and trees one knew so well were not commonplace at all but had, each of them, their own profound mystery. She knew now that she had always suspected this, and she laughed for joy as Tom pulled her hair and teased her, and teased Jacob, and then swung them up on his horse and turned it back again towards the wood.

But then it was the fairytale again, for just within the wood was the unicorn and he had a straight slim boy on his back, dark-haired, wearing a coat of shadowed amethyst, the colour of the maple leaves in the dell, a silver hunting horn slung over his shoulder. On either side of him were two of the most beautiful boys she had ever seen, dressed alike in azure and riding pale chestnut ponies, their bright hair so lit by the sun that they seemed aureoled. Yet sons of the morning though they appeared they did not eclipse the dark boy with the horn.

"He had it as a gift," Tom told Lucy as he led his horse forward. "And nothing would content him but we must ride out from Westminster and let him wind his horn in the woods. Then nothing would content him but we must give Lord Newcastle and his gentlemen the slip. So we did, Buckingham and Lord Francis and I. But, oh lord, the storm there will be when the Earl catches up with us!"

She had known who it was at once. Who else could it be? When the door had opened into fairyland from her mother's bower at Roch she had found Prince Kilhwch, and it was the same door that had opened within the bower of the copse.

"See, sir, the nymph I've caught!" cried Tom. He was excited and breathless, and in his heart a little scared. The Prince was carefully guarded these days both in his own household and at Whitehall, and the Earl of Newcastle had allowed him to come out riding only with great reluctance and after much pleading, and with a considerable retinue. The many armed gentlemen obscuring the view, and making adventure of any sort totally impossible, had vexed the Prince and the boys who were his companions today; the Duke of Buckingham and his brother Francis Villiers, who shared his lessons, Tom Howard and a few others. Following a plan hatched by the Prince they had suddenly broken loose in the fields and galloped away in different directions into the woods. They had reunited at a certain oak tree known to them, where the Prince had changed his black pony for a white one and his crimson coat for the amethyst coat of another boy. A rider on a black pony, wearing a crimson coat, and followed by three more, had then ridden at top speed out of the woods and in again, the gentlemen in frantic chase, and the Prince, the

Duke, Francis Villiers and Tom had ridden off in the opposite direction. But Tom as the eldest of them knew only too well that the punishment likely to be meted out to collaborators in the near future would be severe.

The Prince slid from the white unicorn, who on a clearer view was seen by Lucy to have no projecting horn, and stood waiting, his dark eyes full of merry recognition. The two sons of the morning also dismounted and stood one on each side of him, and at Tom's whispered command Lucy too dismounted and knelt and kissed his hand. Neither then nor at any time did she ever feel in awe of Charles. As she kissed his long brown fingers she showed no emotion stronger than contentment. She had been sore and miserable for so long and now she was healed and happy again. She got to her feet and looked him straight in the eyes, her head back and her hands behind her. Her blue gaze did not put him out of countenance for his own black eyes could probe without blinking for as long as hers could. "I saw you on the bridge," he said. They laughed and his eyes went beyond her to the little creature clinging to the saddle of Tom's pony and chattering with annoyance at being left behind. "Is that your marmoset?" he asked eagerly.

Tom fetched Jacob and Charles took him in his arms, handling him as a boy does who loves animals with understanding and affinity, and Jacob was graciously content to be caressed by him and made no attempt to scramble back to Lucy. The other boys crowded round, and Lucy told them how Robert Sidney had given Jacob to her on the same day that she had seen the Prince come up the river, and it was she and not the Prince who was now the centre of admiring attention. Untidy though she was, with ruffled hair and the usual rent in her gown, she was as unselfconscious as she was untidy. Used as these boys were to demure little girls with careful ringlets and unblemished silken skirts, her tattered gaiety was enchanting. Tom, seeing the impression she was making, was proud to say she was his little wife, but Buckingham interrupted to say that she should be his. "But I am jealous," he said. "Love letters already?"

The letter that she had written and thrust into the front of her gown was showing. The young duke took hold of the protruding edge and pulled it out. "So Robert Sidney is the lucky dog," he laughed. "May I see, Lucy, what sort of love letter you write?"

"You may not, my lord," said Lucy hotly. "The letter is sealed. And it is not a love letter. Mr. Robert Sidney promised to show me the lions at the Tower of London and he has not done so. I have written to tell him he is a perfidious gentleman."

"He has been at Penshurst, Lucy, not in London," Tom explained. "He could not help himself."

"Then he should have written to tell me he could not help himself," said Lucy.

"She must see the lions," said Charles. "I have myself seen the lions and they are very handsome. George," he commanded the Duke, "see that the letter is delivered."

"Command me, sir," said Tom. "I am the more trustworthy." And he took the letter.

"You did not ask me, any of you, whether I wished to have this lady for my little wife," said Charles, and asserting his royal rights he seized her hand and ran with her into the wood, Jacob still in the crook of his left arm. The other three followed slowly, leading the ponies and laughing. It might have been spring, not autumn, in the woods, they were so gay and so forgetful. Winter and retribution had become a double impossibility.

Charles halted where blackberry bushes grew about a fallen oak. They sat down on the tree trunk and ate the ripe berries together, and between bites they talked a little of Jacob and of Charles's dogs, murmuring to each other of this thing and the other thing, a jay with blue on his wings, a toadstool like a scarlet cup that grew upon a twig at their feet. They did not know of what they talked and did not afterwards remember. They had instantaneously loved each other, as two children so often do, without emotion but with complete satisfaction. The wood was warm and golden and together they found rest for their souls. She had known no peace like this since she had sat

in the church with Old Sage. Charles, privacy and quiet
scarcely known to him, marvelled at the silence and having
only the one person beside him, and that person apparently
unaware that he was a prince. Yet she had waved to him from
the bridge and kissed his hand when bidden. He chuckled,
knowing suddenly that if she had not been told to kiss his
hand she would not have done it. He looked round and kissed
her with great simplicity and she returned the kiss with maternal tenderness. "I am four days older than you are," she
explained. She was aware that in spite of all appearances to the
contrary he was not entirely happy. Perhaps he knew too
much too soon, even as she did, about the tangle of this world.
"I would like to comfort you," she said, but before he had time
to answer they were interrupted by the running feet of the
three older boys.

"Sir," cried Tom breathlessly, "we can hear them crashing
about in the wood. They are just about on us."

Charles rose with dignity, less disconcerted than the collaborators, for his would be the lesser punishment, if any. "I
shall command that you be brought to play with me," he said
to Lucy. "Look! Jacob is asleep."

At the sound of his name Jacob woke up, rubbed his small
hands in his eyes and then cuddled back again in Charles's
arms. He was as happy with him as he was with Lucy. This
immature man, his intuition told him, was possessed of a
premature intelligence and knew already that faithful friends
are more easily to be found in animals than men.

Lucy's intuition too was very much alive just now, for she
knew that whatever command he might give she would not be
allowed to play with Charles. The only comfort that she had it
in her power to give him was Jacob.

"Sir, I would like you to keep Jacob for your own," she said.
Then she paused and added, "If your Royal Highness will
deign to accept him it would give me great pleasure."

The words she heard herself saying did not seem her own.
Afterwards she wondered how she had managed to say them,
for the pain of parting with Jacob was very great. Charles was
unaware of the cost of the gift. He was used to accepting pre-

sents wherever he went, usually of an educational character; Mr. Nicholas Ferrar of Little Gidding had lately presented him with a large illustrated bible; a monkey made a nice change. He expressed his delight with his invariable tact and charm and, this time, with sincerity, but his flow of words was cut short by the cracking of twigs and the sudden shout of a very angry man.

"My Lord of Newcastle," said Tom. "Run, Lucy."

She did as she was told and ran fast out of the wood, but not in fear; she ran so that she should not have to see Jacob's velvet face again. She sped across the field and into the little copse and sat down again beneath the gold and amethyst leaves. She did not know how she was going to live without Jacob. She was glad she had given him to Charles, yet together with the gladness there was the loss and the one did not banish the other. She was too miserable even to cry. How could she go on living without Jacob?

The copse grew chill as the shadows lengthened and she remembered her grandmother and Nan-Nan, and that they loved her and perhaps were anxious. She left the copse and went across the field, through the garden and so home. She went straight to the parlour and her grandmother was sitting there alone, doing nothing, and Lucy thought that she looked very much older now that her daughters had come to live with her. Perhaps daughters were a mistake.

"Lucy," said Mrs. Gwinne, holding out her hand, "Where have you been? They have all been looking for you." Lucy came to her grandmother and stood silently beside her, and Mrs. Gwinne cried out, "But where is Jacob? What have you done with Jacob?"

"I have not got Jacob any more," said Lucy.

"But did you not hear me say that you should not be separated from Jacob?"

"I did not hear what you said in all that hubbub of aunts," said Lucy, "and I know that you do not like Jacob."

"It is true that I do not like monkeys, but I would not have let anyone take him from you. He was a comfort to you. Where is he, my dear?"

"I met Tom Howard in the fields with some other boys and I gave Jacob to one of them."

"And you cannot get him back?"

"Jacob was a gift," said Lucy with a touch of pride.

"Who was this boy?"

"A friend of Tom's," said Lucy, and would say no more, for what she felt about Charles was something too strange and private to be spoken of.

Mrs. Gwinne kissed her gravely. "I love you very much, Granddaughter," she said. "I love you more than any other living person. So does Nan-Nan, whom you will find upstairs. It is past your supper time. Goodnight."

"Goodnight, madam," said Lucy. Her grandmother was curiously undemonstrative for a Welsh woman but Lucy understood her undemonstrativeness and respected it. She choked back the tears that Mrs. Gwinne's words had brought near to the surface, curtseyed gravely and went upstairs comforted.

Ten

Lucy's letter was despatched by Tom and soon brought forth an apologetic reply from Robert Sidney. He had not forgotten her but he had been much away from London and the city had been so disturbed this autumn that he doubted if her grandmother would have approved an excursion to the Tower. But when the times were better they would have their outing. Lucy thought this an unsatisfactory letter and showed it to her grandmother. But Mrs. Gwinne upheld Robert Sidney. The Tower was a prison as well as a zoo, and notable political prisoners had been in captivity there since the last Parliament, among them the Puritan leaders John Pym and John Hampden who were so beloved by the people of London. There had been noisy demonstrations not only in the streets but among the Thames boatmen. Lucy must wait.

"It is foolish to keep prisoners and lions in the same place," said Lucy. "For it is in times of disturbance that unhappy people need the comfort of lions."

Mrs. Gwinne looked at her granddaughter and saw that she spoke not flippantly but in sincerity and from inner grief. She was anxious about her father. She missed the animals at Roch and she missed Jacob even more. The lions would have brought true comfort. "Mr. Sidney will take you as soon as he considers it safe for you, Lucy," she said gently.

"I do not wish to be safe," said Lucy. "I wish to see the lions."

November came with skies veiled with thin silver and the trees with thinner gold, a fragile and hushed world imploring peace; and for a while it seemed that the city was in a quiet mood. The Puritan leaders in the Tower had been released. The King's Scottish war had ended for the time being in defeat and armistice, and he had returned to London to call

another Parliament. A letter came from Robert Sidney to
Mrs. Gwinne asking if he might now take Lucy to the Tower.
It was shown to Elizabeth, who said it should have been written to her, and another family storm ensued. But Lucy this
time rode it peacefully. She was going to see golden lions in
silver weather, and with that sense of occasion that had come
with her Welsh blood she said she would wear for the first
time the winter cloak and hood which her grandmother had
made for her and trimmed with beaver fur.

Sitting beside her in the coach, driving through the fields
towards London on the great day, Robert Sidney found her
changed. At their first meeting she had seemed an impetuous
gipsy, though royal withal, but this small maiden seemed a
pensive child who answered his kindly questioning without
shyness but sadly. He could not know that his masculinity, so
close to her, had overwhelmed her with longing for her father.
Depressed by this autumnal mood he pulled her hood back
from her face with a suddenness that startled her, and out
came the gipsy like a jack-in-the-box, rosy and sparkling with
mixed anger and delight, uncertain whether to laugh or spit
like a kitten and dissolving instead into a sudden burst of
tears.

"Whatever is the matter, Lucy?" he demanded, his arm
round her and her head against his shoulder.

"My father does not like me to wear a hood," she sobbed.

"It is a pity, with hair like yours," he agreed, pushing his
fingers through it. "It is like heather, or a dog's coat. And if
you think that sounds ungallant I did not mean it so. I like
heather and dogs. You must miss your father now he's away,
but he's alive and with you on this star, this special green star."
He went on talking at random and she was soon comforted.
He told her that his own father had gone to Paris to be Ambassador there and his mother had gone with him, and his
sister Dorothy, whom he loved very much. There were
brothers and sisters left at Penshurst but Dorothy was the
dearest of them all.

Lucy was interested in Dorothy and wanted to know how
old she was, and Robert said she was nineteen and had a hus-

band and baby, and Lucy was discouraged by such importance and maturity. She had thought Dorothy might be her own age. Then Robert said Dorothy was so pretty that the poet Mr. Lovelace had written songs about her, and that put her instantly into the company of Nest, Olwen, and Fair Rosamund, and the thought of all these lovely ladies brought added brightness to the air, and in no time at all they had reached London.

"We must go by boat to the Tower," he told her, "even though it is on the same side of the river. No one must go to the Tower for the first time other than by water."

They left the coach in the Strand and to Lucy's delight went down the alley way that led to her special place. She looked up at the mulberry tree leaning its arms upon the wall. The leaves were now thin gold, and there were few of them left. They floated slowly down towards the river and when they were standing on the landing-stage Lucy found them rustling about her feet.

"They are mine," she said to Robert, and when this surprised him she told him that the mulberry tree was one of her two special places. "Where is the other?" he asked, and she told him it was at Covent Garden and she would take him there on their way home. Then the boat that Robert's shout had summoned came alongside and she forgot the gold leaves and abandoned herself to the joy of the occasion.

In the care of a stout and jovial boatman they moved down the river with the ebb tide at a splendid and exciting pace. Even on such a windless day there was a cool breeze on the water and the sea birds screamed and dipped around them. They might have been at Roch, only neither the trees of the south bank nor the procession of great houses and autumnal gardens that edged the north bank were like the coast of Wales.

"Look, Lucy!" cried Robert. "Look back at Whitehall." She looked back and saw the famous array of tall buildings rising superbly from the water, crowned by steep irregular roofs, towers and spires, the home and state apartments of the King of England. This royal habitation took the curve of the river in a graceful sweep and was reflected in the water. Past its gateways the white swans floated day by day, and the gulls dipped and rose about the walls. And this was Charles's true home, as Roch was hers. ".Is the Prince there now?" she asked Robert.

"I expect he is, now that the King is home and the new Parliament sitting. Look, Lucy, at the barge coming up-stream. There's a fine barge for you!" Then as it came nearer he exclaimed in astonishment, "That can't be my Lord of Strafford's barge. He is at home in Yorkshire. My God it is! And he is in it. S'death, what a fool!"

The boatman stopped rowing and turned to look. "Black Tom Tyrant, the devil take him!" he growled, and spat in the water. "All the trouble in England is along o' him and the Archbishop. All those goddam taxes. Grinding the faces of the poor. Bringing the Pope over to burn us poor Protestants to death all over again. Hanging, drawing and quartering's too good for them two."

"Hold your vile tongue!" said Robert in sudden fury. "We have a child with us."

Lucy had been aware of their conversation with only one ear, for the other was attuned to the music that came over the water as the barge was rowed powerfully up-stream. A young page was sitting in the prow thrumming a guitar and singing. The music had a noble eloquence that accorded well with the striking figure who stood in the barge, looking at London as though he saw it from the water for the first, or the last, time. He was unusually tall, a lion of a man. Beside him stood a huge Irish wolf-hound. About the man and dog there was a mutual grave affection that was very clear to Lucy.

"Is that my Lord of Strafford, in the crimson cloak?" she demanded.

"Yes," said Robert. "The greatest man in England."

An explosion of disagreement from the boatman was checked by the wash from the barge, which struck them while his mind was elsewhere, and their boat swung into another whose occupants, a couple of city merchants and their wives and boatman, had also been gazing at the barge. An oar was lost; the boatmen swore loudly and blasphemously, the boats rocked madly and the water splashed the ladies' cloaks. They were frightened and screamed, while their husbands shouted and reached for the lost oar, banging their heads together and nearly capsizing the boat. It was a typical Thames fracas. The gulls screamed with the ladies and Lucy, though she laughed, could now understand her mother's reluctance to travel by water. She herself was not frightened but Robert was afraid she might be and rising up, tall and enraged, he roared at the boatmen, beating down the plebeian noise with his aristocratic thunder. Then he turned the Sidney charm on the ladies and soon they were happy and pacified, and with mutual apologies and compliments the two boats continued their journeys.

"I did not know you could shout like that," said Lucy with admiration.

"I can when the situation demands it," said Robert with modest pride.

London Bridge loomed over them and Lucy found it thrilling to look up and see the shops and houses right up above her in the sky. Then their boat shot into the shadows below, where the silver water became suddenly dark and menacing about them, sucking and slapping at the piers of the bridge as the waves at Roch sucked round the rocks when the tide was coming in. There was a booming overhead like the booming of storm and looking down at her Robert saw that she was his little gipsy again, excited by the experience and enjoying it to the full. He was rejoicing in her when suddenly her face crumpled and she was once more in tears. When they came out the other side into the light again it seemed that there had never been a more miserable little girl.

"Lucy, is this just Welsh emotion or is something really the matter?"

"We were just underneath!" she sobbed.

"Underneath what?"

"The shop where you bought him for me."

"The marmoset?"

"Yes. Jacob. I haven't got him any more."

"He's dead?"

"No. I gave him away."

He was surprised but not hurt. He had an intuitive understanding of her and knew there was some good reason for the parting. "Could you tell me about it?" he asked.

Until now she had found it impossible to speak to anyone of Charles, but it was Robert's right to know about Jacob and she must tell him. Controlling her tears with adult resolution and murmuring low as a bee humming in his ear, so that the boatman should not hear, she told him about the meeting in the fairy wood. "I had nothing else to give him," she explained. "Only Jacob."

Robert rubbed his ear, which was tickling with the bee-humming. "I should have done the same," he assured her. "There is nothing that I could myself refuse to Prince Charles. And Jacob will have a good home."

"You forgive me?" she asked.

"Of course I do. True gifts are not given with conditions. They are given for the recipient's pleasure, whatever that pleasure may be. Now look. We are coming along to the Tower."

The great fortress rose menacing in the grey day. Arsenal, zoo, mint and state prison, it was in its last capacity that it awed Lucy. As they drew in to the landing-stage, and she saw above her a flight of steps and a dark arched doorway through which she must pass, fear came over her. It was not physical fear, a thing of which she knew nothing, but a darkness of the spirit. The silver day was unchangeably soft and gentle about her, Robert's hand helping her from the boat was kind and strong, and the face of the man who was coming down the steps to greet them wore a welcoming smile. But these things, dissolving in the chill of the fear, had no reality. Nothing was real but this very terrible spiritual thing that had come to meet her and broken over her like a wave. But like a wave it passed on. She was aware again of her cold hand clinging to Robert's, of stone steps beneath her feet. But the living warmth of Robert, the firmness of the steps, were things that it was necessary for her to test with her own senses, as a man bites on a coin, testing their validity with hers. To have the contact ring true brought the greatest relief she had ever known.

"Is the little maid scared?" asked a kindly voice.

Lucy looked up into the relaxed yet still slightly stern face of the man on the steps and was presented to Mr. Cottington, the Lieutenant of the Tower. Such was the Sidney prestige and his own charm that Robert was able to command even the personal welcome of the Lieutenant when he brought a little girl to see the lions.

"She is cold after the journey on the river," explained Robert.

Mr. Cottington smiled at Lucy, and took her hand. "I have a fire in my library," he said, and led the way through the archway and along a dark passage to a room where the window looked on a green garden that might have been in the heart of the country, had it not been for the grimness of the walls that enclosed it. The library was like that of any country gentleman, booklined and comfortable, with a log fire burning and a collation of cold meats laid out upon the table.

Lucy, with her capacity for enjoyment of the present moment, forgot her fear as her eyes flashed appreciatively from the collation to the two other gentlemen present, or rather one gentleman and one boy, presented to her as Dr. William Harvey and his nephew Smuts. The famous doctor, a Welshman who came sometimes to visit Mr. and Mrs. Gwinne, Lucy knew already but Smuts she did not know. He was on a visit to his uncle and had also been brought to see the lions. He had bright eyes and a sprinkling of freckles over his nose and cheekbones to which he owed his nickname, so he told her later. She knew at once, as she had known with Tom Howard and Robert, that friendship with him was like the end of a long ribbon put into her hand, something she would hold and follow into the future.

Chairs were pulled to the heavy oak table and the cold game pie and roast beef, washed down with ale and London wine, enjoyed to the full. Then the gentlemen sat by the log fire with their pipes but the boy and girl were detained by ginger suckets and rosy apples. Their elders smoked and watched them with amusement.

"There are no children living in the Tower just now," said Mr. Cottington sadly. "There have been so many in the past. Young Watt was here with Sir Walter Raleigh at one time, and Algernon was here with his father the wizard."

Lucy heard and looked round at Robert. "Algernon?"

"Not my brother," Robert told her. "My uncle."

"Was your grandfather really a wizard?" gasped Lucy.

"He carried out scientific experiments; he was a chemist and alchemist. He was looking for a way to turn baser metals into gold."

"Was that why he was put in prison?"

Robert was smiling with private amusement. "No," he said. "My maternal grandfather, the Earl of Northumberland, was mysteriously involved in the gunpowder plot. It was not a serious mystery but it was awkward, and unexplainable, as when one of his chemical experiments went wrong and blew a hole in the ceiling of his laboratory. The final result in both cases was a rather nasty stink." He brushed aside a smoke ring with his elegant hand. "The Gunpowder Plot smell still clings a little."

"I do not think it is right that poor little boys should be imprisoned with their fathers," said Lucy indignantly. "I would not like to be imprisoned in the Tower." For a moment the fear touched her again, but it passed and she added slowly, "Yes, I would, if I was here with my father."

"My uncle enjoyed the experience," said Robert. "He visited the lions daily."

At the mention of lions Smuts who had been intent on his food, swallowed a sucket whole and got up from his seat. "Lucy has finished now," he announced, and Lucy loyally transferred half an apple to her pocket in order to bear out his statement. Mr. Cottington arose to lead the way.

Lucy held Robert's hand rather tightly as they were led along a labyrinth of narrow passages with stone staircases leading up from them. It was all very dark and airless and there was a curious smell everywhere, a stale unhappy smell that she did not like at all. Robert hummed a gay tune as they went and behind them Dr. Harvey laughed with Smuts, and Lucy realized they did it on purpose, and knew that a place where people laughed and hummed on purpose was not a good place. Her heart swelled against the knowledge and gave her a physical pain in her chest.

Mr. Cottington unlocked a big door and they went through and there in front of them, behind the bars of their cage, were the royal lions pacing up and down. While they had been in the dark passages the sun had broken through and now it shone down through a window full upon the lions, turning their tawny coats gold. The first impact of lions is always a fearful yet glorious experience and Smuts and Lucy gasped, then glowed and exulted. One great beast stopped pacing and looked at them, his head up, his great mane so illumined by the light that it surrounded his majestic, dreadful countenance like the sun itself. "That's Leo," said Mr. Cottington.

Leo, the only sign of the zodiac ruled by the sun, a royal sign, its flower the rose, its colour orange and its gem the ruby. For a moment or two the great lion, in his strength and kingliness, seemed not to be an animal at all but a symbol of tragic greatness and a portent of doom. Then, as Lucy's stunned physical senses became active again, she saw with pity the marks of mange upon his body and smelled his smell, and it was as unhappy as the smell in the prison passage, and she knew he would die here. She stood staring at him, oblivious of the others talking and moving about her, and was hardly aware of being taken away, or of the door clanging shut and being locked behind her. As they went down the dark passage a great roar broke out, echoing in the stony place like thunder in a cave. It seemed to come up behind them, to reach, engulf and devour them and to triumph over them. "S'death!" Robert ejaculated. "Thank God the door's locked." But Lucy exulted. They might crash a prison door in his face but Leo had had the last word.

It was Robert's suggestion that they should go up to the ramparts. Lucy, confronting Leo, had looked a little white,

The

and he doubted if his choice of an afternoon's entertainment, regarded as entertainment, had been altogether successful. The tough little gipsy was as sensitive as a princess when it came to a hard pea under the feather bed. She was well aware of what she did not see. She was not to be fooled.

Up on the flat roof behind the ramparts the glory of London leaped to meet them in the sunlight. The Thames flashed and sparkled and London shone as though reborn. The silver mist had not entirely vanished though the sun had thrust a hand through it, long rays of light outspread like fingers, and its ethereal silver gave a unity to towers and trees, ships and gulls and churches, while the fingers of the alchemist sun, turning all they touched to gold, gave to each wing and spire and roof-top its own life within the unity. This marvel, this diversity in unity, the elders saw, but having just experienced the newness of lions the eyes of Smuts and Lucy saw things made utterly new. "What's that word that means things being made again?" she asked him as they hung over the ramparts together.

With the kindly patronage of superior age and sex he told her. "Renewal. Re-new-all. Make all new."

"If you were to put please in front it would be a prayer," said Lucy.

"My uncle says that we are made new with every heartbeat," said Smuts, "as the world with every spring. New birth, he says, is the rhythm of the world."

Lucy could feel the knocking of her heart, pressed against the stone ramparts. "Make us and make us and make us," it knocked and pleaded. "Make us and make us until we come out right." Then she jumped back from the ramparts. "You can't catch me!" she said to Smuts.

"I can," he said, and ran after her as she darted backwards and forwards like a fly-catcher.

"They'll fall," ejaculated their anxious host.

"Sure-footed as conies," Dr. Harvey assured him, and they returned to the anxious adult conversation that had very quickly submerged the first astonishment of the silver and the gold. Scraps of it floated to Smuts and Lucy when presently they leaned again upon the ramparts, getting their breath. Robert was telling the two other men that he had seen the Earl of Strafford. "Why could he not have stayed in Yorkshire?" he asked with passion. "Is he mad? Does he not know his own danger?"

"He knows," said Dr. Harvey. "But the man is a lion for courage. It is my belief that he has deliberately returned to London in the character of the King's scapegoat."

The word riveted Lucy's attention instantly. Another of these scapegoats? But he had not looked like her scapegoat at home. There had been nothing lion-like about her poor old friend. Or had there been just something in him of a fleeting reflection of the gold? She was feeling bewildered and scared when she heard them talking again.

"I think it is his hope to draw the anger of the King's enemies upon himself as much as possible," Dr. Harvey was saying. "He will present himself as the man responsible for the King's policies, and then refute whatever charges the Commons bring against him. He has the skill to do that."

"He will be impeached," Mr. Cottington said gravely.

"He may hope for that," said Dr. Harvey. "He has done nothing treasonable. The law is on his side. If the Commons try to impeach him and he stands his trial, and the impeachment fails, they will have done nothing but make themselves look ridiculous. The result of that to the King will be clear gain."

Smuts was talking to her and Lucy missed the next bit but presently she heard Robert say, "Where was he going in his crimson cloak, with a page singing in the prow?"

"At a guess, to Westminster, to take his seat in the House of Lords without more dallying."

"That will be to set a match to the powder," said Mr. Cottington.

"We will see what tomorrow brings forth," said Dr. Harvey grimly. "Time's going on. Where are those children? Mr. Cottington, we are deeply grateful to you for your hospitality."

2

The return journey was by coach, not by water, and they gave a lift to Dr. Harvey and Smuts, setting them down in the city. As they bumped and rattled up the familiar way from the Strand to Covent Garden Lucy said shyly to Robert, "I said I would take you to my other special place. Please may we go there now? It is in the Garden and Old Sage is in the place. I hardly ever see him now and I love Old Sage."

"Of course we will go and see him. Which house does he live in?"

"He does not live in a house. He has the herb stall in the corner by the church."

"But will not the stallholders have sold out and gone home by this time?"

"Not Old Sage. When there are no more people buying herbs he stays at the stall and reads. He likes reading. He cannot talk because pirates cut his tongue out."

"Cut his tongue out?" ejaculated Robert. He was intrigued. He told the coachman to wait and walked with Lucy towards the sunset that came welling up from behind the church. He felt like a young god, lapped in gold, in the morning of the world. The white pillars of a temple rose up before him and the air was fragrant with the wild thyme of the hills of Greece. There was a yew tree somewhere and he could smell that too, and behind him he was quite sure he heard a flock of sheep grazing the turf; he knew so well the little tearing sound, with its evocation of so much. Then it vanished. The enchantment was so great that he was unaware that Lucy had left him. Then the silence was gradually filled with one of the sounds of power, beginning far off and growing in intensity, his exultation keeping pace with it, until he was ready to shout with joy as Apollo's swans beat their way overhead, their wings lit with gold. They vanished into the sunset and bemused he turned blindly towards the yew. He had been too close to Apollo and needed the tree's earthiness. From its shade a man looked forth at him, and he knew his face so well, the broad squashed nose, the bald furrowed forehead and curly grey beard. Whom else should he find here in the shadows of the Greek temple? Only the man who had spoken with such perfection of Apollo's swans. Only Socrates.

Whatever mystery it might be that had gently withdrawn him from his own place and time returned him with equal gentleness to the reality of the Garden; if where he was now was a place more real than the other. How could he know? But the man was real, and dumb; though it might be that he had an eloquence of being as lovely and moving as the song that the page had been singing as the barge of my Lord of Strafford bore him along to Westminster.

"This is Old Sage," said a voice beside him, and looking down he found Lucy at his elbow. The man rose courteously to his feet, holding a half-closed book in his hand, his finger marking the place, and the herb dust that had been disturbed by his movement was about him in an illumined nimbus. Lucy stood watching. He did not look at Robert as old and poor men so often looked at young and rich ones, with a queer mingling of envy, subservience and contempt, he looked straight in his eyes with friendliness and compassion, as though he were in some way the more fortunate of the two. And Robert seemed to think so too for he looked at Old Sage with respect and entreaty.

"Will you allow me to see what you are reading?" he asked.

Old Sage held the book out to him, and looking up into Robert's face Lucy realized that the language which had been unfamiliar to her was not so to him, for his face lit up. "The Iliad," he said. "I thought that I should find you reading Homer. And Plato? Do you read him too?"

An expression of great sorrow passed over Old Sage's face and Robert divined its meaning. "You no longer possess your Republic," he said. "Is your Iliad the only book now left to you?"

Old Sage bowed his head, and then as though to forestall possible pity bent down to his basket and handed Robert and Lucy a sprig of rosemary each. The brilliant light had faded now and the pillars of the portico glimmered dimly in the twilight.

"I must take Lucy home," said Robert, putting the rosemary away in an inner pocket of his coat. "I have already had her with me for longer than the time allowed me by her mother. When I come back shall I find you still here?" Old Sage nodded, smiled at Lucy, sat down and opened his book, and by the time they turned away he had forgotten them.

"Thank you, Lucy," said Robert as they drove through the dusk towards the village. "I am glad to have met Old Sage."

"He is a very God-like man," was Lucy's surprising answer.

"You are right," said Robert soberly. "We are nearly home. I must come in with you and apologize to madam your mother for having kept you so long."

"If you are coming into the parlour to talk to madam my mother, and my aunt, I shall not be talking to them with you," said Lucy firmly. "I shall be going upstairs to my grandmother. Therefore I will say goodbye to you in the garden."

In the shadowy garden, where a robin was singing a last song in a leafless apple tree, she curtseyed and thanked him very prettily for her entertainment. Then she rose from her formal curtsey, kissed him impetuously, darted into the porch and sounded the knocker. Elizabeth opened the door instantly and while Robert was bowing to her Lucy circumnavigated her mother's wide skirts and escaped upstairs to her grandmother's room.

Mrs. Gwinne and Nan-Nan were sitting before the fire. The candles were lighted and for once Nan-Nan was not busy with the interminable mending. The two sat talking softly together, and the room was so quiet that Lucy regretted the sound of her feet on the polished floor, and the click of the door as she closed it. Sitting at their feet before the fire, with Nan-Nan's hand occasionally caressing her hair, she told her day, reliving it in their company. But it was not until Nan-Nan had left the room, to get some hot milk for her, that Lucy told her grandmother about the fear that had come when she had seen the steps going up from the water, and the dark doorway. The memory of it was disturbing her but she did not want to disturb Nan-Nan. Her grandmother was not easily disturbed. On the stair of life she stood a step higher even than Nan-Nan.

"Do not let it distress you, Lucy," said Mrs. Gwinne calmly. "Many terrible things have happened in the Tower, many griefs have been borne there. These things can remain alive in a building long after they have ceased to trouble those who endured them."

"But it was not the past, it was the future," said Lucy.

Her grandmother looked at her. "Then forget it," she said, and her voice had the firm edge of command. "In this world we possess nothing but the passing moment. Polish it as you would a jewel. It is the only wealth to which you have any right. All your other moments belong to God alone."

3

Robert Sidney was driving back to the Garden and could not hear what she said, yet his mind was busy with the thought of wealth. He was thinking of all the books in his father's library, of the many volumes in his own London lodging. Yet all of them together perhaps gave less pleasure than Old Sage's one volume. And that world which the old man inhabited, and into which he had stepped for a few extraordinary moments, had more tranquillity in it that most men knew from birth to death. He knew, for he had breathed its air. That he would not do so again he was well aware, for these things were never repeated. When he walked back to the herb stall he found what he expected, a corner of Covent Garden, the deserted stalls, bits of torn paper rustling on the portico; the man reading a book by the light of a lantern just another of the poor vagabonds who lurked in London's dark corners after the sun was down. Nevertheless this moment of return had its own richness. Old Sage looked up from his book, and if his face was not now quite what Robert remembered it was striking enough, for all that had seemed lost was still there in his eyes.

Robert came straight to the point. "I have more books at my

lodging than I need. You would honour me if you would accept a few." He paused. "Would you like to come with me now on your way to your own home and fetch them?"

Old Sage without a tongue had nevertheless learned to be explicit. The gratitude in his eyes, the rueful amused smile, the gesture of his hands, revealed all his feelings. He would be glad to accept a few books, and was grateful, but he did not think it fitting that he should come to a rich man's home. What he did not try to express, but what his dignity expressed for him, was his fear that Robert, having him in his lodging, might try and press patronage upon him, and as Hellenists he considered that they must meet as equals or not at all. That he lived in some poor corner where books might be stolen was obvious from the fact that he read here, out in the evening chill, by the light of one guttering candle in a battered lantern. Robert thought quickly.

"Shall I do this," he asked. "Shall I speak with the incumbent of St. Paul's, and arrange with him for you to keep the books in a safe place inside the church? You could perhaps read there in the evenings when it grows colder. Sometimes I could come and join you and read with you."

Old Sage smiled at the young man's confidence, so rightly sure that with a mere word he could arrange matters to his liking. Then he bent his head in agreement and his eyes kindled. Robert held out his long slim hand and Old Sage rose to his feet. He did not kiss the hand, as any other poor man would have done, but gripped it in his great brown fist, looking down at the two contrasted hands with a tender and reminiscent smile. Then he loosed his grip and bowed. Robert also bowed, his bow the humbler of the two, and turned away. Before he entered his coach he looked back. He could see the flicker of lantern-light in the shadows of the yew tree. It faintly illumined Old Sage's bald head and just one pillar of the colonnade.

Eleven

I

Lucy sat sewing on the windowseat of the little room over the porch which was now her bedroom. Nan-Nan was not well and it was she and Elizabeth who now shared a bedchamber so that Elizabeth could look after her. The little room was hardly bigger than a cupboard, and reminded Lucy of her turret room at Roch, and with memories of Roch gathered about her to keep her warm she stitched at her Christmas presents by the last of the winter daylight. She needed to hurry, for Richard and Justus were coming home from boarding school this very evening and Christmas was only a few days away. She was making a satin bag for her grandmother, a posy of silken flowers for her mother, a housewife for Nan-Nan and finely hemmed handkerchiefs for Mr. Gwinne, Richard, Justus, Robert Sidney and Tom Howard. And there was something else, secretly made, though secretly her grandmother had had to help her, so difficult had been the making, a pair of gloves for her father, worked in coloured silks, just in case he would be with them for Christmas. Would he? she had asked a month ago and her mother had flashed out an emphatic denial. But her grandmother had said, "It would be his wish," and had smiled at Lucy, and she did not forget that smile.

And there was still something else, secret even from her grandmother, a purse of soft green leather worked all over with a fragile web of silver threads. It was for Charles. It was impossible to make gifts for the others and not for him. Even if she was never able to give it to him it would still have been made for him, each stitch that she set with such difficulty adding a little strength to the thread that so precariously linked them.

For she had discovered that as well as the evil web there was another. This too bound spirits together, but not in a tangle, it was a patterned web and one could see the silver pattern when the sun shone upon it. It seemed much frailer than the dark tangle, that had a hideous strength, but it might not be so always, not in the final reckoning. Lucy had seen the picture of the silver web one day as she stitched her Christmas presents. She had been remembering what Robert had said about not being separated from people if you were on the same bright star together, and she had seen the silver threads of people's love for each other running all over and around the world. She had tried to make the picture of it on Charles's purse.

Her grandmother's smile and a silver web. They kept Lucy afloat in a sea of unhappiness and fear. The troubles of the time, that had been like a thunderstorm rumbling in the distance, had begun to close in. The day when she had seen the Earl of Strafford going down to Westminster in his barge had been his last of freedom. By that evening he was in prison. On November the twenty-first Dr. Cosin had been arrested and a week later Archbishop Laud had been impeached. There had been much talk of Dr. Cosin's humour in misfortune and the Archbishop's gentleness. Dr. Cosin, bowing to the Committee before whom he had been summoned, had been told, "Here is no altar, Doctor Cosin," and he had replied, "Why, then I hope there shall be no sacrifice." The Archbishop, who had been granted a few hours of freedom, had spent them quietly at Lambeth setting his affairs in order and attending evensong with his household in his chapel. As he passed from his house to the barge hundreds of poor people lined his way praying for his safe return, and he had thanked God and blessed them.

"What does it mean, to impeach a man?" Lucy had demanded of Mr. Gwinne on the day after they had heard about Dr. Cosin. They were facing each other in his library and for once Mr. Gwinne was not submerged in his scholar's serenity. He was irritable, unable to concentrate, his hands continually moving among the objects on his desk.

"It is to accuse him of treason," said Mr. Gwinne.

"What is treason?"

"Violation by a subject of his allegiance to king or state, punishable by death."

His restless movements upset the wafer box and it fell to the ground. The spilled wafers made a red stain on the carpet and they both looked at it and for a few moments could not look away. All the colour ebbed out of Lucy's face and Mr. Gwinne continued hastily, "An impeached man is brought to trial, of course. The trial can last for months and he may be acquitted at the end of it."

Lucy looked up, her colour coming back. "Doctor Cosin will be acquitted," she said. "I remember now that Nan-Nan had a seeing about him. She saw him being kind to me when I am grown a woman." She went down on her hands and knees to pick up the wafers and did not see the expression of scepticism as to Nan-Nan's seeings which momentarily clouded Mr. Gwinne's face. When she looked up again it had passed and his hands were quieter. "I still hope for peace between the King and his Parliament," he said. "A divided state is like a severed body. We cannot be loyal both to the head and the feet and so it makes traitors of us all."

"Or of none of us," said Lucy.

Her grandfather looked at her. He very often spoke his thoughts aloud to her but her understanding of them never failed to astonish him. "I pray that your point of view may prevail in the forthcoming trials," he said gravely. "If it does not, then they will be punished for all of us who are of their opinion."

"Scapegoats," said Lucy, and looked round at the rampart of books which walled them in. "Why should you and I be safe in here?" she demanded.

"We are the lesser mortals," explained Mr. Gwinne. "We are the people for whom it has always seemed expedient that one man should die."

"I do not understand," she said.

"Nor do I," said Mr. Gwinne, and suddenly he abandoned the whole controversy and opened the book in front of him. Lucy could almost see him submerging like a turtle. He would not come to the surface again. He was far more comfortable down below.

But it was not only the realization that terrible things could happen not only to people in the distance but to people whom one knew that was making Lucy afraid, but also the fact that Nan-Nan was not well. She had no illness, they told Lucy comfortingly, there was nothing to worry about, it was just that she was old. But Lucy did not feel happy and was making the housewife in a spirit of defiance. Nan-Nan would get well and do the mending again.

She could no longer see to sew and the growing chill of the room reminded her that in Nan-Nan's room there would be a fire and lighted candles, and the reassuring sight of Nan-Nan herself, smiling at her. She would go and show her the Christmas gifts. Laying aside the housewife she put the rest in her sewing bag, slung it over her shoulder and went quietly down the passage to her mother's bedchamber.

Nan-Nan was sitting propped up in the fourposter. Her tiny face, framed in the white frills of her cap, seemed to be all of her that there now was; and that little would scarcely have been there, Lucy felt, without the nightcap to hold it. Yet her eyes in the candlelight were very bright and alert and her voice, always so light and soft, was scarcely changed, and she went instantly to the point.

"You must be a good girl to madam your mother, Lucy fach," she said. "You will have children of your own to care for in the years to come but now it is your mother who must be your child."

"But oh, Nan-Nan," she cried. "I wish it was my father!"

"Do not separate them in your mind and heart, cariad," said Nan-Nan. "Whatever they do to themselves, and each other, do not you do it to them too. Never take care of the one without remembering the other."

"Will my father come for Christmas?" whispered Lucy.

"It would not surprise me," said Nan-Nan. "Made his gift, have you?"

Lucy spread the gifts out on the bed, the gloves, the kerchiefs, the posy and the silk bag. Nan-Nan was pleased with

them; though she detected crooked stitches here and there.
"Did you make a gift for that boy?" she asked.
"For Justus? You are holding it, Nan-Nan."
"Not Justus. The dark boy on the white pony."

For a moment Lucy was still with astonishment, then she reached into the recesses of the bag and brought out the green leather purse and unfolded the square of silk in which she had wrapped it. Nan-Nan held it for a long time and the silver web sparkled in the candlelight. Seeing it in her hands Lucy noticed for the first time that wherever one thread met another a silver star gleamed at the meeting point. Tears came into her eyes and the silver began to dazzle, and the candlelight set rainbows in the dazzle until it seemed that the little purse was all made of light. Between Nan-Nan's hands it was ethereal as the human soul, its value indescribable, its light reflected up into the intent and compassionate old face. There seemed no sound in the house, no sound in the whole world except the soft settling of ash in the grate. At last Nan-Nan looked across at Lucy and would have spoken, but they both heard something, the sound of wheels coming down the lane, an ordinary sound yet sharing tonight the magic of the light brimming over in Nan-Nan's cupped hands. Lucy wiped the dazzling tears out of her eyes and her cheeks grew rosy. "Justus," she said.

Whatever Nan-Nan had been about to say she did not say it, but gently wrapped the little purse up in its square of silk. "Go down to him, child," she said.

Lucy put her presents away in the bag, kissed Nan-Nan and made up the fire. Then she went out on to the landing. Downstairs doors were opening; the door of the parlour where Mrs. Gwinne and Elizabeth had been sitting, the library door and the kitchen door. It was an exciting Christmas sound. Through the opened doors firelight and candlelight flooded into the dark house, and through the kitchen door came a blast of spicy warmth from the oven where the cakes were baking. Lucy flew down the stairs just as Tabitha came running to open the front door, and saw them standing against the blue twilight, Richard tall and beautiful, his eyes looking over Lucy's head to his mother, and Justus rosy and dumpy and just the same. She had him in her arms whether he liked it or not. But he seemed to like it. He was a little taller and a little broader, and he had a black eye from a recent fight, but he was still himself, still Justus, with his broad wise forehead and clear eyes and wide grin. She took him by the hand and led him straight up the stairs to Nan-Nan and stood him by her bed in the candlelight.

"He's the same," she said.

Nan-Nan touched the black eye with a tender finger. "Witch-hazel," she said. "Of course my boy is the same. Justus will never change."

2

Christmas Eve was fine and frosty and passed into a clear moonlight night. At midnight Lucy put her cloak round her, opened her window and leaned out. Over her head the vast sky was ablaze with stars and she thought they were like the web that had gleamed and sparkled in Nan-Nan's hand. That had been the web of human loving but this was God's web and each star was ablaze with how much he loved it. People said the stars sang for joy of the love, and Lucy listened intently, but all the bells of London began to ring and she heard them instead. She did not know it, but they were ringing in England for the last time for many years, for next year London would be a Puritan city. The sound came over the frosted fields crystal-clear but far away, with the sorrow of distance, and she remembered again that Nan-Nan was old and that her father had not after all come home for Christmas. She felt hollow with longing for him and the tears blinded her so that the starlight ran together and the web of the heavens had rainbows in it, as the little one had done.

Then the bells seemed to grow less sad and reminded her that tonight, at this moment, she and her father were on the same star, the one where the baby had been born. Robert had called it the green star, as though its colour made it special, but it was the baby who made it special for he had come here to stay, never to be driven away while there was one person left upon this star who longed for him. The fact of this, slowly expanding like a flower in the hollow space, filled the emptiness with beauty and she knew it for the central and redeeming fact of human life. She closed the window and went back to bed and after she fell asleep bells and the sound of a trotting horse made magic in her dreams, and her sleep was happy.

Christmas Day passed joyously for the children with nothing forgotten to which they were accustomed; hymn singing in the village church, present-giving, the kissing ring, all the right things to eat, and the grown-ups, at least outwardly, smiling and festive and extraordinarily appreciative of the gifts the children gave them. Nan-Nan made some miraculous effort and sat up in bed lively as a cricket with all her presents strewn over the counterpane, Lucy's housewife between her hands. Aunt Byshfield and her husband and two boys came to dinner and the health of absent members of the family was drunk in Canary wine, not forgetting the health of Uncle and Aunt Barlow in Wales and Uncle and Aunt Gosfright in Holland. William's name was not mentioned and after the last toast Lucy choked over her wine and could not finish it, but looking round she saw her grandmother leaning towards her, and that there was still some wine in the bottom of her glass. She raised it and Lucy raised hers and smiling at each other they drank silently.

And so it was a happy day, with the climax coming after dark when the candles were put out and the children played snapdragon, snatching raisins from the great dish of burning brandy. The four boys were making so much noise that they did not notice when Lucy left them and slipped behind the window curtains. It was the quiet that she wanted, and to look at the frosty stars now they had come back again. They were not so easy to see from downstairs, yet they looked very wonderful shining through the branches of the leafless trees, and they looked much nearer, as though the sparkling web was resting on the tops of the trees. She leaned on the windowsill and she wanted her father. It was still wonderful to her that she

was on the same star with him, yet all the same she wanted him
and pressed her fingers against the bulge in the bodice of her
dress where his gloves were hidden. It had been comforting to
carry them about with her all day, because though ungiven
they were his. She could hear horses on the road coming from
London, and they brought back the memory of her happy
dreams, but there were many riders backwards and forwards
today and so she did not at first connect the sound with herself. Not until she saw the dark shapes of two horsemen pass
behind the trees, and saw them stop at the gate.

Only her grandmother saw her slip from the room, and she
held her peace. The front door had been locked and Lucy's
shaking fingers took a little while to undo the bolt and chain.
When at last she got the door open the crunching feet had
already reached the porch and a tall cloaked man stood in
front of her, light from the hall shining full upon his smiling
face. It was Uncle Barlow of Slebech. The shock and disappointment were for the moment dreadful, but Uncle Barlow
put his hand on her shoulder and bent down to whisper to
her.

"Your father's at the gate," he said. "Do you go down to
him."

Then he took off his hat and stepped into the hall and shut
the door behind him, and Lucy flew down the garden. It was
her opinion, later, that she had really flown, because when she
knew where she was again she was over the gate and on top of
the mounting block, and William was wrapping not only his
arms but his cloak about her to keep her warm, and she had
what she had been longing for all day, his rough cheek against
hers. "Here is my girl," he kept saying. "Here is Bud. It is Bud,
not in dream but in truth. Warm as a glowing coal. It is a
hundred years since I saw my girl. You have grown tall, Bud,
and filled out. You have quite a bosom on you."

"It is not a bosom," said Lucy. "It is a pair of gloves that I
have made for you."

She pulled them out and he examined them in the moonlight and starlight, exclaiming at her cleverness, amazed at
the embroidery.

"Did you think I would come today?" he asked.

"I hoped," said Lucy. "Why did you not come yesterday? I was wanting you in the night."

"We hoped to have been here before but your uncle's horse fell lame."

"Now you have come you can have my room," she said happily. "I will sleep with my mother and Nan-Nan."

"Steady, Bud," said William. "I do not know yet if I will be allowed in the house. Your Uncle Barlow and I have taken a lodging in the city." His voice hardened suddenly. "I have not come back merely for a family reunion, I have come back to fight this lawsuit and see to it that I am not permanently separated from my children. Is Justus here?"

"Yes, and Richard too. Father, did you bring Dewi?"

"No, Bud. While I am away he is with my mother. Loved and well cared for."

"I should like to see Dewi again," said Lucy.

"So you shall, Bud; one of these days when the sun shines for us. Would you like to go back to the house now and ask if I may come in for a few moments? And if not, send Justus out to me."

"Of course you will come in!" said Lucy.

He answered like a boy. "It is Christmas night. Miracles do happen. It is worth trying, Bud. Keep my cloak about you and do not trip over it."

She went joyously to the house but as she opened the front door she saw the back view of Mr. Gwinne retreating into his study, avid for immersion, and knew that something bad had been happening while she was outside. In the parlour the candles had been lit again and the fun of the snapdragon was at an end. Uncle Barlow and Uncle and Aunt Byshfield were looking uncomfortable, and her grandmother was sitting very upright in her chair by the fire and her face looked as it had done when they had heard that Dr. Cosin had been impeached. It had hollows in it, round the eyes and under the cheekbones, the fallen-in look that old people have after a bad shock. But the shock was not because her father had come back. She knew that. It was because of something her mother had said or done. She looked round for her mother but she was not there, and nor was Richard.

"Lucy, go back again and ask your father to come in," said Mrs. Gwinne. "Tell him, please, that it will give me great pleasure to see him." Then she paused and the next sentence came out cut into small pieces, as though she were nearing the end of her tether. "Take Justus with you—in case—your father will want to see him. Take Justus."

Justus had been leaning against his grandmother and she had unconsciously been deriving comfort from the feel of his newly washed head. Now she gave him a little push and he followed Lucy out of the room. In the garden Justus ran but Lucy followed more slowly, impeded by the cloak. She let herself be impeded, for it was Justus's turn. When she reached the gate William was sitting on the mounting block with Justus on his knee and she gave him her grandmother's message.

"Was your mother in the room?" he asked sharply. Lucy knew how desperately it mattered that she should be able to answer yes, and she was silent in her misery. "She had gone out of the room while you were with me?" he demanded, and he shook her arm. "Answer me, Lucy." But Lucy began to cry and Justus followed suit.

William was remorseful. "Christmas night!" he groaned. "Day of miracles. I was a damn' fool to come. Even now, if she had been there. Lucy, thank your grandmother for her kindness. Tell her I will write to her. And stop crying, both of you. I will find a way to see you both. Give my love to Nan-Nan. Do not cry, I tell you. It is Christmas night and I have got you!"

He hugged them both, hard and with joy, and his longing for them, as theirs for him, was suddenly wonderful, a part of that other longing that Lucy had known about in the night. The sound of bells came again from some London steeple and time became this one moment only, a centre of delight at the heart of the green star, and all the shining of it contracted to hold the three of them alone.

Twelve

I

In the dusk of a February evening Robert Sidney found himself unexpectedly in Bedford Street. He had eaten his dinner with friends, stayed late in anxious talk and going home had taken a wrong turning. It was cold, with a crisp sprinkling of snow underfoot, and he shivered even in his warm cloak. There had been a Sidney family reunion at Christmas, he had been away from London for a month and had forgotten how icily the winds could sweep along the London streets. He was unhappy tonight. A peaceable, sensitive man, the increasing bitterness of the tension between the two parties in the country, and the impeachment of Strafford and the Archbishop, had filled him with grief and horror. How could these things end except in civil war, of all things the most horrible; setting men not only against their own countrymen but against their own families? Even his brother Algernon was showing signs of parliamentary sympathies. What if he should presently find himself fighting Algernon? He felt wretched and desperate, and involuntarily looked up as though he were looking for shelter somewhere; not from the wind but from himself, for he was bad company for himself when these moods of black depression came upon him.

There was a light shining through the bare branches of trees, and below the trees there was silence. He turned towards the silence, away from the street where homeward bound coaches rattled over the cobbles and men were shouting to each other, and found himself in St. Paul's churchyard. The lantern was shining in the doorway of the church. The constriction of darkness in his mind became a little less intolerable, for he loved London even when the winds were icy. He loved her beauty and variety and the unexpectedness of her odd corners and crannies; hidden gardens and courts and old

223

graveyards that suddenly confronted one with something un-
looked for and entirely different, something eerie and frightening perhaps, or magical, or lovely, or peaceful. He had had
queer experiences in these places, one of them the flight of
Apollo's swans in the corner of Greece by the herb stall, and
made odd friendships with fantastic people. He liked unusual
people. He was quick to win affection and to give it and his
heart reproached him now that over Christmas he had forgotten his fantastics. He had even forgotten that extraordinary child Lucy; and she had sent him a kerchief for
Christmas crookedly hemmed by herself. And after providing
him with a few books hidden in a chest in the church he had
forgotten Old Sage. He hoped the parson had not forgotten
him but had continued to give him sanctuary.

He wondered if the old man was there now and he went up
the steps and tried the door. It yielded and he went in, to be
greeted by a glimmer of glow-worm light that came from the
recesses of a box pew. He walked to it and looked in. A lantern
stood on the hard seat and by it sat Old Sage, his Socratic face
illumined by the light and a book open on his knees; it was
Robert's Greek Testament. The old man heard nothing and
his absorption was complete. His lantern did nothing to illumine the duskiness all round him but he sat at the heart of
the murk profoundly at peace. Robert could not bring himself
to disturb him, nor could he presume to stand there watching
the old man's face too closely.

He went to a bench at the back of the church and sat there,
but still he saw the face. How did a man achieve a peace like
that? What had happened to Old Sage? What had his life
been? There seemed no likelihood that he could ever know,
but he wanted to know, for it was in the fact of men like Old
Sage that other men found reassurance. From beginnings
older than Socrates, and on to Old Sage, and reaching far
beyond him, the thin line of them stretched out, a girdle
round the green star that alone forbade the final disin-
tegration into evil. One of them, the greatest of them, buckled
them together, his life running through them all like the
strength that made the links in a gold chain secure. What had

Christ looked like? A hundred times he had longed for the
vision to shine out against the darkness of closed eyes. It never
came. It seemed one could not see it. Was that because it was
the face of them all?

Something made him open his eyes and look up. Old Sage
had become aware of his presence, had come out of the pew
and was beckoning to him with his forefinger. Robert joined
him and they sat down together beside the lantern, Old Sage
returning instantly to his reading. He read with intense concentration, his finger passing along the line as he read. He had
brought several books with him into the pew and Robert
picked up his own Republic and opened it at random.

"I mean truthfulness, that is, a determination never to
admit falsehood in any shape, if it can be helped, but to
abhor it, and love the truth. The genuine lover of knowledge
must, from his youth up, strive intensely after all truth."

He was reading of the Guardians. It seemed important to him
that he should know of whom Old Sage was reading. His eyes
followed the moving finger.

"And Jesus said, I have come to bear witness of the truth.
And Pilate said, what is truth?"

His despair, that had lifted, settled on him again, for in his
ignorance he was as Pilate, and Old Sage was dumb. Then it
struck him, for the first time, that the answer to Pilate's question had not been withheld but given on the cross. There alone
could men see and know the truth about themselves and God.
The difference between most men, himself and Pilate for in-
stance, and the Guardians, the links of the chain that held the
world together, was that they had seen, understood and accepted the cross, and the rest had not.

Old Sage had reached the end of his chapter. He turned to
the title page and once more his finger moved. The Testament
had come to Robert from his grandfather, the Wizard Earl,
and his name was written there. Old Sage touched the inscribed name and pointed to himself. Then he turned to Robert, his deep eyes bright with amusement and affection, and

the delight of having found some strong link with a friend. The language of his eyes was extraordinary and Robert grasped his meaning.

"You knew my grandfather?" he asked.

Old Sage nodded and smiled and returned to his reading, leaving Robert no nearer knowing what had happened to him. He did not believe in the story of the pirates. It had a theatrical touch about it that was not in keeping with Old Sage. Then suddenly he was ashamed of himself. A man must not probe the history of another. If he is not told it he must remain in ignorance. The vastness of the story that Old Sage was reading filled the darkness of the church and he was able to lose his lesser darkness in the greater and be comforted.

When Old Sage had finished his reading he closed the book and sat in stillness, his large brown hands folded on it and his head on his breast. He was not asleep, merely at peace. They might have sat there all night, Robert thought afterwards, had it not been for the interruption. The door opened and light steps sounded on the stone floor, children's steps. He got up and went out into the aisle and saw two forlorn little creatures drifting towards him. The girl's green cloak gleamed in the dim light but the boy's brown coat was one with the shadows. But not his face, rosy and solemn, with brown eyes beneath a broad and wise forehead. The face seemed to float towards Robert and he loved it. Then he saw that the boy had been crying, not very much, for his face was not blotched, but a little. His lashes were still wet and his eyes bewildered. Though he was the younger of the two he led his sister protectively. "Please, sir," he asked, "is Old Sage here?"

"He is in that pew," said Robert. And because he had recognized the cloak and hood he bent down and said gently, "Lucy?"

The hood fell back from her face as she lifted her head. She looked blanched and old, no longer a child, but she had not been crying. She tried to tell Robert something and could not. It astonished him that Lucy, of all people, should be bereft of words and needing the help and protection of a younger brother. He spoke for her.

"Our Nurse has died, sir," he explained. "She died this afternoon and we are on our way to tell our father. Lucy wants to tell Old Sage too. She thought he might be here. He liked Nan-Nan."

Old Sage himself was now beside them and he was without surprise. He held out his hand to Lucy, led her back to the glow-worm light of the box pew and shut the door. Robert had the feeling that Nan-Nan's death had been known to him for some hours, and that because of it he had chosen today to read St. John's account of the passion of Christ. He also judged that this was not the first time he had taken care of Lucy in a time of grief that threatened to be too much for her.

He and Justus sat down together on a bench in the shadows. "You two did not walk?" he asked incredulously. In such disturbed times two children walking together in the dusk was hardly safe, and it was a long way from St. Giles.

Justus nodded. "We have to tell our father," he explained. "He loves Nan-Nan and he cannot come to the house because—because—"

"I know," said Robert gently. The gossip about the Walter's matrimonial troubles was known to him. "Do your mother and grandmother know where you are?"

Justus shook his tousled head. "My grandmother is looking after my mother. But we left a message with the gardener."

"When Lucy has finished with Old Sage I will take you both to your father," he said.

They sat silently together, Justus with his head bent, for speaking of Nan-Nan had made the tears well up again and he was ashamed of them. For the children Nan-Nan's death had come as a profound shock. She had been as usual all that morning but during her afternoon's sleep she had died with Lucy sitting beside her. Sitting beside John Shepherd Lucy had known that he was going to die, but no one had realized how near Nan-Nan was to her departure. That any old person could die so suddenly and easily had added a new terror to Lucy's life. It could happen to their grandmother any time, and then there would be no firm ground whatever beneath their feet.

"I go back to school tomorrow," said Justus forlornly. "I am late going back because I had a great cold. But I go tomorrow."

Robert was able to follow his thought. "We will all look after Lucy for you," he said.

"You are not me," Justus said.

There was no controverting the truth of that statement and Robert was glad to see Old Sage and Lucy coming towards them hand in hand. Lucy was still without the relief of tears but her face was now the face of a sad child, not a stricken old woman. Old Sage had eased her. He let go of her hand, smiled at the three of them and went straight back to his box pew, shutting the door behind him. Looking back from the church door Robert and the children found the sight of his glow-worm light wonderfully reassuring. It looked as though it shone out from Old Sage himself.

2

William had found lodgings in Charing Cross, at the top of a tall old house tucked in behind the Palace of Whitehall, and from his attic window he could look between two of the Palace towers over a courtyard and see the river and ships going up and down, and hear the gulls calling. Here he was not too unhappy, and not too far from Lucy or from Westminster, where his wife's appeal for separation was once more being considered. He hoped and believed that he would be given custody of his children. Then he would take Lucy back to Roch. Justus, his heart set on Gray's Inn, would have to stay at school but he would come home for the summer holidays. What Richard would choose to do William did not know. He was his mother's.

He was sitting at the table before his fire of sea-coal, laboriously writing down what he was going to say to their lordships, when he heard a knock on the door below. The rest of the house was inhabited by the family of one of the Palace servants, hospitable folk who had many visitors, and he took no notice, hearing voices only vaguely through the agonies of literary composition. Then to his surprise he heard steps coming up the last flight of stairs that led to his two rooms, and it sounded like the children. But it was only very occasionally that his brother-in-law Barlow, still in London settling the affairs of a dying relative, was allowed to bring his children to see him, and never at this late hour.

Then a knock came at his door, he opened it and Lucy was in his arms; but silently, her face hidden against his shoulder. It was Justus who once again had to put it into words, and doing so for the second time was almost more than he could manage. Having spoken he leaned his head against his father's coat sleeve. William, shocked and bewildered, for Nan-Nan's steadfastness and loyalty had meant more to him than he had known until this moment, looked across at Robert and wondered who the fellow was, intruding himself upon him at this hour. Why the devil did he not go away? William disliked such men, wearing their distinction as they wore their fine clothes, with an assurance that made other men feel rumpled and fuddled and inferior. And he seemed on intimate terms with the children, damn him. Who was he?

"I found Lucy and Justus making their way on foot, sir," said Robert. "I will leave them with you now. My name is Sidney. May I come back later with the coach and take the children home?"

So this was Robert Sidney, of whom Lucy had told him, the fellow who was presuming to play a father's part to his daughter in his absence. "I will take my children home myself, sir," he said stiffly. "I possess a horse. You need not trouble yourself."

"Another evening, may I return? Sir, I am very pleased to make your acquaintance. And I am sorry for what has happened."

His pleasant voice had exactly the right intonations of courtesy and sympathy. These fellows knew how to turn on the charm, William thought savagely. Yet when his angry miserable eyes met Robert's he was aware of assuagement. The man was not acting a part. His grey eyes shone with genuine sympathy and kindness. William mumbled something about

being honoured and Robert smiled and went away so quietly
that they scarcely heard him go. Though the children and
their father instantly forgot him he yet remained with them
as a breath of coolness in the hot uncomfortable misery of
tears. For Lucy, in William's arms, was able to cry.

3

March came with snowdrops in the gardens and the pale
gleam of celandines in the hedges, and though the dawns were
chill the birds sang for joy of the growing light, and when
Lucy opened her window to hear them the air smelt of violets,
though as yet she had found none under the dead leaves in the
unicorn wood. But she found minute buttons of coral buds on
the brambles, and the green of dog's mercury among the
leaves, and when she left the wood and looked back from the
far end of the field she saw how the trees in the silvery sunshine were clothing themselves in pale amethyst and paler
coral, in faint crimson and dun gold, one colour fading into
the other as the colours do on the iridescent breast of a bird.
Who would have believed that bare twigs and the outer
casings of hard buds could have produced this feather softness.
Even when the sun went in, and the light spring rain swept
across them like a curtain, their colour was not quite extinguished but remained tangled in the silver shower like a
lost rainbow.

March passed into April and like a rainbow Lucy's happiness began to reappear through the sorrows of this time. Her
longing for Nan-Nan would be with her for ever, and the di-
latory reluctance of the law had as yet brought no settlement
between William and Elizabeth, only increasing bitterness
that shamed their children, but Lucy was learning to live both
with the longing and the shame, to love her father as her
firstborn and her mother as much as she could, and to pay no
attention to what they said about each other. She was like a
mother with two quarrelling children confined in different
rooms, and went from one to the other with tolerant tenderness.

The circle of her motherliness was for ever growing larger, widening at the end of April to include the royal family of England. It did not strike her that this was ridiculous for she never considered her feelings, she only had them.

It began on the day that Uncle Barlow took her to Westminster Hall to watch the trial of the Earl of Strafford. He had only intended taking her to London Bridge to buy a green girdle, a farewell gift from him before he went back to Wales, but driving home they saw the people streaming to Westminster Hall and Uncle Barlow thought that here would be a show that any child would enjoy. In an impulse of great kindness he dismissed the coach and he and Lucy joined the crowd. "Come on, Lucy," he said, "you will see Prince Charles and the King and the Queen." And at mention of Charles Lucy was alight with eagerness, though she would have gone anywhere with Uncle Barlow for they were fond of each other. He was a burly man, good-natured, jovial and insensitive. He liked Lucy because she was pretty and lively and she liked him because he was kind, and because he appreciated her father.

Near the entrance to the Hall they got jammed tightly in the crowd, and there was so much noise and argument that Uncle Barlow stood Lucy on a mounting block, out of harm's way. The trial, that had been going on for some weeks, was drawing to its close, with the Earl fighting skilfully and with increasing courage as things worsened for him. Black Tom Tyrant was winning admiration and sympathy even from his enemies, and men were saying that there are always two sides to a penny, but the admiration was coming too late and he had been hated for too long for it to make much difference now. The crowd was gay as well as quarrelsome, reflecting the mood of London at this time. Summer would usher in some of the most tragic years of England's history, and London sensed that and realized that within Westminster Hall the tragedy was already in being, but against that dark background there was being played out an exquisite little masque of youth and charm and loveliness; tactfully arranged just at this time to distract public opinion from the thundercloud.

For the Prince of Orange, fifteen years old, was now in

England to marry the Princess Mary, who was nine years old. The people round Lucy were talking of the fairytale procession of fifty coaches that had brought the charming young prince and his father through the city to Whitehall. He went every day, they said, to visit his little bride, and they were as happy and loving together as a prince and princess in a fairytale. A charming prince, he was, yet their own Prince Charles, who was four years younger, was nearly as tall. Ah, he was a wonderful boy! They would see him in a moment. He attended the trial every day, sitting on the dais to represent the monarchy. A woman near Lucy cried out that it was a wicked thing to make a child of eleven attend a trial for treason, Prince of Wales though he might be, but indignant voices shouted her down, the crowd began to move again and Uncle Barlow lifted Lucy from the mounting block.

Westminster Hall, lofty and splendid with its roof of Spanish chestnut, was full. The sun shone down on the rows of the commissioners seated in front of the great west window, on the uniforms of the soldiers standing on guard and on the ranks of ladies and gentlemen who were privileged spectators in the galleries to right and left. The lower end of the Hall was railed off for the citizens of London and the benches were as full as the galleries. Nevertheless Uncle Barlow, softening the impact of physical strength by the charm of personal affability, got himself and his niece to the front. "You can see it all from here, Bud," he said triumphantly. He had adopted her father's nickname for her and she let him do it because he was her father's crony.

She could see it all and would never forget what she saw. She saw Charles first, sitting high upon the royal dais. He sat with a very straight back and still as a statue. His cloak was of dark blue silk and the jewel of the George gleamed upon it. He had changed very much from the boy who had sat beside her in the woods. His brown square face was taut and strained and his dark eyes, fixed upon the face of the prisoner, had a very sombre concentration. Yet grave though he was today the eyes of every man and woman in the hall were continually drawn to him, he was so big and strong and so alive.

Lucy looked where Charles was looking and hardly recognized the Earl as the same man who had stood in his barge with his hand on the head of the Irish wolfhound. He wore the same crimson cloak, but not falling in the regal folds that had seemed a part of his tall dominating figure; he wore it now huddled about stooping shoulders in protection from the draughts that blew through ill-fitting windows. His beard was streaked with grey and his face furrowed with anxiety and illness. He had been for weeks in the Tower and the cold and damp of the place had increased the gout that always racked him. Lucy had not known that human beings could change so quickly. Was this what that terrible Tower did? There were exclamations of pity from the crowded benches, and little gusts of sibilant murmurings ran along the crowded galleries but they could not blot out the voice of the accusing lawyer who was haranguing the court. It went on and on, hard and rasping like a saw with broken teeth at its slow work of destroying some great tree. Then the rasping ceased and the prisoner stood to answer his judges.

He got up with difficulty and was not able to straighten his body to its former height, but his cloak fell about him again in its old manner and his voice was steady and had the same calm dignity as his face. There were no more exclamations of pity and the whispering galleries were silent. Lucy had not understood what the lawyer had been saying, and she did not now follow the Earl's defence, but she was aware of his spirit and courage. She was at the age when new insights were continually flooding her receptive mind; not always comprehended when they came but accepted and treasured for future understanding. And so now the prisoner taught her something new about death, that in John Shepherd and Nan-Nan had been witnessed as a letting go of life. But dying could be something more than that. It could be a piece of work taken up, carried through and accomplished with resolution, something that could atone for life's sins and failures, lifting a man above the tangled dark web to the best he could do, and leaving him there never to fall again.

"Bud, change places with me and you will get a better view

of your sovereign," said good-natured Uncle Barlow, and transferred her to the other side of his bulk. Although she had never seen the King and Queen, and had been longing to see them, Lucy had forgotten they were there. From the moment of coming in only Charles and the prisoner had existed for her. Everyone else had been just a shifting of dim colour and a faint murmuration of sound, like that of leaves on a tree that holds two peacocks with spread tails full of eyes.

Yet when she looked at the royal box she forgot the peacocks and her heart missed a beat, for her King and Queen were so small and frightened. The gilded royal box was bright as a jewel casket, yet it yawned like the mouth of a cave above the little beings who were so much too small for it. They were exquisite, as jewels should be, and as one looked at them they seemed to grow by virtue of their dignity and beauty. The King's white face, framed by the graceful sweep of long dark hair that fell to his shoulders, shone like a clear-cut cameo above the shimmer of his satin doublet but it was stiff, expressionless and sad. The little Queen, though she sat still and upright, was yet restless. Her dark eyes darted from one face to another and she could not keep her right hand still. Her fingers kept touching the pearls at her throat or the curls on her forehead, and once she laid them lightly on her husband's arm; but if he was aware of any comfort in her touch he gave no sign. Her left hand was in her lap, holding the hand of the bride-to-be, Princess Mary, who sat beside her.

The little girl scarcely looked like the happy bride she was reported to be. Her chestnut curls, fastened with a blue ribbon, framed a small face almost as white as her father's, "They bring her day after day," a voice muttered indignantly behind Lucy. "A child like that!" Lucy wondered too why she had to be there. Perhaps because she was so soon to be marrried she had to learn how a princess must behave when life suddenly turns dark and frightening. She was behaving well. Only the occasional trembling of her soft little mouth betrayed her; as did the Queen's restless eyes and the expressionless mask of the King's face. They had expected this trial to lead to the Earl's triumphant acquittal, but their enemies had been too clever for them and things were not going in the way they had expected. They feared for him, and they feared for themselves without him if he should be broken and disgraced. The possibility of his death they were subconsciously refusing to consider and the refusal increased their fear.

It was at this moment that Lucy took the royal family under her maternal wing, quite unabashed by the presumption of what she did. They became an extension of her own family, a nimbus about the moon, separated and mysterious but part of it. But Charles was not mysterious. He sat squarely on the dais, his hands on his knees, sturdy and strong, and his George winked blindingly as the sun caught it.

Thirteen

I

May came in with a burst of warmth, showers and sunshine, birdsong and a sudden wealth of blossom, as though London decked herself for two happy events, May Day and the royal wedding. It seemed that the flowers were all out together. The gardens were full of them and many of the odd nooks and crannies of London that Robert Sidney loved were ablaze with the wild flowers. They grew wherever there was a patch of waste land or a corner with a bit of earth; buttercups, marjoram and pimpernel, bugloss, speedwell and joy-of-the-ground, the wildings that were sweeter to the eye and dearer to the heart than all the tulips in the world.

William brought a bunch of wildings when he came on horseback to fetch Lucy to watch the May morning festivities. It was not often they saw each other now, for since her expedition with Uncle Barlow, which had thoroughly upset her, Lucy was no longer allowed to go into the London streets, and William was never allowed to come to the little house at St. Giles. But May morning was something special and Mrs. Gwinne hoped an outing with her father would keep Lucy's mind off the Earl of Strafford's trial, which had ended in the Commons bringing in the Bill of Attainder.

"What's that?" Lucy had demanded of her grandfather, running to him in his library from the kitchen, where she had heard the servants talking of it.

"An invention of the devil," he had told her savagely, "discontinued since the Wars of the Roses. Who would have believed that they could have raked that up again?" He had been jerked right up out of himself, shouting at her as though it were her fault, a man she did not know he could be.

"But what is it?"

"A parliamentary bill which can be brought in if impeachment fails. Parliament simply decrees a man guilty of treason. Legal proof is not required. Go to your grandmother."

Her grandmother had tried to comfort her. It might not happen. His Majesty, they said, would refuse to sign the Bill of Attainder. She herself was confident the Earl would be saved. No, it could not happen to Dr. Cosin, who had done nothing except speak his mind with more zeal than discretion. Lucy was not to worry and she might go maying with her father.

They left the horse at an ale house and joined the crowd in Drury Lane. The sun was scarcely up and the air was fresh and cool. All the people were carrying bunches of flowers and may boughs were fastened over the doors. The bells were ringing and everyone seemed happy and Lucy managed to be happy too. Her hand was warm in her father's and he was talking to her of the time when they would be together in Roch. And then they heard the violins and saw the milkmaids dancing up the street with their pails garlanded with flowers; as in the years to come pretty Nell Gwynne would see them, standing at the door of her lodging in Drury Lane in her smocked sleeves and bodice, herself observed meanwhile by the kindling eye of Samuel Pepys. Then all the people in the street were dancing, Lucy and William with them, and the sun rose up over the roofs of London and flooded them with gold. When they rode back to St. Giles, through fields of buttercups, the larks were singing in the blue air above their heads.

The next day the bells rang again, this time for the royal wedding. It awed Lucy to think that a little girl younger than herself was being married today. They said she would wear a silver gown, her curls tied up with silver ribbon, her train carried by sixteen nobly-born little girls dressed in white, and that the bridegroom would wear doublet and hose of raspberry satin. She wondered what Charles would wear and all day she saw in imagination the exquisite figures of her other family moving through the ritual of the wedding, and the supper and dancing that were to follow, in that Palace by the river where the swans floated. When she went to bed she dreamed of the wedding and it was a nice dream until there was a rumble of thunder which shattered the pretty thing to pieces, and the charming figures fell away into nightmare and were lost.

She woke up scared in the big bed she now shared with her mother, because since Nan-Nan's death the sorrowing Elizabeth had not wanted to sleep alone. The rumble of spring thunder was dying away into the distance but she remained chill and trembling. The night was peaceful out here in the country but what was happening in London?

The thunder made William think of the waves booming along the Pembrokeshire coast, and he sat and listened to it with restless longing. He had come tonight with Robert Sidney to visit Old Sage in his pew at St. Paul's Church. They had talked to him for a few moments and he had accepted their information with courtesy, but had been glad to return to his books. Robert was reading too now but William, to whom books were anathema, merely sat with his hands on his knees trying to control his restlessness.

The friendship between himself and Robert had been an astonishment to their friends but not to themselves. Robert, a countryman at heart, liked talking about the land, and though William could not quite qualify as one of his fantastics Robert found him sufficiently odd to be attractive. He was a rough-roistering fellow but Robert could see both his younger children in him; Lucy's warm-hearted out-going affection and the simplicity and goodness of Justus. Old Sage, who found all human creatures lovable, had taken Lucy's father to his heart, and William on his side was fascinated by the old man, and had told Robert he would give a good deal to hear the history that Old Sage's tongue could not tell.

The thunder died away but another sound invaded their quietness, the distant roar of an angry mob. William, who enjoyed disturbances within reason, lifted his head like a scenting hound. Light was flickering in the east window, only lightning perhaps, but it might be another fire. There had been several lately. A man could be useful, yelling and passing buckets, and he sighed gustily.

Robert closed his book. He was sick at heart, ashamed of his own helplessness but unaware of anything that he could do to stop this avalanche of tragedy that was descending on them all. "Sit down, man," he said to William, who had half risen. "You know what it is. What we have had all this week. Seamen rioting for pay. Apprentices rioting for Strafford's death. Catholics beaten up in the streets. Catholic houses attacked. Any excuse for a row. They will quiet down when the rain comes."

But William, who had had a dull day, was not disposed to have a dull night, and he lumbered to his feet. Old Sage, his finger marking the place in his book, glanced up at Robert with a gleam of amusement in his eyes. He lifted one expressive eyebrow and his Socratic nose wrinkled briefly, not with distaste for the smell of ale which since William's entry had been effectively banishing the scent of herbs which distilled from his own person, but merely drawing Robert's attention to it. Robert sighed and rose, for Old Sage was quite right. It only needed a few more drinks to get William excitable, and if he went down in the city now he would run into trouble. He must take him home.

Out in the aisle, William already striding down towards the door, Robert looked down at Old Sage. Where did he live? "Can you make your way home through the streets?" he asked. "May I, later, come with you?"

Old Sage looked up at him, smiled and shook his head. The expression of peace on his face was unchanged but he looked weary, and it gave Robert a pang of dismay to see that he was once again reading the last chapters of St. John's gospel. But there was nothing he could do for a man so entirely contented with his situation as it was. He could only shut him in with his glow-worm light and join William in the churchyard.

They went round into Covent Garden and down Bedford Street to the Strand. There was certainly a fire somewhere in the city, and lightning flickered in the dark sky to the east, over London Bridge and the Tower, and the tumult was coming nearer up the Strand. The oppressive darkness, the flickering light and the growing menace of the noise affected Robert not with fear but with a distaste that was near to nausea. How thick hatred was, and how vile the taste of evil in the mouth. His arm, linked in William's in graceful friendship, became a hook of steel. He swung him round and took him relentlessly home but when they reached William's lodging, where the Guards from Whitehall were out across the street to protect the Palace, drenching rain was just beginning. There was no more rioting that night.

2

The next day London was in an uproar. The King, it was said, had tried to save the Earl by means of some dark and terrible plot. He had tried to introduce troops into the Tower. A popish plot. The Gunpowder Plot all over again. All good Protestants would be murdered in their beds. The French fleet was sailing to invade England and would be in the Thames at any moment. The shops were closed and all day the crowds surged through the streets demanding justice and the death of Strafford. He was to blame. Everything would come right, even the hunger and poverty of the people and the quarrel between the King and Parliament, if they could have the blood of Black Tom Tyrant.

The Earl meanwhile, aware that there had indeed been a plot and that it had failed, was more afraid for the King than for himself. The King had publicly declared as a matter of conscience that if the Lords passed the Bill of Attainder he would never sign it, and he had promised Strafford that he would not be sacrificed. If he held to that in face of the appalling clamour he might save the Earl but what of himself? Yet if he broke his promise the crown, and Charles himself, could hardly recover from the shame of such a surrender. On the evening of the next day the Earl wrote to the King the golden letter, so glorious in scapegoat literature, that shone about him for ever. "May it please your Sacred Majesty," he wrote, "I understand the minds of men are more and more incensed against me, notwithstanding your Majesty hath declared that, in your princely opinion, I am not guilty of treason, and that you are not satisfied in your conscience to pass the bill. This bringeth me in a very great strait; there is before me the ruin of my children and family, hitherto untouched with any foul crime: here are before me the many ills which may befall your Sacred Person and the whole Kingdom, should yourself and Parliament part less satisfied one with the other than is necessary for the preservation both of King and people; there are before me the things most valued, most feared by mortal men, Life and Death ... To set Your Majesty's conscience at liberty, I do most humbly beseech Your Majesty (for preventing of evils which may happen by your refusal) to pass this Bill ..."

Having written his letter he gave himself to prayer that he might have strength for whatever should be next asked of him.

The quietness of his cell was not echoed in London. The ports were closed, the quays idle, and the Lords, driving in their coaches to the debate on the Bill of Attainder, could hardly make their way through the crowds. Only eleven had the courage to vote against it and the Bill was passed. The decision now lay with the King alone and next day the citizens gathered about Whitehall. They saw the men arriving whom the King had summoned to advise him, the judges and bishops, and did not know what they were saying to the King. A rumour that the Spanish fleet as well as the French was now entering the Thames, and the knowledge that Whitehall was full of the Catholic servants of the Queen, maddened them, and by nightfall the streets about Whitehall were blocked by a muttering, unsatisfied crowd.

Robert watched them from William's window and did not like the look of them. He knew crowds and this was a nasty specimen. The dark fallen human spirit wanted revenge for all the suffering and frustration of man upon this earth. His own guilt man would not recognize, and he was unable to get his hands on God to punish him for the intolerable act of creation. He would live and sleep with his frustration for a long while, the fires of his hatred so banked down that he hardly knew he had them; and then one day some God-like figure would rise before his eyes and be at his mercy, and the whole thing would surge over like a cauldron come to the boil.

"I hope Old Sage is safe in the church," said Robert suddenly.

William was startled. "What makes you think of him just now?" he asked.

"There is something God-like about Old Sage," said Robert. William shrugged his shoulders. Fatherhood being the gold thread of his being, the thing by which God had him firmly hooked to himself, his thoughts were with the children in the Palace. "Those children," he said to Robert. "The little bride and bridegroom and the rest. If they were to look from a window they would be terrified."

"Their elders will have the sense to keep them on the river side of the Palace," said Robert. "I am going now to see if Old Sage is in the church."

William went with him; not that he could see any reason for concern but two men were better in the streets than one. They pushed their way through the crowd outside William's door and made their way to the church. It was pitch dark inside but again there was a flicker of light in the east window, and there was no lightning tonight. Robert gave an exclamation of disappointment and they went out again.

"I know in which street he lives," said William.

"You know? How?" Robert asked sharply.

"I told you before I would give much to know about the old man. A couple of days ago I asked one of the girls at the Garden, the one Lucy used to buy posies from, if she knew where he lived. She said Fish Street, near the Tower. She knew because she had seen him there one day. But she did not know which house."

"We will go to Fish Street," said Robert.

William groaned inwardly at the contrariness of fate. The other night, with the ale in him, he had been spoiling for a row of some sort and Robert had thwarted it, but tonight when he was dead sober and wanted to keep his eye on the mob outside the Palace in case they did something to the children, Robert was all agog for trouble. Nevertheless he knew he could do nothing to protect the children and he might be able to do a good deal to protect Robert. So he shrugged, loosened his knife in its sheath at his belt and followed Robert down to the river.

It was still early, the hour of the first pale stars, and the watermen were busy; they were busy until after dark these days for with the streets so disturbed the river was the safest and quickest thoroughfare. They had not to wait long for a boat and were soon out on the water. They looked back and saw Whitehall blazing with light. No sleep there tonight, thought Robert. He could not know that inside the Palace the Catholic servants of the Queen were making their last confessions, expecting that at any moment the mob would storm the Palace. What he did know was that for the King, whatever he decided, this would be the most appalling night of his life.

They passed down the river and under London Bridge almost in silence, and it was a strange experience; the tumultuous city was so close to them yet out on the water with the calm pale sky arched overhead they seemed so far removed from it. It was, Robert thought, as though they had already died and were being carried by the great river to an unknown infinity of peace. Then the Tower came in sight and he remembered that, when he had come to it with Lucy, John Hampden and John Pym had just been released from it. There were different men in there tonight, with a new Lieutenant to guard them. That fact alone showed where now the power lay. A few lights lit the Tower walls. Was one of them his? A shock of awareness shattered Robert's peacefulness. For the man in there death was no remote fantasy. It was staring him in the face.

When they came to the Tower steps the twilight had almost faded. There was a glow of fire in the sky and smoke from it almost obscured the faint stars. They landed and fought their way through the mob of apprentices coming in the opposite direction. Intent on getting through they forgot the fire until they became entangled in a different crowd and found themselves being carried towards it. This mob was more dangerous than the other, which had merely been going to shout about its grievances outside the Tower. This one, as far as Robert and William could gather from the shouts about them, was on its way to hound down Papists, the old Armada hatred once more boiling in its blood. They shouted that it was a Catholic house burning, full of Spanish troops who had come up the Thames last night and been landed in the darkness when the rain came down. Robert and William could only link arms and be carried forward, for the impetus of the crowd was so great that there was no escape.

They came out of the bottleneck of the street into a wider space where four ways met at the pillory. One way was Fish Street, blocked half-way down by fire and smoke, another way led down to the nearest water conduit and along this was flung a chain of men and women passing the buckets. They were poor people and for them at the moment nothing mattered except the fact that their own homes were now in danger. It was a quarter of old timbered houses and the fire had already engulfed two of them. But even with the buckets, and the help of a little fire engine shaped like a milk churn with a seesaw laid across it, things were going so badly that with iron hooks and chains men were starting to pull down the two houses on either side of the blaze, to stop the spread of the flames, and the terrified inhabitants were running out of them like rabbits from the last of the standing corn, clutching their children and their few pathetic possessions.

As there were none to be seen the crowd seemed for the moment to have forgotten about the Spanish soldiers, and flung themselves joyously into the work of demolition. But the madness was still in them and they paid no attention to the shouted instructions of the watch. The thing was to destroy, no matter how, without system or common sense. A few had axes and were hacking at ground level at a house to the left of the blaze when a voice shouted, "There is a man up there!" Heads were craned back and an old man was seen to be peering out of an upper window, his face paper-white above the folds of his dark cloak. He did not cry for help but stood there fixed in a strange dignity of fear. "Come down, old gaffer!" a man cried out, but he did not move. "Get him out!" shouted others. And then something about him, his cloak or his dignity, struck a sensitive chord and someone yelled, "Papist! Spaniards!" And hell broke loose.

The old man moved back and disappeared from sight and

the attack on the house was renewed. Jammed in the crowd, swaying helplessly to its movement, Robert and William thought themselves trapped until they saw another man fighting his way through it almost with ease. It was Old Sage, and until now they had not known there was such enormous strength in his broad shoulders and huge brown fists. He seemed at this moment to be compounded of strength, every kind of strength. Even alone he might have reached the house but Robert and William were soon with him. They did not know how they had got there, unless his extraordinary power had simply dragged them in his wake. They used their pricking daggers to get through the mob to the door and then leapt for the rickety stairs. The house seemed now no more than a house of cards that must at any moment crash about them, with the roaring inferno of fire only a short distance away beyond a frail barrier of charred wood. For a moment panic clutched at Robert's throat, but William and Old Sage ahead of him were the one fighting mad and the other as calm as when he sat in his box pew, and their fearlessness brought back his natural courage. Even when a stair gave way beneath his feet he managed to scramble up and save himself.

They reached a landing and found the old man standing upright and trembling, very afraid but determined not to show it more than he must. He had a pointed white beard, a parchment skin drawn tight over delicate bones and fine restless dark eyes. Afraid though he was he had a look of distinction about him, even arrogance, but in his age and weakness he was no longer able to help himself. He seemed to know Old Sage and his eyes clung to him. The whole house was shaking and staggering now and the noise was terrifying. Old Sage opened a door revealing a bedchamber, with a window looking out on a tangled garden. They pulled the sheets from the bed, knotted them together and fastened one end of the improvised rope to the central post of the window; which to William's eye did not look strong enough to support much weight. The rope did not reach the garden but it reached far enough to allow an easy drop. They worked quickly, doing exactly what Old Sage wanted though he could give no orders.

Robert went first, picked himself up and was ready to help the old man, William came next and Old Sage last. It was when he was still holding to the rope that the post above gave way, and Robert and William, confused by the noise as the house started to fall, were not skilful enough to catch him. When they helped him up it was found that he had injured an ankle and could hardly stand on it. In pain though he was he smiled with wry amusement, and then with wide calm gestures continued to direct them. There was an old arbour at the bottom of the small garden, rising out of a jungle of docks and nettles, and to this William and Robert helped him. Inside he was well hidden and out of reach of the fire. Behind the arbour a door opened into a narrow lane and to this he gestured. They must take the old man through it. Robert wanted to stay with Old Sage but he would not have it. Both must go.

Outside in the lane they discovered the necessity, for the old man was hardly able to walk and at first could not think what he must do. They would have to half carry him between them, and it needed all Robert's gentle skill to find out where they had better take him. Had he friends? No. They had fled and he had been left alone there. It was a mistake, he was sure. They had not meant to leave him alone. His cultured old voice had a foreign inflection. "You are French, sir?" Robert asked. The old man shook his head and fear showed again in his eyes. Robert asked no more questions. "I have a friend at the Spanish Embassy," he said. "You will be safe there and that is where we are taking you."

They found their way through lanes that were now deserted and came to the Tower landing-stage. There were a few watermen still about and they hailed one and rowed up river. Robert and William spoke a little to the waterman but the old man sat in exhausted silence, and let the quietness of the night restore him a little to himself. When they landed at the steps nearest to the embassy his courage and poise returned. He found that he could walk now and needed only the help of their arms in climbing the steps, and in his slow progress to the embassy. There was still a small crowd in the street outside but if he felt any fear he gave no sign of it. They went down a side street and round to a back entrance, where Robert summoned his friend, a young Catholic Englishman who was a secretary there, and handed the old man over to his care. But he would not allow himself to be hurried in until he had expressed his gratitude, and his courtesy and dignity had a touch of greatness as he bade them farewell. Looking back as the secretary closed the door Robert and William saw the lamp-light gleaming on his white head, and the folds of his cloak falling from shoulders held now straight and proudly.

"Who can he be?" wondered William.

"No matter who he is, now he is safe," retorted Robert. "Now back to Old Sage. I would offer up all the Spanish hidalgos in the world for the safety of Old Sage."

They had lost all count of time, and almost all sense of fatigue, for the need for superhuman effort had pulled them half out of their bodies; they dragged these encumbrances, aching with weariness, in their wake much as a horse drags a ramshackle plough. When they went down to the river they found no boatmen, and had to walk all the way back to the garden where they had left Old Sage, through a city that grew increasingly quiet as the sky lightened at the approach of dawn, in these May days so early and so fresh. At the last their footsteps seemed to echo in a city of the dead, but in all the hidden gardens, and in all the odd green corners, the birds began to sing. When they entered the wild garden the golden-tongued thrushes welcomed them with praise and they saw the place awash with wild flowers. Between the flowers and the peaceful expanse of shining sky the ruin of blackened houses seemed of no account. They went quickly to the arbour but Old Sage was not there.

William stared stupidly at the empty seat. He was becoming conscious now of burning eyes and a nagging pain at the back of his head. "Where has he gone?" he mumbled, but Robert was already running back into the lane and he stumbled in his wake. Robert did not stop running until they had reached the open space where the four streets met. It was deserted except for one prowling cat and a man in the pillory. Even in his horror and confusion Robert saw the dark figure fastened in the dark wood as though it were the hub of a wheel, with the four streets radiating from it as though to the four points of the world's compass, anchored in it as were the birdsong and the growing light. The centre was still but the wheel seemed turning upon it, and it shone as he had seen a millwheel shine when the sun was caught in its myriad drops of water. The Guardians not only circled the world; they were the still heart of many small wheels.

Old Sage smiled at them as well as he could as they stood on the steps looking up at him, and it was as though they looked at the face of some mediaeval saint or bishop carved on a pillar, for his head and hands, appearing through the holes in the wood, seemed made of the same dark substance that imprisoned them; as though being without rebellion his acceptance had united him most peacefully with what he suffered. It was strange how vividly, for a moment, the carved saint and his peace were apparent, and then the two younger men saw only an old one who had been pelted with filth and stones, his face cut and bruised and grey with pain and exhaustion under the filth. With fury and curses William wrenched at the wood but Robert, as quiet in rage as William was the opposite, said, "Cannot you see it is padlocked? They bribed or threatened the watch. Find him."

"Where?" demanded William.

"I cannot tell you," said Robert. "Knock on doors. Ask anyone. I must stay here."

William shrugged despairingly but loped off down the street along which they had come. He thought he saw a tavern there and when in despair he always automatically made for a drink. Robert did what he could for Old Sage, wiping the sweat and filth from his face and telling him of the old man's safety. Then he sat silently on the steps beside him, for speech seemed to be no longer required. Nor was he any longer capable of it. When he had seen the arbour empty he had thought Old Sage had been murdered in revenge for his rescue of the old man, and had run from the arbour in a mere senseless wish to turn the clock back and find the mob again before they could do what they had already done. But they had not killed him. Had he won their respect to such a degree that though they could punish him they could not kill him? The question was part of the mystery of Old Sage, and that was part of the mystery of all things that yielded up nothing whatever to worrying and probing, but perhaps something, or a shadow of something, to reverence.

It was easy to feel reverence sitting in silence with the old man while the day brightened over London. Sounds from the waking city were heard only distantly and could not invade the circle of stillness that was about Old Sage in his pillory. It was imposed by his suffering yet only Robert's mind recognized that. His spirit was so at peace that he might have been sitting with Old Sage in the glow-worm light of the box pew. That light and the rising sun became one, a sea of light on which in his fatigue he seemed floating away, as on the river last night.

There was a clattering of feet on the cobbles. William, fragrant of a morning draught of ale, was back with the landlord and his wife and a sleepy befuddled gentleman with a bunch of keys. His instinct that a man in distress should make for ale must have coincided with angelic guidance, for the befuddled man was the watch, who had been finishing up the night asleep by the tavern fire. A few sharp questions from Robert did not elicit how it was that his keys had been taken from him and returned again, apparently without his knowledge, but for a silver piece he was willing now to free Old Sage. He sloped off when the padlock was unlocked. He was new to the job, the landlord's garrulous wife told them. He did not know the folk hereabouts. The old watch, now, would not have allowed all the devils in hell to put Old Sage in the pillory, not if it had been the Pope himself he had saved from the burning. Yes, she knew where the old man lived and she would have a care of him till he could walk again. She said that even before Robert slipped two silver pieces into her hanging purse, and he believed she would, for her face was kindly.

The landlord, having helped William free Old Sage from

the pillory, followed the watch, for he too was sleepy and fuddled, and Robert and William carried Old Sage between them, following the still chattering goodwife down Fish Street. He was not a light weight, as the other old man had been, but quite soon she turned to the left through an archway into a square plot of cloistered garden, one of those odd places that Robert loved so much. In the centre was a well with an old rosemary tree growing beside it. From the well and the tree radiated beds full of the herbs that Old Sage sold in Covent Garden. One side of the small square was formed by the stone wall of a warehouse but on the other sides ancient tumble-down cottages leaned about the garden, but no sounds of life came from them. "It's mostly old poor folk live here," said the goodwife. "They can be noisy enough in the evening but they are sleepy in the mornings."

She led the way through a doorway and up a flight of rickety stairs and pushed open the door of a room small as a monastery cell. It was scrupulously clean, with a rough hard bed, a cupboard in the wall and on a chest the few necessities that a man must have if he is to live. They put Old Sage upon his bed and the goodwife examined his ankle and pronounced it no more than a bad sprain. He would be about again soon, she said, and Nan, the girl who sold posies in the Garden, should look after his stall with hers while he was away. She would see to it all and the gentlemen need not worry. Her conversation poured over them in a cataract and Old Sage's eyes twinkled with amusement as he glanced up at Robert and William. But he was growing intensely weary. Struggling up to a sitting position he laid his swollen right hand on the shoulder of first one man and then the other, gratitude and affection lighting his face. Then his hand made a slight but princely gesture. It was as though, having received the accolade from a dying king, they were now dismissed from the presence; yet with humility, for if there was no servility in Old Sage there was no arrogance either.

"And he is not dying, thank God," said Robert as they sat on the steps at the Tower landing place, waiting for a boat. "When I saw him reading those chapters in St.

John I thought it was for himself he read them. It was for another."

William knew of whom he spoke, for sitting so close to the Tower it was impossible not to think of the prisoner there. William, cold and depressed, the cheerfulness engendered by the draught of ale now totally evaporated, did not wish to pursue the subject of the other and returned to Old Sage.

"He must make a fair wage selling his herbs. Why should he live and dress as a pauper?" he asked.

"He needs every penny for his brotherhood."

"Brotherhood?"

"Did you notice the blocked-up doorway in the warehouse wall? It had an arch surmounted by a cross and must have been a door to a chapel. I think there was a small religious house there once, in Queen Mary's day perhaps, and the herb garden was the cloister garth. Old Sage has carried on the tradition but it is my guess that his monks are a company of jailbirds and vagabonds, old or sick men whom no one wants. The goodwife opened that cupboard in the wall as we went out, to get something for Old Sage, and it was stocked as a physician's would have been."

"He often came late to the Garden," said William. "He was always erratic in his comings and goings."

"He would be," said Robert. "He would have to see to his brothers before he left and if any were dying he would not be able to leave them. What a devilish clamour they must make about his silence! Those hours of reading alone in the church must mean much to him."

The river traffic was beginning now and they hailed a boat. Their waterman chuckled at their disreputable appearance, but he was not in much better shape himself with one eye closed up and his clothes filthy and torn. Mercifully he was as tired as they were and not disposed for conversation. The river, flooded now from bank to bank with brimming gold, received them with calm indifference and six o'clock struck from the church towers. Three swans were flying high, their wings lit by the morning.

Fourteen

That dawn was the last but one that the Earl of Strafford would see. The King had given his consent to the Act of Attainder and he would die at noon on the following day. In his cell he received the news calmly, but Archbishop Laud, in his, heard it with despair, and wrote in his diary that this King whom he and the Earl had served so faithfully was not worth serving. Yet the King made one more attempt to save the Earl's life. He wrote a letter to both Houses of Parliament begging that the sentence of execution should be changed to imprisonment, and at the Queen's suggestion Prince Charles was sent to deliver it. How could they refuse anything to Charles? Everyone adored him. By that evening all London knew what had happened. The boy had been driven hurriedly through back streets to Westminster and had entered the House of Lords quite alone. He, the darling of the nation, used to cheers and adulation wherever he went, was received with coldness. No one smiled at him and when he tendered the letter it was returned to him unopened to take back to his father. Then he was dismissed.

Lucy had heard the story by the evening and when she was in bed that night, afraid even to try to go to sleep in case she had a nightmare, she wondered what it had been like for him, getting out of the coach and walking alone into that awful place, he who never went anywhere alone, and meeting not the usual wave of love carried up to greet him by the cheers but only silence and cold dislike. Had he pleaded with them as he presented the letter, or had he just stood in silence watching their faces to see how they would look when they opened it and read it? He would know by their faces what they were going to do to the Earl. But they had not opened it. They had just told him to take it back where it had come from. She could see him walking out of the silent place, the unopened letter in his hand, his back straight, but transfixed by all the hostile glances that drove him away like a shower of arrows. She could feel in her own body the coldness that had made him shiver all the way home in the coach, though the day was warm, and the numbed feeling in his feet as he went up the stairs to return the letter to his father.

And now he was lying awake, just as she was, listening to the clocks striking all over London. Their own church clock had just struck one. It was morning now. In a few more hours the birds would be singing and when the sun was high the Earl would be coming out of the Tower to die. Unless somebody thought of something else they could do. Children are never quite without hope and she at last fell asleep, but her nightmares were not of the Earl. She dreamed that Charles, with the body of a boy, came running to meet her, but when he came close he had a man's face with deep lines in it, and when the eyes looked into hers they were dark and unhappy as the face. It frightened her that such a young body could have such an old face; the contrast was grotesque and horrible. The fear remained with her the next morning and was perhaps merciful, because it was not until she heard the distant boom of the gun at the Tower, and saw her grandmother's blanched face, that she fully realized that no one had thought of anything and the Earl was dead.

The scapegoat had finished out the ritual until the end with composure and dignity. The two men who had once shared a vision of England's greatness, and together had loved their King and worked for him in the faith that he too could be great, were allowed no last meeting, but when the Earl went out to die he passed beneath the window of Archbishop Laud's cell and the old man thrust his hands through the bars and blessed him. On the scaffold at Tower Hill, a tall black figure sombre in the spring sunshine, he looked out over the vast crowd of his countrymen who had come to see him die and made his last profession of loyalty to them and to the King. "I had not any intention in my heart but what did aim at the joint and individual prosperity of the King and his people."

Then he turned to the block and was offered up. There was a roar of exultation when they saw that he was dead.

2

The next day a queer peacefulness fell upon London. The rioting was over, the anger and hatred spent. The shops opened and the docks came to life again. People went about their business as usual, but with an exhausted gentleness, as though they were convalescing after a long illness. For the moment at any rate the Earl's friends were too grief-stricken for hatred, and his enemies too uneasy for gloating. The shadow of yet another dream shattered, and yet another great man dead, lay over them all and was dumbly recognized as a recurrent shadow of majesty. They felt in some way purged, as though the majesty had divinity in it and had carried away their sins. And they felt pity for the little King, left now to carry for the rest of his days the guilt of the survivor for whom another man has died. They wondered if he was strong enough to do it or whether it would break him. For a short while the royal family became almost popular again, and when at the end of the month Prince Charles escorted Prince William in state to Gravesend, to see him off for Holland, the two young princes were cheered almost in the old style.

It was during this interlude of gentleness, two days after the Earl's death, that Robert thought it his duty to go to the Spanish Embassy and enquire after the health of the old man sheltering there. He was ushered up to the old man's bedchamber and found him sitting before a small wood fire, wrapped in a furred gown against the chill of the east wind. He was not yet physically recovered from his ordeal but his spirits were lively and he was disposed for conversation. He had been told Robert's name and expressed himself as honoured by a visit from a member of the Sidney family. His own family, he was able to convey without actually saying so, was equally noble. The formalities of greeting over, Robert experienced at once that sense of magnetic suction known to good listeners who have strayed too near the web of a compulsive talker. He still felt dazed with weariness and sorrow but he need do little more than listen to give the old man a happy afternoon; and in a very few moments he knew that he would want to listen.

"As no doubt you have guessed," said the old man, "I am a Catholic priest; Father Ignatius of the Society of Jesus. We do not wear the habit in times of trouble such as these."

"You honour me by trusting me with the information," said Robert cautiously.

"Ah, I knew your distinguished grandfather the Earl of Northumberland," said Father Ignatius. "Naturally I should trust his grandson. And also naturally I should trust a friend of Isaiah Fuller." Then seeing a blank look on Robert's face he added, "Possibly you only know Isaiah by the name given him after he became a seller of herbs."

Robert smiled. "Old Sage! In my mind I have always called him Socrates, but Isaiah is equally suitable." Then he sheered away from the subject of Old Sage to another, still unwilling to know what Old Sage could not tell him. "The mob who attacked the house where we found you expected to find Spanish soldiers hidden there. Had it at one time been a Catholic house?"

"Many years ago it was owned by a house of Augustinian friars across the way," said Father Ignatius. "When they were driven out at the Dissolution of the Monasteries a few of them lived there as laymen for a while. One of them, a novice at the time of the Dissolution, later married and lived there for the rest of his life. He was Isaiah Fuller's grandfather, which is why Isaiah is so attached to Fish Street. This was told me by Isaiah himself before his accident. In the time of the late king it came into the hands of a Catholic family who in their devotion are always ready to give refuge to priests in hiding. I went there for shelter a week ago, feeling myself in danger in my own lodging, and found them away from home, but their two old servants were there and took me in. The night of the fire I got up and dressed and then found that they had already fled. They had, I feel sure, forgotten in their fright that I was there. The back door was locked and I feared to go out from the front door because of the crowd. I remained in the house hoping the fire would not spread to it. The rest you know. But what you do not know is how I became acquainted with your grandfather and Isaiah Fuller."

So it had come back again and now Robert must know about Old Sage. He did not change the subject again. The talk that followed was interrupted only by a servant bringing them fruit and wine, and fresh logs for the fire, and by the fitful gleams of sunshine that came late in the afternoon. Whenever for the rest of his life he thought of the story he would smell again the burning apple logs and see the pale sun sparkling in the golden wine in the goblet he held between his hands. For throughout the story he did not drink his wine. He held the goblet much as David must have held the cup of water in the cave of Adullam, as though the sparkle within it were the sparkle of heroism.

"I was at one time engaged with your grandfather in scientific work," said Father Ignatius. "Science has always had an overwhelming fascination for me. Science is exploration. Geographical, mystical, scientific exploration are the three prongs of man's thrust forwards into the mystery of things. What you are doing may become eventually sacrilege in regard to the Almighty, exploitation in regard to man, but the explorer is like a creature tunnelling underground towards the light, with the tunnel closing behind him as he goes, and he cannot turn back. We are ruthless, you will say. Possibly. But we have our honour. We never betray each other. Your grandfather never betrayed the Catholics who worked with him."

"Was old Sage one of them?" asked Robert.

"No, Isaiah Fuller was never a Catholic. I imagine he would have called himself a Protestant, perhaps still does, but like so many mystics he found it difficult to accept any particular religious allegiance. It was difficult for him to tolerate the pettiness and intolerance of religious controversy. But his greatest friend, Patrick O'Donovan, the man whom I imagine he loved better than any other human creature—and Isaiah has an enormous power of love—was a Catholic, and I imagine it was for his protection that he joined our scientific circle. For his own way of exploration was the mystical one. He was a good scientist only because his fine mind could encompass all intellectual concepts with ease."

"Tell me about Patrick," said Robert. "If Old Sage loved him so much he must have been a remarkable man."

"He was intellectually remarkable, a very promising young lawyer, as was Isaiah himself. The friendship had started when they shared rooms together at Gray's Inn. Patrick was the only son of an aristocratic but impoverished Irish Catholic family. His parents died and he came to live in London with his uncle, who decided to make a lawyer of him. The uncle also soon died but at Gray's Inn Patrick found Isaiah, a young man slightly older than himself, and held to him like a limpet to a rock. Isaiah is, I think, a largely self-educated man. But what a scholar he is! In the days when he had his speech it was a delight to talk with him. He had a golden voice and a clear and balanced mind, and those combinend with an extraordinary winning charm made him a brilliant advocate. We used to say among ourselves that he would be Lord Chancellor one day. He would have been the best Lord Chancellor since Thomas More."

"And Patrick O'Donovan?" asked Robert again. He was already aware of Patrick as one of those men of fascination and weakness who bring down stronger men into ruin in their defence, as the King had just destroyed the Earl of Strafford.

"A very different proposition," said Father Ignatius. "I think his mind was actually more brilliant than Isaiah's, but he was without Isaiah's strength and balance. He was strikingly beautiful to look at, tall and slender, full of fire and enthusiasm but physically delicate, abnormally sensitive and highly strung. The sort of young man who catches a fever and dies before his prime, mourned and lamented as a dead Adonis. Those whom the gods love die young, men say, and often say it with relief. Such men as Patrick, living so often in a world of their imagining, are ill equipped to face the world as it is."

"Did Patrick die young?"

"I cannot tell you. After he had been the ruin of Isaiah he disappeared." The old man was silent while Robert sat patiently yet intently waiting, and then he sighed and continued. "And with no word to me. I would have helped him if I could, for I was more intimate with him than any man except Isaiah himself. But I am passing to the end of it before I have told you the crux of the matter. As a scientist Patrick was very helpful to us. Your grandfather especially thought highly of him, and would have made him his personal assistant, but before he had time to speak of it to Patrick the young man passed through a crisis in his spiritual life, and believed himself called to be a priest dedicated to the mission of England. He was beside himself with fervour. Isaiah, knowing Patrick's emotional, unstable temperament, opposed his resolution; and this was the first rift between them. Patrick's confessor and I myself were also uneasy. No one in those days, or in these either, could or can be a Catholic priest in England without risk of persecution and Patrick was not the stuff of which martyrs are made. But he held on with such tenacity and passion that he finally won the two of us over, and arrangements were made for him to go to the English college at Rome as soon as there was a vacancy. But Patrick did not convince Isaiah, and was so angered by his opposition that he broke off the friendship completely and went to live with a Catholic friend, a member of our scientific circle. It was one of those heartless actions of which men of his type are so strangely capable when their pride is stung by opposition. Isaiah left our circle, in which I think he had never been at ease, and we did not see him again, and a short while after I left it too owing to illness. But Patrick did not go to Rome. The Gunpowder Plot intervened."

A slow smile spread over Robert's face as he asked the question to which the avid curiosity of the Wizard Earl's descendants had never received a satisfactory answer. "What exactly had my grandfather to do with the Gunpowder Plot?"

"No one knew," was the careful reply. Father Ignatius had placed his fingertips together and he too was smiling. "Your grandfather was a very astute man. I think myself that his only connection with it was his refusal to inculpate one or two members of his circle, upon whom suspicion rested. Your grandfather was not only astute but, as I said before, loyal."

"Hardly so to king and parliament," said Robert. "But loyalty is one of the most difficult of virtues, a flower with all its petals pointing in different directions."

"Looking back," said Father Ignatius, "it must seem to you, as it now seems to me, almost incredible that Catholic gentlemen, good men it would have been said at the time, could assent to such a murderous affair as the Plot. They were enraged, of course, by the king's inconstancy, promising relief from recusancy fines and then reimposing them, and by the continuance of persecution. You know the dismal story. It would seem that some evil will inspired them with great subtlety. They brooded long, in a manner calculated to twist reason. They were so wrought upon that the destruction of such a king, and such a parliament, appeared to them an action both of necessity and nobility. The plans were laid by men who had served in the Spanish Netherlands and knew war, dependable men. But not all who knew of the affair were dependable, least of all Patrick, on fire like a torch, seeing himself as an avenging angel, half out of his mind with enthusiasm."

How did the old man know all this, Robert wondered, if he had been ill at the time? How did he know that the plotters had been subtly inspired? Had he been supplied with information upon his sickbed? He did not ask but waited for more.

"You know the outcome," said Father Ignatius. "The conspirators were betrayed by a man of tender conscience."

"Patrick?" asked Robert.

"It is not definitely known," said Father Ignatius. "All I know is that after the collapse of the conspiracy Patrick disappeared from his lodging, and was found later hidden in a church outside London, in a state of terror and collapse. He feared vengeance, perhaps, of God or man or both. But he was in no state to explain what he feared. He was arrested, imprisoned and later tried for complicity in the Plot. Isaiah was the

THE CHILD FROM THE SEA

defending counsel. I was about again by that time and was at the trial, and I never heard Isaiah speak more brilliantly or persuasively. Nothing could be proved against the poor devil and he was acquitted.

Isaiah took him home and nursed him. I went to see him several times and found him pathetically deranged, believing himself already to be a priest; but one with a lost soul, guilty of every crime in the calendar. Isaiah looked after him with devotion and forgiveness. He might have nursed him back to health had not his own tragedy intervened. His golden-tongued advocacy was not forgotten and had increased his reputation. Jealousy, perhaps, as well as his devotion to Patrick, caused it to be put about that he himself was secretly a Catholic. England was understandably seething with anger and fear after the Plot. Going home one night he was set upon and we will not speak of what they did to him. He would defend no more Catholics."

There was silence. Robert looked at the wine in his glass. So Old Sage had given his life, his professional life, for the wretched Patrick. Yet Patrick could not have been entirely worthless, or Old Sage would not have loved him so much. He could see Patrick in his mind's eyes; a man of charm and delicacy but without the humility to know his own weakness. A man who would mistake euphoria for courage and rush on undertakings he could not hope to sustain.

"What happened to him?" he asked.

"Patrick? I told you before. He vanished. It would appear that seeing Isaiah when friends brought him home must have finally destroyed his reason. That night he locked himself in his room and by the morning he had disappeared. He took nothing with him except an old priest's cloak that Isaiah had got to pacify him. It was rumoured that he had gone to the west and embarked on a ship bound for Ireland, that was later reported lost at sea, but nothing is entirely known. To Isaiah in his grief we stressed the likelihood of the loss at sea, and Isaiah believes that his friend has now found peace."

Robert lifted his glass and drank the wine. David, he believed, had been wrong to empty the cup on the floor of the cave. The life of the Guardians, poured out for other men, should be accepted with humble gratitude.

"Was it then that Isaiah became a herb seller?" he asked.

"Soon after. But first I took him to the house in Fish Street that had been his grandfather's. He had been maimed in defending a man who was a Catholic and we looked after him until he had recovered his strength. The old religious house opposite was then more or less in ruins, apart from the chapel which had been turned into a warehouse. Men and women of the disreputable sort sheltered there. You could have described it as a rabbit warren of vice shunned by respectable people. I think Isaiah saw it as something of a challenge. He had lost his tongue but he still had his immense physical and spiritual strength and the place called for both. Against the persuasion of all his friends he went to live there.

"Had he been a whole man the inhabitants would doubtless have flung him out at once, but his condition aroused their pity. Moreover, a dumb man could not preach to them upon the subject of their sins." Father Ignatius paused and chuckled. "That must have been his greatest asset in their eyes! He cut himself off from his old friends that he might be one of them. He even covered up his tracks so that no one should find him or know how he lived. It was of course the only way to win their acceptance. What he had he shared with them and when it was gone, perhaps even the last book sold, I imagine that he more or less starved with them, for it took him some while to establish his herb business. But he so won them that they helped him clear the court and lay out the garden, and make the ruined place more habitable. As the years went on it gradually changed. There was less vice. It has now the character of an almshouse for the sick and unfortunate, and is one of the most attractive corners in London, as Isaiah is one of the most remarkable men. Yet few know of either. The yeast is hidden. Old Sage has no tongue with which to ask you and your friends to keep it so, but I am sure that his desire in this matter is as obvious to you as it is to me."

The old man was tired, and there was no more to say. Robert made his courteous farewell and went away.

3

Lucy did not see Prince Charles and Prince William as they processed through the city for on that very day her father once more left London. He and Elizabeth had failed to win their separation. Their lordships could see no adequate reason for it and Elizabeth was commanded to return to her husband. She refused, and the court washed its hands of the matter, but did not give William the custody of the children. In his fury he said that nevertheless he would take Bud home with him. Justus he could not take because of his schooling, but Bud should come. And then to his astonishment Lucy refused to go with him. They fought it out in the field by the unicorn wood, sitting in the deep grass that was now fragrant with clover, Lucy sitting upright and whitefaced, afraid even to look at William in case she should cry.

"While my mother is unhappy she is my child and I must look after her," she said for the tenth time. "I promised Nan-Nan. I love you more than my mother, you are my firstborn, and when she is happy again I will come to you. But I cannot leave my mother while she cries in the night."

"It's the crying of a spoilt child," said William, nearly choked with his anger and disappointment. "Nan-Nan has been dead for months."

"Nan-Nan dying is not the only reason why my mother weeps," said Lucy.

"Hold your tongue, Bud!" said William angrily. He knew what she meant and he did not want her to put it into words. The man whom Elizabeth imagined she loved had grown tired of her. He had gone to his country home and taken a fancy to his wife. Somehow the whole household knew this, even the children. To William it was intolerable that the children should know. He looked at Lucy and the adult compassion in her eyes horrified him. What had he done, what had Elizabeth done, that this child was already a woman?

Then self-pity overwhelmed him. Why should Bud punish him for her mother's disappointment? It was he who deserved comforting, not Elizabeth.

He got up, flung away from Lucy and went to find his mother-in-law; Elizabeth was spending the day with her sister and he had the run of the house. But Mrs. Gwinne upheld her granddaughter. If war came and he turned soldier, what would happen to Lucy? He must look at things from the point of view of the welfare of his daughter. Poor William tried to. "But I will be back," he warned his mother-in-law. "I will get the custody of my children or go to hell."

"An unpleasant alternative," said Mrs. Gwinne drily. "I should prefer you to have the custody of your children. When you have won it then the matter will be settled. Until then it is best for Lucy to remain here."

William went back to the field, took Lucy in his arms and kissed her, and went away again, the tears running down his face. It was a long time before Lucy went back to the house and she hated the smell of clover for the rest of her life. She hardly knew how to live through the next two days. Her eyes saw nothing but William's lonely figure riding back to Roch without her, and her ears heard nothing except the queer sound, half sob and half curse, with which he had turned away from her in the field. But on the evening of the second day alleviation came. Dr. Cosin's trial, that had started after the Earl's execution, had gone well. He had defended himself with great skill and humour and was acquitted.

But when they saw him again he was not the same man. His wife had died and his private grief had deepened his awareness of the tragedy gathering over them all.

Just once more a sunburst lightened it. In August the King had gone north on another fruitless expedition into Scotland and when he returned London gave him a civic welcome. Robert Sidney took Lucy and her mother by coach to see the show, and Tom Howard came too. The King, the Queen and the three elder children were to drive from Stamford Hill to Moorgate, where the mayor would welcome them. They would watch the ceremony at Moorgate and then see the King ride into the city to the banquet at Guildhall. They had to abandon the coach before they reached Moorgate, the crowds were so great, but Robert and Tom made a way through for them and they reached the spectators' stands in safety. They were scarcely settled when there was a burst of cheering. The Lord Mayor, attended by the aldermen, had come to the city gate to receive the King and leaning forward they could see the gilded coach approaching, with horsemen riding on either side, for the King was escorted by the Sheriff of London and a company of noblemen. The coach stopped, the coach door was flung open, the steps adjusted and the King stepped down to greet the mayor. Then the Queen was handed down, and the three children.

Since the trial Lucy had seen the royal family only in her dreams and imaginings, and she dreaded to see the King again, afraid that she would hate him for what he had done. But she did not, for he and the Queen still seemed to belong to her, and standing they were like little people made out of china, too fragile to be expected to bear up the burden of the world without cracking here and there. The jewels of the George flashed on the King's dark cloak and the Queen had diamonds in her hair, and their regal bearing, still and gracious, had something luminous about it. But the light was too gentle to give much protection; it seemed only to accentuate their loneliness. It seemed to Lucy at this moment that they had not even the protection of each other. Was everyone as lonely as this?

She returned to knowledge of her own heart to find it lurching in fear. Then she saw Charles and her whole awareness flowed out to him, at first protectively, aware of menace, then in amazement that she could have even seen the King and Queen when he was there, he was so glowing and so strong. The three children stood beside their parents, Charles and the Princess Mary holding the hand of the little one, the Prince James. The Princess, so soon to be sent away to Holland to her bridegroom, looked like Justus on the last day of the holidays, a stiff smile on her face but her eyes looking in all directions for something to happen, plague or fire or storm, that would make travel impossible. James was frankly scared by all the people and Charles towered over him like Jove, protective and confident. But his smiling face had a new maturity. They might be cheering now but he would not forget how they had treated him in the House of Lords.

Then it all turned into a fairytale. The mayor, marvellously dressed and attended, made a speech of welcome and the King made a stammering courteous reply. Then the mayor knelt on one knee and was knighted by the King, the sunlight flashing on the sword. Two beautiful horses, gifts from the city to the King and Prince Charles, were led up and while the Queen and her younger children returned to the beautiful coach, a gift to her, they mounted them. Good horsemen as they were they both mounted gracefully, but the Prince came up into the saddle with all the joy of a boy with a new and glorious gift. Laughing, he waved his hat to the people and they cheered him and some of the ladies threw flowers to him.

Lucy had no flowers but she took from her hanging pocket a treasure she had been holding there. Bowing first to one side and then the other, as his father was doing, he suddenly saw her. Mounted on the stand she was on a level with him. Their eyes met and for a moment he looked at her with great seriousness. She threw the purse she had made for him, her aim so accurate that he caught it easily. He laughed as he had done when he looked up at her from the barge on the river and flung her the white rose he was holding. Then he rode forward with his father and passed into the city, the coach following. Within the city the cheering rose as the cavalcade passed along to Guildhall, but without the gate silence fell for a moment or two before the people started to climb down from the stands. For Lucy the bright day was suddenly dark as though a curtain had fallen. Her childhood was over and it would be years before she would see Charles again.

BOOK II

The Idyl

One

8

The bees were humming in the warm Devonshire garden and the flowers burned in the drowsy September heat. Nicholas Chappell, Lucy's paternal step-grandfather, was as fanatical about his garden as her maternal step-grandfather was about his library. Each flower was as dear to him as each book to Mr. Gwinne. And how dear, Lucy thought with a pang of gratitude, were step-grandfathers. She straightened herself from her weeding and looked with affection at his extraordinary figure, bent now over the bush that he was pruning. His gardening wear on a hot afternoon was a pair of patched and mud-caked old breeches topped by an exquisitely embroidered linen shirt, the sleeves rolled up above the elbows. No matter how great the heat he never wore a hat and his bald head was burned a rich brown by the sun. He was immune to any sort of weather a man can encounter in his garden, and paid no attention to such physical infirmities as rheumatism and increasing rotundity of figure. While he could stand he would garden. His annual prayer to the apothecary who attended him through the attacks of bronchial asthma that came upon him each February was always, "Give me one more spring if you please, sir. One more spring."

Feeling Lucy's eyes upon him he straightened himself and smiled his charming toothless smile. "Do not get tired, my maid," he called to her. Though equally fanatical he was a less selfish man than Mr. Gwinne. Faces that bent over his flowers were for ever dear to him, and those who sat about his hospitable board eating his apples and drinking his home-brewed wine were never forgotten. And he would sacrifice himself for them; as witness the occasion when to oblige his wife and stepson he had torn himself from his garden to sojourn for a whole mortal winter at Roch, where the salty winds were enough to

break the heart of any gardener. Seeing Lucy rosy and unharmed by her efforts he nodded to her and returned to his,
but knowing he would not blame her she sat down on the
wooden seat beside the michaelmas daisies and took a rest.

Michaelmas daisies had only recently arrived in England
and those in the garden were Mr. Chappell's pride and joy.
They also gave joy to the butterflies. Their delicate and jewelled wings shimmered over the daisies as though they were
flowers themselves; yet the wings trembled a little now and
then, opening and shutting with a fanlike motion, showing
them to be free of the air as birds are. Yet not quite birds, as
they were not quite flowers, mysterious and fascinating as are
all indeterminate creatures. Lucy held out a brown hand and
one drifted to her finger like the bird at Roch. Her delighted
heart seemed to tremble in rhythm with the faint movement
of its wings. She was an indeterminate creature herself just
now, neither child nor woman, feeling adrift and lost, without
either anchorage in the earth or resting place above it. A solitary tear fell and alighted on her finger beside the butterfly. It
was scared half out of its wits and flew away.

"Serve me right," thought Lucy, feeling for her handkerchief. "Why cry? We are all alive."

She knew herself to be fortunate indeed that all whom she
loved were still alive after two years of civil war. So many men
whom she had known were not now alive, or badly wounded
like Algernon Sidney, or fighting their brothers, or homeless
like her own father. Roch Castle had been practically destroyed. The Earl of Carbery had garrisoned it for the King
but a year later it had fallen to the Puritan Roland of Laugh-
erne. A few months ago, when she had heard the news, Lucy
had known she must go to her father. He had not yet won the
custody of his children, and would not do so for another three
years, but Elizabeth was happy now and he was grief-stricken
and not even the thought of leaving Justus behind in London
had held Lucy back, for her father was still her firstborn. By
what Mrs. Gwinne had considered to be heaven's mercy an
Exeter family were returning there from London and Lucy
travelled with them, dangerously but in the event safely, and

now they were here together with William's parents and Dewi. And it was peaceful here for Exeter was still in Royalist hands, as London was in the possession of Parliament. There was no fighting here and none in London and Roch Castle, though so passionately loved, was not actually a person. So why weep?

But still there was that other family, that nimbus about the moon of which she was still deeply aware, and all was not well with them. They were scattered now, the King and Charles with the army, the younger children in a place of safety, the Queen in France. The past April, with the tide turning against her husband's cause, she had taken leave of him at Abingdon and come, ill and discouraged, to Exeter. Her youngest child, little Princess Henrietta, had been born at Bedford House in Exeter last June and was still there in the care of Lady Dalkeith, but the Queen had fled to France. She had been heroic through two years of war but her health had been broken and her nerves shattered. When the King himself came to Exeter expecting to find her he found only the fragile little princess and his wife's goodbye letter. 'Adieu my dear heart. If I die believe that you will lose a person who had never been other than entirely yours, and who by her affection has deserved you should not forget her." Forsaken, tormented in mind, he had become ill in Exeter. But he was not there now. He was back with the army.

And Charles? When he was only thirteen he and James had marched with the army in the care of Dr. Harvey, Lucy's friend of the Tower, and had watched the battle of Edgehill. For a short while Charles had managed to escape Dr. Harvey and get into the fight. Lucy had been told this and thought it must have been a very vile battle for a boy's first. She remembered how he had had nightmares as a child and remembered her own nightmare of the boy with the child's body and the man's face. And what were they all fighting about? It had seemed clear at the beginning but was becoming more and more confused as time went on. War was like that, Grandfather Chappell had said. At the end men were hanging on to each other's throats as dogs do out of sheer obstinacy. She found she was crying again, not for the obstinacy but for Charles. But how ridiculous. For what was he now to her? What could he ever be? Only a mixed-up memory of a bridge and a barge on the water, a white unicorn and the love of two children. Yet she still had the rose he had thrown her, pressed between the leaves of her bible. And the thread that united them still held.

The wooden bench faced a grass path that vanished at its farther end under an archway cut in a tall hedge of clipped yew. Lucy, sundrenched and now a little sleepy, saw a fairy creature appear in the archway, a russet-clad brown thing with a feather in its cap. It danced like a March hare upon the grassy space before the archway, then bounded towards her. She held out her arms and Dewi flung himself into them.

He was eight years old now, with rosy cheeks and eyes black and bright as a blackbird's. He had a flaming temper when crossed but in a good mood he was a nice small boy, gay and loving. He let Lucy hug him and then struggled free with sudden arrogance, for he was an indeterminate creature too, midway between child and boy, at one moment wanting the protection of arms about him and at the next disdaining them. He picked up the fallen cap with the pheasant's feather with one hand and with the other grabbed Lucy's skirts, pulling her off the seat.

"Cavalry," he said. "Down in Exeter. Quick."

Horses were his life just now, especially the glorious horses of the King's army, but when His Majesty had ridden in from Exeter three months ago he had been confined to his chamber with contagious spots, and though he had bitten the hands that fed him, and hit out with his fists at the kind faces about his bed, he had not been allowed out. Now he was not to be defrauded of his pleasure, and nor was Lucy of hers; though with her it was something more than pleasure that set her heart beating madly against the detested corsets into which she had been thrust on her fourteenth birthday. But she was all child as she raced with Dewi to the stable. Mr. Chappell saw them go but did not enquire where they were going, for as a mere step-grandfather he refused to be associated with disciplinary measures. He was pleased to have William, Lucy and

Dewi under his roof, and not unwilling to pay for the education of Richard and Justus, but he declined responsibility for the children's misdemeanours; it was not he who had begotten their father.

Sitting side-saddle on her grandfather's chestnut mare, with Dewi beside her on his rough little Dartmoor pony, riding towards Exeter, Lucy found herself lifted on a sudden wave of pleasure and relief. She had delighted in London but here in the country she had captured once more the peace she had known at Roch. And she was her father's daughter. The smell of Mr. Chappell's farmyard was as good to her as the smell of cowslips, and no golden chair in the world was as fine to sit on as a horse's back. This countryside was not Wales but it was near enough. She loved the round green hills of Devon, the deep lanes where the white violets grew in spring, Exeter Cathedral and the river that wound its way under the bridges of the old town to the meadows where the sheep were feeding, and on to the sea.

"There's Exeter," she cried to Dewi as they reached the turn in the lane from which they could see the city.

"Of course it's there," said the practical Dewi, and he cantered on, afraid to miss the cavalry. But Lucy stopped to look at the city, for if Roch Castle could be practically destroyed, with the tower fallen and the great roof of the hall burnt to cinders, so could the houses with the tall chimneys from which the smoke crept up so peacefully and lazily. It was not men alone who died in war. There was a mist over the river and the sun had combined smoke and mist into a golden haze from which the towers of the cathedral soared clear. With a feeling of reassurance Lucy rode after Dewi. The mare's long graceful stride soon overtook the bustling hurry of the little pony, to Dewi's annoyance.

"You were told not to take the mare without permission," he reminded his sister.

"I never ask for what will be refused," retorted Lucy proudly.

When they reached the city they found the narrow streets crowded and the noise and confusion stupendous. Officers in plumed hats, with the royal ribbon across their breastplates, were riding hither and thither trying to find billets for men and horses, and the tired troops were making for the alehouses or for flights of steps where they could sit and rest, while the citizens who were not in the streets were leaning out of the windows demanding to know where the Prince was lodging.

"The inn, Fore Street," a soldier answered them and the tide of rejoicing humanity flowed instantly towards Fore Street, carrying Lucy and Dewi with them. In the Royalist west the King was admired but it was the Prince who was still the chief darling of the people.

The Cavalier Inn, a timber-framed house with mullioned windows, was one of the loveliest in Devon and today confronted Fore Street with pride, the sun sparkling on the newly washed windowpanes. A group of officers lounged about the doorway and the space in front of it was being kept clear by the pikes of an armed guard. Grooms were holding horses in readiness to the right of the door, and expectancy rippled through the crowd for it had been rumoured that the Prince might be coming out at any moment. "We will stay here till he does," Lucy said to Dewi. They had manoeuvred the mare and pony to a position exactly behind the guard and discontented persons called out to them, some of them not too politely, that they should take their mounts round to the stableyard, but Lucy and Dewi had expended much charm and force getting themselves where they were and they refused to budge. "I wish to honour the Prince of Wales," Lucy called back. "I am myself a Welshwoman and I will not be dissuaded." Some of the remarks had angered her, her colour was up and her head held high. She was aware that she had no hat and that her gardening clothes, an old shabby kingfisher blue skirt and a faded orange bodice, were not suitable for riding, but what did that matter? She was a gentlewoman however she was dressed, with the blood of princes in her veins, and Dewi with the feather in his cap was the finest little boy in the world; they were here and here they would stay, for the glory of Wales and the honour of its Prince.

They waited for a while and then there was a burst of cheering and heads were tipped back, for a window above had been flung open. Lucy looked up too and saw Charles there leaning out and waving to the crowd. She had often wondered what would be in her mind if she saw him again and strangely it was a fall of music, the chiming of familiar words.

> *The white upturned wondering eyes*
> *Of mortals that fall back to gaze on him,*
> *When he bestrides the lazy pacing clouds*
> *And sails upon the bosom of the air.*

And indeed for a few moments he looked like a young god leaning from the window, his dark eyes alight with laughter, for he could look handsome when he laughed and his vitality and grace had a startling charm. He was royally dressed in a scarlet doublet, the lace of his cravat falling on a cuirass so brilliantly polished that it shone like silver. The boy who had come up the river in the Royal barge had acknowledged the cheers of the crowd with anxious carefulness, but this much older boy responded with the ease of a cat rearing its head to the stroking hand. He had grown to like acclamation and just now it was a needed balm. He saw Lucy and stopped laughing, and in his sudden gravity she knew his need. Serious and puzzled he was no longer a young god, scarcely any longer a boy, for his face had a look of strained fatigue that had nothing to do with youth. To make him laugh again she smiled up at him herself, and he responded, but uncertainly, groping for a lost memory. She knew what it was. London Bridge. Only it was the other way about now. It was he who leaned from above and she who looked up from below.

He drew back from the window and a moment later he appeared at the door, his plumed hat in his hand. He was now in his fifteenth year, so tall and strong that he looked much older. His black horse was led up and he mounted quickly and gracefully. He was facing Lucy, looking at her over the heads of the guards, and now he noticed Dewi in his feathered cap and grinned at him, for already he loved children. "Will you ride with me?" he asked them both, and then turning to his gentlemen he said, "I am acquainted with this lady. She and her brother shall ride with me." There was no more to be said but Lucy as she wheeled her horse to ride out into Fore Street beside the Prince was aware of profound disapproval rising up about her thick as fog. Charles felt it too, for trained in discretion as he had been, and not impetuous by nature, this was the first time he had been guilty of such an unsuitable and erratic action. But it was too late to turn back now, the girl was beside him, the small boy following, and he forgot his anxiety in sudden joy.

Out in the street it appeared that he had pleased the crowd if not his gentlemen. They were delighted to see a West Country girl riding beside the Prince and roared their approval. And indeed the boy and girl in their bright clothes, sitting their horses with very straight backs, the little boy riding behind like a small esquire, were a sight for sore eyes, so clear-eyed and innocent as to appear untarnishable, so young it seemed they could never be old. The moment was lifted up out of time, not to be forgotten by those who watched and cheered, or by the three fairytale figures who rode through the sunshine as though it were a sea of light flowing in from another country. Beyond the cheering they could hear the cathedral bells.

As well as laughing and waving to the people they found they could talk a little. "I said I knew you," said Charles. "But do I? You are familiar but I don't know why." And in his heart he wondered if that was what every man thought when for the first time a woman came up over the horizon like the sun and struck him between the eyes.

"Sir, I gave you a monkey," said Lucy. "His name was Jacob."

Charles's eyes lit up. "Jacob. So you did. And a little purse. I have it still." Actually he had lost it but he had a beautiful voice, already deep and caressing, and he made it sound as though the purse were against his heart at the moment of speaking.

"And once, sir, I waved to you from London Bridge." She wanted him to remember how he had looked up at her as she just now had been looking up at him, but he replied to her only with a smile and she knew he had forgotten. How could he possibly remember? Yet all the same she felt a slight chill at her heart and was aware again of the disapproval of the gentlemen riding behind them, and knew that her immortal moment was slipping from her.

"You are riding to the Guildhall, I believe," she said. "I will leave you, sir, at the next turning. It will be more suitable."

"What is your name and where do you live?" he asked her hastily.

"My name is Lucy Walter. I live with my grandparents at the house of Brock Hill in the village of Broad Clyst."

"Is it far?"

"Only a couple of miles. Goodbye, sir."

She had seen the lane leading off Fore Street between two houses. She bowed to him and turned her horse and the people let her and Dewi through. She rode some way down the deserted lane before she stopped and looked back. Above the heads of the people, framed by the leaning houses, she saw the plumed horsemen going by as though they were far away, she herself a lonely onlooker, and felt a pang of unexplainable desolation, as though she had been cast out.

"Are we going home now?"

She had forgotten Dewi. She smiled down into his brown mischievous face, "As quick as we can. It may be they will not know I have taken the mare."

2

That however was too much to be hoped for and at supper that night Lucy sat with her back very straight and her cheeks very rosy, for not only her grandmother but her father too was seriously displeased. Indeed William was at the moment a very worried man. The landlord of the village inn had been in Exeter that afternoon and had seen Lucy riding with the Prince, and his daughter was now being talked about in every house in the village. And not for the first time either, for Bud's escapades followed each other in rather close succession.

Harmless in themselves they were always spectacular, as when she had plunged fully dressed into the river to rescue a drowning puppy, or sat all day beside a village lad who had been put in the stocks, feeding him with her grandfather's strawberries, or worst of all when she had seen a felon marched by to his hanging and had tried to walk beside him; she would have gone with him to the gallows, William believed, had she not been forcibly removed. And now riding brazenly beside the Prince who had been going neither to the stocks, nor the gallows, nor the block. Not at the moment. The ghost of a smile softened William's eyes as he looked at his daughter. If it had been the block to which Charles had been riding she would not have left him. Lucy saw the smile and knew herself once more forgiven. Her father, whatever she did, would always forgive her.

"What's that?" asked Mrs. Chappell suddenly. The clatter of horses' hoofs in the lane beyond the house was so loud that it reached even to the quiet dining parlour, and she turned her eyes accusingly upon Lucy. What had her scapegrace granddaughter brought upon her this time? She was a different type of grandmother from Mrs. Gwinne, a wiry little woman, bustling and kindly and a notable housewife, anxious to do her duty but seeing it more in terms of food and shelter than of love and understanding. She had affection for her legal grandchildren but there was no love lost between her and Dewi, and for this latter reason there was not very much love between her and Lucy.

"If a detachment of cavalry is to be billeted upon you, madam, it is none of my doing," she said to her grandmother and held her chin in the air rather naughtily.

"Bud, Bud," chided her father under his breath, for she was wearing a gown of sea-green that her grandmother had given her, and the little pearl drops in her ears had come from Mrs. Chappell's treasure chest, and the small holes in the lobes of the ears from her expert surgery with needle and cork. Lucy flushed with shame, for Grandfather and Grandmother Chappell had been very kind to them all. Where would they have been without them?

"The men pass by," said Mr. Chappell. "They are going to the inn." But his optimism was too quick for the silence that succeeded the dying away of the clatter was presently shattered by a vigorous attack upon the knocker of the front door. A Captain Symonds was ushered in, a smiling young man with a couple of front teeth knocked out. The homeliness of his appearance, his Devonshire speech and the slight difficulty he was having with it in consequence of the accident, made his request for stabling a few horses, the accommodation at the inn being insufficient, less of an affliction than it might have been. Supper awaited him at the inn but he sat down and had a glass of wine with them, and talked a little of the war. He talked hopefully yet his broad good face was now unsmiling. It was Lucy's first real intimation of a tide going out and she longed for reassurance; so much so that when Captain Symonds rose to take his leave she got up too and said she would show him the way to the garden door, that was nearer to the inn than the front entrance.

"The hussy!" murmured her grandmother as the two left the room.

"Bud is not a hussy," said William, breathing hard. He was not able to tell his mother what he knew so well about his daughter, for the necessary words would not come to his mind, but Grandfather Chappell the gardener was able to do his explaining for him.

"The maid has long tap roots," he said, "and finds her nourishment far below the usual vanities of maidenhood. Therefore she is not self-conscious and not, I think, as much aware of the difference between men and women as maidens mostly are."

"No?" asked his wife drily.

"All innocent maidens make instinctive use of their natural charm," Grandfather Chappell conceded. "Men also in a different manner. But down below the surface where the tap roots are humanity is of one stuff of love and sorrow."

He spoke so sadly that his wife's face softened and William, the remembrance of his shattered home and his broken marriage bitter within him, poured himself another glass of wine.

Of one stuff. Deio! Deio! If men could only know that before it was too late.

At the door in the garden wall the man and girl stood talking. The door opened on a narrow lane leading to the inn. A small stream rippled down the farther side of it, its voice interwoven with the song of the thrush in the garden. Beyond the stream a ferny bank rose to a drystone wall and beyond it was the Chappells' orchard, reached by stepping stones across the stream and an ancient stone stile in the wall. The dew was falling and the smell of wet moss and ferns was cool and fresh. "No smell in the world like the West Country smell," said Captain Symonds. "I have been on the march since Naseby. I wondered if I would ever smell Devon again."

"Wales smells better," said Lucy.

He laughed. "Wales is the West Country too. We are compatriots."

She could not have disagreed with him more profoundly but politeness forbade her to say so, and she had not brought him to the garden door to discuss moss. "Are they far away?" she asked abruptly. "I felt when you were talking just now that they were not far behind him." Then seeing his puzzled look she added with grave dignity, "I speak of the Prince."

He had been told of the bold girl who had ridden with the Prince. Was this the maid? He looked round at her with mischievous enquiry, his eyes twinkling, but he was instantly sobered. She seemed to have aged since he had last looked at her and her face was a woman's in its controlled anxiety. He had seen so many women look like that during the past two years; longing to cry out for reassurance but too proud to do so.

"We will never permit them to capture the Prince," he told her. "Wars always sway backwards and forwards and if the tide is against us now it will turn again, we hope and believe. If not, and we are forced back into Cornwall, remember that there is the sea and France."

She was comforted and grateful and a girl again as she picked a sprig of rosemary from the bush by the door and put it in his coat. "Goodnight," she said, and was gone as soundlessly as a moth. He was out in the lane, he found, with the door shut between them, and he laughed ruefully for he had not wished to leave her. They would have six days' rest here, he had been told. It was a pleasant thought. He would look for her in the garden tomorrow.

3

It was not in the garden that he found her but in the orchard picking blackberries for bramble jelly. A hedge separated the orchard from the Exeter Road, and here the brambles grew so thick and tall that it was only possible to see passers-by if they were on horseback. It was a place both enchanted and enclosed, the windless warmth giving to all it pervaded a dream-like eternal quality. All things had reached their fruition and were contented with it. The voices of the sheep in the fields, and the humming of the bees in the wild flowers that grew along the hedges, seemed not so much sound as the gentle breathing in and out of this contentment. Pressed into blackberry picking slightly against his will the man soon found himself lazily happy with it, since it was what the girl wanted him to do. In her shabby clothes, her fingers stained with blackberry juice, he found her even more desirable than she had been last night in the silk dress, sitting a little stiffly in the formal parlour.

"Do gipsies have queens?" he asked her. "I ask because if they do you are one of them."

She laughed but did not reply. It was a day well calculated to melt masculine minds to lazy nonsense but she must get on with the blackberry picking. She had vexed her grandmother last night and she wanted to make up for it. The blackberries fell from her fingers to her basket almost as fast as beads from a broken string and she was so absorbed in her picking, and Captain Symonds was so absorbed in her, that neither of them took any notice when they heard a horseman riding by towards the inn. But they did look up when they were suddenly hailed in the high excited voice of Ensign Haynes, aged fifteen. He was standing on tiptoe on the other side of the hedge, only visible from the chin upwards, his freckled face flushed and his eyes sparkling.

"Come back, sir," he commanded his superior officer. "That fellow came with a message. The Prince is to ride out on a visit of inspection. He may be here at any moment."

Captain Symonds was annoyed. " 'Sdeath! Why must we be inspected? We are resting."

"Not now. Come on, sir."

"He is a lay-abed," temporized Captain Symonds. "God-a-mercy, he will not be here for hours."

"If you are not ready for them, they come," said Ensign Haynes out of his vast experience of military commanders. He looked at Lucy and grinned. "But I am not needed. I will stay and help this lady."

"You will not, you jackanapes," said Captain Symonds hotly. "You will come with me and do what you are told." He sighed and turned to Lucy. "Army life is hard on a man."

"All life is hard," said Lucy. She had not ceased picking blackberries while they talked but Ensign Haynes had seen the sparkle in her eyes and it belied her grave words. He chuckled and looked at her again, but she was dismissing them both with a queenly inclination of the head and a peremptory gesture with a blackberry-stained hand. He continued to chuckle.

"Who does the maid think she is?" he asked Captain Symonds as they went back to the inn.

"Who knows what maids think," said Captain Symonds disgustedly, for the dismissal had hurt his pride. "Above all that maid."

But left alone Lucy knew no more than they did who she was or what she thought. For a short while she felt crowned with glory, and wild fantasies circled in her mind like exploding stars, but then came hope and fear tearing her apart, and leaping between them a mocking spirit who laughed and jeered at the fantasies so that they fell down and turned into tears lying on the blackberries in the basket. Laugh at yourself, you little fool, he said to her. Fall in love with a prince? Fool! Come away into the woods with me and laugh at your-

self there. But I cannot run from love, she said, for it is glory.
To run away is only worldly wisdom. But I will not run to it. I
will wait and be still.

She filled her basket and carried it into the kitchen and she
said no word of the Prince to her grandmother who was pre-
siding there.

"Wash the berries, Lucy," said Mrs. Chappell. "We will get
the jelly on the boil immediately."

Mrs. Gwinne had left the kitchen work to her servants and
so household chores were new to Lucy, but she was anxious to
learn because William hoped that one day, after he had helped
his step-father with the farm for a little longer, they would go
back to Wales. The castle was in ruins but they would find a
home somewhere and Lucy should keep house for William
and Dewi; and when the war was over for Justus too in his
holidays. Until today this had been for Lucy a thing so longed
for that her thoughts had been always busy with it, but now
her mind was a confusion of other images; the curve of a boy's
smooth cheek, a fall of dark hair, brown hands holding the
reins. She knew his face by heart, she found, and knew where
the reins had hardened the palms of his hands. "I will not go
to meet it," she vowed again, and tied the strings of her cooking apron so hard that it was as though she had tied a knot
upon the vow. Mrs. Chappell found her a good worker that
morning though she did not always answer when she was
spoken to.

When their frugal dinner was over her grandmother was
ready with another task for Lucy. "I always give a pot of my
bramble jelly to Granny Miles," she said. "And I have some
pasties for her too, poor old soul. Take them now, my dear,
and see that you are tidy before you set out. Change your gown
and put a hat on your head."

Mrs. Chappell was patronizingly generous to the poor of the
village and though Lucy loathed the patronage she could co-
operate wholeheartedly in the generosity. But not today when
she wanted to be by herself. However there was no help for it
and presently she was walking up the lane with a basket on her
arm. Her grandmother, glancing from a window, saw her go

and sighed in despair, for her bareheaded granddaughter had not only neglected to change her gown but had forgotten to take her apron off. Yet no one would have taken her for a village maid, for she moved with grace and dignity. She rounded the corner and disappeared and the quiet autumn scene appeared for a moment or two empty and colourless.

4

Granny Miles lived in a small cob cottage next to the church and Lucy loved her because her tiny stature and snowy cap and apron reminded her of Nan-Nan. She was not so great a woman as Nan-Nan but she had wit and gentleness and unquenchable vitality still burned in her sunken dark eyes. Sitting and talking with her always eased Lucy's longing for Nan-Nan, a thing that had become bearable with time but would not leave her, and today more than most days it was good to rest against the serene strength of an old woman who has weathered all the storms and not been broken by them.

She stayed with Granny for a little while and then crossed the lane to the churchyard thinking of Nan-Nan. Was it true that the dead do not die? Because of the war the grass had grown long in the churchyard. Members of the Chappell family were buried here. One was Nicholas Chappell who had died aged seventeen. His hour of life had held his livingness as a cup holds wine, but now nothing was left of either except a few bones beneath the earth. And she stood here beside his bones with her own cup sparkling to the brim. He was not of her blood yet he seemed to be so at this moment. Had he even had time to love a girl? And what had he felt when he had come to know that the cup was cracking in his hand? Despair? Bitterness? Or that pure grief and pure bright anger that could spring like a flame from the dark web? She could not know but for a few intense moments he was so vividly real to her, and her longing to give him all that he had missed was so great, that his presence beside her brought neither astonishment nor fear, and when he slipped his hand into hers she held it closely to comfort him and was not surprised to find him warm. She thought only, yes, it is true what people say, the dead do live on.

Then she turned towards him and it was Charles. She stood speechless, holding his hand and looking up into his face, and though he was not Nicholas she gave him her sorrow, and the gift of herself entirely. He was not Nicholas and yet he was. He might not see his eighteenth birthday. "Golden lads and girls all must as chimney sweepers come to dust." To one kind of dust or the other, the death of the body or the death of love. Her thoughts were not formulated, they were part of the confusion that had been in her mind all day, and they made her eyes look large and lustrous with sorrow and her mouth soft and compassionate.

Charles flung his arms round her and hugged her. At first it was a boy's awkward hug but it strengthened as he got the feel of this girl in his arms for the first time. They grew as they stood together. They were a year or two older when she sighed and he released her. Hand in hand they wandered under the tall trees, not knowing where they went and surprised when the cool darkness of the church porch enclosed them. But it held the promise of a greater privacy and they pushed the door open and went in and sat down on a bench. Peace held them both and presently Lucy remembered the church at Covent Garden. She had been able to go there so seldom after she went to live with Mrs. Gwinne and then at last, growing older, she had not gone there at all and had ceased to think of Old Sage. She was ashamed. How could she have forgotten him even for a moment? "Touch God in the fair temple." She had done that with him and through him and she was doing it now through the peace that held her and Charles. She had not known that glory held this peace. "All true glory, while it remains true, holds it. It is the maintaining of truth that is so hard." The words came to her in Old Sage's voice. Yet she had never heard his voice, for he was dumb. How could that be?

The church clock struck over their heads and Charles got up, pulling her with him. His face that had been still as a dark carving, so that she had wondered what thoughts held him, had broken up into life and mischief and he ran her out of the church into the sunlight. "Not by the graves," he said. "What made you stand by that grave? Come round here. It's warm here."

In a sheltered corner by an old buttress, behind a yew tree, they could not be seen from the path, and a sweep of golden branches hid the graves. The sun was trapped in the warm place and a couple of butterflies sunned themselves upon the wall.

"It was the grave of Nicholas Chappell," Lucy said. "He was seventeen when he died."

"That has nothing to do with you and me." He pulled her towards him and they leaned together against the wall beside the butterflies. She could make no answer. She could not tell Charles that if she had not turned to comfort Nicholas she would not have found herself so suddenly in his arms. She would not have run to her glory. "How do you manage to be here, sir?" she asked.

"I have my methods of escape," he told her. "The churchyard, I thought, was a short cut to the orchard."

"Ensign Haynes told you I was there this morning?"

"He is a nice lad. He shall have promotion."

Their low murmuring was of nothing at all yet it seemed the wisdom of the ages. Everything about them had taken on a new depth of significance. The butterfly wings, lazily lifting on the warm stone, had a beauty so heartbreaking that it brought them near to tears. The sweep of gold was music, the song of a thousand tongues, and the warmth of the sun on their bodies was divine blessing. These things were still themselves, butterflies, leaves and sunshine, but they were also transmitters of glory from beyond themselves. Lucy found that she could no longer look at Charles and the feel of his coat sleeve against her bare arm made her breathless, so full of awe was she in the magic of his presence. Beyond this place of blessing the loneliness was vast, for no one out there had the slightest meaning now. Only Charles existed. And she only because he did. There was an old story that woman had been taken from man's side. She could believe it.

Charles moved, turning his hand to take hers again, and she

was able to look up at him, searching his face anxiously. His eyes were bright and laughing but the grip of his hand was crushing hers to pulp. "I did not know it could happen so quickly," he said. So for him too it had not happened before. That each was the first for the other was their especial blessing, their incredible and glorious luck.

They turned into each other's arms again with the easy movement of the two halves of an opened watch being pressed shut by some unseen hand. The pressure of the hand could be felt, and the rightness of it, and the disappearance of time. They did not know how long they stood there before fear took hold of them both. Without actually seeing them Lucy became aware of two butterflies fluttering perilously over the surface of a dark sea. No, not sea. It was the dark web. How could they keep above it? How could they not fall in? Trying not to fall in she found herself struggling out of Charles's arms, and because his fear had been a different one he pulled her roughly back, terrified to lose her.

"I know what we will do," he said quickly. "You know where my baby sister is lodged? You know? I am to visit her tomorrow morning at ten o'clock. Go down the lane between the walled garden and the stables, a cherry tree leans over the wall there with a door beneath it. Wait there in the lane for me."

"I will wait," said Lucy, and withdrew herself gently. A gust of wind had come into the churchyard, making the gold leaves restless, and the butterflies had gone from the wall. With the intuition of a country girl she knew that the weather was about to turn around and because weather changes had often been important at Roch, demanding action of some sort, she took action now.

"Go straight back to the inn, sir," she commanded him. "I will stay here for a while and then go home."

He obeyed her. In the hidden corner she could not watch him go away but she listened intently. He walked with a long easy stride and she realized he would never allow himself to be hurried. She laid the piece of knowledge away in her mind with the few other things she had come to know about him during the last hour; the ability to be at peace, the still untarnished idealism, the determination to have what he wanted; the first few bits of the mosaic of understanding that she would build up as love increased. But could her love increase? It would change its character but it could not be more peerless than it was at this moment, untouched by the dark web.

Presently she went home and found everyone there, even her father, like figures in a dream. Besides the reality of Charles they hardly seemed to exist.

5

The changing wind that had disturbed the golden leaves brought rain from the south-west by midnight, and delight to Lucy because it had swept over the cliffs of Roch before it reached the hills and valleys of Devon. The sound of it rushing in the trees brought the Roch music tumbling about her ears; all the magnificent tumult that had terrified her mother and through its mere memory would for ever fill her with joy. By morning perhaps the dogs of storm would have passed on but she thanked them for coming just now, bringing her a night of Roch on the heels of a day that had brought her Charles. All through the wakeful hours she saw him against the background of Roch. To picture him against his own background frightened her, to see him against hers brought peace.

In the morning only the stableboy and Dewi, who helped her saddle the mare, saw her ride out of the stableyard, and though they were pledged to assure the family of her safety when she was missed they did not see which way she went. But they noted that for once in a way she had dressed with care in her dark blue riding habit, and her hat with the white feather that she never wore if she could help it, for her springy hair hated hats and always tried to push them off. And the stableboy also noted the loveliness of her glowing face. Himself appreciative of curves in a woman he had hitherto thought Miss Lucy too brown and bony for beauty, but today he changed his mind. It seemed cold in the stableyard after she had gone.

She had to hold her hat as she rode for the wind was still high, the clouds sailed with billowing white crests lit with silver, the trees bent before the wind and the leaves streamed upon it. When Lucy and the mare reached Exeter they found the houses alive, flinging their chimney smoke up like banners, walls flickering with the patterns of dancing leaves, windows now bright with the sun, now shadowed. At the street corners the housewives going to market had their skirts blown out like balloons by the wind, and the children ran before it with cries of delight.

But in the lane, sheltered from the wind by the high walls, there was stillness. The bright leaves on the tall cherry tree scarcely stirred. The door below under its arch of stone looked as though it had never been opened. Lucy did not dismount but sat upright upon the mare beneath the cherry tree, waiting. A robin upon the garden wall flew up into the tree and disturbed the leaves there, so that a shower of them scattered upon her dark skirt and lay there scarlet as blood, and for a moment she was frightened. Then the fear passed into the first genuinely feminine flutter of nerves that she had ever known. Was she tidy? Was she pretty? She had never enquired and no one had ever told her. She dropped the reins and put her hands up to straighten the unaccustomed hat and smooth its creamy feather. Then the robin over her head suddenly shrilled out a stave of song, sharp as a warning, and she gathered the reins again, her heart pounding. She should dismount to kiss his hand, she knew that, but even when she heard the bolt being drawn from the inside of the door she could not move.

And so it was as queen, not subject, that he saw her and he was startled, and halted under the archway. He had been thinking of her most of the night; the child laughing down at him from London Bridge, the motherly little girl in the woods, the gay untidy gipsy riding beside him down Fore Street, the loving and gentle girl of the churchyard. But here was someone different again. The tall motionless mare, the tall dark figure so erect in decorous clothes, the height of the scarlet cherry tree above her. His eyes had to climb a long way to find the face of this aloof and queenly creature, and then it was shadowed by the fine hat. He took three strides towards her and stood by her stirrup looking up at her. "I cannot find you," he said in puzzlement.

She looked down at him standing by her with his hat in his hand and she was puzzled too. He had dressed himself in the plainest clothes he had and looked sober as a brown thrush. But for his height and grace he might have been a country boy, uncertain of himself and in need of reassurance. She saw that he was not certain of himself. For some reason that she did not know he was afraid this morning and not certain of anything. She slid off the mare's back and down into his arms so suddenly that he staggered, and holding to each other they rocked together in a sudden gale of laughter. Her fine hat fell to the ground and her hair, tangled by the wind, fell about her glowing face. They laughed and then grew suddenly serious again.

"Now you're the same," he said. "What made you so different?"

"I was afraid," she said. "What made you so different?"

"I was afraid too."

"Why, sir?"

"Even though I thought about you while I lay awake I hated that wind last night. It moaned under the door like a dying man and when I got up the shadow was on me. Do you know what I mean? It falls on you from what is still to come." She knew but she would not say that she knew. "Sir," she said shyly, "this is my day of glory and I do not look beyond it. Do you wish us to ride together?"

"No, I should be too conspicuous. We will walk. I will take your horse to the stable. Wait here for me."

He led the mare away and she waited under the cherry tree. Charles thought she looked strangely mature when he came back to her. "How old are you?" he asked abruptly.

"I am the same age as yourself, sir. I was born under your star. Did not the people of London say that a special star danced in the sky when you were born?"

"It was your star, not mine," he said. "I would not have a

290

dancing star. You should have been called Beatrice. Shall I call you Beatrice?"

"Call me what you like, sir."

"No, I prefer Lucy. Beatrice sounds fat and I do not like fat women."

His mood had changed again and he was whirling her up the lane, striding fast and laughing, his arm tucked tight into hers. Breathless, and laughing too, she was carried along by his speed. They seemed flying and a memory flashed into her mind; the man and girl she had seen in Covent Garden, speeding along on the wings of their joy. Now it was her turn, her day of glory. They came to a busy street. Carts and coaches rattled over the cobbles and they must dodge the pedestrians, housewives with their baskets, itinerant pedlars with their wares, soldiers with their girls, children, dogs and cats. They were excited, and thrilled with a delicious fear.

"Pull your hat forward, sir," whispered Lucy.

"You dare call me sir," he whispered back. "My name is Charles."

"That is not your name today."

"What then?"

"You are Kilhwch today."

"Who?"

"Kilhwch."

"What an outlandish tongue!"

"Do not insult my language. Princes spoke it and I am descended from them."

"Who was Kilhwch?"

"A very grand man. He had a gold-hilted sword with the hue of lightning and his greyhounds wore collars of rubies." She smiled up at him as he bent his head down to her and whispered very low, "He was a prince of Wales."

It seemed a huge joke. Laughing they bumped into an old woman and bounced the apples out of her basket. Charles picked them up for her and she berated him soundly while he did it. After that they laughed more than ever, but the little incident had made people turn round and look at them and Charles whispered, "We will go to the Cathedral."

He whirled her round a corner into a side street, in sight of the towers that soared up towards the racing clouds, and on to the Cathedral Close. The wind blew them in through the west door in company with a shower of autumn leaves, and put them down in a cavern of silence so vast that it shocked them into complete stillness. The leaves rustled for a moment about their feet and then lay quiet. They no longer heard the wind or the rattle of carts, nor the voice of humanity. They had been flying together, now they were still together. They were spirits who had been blown out of time into eternity.

Lucy looked up at Charles and saw him rapt and astonished; even, she thought, forgetful of her. But her eyes on his face brought him back to her, as they would always do, and he looked down into her face. He had noticed already how penetrating her gaze was, and that her eyes were not easy to meet. They seemed to demand the truth and the human desire to be understood is never quite sincere. It is on our own terms that we desire to be understood, not on the terms of truth. The acknowledgment of truth, like the maintaining of it, is too hard for us. But he forced himself to hold her gaze, even to beat it down if he could, for he was not going to be governed by a girl, even when she was his first love. But he could not do it. It was she who deliberately lowered her eyes, releasing him, and he was a little angered, as he would have been if a servant had dismissed himself instead of waiting for the royal permission to retire. Then he was amused, for she had released him with quite a royal air. What was that she had said about her royal descent? But he did not ask her yet for they were strolling down the nave together, hand in hand, and though he knew it well the awe of the great fane was still upon him.

"I have been in so many great churches," he told her, "Westminster and St. Paul's among them, but never in quietness like this. Wherever princes are there are crowds, trumpets and music. You must be alone to feel the mystery of things and princes are never alone."

"You are not alone now," said Lucy. "You are with me."

"I love you," he said simply. "I love you in the way that makes two people one person." And he kissed her.

"Would Nan-Nan think we ought to make love inside a church?" Lucy wondered. "We should be saying our prayers."

"I cannot say my prayers unless I shut my eyes and I will not insult your beauty by doing such a thing. Who is Nan-Nan?"

"She was my nurse. She is dead now but I love her very much and I try never to do anything of which she would disapprove."

Charles looked at his love in some dismay for he was well aware that she meant what she said, and she spoke of Nan-Nan as though the dead woman still lived. He turned from the thought of Nan-Nan, and from the sight of Lucy's obstinate chin which told him this was no pliant maid and that there might be rocks ahead. "These Welsh princes from whom you are descended," he asked, "who are they?"

They were standing in a little chantry now, beside the tomb of a knight in armour, and Lucy was reminded of the tomb of Rhys ap Thomas in the church at Carmarthen, and all that her father had said to his children there. With her head up she recited the deeds and virtues of the greatest Welshman since Owen Glendower and gave an account of her own lineage. Then looking up and flashing blue fire at him she said, "Sir, there is more true royal blood in my veins than there is in yours."

"Then why do you insist on calling me sir?" asked Charles, and he was nettled.

She pondered this in silence for a moment or two. "Because I acknowledge that I am King Corphetua's Beggar Maid," she said at last. "If my father ever gives me in marriage he will give no dowry with me. He had a castle in Wales, Roch Castle, but now it is in ruins. It was garrisoned for your father and destroyed by his enemies. But a maiden, just because she is poor, need not sit on the bottom step of the throne looking at the ground. I despise such maids. I will call you sir, for that is my duty, but I will never say yes sir, or no sir, at your whim, and I wish you to know this."

Charles saw that he had been right about the rocks, but

what she had said about her father's castle had banished his anger. He had a compassionate heart and those who suffered for his father found instant place in it. He took her hand and led her to a bench. "Tell me about Roch Castle," he said gently.

She sighed, for it was hard to speak of Roch. "It stands, I mean the ruins of it still stand, on the brow of a hill. From the windows you could look out to sea, and you could look across the land to the mountains. It was built upon volcanic rock."

"Ah!" said Charles. "Roch. Were you born there?"

"Yes, I was born there."

"Listen, Lucy. When the war is won my father and I will build up your castle and give it back to you again. That is a promise. I would like to see Roch."

"To show you Roch would be such happiness," she said. "I would show you the bay where the seals come, and perhaps they would sing to you, and the Valley of Roses at St. Davids, where the stream is so cool. We would stand on the cliffs when the wind was blowing and hear the gulls screaming and the waves roaring all along the coast."

"You love the sea?"

"I belong to it."

"You shall show me Roch," he promised her.

"It is only a dream," she said.

"No. You shall show me." They were silent and then he said, "We must go now."

"Why?" she asked. "It is so peaceful here. Can we not stay longer?"

"No prince can ever stay anywhere," he told her. "There is forever something else we must do. I cannot disappear for an hour without a hue and cry after me. But you shall come back with me to Bedford House and I will show you my little sister."

"Will not people see me with you?"

"They saw you when we rode together."

"But a second time?"

He got up from the bench and held out a hand to her. "They will hardly trouble to chide me, for tomorrow I leave Exeter. We must go now."

He put his arm into hers again and took her down the nave and out into the Close where the wind from Roch met them again and the leaves once more danced about them, but there was no airiness in their movement now as they walked away. He held her tightly because she was trembling, not because he thought that she would float up into the air at any moment.

"To the war?" she asked.

"Yes. Do not tremble, love."

"No, I will not," said Lucy. "There will be other men and girls saying goodbye today. It is no different for us than for them."

"It *is* different," said Charles bitterly. "They can make plans. They can say, when the war is over we will marry and have a butcher's shop. But what can we do? You will show me Roch, I said to you, and that was all I could say, and now I do not feel certain even of that."

Like all lovers faced with the first parting they were like two children on a see-saw. When one was down the other was up. "I think it could be gain to have no certainty," said Lucy. "Suppose that night came and you were not sure the sun would rise again, and then after the dark hours you saw the east beginning to glow. What joy! That is how we will feel every time we meet. Each time we are together it will be an unexpected wonder. A present. I have had five already."

She felt his fingers counting on her arm. "Four," he said gloomily. "And you had to remind me of the first."

"We were together in Westminster Hall," she told him. "It was when the Earl of Strafford was standing his trial. I wished I could comfort you."

"Do not speak of it again," he said. "If there is justice anywhere we shall pay for that, my father and I."

"Not you!" she said quickly.

"I am one with my father," he answered and she knew he was right. He loved his father and so must share in guilt and retribution. And she must share in all that happened to Charles because she loved him. Not only the dark web but the golden web too demanded it, the one of necessity, the other by reason of its own nature.

They had come through the streets without knowing where they went and were in the lane again. Charles unlatched the door under the cherry tree and they went in. There were tall trees in the garden, the vividly green grass of the West Country and along one wall a tangled rain-beaten border of flowers. A lady with her skirts tucked up and a kerchief tied over her head was dealing with the tangle. "It is Lady Dalkeith, my mother's friend who is looking after the baby," said Charles.

She had turned at the sound of the closing door and waited for them on the path. Her worn but still beautiful face was severe as the couple approached, but not unsympathetic, and Charles knew how to forestall displeasure. He presented Lucy with the information that her Royalist father's castle had been destroyed by the King's enemies. "And so may I take her to see the Princess Henrietta?"

Lady Dalkeith did not relax her severity, though there was a quirk of amusement at the corners of her mouth as Lucy rose from her curtsey. An untidy girl, but pretty and not predatory and in any case Charles was leaving Exeter tomorrow. "As you wish, sir," she said. "Only if the princess is asleep do not wake her."

Servants came forward as they entered the house but Charles waved them aside and took Lucy up the winding staircase, warning her to be careful at the trip step, that was shallower than the rest so that a man running up the stairs with evil intent would stumble at it and give warning of his approach. In the nursery the nursemaid who was watching the baby was also waved away and there was no one to see them as they knelt down beside the cradle. It was not, Lucy thought, quite so fine a cradle as the ones they had had at Roch, but the Royal Arms surmounted the carved hood and a little bunch of golden balls hung from it on a white ribbon to amuse the baby. But inside the cradle there was a royal grandeur of lace-trimmed pillows and a silken coverlet embroidered in gold.

The Princess Henrietta was a fragile baby and there was no colour in her delicate face. Her short hair lay in rings of thin gold all over her shapely little head and her minute fists were doubled up under her chin. The peace that emanates from a sleeping baby filled the room. She was white and gold like the rose at Golden Grove and as she looked at her Lucy's heart turned over. Then she looked at Charles and marvelled that this tall, vital boy could be the brother of this little moth of a child. It was the difference between a child born in sorrow and despair and one born in joy and hope. Yet his face was as mobile as hers was delicate and the tenderness and sorrow he had for her trembled over it almost like a reflection of her fragility. Lucy got up from her knees and came to him. "You are sad for this baby," she said.

"She is like my sister Anne. I liked Anne. When they told her she had to die and that she must say her prayers she said, 'I cannot say my big prayer but I will say my little one.' And she did. She was not afraid to die though she was only five."

"This princess will live to grow up," Lucy said steadily, and as if to assure him the baby woke up. They made the bells swing and she laughed and condescended to hold her brother's finger and bestow a smile on Lucy. She was very much alive, full of Stuart charm, and sorrow vanished.

"I call her Minette," said Charles. "She is so tiny."

The nursemaid was back again, murmuring something about Lady Dalkeith not liking Her Royal Highness to be overstimulated, and they left the nursery and went back to the garden. Lady Dalkeith was still at work in her border but she was an ardent gardener and was now too absorbed to know or care what went on behind her bent back. Time had stopped for her and only the crying of Minette would have brought her back to awareness of it.

A mulberry tree, its aged limbs propped up on crutches like those of an old man, protected a narrow path from the eyes of the house. They wandered up and down for a few moments and tried to talk and could not. "We must say goodbye now," said Lucy with sudden decision. "Having to say it is a shadow over us and we will not be happy if we stay longer together. Let us say it and be done."

"I will come back," said Charles urgently, his hands on her shoulders. "Exeter is my base and I will come back as soon as I

NT FROM THE SEA

can. Stay here. Do not you dare to leave Broad Clyst! Promise me!"

"No," said Lucy.

His hands tightened on her shoulders. "Why not?" he demanded. "I do not ask it. I command it."

"Sir, you have no right," said Lucy. "You are not the only person in the world I love. All I can promise is that I will stay at Broad Clyst if my duty permits it."

"Lucy, you are the most arrogant girl I ever met!" he exclaimed angrily. "Your duty is to me, your prince."

"As to that I am not sure," said Lucy. "The Welsh are subjects to the King of England by conquest only and if Owen Lawgoch should suddenly come up out of his cave, as he has promised to do, and unite all Wales against her enemies, England will be one of them."

Even in his anger and unhappiness Charles began to laugh. "You are right," he conceded, and took her in his arms. "And who can make promises in wartime? I cannot. Nor you. Goodbye."

"Now, it would break my heart to leave Broad Clyst," said Lucy, and began to cry with a wild heartbreak that took him as much by surprise as the indignation of a few moments before. Would he ever understand this girl of his, so sturdy and yet so temperamental? But at the moment he had not to understand but to comfort. He flung her hat on the path and kissed her and tried to stroke her hair, but it rose under his hand like an indignant cat. "Your hair is alive!" he ejaculated.

"Of course it is alive," said Lucy through her sobbing. "I am alive am I not?" Then abruptly she controlled herself. "Take me out of this garden," she implored him, "and find my horse and send me away."

He hugged her close for a moment, then let her go and did what she had asked him to do. He picked up her hat and handed it to her and then walking hand in hand they went out of the garden. He left her standing under the cherry tree while he fetched her horse, then helped her up into the saddle.

"Goodbye, sir," she said, looking straight in front of her.

"Goodbye, Lucy," he said, and went back into the garden and shut the door.

6

She did not go straight home. She and the mare spent the next few hours wandering through the woods and the country lanes near Broad Clyst. Waves of desolation kept coming at her and breaking over her. Sometimes in a moment of respite she would hear a bird singing or notice the tracery of a fallen leaf, but then another wave would come and she would know only that she could not live without Charles. But she had to live without him, perhaps for a short time, perhaps for always. That was the way it was. "My father is my firstborn." Had she said that? It was no longer true in the sense in which she had once said it but in another sense it was true. In time he had come first and her love for him was no less than it had been; perhaps greater because she had grown five years in the last few hours. She turned the mare's head towards home.

Her reception was hardly loving. William was in the stable-yard when she rode in and he lifted her down from the mare with a face black as thunder and eyes miserable as sin. With his right hand clamped on her arm he marched her straight into the empty harness room and banged the door. Then he sat down on the bench and she stood before him bolt upright, her eyes on his. "No privacy indoors with your grandmother and her maids prying and peeping everywhere. Damn you, Lucy, where have you been?"

That he should swear at her even in displeasure, that he should call her Lucy and not Bud, was something entirely new. She remembered the days of her childhood at Roch when he would put her across his knee to punish her and afterwards give her a hug. There was no chance now that this coldly furious man would give her the comfort of his arms about her. "The little cane you used to use was burnt at Roch," she said sadly, "but some fathers horsewhip their grown-up daughters. The whip is hanging there by your hand."

In the dimness of the room her eyes seemed burning into his

head. "For God's sake do not stand there looming over me," he shouted at her. "Sit on that stool. You know I would never lay a hand upon you. But what I will do is to sit here until you tell me where you have been and with whom."

"I have been in the cathedral with the prince, and for a short while at Bedford House with him to see the baby princess."

"It was an arranged meeting, for you took the mare and left a message. When did you make the arrangement?"

"Yesterday. I met the prince by accident in the churchyard after I had been to see Granny Miles."

"Accident, begod! You told him to find you there."

"No, sir."

He dropped his face into his hands and groaned from behind them, "That is a lie, Lucy."

"I would never lie to you."

He took his hands from his face. "As a child you would not have lied to me but as a maid you do. You have been out most of the day and you have not only been in Exeter. You have been in the woods. The mare is mud to the fetlocks and you have leaves in your hair."

"I have been in the woods and lanes all the afternoon but I have been there alone, and if you think I would lie to you then all the love I thought there was between us has been a sham on your part."

"Bud!" he cried out. "For that last sentence I would whip you, but for nothing else." She was Bud again. She slid off the stool to the floor at his feet. "I believe you, my girl. But why alone all those hours in the woods?"

"I was too unhappy to come home."

"Unhappy, were you? Do you imagine yourself in love with that ugly arrogant boy?"

"I do not imagine things."

"Bud, Bud!" groaned poor William. "What do you know about love? You are a child."

"No," said Lucy. "I am older than my age and so is Charles. We have both suffered so many things that we are not young now."

The truth of this plunged William into sadness and the familiar use of the prince's name appalled him. She spoke as though she had known the boy for years. "Bud," he said, "do you know to what utter misery this may lead you? Who do you think you are?"

Lucy looked up and smiled at him. "You have told me often, sir. A Welsh lady of royal descent and I am not to forget it."

"I was a fool to tell you so," groaned William. "Here in England you are a nobody. Do you hear? A nobody. Listen to me, bud. The prince leaves Exeter tomorrow, I am told, but when he is back he will not find you at his beck and call. I must have your promise."

"No," said Lucy. "I cannot promise not to see Charles again."

William struggled for the right and incontrovertible words that would never come at his call. "Bud," he said at last, "you are living in a fairytale. It is no use, my girl; in this world that we actually live in there are no happy endings this side of the grave. All a girl like you can expect, if a prince takes a fancy to have his pleasure of her, is—well—begod it is no fairytale." He paused, breathing heavily, crimson with effort and misery. "God forgive me, but there have been days lately when I have found it mighty peaceful being quit of your mother; but I wish she were here now to deal with you."

Lucy leaned her arms on his knees, her eyes once more holding his, and they were so limpidly blue that he could fancy he was looking down into a well of clear water with truth at the bottom of it. Her eyes gave him more comfort than what she actually said. "Sir, I will never willingly do anything of which you or Nan-Nan would disapprove, but I cannot give you my promise not to see the prince when he comes back to Exeter And as for my future, sir, and all our futures, what we do today determines them, so it is just to be honest and loving for today and look no further."

He was put in his place. She laid her head down on her arms and his hands moved clumsily in her hair, mechanically picking out the dead leaves. He felt unutterably wretched. This business of begetting children, that was forced on a man merely because he was a man, how it could harrow his very soul. A small child in your arms beside the fire was one thing, food and shelter and love were all it asked for, but that child grown was another kettle of fish altogether. Once escaped out of his arms children broke a man's heart, if his wife had not broken it already. Richard estranged from him, Justus forgetting him he could bear, but Bud lost to him would be a thing past endurance. The harness room was growing dark and cold but he could think of nothing more to say to her. Yet he could not take his hands from her hair. If he did she would go out of the door and be lost to him. He could not relinquish the feel of her, the warmth of her against his knees. What was she thinking that she was so silent, her face hidden? He sighed; a sigh of hopeless dejection.

She stirred and looked up at him and he could just see the pale glimmer of her face. "You made a promise to me once," she said.

"Eh, Bud?"

"That we should ride back to Roch together."

"Bud!" he gasped.

"Shall we go soon? You and I and Dewi?"

"Bud! We thought to wait till the war was over. There will be no comfort for you there."

"There will be a corner of the castle we can make habitable. Or a cottage somewhere."

"The travelling may be dangerous, Bud."

"You and I do not mind about danger."

With a gasp of relief he dropped his hands to her shoulders and held them tightly. Yet he sensed that she was at a distance from him. He would never know what her thoughts had been while she sat at his feet so motionless. He would not know what they were when they rode home together. She would love him and laugh with him, and it might be that they would share a last paradise together, but he would never know her thoughts.

Two

Lucy scarcely knew what they were herself when she sat at his feet, struggling to turn home to Wales. Roch, and her father with her there, had always been her magnetic north, but now her being swung towards a boy on horseback who was homeless, and it seemed that his homelessness was now her north. Yet here was her father, his knees hard and firm under her arms but his thoughts a torment of anxiety, of which she was the cause, and for him Roch with herself at its heart was still the magnetic north. There, if she were with him, he would be himself again and at peace. He would think her safe from Charles there and it was the knowledge that he might be right that made it so hard for her to turn home. Charles would come back to Exeter and find her gone and how, in wartime, could he follow her? But the war would end some day and if he loved her with something more than a passing infatuation he would come to Roch to find her. She could not now give any happiness to Charles but she could give it to her father. And so she looked up at him and reminded him of that old promise.

Mrs. Chappell made heavy weather of their going. She had considered their presence a cross which she must bear with Christian fortitude, and had repeatedly told her husband how she longed for their departure, but the realization that William and Lucy had had an equal longing for departure was a wound to her pride. "Have you not liked being here?" she demanded. They assured her both of their past happiness and their eternal gratitude but her hurt was not assuaged. To venture forth on a dangerous wartime journey with winter coming on, hardly a penny to bless themselves with and no roof over their heads when they got there, was the action either of raving lunatics or the most ungrateful creatures God ever made. There had never been mental instability in her family, nor in William's father's family, therefore they were ungrateful and she was exceedingly angry with them and, perversely and with an unconscious wish to punish them, determined they should not go.

William, loving his mother and grateful to her, might possibly have yielded but Lucy stuck her chin out and began to pack the saddlebags. William had no servant of his own now and they were to ride alone. They would be murdered, Mrs. Chappell assured them, but Mr. Chappell said they would be just as likely to get through safely three as four, and servants were often a liability. He would miss William and Lucy but he was in agreement with them. Being a gardener he knew how deeply William felt about his land; such a man is only happy when his own mud is on his boots. And as for the pretty maid she was too pretty altogether and it was better she should be out of the Prince's reach. To his wife's subsequent fury, for he did not consult her, he gave Lucy the mare for her own, and Dewi the Dartmoor pony, for though he might slow them up a bit he was a stout little creature and would enable them to carry a few more saddlebags. He also gave Lucy a little purse of soft leather, and in it a few precious gold pieces, "For when you get married, my maid."

They set out early in October, St. Luke's summer already golden about them and the moon a faint but growing crescent in the sky. "Remember, Lucy, I wish you never to ride after dark!" was Mrs. Chappell's last injunction to her granddaughter as she embraced her at the front door. "Madam, I will remember," was all Lucy said, but she hugged her grandmother with warmth, remembering her many kindnesses and touched at feeling real tears on her cheek. They were on hers too when she said goodbye to Mr. Chappell. His arms on her shoulders trembled and when he tried to take her face in his hands they would not hold it. Looking back as they rode away she knew she would not see him again. Her grandmother was weeping and wiping her eyes but the old man watched them go with a look of bewilderment on his face. It must, she thought, be very bewildering to be so old and know yourself no longer able to hold what you love. The three of them rode silently away and Lucy and her father did not look at each other. How strange it was. Here was their dream coming true at last and they were not as happy as they had expected to be. Would it always be like this with one's dreams?

"Look!" yelled Dewi. "A kingfisher."

There was a stream near and the music of it had been in their ears for some while. The glorious creature flashed like lightning right across their path as they rode and suddenly they knew that they were going home.

When they reached Wales they were greeted with the sights and sounds and scents that spelt heaven for them. The sound of the streams and the smell of the wet ferns and moss, the sight of a falcon sailing up from the woods to hang a quivering speck in the blue above and the mountains faded purple and dull gold like the shoulders of an aged king. And there were the nights spent in rough inns, eating bara ceich and drinking buttermilk once more, hearing the Welsh tongue spoken again and the old songs sung before the fire.

They had a few adventures. Twice they were set upon by thieves and William had to lay about him with the butt of his pistol and Lucy with her riding crop, and once Dewi, very tired with much travelling, fell off his pony and bumped himself so severely that they had to stay four days at an inn to nurse and rest him. But the plain clothes they wore made them inconspicuous, and when they met enemy cavalry, or small weary detachments of infantry on the road, no attention was paid to them beyond whistles of appreciation when Lucy's pretty looks were perceived. Little did they know, she thought, that in one of her saddlebags she carried a sea-green dress and two little pearl earrings; and in her veins the blood of the Plantagenets. On this journey her childhood's dreams came back to her and many times William and Dewi were slightly daunted by the hauteur of the Princess Nest, or set to a flying gallop by the buccaneer. It was a long journey, for William could not press his children too hard, but strangely they were in no hurry to get there. Journeys can be a respite from living. The problems left behind by the traveller, and the problems that will confront him when he arrives, fall away in a strangely dreamlike manner. They will link up when he arrives but while he is on the wing they are almost non-existent.

On a windless pearly-grey afternoon, with dusk not far off, they seemed to come quite suddenly into their own country. "Remember, Lucy," said William, "that when you have the first sight of the castle it will not look as you remember it." Lucy nodded, speechless. William and Dewi had not been away from Pembrokeshire for long but she had been away for six years, and they had changed her almost beyond her own recognition. She felt a stranger even to herself.

But the country had not greatly changed, though they passed burnt-out farms and hedgerows broken down by the passage of guns and troops, scars left by the recent fighting that had now left this part of Wales peaceful but in Puritan hands. Landmarks that Lucy remembered soon came thick and fast. They turned a corner and saw the old bridge that spanned the Brandy Brook and except for a broken balustrade it was unharmed. The brook sang under it in just the old way and looking to the right she saw a proud heron standing among the reeds, just as she had done when they went away. She looked up to the castle on its hill and saw the tower stark and torn like a tree that has been blasted by lightning, a cascade of fallen stones about its base. Yet it was still grand, perhaps even more so than it had been before, and for a moment her spirit leaped up to meet it, hot with the heron's own pride. She looked at her father and smiled and as they rode up the steep hill the sun broke through the grey clouds behind the tower.

2

It was another good omen for their homecoming, for the next weeks were not unhappy ones. The first joy was the welcome they received from Parson Peregrine, the Perrots, Old Parson and William's men. They stayed at first at Brandy Mill with the Perrots and Old Parson, and they were happy, though Lucy grieved to hear of the death of the sin-eater. Old Parson had taken it to heart greatly. One cold winter when he had

himself been sick and not able to climb up the mill woods
the sin-eater had been found lying dead, thin as a starved spar-
row but free of the sins at last.

After Christmas they moved to an empty cottage in the
fishermen's bay. The people there were rough and independent but they made them welcome because they were unfortunate, and though life in the primitive little cottage was
hard it was happy. William's sorrow over his wife and Lucy's
longing for Charles were always there, and they learned to
hide a great deal from each other, not least their mutual bed-
rock knowledge of the precariousness of their state, but they
found that joy cannot live at all unless the sense of eternity
inherent in each moment, each now, is protected from the pressure of yesterday's remorse and tomorrow's fear and they
learned the art of this protection. And they worked so hard,
William on the land, Lucy in the cottage, Dewi as Parson Peregrine's pupil, that their sleep at night was that of drugged
dormice. But Lucy could not recapture her first pride at sight
of the undefeated castle tower. William and Dewi went there
occasionally but she did not. Brave though she normally was,
over this one thing she was a coward. She could not face the
emptiness.

And then one morning in the new year she did. It had been
cold and stormy since their return but at the end of January
there came a strange foretaste of spring. The sea was quiet and
the gentle wind blew from the south, and in the mill house
garden the snowdrops stood bolt upright, a flash of white
gleaming in the sun at the point of each spear. She got up early
one morning and wrapped in her cloak climbed up through
the leafless wood behind the fishermen's bay to the cliff. It had
been dark in the wood and her feet rather than her eyes had
found the path, but out in the open a few stars and the crescent moon floated in a clear green sky. The sea was calm, the
wash of the waves below the cliffs a sound so peaceful that
Lucy was only aware of it as a quietness in her own mind. As
she walked slowly along the cliff the lightening sky called
forth the cockcrow; the trumpets of the birds of dawning
sounded as though one after the other, as they saw the light

grow, they cried the news all the way from the eastern mountains to the western sea. Yet down in the woods the owls were still calling.

Looking out over the sea, watching the gleams of light that floated like pale lilies on the dark flood, Lucy listened to the faint trumpet calls behind her and knew that she must turn round. She did so and saw the ruins of the castle standing out starkly against the sunrise, and though no fire burned now in the roofless hall the rising sun shone through the empty windows as though the logs were still glowing on the great hearth. Lucy looked for a long time and it was as though the emptiness were slowly filling up with warm welcome, and hardly knowing what she did she walked towards it. And presently she began to run.

In the lane she felt almost joyous, even when she found that the garden door was broken and hanging loose on its hinges. She pushed through and found herself in a beautiful wilderness, with bright green moss growing where once the smooth grass had been and the rose trees exulting in wild and thorny freedom. The herbs, the mint and southernwood and thyme, had spread everywhere and their pungent scent was sharp in the cool wet dawn. The rosemary tree was unharmed and she buried her face in its cloudly greyness. The leaves pricked against her skin and the invigorating tang of it seemed to go through her body like sharp wine. Behind her back a stormcock tried out a few bars of his dauntless song.

She went up the steps to the hall, and found it carpeted by the leaves that had blown through the empty windows in the autumn gales. They were sodden under her feet and smelled of death, but when she looked up at the space that had once been arched over by the glorious wooden roof she saw it pavilioned by a sky of flame. She must have been in the garden longer than she knew for there was no more night. She stood almost breathless and gazed up and up into a vault of extraordinary glory. This was the way to see sky. There were no distances to distract the eye, no distant hills or glittering sea, just this concentrated splendour of light, held up, it seemed, by the stark walls of the ruined castle. Had they not reared up their strength towards it surely the weight of glory would have fallen on her head. She was blinded and covered her face with her hands.

When she opened her eyes again she found herself looking at the tumbled ruin of the hearth, and the question she had not dared ask of anyone was answered. The heron was gone. Though she felt a pang of sorrow it passed quickly. The scent of the rosemary, the stormcock and the flaming sky had given her a new awareness. She could not put it into words, no one could, she could only say to herself that scent and music and light, intangible things, were symbols of spirit, and while the symbol of the world still circled round the symbolic sun, like the spirit of a man about the glory of his God, they were indestructible.

She did not today go up to the dais to face what had once been the nursery and the bower and the great bedchamber, instead she went down the stone stairs to the great kitchen. It was hardly changed for it was so deep in the earth that neither guns nor fire had touched it. Grey ashes lay on the hearth and there was wood piled beside it. There were still a few pewter plates on the dresser, a dish of withered apples on the oak table and a couple of buckets beside the well. She sat on the floor beside the buckets, as she had done so often as a child, and for a long time looked down into the darkness of the water. As she watched the rising sun sent an arrow of light through the slit of an eastern window and it fell into the depths of the water. The dark face, receiving the arrow, quivered very slightly, or seemed to do so, as a very sensitive human face will do when the heart of the man has to receive a hurt. For it was living water and somewhere down in the rock received its life from the depths. Here were the roots of being, the stone, the water and the fire.

For there was now a fire on the hearth. It did not surprise her when she turned her head to see a glow of flame, or to see an old man bending over the fire that he had lit, feeding it with fir-cones from a basket, and dry bits of lichened stick. It would not have surprised her if he had turned out to be John

Shepherd, so much was John in her thoughts in this place. But he was Old Parson. He looked back over his shoulder and smiled at her and she got up and went to kneel beside him and help him. Kneeling like a couple of children, feeding the fire, the barrier that had been between them since she had come back suddenly vanished.

He had been a little afraid of her until now, unable to find the child he had loved in this tall maiden. And she had been awed by the change in him, by the deep lines scored in his face and by the frailty of his body. But chiefly she had been awed by a deeper change. He was happy, she realized, but it was a happiness remote from any she knew herself. Perhaps if she were to sin in a manner that seemed to her unforgivable, and yet were to find herself forgiven, and suffer in a manner that seemed unbearable and yet find herself surviving, she would know this sort of happiness. Like the living water it welled from unknown depths. But his fear and her awe vanished now. He had once been as young and ignorant as she was, she would one day know what he now knew, and his past and her future somehow came together in this timeless old kitchen. They sat before the fire and laughed together at the flowerlike prettiness of the burning cones.

"I come here every day that I can," Old Parson told her. "Not in the snow because of my rheumatism, and not when the dogs of storm are out for I cannot stand against the wind, but the other days. And whenever I come I light the fire to keep the castle warm for you."

"And I have not come until today," said Lucy. "Why did you not tell me you were keeping it warm for me?"

"You were not ready to come until today. I knew you would come when you were ready. Get up, child, I have something to show you."

It was the first time he had called her child since she had come back and in her relief she put her arms round his neck and hugged him as she had done so often in the old days. "Your face has the same feel to it," he said with equal relief. "I always liked the feel of your face."

Would any man, even Charles, ever say anything nicer to

her, she wondered, as she helped him to his feet. She doubted it.

"I have something to show you," he repeated, and he took her hand and led her to the little room with the spiral stone staircase where John Shepherd had lain after he had died, and that dreadful day when the sin-eater had taken the burden of another man's sins on himself came back from the past and was once more a present anguish, so that pulling at Old Parson's sleeve she asked urgently, "Is it true that one man can take upon himself the sin of another? Can he save him that way? Is it really true?"

Old Parson did not know what scene she was remembering so vividly in this place but her question was one he was now able to answer. "Yes," he said slowly. "If the sinner will accept salvation, it is true."

"How do you know?" asked Lucy.

"I was told so," said Old Parson.

"Who told you?"

"My friend who died. I did not hear him speak, since he is dead, but just as I woke one morning he told me without the use of words. He was well able to use such speech for on earth he had been dumb for years." Lucy looked at Old Parson, astonished not only by the strangeness of what he said but also by the serene and confident way in which he said it. At the mill at Christmas he had still seemed the muddled old thing that he had always been, but now it seemed that a measure of mental clarity had come to him, if only fitfully.

"Waking dreams can be true, Lucy," he went on. "You can know when they are true by the joy they bring. That is the hall mark. Joy."

But Lucy's mind had jumped back to a word that he had used. "Dumb?" she said. "Your friend was dumb?"

"For a long while I believed that I had cut out his tongue myself," said Old Parson. "But I could never remember how it was that I did it. Or whether perhaps I had not done it with my own hands but had been the cause of its being done. Sometimes I would remember one dreadful thing and sometimes another but I could never fit them together to tell me how it happened. I ran away, you know, but it did me no good because the sin came too, fastened to my heels like a shadow, and a man cannot get rid of his shadow. It would crawl up my back sometimes, I would feel it crawling and go cold, and then it would fall over my face and all the world would go black. But it would not show its face to me, and so I thought I could not be forgiven. And then the man at St. Davids said I could and I believed him. But I did not know why. And then my friend died and told me why. The man who is the cause of the suffering can be saved by the man who bears it, he told me, if the tortured man for love's sake takes the sin upon himself together with the pain. That's the way it is, he told me. It is quite simple, if the sinner for love's sake will accept his salvation."

"How do the dead speak?" asked Lucy. "What voice do they have?"

Old Parson pondered this. "I think their voice is the utterance of what they are," he said at last. "They may say nothing. They may merely forgive. But if it is knowledge you need then what they know can touch your mind like fingers on a keyboard. Then your mind may perhaps give you words and a voice, but perhaps not. It is no matter if you have the knowledge." He had stumbled in his speech as though still unaccustomed to his new clarity, though with conviction, but now his mood suddenly changed. "Look, Lucy. There is the thing I wanted to show you. Look."

Lucy had been so intent on what he had been saying that she had not looked about her, but now her eyes followed his and there on the sixth step of the spiral staircase, just before it curved out of sight, like a statue in a niche, was the stone heron. She gasped and her face was as radiant as though she looked into heaven. Old Parson, watching her, smiled. He had waited long for this moment and it was not disappointing him. No one who prepared a surprise for Lucy would ever be disappointed by her reaction, for if her power of appraising the material value of a gift was nil her power of looking through it to the heart of the giver was great. For her all the symbols were translucent. She gave Old Parson a quick joyous hug but words were for the moment beyond her. Then she went to the foot of the steps and stood looking at the heron.

He was not what he had been for the tip of his beak had broken off and his wings were chipped. Yet it seemed to Lucy fitting. The castle was not what it had been, and nor were any of them, and he their spirit was bound to be broken too. But his long neck was as proudly curved as ever and his expression as tolerant. He had seen much. He would see more. What he thought of it all he did not say, but if his beak was closed so were his wings and he would not desert them. Lucy gently stroked the curve of his silent beak, but she did not go too near the broken tip. As a small girl, when William had lifted her up to stroke the heron, she had always had a feeling that he might mistake her finger for a fish.

"You have brought me right home," she said to Old Parson. "I might never have been away."

3

Later, after she had left the old man at the mill and was climbing down through the wood beside Brandy Brook, Lucy remembered what he had said about the speech of the dead. "What they know can touch your mind like light fingers on a keyboard. Then your mind may perhaps give you words and a voice, but perhaps not. It is no matter if you have the knowledge."

That was what had happened to her in the church at Broad Clyst. So Old Sage was dead too. He had spoken of peace. What had he said? "All true glory, while it remains true, holds it. It is the maintaining of truth that is so hard." It was strange that Old Parson's friend as well as hers should have been dumb.

The fishermen's hamlet curved like a horseshoe about the rocks and pebbles of Brandy Bay, the curve of the horseshoe broken at its apex by a rough stone bridge beneath which the brook foamed steeply down to the beach. People did not come here to spend a pleasant afternoon. Those who had made it their home liked it, but those who did not live here and had not been accepted by the tough spirit of the place were frightened by it. There was hardly any sand and the shelving beach was bony and inhospitable, the fishing boats lying upon it like stranded whales. Rough flights of stone steps led up from the beach to the rocks where the stone-walled cottages had been built. They were roofed with stone tiles, for no thatch would have stayed on when the gales came from the west, and their windows were tiny in the thickness of the walls. They had no gardens to speak of, though a few tamarisk trees and fuchsia bushes grew here and there, but behind them the stunted trees of the wood's ending rose steeply, and hidden in the wood in springtime were primroses and violets.

So steep was this wood that Lucy, climbing down beside the brook through the thinning trees, had the smoke from the cottage chimneys rising up into her face. She ran across the bridge and came to the door of their cottage. How quickly human beings can make a home, she thought. All they need is a roof of their own over their heads, preferably sound though that is not essential, a fire of their own to sit by and a family of their own to love. She and William and Dewi were a family and they lived and loved in this cottage with no prying eyes upon them. Broad Clyst had never felt like home to Lucy. The castle had been home and now this.

She went inside and closed the door and the room seemed for a moment almost dark. Then as her eyes grew accustomed to the dim glow of the firelight, and the sea light that came through the two small windows, she saw again the small oak settle, the table and stools and her few pots and pans and dishes. Friends and neighbours had given them these things and they were precious as gold and silver. There were no rooms upstairs, only a loft in the roof, but two little rooms opened out of the living room. William had one and she and Dewi had the other. She peeped into both rooms and saw unmade beds and disorder that was incredible when one considered how few possessions William and Dewi had to be disorderly with. She smiled tolerantly, for she had not been there to wake them up this morning and they had had to rekindle the turf fire, get their breakfast and go to their work, William to his land and Dewi to his lessons with Parson Peregrine, with no help from her. But they had not forgotten her for a pail of water stood by the fire and the bara ceich and the jug of buttermilk had been left ready for her on the table.

She had her breakfast and then went singing about her work, sweeping the floors, washing the dishes, making the beds and preparing a rabbit stew for dinner. By the time the stew was on it was so warm that she could open the door and sit there with her darning as though it were April, calling out greetings to the other women who came to their doors to knock the dust out of their brooms, or spread their washing to dry on the tamarisk tree and fuchsia bushes. She greeted the men too, coming in from a night's fishing or sitting in the lee of upturned boats mending their nets, and they wished her good-day with smiling respect. They liked her. She was the girl from the castle yet she had been able to make herself one of them without condescension. It had not been difficult for she loved people so much that her pride of birth, which she had in full measure, was never a personal pride. She could have as easily fallen in love with one of the young fishermen as with Charles, and whatever trouble it might have brought her she would have been as loyal to one as the other.

A familiar little cry came from a tamarisk tree that grew near the door. It was the cock chaffinch, mistaking the warmth of the day for spring and mating time. Long ago Nan-Nan had taught her the words of his song. "Sweet, sweet! O bring my pretty love to meet me here!" he sang. "Meet me *here*!" She bent her head over her darning and began to cry. Mostly it was only at night that she cried, her face buried in the pillow so that she should not wake Dewi, but the chaffinch had too suddenly assaulted her control. She wanted Charles so appallingly. She had made the discovery that to lose one's heart suddenly and entirely, and then to have what should have been an unfolding and progression of love suddenly cut short, was a sort of death. But Charles was alive, the sort of death was not real death. What if it had been? There would have been no happy moments and she could not have endured to sit and listen to the cock chaffinch, not even with tears.

THE CHILD FROM THE SEA

There was far more command than entreaty in the way he
sang and he was so sure of being obeyed that she began to
smile.

The singing ceased and she could distinctly hear some
young creature bounding down through the wood. For a mad
moment she wondered if it was Charles, but he would not have
been so sure-footed, and would not have known the airy leap
that could bring a headlong runner from the wood
path to the bridge as though he flew. She heard the soft
thud of arrival, and there was Dewi, home from his lessons
with Parson Peregrine an hour too soon. "Where is our
father?" he demanded.

"They are harrowing the mill field. No! Stop! Tell me first
why you have run away from Parson Peregrine."

"I have not run away," said Dewi indignantly. "He kicked
me out."

"What for? Did he cane you first?"

"No, you horrid girl," said Dewi with fury. Lucy, now that
she was the mistress of the household, was tending towards
authoritative airs, not permissable in a mere sister, and he was
in no mood to put up with them. "I am going to my father. It is
men's business. You would be scared." And he leaped around
with the swiftness of a puppy pouncing on its tail and would
have gone but for Lucy's hand suddenly twisting in the slack
of his doublet. If he could be quick so could she. With a wrist
of iron she spun him round to face her, pressed tight against
her knees with her hands linked behind his back.

"You will tell me what has happened, David Walter, or I
will pull your hair out." The tears of the lovelorn maid had
evaporated from her hot angry cheeks and in her burning
curiosity she had for the moment forgotten that Charles existed. "Scared? When have you known me to be scared? What
has happened?"

Having succeeded in making her angry Dewi's own rage
vanished and he began to tease instead, leaning back against
the grip of her hands, his dimples showing and his head on
one side. In this mood he could be maddening.

"The post came. We heard him down by the bridge and he

316

cantered all the way up the hill. When Parson Peregrine had read the letter he kicked me out and went to the church to get a musket."

"You lie, Dewi!" said Lucy. "There are no firearms in the vestry now. They were taken out when the castle was garrisoned."

"Parson Peregrine hid one or two," said Dewi. "He told me so. For now."

"For now?" gasped Lucy. "Dewi, what was in the letter?"

"I am telling my father," said Dewi. In her anxiety she had relaxed her hold and with a sudden twist he escaped from her and ran off across the bridge. Quick as lightning she ran after him, but in the scramble up through the wood her skirts impeded her and she did not catch up with him until he reached the road and the bridge above. They ran across the bridge to where the mill field rose up steeply from the St. Davids road. Here William and the old horse were toiling up and down with the harrow, preparing for the spring sowing. "Father! Sir!" yelled Dewi.

"What now?" demanded William, but he went on to the top of the slope and turned the horse before he stopped, for just now the harrowing of this field was more important to him than anything else upon earth. His children panted up to him.

"Parson Peregrine has had another letter," gasped Dewi. "He is to be evicted if he does not change his ways."

"God-a-mercy!" ejaculated William. "Llewellyn!" An old man popped up from behind the hedge and William commanded him to take over the horse and harrow and made off down the hill. "If you are going to the parsonage I am coming too," called Lucy as she and Dewi ran after him.

"No, by cock," said William. "I have no mind to have my dinner burnt to a cinder. Attend to your woman's affairs."

Without a backward glance he strode across the bridge with Dewi at his heels.

Woman's affairs! Lucy seethed with anger all the way down through the wood but back with the stew she calmed down. Men's affairs were more exciting, and she had always wished she was a boy, but Charles would not have fallen in love with a boy. She smiled as she set some apples to roast before the fire, for the first time consciously contented with what she was.

The Puritan victory in Pembrokeshire had ended the physical fighting but not the religious wrangles. There were bitter arguments as to whether the altar was to be at the east end or in the body of the church, whether it was to have a cross and candles on it, and were images and pictures and stained glass windows of God or the devil? And should a priest wear vestments in church or a plain black gown? Lucy could not see that such matters were important, and she doubted if God could either, but the Presbyterian Parliament now sitting at Westminster regarded them as symbolic of deeper matters and permitted Puritans all over England and Wales to wreck the insides of churches, and turn the priests and their families out of their houses and treat them just as they pleased.

Some priests, afraid for their children, gave in. Parson Peregrine, though he had been warned again and again by Puritan gentlemen of the neighbourhood, had no intention of conforming. In old days he had sometimes forgotten to light the candles on the altar but he never forgot now, and he had found somewhere a little statue of Our Lady and put it on one of the window ledges, and had taken no notice of the recent parliamentary command to cease using the prayer book and use the Directory of Public Worship instead. He had been issued with the Directory and had stoked the kitchen fire with it. And now he was to be evicted. He was a very courageous, angry and obstinate man, not a man to placate his enemies. What would they do? Lucy had heard some terrible stories and she was afraid for him.

She began to lay the table for dinner and her thoughts passed on to Dr. Cosin, for there was another brave and loving man capable of great anger. Where was he now? She knew that both his deanery of Peterborough and his mastership of Peterhouse had been taken from him, and she knew too that it had taken the Puritans a whole fortnight to wreck the treasures of his cathedral. Where he was himself she did not know but she did not believe that he was dead.

There was the sound of footsteps and the light of the door-way was blocked by the dark figure of William. He came in heavily and with anger, Dewi behind him. "A foul anonymous letter," he told Lucy as he kicked off his muddy boots. "If the old man does not do as he is told this time we will have the church wrecked, and Peregrine himself with his ears cropped and the parsonage burned over his head. And so I told him. Does it matter a damn, I said, where you put the table or the candles? Does it matter a damn if you have them at all? And that pretty little female you have put on the window ledge, she is nothing but a distraction to a man's thoughts. And you might just as well groan prayers out of one book as another. Better give in, I told him. Let us have a bit of peace, I said."

"What did *he* say?" asked Lucy.

"Lost his temper and was most insulting to me. Dared to ask if I had turned Puritan myself. Aye, by cock! He is a damned impertinent fellow and deserves what is coming to him. I have never liked him. I wash my hands of the whole business. That stew done?"

"You do not deserve it, sir!" said Lucy hotly as she ladled it out.

"What has the arrangement of furniture or dolls on window ledges to do with religion?" demanded William.

"Nothing," said Lucy, "but taking the little statue down from the window would be yielding to the enemy and no man likes to do that. Would you have liked it if they had taken the Royalist flag down from our castle tower when the fighting started? It was nothing but a bit of silk, and taking it down might have saved a lot of trouble, but would you have approved?"

"You hussy, to put such a question to me!" roared William.

"It is just the same," said Lucy. "Now eat your stew."

William began to laugh, for Bud was so patronizingly maternal, and he ate his stew, but for days he did not cease to mutter that if trouble came Parson Peregrine could expect no help from him. And all the villagers said the same. Their loyalty to the King was not in question but it would soon be lambing time, and then it would be the spring sowing, and it was not to be expected that a countryman could attend to quarrels of Church and State when land and beasts needed attention.

It was possible that the enemy had the same idea for it was after the lambing, but before the spring sowing, that it happened, and the first that William, Lucy and Dewi knew of it was a banging on their door in the first light of a spring morning. They all three bounded from their beds and opened the door to Bowen the Beadle. "Come quick, sir!" he cried to William. "They have tied Parson Peregrine to his bedpost and are smashing up the church."

William rushed back into his room and began pulling on his clothes. "You children stay here," he called to Lucy and Dewi. "If you dare follow me I will thrash you both to within an inch of your lives when I get back."

"I am coming!" cried Dewi.

"You heard me," said William.

"We will follow," Lucy whispered to Dewi, who instantly subsided, and as William ran out of the cottage with Bowen he spared a moment to congratulate himself on his children's obedience. He had trained them well.

Lucy and Dewi dressed and climbed up through the dark wood by Lucy's short cut that brought them to the cliffs. At first, running and stumbling over the tussocks of grass and heather was exciting but as they came nearer the churchyard and heard the noise excitement vanished in fear, for the angry shouting had in it real hatred; and these men were of the same race and the same countryside. And it was not fair. That was her first coherent thought as she and Dewi ran down the hill towards the church. For the Puritan gentry had brought their men, well prepared and primed with ale, down upon a sleeping village, while the men of Roch had had to tumble out of their beds to the defence of their church and parson. And they were outnumbered, with no stiffening of troops among them as the enemy had. But anger stiffened them. They had forgotten now that they had said they would not defend Parson

Peregrine. While their blood stayed hot they were ready to die for him, for who were these damn' fellows, not even born upon the soil of Roch, that they should dare to come down like wolves on a fold that was not theirs, and with the lambing scarcely over? Was there no liberty now in this land of Wales? Could not a man do what he liked in his own church? Their parson was a good old fellow and the roaring that came through his bedroom window, where he was tied to his four-poster, was a trumpet call to which they rallied with all the strength they had.

Lucy heard it as they ran down the lane and she swerved aside towards the parsonage. "We must undo him!" she called to Dewi.

"Let him be, Lucy!" shouted Owen Perrot, running to her. "He is out of harm's way there." And he snatched her up in his arms, and then Dewi, and deposited them as high up as he could in the oak tree by the lynch-gate. "You plaguey children!" he shouted at them. "Stay there." Even in his anguished state he knew it would be useless to tell them to go home. They would not go.

Lucy was so frightened that she felt only a passing anger at being called a plaguey child by her father's bailiff, she, a maid nearly fifteen years, beloved of a prince. Dewi was frightened too. They clung to each other in the oak tree and watched the destruction going on below with horror. A bonfire had been lit in the churchyard and the communion table had already been flung upon it, together with Parson Peregrine's surplice and the prayer books from the vestry. Men were coming from the church now carrying the altar rails, and the chairs upon which William and Elizabeth had sat in the happy days of peace. They were having their will because there were so many of them, and because their discipline told against the confused anger of the men of Roch, but they were getting plenty of savage kicks, bloody noses and black eyes. It was not them Lucy hated so much as the men who had set them on to do this, the Puritan gentlemen in their tall hats who kept at a safe distance while they issued their orders and laughed and jeered, their swords drawn to defend themselves, their pistols ready. They were the only ones who had effective arms. The rest only had sticks.

The wind was from the sea and carried to Lucy a whiff of smoke and the scent of burning. She looked round. "The parsonage!" she cried to Dewi. "It's on fire and Parson Peregrine is tied to the bedpost!"

No one saw them scramble down from the tree and run across the lane to the parsonage. It was not the cottage itself but the pile of wood that Parson Peregrine had stacked against the rear wall that had been fired, but the wind was rising and it would not be long before the cottage was on fire too. The door had already been broken open and they ran across the living room to the kitchen, where Lucy snatched up a knife before they dived into the cupboard in the corner where the stairs were, and climbed up to Parson Peregrine's bedroom above. The old man was dressed except for his coat, for he was an early riser. He had been strongly roped to his fourposter and even his colossal struggles had not been able to get him free.

"Give me that!" he shouted to Lucy when he saw the knife.

"I cannot give it to you while your hands are bound," she pointed out. "Keep still and I will cut your ropes. Keep still. Dewi, hold him still."

Something of the calm that had descended on Lucy with the need for quick action came to the frantic old man too as he felt the light hands of the little boy trying to hold him still. Except for his angry panting he kept quiet while Lucy freed his wrists. Then he snatched the knife from her and hacked at the ropes round his ankles so madly that he cut himself. "Come quickly, the parsonage will be burning in a minute," said Lucy. But he did not hear her. He went instantly to the window. He had seen something of what was happening from his bedpost, but now he could see the west door with ease and just as he looked one of the Puritan gentlemen came out laughing, carrying the little statue of the Virgin upside down by her feet as a man would have carried a dead rabbit. He was a magistrate from Haverfordwest, a man Parson Peregrine

had always disliked and whom now he hated, because it was he
who had written that last vile letter. Cold with fury he reached
for the loaded gun that lay on the chest against the wall and
took careful aim. He did not intend murder and even in the
extremity of rage he was a good shot. The bullet passed
straight through the man's tall hat. But the report turned
what had hitherto been no more than a nasty scrimmage into
bedlam.

Lucy never remembered clearly what happened after that.
She remembered getting safely out of the parsonage before the
roof went up in flames, and trying to hold Parson Peregrine
back as he stormed across the lane to the lych-gate, her feet
dragging on the road as he pulled her with him. Then someone, she thought it was William, pulled her away, lifted her
over the parsonage wall and dropped her roughly in the
garden, where she and Dewi crouched sobbing among the cur-
rant bushes. But she must have looked over the wall because
confused memories of what she saw fluttered like bats through
her nightmares for months afterwards. Only two of them were
touched with greatness. Almost at the end of it all she saw
Parson Peregrine mounted on a horse, his feet roped under it.
His face was bruised and bleeding and one arm was hanging
down as though it were broken. But he held the reins with the
other and his back was straight. All anger had passed from
him and his face was strong as stone and in spite of the pain he
was in, peaceful. Other horsemen gathered around him to prevent rescue and the cavalcade rode quickly away. The sound of
the horses' hoofs going down the hill, and the hollow sound
they made as they passed over the bridge that spanned the
Brandy Brook, sounded in Lucy's ears all through the days
that followed. The other picture was of Old Parson standing
beneath the walls of the ruined castle, his hands held palm to
palm together as though he prayed and the tears running
down his face. Weeping and the hollow sound of death. That
was the end of it.

Three

The August afternoon was hot and breathless in the garden
of Bedford House and Charles sat inert beneath the mulberry
tree, his back against its trunk, an open book on his knees. But
though he kept his eyes lowered he was not reading. Occasionally he turned a page so that kindly persons watching him
from the windows of the house should think he was and leave
the scholar alone. A scholar! What elaborate parts princes
played in order to be left to stew in hell by themselves for one
stagnant hour. 'Sdeath, it was hot! His head ached and his
shirt stuck to his skin. He was tired to the bone and his mind
was filled with a queer blank dismay. It was neither fear, despair nor grief, but the sort of feeling a man would have who
opened his front door one morning and saw not the familiar,
sunlit garden but some blackened landscape utterly unknown
to him. For he had always been sure that it would end right.
He had never doubted the ultimate victory and the triumphant return home to Whitehall; where in the evening the
air came freshly off the face of the river and the swans floated
cool as lily petals.

The defeat of Naseby, two months ago, had marked a disastrous turning of the tide, and after it the note of foreboding
had sounded so constantly in his father's letters that he had
dreaded to see the familiar handwriting on an envelope. If
only he had been with his father and Rupert at Naseby. If
only they had kept together! His father's superb courage had
very nearly turned defeat to victory that day. The King and
his nephew Prince Rupert had become separated in the
fighting, with the main battle raging in the valley between
them and going badly for the Royalist troops. But the King
had seen clearly that he had only to lead his own guard in a
charge downhill to meet Rupert, and Cromwell would be

trapped. "One more charge, gentlemen," he had cried, "and the day is ours," and his troops had rallied as he drew his sword and rode to put himself at the head of the cavalry. Then one of his gentlemen had cried out, "Sire, will you go to your death?" and snatched at his bridle and turned his horse aside. The King, always irresolute, had hesitated, then had yielded and ridden from the field.

"If I had been there I should have cut the bastard's hand off the bridle with my sword!" Charles muttered to himself for the hundredth time. But it was too late now. He was separated from his father, who had marched north to try and make contact with Montrose, and from his cousin Rupert who was holding Bristol. His own commanders here in the west were quarrelling with him and with each other and he did not know what he should do next. He had not been well and had been sent to Exeter to visit his little sister. It was a time of stagnation and there was nothing he could do except sit here in this hellish heat, and try not to think what might have happened if he had been with his father at Naseby.

But it did not mend matters to think of Naseby. Nor to think of the girl. He had ridden to Broad Clyst to find her but she had gone. Little bitch! She had run away to Wales. He was furious with her yet in this garden where they had been together he ached for the sight of her, the comfort and feel of her. There was not a breath of wind under the mulberry tree. Exeter was in the valley and such low-lying, airless and damp places always made him feel ill and depressed. And Sir Edward Hyde, who had been his father's faithful friend and adviser and was now appointed to be his, was driving him mad by watching over him like a clucking hen and lecturing him like a maiden aunt. It appeared likely that they would be stewing and quarrelling here for a month or more, while the war in the north fell into its new pattern.

He sat without movement for a long time and forgot to turn the pages. Then a slow smile spread over his face. The idea was both mad and reprehensible. The commander of the army in the west had no right to leave his army even in a period of stagnation. If it were known to more than a few his father would never forgive him. But why should it be known? He was supposed to be resting, and Exeter was where the Stuart family went to earth. His mother had come here to have Henrietta. His father had been seriously ill here for some while. Why should he not burrow down too? Only the end of *his* burrow should come up in Wales. With luck he should get there and back in a month. With incredible luck. It would be the biggest gamble he had ever taken on but he was at the age when a gamble is the breath of life, and it was air he wanted now, air and life. God alone knew what the future held for him; probably ruin and death both for himself and his father. Why not live first? Why not? The faintest breath of wind stirred in the hot garden and something soft touched his face in passing; almost as though a girl had bent to flutter long eyelashes against his cheek in what children called the butterfly kiss. He looked up, startled, and saw two butterflies floating by. They settled on the low branch of the mulberry tree close behind him and basked there, slowly fanning their wings. He had his sign. The luck would be incredible.

He got up instantly and went into the house to his room and wrote two letters, to Lady Dalkeith and to Hyde. He badly needed sea air, he told them, and was going sailing, a trip down the river to the sea, and he might be away three weeks or more. All arrangements had been made for his safety and he would be excellently cared for and they were not to worry. They were to say he was ill. Everyone knew his family were always ill in Exeter. Having written his letters he put them in his pocket and strolled to the stables to find a favourite, trusted groom. Ten hours later, with moon and stars to guide him, he was riding alone across Dartmoor dressed in his groom's clothes. His luck in getting away unseen had already been fantastic, and a singing south-easterly breeze caressing the back of his neck told him it would continue so. For the south-easterly was what he wanted. He was bound for Torrington and from there to Bideford. There were always ships in plenty at Bideford and he would be certain to find one bound for a Pembrokeshire port and willing to take a passenger. He had money in his pocket and money accomplished most things. If the south-easterly were to sing a little more powerfully he would be in Pembrokeshire in a few days' time. There was heather now under his horse's feet and he began to sing himself. His breed were always at their best and their happiest when they took to the heather.

2

"I have to ride to St. Davids today, sir," Lucy said to her father at breakfast, "and so I fear you cannot borrow my mare." She spoke in a queenly manner, tilting her chin, and William and Dewi exchanged glances. Bud was in one of her moods. "God-a-mercy," said William. "Marry-come-up! The Princess Nest! Nevertheless I must have your Highness's mare for my nag is lame. Do you expect me to ride to Haverfordwest on one of the plough horses, or Dewi's pony?"

"No, sir. But I expect you to postpone your visit until to-morrow, when I shall be pleased for you to borrow my mare."

They were breakfasting outside their cottage very early on what would soon be a fine hot morning. Lucy was wearing a plain green gown, such as any countrywoman could have worn, but it was fresh and clean and a last late rose that had bloomed in the castle garden was pinned at the neck of the bodice, the creamy petals reflected under her tilted chin. How astonishing, thought William suddenly, to have a skin so satin smooth that it could reflect a flower. He could almost fancy that the slow movement of the sea was reflected in waves of light passing across his daughter's face, as its colour was trapped in her eyes. She was his for the nonce but for how much longer? He took her hand, spreading out her thin brown fingers on his own hard and earth-encrusted palm. It gave him a shock to find it a woman's hand, not a child's. Bud was grown-up now, in her sixteenth year. Who had told him that there was no love so poignant as that of a doting father for a grown-up daughter? Whoever it was had spoken the truth, as his sudden anguish told him. The shadow of parting was on him and it seemed upon Lucy too, for her arrogance melted away and her hand closed upon his. Their eyes met. They looked at each other for a moment and then looked away.

"Must you ride alone to St. Davids?" asked William gruffly. "When the nag is mended I could ride with you."

"I shall be safe," said Lucy. "I have not been to St. Davids since I came home and I have a great longing on me to ride there alone."

"Then you shall," said William, and he kissed her hand and put it back on her lap.

3

Why did I feel I must come today, Lucy wondered, as she rode quickly along the pilgrim way that she had last travelled more slowly with Old Parson. She was feeling wonderfully happy, so happy that even the remembrance of Parson Peregrine in jail had no power now to sadden her. That was wrong, she thought, but her happiness today was something that could not be gainsaid. She had brought it with her from last night's sleep, from one of those deep dreams that cannot be recalled on waking because the conscious mind is not able to record the experience of them, only remind the dreamer that he has known something beyond waking knowledge. The flavour of such a dream, sometimes vile and terrifying, sometimes fresh and joyous, could linger all day. What had she known that now everything about her, fields, clouds, trees and birds, should seem to be flowing in and out of each other as though they danced together, as sunbeams and raindrops seem to do when a rainbow spreads across the sky? Something so real that the suffering of an old man she loved could become more dreamlike to her than this strange and lovely dance. Will all suffering seem a dream one day, she wondered? Will it be as they say it is when a woman bears a child, that she forgets for the joy? But why is a forgotten dream sending me to St. Davids? She remembered that the Valley of Roses was one of the shrines. In it one came near to mystery.

The wind that for so many days had blown from the southeast was from the west today and riding along the cliffs its coolness tempered the heat. Lucy was still wearing the green dress, for her riding habit was too tight for a warm day, and a broad-brimmed straw hat to shield her from the sun was tied beneath her chin with scarlet ribbons. Her saddlebag had food in it, wrinkled apples and bara ceich, for she seldom found her appetite much diminished by hot weather. The people of St. Davids looked up at her and smiled as she rode through the village, for they found themselves, even the dourest of them, as much aware of her golden happiness as they would have been of the wealth of a royal lady, had such a one passed by scattering her largess. Even the saturnine hostler at the inn, whose dark and ancient face had never been known to smile, suffered a curious spasm of the features as he took her horse. It had passed in a moment but not before it had revealed to a startled Lucy that his dark cavern of a mouth had but two teeth in it.

Somehow this intimation of mortality was sobering, and as she walked to the gatehouse she was for the first time aware that the rose she had picked last night in the castle garden was dying on her breast like a neglected child. She took it from her dress and held it against her face and its scent was still sweet and without reproach. The happiness drawn from beyond time can be precarious and she had almost lost it because earth, the green star, with its flowers and its creatures, lies so helplessly before human greed, and she was under the archway and standing at the brink of the Valley of Roses before she knew it.

Then instantly it flooded back. Down there was the stream and in the cool water her flower would revive. She ran down the steps and soon was in the green grass below the bridge, and then pushing through the rushes to the stream. It was shallow, because there had been no rain for some while, but still clear and cool because it ran swiftly. In a moment Lucy had pulled off her hat and shoes and tossed them down with the saddlebag, gathered up her skirts and waded out to a large stone in the centre of the stream. Here she sat with the coolness lapping about her ankles and held her flower with its stalk in the water, drinking in life. She drank life too; from the great cathedral beyond the bridge, the tall motionless trees, the stillness and silence, broken only by the music of the running water and the chiming of the hour from the cathedral tower. Such music does not profane silence and presently she began to sing too.

"Lucy! Lucy!"

At first the voice distantly calling her name seemed a part of the music, a part of herself, making no more demanding claim upon her than the remembered dream had done, the response of total joy within herself. Then the voice called again, coming nearer, and the joy streamed out from her in the manner of sunlight pouring through a rent in a cloud, taking all that she was with it and leaving her for a split second still as the stone she sat on. Then she turned her head and saw him running and stumbling through the grass beside the stream, laughing and calling her name. There was no longer any question in her mind about running to meet her glory. All that she was had run already and if she did not go to him now she would have lost not only him but herself. She jumped from her stone to the bank, leaped again and was in his arms.

"You jump like a green frog," he gasped when he could speak for laughing. For there was no fear in this meeting, no awe or uncertainty, nothing but a joy so extraordinary that their mutual possession of it seemed to them almost ridiculous. Lucy lifted her face from his shoulder to wipe the tears of laughter from her eyes and found that the dance had begun again, only now the dancers were not nebulous but as vividly alive as characters in an immortal fairytale. Her rose, that she had forgotten to take from the stream, went dancing by on the water with its refreshed petals rounded like the sails of a small ship. The tall trees that a short while ago had been motionless and weary with August heat were now alight with green fire, swaying in the dance, and all the birds in them, looking down at the lovers with eyes bright as diamonds, clapped their wings, then rose up like the sons of the morning and sang for joy. A swan came down the stream and he had a gold crown on his head and was singing. But it was not his own death song. He sang of the death of fear.

Charles was also changed. Prince Kilhwch, who had ridden

alone in magnificence, had vanished, for like all the great ones
he had put on disguise for the wooing of his love. He was a
mendicant now, and a suppliant. His doublet was stained with
seawater, his hair tangled, his dark sunburned face orna-
mented with a black eye and still wet with the water with
which he had been trying to remove its dirt. He had been
bending over the stream, cupping the cool water in his hands
and splashing it into his hot face, when he had turned his head
and seen a girl sitting on the stone. Even seen through the
glinting water, at a distance, there could be no doubt that she
was *the* girl. Who else could be the only human being except
himself alive in this dream at the world's end? For that was
how it had seemed to him as he cried her name aloud and
stumbled over the grass towards her. It had been a difficult
journey, and a frightening one, but now it had ended; at the
world's end or at its beginning, he did not know which.

They sat down in the grass by the stream and he told her of
his adventures, and now they seemed not frightening but
funny, so that they both laughed as he told of them. He had
left his horse at a stables in Bideford, found a ship bound for
Milford Haven, paid his money in advance as requested, been
given a good meal and slept the sleep of exhaustion through
the night as the ship ran fast before a fair wind. But Milford,
like Pembroke, was in Puritan hands, and the military had
been everywhere, he had been stared at and had felt afraid to
go into the town and try to hire a horse to carry him to Roch
lest he should be recognized by some officer who had seen him
before. Instead he had wandered round the docks, asking questions of the seamen, until he found a small boat bound for
Solva Bay.

Her sailors were rough men but they took him on board in
comradely fashion, and finding he knew how to handle a ship
let him have his fill of work as the little boat pitched and
tossed along the coast to Solva. He had promised payment on
landing, pleased that they had trusted him, but when at the
quayside he felt for his wallet it had gone. He had slept rather
too well on the journey from Bideford to Milford Haven
Then they had turned threatening and abusive, but his wits

told him what to do and as they gathered round, closing in on him, he offered to fight the mate in payment. Their anger turned to laughter and appreciation and on the quayside he fought the mate, not with much skill but with pluck and determination and the advantage of height and agility. It was not a fight to the finish but it won their hearts. They let him go with a black eye and many bruises and a few friendly kicks to speed him on his way. He had made his way to St. Davids and remembering what she had said about the coolness of the water in the Valley of Roses he had gone straight to the stream to wash himself.

"And what now?" he asked Lucy. "I promised you we should be together at Roch and I have come to keep my promise while I can."

"I shall love you for ever and ever for keeping your promise," said Lucy. "I should have loved you for ever in any case but now it is for ever and ever. What now? I have food in my saddlebag and we will eat it. Then we spend the happiest day of our lives here at St. Davids. Then I take you home."

"What will your father say?"

"I hope nothing. I will keep you hidden if I can for he would not like you coming here. When I said home I did not mean the cottage where he and I and Dewi are living now, I meant my real home, the castle. The kitchen down among the roots is still habitable. If we are lucky you can live there for days and no one will know. There's my saddle bag in the grass."

He fetched it and the homely fare tasted like the food of the gods. But half-way through Lucy snatched it away. "In another three hours you will be hungry again. You eat like a wolf and there will be nothing else until we get home."

"Until we get home," repeated Charles slowly. He had heard the four words spoken so often and they had always been pleasant words but not magic until now. Down among the roots, she had said, and his inward eye saw tree roots spreading out in protection, and hidden among them the warm secluded dwelling-place of two small furry animals, with nuts stored in plenty and a bed of dry moss. A slowly spreading grin warmed his sombre face to delight. That would be home indeed. Not a procession of palaces but just the one hidden and private place. "You look like a tinker," said Lucy.

"They are respected members of a reputable trade," he told her.

"I respect you," she said, suddenly sobered. "I could not love a man I did not respect."

"You said you would love me for ever and ever but if one day you can no longer respect me, what then?"

She looked him straight in the eye. "You must know that I will never change and of that you must always feel certain, even if one day *you* feel that you can no longer respect *me*. But I do not see how respect, once given, can ever be lost. If you have ever seen the true metal in a man or woman you must believe that it is still there, however tarnished it becomes. Tarnish hides but it does not destroy. But truth is the glory of love, Charles, and unless we remain true to each other we shall lose our peace."

"How do you know these things?" he asked her.

"I do not know them by myself, how could I? I am told."

"The maintaining of truth is so hard," he said.

"There is very little peace in the world," she replied.

The world! A cold wind seemed to blow down the Valley of Roses and he got up quickly, pulling her with him, for he did not want to remember what men called the real world but only to experience this one. And was not this one as real as the other? It had seemed slipping and he pulled its protection quickly about them both again. "Show me this place," he commanded her.

"You must come as a pilgrim," she told him. "King Henry did, the second Henry who loved Fair Rosamund. He landed at Solva, as you have done, on his way home from Ireland, and he came dressed as a pilgrim and leaning on a staff." Suddenly she laughed delightedly for here was a second royal pilgrimage on a second day of great happiness, and a second prince in love with a Welsh girl. Treading in former footsteps gave one a feeling of reassurance and stability. "And you landed on the shore of Milford Haven as Henry the Seventh did when he came from Brittany to win the crown of England. He was born in Pembrokeshire. Did you know? You have done all things just as you should."

"Only by chance," laughed Charles. "But I knew the luck would be incredible. Did Henry the Second cross the stream by this bridge?"

"Not this one. When he came the stream was spanned by a marble slab, wonderfully polished by the feet of all the pilgrims. It was called Lachavan, the talking stone, because once when a corpse was being carried over it the stone cried out and cracked itself with its cry."

"I will have nothing to do with corpses or cryings," said Charles firmly. "No bad luck shall touch you and me. We will not cross this bridge. We will jump the stream."

"It is wide here," Lucy warned him.

"Are you afraid?"

"Me? Afraid? No!"

"Then take my hand."

They threw her hat and saddlebag across the stream, moved back and took hands, ran and jumped. Impeded by her skirts, even though she gathered them up in her free hand, she would have fallen short, but Charles leaped with the strength of some great long-legged hound and though her arm nearly came out of its socket he brought her flying through the air to safety. They fell flat on the grass on the farther side, laughing and triumphant. Now they were secure in good fortune. Now nothing could ever go wrong.

Lucy picked herself up and tied her hat on. "This is where Henry was met by all the cathedral dignitaries walking in procession," she said.

"They are not meeting me, God be thanked," said Charles. "They are not even in existence. No one exists here today but you and me."

As the hours passed it seemed true. They walked round the cool, echoing cathedral as they had walked round Exeter Cathedral, hand in hand and quite alone, visiting the altar tomb of Henry the Seventh's father and the tomb of Rhys ap Griffiths, and kneeling together at St. Davids shrine. Then they visited the ruined palace and sat and talked among the flowers that carpeted the old banqueting hall. And they went down into the vaults below to find the wishing well. To make a wish it was necessary to drop a pin into the water and Lucy, always careless about her clothes, had that morning pinned up a torn petticoat hem rather than bother to mend it, and she produced two pins. They leaned over the well side by side dropping the pins, and wished in silence. Their wishes were substantially the same. "To maintain truth," was Lucy's, and "To love this woman, and no other, all my life long," was Charles's confident and hopeful desire.

"In all the years, so many hundreds of wishes and so many hundreds of pins," whispered Lucy, staring down into the black water. Then she raised her head and cried aloud, "Charles!" and he cried, "Lucy!" There was a strange echo down in the vaults and the two names echoed on and on, seeming to chase each other. Then they cried both together and in the echoing triumphant shout the two were not distinguishable.

They climbed out of the Valley of Roses and went down to St. Bride's Bay and sat among the rocks with the sea wind in their faces, and paddled in the pools, and Charles saw his girl with the wind blowing her hair about her face and the sea water green about her ankles. She told him about St. David's birthplace up on the cliffs, where a well had gushed forth, and stones risen up to protect the blessed mother, and about the chapels along the coast where passing sailors left votive offerings. She talked enchantingly of what she loved and enjoyed and not of what wounded or saddened her; these things were many but she did not speak of them. Yet Charles was aware of them and aware of the selflessness of her occasional little brooding silences. That they were selfless, and as natural to her as her merry talk, he knew because they lay so gently on his mind. He was also almost dumbfounded by the knowledge that she was flowering into all he had believed her to be. His sudden journey in search of her had had about it the elements of an act of faith and to find faith justified always seems too good to be true.

They were hungry and ate the last of the food. Then it was

time to be turning home and Lucy left Charles on the cliffs
while she fetched the mare. It was hard on the mare to have to
carry the two of them on her back, Lucy riding pillion, but
often they let her walk while Charles dismounted and strode
beside her, and often the three of them rested in the shade.

"It is not going to be so easy as you think to keep me
hidden," said Charles. "I cannot spend all my time skulking in
your castle vaults. So what do we say when I am seen?"

"That you are an escaped Royalist, a prisoner in hiding. For
the moment the Puritans have got Pembrokeshire but my
father's people are Royalist at heart and no one would tell of
you."

"What is my name?"

"Tomos Barlow."

"But I do not speak as the Welsh do."

"You had better not speak at all. If you are spoken to smile
and nod your head."

For the rest of the ride home they laughed often, but in the
midst of their laughter they would fall suddenly silent, for
they both knew that they were approaching a climax in their
lives. An act of faith could lead to nothing else. When they
looked at each other they smiled encouragement.

In the westering sunlight they reached the bridge below the
mill and dismounted. "I must stable the mare and get food for
you," said Lucy. "You go on to the castle. It is at the top of that
hill. Go down the lane to the left and you will find the ways in
through the garden."

When she reached the cottage Lucy found that her father
had not come home yet. Dewi was winkle-picking down on the
rocks but he was too absorbed to notice her for winkles cooked
in ashes were his favourite supper. She put food in the saddlebag, took two blankets from the chest and the little mattress
stuffed with dried bracken from her own bed, bound them
together with rope, loaded them on her back and toiled up
through the wood, and up the hill, burdened like the man
in the moon. But the joy of what she was doing had a sharp
intensity. This burden-bearing for Charles was the true beginning of her womanhood.

She found him in the great hall. He was on the dais and called out to her as she came in. It was sunset now and once again the hall was roofed with glory. She dropped her burden, straightened herself and turned towards him. They each saw the other lit with gold like a little royal figure in the margin of a painted manuscript. Then they ran to each other, growing in size as they ran, and in the centre of the hall were in each other's arms.

"Why are their tears in your eyes?" Lucy asked.

"Because this castle is lost to you and your father for my father's sake, and my sake."

"Why do you mind so much?"

"Would not you mind? The very birth of a prince means conflict sooner or later; homes destroyed, men wounded and dead, women bereaved."

"You are not a prince here in Roch," Lucy comforted him. "You are only my lover Tomos. And you are tired and need your supper and bed."

But Charles was not to be comforted. "I shall have nightmares sleeping in this ruin," he said. "Is there a haystack somewhere?"

"Down below, where the kitchen is, there are no signs of ruin. It will make you happy to sleep there. Look, you must carry your own bedding down. I am not going to wait on Tomos." She looked up at him, her eyes sparkling with mischief and a touch of anger. "I am never going to wait on you more than any wife should wait on any husband; nothing extra."

He flushed with sudden shame and instantly shouldered the mattress and blankets and bag of food; because just for a moment he had stood aside to be waited on just as he always did. But following her down the steps an enormous question mark loomed up for the first time in his mind. Wife, she had said. Wife. And the shadow of Nan-Nan fell upon him.

"Did she always live here with you?" he asked.

Lucy glanced back over her shoulder, surprised. "Who?"

"Your old nurse."

"But of course she did. She was here before I was born. She is a part of Roch."

"I thought so," said Charles gloomily.

But she had not heard him in her pleasure at showing him his hiding-place. The sunset light was pouring in through the west window and gave warmth to the pots and pans, the table and stools, the well and the great fireplace. There was no suggestion of ruin here, only of strength and peace. "Ruin is only temporary," she told Charles. "Down below it is like this. Are you happy now?"

"Yes," he said. "This is the most comforting place I ever saw."

"Look here," said Lucy, and she led him to the little stone figure. "He is our family crest and he used to stand over the fireplace in the hall. He is a stork really, but we call him the heron because there are herons down by Brandy Brook and we love them."

"Arrogant and undefeatable," said Charles. "Like you."

"But I am not sharp-beaked," pleaded Lucy, a little hurt by the "arrogant".

"No, you could never say sharp things, dear heart, but you could say hard things. Truthful things. And I love it in you."

He went thoughtfuly back to the kitchen for he had just called her dear heart, which was what his father called his mother. The words had come most naturally to his tongue.

Lucy said they must light a fire. It was aways cool among the roots, the light was fading and the air from the sea came freshly through the window. And besides, she told Charles, this was their home just for now and every true Welsh home has a fire burning on the hearth whatever the weather. They became merry as children arranging the logs and fir-cones and getting the fire blazing, and then they sat and talked by it for a while.

"I must go," said Lucy suddenly. "It is getting dark and my father will be home. I will come in the morning and we will think what to do next."

He did not want her to go and hugged her so hard that she had to use her strength to get free. He dropped his arms and let her go.

Four

I

It had without doubt been decided in some other world than this that the luck should be incredible. Not in heaven, whose concern seems to be not with what men call good fortune but only with pure good, and that interpreted on its own terms, not ours. No, not heaven, but the world of legend and myth that coming up over the horizon like moonrise put a magic protection about a few hours, a few days, a whole week it may be of human experience. Climbing up through the wood in the first light of the next morning Lucy wondered to which world her unremembered dream had belonged. Perhaps to both, since both were in the depths of herself. It did not matter. What mattered was that William and Dewi had been too deeply asleep to hear her getting up and putting their breakfast ready, and that upon going to the mill house last evening she had found Old Parson not very well in the heat, and in no mood to climb the hill to the castle as he so often did.

A sea mist made the dawn mysterious today. The birds were hardly awake yet and in the castle garden there was silence and stillness. Motionless rose sprays, half seen in the mist, looked like arabesques faintly traced on silver, and the castle, its scars hidden in wreaths of vapour, seemed to rise to an immense height. As she climbed up the steps to the hall she heard faint unearthly music and stood still, her heart beating. "Where should this music be? In the earth, in the air?" She did not know and she went on to the hall thinking that it came from neither earth nor air but from the depths of which she had been thinking. She went slowly and softly down the stone steps to the kitchen and the music, while losing nothing of its beauty, became something homely. Charles was down there playing the flute.

For a few moments she sat at the bottom of the steps and

listened. He must have awakened very early for he had already lit the fire and now he was sitting on a stool beside it playing the flute with extraordinary skill. Now she knew something more about him. He was a musician. Oh joy, oh joy! For so was she. He was playing the air of Greensleeves. She stood up against the wall and began to sing to his accompaniment. They took it from beginning to end and then looked at each other and laughed in delight.

"You sing like a thrush," said Charles. "Why did you not tell me?"

"Why did you not tell *me* that you can play like that? And where did you find that flute?"

"Have you never been up the staircase behind the heron? There is a little room up there, a storeroom I should think. It is unharmed. There was a chest there and I opened it and found a guitar and this flute, both carefully wrapped up. Both unhurt."

The tears rushed into Lucy's eyes. "They belonged to my father and mother," she said. "We left them behind by mistake when we went to London and one of the servants must have looked after them and put them there for safety. It must have been old Gwladys. She is dead now."

"Do not cry," said Charles.

Lucy wiped her eyes on the back of her hand. "No. But on Sundays we used to make music in the arbour, my father and mother and we children."

Charles came to her. "Have you brought me any breakfast?" he enquired in her ear. He was not heartless but he was intensely hungry and he had seen the bag slung over her shoulder. She was dressed as a boy today and he was amused to see how well her father's breeches became her.

"You shall have it later," said Lucy. "Now you can only have a bit of bara ceich to eat while you come with me."

"I do not want to go anywhere. Only to eat."

"Very early this morning I heard something that you have got to hear too. That is why I got up so early. Come quickly."

Hand in hand, munching bara ceich, they walked towards

340

the cliff. The mist was slowly yielding to the rising sun, and encompassed them mysteriously, as though peopled by spirits. Each faint movement of the veil seemed to promise the revelation of some secret thing, perhaps the very meaning of the world, but there was no fulfilment. Always as the curtain stirred it dropped again and from somewhere far away there came a cry that sent a shiver down the spine, a wild heart-broken voice, all humanity crying out in outrage at this thing. Must we suffer so, and never know why? Never from the beginning to the end of the world know why?

"For God sake!" cried Charles, and dropped his bit of bread in the wet grass. "What in this world or out of it was that?"

"You will soon know," said Lucy placidly, and she steered him a little towards the right. "But you must keep very quiet." She knew exactly where she was. She could have found her way to either of the three bays of Roch blindfold. Yet it gave Charles a jolt when she suddenly pulled him to a standstill and he found himself standing on the edge of the world, with nothing below him but a great cavern full of mist. One more step and he would have plunged into it.

"You are quite safe," whispered Lucy, as to a child, her hand gripping his tightly. "I have got you."

But from somewhere in the bowels of the earth, right under their feet it seemed, the cry came again, louder and more dreadful and he did not agree with her. Safe? In such a world? Nothing was safe, neither love nor life nor fortune. Only death was sure. And then a softer cry came, not beneath their feet but a cry in the mist, a flute-like cry that was sad but not hopeless. And then to the left another, and this time Charles thought of the god Pan and his sorrow now that no man believed in him any more. After that there was silence, the sort of silence which cannot be broken. The mist thinned and Charles thought he could see a glimpse of water, and dark rocks in the sea. And then what he thought he had seen was hidden, and then revealed; only one of the rocks moved. He was glad when Lucy at last softly broke the silence.

"The first cry and the second must have come from one of

the caves. The voice echoes so in the caves. The others are down in the cove or out at sea. They are the morlos."

"Morlos?" whispered Charles. The strange name seemed entirely appropriate to whoever they were down there. The sweat had started out on his forehead. He was ashamed of the fact and wiped it away with his wrist. "Morlos?"

"The seals," said Lucy.

"Oh, the seals!" Caught amid shame and amusement he flung back his head and began to laugh his great laugh but Lucy, in a perfect fury with him, slapped her hand so hard over his mouth that he staggered and was instantly silenced. "I told you to keep quiet!" she muttered. "If they hear us they will go away. This is a chance of a lifetime. Follow me and do not dare make that noise again!"

The mist was thinning very fast and already they felt the warmth of the sun. He could see now that the cliff fell from their feet in a savage rocky mass. She began to climb down and he followed her with his heart in his mouth. She climbed like a mountain goat and the education of Charles Stuart had not as yet included rock climbing. Presently they reached a wide rock-ledge where rough grass and heather grew. There to his relief they could lie flat and look down into the bay below, and gradually, as the veils of mist withdrew over a sparkling sea, the bay of the seals lay clear beneath them.

It was a small bay of sloping shingle and flat rocks. Several marbled cows were lying on the rocks with their ivory-coated pups beside them, and a little way out in the water were five bulls. Lucy leaned close to Charles and began to whisper to him, but he hardly heard what she said for the burning sweetness of having her so close, her body stretched beside his, her hair tickling his cheek. "They are the grey Atlantic seals that breed on the Pembrokeshire coast. There are black seals too, my father says, but they come from the North Sea and the Baltic and you find them only in Scotland. The pups have soft brown eyes that fill with tears when they are hurt. You must never hurt a seal for they were human once. That dreadful cry is because of something they did long ago that banished them from the world of men. But they can sing too, like flutes. You heard them. The grey seals sing a better song than the black ones, they say."

She was so young that her hair still had that faint delightful scent that children's hair has. He edged a little away from her and tried to concentrate his mind on flutes. He had heard that last bit, musician that he was. "Have you ever played the flute to them?" he asked.

"No!" Lucy sat up, her whole face sparkling with delight. "I never thought of it. But we could not get near enough. They would hear us scrambling down the scree below the rocks. It is so steep there. It is not possible to be silent."

"We could come in very quietly from the sea at dusk," said Charles.

"So we could!" She was like a child delighting in a new game. Biting her little finger she wondered how they could manage it. "We cannot set off from the fishermen's bay for we would be seen. But there is a boy there who would do anything for me. I will get him to take a boat round to the castle bay and beach it there. I will say I am going fishing with my father."

"Who is this boy who would do anything for you?" demanded Charles.

"Just one of the fisherboys. They would all do anything for me but this one especially because I bandaged his arm when he cut it badly. His name is Iolo."

"What an outlandish name."

"No more outlandish to your ears than Charles would be to his. Are you jealous?"

"Jealous? No! Why should I be jealous of a fisherlad?"

But his face was dark with it and his eyes hot and she remembered Othello. "Dear General, I never gave you cause." Who had said that? Someone in the same play. She must never give him cause.

"You only for ever and ever," she reminded him. "I will fetch you at dusk tonight and we will go to the castle cove and row round the headland and play to the morlos. Take another look at them for we must go now. My father's men will soon be about in the fields."

They looked down again at the bulls in the water, the gentle cows and their pups on the rocks, and climbed back to the cliff top.

"I will not be able to be with you again today, not until this evening," said Lucy, "for my father said I must ride with him to see the new parson and his wife who have been sent to look after us now that our old parson is in prison. They are Puritans and we do not want them but my father says we must be civil. You will not be lonely till I come?"

"No, I will sit in the garden and read the book I found in the chest."

"A book? Did Gwladys hide a book there?"

"The Mabinogion. A lovely book, safely wrapped in a blanket like the guitar and the flute."

"Oh, dear Gwladys!" cried Lucy in joy. "I thought the Mabinogion had been burnt with all the other things in my mother's bower. Gwladys must have known inside herself what was going to happen. The Mabinogion has all the stories of our beginnings. Read about Prince Kilhwch and Olwen. Read about the giant who propped his eyelids up with forks."

He laughed and said he would and then he asked about the old man who was in prison and made Lucy tell him why he had been taken away. It grieved him and there was nobility in the sadness of his face when he grieved for those who suffered for his father. It banished the memory of his sudden fit of jealousy, and saying goodbye to him at the garden door Lucy felt her love for him burgeoning like a tree in spring. That it should be drawing strength from the soil of Roch seemed a happiness almost too great to bear.

2

It was twilight when they came down the lane to the castle bay, and there was no sound except the murmur of the little stream running to the sea. The rock that had always been Lucy's special place loomed up with benign strength and Iolo had beached the boat beside it. Barelegged and laughing they pulled it down to the sea, pushed off and jumped in. Charles took the oars and Lucy steered, the flute lying in her lap. Birds were about them for the gulls who had flown inland today were coming back to sleep within sound of the sea, and the cormorants and guillemots were settling down for the night. The sky over their heads was deep and clear, but wisps of mist floated over a sea so still that it scarcely seemed to breathe. Charles rowed so skilfully that his oars in the rowlocks made only a whisper of sound. The blades dipped into the clear water and rose again so rhythmically that they seemed themselves to be the slowly moving wings of some majestic bird. "The swan that went down the stream with a crown on his head," said Lucy to herself. "These days are crowned with joy. They are not earthly."

It was a fairly long row round the headland that separated one bay from the other, and they took it slowly, for they wanted it to be a little darker when they reached the seals. A few stars pricked out in the sky and starry drops fell like diamonds from the blades of the oars to the water. The last lights were fading from the western sky but as they came out beyond the headland and saw the faint shine of the coastline, and the islands rising silvery out of pools of diaphanous mist, they knew that the moon was rising and would soon flood the sky with light. "I think we should go in now," whispered Lucy.

Charles brought them round to the bay and then shipped his oars while Lucy cast out the floats. They could see the morlos, lulled by the same gentle breathing of the sea that peacefully rocked their boat, and they sat for a long time without movement or speech, anxious to become so much a part of the beauty about them that they would not disturb the morlos. This, they felt, was important. Creatures are not afraid of something that has for long shared their rhythm and their peace. "Now," whispered Lucy at last. "You play the flute better than I do."

He began to play, hardly knowing when he started what he would play, but the right tune came. It was a Hebridean lament and he wondered for the moment what he was lamenting about on this night of joy. Then he remembered that the morlos had been banished from the warm life of men. It must always be in the cold sea now that they must fight for life, their only hiding-places the lonely caves that thrust in like fingers under the earth. Here they must lie in darkness and when they cried out to the men above them be heard only with fear. He would laugh at himself afterwards but while he played Charles almost believed the old story, and yearned after those seals as though they were his kith and kin.

He ceased playing and listened, and from over the water was answered by a low fluting cry. It was so mysterious, so beautiful and yet so eerie that when Charles took Lucy's hand he found it was cold and trembling. He was pleased to cherish it with his own superior warmth, but his heart was beating none too steadily. He laid Lucy's hand gently down and took up his flute again. He played a few notes like a call and was answered. He did it again and again and each time like an echo his music came back to him, now here, now there, now near, now far. It was not easy to see, with the moon not fully risen yet and the faint haze of mist on the water, but they were aware of movement. Were they wanted? Was their companionship desired, even yearned for? Lucy, who had been so happy, felt heartbroken now. They were so close to the seals, they loved them so, yet could tell of their love only with these wordless cries, and heartbeats that could bring no comfort. Some great mystery united them and some other mystery divided them. Why is love not enough, she wondered. Why is love never enough to break down separation? If love could become strong enough for that then there would be no more weeping, no more death. Then would come the time for dancing. And there was already a dance. She had been aware of it twice now. One could dream that it might one day sweep over the whole universe in a thunder of rejoicing. "Play something merry," she whispered to Charles. "Play a dance tune, but very softly so as not to frighten them."

He played the air of a country dance, one of the lilting tunes to which Lucy and William had danced on May morning. There was no reply to this but the moonlight was brighter and they could see that the morlos were on the move. It seemed to

Lucy that in their own way and in their own manner they moved in the slow mazes of a dance.

"Look at those two!" gasped Charles. "They are flying to us!"

Lucy had heard of this marvel but never seen it before. The heads of the two seals were reared high up out of the water and they were moving so fast towards the boat that in the uncertain light they seemed flying. Then they disappeared and left Charles and Lucy wondering if they had really seen what they had seen, or merely dreamed it. They waited a little longer, but there was no more movement, no more music, and the moon grew bright and hard above the cliffs. It seemed all over and they turned the boat and rowed slowly away.

They were just rounding the headland when it happened. A great head streaming with water came out of the sea beside the boat, and a face looked at them, old and furrowed and wise, with great eyes of love and sorrow and wet whiskers silvered by the moon. Then another head rose behind the boat and cried aloud to them. Then suddenly both were gone. They waited a long time but they did not come back.

"They were saying goodbye to us," Lucy said at last, and began to cry.

"Do not weep, little love," said Charles. "It was great, it was beauty, and it was true. And now it is over. Let us row home."

They beached the boat in the castle cove and walked home under the stars, hand in hand but in silence. Out at sea with the morlos they had been aware of being together in a world alien to their own, among beings whose ways were a mystery to them but yet whom they had loved, and left only with sadness, and it deepened their union with each other in a way that belonged to the spirit alone; but each step nearer home brought them closer to their own mystery, the human mystery and predicament of loving so much that the condemnation of separateness laid upon human creatures becomes too great a burden. There was no predicament for the morlos, but simplicity had gone from human loving. For the humankind, tangled in the complexities in which experience of good and evil had bound them, complexities that grew ever worse the longer men stayed upon this earth only to corrupt it, there was no more simplicity. The morlos mourning for their lost heritage did not know that man had lost his too.

The man and woman reached home, the old safe hide-out among the roots of the trees, and the intensity of his sense of homecoming overwhelmed Charles. Here it was, the lost simplicity, not entirely lost after all but still to be found for the delving. Here was the deep well of water, and the fire and the bed of bracken beside it, and the girl who was his girl and must belong to no one but himself alone. All through these hours of enchantment his persona and his duty had seemed no more than echoes of thunder beyond a lost horizon, but now with his arms round Lucy even the echoes vanished. There was only silence.

But he did not carry Lucy with him into its depth. Her childhood had not been the ceaselessly moving, over populated pageant that his had been and the few events that had struck hard upon her mind and heart had struck like a carver's chisel, and she acted now out of a simplicity of grief and loyalty unknown to him, and without premeditation. She twisted out of his arms and standing back with her hands behind her delivered her blows. She spoke as a small child might have spoken, so that in spite of his anger and desperate hurt he could almost have laughed; she was so resolved.

"I promised Nan-Nan I would not do it. I know how a bastard child suffers and I will not bring one into this world to die as Betsi died. Nor will I bring shame upon my father. I loved Nan-Nan and my father before I loved you. You have tonight to choose what you will do. If when I come in the morning I find you gone—" She stopped, for suddenly scalding tears were boiling up, almost choking her, but she fought them back and went on. "If you are gone I shall know I will never see you again. But if you are here I will know that I am to be your wife."

"You speak as though marriage between us were an easy thing," he said bitterly.

"No, it will be hard," said Lucy, "for as soon as you have

348

married me you will have to leave me. Then one of three things can happen. You may be killed in this war. Then I shall break my heart but the child, if there is a child, will not suffer as Betsi and Dewi did. Or you may be exiled and never come to the throne. Then I shall share poverty and exile with you and I shall not mind at all because we will be together. Or you may come to the throne and then you will have to decide what to do with me, and it will be hard for you but less hard for me because if my children are safe in honour I shall do exactly what you want. But it feels so distant, that third thing."

And suddenly she could not hold the tears back. It was the first thing now that seemed to her the most likely. So many princes died by violence. One after the other right back through history, the sword had got them. The fairytale in which they had been living had collapsed and vanished and it seemed that death and parting had taken its place. She turned and ran away up the steps, so quickly and so deafened and blinded by her storm of tears that she never heard the cry that Charles sent after her.

3

The sun was high when Lucy arrived the next morning and Charles was out in the garden, rooting up weeds by the savage handful to find some outlet for the fiery longing and impatience that were driving him nearly out of his wits. Lucy, who had run all the way up the hill, arrived breathless and as though carried by the wind of her eagerness. She had information to impart but having landed on Charles's chest was too winded to get it out. It was he who spoke first, his earthy hands pressed against her shoulder blades. "We will get married as soon as possible," he whispered into her right ear. "And to hell with what happens after."

If he expected gratitude for this humbling of a princely will he did not get it, for Lucy considered he was doing no more than his duty in the circumstances, and she never praised anyone for doing their obvious duty. "I knew you would say that," she told him, leaning back against his hands to look him straight in the eyes. "I knew it soon after midnight, I think. I had not been able to sleep, I was so stiff and stretched with wondering if it was true that you loved me as a man should love a woman, not for yourself but for myself, and then suddenly I knew it was true, and I went to sleep as though knowing it were a mattress stuffed with real feathers."

It went through Charles's mind that her present mattress, which she had given him, was stuffed with bracken. And what was she sleeping on meanwhile? A blanket on hard wood? "Do I love you for yourself and not myself?" he asked her. "Is love ever as selfless as that?"

"Yours was last night."

Yes, that was true, he thought. Last night he had wanted for sheer love of her to do what would make her happy and had not remembered until now, when he felt the steel of her in his arms, that if he wished to have her he would have to do so in her way since her will was stronger than his.

"Now listen," said Lucy. "I have much to tell you."

"Come inside, down to our own place. Have you brought me anything to eat?"

"No. There was no time. You must learn to do without food occasionally. You may be on the run one day and you should learn to starve."

They went down to the kitchen and sat on the floor beside the hearth. A glow of warmth still came from the ashes of the fire Charles had kept going through a sleepless night, and it comforted them like the glow of the new trust in each other they felt now that they had taken their decision.

"My father was very angry when I got in last night," said Lucy. "I was too late back, he said."

"What did *you* say?"

"The truth. That I had borrowed Iolo's boat to be with the seals. That is the sort of thing I would do and he accepted that. I will not tell lies to my father and so we must be married tomorrow."

"Is your father going away?"

"He went early this morning to Haverfordwest for perhaps two or three nights. We have an old cousin who lives there and my father very often visits him, for he loves him, and last night a message came to say that he was dying and asking for my father."

"So we can get married without telling lies to your father. You will tell him afterwards?"

"Of course. As soon as he gets back."

"Will your new Puritan parson agree to marry us?"

"That man!" cried Lucy in scorn. "I would sooner be married by the devil himself. No. If we cannot be married by Parson Peregrine then Old Parson shall marry us. You do not know about him. I will tell you."

She told him and they made their plans, very seriously and soberly, and Lucy had no doubt at all of the legality of what they were doing. They had passed the age of fourteen, the age of consent, and would be married by a real priest in a real church, with a real notary present. Charles, while he was being watched, would sign the church register and the marriage certificate with the name of Tomos Barlow, but later he would write his own name beneath that of Tomos. Today they had their preparations to make. Charles must ride to St. Davids to make arrangements with the notary who lived there. He could be a troublesome man, Lucy had heard, because he sometimes drank more than was good for him, but she hoped that a couple of gold pieces from the purse her step-grandfather had given her would make him not too difficult to deal with. And he must bring his clerk with him, Lucy impressed upon Charles, because she had heard there must be two witnesses present at a marriage. They would be married very early in the morning so that no one should see them. She concocted the story that must be told to the notary. Lucy and Tomos had been promised to each other from childhood by the wish of their respective parents as well as their own, and now that Tomos had escaped from prison Lucy could not face another parting from him unless they were married. Her father was away but when he came back he would understand her feelings and not be angry.

Charles thought it sounded a childish sort of story and remembered that the lies of those unaccustomed to dishonesty are invariably puerile; he hoped the notary would be drunk enough to swallow it. And he also doubted the legality of what they proposed to do but he did not tell her so; if it turned out later that there had been a hitch somewhere then they would be married again.

"You must tell exactly the same story to your Old Parson," he said to Lucy.

"No!" she cried in sudden distress. "I must tell the truth to Old Parson!"

"Are you mad, Lucy? He gets confused in his head, you said, and he might give me away to the other parson, the Puritan."

She was silent, for he was right. She had a sensation of panic, and then of helplessness, as though the dark web was starting to tangle about her. She jumped up quickly to get rid of it. They were doing what was right, she insisted to herself, and sometimes to do right one had to do a little wrong. She had heard people say that. One had sometimes to tell a lie for kindness' sake, and it would be kinder to Old Parson not to tell him the truth. But she was not entirely happy and she thought that Charles was not, for he pulled her to him and kissed her hard and a little desperately, as though to reassure them both.

"I will go and saddle the mare for you," she said. "Meet me in half an hour in that thicket of trees beyond the bridge."

She did not have to wait long for him but when he came he looked serious. "Two of the village men saw me and shouted after me to know who I was," he told her. "I did as you said I should do; said nothing and grinned like a village idiot. I had better not come back from St. Davids till after dusk."

"I will be waiting at the castle for you," she answered.

She watched him ride away and then went straight to the mill to find Old Parson. She was met by Damaris, who told her that the old man was better now but not himself. Lucy found him sitting at the door of his little room, where it was shady and he could hear the hum of his bees, and when they had talked for a few minutes she realized that his new clarity had for the moment deserted him. He was very muddled indeed and at first she thought that would make her task easier, for when he was muddled he was usually obedient. But he was not entirely so this morning. She was able to convince him of the truth of the story of Tomos, but she could not convince him that it was right that he should marry her when her father was away. "I will have no hand in it if your father is not present," he said over and over again. Nor would he marry her without the consent of the present parish priest. "You will go now, maid, and ask Parson Gryg for his permission."

To pacify him she did so. And perhaps, she thought, that was legal and right. The burnt-out parsonage had not been rebuilt yet and the new parson lived at a cottage a half mile from the church. As she walked there she had to rearrange the story of Tomos for he could not now be a Royalist. He must be a Puritan or he might be denounced. She had quite a likely story fixed up by the time she found herself sitting opposite Parson Gryg in his kitchen, but she found his grey eyes penetrating and increasingly she hated her own lies. The mocking spirit had been muttering inside her all the morning, and he now reared his head and suggested nastily that if she had let Charles have her without her marriage lines she might have been less dishonest in the long run. But then what of her promise to Nan-Nan? she asked him. If she had broken that it would have been the worst dishonesty of all. And she had been brought up to keep the ten commandments. How could she, he asked? The third and the ninth both referred to lying, so if she kept seven she would break three and nine. With a sense of hopelessness she pushed him down out of hearing and managed with great skill and charm to convey to Parson Gryg, without actually saying so in words, that the marriage was not to take place immediately. It was just that Old Parson wanted the permission of the parish priest before they went further with their plans. Parson Gryg gave it, but he was surprised, he said, though gratified, to find the Walter family allying themselves with the Puritan persuasion.

"When you love someone politics, and different thoughts about religion, do not matter," Lucy explained.

"At your age it is natural to think so," Parson Gryg

answered, "and it is my hope, Mistress Lucy, that you will reap only happiness from your decision."

He was not a bad man, she thought, as she walked home to get Dewi's dinner, and there had been kindness in his eyes as well as that sharpness.

In the afternoon she went back to Old Parson with the news of Parson Gryg's permission, and also with the worst lie of the whole day. Her father, she said, had come home unexpectedly and would be there in the morning. Instantly Old Parson was reassured. Yes, he said, he would be there at the time appointed, early though it was, and he would not bring Damaris for he realized that secrecy was the only way to protect Tomos. He was entirely happy now and delighted that it should be he who was to marry Lucy.

At dusk she was in the castle garden waiting for Charles and the quietness brought peace. And tomorrow Charles would be her husband. She realized it suddenly and the anxious, hot, dishonest day seemed to disappear behind her like a stone dropped into a pool of water. That the pool of the past always dries up in the end, leaving one to reckon with what lies at the bottom, she knew, but she let the knowledge drop also, so that the surface of the pool mirrored nothing but quietness. In the silence she heard the hoofs of the tired mare clip clopping up the hill and it was one of the best moments of her life. But all she could find to say when he was with her was, "I have brought you more food and it's in the kitchen. Has it gone well with the notary?"

"He was fuddled enough to swallow every word of your story, and he accepted a gold piece with a promise of another tomorrow. And I gave another to the clerk who will have to get him here on time. There will not be much left in your purse, dear heart, by the time we are safely married." He laughed his great laugh. "This must be the first time in English history that the heir to the throne has had his wedding paid for by his bride. I should be ashamed if it were not so comic."

"It is good for King Corphetua," said Lucy. "It will teach him not to get his wallet stolen." She broke off abruptly as a sudden thought struck her. "We have no ring! That is the most important thing of all and we have forgotten it."

"No," said Charles. "I have a ring my father gave me that I always wear. When I came to find you I hung it round my neck on a cord, for I could not leave it behind. It is part of me."

"Can you bear to give it to me?"

"I have given it to you already, when I gave myself in the Valley of Roses. You will see it tomorrow."

"Thank you," said Lucy simply. "I am going now for I have so much to do at home. I will send Dewi to wake you in the morning. It would be dreadful if you overslept."

"You are telling Dewi?" asked Charles, astonished.

"In the morning. I cannot have my father so I must have a brother with me. I wish it was Justus, but I love Dewi."

She spoke a little sadly but he knew she was not unhappy. She was not a woman who would ever waste her time longing for the impossible perfections when the imperfections of this life could be so unbelievably lovely.

Five

Early the next morning, while the hot day was still tempered by the sea's cool breath, Lucy and Old Parson went up the hill together, and Lucy told her last lie. Her father had developed a fever and could not be with them.

"The same fever that you had. It seems an intemperance that this hot weather brings."

Old Parson accepted this. He found himself very serene this morning, weak after his illness and not able to think or remember clearly, but serene. He had read the marriage service carefully in the Perrot family prayer book, he had the book with him and knew what he must say. He was wearing his black gown. His mind fumbled at what Lucy had said and arrived at a peaceful conclusion. "Then, my child, I must be to you father as well as priest."

"Thank you," said Lucy, "That is just what I want. My father and I will always be grateful to you."

They had nearly reached the top of the hill and she looked up just as two punctual figures came out of the castle lane and turned towards the church, Charles striding quickly, tall and straight, Dewi running at his heels like a small esquire. A gush of joy broke over her and she laughed as she said to Old Parson, "Look sir! There he is. There is Tomos."

Old Parson blinked feebly as the couple swung round the corner and disappeared. "The young travel so fast, my dear," he said. "One scarcely sees them. I wish the young did not travel so fast. It bewilders me."

They in their turn turned the corner and Lucy saw two horses tied at the lych-gate. So the notary and his clerk were there already. The church was not locked in these days since it was stripped bare and there was nothing to steal. And how bare this royal wedding was stripped! But she did not mind since she was being married at Roch, in the church where she had been baptized, and the music of birds and leaves talking together in the arching boughs above her head, as she walked through the churchyard, was all the music she wanted. "Father, Mother, Justus and Nan-Nan," she whispered to herself as she came into the porch, and she felt a great pang. But they were here in her heart, she told herself.

Charles was waiting just inside for her, by the old low font. He had got used to seeing her dressed as a boy and it startled him to see how tall she looked in the long sea-green gown, pearls in her ears and her hair tidier than he had yet seen it. There was no girl in the world, he thought at this moment, so fit to be a queen. He took her hand and led her up the church to the chancel steps, Old Parson and Dewi following placidly behind them. The church was full of cool emptiness and the shimmer of early sunshine. There was something about this wedding, some quality of stillness and order, that awed the notary and his clerk to unobtrusiveness, and Charles and Lucy hardly noticed them where they stood by the pulpit. Old Parson stumbled placidly through the service, prompted here and there by Lucy, the vows were spoken and the ring with its dark ruby glowed on Lucy's finger. It caught the sunshine like fire.

In the vestry, at the signing of the register and the marriage certificate, the notary pulled himself together and endeavoured to be facetious, but was silenced and bewildered by the extraordinary dignity of the young bridegroom, and the shining beauty of the girl. Moving in her own world she yet seemed to wish that her light should grant blessing, like Hesperus at the first hour of eve. She smiled upon the four men, and had indeed been in control of them throughout the strange little ceremony, but in her starry world there was actually only the one. Yet with grave friendliness she led the notary and his clerk out to the churchyard to show them the beauty of it, so enchanting them that it did not strike them as odd that the bridegroom should stay behind in the vestry. For the notary the whole thing had by this time taken on something of the progression of a dream; all but the gold pieces upon which his hand was clamped in his pocket. They were real enough, but so in a queer way was the dream. As he rode away he was still enclosed in it, and disturbed by it, as though some door in his own being, long closed, had been wrenched open again. But his dim eyes allowed him no vision and his confused memory, groping back to his childhood, could not find what it groped for. It took a few days of familiar routine, and much good ale, before he could shake off the vague sadness and confusion engendered in him by the beauty of that early morning wedding in a bare church.

And for the rest of that day Old Parson was even more confused. He sat at the door of his little room and his hands trembled on his knees. It had been a dream of beauty but what had been his part in it? What had been the actual meaning of his priestly action? He tried to think but the mere physical exertion of the morning had been too much for him, and by the evening he had a fever again and the dream was lost in the mists of his imaginings.

2

Lucy woke first and looked straight up through the great rent in the ceiling to the sky at dawning. It had been her wish that she and Charles should spend their wedding night in her parents' great bedchamber, though what was left of the ceiling was likely to drop on them at any moment and the floor was littered with the fallen stones of the tower. The fourposter was more or less intact and no harder than the kitchen floor when spread with blankets. To sleep here had seemed to Lucy an act of reparation to her father, and since Nan-Nan had said that her mother and father must always be held together in her love, to her mother too. They had been excluded from her wedding day but they should have a link with her wedding night. Where they, in the early happier days of their marriage, had lain and loved, she and Charles would also lie, and in the very depths of her bliss last night she had not forgotten them.

It was not a flaming dawn, it was pale silver, and so still that the sleepy birds in the garden seemed murmuring at her very ear. But she could not hear the sea and she knew it must be lying still as a polished shield, as still as she and Charles had been lying for the past few hours, only their breasts moving as they breathed, as the sea's breast had moved all night.

She lifted herself on her elbow and looked down at her husband's dark face. He lay as she had so often seen Dewi lie, on his back with one arm behind his head on the pillow, his lashes dark on his cheeks, relaxed and defenceless in sleep, young as a fledgling. Was this a man she had married, or a child? He seemed remote from her in the mystery of his being and his sleep, and yet she was now bone of his bone and she had no existence apart from him. Down through her body to her mind and soul she had taken the stamp of this man, as though a seal had been pressed on soft wax. She had thought, when the whole of her had seemed to go out to him in the Valley of Roses, that she had given all she had. She had been wrong. She had given more last night because she had also taken. She knew now that no giving is greater than when it is mutual, since to be able to take deepens the power to give. Her eyes on his face would always bring Charles back to awareness of her. He opened his own eyes and looked up into the deep blue of hers. A slow grin spread over his face. Then something wet fell on his cheek.

"Lucy! What are you crying for? What weepers you Welsh can be."

"O Dduw, y mae yr hapusrwydd yma yn ormod yw ddal. Dear God, this happiness is too great for me to bear," Lucy murmured.

She spoke only in Welsh and he did not understand her, but he did not just then ask her the meaning of what she said for the strange sonorous phrase seemed to express so perfectly the shock of joy that each had experienced as he returned to her from his deep sleep.

"Did you sleep?" he asked.

"I slept like a bee sipping honey. I would drop into the sweetness of it for a little while but I would have to come up again to the sun; to my husband warm and alive beside me." She sank down again to her pillow and lay beside him, her hand feeling for his. "I do not think Dewi woke all night. I did not hear him."

She had not wanted Dewi to spend the night alone at the cottage and they had brought up her little bracken-stuffed mattress and laid it on the dais not far from their door.

"I like Dewi," said Charles.

"Nan-Nan said you would."

"Nan-Nan! But she never knew me."

"She had a 'seeing' one day and said that Dewi would be beloved of a king." A sudden thought struck her and she raised herself on an elbow and gazed at Charles with shining eyes. "So you *will* be king! Nothing dreadful will happen to you. I never thought of that before. Why did I not remember Nan-Nan's 'seeing' when I felt anxious about you?"

Charles opened his mouth to say that Nan-Nan might have been referring to another king but thought better of it because Lucy was so full of relief and joy. He said instead, gazing up at the sky, "Why has it not hung out its banners for us?"

"The weather is on the change," said Lucy. "I think I am glad. I would like us to stand on the cliff together when there is a gale blowing from the sea. We must do that before you go." She paused, her voice catching. "Charles! You cannot go! You cannot!" Her few waking tears had been as nothing to the storm that broke now as she clung to him and sobbed her heart out. "Now look, Lucy," he implored, "I did not come all this way, I did not marry you, to be drenched to the skin on the very first morning of my married life. Stop it, Lucy."

He was annoyed and she struggled to stop crying. The Welsh cried easily, the English did not. She was English herself now and she must not annoy her husband. She held up her hand, looking at the beautiful ring, and the tears in her eyes splintered the ruby into a five-pointed star of flame.

"It is beautiful," she murmured, "and so different from the first."

"The first?" demanded Charles sharply. "The first what?"

"The first ring," said Lucy. "I have been married before, you know."

Charles had only just emerged from sleep and was in no state to receive a profound shock. He sat up like a jack-in-the-box, leaned over and pinned her down in the bed with all his strength, his hands pressing hard upon her shoulders. She gloried in the power of his grip, though she was sure her shoulders would be bruised for weeks to come. She smiled fearlessly up at him and did not move. "I was married to a bird," she said.

"A bird!" he ejaculated, his fingers biting more deeply into her shoulders, his bewilderment profound. Her eyes were sparkling with teasing mischief now, yet the wet track of tears still ran back from the corners of them to lose itself in the cloud of dark hair on the pillow. She was enough to drive a man mad, he thought, with her bewildering changes of mood. But how lovely she was even with her hair in a tangle and her face tear-streaked; shed tears made her eyes more intensely blue and the tangled hair lay in a pool of darkness that turned her face into a floating flower. He must be hurting her but her smiling mouth would not acknowledge hurt. He bent over and kissed it, and the hollow at the base of her neck, and the tear-damp patches in front of her ears. "Could you tell me about this goddam bird?" he asked humbly.

Because it had meant so much to her she was shy as she told him of the migration that the storm had halted, and the small birds dropping from the sky like autumn leaves. "It felt so strange, his claw round my finger just for the moment like that. It married me for ever to all wild things, birds and morlos and the field mice in the hedges."

"Do you remember when we ate blackberries together in the wood?" he asked her. "I would like to see you again with blackberry-stained lips, for they suited the gipsy in you."

"I love the true wildness," she told him. "The winged part of a man or woman beats against conformity like a bird against the bars of its cage. I think that people who do not sometimes bruise their wings are not truly alive. You will not mind if I go wild sometimes?"

"I will never mind," he promised. "I will always love you as you are."

It was to be a poignant day. and the first stab of poignancy came after they had dressed, and removed the battered remains of a door that had closed their room through the night, and found themselves looking down upon Dewi lying asleep at their feet. Lucy had laid his mattress against the wall but he had pulled it across the threshold that he might guard them. He lay curled up like a puppy and beside him was a stick that he had found in the kitchen. Charles had wondered if it was safe to entrust Dewi with the knowledge of his presence at Roch, for the little boy had ridden with him at Exeter and knew who he was, but Lucy had said Dewi was as trustworthy as her brother Justus and Charles believed her now.

"Dewi! Dewi!" whispered Lucy, and then to Charles, "He will serve you well one day."

Charles bent down and picked the little boy up in his arms. Carrying the child they went down into the kitchen that was home to light the fire and draw the water from the well.

3

The great heat was past and the day was clouded and cool. The weather was changing not with the cataclysm of a thunderstorm but with the gentle movement of a drifting leaf, and in spite of the singing joy in their hearts, that created an island of immunity all about them, Charles and Lucy were aware of a distant sadness. It was at the rim of the wheel of the world and they were safe at the heart where no harm could touch them, for the wheel had lost its spokes. Yet in spite of this safety they were reluctant to leave the castle and to part from each other for even a bare half-hour seemed impossible. Yet Lucy and Dewi must go back to the cottage and see that all was in order there, for William might come back at any time. Besides, they had finished all their food at breakfast and if there were men who could live on love alone Charles was not one of them. It was already mid morning by the time he and Lucy could bring themselves to say goodbye in the castle garden, and even then Charles had to come with them up the lane and out to the road where he stood to watch them go.

Lucy applied herself to baking and scouring while Dewi went fishing in Brandy Brook. Sea fishing was not yet for him, though he hoped to attain to it, but hanging over the bridge with a bent pin on the end of his line kept him happy for hours whether he caught any minnows or whether he didn't. The water rippling under the bridge fascinated him and he could watch for the kingfisher. Presently Lucy joined him with a bit of bara ceich warm from the baking and while he munched she too leaned on the balustrade to watch for the kingfisher. The hollow by the stream still held the warmth of yesterday and she was so drowsy with her bliss that it was Dewi who heard the horses' hoofs first. "Look!" he shouted to her.

There were three horsemen riding down the hill, William and his two sons.

"Justus!" gasped Lucy. "Richard!"

She could not believe her eyes. She did not even know that she moved, only presently she was a little way up the hill and Justus was in her arms. And then, with surprising gladness, she was in Richard's, and then in her father's, laughing and crying together in a state that was half ecstasy and half nightmare. She had not yet really faced the meeting with her father, and now she had two brothers on her hands as well. It did not seem true. It could not be true and yet it was, and presently she found that the horses had been stabled at the mill and they were going down through the wood together, William and his four children. She hardly heard the happy excited talk that buzzed about her ears, but she did know that Justus had his hand through her arm, holding it against his side with a man's strength. Yet when she looked sideways at him he was still a boy, a stocky fourteen-year-old, and just the same. It was Richard who was the man, tall and self-assured, with all his mother's beauty. For some reason that she was too bewildered even to try to fathom she was at first afraid to look at him, yet when she did look his smile met hers with charm and friendliness.

"They overtook me," William was saying with incoherent delight. "I had not left Haverfordwest a couple of miles behind before they overtook me on the road. My sons."

"Has Cousin Llewellyn died?" Lucy heard herself asking

"Who? Llewellyn? Last night. Poor fellow. My two sons, Lucy! Overtook me on the road home. It was Richard who thought of coming to visit us. It was Richard thought of it."

Lucy realized that he was almost stupified with joy. The son he had thought lost was home again. "For this my son was dead and is alive again, was lost and is found." A sort of weeping started up inside her. Richard had brought this joy to their father but what was she going to bring him? Not shame, she had spared him that, but at the very first sight of his face as he rode down the hill she had known it would not be happiness. She had been drifting on a sea of joy and had let the tide carry her whither it would, but now the shore was rocky. She and Charles had seemed immune in bliss only a short while ago but it had been a false immunity, and now they were united once more with the sorrow of the world.

Yet she played her part and in the cottage, as her brothers devoured the food she had prepared for Charles, her loving welcome was all that Justus had longed for and Richard had expected.

"Justus had put his eyes out over his law books, and I found myself temporarily out of employment," he said. "I have, as perhaps you know, been working as secretary to a certain noble lord, a member of the government, who has died, God rest his soul, and it seemed a good opportunity for us both to take a holiday and come and see you and my father. It has been a difficult journey but well worth every effort to see you both so blooming."

He paused, crossing one elegant leg over the other, and smiled at his sister, whose adult beauty he found both astonishing and gratifying; positively Bud had developed into a sister to be cultivated. She was equally astonished by the change in him. In the past he had not been much of a talker, preferring to listen cynically to other people making fools of themselves rather than risk anything of the sort himself, but now he talked easily and with charm. But not, she thought, out of genuine friendliness, for his fine eyes had still their old coldness. He was still Richard, not really the stuff of which prodigal sons are made. Why had he come, she wondered? Then she returned his smile with a rush of grateful affection, for he had made their father happy ... And she must make him unhappy ... Abruptly she turned her face towards the open door and the sea, afraid that Richard would read in it the mingled joy and dread that were tearing her apart.

"Could we go now, sir?" It was Justus speaking to his father. His endearing homeliness was now intensified by the fact that his voice was breaking. Its alternate squeaks and organ notes were making William laugh, and as Justus never minded being laughed at he was laughing himself; and a further sign of his maturity was the deep warm chuckling laugh he was developing. Then he and his father suddenly sobered. "I have been thinking of it all the way home; next after you and Lucy and Dewi. Well, it is home, whatever has happened to it now."

"You will have a shock when you go inside," his father warned him.

"Let us go now!" Justus pleaded.

"No!" Lucy cried in panic, swinging round to them. "No, sir. No, Justus. Not to the castle. Not yet. I must talk to my father first, and you and Richard shall know later. But my father first. Please, sir, I would talk to you alone."

They had finished their meal and Richard instantly got up, suave and a little mocking. "My very beautiful sister, I have been wondering for some while who gave you that handsome ring. Justus and I will go down to the beach. When you are ready to receive our congratulations, shout."

Justus, as unobservant as his father of such matters, had not noticed the ring. He gazed at it for a moment, astonished, and then as he followed Richard gripped Lucy's hand without looking at her. It was no longer a little boy's hand, slipping into hers for protection, but a man's hand giving her re-assurance. Yet it felt rough as always, for Justus never bothered to dry his hands properly. He had not changed. Because of him she could turn to face her father in control of herself, and not weep at sight of his suddenly old and stricken face. "I am married," she whispered to him, her arms round his neck. "Do not you know that I would never disgrace you?"

It was one of the worst half-hours of her life for she could not understand the depth of his anger and grief. That her deception and secrecy should distress him was not surprising, for there had never been anything but honesty between them, but even more it was the mere fact of what she had done that overwhelmed him with anger. And what *had* she done, she asked him at last? Married a good man in honest wedlock, and he was behaving as though she had become the mistress of a thief or mountebank. Did it make so much difference that he was a prince? Were they not fighting a vile civil war? Charles might be dead in a month. Her voice broke and William braced himself for the expected storm of tears, but it did not come, and by this he knew the depth of Bud's hurt. She had never cried when he whipped her.

There was a long silence while he struggled with himself and then he said gently, "Well, Bud, what's done is done. I can only pray for your happiness. We are, as you say, at war, and can only live for the day. But Bud, Bud, I looked to see you the wife of some country gentleman of our own walk in life, secure and comfortable in a life you know."

He broke off, for she was in his arms, and beginning to cry a little. "You do not know Charles," she said through her tears. "You do not know what he is. The dearest and the best. Will you come now and see him?"

"No, Bud, no!" poor William said in horror. "He does not know I am here. You go now and tell him of my coming and then let me know his wishes. I am stunned, Bud. I cannot get my bearings at all."

"You will tell my brothers?" asked Lucy.

"I will tell them."

She left him and climbed the hill to the castle. Why must her father spoil it all with his distress? Why could he not see that she and Charles hated the dishonesty and secrecy of what they had done as much as he did, but had not been able to help themselves? Why could he not rejoice with her in the glory of this happiness? Why must parents always be so difficult? At their ages, poor things, she thought, they lacked courage and

hope in the future. They had lost the power to step out bravely. But they must know they were like this so why could they
not put their trust in their children?

In the garden she found Charles weeding, and Dewi with
him. She had not realized that Dewi had left the family party,
but she remembered now that he always absented himself at
the first hint of family disagreement; especially if the food had
already been finished. He disliked fracas unless he was himself
the centre of it and had scampered off to his hero Charles.

"Dear heart, Dewi has told me," said Charles straightening
himself. "I am very sorry."

"My father is very distressed. What shall we do?"

"Is he very angry with me?"

"No. I do not think so. But he would not come with me to
see you. He asked me to discover your wishes first."

Charles had been trained from the cradle to the tactful
smoothing out of difficulties and rubbing his earthy hands up
and down his shabby breeches he considered this one. "We
will ask your father and brothers to our wedding feast," he
said. "Dewi shall take the message now and you and I will go
down to the mill and collect some food for it."

"Not you," said Lucy.

"Yes. The village know I am here now. You remember I
stood out in the road this morning to watch you go down the
hill? When I turned back again there were two men coming
from the direction of the church. Good-looking men, not villagers, but evidently at home on their own ground. I saluted
them and came back into the garden. They looked dumbfounded but they did not follow me; I think they had seen me
waving to you."

"They were Howell and Owen Perrot," said Lucy. "Owen is
my father's bailiff and they live at the mill." She smiled.
"Well, Tomos can now go free."

She was pleased, she found, and so was Charles, for they
were relieved of some of the pretence. They went down the hill
together with clasped hands swinging and Dewi strutting in
front like a bantam cock. It was with tremendous pride that
Lucy presented her husband Tomos Barlow to the family at

the mill, but they were not so surprised as she had thought they would be. Damaris knew very well all that happened on the road beyond her home for she had a species of second sight that brought her to the window, or out into the garden, the moment there was anything to be observed. She had seen the notary and his clerk riding by and she had seen Old Parson leave the house and Lucy waiting for him. She had seen the notary and his clerk riding by again, and the return of Old Parson, and the reappearance of Old Parson's fever had needed accounting for too. She knew there had been a wedding and when her husband and his brother had told her of the tall dark young man skulking in the castle garden she had merely remarked, "Fancy!" Confronted with Tomos she was at first a little stiff because she had not been told before, but she fell quickly under his spell, rolled up her sleeves and ransacked her larder.

At the appointed hour the wind was rising, with the promise of rain in its chilliness, but the old kitchen looked capable of defying any kind of storm or sorrow. A log fire was blazing and the candles Damaris had given them were alight on the table and dresser. There was good food and two bottles of home-brewed wine, and Lucy had picked an armful of traveller's joy and honeysuckle starred with red berries to soften the stony places with feathery snow and royal crimson. Dewi was sent running through the wind down to the cove to fetch the guests when all was ready, and Charles and Lucy were standing in the hall to welcome them when William and his sons came up the steps. For a moment Lucy was surprised to see that her father and Richard and Justus were wearing their swords, and then she remembered the old ceremony of loyalty that was to come and she smiled with a great breath of relief, realizing that her father had himself in hand and was ready to play his part. Without a glance at her he pulled off his cloak and stepped forward to kiss the prince's hand. But Charles forestalled him. In a flash he was kneeling before his father-in-law to ask his blessing.

It was a good beginning and a feeling of ease and timelessness fell upon them all as they sat together round the old table beside the well. Even William, though his nagging anxiety was very precariously battened down, relaxed and let a gentle glow of pride take slow possession of him. For Bud in her radiant happiness was looking more lovely than he had ever seen her, and was it a small thing that she had won the love of a prince? Had he not reason for pride as well as anxiety? And that her husband loved her he had no doubt. Charles was intent on bringing reassurance and happiness to his father and brothers-in-law but his dark eyes always came back to Lucy, and whenever he looked at her his face lit up in a way to which William's heart responded with a lurch of sympathy. What else could any young man have done? Not to have followed Bud would have called for a resolution of which only maturity could have been capable. At his age I would have done the same, thought William, and under the influence of his son-in-law's charm, and the warmth, and the wine brewed by Damaris from wild mountain raspberries, he began to melt into a state almost bordering on happiness.

Justus took longer to melt. Knowing his brother he could not believe Richard had undertaken a dangerous journey out of family affection alone. Richard declared that he had no politics but his late employer had been a member of the Puritan government. What was Richard doing in Wales? Was he a danger to the prince? At the moment Justus thought he was not. Until the war was actually over, he had said upon the journey, one could not rule out a final swing of the pendulum. A Parliamentary victory now seemed certain but dying fires could spring into life again. One must remember that, he had said. He was remembering it, Justus thought and hoped, and regarding the heir to the throne as a secret investment that might yet prove useful. Justus too, like his father, began to feel happier. He lifted his dormouse head and said to William, "Sir, we never thought we should all dine together again under our own roof. And with the Prince as our guest." He paused and smiled shyly at Charles. "It is a marvel."

The meal was finished and they rose to their feet. William filled the largest of the horn cups with the last of the wine and the men drew their swords. Dewi had no sword but he grabbed a knife instead. In a large assembly it was the custom as the cup was passed round the circle for two men at a time to stand while the health was drunk, so that each man as he lifted the heavy two-handled cup was defended by his neighbour, who stood beside him with raised sword. But with the Prince present, though the swords were raised turn by turn, they all stood. "I am sorry, sir," said William, "That we must drink to His Majesty from a horn cup. It should have been my very best silver standing cup but my silver was taken from me." Then he gave the toast, "The King". They drank it in silence and Charles as he drank to his father was defended by William's sword, and Lucy stood upon his other side.

"The Prince," said Richard, and they drank again. Charles glanced from one to the other and for a moment he saw these people as they might have been, standing on the dais of the great hall, their beautiful roof sound and strong over their heads, the long table gleaming with the silver cups and dishes. And now they stood in an old smoke-grimed kitchen, and above was the desolate hall, the roof open to the sky and the wind moaning through the empty windows and rustling the dead leaves on the floor. And they must drink to his father from a horn cup and receive into their family a prince who had nothing to bring them but added anxiety, more sorrow, increased poverty. That for a moment was how he saw it and he was speechless, unaware of the tears on his face until he felt Lucy's hand in his and knew it was there for comfort's sake. He looked round at the one girl of the party and saw her radiant, her blue eyes alight with encouragement and hope.

"The bride and bridegroom," said Justus, his voice beginning as a frog's croak and ending in a falsetto squeak. The comedy of it broke the tension and they dissolved into laughter. When it was found that there was no more wine and they could not drink the toast the young ones were laughing too much to be disturbed. But William minded that there was no wine left in which to drink to Bud's happiness.

Afterwards Lucy fetched the flute and the guitar, all that was left now of the family treasure, and they sat before the fire and made music. Giving himself to the enchanting of his new relatives, and changing from the flute to the guitar that was his favourite musical instrument, Charles sang one of the songs that in happy days they had sung at Whitehall. His voice was not very sure of itself yet but it was a musicianly performance. Listening to him, trying to glean some knowledge of the boy who now had Bud's happiness in the hollow of his hand, William remembered that evening in London when the guards had been out to protect the palace and he had worried about the safety of the royal children. The boy now singing was one of the children. How closely human lives were interwoven one with another, and also, it seemed to him at that moment, wonderfully. He was aware of wonder in the air and it comforted him. The wonder of first love, the wonder of music and the flames on the hearth. Wonder was a most comforting thing. It bore witness to realities beyond human understanding, even to the supreme reality that controlled the end.

"Your turn, Father." Too much ale had impaired the fine tenor voice William had once possessed, but he could still play the flute like a master and he played the airs of old Welsh dances until he had the feet of his children tapping on the floor.

But it was Richard who brought the evening to a climax. He had inherited his father's voice, though no one had known it until tonight. Nor had anyone known that he cared enough for the songs of Wales to have committed *The Grove of Broom* to memory. Yet he had, and with apologies to Charles because the girl's hair was the wrong colour, he sang the golden song with a perfection to match its own. "I will remember him like this always," Lucy thought to herself. "Whatever happens afterwards I will remember him like this."

> *There for me and my sweetheart*
> *Is life, a fresh saffron field.*
> *I've a house, a good dwelling*
> *Made of Arabian gold.*
> *Tent of the firmament's Lord,*
> *Cloth of gold, the roof's speckled;*
> *A fair angel of heaven*

Embroidered it for May's bed:
Gold gossamer, wondrous bees,
God's glow-worms, gems of sunlight.
What bliss, on the vine-clad hill
To have the young twigs gilded,
And the tips of bushes seen
Like the stars, golden bullion.

Thus have I, all one colour,
Flowers of May like small birds.
What a joyful thing it is,
The grove veiled like an angel!
I keep the grove and the glade,
Fine custom, for my sweetheart.
My bond's good, I'll not go from
The grove with its gold-speckled veil
Without, this summer, one tryst,
Gold-haired girl in the greenwood.
Let her come, where none part us,
Fair slim girl, beneath fresh broom.

Into the silence there came a rush of wind, the flames of the fire staggered and Dewi, who had been curled up on the hearth fast asleep for the last half-hour, woke up and with his fists stuck in his eyes began to whimper. He had been dreaming that something was after him and the rush of the wind had been like a pounce. They picked him up and comforted him, but their hour of harmony was over and William rose wearily to his feet and turned to Charles. "Son, you must be gone tomorrow. It is not safe for you to be here." Charles had smiled in delight that he had been called "son", but now panic wiped the smile from his face. Leave his fair slim girl after only two nights with her? No, begod! "No, sir! I cannot possibly go tomorrow."

"Too many people know about you, son. I have myself been looking at the register in the church and I may not have been the only one to do so. You have written Charles Stuart very firmly under the name of Tomos Barlow. I honour you for it

372

but I will not be responsible for your continued safety in a part of the world that is now in the hands of your enemies."

"I cannot go tomorrow," said Charles, "and I will not." He spoke with a touch of arrogance and William frowned. "I will not be responsible for your safety," he repeated.

"One more day," pleaded Lucy.

William shrugged his shoulders.

"I will stay two more days," Charles decided. "Only two. Will that satisfy you, sir?"

"Son, son!" said poor William, all his previous comfort gone from him, "I have little satisfaction in any of this business. Your will is your own, and royal. I can only obey."

They went silently up the stairs and found the great hall now booming in the wind and the rain falling in fierce slanting spears. It hurt Lucy to see her father and brothers huddle their cloaks about them and with the sleepy Dewi carried pickaback on Richard's shoulders go from their home into the stormy darkness. It was as though they went out of her life. But in five minutes she was in bliss again, as she and Charles ran laughing downstairs to the kitchen. Their bed must be made in front of the fire tonight for the great bed-chamber would be awash with rain.

4

The next day was walled about with rain and Charles and Lucy felt as protected by it as by the spears of a friendly army. After a morning visit from Justus no human being came near them, but Justus had been welcome in that he brought food and wine, and cloaks to protect them from the weather; for well he knew that Lucy would not stay indoors in a storm. He also brought the unwelcome news that William was making arrangements for his son-in-law to start his journey back to England on the day after tomorrow, and that was not so good. Yet when Justus disappeared again into the rain he seemed to take the unwelcome tidings with him, while the food and wine remained.

Until now Charles had looked upon bad weather as something to be endured until the sun shone again but today Lucy taught him to glory in it. The boom of the wind thrilled and awed her, as though some great master were playing the organ, and the elemental power of water, so dreadful when it was unleashed, was yet glorious to her because it was as much the source of life as the sun itself. "It is as though the sea were pouring in," she whispered happily to Charles, as they stood at the top of the kitchen steps and watched the rain drench into the roofless hall. It cascaded down the wide steps to the garden but not so much down the kitchen steps where the entry was narrow. "Our home is down at the bottom of the sea," she said contentedly. "It is Cantre'r Gwaelod. We live in Cantre'r Gwaelod."

"Explain to me," said Charles.

They went back to the kitchen again and sitting in front of the fire she told him about the town under the sea. "When I was a little girl I used to think I had come from there. When I was small I did not think I was really the child of my parents. I thought I had run away from one of the houses in Cantre'r Gwaelod, where people still lived, and that the sea had washed me up in castle bay, and I used to picture myself crawling up the sand on all fours like a crab because I was too small to walk, and that my father had found me there and carried me home in his arms. I thought that is why I love the sea so much and why I always have a feeling that I must return to the sea. Do you think that souls come back to this world again? Do you think I was once a little girl living in Cantre'r Gwaelod before the sea swallowed it?"

"I could believe any such tale about you," said Charles. "For you are an enchantress. And I like those old tales of earth men who fall in love with water maidens. Water is mysterious, and first love is so mysterious it is like rainbows in waterfalls, and the wonder world of jewelled fish and forests of swaying flowers that one sees down at the bottom of the sea. If I could have chosen my first love I would have chosen a maiden from the sea."

"And I would have chosen an earth prince with sunburnt

dusky skin and eyes like agate, and a laugh that makes me think of cornfields when Sirius dances in the sky, rich and golden corn. Was Sirius the star that shone when you were born?"

They went on talking nonsense until Charles said, "I am hungry. Are you?"

"You had a large breakfast," said Lucy, "and you cannot eat more till you have been out on the cliffs and down to the cove with me. Then we will come home and eat the pastan that Damaris made and drink the wine and make music."

Wrapped in their cloaks they fought their way to the cliff's edge and stood clinging together, leaning against the wind. All along the coast the waves were roaring in, line upon line of galloping horses with flying white manes. They were very powerful yet when they sprang upon the silent, motionless enemy they could make no progress. Every rock, every island, the whole great rampart of stone that defended the inland treasure of fields and valleys stood firm as iron. The islands were almost hidden at times by the tossing manes and moon-white bodies of the leaping horses, but they always fell back shattered. Their courage and beauty could gain no victory over the old crouching rocks.

"The sea was here first," Lucy called exultingly to Charles through the roar of the wind. "It was all the pasture of the white horses before the earth pushed up. And so it will be again."

He smiled but did not speak. He thought she was identifying the peerless white horses with goodness and truth, and the black rocks with evil, but with nature one could not press these parallels. The black rocks protected not only the fields and valleys but human life and love. They protected Lucy and himself. Nature was too wild a thing to let man bend her about in a chaplet of his own fantasy.

They went to the cove and here they looked not down at the waves but straight at them as they leaped and reared and crashed on the shore, flinging their great half-moon curves of shattered whiteness racing over the sand towards the human creatures, as though they flung a silver net to entrap them and drag them back to the sea from whence Lucy believed she had come.

But the human creatures did not want to go. They ran back laughing out of reach of the silver net, only to run back again to watch the next wave sailing in and try to see through the spray and rain a glimpse of the incredible blue-green of its arching throat. It was the blue of the sky and the green of the spring trees washed together. It was the colour of the green flash that is seen when the sun goes down below the rim of the sea. It was perhaps the colour that the dying speak of when they murmur of "the green peace".

They went back to the castle and feasted on the pastan and drank mulled wine, and for the rest of the day they were warm and contented in front of the fire, making music sometimes, and telling each other stories of their childhood. The tales were so utterly different, coming as they did from such contrasted lives, that they sounded like fairy stories to the one who listened. They spoke only of amusing things and often their laughter echoed in the kitchen's vaulted roof. Lucy loved the tales of Charles's tiny mother and her love of dogs and monkeys and dwarfs, and all creatures that were small and odd and different, as she was herself. "Jeffrey Hudson was my mother's favourite dwarf," said Charles. "Poor Jeffrey! We have lost him now. He shot a gentleman who insulted him and had to fly overseas. My mother cried when he went, he was so gentle and he never murdered people he liked. He was only nine years old when my mother first had him, and eighteen inches high. He came in a pie."

"A pie?" gasped Lucy. "I thought we said we would only tell each other true tales."

"This is a true tale. My lord of Buckingham, the father of those two boys who were with us in your unicorn wood, gave a banquet for my father and mother and a huge pie was brought in and set down upon the table, and when the crust was removed out came Jeffrey. But I never liked my mother's dwarfs so much as her Negro servants. I have always been very conscious that I alone of our family have this dark skin that comes from my mother's Spanish blood. "He is so ugly that I am

ashamed of him," she said when I was small. And so I have a
fellow feeling for the Africans and I liked their dark sad faces.
They had lived so near the sun in lands where the sun's heat
can kill that they had the shadow of death upon their faces. At
least when I was a child I thought that was why they were so
sad. Perhaps they had other reasons."

"They were homesick," said Lucy compassionately. "And
there was the wind and the rain. What was that song Will
Shakespeare wrote? Hey ho the wind and the rain."

Charles sang it to her with the distant music of the storm as
accompaniment. The dying cadences still echoed in their ears
when they fell asleep that night beside the fire, but when Lucy
woke in the dead of night there was no sound, and she saw a
star in the window.

The next day was so different it was hard to think they lived
it out in the same world. There was no rain to protect them, no
bombardment of the wind. For all its length the day was grey,
cool and quiet, and the rain-washed distances opened out to
long perspectives of sea, sky and mountains, speaking of parting and of time.

The quiet was with them even in the first moment of
waking, so that they turned into each other's arms not with
the laughing delight of the morning before but silently,
trying, since silence alone seemed possible, to give each other
strength through the mere fact of it. There is no emptiness in
silence, they thought. Neither a windless dawn nor the silence
when one can find no words to speak are empty. Outside is the
growing light, the air becoming warmer, and when one cannot
speak silence need not be empty of love. So, wordlessly, they
strengthened each other and then went about the business
of the day, lighting the fire, getting their breakfast and washing the plates and dishes with the water that Charles drew
from the well.

But the same thoughts persisted and presently Charles said,
"There is something that John Donne wrote. I may not remember it quite rightly but I think it went like this. He said
that two lutes, being both strung and tuned to an equal pitch,
and then one played upon, the other laid upon a table at a fit

distance, the second will, like echo to a trumpet, warble a faint audible harmony in answer to the same tune, yet many, he said, will not believe that there is any such thing as the sympathy of souls. We will be like that, Lucy. Even though many miles part us we will learn to call music from each other."

Lucy pondered this. "What sort of music?"

"Remembrance and trust. We will remember our love and trust each other. It may be a short time that we are parted, it may be a long time, but I will never forget you and I will send for you to be with me as soon as I can."

"However short the time is it will seem long," said Lucy. She seemed in no danger of weeping but she was quieter than he had ever known her and there was a heavy dullness upon her. He realized that she was bewildered. This parting which was creeping nearer seemed an impossible thing. They had been able to forget it yesterday but they could not today. She folded up the blankets and found that the housekeeping tasks were ended. There was nothing more that she could do so she had better say something. She struggled with herself and managed a few sentences. "My grandmother took me to St. Paul's Cathedral and the choir sang a hymn John Donne had written. And we saw his effigy. He did not look a happy man. But then he was supposed to be dead. He had his graveclothes on."

Suddenly Charles laughed, for her precise and dismal tones became her so badly that they were an absurdity. "And we are alive!" he cried to her. "Alive and in the same world."

"The same green star," said Lucy, and her cheerfulness leaped up again. "Green fields and green woods, and sometimes the sea is green as spring wheat. If you have to go beyond the sea then when it is green I will run across it to you and come into your dreams."

"We will go and work in the green garden," said Charles. "I would like to see it tidied up a bit more before I leave."

He had found rusty gardening tools in the arbour and was delighted, for he had inherited a love of gardens from his mother. Wet though it was in the garden they attacked the briars and weeds with a will. They were disturbed only twice, by Damaris bringing them custard tarts and cold chicken, and later by Justus who came to tell them that arrangements for tomorrow morning were complete; William would be at the end of the lane at six o'clock with horses for the journey. Justus would not stay. He looked at them with shy compassion and went away again.

When the evening turned chill they made a good fire and ate the chicken and tarts and drank the last of the wine, and then healthy tiredness, food and drink and warmth brought comfort. The thought of the parting had been leaping on them in all the intervals of the day, as toothache leaps, gripping harshly then relaxing only to grip again. But now it was as though they had taken laudanum. The pain was there all the time but they could talk of how Charles would try and get letters to her now and then, and she to him, and at what hour each day they would think of each other and of how they would always remember the home in the castle when they woke in the night. And presently Charles said to her, "I have one more song for you. John Donne wrote it. I found out things about him and read things that he wrote because my grandfather was fond of him. It was my grandfather who made him Dean of St. Paul's. He had a young wife whom he loved and once when he had to go on a long journey and leave her behind he wrote this song for her. I would write it down if we had paper and pen, but we have not, so I will sing it, and then I will say the words over and over till you know them by heart." He wanted her to think cheerfully about him. He did not want her to weep.

Lucy rather thought she would not be able to bear it if Charles sang, yet when he had fetched the guitar, and tuned the strings and began to sing in the firelight she was comforted. Music was timeless as wonder. It could for the short while it lasted even transform the sorrow of which it spoke.

Sweetest love, I do not go
For weariness of thee,
Nor in hope the world can show
A fitter love for me;
But since that I

At the last must part, 'tis best,
Thus to use myself in jest
    By feigned deaths to die.

Yesternight the sun went hence,
    And yet is here today;
He hath no desire nor sense,
    Nor half so short a way;
    Then fear not me,
But believe that I shall make
Speedier journeys, since I take
    More wings and spurs than he.

When thou sigh'st, thou sigh'st not wind,
    But sigh'st my soul away;
When thou weep'st, unkindly kind,
    My life's blood doth decay.
    It cannot be
That thou lovest me as thou say'st,
If in thine my love thou waste,
    That art the best of me.

Let not thy divining heart
    Forethink me any ill;
Destiny may take thy part,
    And may thy fears fulfil.
    But think that we
Are but turn'd aside to sleep.
They who one another keep
    Alive, ne'er parted be.

He put the guitar aside and taught her the words. She was quick to learn and could soon repeat them to him. "You understand what he means?" Charles asked. "If we do not think happily and hopefully of each other we may hurt each other."

Lucy nodded and then smiled. Such a way of thinking suited her natural optimism. "Yet it is so hard not to be afraid for one another," she murmured.

"Fear and unhappiness chase each other round and round

in a circle. From now until I go we are going to be happy. And afterwards."

They sat late by the fire, talking and building castles in the air and trying to believe in them. But when they at last went to bed it was not easy to sleep. They had no clock and Lucy had to watch for the changing of the light and listen for the sound of the cocks crowing, for they must get up at five o'clock.

At the appointed hour she woke him and he looked up into her face and said, "They who one another keep alive, ne'er parted be." She smiled and he saw to his intense relief that she was still tearless. They got up and dressed and had breakfast, and then went through the sleeping garden and up the lane to the road. They stood waiting hand in hand, two silent children, and presently they heard the horses.

William had planned as well as he could. It had been useless to hope for a boat at Solva, for the wind was contrary, but he had spent the two past days in riding to Carmarthen, where he had Royalist friends, and with their help had found a boat ready to sail to Devon as soon as the wind was favourable, and prepared for a consideration to carry his son-in-law Tomos Barlow to safety. It had taken almost the last of his ready money but that he would never tell Charles. He looked grim, worn and tired, but he had determined that he and Richard should ride with Charles and never leave him until they saw the ship sail away down the tideway.

Justus, who had ridden Lucy's mare up the hill for Charles, dismounted and Charles mounted in his place. It seemed all to happen very quickly. Lucy was conscious for a moment of being in Charles's arms, gripped hard and then quickly released, and striving for speech and finding no word of love to say, no response even in her limp body, and then all she heard was the sound of the horses trotting quickly away. The clear morning seemed dim and there was a hard pain round her chest as though an iron band were tightening there. She began to murmur little endearments and then realized it was too late, Charles could not hear them. And she had not, as far as she could remember, even kissed him. She could not weep because of the iron band and all she wanted was to get back to the kitchen, and the blankets before the fire, and lie with her face in Charles's pillow. She turned to fly there but something held her, a rough hand holding hers and refusing to let go. It was Justus holding her hand. She gazed at him stupidly. Justus. Tousle-headed and owl-eyed, for sympathy had kept him awake all night, he looked at her with bewilderment and dumb sympathy, and she was back in the church at Covent Garden and they were going hand in hand to tell Old Sage that Nan-Nan had died. Suddenly she realized Justus. He had been no one's best beloved. His mother had scarcely loved him at all, William only second to herself. He had been left behind when she went to join William and Dewi. He was plain and homely and perhaps he would never be loved very greatly or noticed very much. All the loves of Lucy's life had been, and always would be, three parts maternal, for maternity was the strongest passion in her. The germ of her love for Charles had been pity for a small boy who had nightmares.

"Where is Dewi?" she suddenly asked Justus.

"Asleep in the cottage. We did not wake him up to bring him. We thought he would howl if he had to say goodbye to—to—Charles, to the Prince."

He stammered a little in speaking of Charles and he did not look at Lucy, for he was sure he was nothing to her now. He had been looking forward to Dewi, thinking that the little boy might perhaps be fond of him, but Dewi had given his devotion to Charles. Neither fact surprised him and he was overwhelmed to find himself suddenly gripped in one of the bearlike hugs to which Lucy had so often subjected him in their childhood.

"There is no one like you, Justus," she was saying. "And now we are going to be alone at the cottage with Dewi for three or four days. I will look after you both. We had better go and get Dewi's breakfast."

She began to run and he ran with her, but presently she could no longer run because she was sobbing. They walked slowly to the cottage, Justus with his arm round her. Her hard sobs scared him a little but he was glad she should be with him and not alone in the castle.

BOOK III

The Woman

One

1

I am here again, thought Lucy, and it is autumn as it was before, but last time I was here with Nan-Nan and now I am alone, a woman and not a child.

She was standing at the window of her bedchamber at Golden Grove and she was feeling tired and discouraged, for her arrival had been a lonely one. She had travelled with friends but they had left her at the gate and she had ridden through the park by herself, to find only servants to greet her in the great hall, for she had arrived earlier than she had expected and Lord and Lady Carbery had not yet returned from an afternoon's visit. She had been shown her bedchamber and the maidservant had brought her warm water in a silver ewer, and told her the hour at which the family dined, and smiled and left her.

The window was closed and the leaded panes seemed like bars between her and the outdoor world she loved. A little desperately she wrestled with the latch and pushed the window open, and the golden warmth of St. Martin's summer flowed in and took possession of her almost as though Golden Grove took her in its arms. She pulled a stately chair to the window and sat with sunshine lying on her tired eyelids, the warmth soaking into her aching body and taking her back over the years to the day when she had looked into the heart of the rose that grew on the terrace. "I'm glad I have come," she told Nan-Nan. "I'm glad, after all, that I have come."

2

When a month ago Lord Carbery had asked her to come she had not known whether to say yes or no. He had arrived at Roch unexpectedly one day, having ridden from St. Davids,

and had found her and her father and Dewi sitting in front of
their door gutting fish. Serene upon their own ground Lucy
and Dewi had been unabashed, and William very nearly so.
Seating their distinguished relative upon an upturned bucket
in the sun they had finished the gutting, washed themselves,
cooked the fish and then entertained him to dinner.

It was Lord Carbery himself who had been abashed. With
the war in Wales apparently ended he had returned to Golden
Grove, with no intention of getting mixed up in any fresh
flare-up of fighting, should it occur, and so comfortable that he
had been a little slow in enquiring into the welfare of less
fortunate relatives. The sight of the ruined castle, which he
himself had garrisoned for the King, had appalled him and
when he had arrived in the middle of the fish gutting, a
process which he had not hitherto beheld, he had been more
than appalled, he had been ashamed. His own relatives had for
months been existing in a condition of smelly squalor and he
had done nothing whatever to help them.

But William was proud and had wanted no help. An offer to
provide himself and his children with a home at Golden
Grove, the charm of it slightly overstressed because the Earl's
lower nature could be coupled with his higher one only with a
good strong haul upon the harness, had been courteously refused because the manoeuvre was apparent to William. A tactful offer of financial assistance, in which there was no division
of personality because the Earl was still so wealthy that he
could be generous without suffering any change in his habits,
was also refused; less courteously. Lord Carbery, noting that
the child who had twisted him round her little finger had
grown into a charming young woman, had wondered if Lucy
would like to pay them a visit? This offer William had referred
to Lucy.

But he had encouraged her to accept it. He and Dewi would
flourish, he had said, if she did not stay too long. Damaris
would look after them. A little change would do her good. But
Lucy had jumped at the offer. She would like to think it over,
she had said, and had left them and gone down to sit on the
rocks; and had sat there so long that William had been hard

put to it entertaining the Earl while she made her mind up. But at last she had come back and accepted the offer with gentle gratitude.

Sitting now in the open window at Golden Grove her thoughts went back to Roch. Life with William, after Charles had gone away, had been difficult for them both. She was no longer single-minded, for Charles possessed her and not for one moment could her thoughts leave him. She would talk and laugh with those she loved, and her hands would serve them, but afterwards she would not remember what she had said or done, for at the back of her mind Charles lived and moved and spoke, and her true colloquy was with him alone. She had had two letters from him and then no more. In the isolation of Roch little definite news reached them. They knew only that the defeated army of the west had fought its way back to Cornwall, until finally the Royal Standard floated from the last outpost of Tintagel Castle. On a dark March night, Charles had escaped to sea and sailed to the Channel Islands. Two months later his father had yielded himself a prisoner to the Scots.

The news that Charles was safe had at first brought relief to Lucy, and the cessation of the nightmares of wounds and death that had haunted her, but something in the last of his two letters had frightened her. He had asked her never to speak of Tomos Barlow beyond the circle of her family, and never to wear her ring. She had obeyed him to the point of taking it from her finger and wearing it round her neck beneath her dress on a gold chain, but though the feel of it between her breasts sometimes comforted her it brought too the fear that Charles might try to hide her away out of memory in the same way as he had told her to hide her ring. She had grown thin and pale and William had been greatly troubled, but they could make no real contact with each other now, for she knew her father's terrible hopes and fears. He took a gloomy view of her prospects and wanted her marriage terminated; and before the escape to the Channel Islands his secret thoughts had not stopped short of the death of Charles in the last battle. Above all he had hoped she would not bear a child as passionately as she had hoped she would. And he had had his wish for there was no child. "You are full young yet," Damaris had said, trying to comfort young Mrs. Tomos Barlow. "When you are older you will bear as many babes as your granny Mrs. Gwinne." But William's relief had cancelled out Damaris's comfort and it had sometimes seemed to Lucy, in the sleepless hours before cockcrow, that her father's unspoken thoughts had denied life to her child and might deny it to Charles. Had thoughts such terrible power? The song of John Donne's that Charles had taught her had suggested that they had, and she had grown afraid of her father and estranged from him.

Sitting on the rocks she had thought, it will do us both good to be parted for a while. And she had also thought, at Golden Grove they will know all that has happened in the world. They will tell me about Charles.

3

In the passage outside her room a board creaked under a light step and a silk skirt rustled and suddenly Charles, and news of him, were so near that her heart beat to suffocation. Hardly knowing that she had moved she had opened the door, curtseyed to Lady Carbery and was in her arms.

They were of the same height now and Lucy found herself looking into the tired eyes of the older woman with a new sense of recognition. On her previous visit Lady Carbery had been to her no more than a background of pervasive kindness against which the Earl had stood out a little larger than life, but now, here was another woman who felt as weary as she did herself; not with physical labour, for Lady Carbery's shapely hands had never made contact with a saucepan, but with the perpetual guidance of a great household, the unending drain upon the compassion that had made Golden Grove the refuge that it was. She lives her real life hiddenly, thought Lucy, looking into her hostess's face, like I wear my ring. Do all women do that? Must I?

She looked searchingly at Lady Carbery, slightly discomposing her hostess by what Mrs. Gwinne had called "that dreadful blue stare". The poor lady detached her own gaze with difficulty and pulled a second chair to the window.

"I must tell you, my dear," she said when they were seated, "that our household is now larger than it was. We have a resident chaplain now. He lives here with his wife and young children. I will present you to Dr. Jeremy Taylor and his lady at dinner. He has lately been released from prison and it is a source of thankfulness to the Earl and myself that our home can now be a refuge for him and his family."

"Prison?" asked Lucy with interest. "What did he do?"

"He was a prisoner of war," said Lady Carbery hastily, for the sharp turn of Lucy's head had suggested a reprehensible interest in crime. "An imprisonment of honour in Cardigan Castle."

"Ought priests to fight?" wondered Lucy. "Parson Peregrine shot at a Puritan's hat, but then he is a hot-tempered man and he was goaded to it."

"Dr. Taylor served with the army in a priestly capacity, as a chaplain," explained Lady Carbery. "He was with the army in Wales at the time of our sad defeat. I must tell you, Lucy, that he is a very distinguished scholar and Christian. He was a friend and protégé of our beloved martyr Archbishop Laud. He is a Fellow of All Souls and was with the King at Oxford."

With the King at Oxford? thought Lucy. Charles was with the King at Oxford. If I am very careful I can speak to him of Charles. Aloud she said to Lady Carbery, "I shall be honoured to meet him."

"There will be two other guests present," murmured Lady Carbery. "Mr. Wyatt and Mr. Nicholson. Mr. Wyatt is our rector at Llanfihangel Aberlythch. They have a private school for young gentlemen at the Rectory."

"I shall be honoured to meet him, madam."

Lady Carbery's eyes were resting on the skirt of the shabby blue riding habit that Lucy was still wearing. She had grown considerably since it had been made and the hem had been let down and adorned in two places with patches of a lighter shade of blue, one having the shape of a star and the other of a crescent moon. There was a light-heartedness about Lucy's repairs that would have delighted the Earl but Lady Carbery had little sense of humour and was saddened. "You have a gown for evening, my love?" she asked tenderly. "Anything I have is yours, you know."

"Thank you, madam," said Lucy, "but my grandmother gave me a sea-green silk gown and pearl earrings. I think you will not need to be ashamed of me."

She spoke with gratitude but there was a sparkle in her eyes that might have been due to a touch of anger. Lady Carbery could see that she had been something less than tactful. When one spoke to her first the girl had her mother's gentleness but Lady Carbery feared that she might also have something of her father's wilful spirit.

She did more than fear when Lucy entered the parlour. It was not by intention that she had kept the distinguished company waiting, for her unpunctuality was congenital, but the proud carriage of her head made it appear so. And she should have accepted the loan of a dress; the sea-green gown had seen better days. But the girl had arranged her unruly hair as carefully as she could and the curtsey into which she sank before Lord Carbery was graceful, and when he raised her and kissed her Lady Carbery perceived that though she was smiling she was also trembling. Poor child! If she must face misfortune with defiant pride, well, that was her way, but it could be a dangerous way and Lady Carbery's heart ached as she presented Dr. and Mrs. Taylor, and Mr. Wyatt and Mr. Nicholson. Three strange men black as crows, thought Lucy, very reverend and very learned, and a woman with a kind smile, a little startled by her, and Lady Carbery not approving of her. But Lord Carbery was just the same and seated her by him at the dining-table, his amused eyes telling her that he and she were the black sheep in this grave company and must be a comfort to each other. The hurtful defiance left her, she was herself again and presently very much aware of Dr. Taylor.

He was one of the redeemers, she realized, and was suddenly

happy as well as relaxed. They were good company; like the sun of which she had drawn pictures as a child, rays shining out from a courteous face, and a small blessing hand at the end of each ray. She did not know she was looking at a man who in his youth had been described as "no less than the son of Apollo, the god of wisdom and eloquence", but she would have accepted that as an apt description. His wife looked worn though content, as the wives of such men so often do. The strength of his power to cheer and carry others had its corresponding reaction of fatigue in the home circle, and her own supporting role was arduous; yet that she adored him Lucy realized instantly. And she was also aware, now that she herself was a wife, of how greatly Lady Carbery loved her husband, even though he was not really as serious-minded as she could have wished or as he for her sake endeavoured to appear. To fall in love had seemed the glory of the world, but she saw all over again that there was no true glory unless the maintaining of faith worked upon the sparkle and moulded it to the durable diamond. These two women possessed that. Charles, she thought. Charles! Charles!

Dr. Taylor was sitting opposite her and instantly, with boldness, for her conversation should have been directed to Mr. Wyatt at her side, she asked him, "You were with the King and the Prince at Oxford I believe, sir. What do you think of the Prince?"

There was a second of stunned silence and Lady Carbery actually blushed for her young relative, but Dr. Taylor's laugh came to the rescue. "Every young lady asks me that," he said. "And not young ladies only, since all our hope hangs upon him."

"Could we get him back to England and on the throne, a young man of humour and tolerance, our troubles would be over," declared Lord Carbery.

"And what of our divinely appointed and most gracious King?" asked Lady Carbery gently. It saddened her that this heretical notion of the Puritans, this diabolically-inspired suggestion that kings were not necessarily the vice-regents of God, was now spreading even to good Royalists. That, she thought, was the dreadful thing about wrong notions. They had a power of insidious growth that seemed denied to good and proper ways of thought. She must talk to her husband about this in bed tonight. She never corrected him in public.

"Graciousness does not rule out fanaticism," said the Earl firmly, "and if our sovereign is king by divine appointment then here is yet another case where I fail to see eye to eye with my Maker. I think the King should abdicate and join his sick wife. The Scots would gladly give him up to connubial duties in foreign parts."

"Your suggestions are exactly those that were put before the Prince in the Channel Islands," said Dr. Taylor, "and he would have none of them. In his own way he is as obstinate as his father, and loyalty to his father is one of the notions he is most obstinate about, and may God bless him for it."

"So there's now little hope of his return to England," said Mr. Wyatt.

"None," said Dr. Taylor. "Were he to return now, thinking as he does, we should merely have him in custody with the rest of the royal children. There is nothing for him to do now but go to France."

"The outlook for us is that of a ship at sea in a thick mist," said Mr. Nicholson gloomily. "We do not know to what we are drifting and until the wind changes we are helpless."

Lady Carbery resolutely changed the conversation. "You have still not told my young cousin your opinion of the Prince, Dr. Taylor," she said. "Is his countenance pleasing? Are his manners charming?"

Dr. Taylor laughed. "I am no judge of a man's looks," he said, "but I believe it is said that the Prince's manners redeem his face. But talking to him you are too enamoured of the boy himself to think of his looks. One even forgets his youth. Can one give a young man or woman higher praise than that? Youth is itself so radiant a garment that a personality that can outshine it must be captivating indeed."

He smiled across the table at Lucy with an admiration so honest and delightful, and so obviously linking her to Charles in his thoughts, that suddenly she felt very close to her husband, warm and happy. Yet she was in confusion too, feeling that they must all see the ring between her breasts shining through her gown like a flame. The colour crept up her face but Mrs. Taylor's kind smile steadied her. It told her that Mrs. Taylor knew quite well that she had a lover but was making no guesses as to who it could be.

Once again the talk turned to the troubles of the time for it was hard for these people to discuss anything else. The new ways of thinking threatened not only the form of religious faith in which they had been trained but their material way of life too. All that had seemed stable as the ground beneath their feet was now under attack, and so rooted are human beings in the seeming security of custom that their quaking foundations had communicated tremor to the very world itself. About this table, as about so many all over the country at this time, there was talk of the Last Things. Though they hardly realized it they secretly found it easier to contemplate the last trump and the final judgment than having all their habits upset.

Lucy and Dr. Taylor were more free from the prevailing anxiety than the rest, and both of them because they were in love. Lucy longed for no security except that of Charles's love, and nothing frightened her except the non-appearance of his letters and the sea between them. Dr. Taylor had been with the army, he had seen his friends die and had buried them, and from the window of his prison he had seen fellow prisoners led out to execution and wondered when his own turn would come. In a puzzling letter written at this time he had spoken of a storm of "so impetuous a violence that it broke a cable and I lost my anchor, and but that he who steadies the raging of the sea, and the noise of his waves and the madness of the people, had provided a plank for me, I had been lost." Only he could have explained his meaning but Lady Carbery wondered if the anchor of his first faith had been secured by nothing stronger than training and tradition, and if disaster had smashed that cable, leaving him anchorless in darkness. If so, as he came in desolation to its heart, he had not found it empty but discovered with the Psalmist that darkness is the garment of God. "He made darkness his secret place, his pavilion round about him was dark water, and thick clouds to cover him." He was a man now so greatly in love with God that he could be entrusted with the ransom of souls; since he wanted so little for himself that he was prepared to pay the price. This was how Lady Carbery had come to think of this man who was slowly revealing to her, more by the thoughts of him that his presence aroused than by anything he said, the first contours of the hidden life.

Two

The days went by and Lucy was as contented as a girl can be whose lover does not write to her. That the female passion for letter writing is seldom shared by the male of the species was something she had not discovered yet, so her comfort was merely in the thought that it was not possible for him to write, or that his letters had been intercepted and destroyed. At night when she tried to reach him she could not find him, could not know if he was ill or well, happy or miserable, and she was deeply unhappy. It was bitter to her to discover that embodied spirits are not so free as she had thought, that even when loving greatly they can be so ignorant, crass and floundering in their prison of flesh.

But at Golden Grove the days could not fail to bring peace. She went riding with the Earl, or sat in the parlour with Lady Carbery and Mrs. Taylor, reading aloud to them as they stitched at their embroidery. She read aloud very badly but Lady Carbery thought she should learn, deficient as she was in ladylike accomplishments. When the hour of instruction was over she escaped gladly to the chief joys of this visit, playing with the children in the garden or talking to their father in the gazebo at the end of the terrace where he was writing a book.

Of both these activities Lady Carbery disapproved. Until Lucy arrived the children had been well-mannered and quiet, a little depressed by their father's learning and their mother's piety but able to smile very sweetly when spoken to. But Lucy, her skirts tucked up, led them scampering round the garden in wild games of bear-leader and catch-who-can. Lady Carbery apologized to Mrs. Taylor for the children's racket, and even more for the disturbance of their father's peace. "This immortal book!" she mourned. "How is it to progress?

Lucy is a naughty girl. I will get the Earl to speak to her."

But Mrs. Taylor prevented this with the nearest thing to a flash of anger that her gentle nature could produce. "Playing with my children comforts Lucy," she said, "and talking to my husband is a strength to her. She needs both at this time."

"Is Lucy unhappy?" wondered Lady Carbery.

"She is in love in wartime," said Mrs. Taylor.

"Has she told you so?"

"No," said Mrs. Taylor.

Not for the first time Lady Carbery was astonished by her guest. Apparently devoted to her husband she yet displayed no wifely zeal either in defending him from intrusion on the one hand or in persuading him to work less arduously on the other. It could not be that she was indifferent to his welfare. Could it be that she took a deeper view of it than is usual with wives? Lady Carbery had thought lately, as Dr. Taylor led her more deeply into the life of the spirit, that she would have delighted to be the wife of a priest. Now she changed her mind. Lord Carbery was always delighted to be defended from intrusion and encouraged in the life of dignified leisure that was so suitable to his age and temperament.

It was not at first entirely for her own sake that Lucy had dared to sit quietly down on the steps of the gazebo, to wait until the tall quill pen had come to a good stopping place. She was prepared to wait half an hour but it stopped in mid-sentence, for Dr. Taylor was a priest first and a writer second.

"Can I be of service to you?" he asked politely.

"When you were in prison could you talk to other prisoners?" she asked abruptly. "Were there other priests there with you?"

"I was always alone in my cell," he said, "but we were allowed to be together in the prison yard once a day for a short period of exercise. We tramped round and round like squirrels in a cage under the eye of our guard but we could exchange a few words. As far as I know there was only one priest besides myself among us."

"Did he tell you his name?"

"Yes. Nathaniel Peregrine."

"So he is still there. He was our vicar at Roch. Did he tell you how he came to be in prison?"

"Yes. He told me. But he is no longer in Cardigan Castle. He was sent to another prison."

Lucy sensed that much was not being told her and she said, with a flash of autocratic authority that in another context would have amused Dr. Taylor immensely, "I wish to be told how he was and where they sent him. I do not wish to be spared."

"I was on terms of friendship with the officer in charge of the prisoners," said Dr. Taylor. "He was the son of an old friend. That is one of the strange quirks of civil war, Lucy You can suddenly find that the enemy confronting you is well known to you. It can present puzzles to loyalty and it did so with this young man, but he came down upon the side of friendship and I probably owe it to his pleading, as well as to that of Lord Carbery, that my imprisonment was so short. But while I was still waiting for release I persuaded my friend to let me minister as priest to those under sentence of death. For a few days, until the authorities could be persuaded to commute his sentence to a further term of imprisonment, Nathaniel Peregrine was one of these."

"Why?" demanded Lucy indignantly. "He tried to defend his church from sacrilegious handling. That was all."

"He fired from his window at a Puritan gentleman of some importance. I had hard work to persuade the authorities that the fact that the shot merely pierced the man's hat was not an accident but a matter of deliberate aim and fine marksmanship. You see, Lucy, our friend, even in his suffering, remained a man of choleric temper and his endurance in prison was too much mixed with heroic anger to do him good. But to me he talked quietly and I was able to persuade his enemies of the truth of what he said to me."

"You said he suffered," murmured Lucy.

"His broken arm was never properly cared for and his rheumatism was not improved by the dampness of our prison, but his spirit remained unbroken and his anger was never in connection with himself. Injustice as such aroused it, the treatment he saw meted out to other men. He had no fear of death but he wished he might live a little longer, he told me, so that he might attain humility and finish the book he was writing." Dr. Taylor smiled at Lucy. "You would be surprised how much we writers are prepared to suffer in order to complete a book. The travail of creation of course exaggerates the importance of our work while we are engaged in it; we know better when the opus is finished and the lion is perceived to be only a broken-backed mouse. I understood him, and so I pleaded for his life. But where they have sent him I do not believe even he, with all his courage and concentration, will be able to finish his book." His hands had been lying loosely on his knees and Lucy saw them suddenly tighten. "I did no good service by saving his life," he finished.

"Where *did* they send him?" Lucy asked sharply. She was caught up in a state of confused rage, hardly knowing with whom she was so angry; with men in general for their idiocy in going to war at all, and their cruelty to each other once they had gone there, or with Dr. Taylor for blaming himself because his merciful action had failed to help his friend. "Was it your fault if doing right went wrong?" she demanded. "And where *did* they send him?"

"To one of the hulks. One of the prison ships on the Thames to which they are now sending recalcitrant priests."

By the flat deadness of his voice she knew without being told that conditions on the hulks would be worse than other prisons. She was appalled but the rage was dying away and she could try and find words to comfort Dr. Taylor. "Could a man find humility in hulks? And God? If Parson Peregrine does that he will be comforted and not grieve so much if he cannot finish his book."

Dr. Taylor smiled at her optimism. Not even the most imaginative can conjure up the reality of hulks. Then he remembered his own experience in a lesser trial. "It is possible," he said. "I have just written something about comfort in tribulation. I will read it to you. 'He who promised his spirit to assist his servants in their troubles will not, because they are in trouble, take away the comforter from them; who cannot be a comforter but while he carries our sadness, and relieves our sorrows, and turns our persecutions into joys, and crowns and sceptres.' "

The children came running to call Lucy to play with them and they said no more that day, but on other days she told him of some of the things that had happened to her in what seemed so vast a period of time, and he listened with so much attention that it would appear he thought her ups and downs very important and sixteen years a long time to have been alive. She told him she thought she had come from the sea and he agreed that indeed she had. "The sea is a picture of the divine mystery from which we came and that laps for ever on the shores of our being, and sounds about us when the storms come. The mystery is within us also and in all that lives, even in the bodies of the small fishes in the sea-pools, the mystery of the being of God. There is no creature that breathes but the breathing is the rhythm of his love, no flower that glows with any other light but his, no voice that speaks in kindness but the cadence of the compassion is his own."

Shyly she told him about her last visit to Golden Grove and how she had seen the golden-hearted rose and how it had seemed to glow inside her in the cave. "There the small child touched the deeps of prayer," he said. "The adoration, and then the experience of divine rescue."

"But I am not a religious kind of person," she told him, "and I do not know how to pray."

"You will know when the storms come. It is then that God goes out of his way to meet his children. Until that time comes keep in memory that which you have found to be within you, and without you in the world's glow. When the clock strikes, or however else you shall measure the day, it is good to turn to God, that the returns of devotion may be the measure of your time. And do so also in the breaches of your sleep. You do not even need to speak. To turn is enough."

"Are you writing these things in your book?"

"I have not yet progressed very far in my book. But I am

399

sure that as I progress I shall remember my talks with you."

"What will you call your book?"

"I think I shall call it *Holy Living and Holy Dying*."

"What is holiness?"

"Lucy, what questions you ask me! To grow in holiness is to grow in the power of turning from yourself to God and his children. When there is no more turning back to yourself, that wounding of the soul of the world, then you are whole."

"Yet I would like to have some words when I turn. Could you write some for me? Only a few, please."

He picked up his pen and wrote, and handed her the paper and she read what he had written. "Keep me, O Lord, for I am thine by creation; guide me for I am thine by purchase; thou hast redeemed me by the blood of thy son and loved me with the love of the Father, for I am thy child by adoption and grace; but let thy mercy pardon my sins and thy care watch over me. Holy is our God. Holy is the almighty. Holy is the immortal. Holy God have mercy upon me."

"Thank you, sir," she said. "It will be a secret thing, this life of turning."

"Secrets and yet shared," he told her. "You will share this with every man and woman who has ever tried, however feebly, to love God and his neighbour."

She looked up at him, her eyes shining, but her mind had suddenly gone elsewhere. Dr. Taylor smiled, for that this was a girl in love he knew very well. Now, he thought, she would forget instantly all that he had told her. But in this he wronged her for she never forgot.

2

The next day the letter came. The postboy was heard winding his horn as he came cantering through the park and a faint tremor seemed to pass through the house from top to bottom, for in time of war especially life or death was in the postman's bag. Every heart from that of the Earl to the youngest little maidservant, whose lover was in the army, either missed a few beats in dread or quickened in expectation. But the great folk in the front of the house kept an unruffled surface; though the Earl strolled out from the library to remind his wife of some small matter and Dr. Taylor came in from the gazebo to find a book he had mislaid.

Lucy did not count herself one of the great folk and she joined the children in their headlong rush to the terrace. But she did not at once run down the steps as they did, she halted at the top suddenly aware that Charles was near her. For the first time in all the months of parting she felt him near. And he was coming closer. It was not he who rode the cantering white pony but the postboy had a summons for her. She did not use her reason, she did not stop to think that any letter from Charles would not be sent to her at Golden Grove, but as soon as the postboy emerged from the trees jumped down the steps, pushed through the children and ran to him. He had been about to ride round the house to the side door where letters were delivered, but he reined up at sight of her and gave the precious packet into her hands.

She had no recollection of going back up the steps. The next thing she knew she was standing with the others in the hall and the Earl was unfastening the packet with dreadful deliberation.

"The letters would have been brought to us, Lucy. You are very impulsive, my dear." It was Lady Carbery speaking with gentle reproof. Lucy trembled but looking round she was aware of the amusement in Dr. Taylor's eyes and was steadied. But there was no letter for her and with his own unopened Dr. Taylor put his hand through her arm and led her out to the terrace. "I did not really expect a letter," she told him.

"We always expect a letter," he answered. "It is the human condition to be always listening for the voice when we cannot see the face. But they are never as far away as we think they are, merely on another path through the same wood, and all the paths wind inward at the end."

"Lucy, I have a letter from your grandmother. Will you please come to me in the parlour." It was Lady Carbery calling from the door behind them, Lucy dropped a curtsey to Dr. Taylor before she obeyed and his answering smile was sympathetic, for he knew that it was not her grandmother's voice she wanted to hear.

It was however the right grandmother, it was Elenor Gwinne, writing to inform the family at Golden Grove that her daughter Elizabeth was unwell. "The apothecary thinks gravely of her illness," Lady Carbery read aloud to Lucy, "though he does not put a name to it. He is, I think, unable to do so, and the treatment he prescribes, rest and warmth and light diet, I was putting into practice before he came. But to a household of women the mere presence of a man in the house is of itself remedial and Elizabeth is always slightly better for his visits. But she frets for Lucy. The final decision in that tedious lawsuit was that William should have the custody of his children, and it has given Lucy entirely to her father who was always her favourite parent, and is a source of great bitterness to Elizabeth. She is too proud to ask William if her daughter may visit her, or to allow me to do so. I therefore without her knowledge write to you, for I think it probable that you see the little family at Roch from time to time and might be able to persuade William to allow Lucy to visit her mother."

"Madam, I will myself persuade my father," said Lucy. "I am a woman now and make my own decisions. He knows that. He loves me and he will not withstand my knowledge of what I must do."

Lady Carbery felt put in her place and was astonished at the flash of fire in Lucy's blue eyes. It was directed, she believed, against herself; the girl would allow no go-between in anything that concerned herself and her father. Lucy had intended no discourtesy but resolution was flaming through her whole body, for behind the immediate summons there was another. Charles wanted her, she believed. He wanted her and London was nearer to him than Roch. Under cover of the dark so many ships sailed down the Thames to France and the Low Countries. Her flashing thoughts carried her no further than that. Just to be a little nearer was great gain.

Travel was easy for the well-to-do. Instantly Lady Carbery was busy, horses were groomed and servants leaped to attention. William was summoned from Roch and Lady Carbery's friend, Lady Lewis at Llanelly, was told to postpone her departure to her daughter's lying-in at Richmond until Lucy could be brought to her to share her journey. She obeyed, only reminding Lady Carbery that though a first baby was generally late it could also be early, and the young lady must make haste. Great haste was made, Lady Carbery's maid working half the night as well as by day altering a selection of her mistress's dresses to fit Lucy, so that Lady Lewis should not be ashamed of her travelling companion. By the time William arrived, having left Dewi with Damaris, the last stitch had been set in place and he wondered why they had bothered to send for him at all. Why ask permission for a *fait accompli*?

"Because though I knew you would not refuse it I would not go without it," said Lucy. "Nor without your love to carry with me."

They were standing together in the little room near the front door, safe from interruption because no one ever used this room. The window looked out on the terrace and at the bottom of the steps a groom was holding William's horse in readiness for his journey home to Roch, and somewhere out of sight the Golden Grove coach was waiting to take Lucy to Llanelly. The fine weather had broken and a curtain of drizzly rain was swaying over the park, slowly erasing all the colour and warmth of the past weeks. When it stopped its work then the skeleton shape of winter would be seen upon the trees. The walls of the little room were lined with books the Earl no longer wanted to read, and they seemed to know it for they smelt musty and sad, like old men who have outlived their usefulness, and their bindings seemed to have all faded to the same dun colour, the colour of William's shabby coat. Lucy looked at her father and a sudden dizziness made her put her hand out to the windowsill to support herself. He had grown thin and in the grey light he looked like one of the books, a grey-faced man whom no one now wanted. "I will want you till I die," she cried out impetuously. "And so will Dewi and Justus."

"It is not in nature that children should need their parents for long," said William. "Some men have wives who stay by them, but not all. Why complain? All men are lonely and again it is the nature of things that loneliness should deepen with age."

Lucy flung her arms round his neck. "It is my duty to go to my mother for a while but I will come back to you at Roch." And then her voice broke with the sharpness of her realization that she did not now want to come back either to Wales or William. She wanted to go on, not back, on to another country and another man. She clung to her father and sobbed in guilt and shame.

"Stop crying, Bud," commanded William, unwinding her arms from his neck. "You and I have had too many emotional farewells already and I cannot stand another. And speak the truth, if you please. Your mother is the excuse but you have a deeper motive. You have no need to ask for my love because you have possessed it entirely since the day you were born, and will not lose it while I live. But I was wrong to speak of loneliness as I did because as long as a man has a patch of earth to dig he is not lonely. You have no need to think of me as an unhappy man."

His voice died away as though over the rim of the world. She did not hear the door close but she heard him go down the steps. She was in the chair where he had been sitting when she came into the room, and was clutching the cushion in her arms, for it seemed to give out the faint scent of tobacco and leather and horses that was his especial smell. Her firstborn was entirely gone and the goodbye had been cold, loveless and horrible. For the moment that seemed almost the worst thing; not having a goodbye that she would be able to bear to remember. But presently a queer thought jerked itself into her mind. He does not get drunk any more, she thought. When did he stop? How strange that I did not notice when he stopped. And then the steely strength of his words crept into her and she quietened. He is greater than I knew, she thought, he has grown bigger all these hard years. He will dig, like he said, and grow into the earth like a tree, and live for the crops and the beasts. He will not forget me and I will not forget him.

Three

"Spring!" said Lucy to herself. "It is really spring now."

She was in her grandmother's garden listening for the sound that just now was for her the most longed-for, the clip-clop of Moses, the old nag which she and Justus, strolling along Cheapside together just before Christmas, had seen being led to the knacker's yard and had bought for the few pence in Justus's purse and her pearl earrings. Stumbling over the cobbles on his way to death, half-starved, Moses had reminded Lucy of the sin-eater and she had cried out in distress. The rascal who was dragging Moses along by his rope halter had known how to exploit a lady's pity, and how to catch a glimpse of pearls through a tangle of untidy hair, and it had only taken ten minutes of bargaining for the old horse to become Lucy's Christmas present to Justus. Well fed, groomed and adored Moses had renewed his youth, but still he reminded Lucy of the sin-eater. He had the patient yet apprehensive expression of a burden bearer who has not yet attained to sainthood.

The April day was warm and scented with flowers, and the birds were singing in a tumult of delight. Suddenly it seemed to Lucy that she could not get her breath. It was spring again, the second spring since Charles had gone away, but she was no nearer to him for he had neither written to her nor sent for her to come to him. And yet that day at Golden Grove he had been so close. Surely it could not be that the man who had made her a woman could forget what he had done, could not know that it was winter for her until she was with him again?

The sound of Moses in the lane relieved her pain in a little rush of tears, as quickly over as a spring shower, and a moment later she was riding pillion behind Justus and jogging to

London upon an errand about which their mother knew nothing; for she had forbidden her lovely daughter to ride that terrible old horse.

Justus had filled out in the last year and his back was broad. He would not grow taller, he would always be a strong stocky man without grace of body but with so much grace of spirit that he would never seem an unattractive one. Leaning her cheek against his back Lucy sighed and was at peace. Though not himself demonstrative he allowed his sister to express affection. Women were demonstrative, that was a fact of nature, and he had early decided that rebellion against facts of nature is useless and a waste of time.

"Is our mother worse?" he asked gently, for he knew she had been crying.

"Not worse," said Lucy, "but not better. I do not think our mother has ever been really ill. She had a fever to start with and then she kept it with her for company."

"Lucy!" chided Justus. "Our mother has looked very unwell to me."

"Unwell, yes," said Lucy. "Nothing is well with a woman who has parted from her husband. Have you not noticed that? If she has had him for a long time she is lonely, even if she did not like him, and an illness, even if she does not like that either, fills up the empty space."

"She may be worrying about you," said the charitable Justus. "Does she know?"

"About Charles? Yes, and so does my grandmother. I could not tell my father and brothers and not tell them."

"Are they glad, or not?" asked Justus. He wanted to know because he himself was not.

"When I told them it was as though I had stunned them," said Lucy. "Then my mother was so excited that she made herself quite ill. Now I think she is pleased and she builds castles in the air like a child, talking of all the wonderful things that will happen to us when Charles is king. But my grandmother was awake all night, I think, after I had told her, for in the morning she looked so old. She asked to see my marriage lines and she wished me joy. But she has not spoken of it again. They both know that Charles does not wish me to speak of our marriage outside the family. You and Richard remember that?"

"We promised our silence," said Justus. "I will not break my promise and I do not see that Richard has anything to gain at present by breaking his."

This comment on their brother's character Lucy heard in silence. Richard was now a very prosperous young man, an able and trusted secretary of his influential employer, but it was hard to love a man who would never commit himself. Even his loyalty to his mother, Lucy suspected, was conditional and his service to Parliament certainly was. The King was now a prisoner in Carisbrooke Castle and he had the sympathy of a great many of his subjects. Below the apparently strong surface of parliamentary power there was anger and discontent, and occasional demonstrations for the King in the London streets. The smell of war was in the air again. The matter was not yet decided and nor was Richard's mode of dress; it still kept the balance between the two parties. But he was a kindly brother in his prosperity and he had taken considerable trouble to find out for Lucy and Justus in which prison ship Parson Peregrine was confined. It was not possible to get permission to go on board, but Lucy hoped that from a boat on the river she and Justus might catch a sight of the old man and that he too might see them and know himself loved.

The hulks were not far from the docks though on the other side of the river. They left Moses in the stable of an innkeeper of whom Richard had told them and walked to the nearest steps. There was a good deal of shipping on the water and they could not at once get hold of a waterman. Lucy did not mind for she loved ships of every kind, from a Welsh coracle to a man-of-war, and she almost forgot the sadness of their errand in her delight in the sights and smells and sounds all about her. The world of ships was a man's world and the buccaneer in her was at home in it.

"Look at that one!" she cried to Justus. "Look at the figure-head. Why, it is a sea-horse! The proudest little sea-horse I

ever saw. It is a Dutch ship from Rotterdam. From Aunt Gosfright."

Justus laughed. "Just a little merchantman. Look, they are
unlading now. And what makes you speak of Aunt Gosfright?
You never liked her."

"I have thought of her a good deal lately," said Lucy. "She
has been ill, you know. Justus, that is a lovely ship. I would like
to sail in her."

"I would be proud to have you on board, madam."

Justus had seen a free waterman at last and had raced off to
get hold of him, and Lucy found to her surprise that she was
talking not to her brother but to a young man who stood
solidly planted beside her as though he had been growing
there for a long while. She liked him instantly for that was
the way that Justus stood, thoroughly rooted in his own
peace. He spoke English well, giving to it that special charm
that any language has when a foreigner speaks it, lighting up
the music of it with the freshness of contrasting stress and
intonation.

"You see my ship's name painted on the hull?" he asked. "I
will turn it into English for you, though if you have noticed
the figurehead it is not necessary. The *Sea-Horse*. A good little
ship and the motion is easy when she jumps the waves. Will
you sail with me?"

He was saying any nonsense that came into his head, merely
to keep this pretty girl beside him for a few moments longer,
and falling into his mood she answered laughing, "When do
you sail, sir?" But he found himself answering quite seriously,
"I have business in the city. But any day after next Wednesday
when the wind is favourable I shall be sailing back to Rotterdam."

Justus had captured a boat and was dodging through the
crowd towards them. "Lucy!" he called. "Lucy!"

"May I know your name, sir, please?" she asked.

"Captain Axel, madam."

She gave him her hand impulsively and then turned and
ran to Justus. He helped her into the boat with chilly courtesy.
Few things upset his equable temper but one of the few was

the headlong way in which Lucy struck up sudden friendships. Anxiety mixed with unrecognized jealousy emerged as
irritation. "What did that fellow say to you?" he asked when
they were out on the water.

"He invited me to sail with him to Rotterdam," said Lucy.
"And I asked his name and when he sailed."

"What for?" demanded Justus and a sense of dread made
his heart lurch. He loved his sister so much that though he was
now at the age to have his eye taken by other pretty girls he
was hardly aware of their existence. "And have you forgotten
what we are supposed to be doing at this moment?"

Lucy's heart also lurched, not in dread but in self-reproach.
When would she learn to keep her mind centred upon one
person at a time? This was Parson Peregrine's day and neither
the captain of the *Sea-Horse*, nor Justus, nor even Charles himself must usurp it.

"We have not a chance of catching sight of old Peregrine,"
said Justus. He was no longer annoyed, for his rare irritations
were always short-lived, he was merely stating a fact. "And I
do not know what good you think we are doing by coming at
all."

"When people are in tribulation I try and come as near to
them as I can," said Lucy.

"What is the use of that if they do not know you are there?"
asked Justus.

"They may feel happier because I am near."

"You think a lot of yourself, surely?"

"No, but he loved me when I was a child and he does still. I
know when I am loved."

"Do you now?" said Justus, smiling. "That is pleasant for
you."

"It is," said Lucy.

A sudden chuckle from the waterman reminded them of his
presence. "Them's the hulks," he told them. They looked
round and saw the prison ships blocked starkly against the
blue and silver of river and sky, and they seemed to Lucy and
Justus a blasphemy sprawled upon it. They looked in silence
for a moment and then Justus said to the boatman, "We want

to come as near as we can to the third in line. We have a friend
there."

The waterman nodded. They had his sympathy and his
muttered maledictions upon prisons of any sort or kind, the
Tower, the Fleet, the hulks, the whole stinking lot, was a brief
comfort so strengthening is it to realize afresh the right thinking of the men of labour and poverty who are the foundations
of the commonweal. Like a darting moorhen their boat shot
this way and that through the intervening shipping until with
a quick twist the waterman had it right under the hull of the
third ship. Its dark shape rose above them growing in height
like a mounting wave, and Lucy was suddenly cold with
horror. She had wanted to come near, she had said in the
immunity of distance. But now she was too close to be
immune. She knew as yet next to nothing, in her own body
and mind, about the horror of human suffering, and now here
it was looming over her in stifling darkness. It was partly the
smell of it that made the hulk so dreadful and gave it this
density. The small port-holes were open and gave forth the
stench of human misery.

"Watch them as they pass!" commanded Justus angrily
and sharply. "Turn your face to them. He might, perhaps, see
you. Turn your face up, I tell you. Watch them."

The boat was slipping slowly along the hull. She controlled
her trembling and with all her heart and soul she watched the
port-holes and drew their dreadful breath into her lungs. She
was aware of human life and endurance within the darkness
but she could distinguish no lineaments of it. It seemed a face-
less thing. The misery of men was so vast that it could bear no
single face, only the face of humanity itself, the face of Christ
that is marred more than that of any man. Searching the dark
eyes of the port-holes in vain, she could feel nothing but fear
and hopelessness, and when the boat had drawn away a little,
and rocking gently on the water they looked back at the ship, she
hardly understood Justus when he said, "You were quite right to
come, Lucy. Those port-holes look blind but they are not and
there is light in the eyesockets. Stand up and wave. And do not
look so sad. Stand up and laugh with the man who is there."

She let him pull her to her feet and hold her steady in the rocking boat, and she smiled obediently as she waved, and so did Justus, and the waterman did the same, though he thought the couple crazy. And inside the darkness a tremor of happiness shivered from prow to stern of the prison ship, and one old man, though the tears were running down his face, was laughing, so joyous is it to know that you are not forgotten. But this he could not tell them, and by the time they got back to the quay Lucy and Justus could have wept because they would never know if they had done anything or nothing for Parson Peregrine.

Lucy, going first up the stone steps against the river wall, was too bewildered with sorrow to look where she was going when she reached the top and it was not until she had bumped into the burly man coming quickly towards her, and he had gripped her arm to keep her from falling, that she gasped, "Uncle Barlow! I thought you were in Ireland with Lord Glamorgan."

"Not so loud, my girl!" he said. "Is it Lucy? It must be, since that is Justus. He is not changed so much. But you, Lucy! Who would have thought you would have turned out so pretty? Who is the lucky man? Begod, if I were only younger and not married to your poor aunt! Would you have liked to be Mrs. Barlow?"

"I like to be your niece," said Lucy politely. "Where *is* my poor aunt?"

"With friends in Fishguard. I visited her before I came to London with Lord Glamorgan."

Justus had joined them now. "You had a pleasant journey?" he asked.

"Pleasant!" ejaculated Uncle Barlow with sarcasm. "Just the two of us, with my lord travelling as my servant and in as vile a temper as ever I have known him. Pleasant, by cock! Tell your grandmother, if you two children are with her now, that I will give myself the honour of waiting on her in a day or two."

"If my lord is going overseas there is a ship down there bound for Rotterdam," said Justus.

"Do not speak so loud, boy! My lord has business in London."

"The ship is called the *Sea-Horse*," whispered Lucy, and her captain looks trustworthy. His name is Axel. Do you sail with my lord?"

"That is as may be," said Uncle Barlow mysteriously. "And not a word of this outside the family."

He left them, pulled his hat over his eyes and ran down the steps, and they retrieved Moses and rode home laughing together at Uncle Barlow's cloak-and-dagger manner, and his boyish delight in his adventure.

"It is a game to him," said Justus.

"Thick-skinned, stout and jovial men are lucky," said Lucy. "Who would think to look at him that he had lost his home and fortune? His surface is not even dented. Yet that may be their way," she added.

"Their way?" queried Justus.

"With misfortune. They may deliberately train themselves not to care too much."

"You might try practising that way yourself," said Justus gently. "Try tonight. Try being a cloak-and-dagger girl."

She laughed but that night in bed, after sleepless hours thinking of Parson Peregrine and the hulks, she tried to find happiness and normality again by remembering Uncle Barlow's undented surface and Captain Axel's laughing eyes, and the contours of the little *Sea-Horse* whose motion was so easy when she jumped the waves. She slept at last, and dreamed that she was herself on board the *Sea-Horse*, in the bows of the ship with a keen wind blowing. It was night but the stars were brilliant and the light of the ship's lantern showed her the outline of a tall cloaked figure standing beside her. "Charles!" she gasped, but just as the heavy dark head turned towards her she woke. All day she longed for the unseen face and remembered vividly the brilliance of the stars, the wind and the surge of the ship. All day it seemed to be carrying her with the movement of life itself and the movement of her own longing. Had it been Charles?

That evening Uncle Barlow came to see them, and Justus.

came with him, and they sat before the wood fire in the spring twilight and talked in low voices of the family and its doings and of the sorrows of the time. Uncle Barlow said nothing of Lord Glamorgan but he told Mrs. Gwinne and Elizabeth in strict and portentous confidence, enjoying their amazement and curiosity, that in a few days time he would be sailing for Rotterdam on secret state affairs. "In order that I may bring you word of her I shall make it my business to visit poor Margaret Gosfright," he told Mrs. Gwinne. "I hear she has been ill. I trust she has not ailed seriously?"

"My sister and I have both been unfortunate this year," murmured Elizabeth, and her eyes travelled sadly to the transparency of her thin hand held fanwise between her cheek and the flames. She was looking very beautiful.

"They are both mending now," said Mrs. Gwinne with firm gentleness. "Elizabeth still lacks confidence and Margaret frets because she is unable to visit me. She has never put down roots in Holland. Her heart is incurably Welsh and she is homesick."

"Poor Aunt Margaret!" said Lucy with a rush of sympathy. "Could I not go with Uncle Barlow and visit her?"

The words were out before she knew she was going to speak them. For a moment she seemed to be standing outside herself, watching the surge of her own longing, and the movement of the ship. Then she was back within herself again, folding her longing in resolution about a heart that had become oddly unaware of the beloved people who shared the quiet room with her. She looked at them and saw them as misty dream-like figures. Only the tall man whose face she had not seen was real, and he wanted her.

"Lucy, I cannot possibly be left!"

It was her mother crying out in outrage. But the cry raised no pity in her. Not even her grandmother's hand laid upon hers, or Justus's pleading eyes burning for a moment through the mistiness of his face, moved her to more than a passing sensation of pain.

"I do not know you, Lucy," said Mrs. Gwinne. "Your face is strange to me."

413

"I feel a stranger," said Lucy. "I love you but I feel I have to go away for a while."

"If you think," said Uncle Barlow, "that I am going to saddle myself with a pretty maid like you on an important journey like mine you are very much mistaken. You will stay where you are, my girl. At home under the authority of a good mother is the place for you."

"Not just now," said Lucy. "Aunt Gosfright is ill. She needs me."

"So am I ill," said Elizabeth. "So do I need you."

"Not now, madam my mother," said Lucy. "You could be well now if you wished to be."

"Lucy!" cried Elizabeth, and began to weep.

"There is no need for argument, ladies," said Uncle Barlow firmly. "I do not either hamper my movements or endanger my reputation by travelling with a little hussy."

He was annoyed now, for he disliked female tears, but Lucy knew what to do; no annoyance of Uncle Barlow's was ever proof against a good laugh. "We will talk it over with my grandfather," she said, and taking his arm she led him out of the room and into the passage before he knew what she was doing with him. "There will be no danger to your reputation if I travel with you as Mrs. Barlow," she said. "You asked me yesterday if I should like to be your wife. For a short while, yes, I would." She paused. "Only nominally." she added firmly, and knocked at the study door. "It is Lucy," she called to Mr. Gwinne.

The old man shuffled to the door and unlocked it. When they entered they beheld his back view, a large handkerchief trailing from his pocket, shuffling away from them. Mr. Gwinne had become more eccentric of late. He had built a little house of books all round his chair and table, with a gap in it just wide enough to admit his thin figure, and inside this he sat and read all day. He went inside now, sat down and was instantly lost again in the book he was reading. Lucy, as thin as he was, followed him in and stood beside him but he took no notice of her. Uncle Barlow, too stout to pass through the little door, stood outside chuckling. The situation had tickled his sense of humour as Lucy had known it would. She gently closed her relative's book, removed the spectacles from his nose and knelt down beside him, her free hand on his knee. He looked round vaguely for his spectacles and saw her face raised to his and smiled in childish pleasure at the sight of it.

"You know that Margaret Gosfright has been ill, Grandfather? Yes, you do. We told you. And as she cannot visit us now it is only right that one of her family should visit her. Uncle Barlow is willing to take me. Have I your permission to go?"

"Where are my spectacles?" asked Mr. Gwinne, hunting through the papers on his table.

"I will find them for you when you have answered my question. Have I your permission to visit my Aunt Gosfright? Uncle Barlow will go with me and look after me."

"Yes, yes. Do what you like. Do you see them anywhere?"

"Here they are," said Lucy, replacing them gently on his nose. "Thank you, Grandfather." She got up, bent down and kissed him in farewell, opened his book for him and found the place. For a moment he took her hand and held it, but he had forgotten her by the time she had rejoined Uncle Barlow. She pulled him over to the window and looked up into his face, her hands on his shoulders. "Uncle Barlow," she said, "I have to go. You must understand that I have to go. We have my grandfather's permission."

He no longer refused her but he answered soberly, "I must have your mother's permission too."

"She no longer has authority over me," Lucy reminded him. "My father now has the custody of his children and he is in Wales."

"Then I must have your grandmother's," said Uncle Barlow.

They went back to the parlour and found Mrs. Gwinne alone. "Your mother was crying so much that Justus took her to her room," she said. "Lucy, come here; you too, son Barlow. Lucy, you must give me a truthful answer to my question. Is it your intention to force yourself upon a husband who in his present circumstances may no longer want you with him?"

"No," said Lucy steadily. "But I must know what his pleasure is."

"And how are you to know it? He is in Paris, they tell me, and you will be in Holland."

"The Princess Mary is at The Hague. He is sure to go there soon to visit her. Then I will try to find some way of seeing him. If he wants me I will stay with him. If he does not I will come home again, as soon as Aunt Gosfright is recovered."

"You think he wants you?"

Lucy remembered her dream and her face was illumined. "I know that he does," she said.

Mrs. Gwinne turned to the astonished Uncle Barlow. "Lucy's circumstances are difficult," she said. "Her husband is the Prince of Wales."

At first Uncle Barlow was deprived of the power of speech, then a flicker of excitement came into his eyes and his lips slowly parted in pleasure. "Is he, by cock!" he ejaculated.

Lucy was speechless too, in horror at her grandmother. Surely she knew that Uncle Barlow, the cloak-and-dagger man, was not to be trusted with a secret like this? She flushed with sudden anger and Mrs. Gwinne knew why. "He must know, Lucy," she said sharply. "He must know your real reason in this. He is your uncle and he will not speak of your marriage outside the family. That, son Barlow, is the Prince's wish at present."

"I understand perfectly, madam," said Uncle Barlow solemnly. Then he roared with laughter and slapped his thigh. "You clever girl, Lucy!" he ejaculated through his mirth. "You clever little girl!"

"Son Barlow, I beg you will be silent," said Mrs. Gwinne, and glancing at her he saw that she was looking grey and old and he stopped laughing. She went on in a tired voice, "Tell us, when you can, the day and time when the ship will leave the docks and her brother will bring Lucy to you if she is still determined on this course. But I hope that Justus will go alone to tell you that my granddaughter remains with me. You had better go now."

Lucy found she was alone with her grandmother and she

knelt on the floor, her face buried in the arms she laid across Mrs. Gwinne's knees. "You cannot do this, Lucy," said the old woman. "You may know great bliss in the reunion but the end can only bring you grief."

Lucy began to cry a little but she did not answer. Not even her grandmother's grief seemed real to her. She could weep for it but it could not pierce through her resolve to her heart.

2

Lucy packed her few belongings secretly and hurriedly. No one saw her do it and her mother did not know whether when the summons came she would go or not, but her grandmother knew that though she was gentle and tender to her family she had withdrawn her true self from them. But not because she feared the shaking of her resolution. Mrs. Gwinne, who in her own life had loved deeply, recognized now the depth of Lucy's love for her husband.. It had been growing, not lessening, through the months of absence and now that the time of crisis had come it so possessed her that it was her only truth. Mrs. Gwinne knew it all so well and through the sleepless nights acknowledged her helplessness.

Two days later the wind moved into a new quarter and early the next morning a message came and Lucy herself received it. Mrs. Gwinne knew it had come but she said nothing and it was not until dusk had fallen, and the stormcock was singing on top of the apple tree, that Lucy said to her mother and grandmother, "As soon as it is dark Justus will be here with a hired chaise to take me to the ship. My uncle will come later on foot and then we shall sail."

There was no time now for anything but the last flurry of preparation. Mrs. Gwinne herself went to the kitchen to prepare a final meal for Lucy and Elizabeth went upstairs to find two gifts she wanted to give her daughter. Lucy ate what was put before her but now at last realization of what she was doing to the two women was coming to her, and it was hard to swallow the food and listen to the composed messages that her grandmother was giving her for Margaret Gosfright.

"I may be back quite soon, Grandmother," she whispered.
"You may, my love," said her grandmother.

Elizabeth came in with her own blue cloak and hood over her arm. "It is warmer than yours," she said to her daughter. "And not so shabby. And you always loved the crocus-coloured lining." She put the cloak round Lucy and handed her a small leather case. "Put it in one of your bags and look at it later. It is something I would have given you on your wedding day had I been with you."

Lucy put the case in one of her saddlebags and put her arms round her mother and thanked her, and in this moment of parting she felt deep reverence for her. This was her mother who had given her birth and even a selfish woman is selfless in giving life to another. There could be no greater gift and no greater bond between two people. Too late, Lucy knew it. "I have never loved you enough," she said to her mother.

It was all she did say by way of farewell and to her grandmother as she clung to her she said nothing at all, for the chaise was already at the gate and Justus was getting out of it. After that there seemed a blank in time and the next thing she knew she was sitting beside Justus driving to London. He said nothing but he was holding one of her hands and examining her fingers as though he had never seen them before.

In the bustle of the docks, in the alternate darkness and confused light of swinging lanterns, no one noticed the boy and girl making their way to the Sea-Horse. They went up the gangway and were met at the top by Captain Axel, who took them instantly to Lucy's cabin. "Mrs. Barlow," he said formally, "I have a message for you from your husband. He wants you to stay here until the ship has put to sea. If you should hear him come aboard with his companion he begs that you will not leave your cabin to greet him."

"Does my husband's companion know that I am sailing with them?" asked Lucy.

Captain Axel's eyes twinkled suddenly. "I gather that he will be informed of that fact when we are well out to sea," he said. "Now I will leave you to take leave of your brother."

In Justus's arms, gripped with all the strength of his grief, she was fully aware of him again. Their oneness with each other had been deeper than she knew. They had shared life from the beginning with complete trust in each other and dependence upon each other's love. It was worse than the parting from her father for he had turned from her to the satisfactions of loneliness but Justus had yet to find these. Ever since the parting between their parents all his security had been in Lucy. He let go of her and slipped something into her pocket.

"I will see you again, Justus," she gasped. "I know I will. It is not goodbye. I will see you again."

She was talking to emptiness, for he had gone, taking her childhood with him. Under her feet the boards were uneasy and she was aware of the flow of the dark river. Feet tramped past her cabin door and she heard rough voices talking in a tongue she did not understand. She was afraid, and the hand she had slipped unconsciously into her pocket tightened on what Justus had put there. She took it out and found it was one of his most cherished possessions, a sea-shell which when held to the ear gave one the sound of the sea. She listened, and heard the sea at Roch. He had given her back her childhood in a shell.

Then she remembered that her mother had given her a gift too and she unfastened the saddlebag and found the leather case. Inside was the miniature of William that had been one of Elizabeth's wedding presents. She sat on the floor and held it cupped in her hand, the light of the lantern showing her a young and happy bridegroom, his smiling face surrounded by a gold frame set with pearls. That her mother could have sufficiently conquered her jealousy of her daughter's greater love for her father as to give her this miniature took Lucy's breath away. It was her first experience of the great gusts of nobility that can spring at times from even the most self-centred of human beings. She wished she could cry but she was too taut with grief to do that. "I have never loved you enough," she said again to her mother. "Never enough." Then she put the miniature away and turned herself back to her presently loyalty. "Charles," she said to herself, and taking

419

her wedding ring from the chain round her neck she put it on her finger.

There was a knock at the door and a man entered with a bowl of soup for her. There was a small bunch of violets beside it on the tray and though she could not understand what the sailor said she knew that Captain Axel had seen Justus leave the ship and had sent both to comfort her. By the time she had eaten the soup and fastened the violets in her dress she could smile a little and wondered if he had been disappointed to find her the wife of that stout elderly man her uncle Barlow.

She was tired and lay down on her bed, listening to the sounds of departure, the shouted orders, the tramping feet, the rattle of the hawser as the anchor came up. Uncle Barlow and Lord Glamorgan were on board, she supposed, though she had not heard them come. Then came the gliding of the ship and the thrill of the movement went through Lucy's body too and the vividness of her dream came back. She was moving to Charles. She laid her left hand flat on the pillow beside her cheek and the glow of the ruby gave her courage. It was the first time that she had experienced the almost mystic power of jewels, that from the beginning of time had symbolized the exchange of love.

Uncle Barlow came in once and patted her shoulder in satisfaction, very pleased with her. He had feared tears and was delighted to find her so serene. "That is a good girl," he said. "Sleep well."

Then he straightened his shoulders and braced himself for the unpleasant necessity of telling his lordship that his niece was travelling with them to visit her aunt; called Mrs. Barlow for her added protection and safety.

She dozed fitfully for a few hours and when at last the ship seemed quiet she went out on deck. They were still in the tideway but it seemed that the sea was coming to meet them for there was a strong tang of salt in the air and the few shore lights were so distant that they might have been stars low on the horizon. Overhead was a blaze of constellations but no moon. The ship's lanterns showed the water in exultant movement, tossing the lights from its shoulders as it raced to the sea. With her mother's cloak wrapped warmly about her she stood in the bow of the *Sea-Horse* and looking up saw the carved poop above her and the figure of its captain standing beside the helmsman at the wheel, and overhead the sails were full of wind, curved like the petals of magnolia blossoms. The buccaneer was awake in her and she could have laughed for joy.

She did not hear footsteps and when she turned and saw the tall cloaked figure of her dream standing beside her she was startled and even frightened when the heavy head turned towards her. A lantern faintly illumined the long melancholy face. She could not see the eyes in the pits of darkness but she sensed that they were not softened by the sight of her. The wig increased the ponderous weight of the head that seemed now to be hanging over her like some portent of doom. The grim mouth opened like a dark cavern and let out a gusty sigh. "Mrs. Barlow," said Lord Glamorgan in tones of deep despair. "Your servant, madam."

Lucy was abruptly set free from the whole gamut of emotions that until now had made her feel like a quivering harp plucked by more hands than she could well endure upon her spirit. Her natural laughter came back. Poor Lord Glamorgan! He had looked forward to the peacefulness of an all-male journey and now a giddy girl was to be his travelling companion.

"My lord," she said gently, "I will not incommode you. Even if we encounter storm and are long at sea I shall give no trouble. I am strong and healthy and I know when to hold my tongue."

Something faintly resembling a smile creased Lord Glamorgan's gloomy face. "That, madam," he said, "is a priceless gift in a female. Are you returning to your cabin? I wish you a very good night."

She was still laughing inside herself when she lay down again on her bed. Then came a tremor of fear. So that dream had not been a summons from her husband but merely that queer thing, dreaming forward. The rest of the night she could not sleep.

Four

I

Lucy was leaning on the parapet of one of the bridges of The Hague, lulled to tranquillity by the stillness and peace of the July morning. The sun had only just risen and when a short while ago she had ridden through the sleeping city she had felt as though she alone were alive.

It was something new to feel tranquil for the two months she had spent in Holland had brought her no nearer to a meeting with Charles, and into close companionship with Aunt Margaret in the Gosfright house at Rotterdam. That her aunt, ailing and irritable, had not driven her distracted she had put down to the extraordinary fact that she had fallen in love with Holland. That she, who so loved mountains and wildness, could so delight in a flat, tidy landscape surprised her. It was the nearness to the sea, she thought, and the rivers that brought the shipping so far inland, and the quantities of seabirds that pleased her. At Rotterdam the deep canals came right through the town and sea-going ships sailed past the doors of the houses. The *Sea-Horse*, after sailing up the River Maas to Rotterdam in the dawn of a May day, had glided close to the windows of Uncle Gosfright's house before she docked, and those windows had been for the next two months Lucy's comfort.

But Aunt Margaret was better now and for her convalescence they were staying at The Hague with her husband's sister Wilhelmientje Vingboon. Ardent gossips as they both were Margaret and her sister-in-law got on well, and when they were settled with their needlework Lucy was able to escape, ostensibly to her chamber to write to her mother but often out through the back door to the streets and canals of The Hague. But to this bridge on the outskirts of the city she could only escape in the early morning, with the collusion of

Wilhelmientje's husband Herman, who had shown her where to find the key of the stable and had put one of his horses at her disposal.

This bridge was another of her special places. Here she could look out over the fields and marvel at the windmills. She liked it best when the vast sky was full of hurrying clouds and the wings of the mills turned swiftly, but when the day was still and blue like this one the extraordinary clarity of the light made her think of Pembrokeshire. The fields were intersected by canals. The big ones were the roads of Holland where the barges and sailing ships passed and repassed in dreamlike silence, the small ones, made for drainage and division of the fields, were carpeted with waterlilies, their banks gold with kingcups in the spring. The herons loved these fields and canals as the storks loved the town, building their nests on the chimneystacks. Lucy would never forget her arrival at The Hague for almost the first thing she had seen had been her family crest, the stork, surmounting the church towers and public buildings, and Herman Vingboon had told her that every ounce of plate wrought by the famous silversmiths of The Hague bore the emblem of the stork.

There was no sound, no human figure in all the vast landscape. She had always liked to be alone but now that Charles had made her a part of himself she liked it less, for the loneliness passed so quickly into longing. Her husband was still so far away. She knew something of his movement for since he was the brother of their princess there was often talk about him at The Hague, and especially at the Vingboon house, for Herman was in charge of the horses at the royal stables and he heard the latest gossip. The Prince was in Paris with his mother, Lucy had been told, and it had been rumoured that he was to marry Mademoiselle de Montpensier, a great heiress and the French king's cousin. Her heart had beaten to suffocation when she heard this but when she learned that Mademoiselle was much older than Charles, a large lady with a large nose, it had quietened.

Then had come the tidings she had been longing for; Charles was coming to The Hague. For a few days she had been wild with hope, and then Herman had come from the palace with the startling news that the greater part of the English fleet had mutinied and sailed for France and the Prince of Wales, and Charles had left Paris for Calais. After that, no news, and she had been so restless and anxious that this early morning peace seemed very strange. Unless he was nearer to her than she knew? She looked round involuntarily, but there was no one there and nothing to feel but the ache of longing.

Suddenly the air was trembling with distant music. It was six o'clock on a July morning and all the bells of The Hague were ringing out the news. The bells of the city of London had been a delight to hear, borne on the wind to the garden at St. Giles, but the bells of The Hague rang carillons, clear as the air of the great skies swept by the sea winds. Away from The Hague Lucy would always remember it as a city of bells and birds, surrounded by a necklace of trees, and beyond the trees the flat green meadows and the canals with their floating carpets of lilies.

The city would be stirring now and she must go back. She had tethered the chestnut cob to the parapet of the bridge. She mounted him and rode back to the city and along the cobbled lane that led to the Vingboon home. The canal was on one side of her and on the other towered the tall red-roofed houses. Many of the older houses were crooked because of the subsidence of the soil, and they seemed like aged people holding each other up. This watery country was much afflicted by rheumatism and it was not difficult to think that the oldest houses had it too. She rode slowly because maidservants in white caps and wooden sabots were going backwards and forwards to the canal fetching water, and storks were stepping daintily and arrogantly here and there, entirely at home and unafraid. No one would ever harm a stork for they were regarded with almost superstitious reverence. They were lucky birds and to have storks build a nest on your roof was to be protected and safe. The wings of the gulls flashed overhead and when Lucy opened the door in the wall beside the house and went into the courtyard the doves rose in a cloud to greet her. They again were birds that brought luck and there were few families who did not own at least a pair of turtle-doves as a charm against the rheumatism.

Lucy led the cob through the courtyard to the stable and then went into the house to get ready for yet another decorous day. The stableboy and the indoor servants greeted her with broad smiles, for they knew all the ways by which she escaped from decorum and like Herman kept her secret.

One of the servants, Betje Flinck, who especially attended upon the ladies of the household, was a good friend to Lucy. She was an intelligent girl, soon to be married to one of the French chefs at the palace, a man called Louis Fragonard. She had picked up a little English from her mother, who in her youth had been a maidservant at the house of the English ambassador at The Hague, and Lucy, equally intelligent, could now speak some Dutch. They liked each other. Betje was older than Lucy and mothered her. Her home was at Scheveningen, a village by the sea a few miles away. Her mother and father, she had told Lucy, lived in a farmhouse there. Her father and elder brother were fishermen and had a stall in The Hague fishmarket. Their business was a prosperous one and they provided the palace with fish. The younger brother helped his mother with the cows and dairy. If at any time Lucy wanted a breath of sea air, Betje had said, she would be welcome at the farmhouse. Lucy had told Wilhelmientje and Aunt Margaret of this invitation and Wilhelmientje had said that the Flincks were highly respectable people and Lucy would be safe with them. Aunt Margaret had said frigidly that they would consider the question if the invitation was repeated.

But this day was not destined to be one of the dull ones for at the midday meal the three ladies were joined by Herman Vingboon in a state of great excitement. He was a jolly man, tall and handsome, with a small pointed black beard and twirled ends sharp as needles to his waxed moustaches. Lucy liked him because he was a horseman. There was nothing he did not know about horses and all the love of which he was capable was bestowed on them alone. Though perhaps capable

CHILD FROM THE SEA

of cruelty in other directions she knew he would never harm a horse. Between large mouthfuls of roast beef and great draughts of beer he communicated his excitement to the ladies.

"The English fleet that ratted to the Prince of Wales is at Helvoetsluys," he told them. "The Prince and his brother the Duke of York are with them, and Prince Rupert. The Duke, they tell me, has just escaped from England in women's clothes. There's a plucky young fellow for you. Only fifteen years old."

"When did you hear this, Herman?" asked Margaret.

"Early this morning at the stables," said Herman. "The horses had to be groomed and got ready early to take their highnesses to meet the Prince. A busy time I have had of it this morning I can tell you." he reached for more beer. "And I will have a busier few hours this evening when they all come back and I have the Englishmen's horses to see to as well as my own."

"But how can Prince Charles come back to The Hague with Prince William and Princess Mary?" asked Lucy, who was sitting bolt upright with a flaming red spot on each cheek. "He must set sail at once for England. If he does that, with the temper in England what it was when I left, the whole country will rise to him and the King will be set free."

"Ships have to be refitted, my dear," explained Herman patiently. "You cannot start a campaign without making plans for it. You must have food and water, men and arms. You must also have money to pay for these things. Where's that to come from?"

"I do not see why Holland should finance an English war," said Wilhelmientje.

"Our Princess Mary is your Princess of Orange." said Lucy hotly. "Families should help each other."

"It is the duty of France to help our cause," said Aunt Margaret, pouring oil on troubled waters. "Queen Henrietta Maria is a French princess. Better still, Prince Charles should marry his heiress with no further dilly-dallying. Then as regards finance there would be no further difficulty."

26

Lucy had not yet told Aunt Margaret about her marriage and so no one knew that she sat there with her blood turning to ice. Present with her at the table now were two of the three demons that would torment her for the rest of her life; wrangles about money and the fear that Charles would commit bigamy.

Herman broke into a roar of laughter. "The Prince is a lad with an eye for a pretty woman," he told his ladies. "He will hardly take la Grande Mademoiselle to his bed while the Duchesse de Châtillon continues to smile on him. There's beauty for you! They say that—"

"That will do, Herman," interrupted his wife severely. "The gossip of the stables is not a suitable subject for our table."

Lucy's third demon entered and stood with the other two behind her chair, the demon of malicious gossip. With her head high she spoke out instantly, reiterating to herself her faith in Charles. "The Prince has always borne an unsullied reputation," she said coldly. "At what time will they be returning to the palace?"

"I could not tell you," said Herman. "In time for the banquet this evening. Five o'clock perhaps. Six o' clock."

"You cannot be out in the streets to watch them ride by, Lucy," said Aunt Margaret firmly. "You might have to wait for hours and Wilhelmientje cannot spare a servant to attend you for so long."

The meal was finished now and Herman pushed back his chair, his eyes twinkling. "Lucy can ride back to the palace with me," he said. "We shall be told when they are on the way and I will take her to a good vantage point for seeing the procession. Make haste, Lucy. Put your habit on."

No one could object and Lucy ran upstairs to put on her riding habit for the second time that day. The three demons had vanished and she was madly happy. She would see Charles again and that at the moment was all that mattered. Her habit was the colour of the swallow's wings and a bird could hardly have flown down the stairs into freedom more quickly than she did.

Their way took them past the Wassenaer Hof, the residence of the widowed Queen of Bohemia, Charles's aunt and Prince Rupert's mother, and she turned her head to look with interest at the gateway in the courtyard wall, with rising beyond it the tall red brick building with its towers and gables. Charles's family was still for her an enlargement of her own, the nimbus about the moon, and for no member of it did she feel a more lively affection than for the Queen of Bohemia, who was never so happy as when she was on horseback.

She was a woman of courage and character; so much of the latter that she had become "a character", horrifying the careful Dutch ladies by the extravagance and eccentricity of her housekeeping and the troops of monkeys and dogs who accompanied her wherever she went. And even now, after bearing many children, she was still so beautiful that men called her the Queen of Hearts. At other times she was called the Winter Queen, for her brief and tragic reign had lasted for only one winter.

The gossip about this extraordinary woman was neverending and Lucy had heard some of it when she listened to the talk of Aunt Margaret and Wilhelmientje, and had boiled with anger. The jealousy that could do its best to harm the reputation of a woman of spirit and beauty, merely because she had a power to charm and delight that others did not have, seemed to Lucy a vile thing. Sometimes she had a strange sense of kinship with the Winter Queen; almost as though they were sisters in adversity. But that was nonsense, and audacious nonsense too. Yet she answered Herman absently as they rode past the Wassenaer Hof, and he was piqued by her lack of attention.

"The Queen will have ridden out to Helvoetsluys with the rest," he told Lucy. "Any excuse to ride abroad, and I must say that she has a good seat on a horse. They call her a beauty but she is too gaunt for my taste. I like a bit of flesh on women and horses." He eyed Lucy. "You could do with a good bran mash, yourself, my girl."

Lucy withered him with a glance yet in a moment she had relented and was laughing with him for he was being very

kind to her today. Was he not helping her to a sight of her
own husband?

2

Herman obtained permission for his niece to sit in the palace
gardens with the proviso that she must be out of them before
the royal family returned, and he left her on a seat beside a
small lake where swans were elegantly floating, their whiteness mirrored in the blue water between the lilies. Not far
from the lake was the newly completed Mauritzhuis, built by
the Prince of Orange to house his splendid collection of pictures. She glanced towards the palace and it looked to her very
splendid, and the garden was so large and it awed her. What
wealth these people had! And what power. They could crush
you or make you just as they pleased. She felt scared beneath
her joy and taking her ring from round her neck she put it on
her finger, and the fear was gone. She got up and wandered
about the garden, finding hidden grottos, fountains and
marble statues, but she kept returning to the swans' lake lest
Herman should waste time looking for her when the message
arrived.

It came earlier than they had expected, about five o'clock.
Herman fetched her in a hurry and disregarding the command that she must leave the garden took her to where a flight
of steps led up to a little Greek temple built against the wall,
beneath the spreading branches of a tall yew tree. Here it was
easy for him to lift her to the top of the wall where she could
sit hidden by the sweeping shadow of the tree. He laughed as
he turned to leave her. "There will be the devil and all to pay if
you are found there but in that habit you look like a dark
bird hidden in its nest. But mind, Lucy, do not you dare come
down till I fetch you. I will not forget you. Stay where you
are."

She gave him her promise, for he might be in trouble if she
were found, and settled herself within the friendliness of the
tree, feeling as though she drew its shadows about her like a
cloak. She had a growing sense of silence and of sanctuary; yet

she was looking down a broad tree-lined avenue where a laughing crowd of people was gathering to line the way beneath the linden trees. The silence came not from about her but from within, from her past. She was remembering the yew tree beside the portico of the church at Covent Garden, and Old Sage. "The maintaining of faith is so hard." She had forgotten him again, but it seemed he did not forget her. For the flash of a moment she knew that the maintaining of faith was what supremely mattered to her. It was for her the hidden life.

Time flies when the mind turns inward to the past it treasures and it seemed only a few moments later that she heard the distant cheers and the sound of an approaching cavalcade beat in her blood. Processions of any kind always excited Lucy; kings and princes coming and going, wild beasts on the move, the migration of birds, ants upon the march and the passing of clouds across the sky. They thrilled her with a sense of some vast purpose to be achieved and some great haven to be reached. Even when they were caught up short, abortive, or satisfied with some minor goal, the echoes seemed to sound on through time. And this procession was bringing Charles once more from his world into hers. They were swinging together again like two clock figures who can meet only briefly at the striking of the hour.

They were coming under the linden trees, the summer dust rising under the horses' hoofs, the sun piercing through the leaves to illumine the colours of plumes and doublets and the sparkling points of the swords and halberds. They were passing her, a detachment of cavalry first and then the young Prince and Princess of Orange whom she had seen last as children, the Queen of Bohemia and her two dark eagle-faced sons, Rupert and Maurice, Charles and his young brother James and the ladies and gentlemen in attendance upon them. She watched them from the depths of her dark tree as once she had watched the procession at Exeter from the narrow street down which she had turned back to her own world. Now, as then, they passed by and she was alone again.

They were gone and only three of them seemed still with her. The Queen, gaunt in face and figure but still a woman of grace and beauty, holding herself proudly and sitting her horse superbly. And Charles, no longer the boy she had married but a confident young man with a new pride in his bearing as well as a new hardness in his face. And the third was Robert Sidney, with the same dignity and gentleness that she remembered. To know he was here at The Hague brought comfort; for Charles had changed so much in so short a time.

Yet it was his face only that she saw when they had all gone and the road emptied and she was alone in her tree, for he was her husband and she wanted him intolerably. Yet how could she come to him? What could she do? At this moment, nothing. Only sit here and wait for Herman to fetch her.

But he did not come. She heard the church clocks strike six and the shadows lengthened on the grass. Two storks flew over the tree and she heard the gulls calling. She saw and heard these things but her mind grew numbed as her body grew stiff with fatigue. She supposed that Herman, the most casual of men, had forgotten her, yet she did not want to leave her tree because she did not know what to do if she did. Having seen Charles existence no longer seemed possible without him, and yet there was no way to come to him. So there was nowhere to go and nothing to do.

There were laughing voices in the garden and she saw a group of young men and girls standing beside the lake watching the swans, and Charles was with them. They had come out to enjoy the coolness of the garden before getting ready for the banquet. She had not expected this. She had no experience yet of how Charles behaved in his own world, they had been together only in hers, and she did not know that he would always be where there was fun going on. The aloofness, the cold and royal dignity that was his father's, would never be for him. She did not move from her tree, for she could not; but she did not take her eyes from his face until Robert Sidney came from the palace, it would seem with some message, for he and Charles drew away from the others and walked down the long path towards her, talking together.

She would never know what would have happened if at that

moment the two storks had not come flying back. Perhaps she
would have made no sign. Perhaps she would never have been
united to Charles again. But they came back and being tame
storks alighted fearlessly together on the roof of the Greek
temple beside her tree. Charles and Robert, new to Holland,
were not yet accustomed to the charms of the storks of The
Hague. They broke off their conversation and looked up with
delight at the two birds. It was Charles who saw her first and a
mischievous grin broke across his face. He saw only that there
was a girl in the tree, not who she was. "There is another bird
up there," he said to Robert, "A swallow." And he ran up the
steps beside the wall. "Lucy!" he gasped.

For a moment the expression on his face was one of blank
dismay, then as she stretched out her hand to him and he saw
his ring on her finger his face seemed to break up, the man's
hard mask dropped away and the boy behind came back. He
gripped her hand and love poured from his face like light.

"Sir!" gasped Robert from the foot of the steps. What next?
He had recently been appointed a gentleman of the bedchamber to the Prince and found the appointment no sinecure. Charles swung round to him and was instantly a man
again, rapping out the royal orders. "Go back to the others and
say I have gone into the palace. And please see to it that my
devotions in this temple are not disturbed."

"You are acquainted with this lady, sir?" asked Robert
coldly.

"Since my childhood. She is Mistress Lucy Walter."

"Lucy Walter!" Robert forgot he was a mere gentleman of
the bedchamber and leapt up the steps to stand beside the
Prince. "My little Lucy! Marry come up! I'd not have known
you, Lucy." He laughed, his old unchanged kindness pervasive
as some astringent herb. It saved Lucy from the disaster of a
storm of weeping and she smiled and held out her other hand
to him. Her husband's hand was cold from shock and shaking
a little but Robert's grip was warm and reassuring. Jealousy
surged in Charles and he struck his free hand down on
Robert's wrist. "You have my orders," he said, and Robert
bowed and left them.

Charles lifted Lucy down from the wall and they went into the little temple and clung together as though each was welcoming the other back from the grave. And so indeed it seemed to them. The stretch of time that had brought them from the kitchen at Roch to this hidden place at the foot of the yew tree had seemed endless, but now it had doubled round in a circle and brought them to the roots of being again and in so doing had vanished. For a moment or two the westering sun, slanting into the little temple, seemed the warmth of the flames on the kitchen hearth. All the bells of The Hague rang out their joy as the new hour dawned and for the man and woman life began once more. "The maintaining of truth is so hard." Not now. Never again, thought Charles. There was only the one woman and there would never be another.

They found themselves sitting on the seat inside the temple. Looking out they could see no more of the world than the flowers growing against the wall and it was easy to forget the dangers that threatened them beyond. Lucy, who need hide nothing from her husband, talked most. The question she had come to ask him, whether or not he wanted her, she did not ask for there was no need. The love that had shone from his face had banished the memory of that first look of dismay. She told him how she had come to be here, and going back a little she told him about the visit to Golden Grove and of her conviction, on the day the post came, that he had wanted her. "Did you want me then?" she asked.

"It was in October?" he asked.

"Yes. I think in the second week."

"I did want you then," he said thoughtfully. "It must have been the day when I told my mother about our marriage."

"What did she say?" whispered Lucy.

But it seemed that he wished he had not spoken for he suddenly changed the subject and began to tell her about little Minette who had been brought out from England to be with their mother, and how enchanting she was, and then he said, "Lucy, I have only a week before the fleet puts to sea again. What are we to do?"

433

"You do not wish your family here to know about our marriage?" she asked.

He seemed horrified at the very thought. " 'Sdeath, no! That would wreck all. And you are not to speak of it to a soul, Lucy. Where can we find another hidden home like the one at Roch?"

Lucy thought a little. "There is a fishing village on the coast called Scheveningen," she said. "People from The Hague go there to watch the wind chariots on the sands. The parents of Wilhelmientje's maid Betje live there. They have a farm and Aunt Margaret said I might go and stay there when I liked. Shall I do that? You would not mind being Tomos Barlow once more, my sailor husband from one of the English ships?"

Charles laughed. "Would I mind? I wish I were really Tomos, not heir to the throne of England but just your husband Tomos."

"That is not true, Charles," said Lucy soberly. "The throne of England is what you want. Even as a little boy you desired it. You wept when you thought your father might lose what you wanted."

He was silent and for a moment angry, for it would always vex him when she put her fingers on the truth, and to punish her he got to his feet. "I regret that I must leave you now," he said formally, but looking down into her vivid brown face with its blue, deep eyes he was overwhelmed again by his love for her and pulled her into his arms. "Make the arrangements," he whispered to her, "and then send a note to Sidney. He is trustworthy."

"I would like him to know that we are married. He was fond of me when I was a child."

"You may not tell him," said Charles shortly. "He will think none the worse of you. Do you not know that to be the mistress of a prince is to occupy a position of honour?"

"I did not know," said Lucy with equal shortness.

For a moment or two they were both taut with obstinacy, but they did not pull away from each other and presently Lucy relaxed with a willed gentleness that acknowledged no defeat. "If I have my integrity inside myself I can learn not to care too much what people say of me," she said.

"Did you expect me to proclaim you as my wife, just at this moment when the tide is turning and I am about to sail for England to recapture it for my father?" demanded Charles.

"No, merely to acknowledge me for what I am if and when we are seen together. But I have yielded now, for I did not come here to embarrass you but hoping that I might be with you sometimes to love and comfort you. And so I choose to be at your command to honour and obey you in all the ways that are possible for me."

The relaxation that was in her body was still not in his for he knew he had won no victory over her. The right of choice was something she still retained; and he wanted her to hold nothing back. Then the gulls flew over, returning from the inland feeding places to the sea to sleep, and their voices brought back memories of Roch and he knew that if fortune should be good to them, and if he could match this girl's integrity with his own, he might yet find all his happiness in her love.

"You will not be sorry, Lucy," he whispered. "One day I will make it all up to you."

For a moment or two they were in bliss, then Lucy heard Herman striding up the garden path and withdrew herself gently. "Stay here," she said. "I will go with him before he has time to see you."

Charles stepped back and sat on the seat in the shadows as she ran down the steps. He heard her ask Herman, "Had you forgotten me?"

"No, my girl. But Prince William's horse has fallen lame and I was delayed. Come quickly now. It is late."

Their footsteps died away and Charles sat on in the little temple, for he found that he had their bliss with him still. The two years of their parting that she had passed in the quietness of familiar places, cherishing her love for him and pondering upon it, had been for him years of turmoil and anxiety. At first the longing for her had been acute, then it had gradually become merely a dull sense of loss, and the acute longing had returned only once, on that day in Paris when his mother had tried to make him promise to marry Mademoiselle de Montpensier. He could never see La Grande Mademoiselle, jewelled and elaborate and looking always a little coarsened by her wealth, without a haunting memory of Lucy's simplicity and grace and that day, goaded beyond endurance, he had suddenly longed for her with such passion that he had told his mother he was already married and had shown her his copy of the marriage certificate.

After her first stunned silence the Queen had flown into one of her famous tempers and behaved like a little wild cat. After that she had wept herself exhausted and taken to her bed, made a remarkably quick recovery and summoned her chamberlain Harry Jermyn to a conference in her bedchamber. Jermyn had then tackled Charles. Their relationship was difficult. Charles disliked the large fair smiling man who for years had been his mother's favourite servant. Even in England the usual rumours had circulated and here in Paris it was the same. Yet the Queen was most easily approached through her chamberlain and her son dared not quarrel with him. But he could talk good sense and he had talked it then. He had told Charles that to acknowledge his marriage at this juncture would gravely prejudice his succession, and would give his enemies yet another weapon against his father. "Hold your tongue, sir, I implore you," he had said. "The Queen and I will do the same. The time of revealing this foolishness is not yet."

Privately Jermyn had trusted it would be never. He had a keen nose for rats and he thought he smelt one in that marriage certificate. Enquiries must be made. There was that man Prodger who was always about the Prince. Not a man he cared for personally but a useful type. But at this point he had realized that the Prince was speaking.

"Then if Lucy joins me here it must be as my mistress and not my wife."

"Join you here!" poor Jermyn had ejaculated. "God have mercy on us! I trust there is no danger of that, sir. Is she likely to follow you?"

"Only if I send for her."

"Sir, I must ask for your promise that you will do no such thing."

"I will think it over," Charles had said with hauteur.

But he had not thought it over for there had been too many other things to think about. And now here was Lucy. His confidence that she would not come unless he sent for her had been misplaced. Sitting in the little temple he had a moment of reaction and was a little angry with her; she was too proud, too independent, and she could not have come at a more awkward time. This mutiny of the fleet and its desertion to him was the opportunity that they had all been praying for. How could he think of Lucy when his mind was seething with anxiety and excitement? Yet when she had been in his arms she had seemed his world. He sat up straight with sudden resolution. Why should he not have this small world of home hidden secretly at the roots of his life? The French court was cautiously hospitable at present but exiled penniless princes were always felt to be a liability sooner or later. The same was true of the Dutch court who already had his exiled aunt of Bohemia upon their hands. He had no home and though he would have admitted it to no one he often felt lonely, rootless and insecure. Lucy had come and she should stay. He got up and ran down the steps of the temple light of heart.

3

Hesitation was never a part of Lucy's temperament and that same evening she had a conversation with Betje, and told her of her husband Tomos Barlow in the English navy, whose existence was not known to her Aunt Gosfright. Her explanations bore little relation to the truth but Prince Kilhwch-Charles Stuart-Tomos Barlow had such a radiance of fantasy about him now that the fabrication of fairytales was not as difficult as it had been. Passing on to Aunt Margaret she beat down her objections with her superior willpower and going to her bedchamber wrote a letter to Robert Sidney that Betje's father would deliver at the palace with the fish.

The next morning one of the Vingboon servants rode with her to Scheveningen. Joy came to her when leaving the woods behind them they crested a little rise and she saw the North Sea brilliant under the summer sun. The famous sands of the wind chariots looked from this distance like a gold pavement laid down for the containment of the sea, and behind it was a protective stretch of sand-dunes. Sheltered behind this rampart was the village of low red-roofed houses standing in small trim gardens.

The Flincks's house looked seaward across a small flower-filled garden with a sandy path leading from the wooden gate to the door. The square one-storey building was the largest in the village for the Flincks were well-to-do. The kitchen-living room, called the huiskamer, was in the centre of the house and the other rooms opened out of it, a bedchamber to right and left, with behind them a dairy and cow-house also opening from the huiskamer. A ladder led to the loft above. Across the yard at the back of the house was the stable and in the green fields beyond the black and white cows were at pasture.

The huiskamer was not like the Roch kitchen but it had the same atmosphere of work, warmth and hospitality. Vrouw Flinck was a friendly, motherly woman. Her hair was hidden away inside a snow-white cap and a white apron covered her voluminous blue skirt. Upon a hook behind the door hung the vermilion cloak which she like all the women of the village wore when she walked abroad. The fishermen wore jerseys of blue or red and it was a memory of colour that Lucy carried away with her from Scheveningen; golden sands and blue sea, the red roofs, the brightly painted fishing boats and the gay clothes.

The huiskamer gleamed with light reflected back from shining utensils and highly polished heirloom furniture. It was a low-ceilinged room scented by the bunches of herbs hanging from the beams of the ceiling, the peat fire and the strings of dried fish that hung within the huge chimney-place. The floor was of stone scrubbed to snowy whiteness, and never soiled by mud for sabots were left at the door and the family moved about their spotless home in stockinged feet. Vrouw Flinck herself knitted the stockings in thick, strong homespun yarn.

"Even in winter our feet are not cold," she told Lucy, "for when we are eating round the table or sitting to read or sew we have our stoofs," and she showed her the wooden footstools with perforated lids that in winter held earthenware vessels full of burning peat. "And it is with stoofs that we keep our babies warm." And she pointed to a corner of the room where there stood beside her spinning-wheel the baby-chair that her children had used, a beautifully carved wooden chair on wheels with a little cupboard underneath it for the stoof. Lucy almost cried out because for a flash of a second she saw a little boy sitting there, kicking his legs and laughing.

"You feel well, dearie?" queried Vrouw Flinck.

"Yes, madam," said Lucy, quite unconsciously using the title she gave her own mother and grandmother. "It is just that my husband and I have no child and what I want most in the world is a son."

Vrouw Flinck put her hand on Lucy's shoulder. "Many babes have been conceived and born in this house," she said. "And many children have sat laughing in that chair. So keep your heart up, my love. Is it tonight your man comes?"

"Tonight or tomorrow night," said Lucy. "I do not know. He is a sailor with the English ships. His name is Tomos Barlow."

"How strange are these English names!" murmured Vrouw Flinck.

"It is a Welsh name," Lucy corrected her with severity. "Tomos and I are Welsh, not English."

"I ask your pardon," said Vrouw Flinck humbly. "And now come through this door and I will show you the cow-house."

It was a large apartment, spotlessly clean, the walls lined with coloured tiles. The beams overhead held the overplus from Vrouw Flinck's china cupboard, Delft plates, glazed brown bowls and pots and pans. And from the beams hung bunches of peacocks' feathers. "This lovely place for the cows!" gasped Lucy.

"Our cows are our greatest treasures," explained Vrouw Flinck. "Are they not treasures in Wales?"

"Yes," said Lucy, "but we do not give them parlours to live in."

"I have heard that the English regard their dogs and horses as members of their families but not their cows," said Vrouw Flinck, "the Welsh are perhaps the same. If the dogs and horses why not the cows? What should we do without our butter and milk and cheese? The poorer people have but one cow but we have four. When the weather is cold they are brought in here to their own house and kept warm with blankets."

Lucy was gazing at the peacocks' feathers. "Do you think as we do that they are magic things?" she asked. "We have an old song in Wales which tells how a girl made a garland of peacocks' feathers for her lover."

"They bring good fortune," said Vrouw Flinck. "The peacock is to be revered, you know, like the stork, the heron and the swan. We do not know from whence they come on their great wings. They are to be revered."

"I revere all birds," said Lucy gravely. "Even the little ones with claws so tiny they can fit round your finger like a ring."

The dairy upon the other side of the living room was spotless as the cow-house and tiled with the same gay tiles. Lucy looked with admiration at the churns, the cheese press and the bowls of milk. There had been a dairy at Roch but as a child it had always been to the stables that her feet had carried her. "You have horses?" she asked.

"We have Nico who pulls the fish cart to market. We need horses in a fishing village for the boats are drawn up on the sand for safety by horses and pulled by them to the wharves for repair. And now I will show you your bedchamber. My two sons sleep there as a rule but they have moved to the loft while you and your Tomos are with us."

The little room was simply furnished with a chest for clothes and two carved oak chairs that must have been brought from the living room. The bed was a cupboard in the wall. There was a pot of flowers on the windowsill and the smell of the sea was in the room. Tears came into Lucy's eyes. "You have taken so much trouble for two strangers," she murmured.

"My daughter Betje loves you," explained Vrouw Flinck simply. "There is your saddlebag upon the floor. My husband brought it in for you. I will leave you now. Make this room your home."

Lucy unpacked her bag and changed her riding habit for an apple green gown. She dressed in the style of a Dutch huisvrouw now with a white cap over her hair and a little white apron. There were hooks in the wall and on one of them she hung the little mirror that her father had given her when she first grew old enough to need such a thing, and on the other his miniature. She flung her mother's cloak over one of the chairs, crocus-coloured lining outwards. The shell Justus had given her she put on the windowsill beside the pot of flowers. And she slipped Charles's ring on her finger.

Presently Vrouw Flinck called her to the kitchen for the midday meal of black rye bread, cheese and buttermilk, and then she went back to her room and sat with her sewing at the window to watch for Charles. She was making a shirt for him out of fine linen embroidered with scarlet thread hardly coarser than gossamer. She still did not exactly love her needle but she had mastered it and the pains she took were so infinite that the result was almost perfection.

She was so happy that she was not impatient and it was almost with surprise that she looked up at the click of the gate and saw a tall young man walking up the path in the dazzle of the late afternoon. He wore the rough clothes of a common sailor; a kerchief was bound about his head and he had a bundle hung over his shoulder on a short stick. He wore sabots and walked with a seaman's rolling gait, and it was not until he lifted his head that she knew who he was and flew out of the house and into his arms. In full view of the little world of Scheveningen but oblivious of it they clung together in fits of laughter, the tension and pain that had been between them in the palace garden entirely gone. This was Tomos again, delighting in the fun of masquerade, and there would never be tension when Charles was Tomos.

"How did you get here?" asked Lucy.

"I rode as far as the woods with Sidney and then changed into these clothes he got for me. It was easy to get away. My sister thinks I have ridden back to Helvoetsluys. There can be only this one night, dear heart, for there are great doings of trouble and hope in my world just now."

"Forget your world for this one night," pleaded Lucy.

"I have forgotten it," he said. "I will not even speak of it."

But later, sitting on the sand-dunes watching the strong colours of the dazzling day fading slowly to exquisite echoes of themselves, like flowers reflected in pools of pale water, he did speak of it and she was glad, for she wanted to share as many of his anxieties as she could; his father in prison and Princess Elizabeth, the most sensitive of all the children, and little Prince Henry still in the hands of their enemies. "But if this invasion succeeds it will be the turning of the tide," said Charles. "And by God it must or what will become of my father? Buckingham says I have only got to land and the country will rise for me. He has just come from England where he led a rising himself. It failed but he says had I been with him it would have succeeded. Do you remember Buckingham? One of those two fair boys in the unicorn wood? Francis, the other, was killed in the rising."

"I am sorry," said Lucy steadily but she felt shaken. So soon now Charles would be fighting again and she would be back once more with the nightmares and the fear. "You sail soon?" she asked.

"Quite soon," said Charles cheerfully. "I will be on board the *Satisfaction*. I will have Rupert with me, and Buckingham and my brother James. I will be glad to be fighting again, whether by sea or land. Inaction drives me mad."

"We were together before you went to that last retreat in the west and I thank God we are together again before this new fighting."

He took her hand and they sat silently watching the extraordinary peace of the scene around them. The dunes cast long shadows of heliotrope over the sand and coarse grass, and the calm sea was pale blue silk streaked with silver. From the red-roofed cottages of the village the peat smoke from cooking suppers curled up in wreaths of blue. They watched for the first few stars to come out and then saw the fishing boats pushing out one by one from the shore, going off for a night's fishing. There was no wind inshore to fill the coloured sails and they could very faintly hear the sound of the oars in the rowlocks and the men singing.

"At night the watchman on horseback keeps a look-out for the boats," said Lucy. "He sounds a trumpet when they come in, for there is no harbour and men go down with the horses that pull the boats in. On stormy nights, Vrouw Flinck told me, the women are so anxious that they are all down waiting on the sands. The seas here can be very wild."

"It is difficult to believe it tonight," said Charles. "When life is full of peace it always seems impossible that it can vanish. One can realize that beauty will pass and knowledge decay but not peace. Why is it?"

"I do not know. Perhaps peace is the air of eternity, its very breath, without which no other thing could exist at all."

Presently, still hand in hand, they walked slowly back to the farm and found the family just sitting to supper. They were all there for the two fishermen were not going out that night. Mijnheer Flinck had a face that seemed made of dark folded leather, and far-seeing eyes. A thatch of white hair fell round his face, contrasting vividly with his bright red jersey. His sons were not much older than Charles but the spring of youth had gone already from their slow and heavy movements. They stood up and greeted their guests with simple dignity, and with a special delight in Charles as another seaman. But when they were settled again Lucy saw the old man looking at his guest's smooth hands, and then the far-seeing eyes rested with wonder upon his face. But the wonder did not pass into curiosity, which is not becoming in a host; and this family practised still the ancient hospitality that takes a guest on trust from God, to be fed, warmed, defended with one's life if need be, but never questioned, doubted or criticized.

Nevertheless Lucy thought it was as well that Charles's Dutch vocabulary was at present limited for she doubted if his knowledge of fish was extensive. But the few words he had learned, though he did not always know what they meant, his charm and laughter delighted his hosts. The simple meal in the long room, now full of shadows, the windows opened to the darkening sea and the candles burning on the table, was for Lucy and Charles no interruption of their joy but a part of it. This did not surprise them for they were both aware of the ancient hospitality. They felt it as a prolongation of the peace they had known on the dunes in the sunset.

"You have made it look like home," said Charles when they stood together in their room. The moon was up now and they hardly needed the candle he carried. He put it down on the chest and looked about him. "What have you done?"

"It is my mother's cloak over that chair and my father's picture and my little mirror on the wall, and the flowers and the sound of the waves at Roch." And she picked up the shell and held it to his ear. "Do you hear? That was the sound that was in our ears on many of our great days at Roch. Do you remember?"

"I do not forget Roch," he said with his arm round her.

"Do you speak French as well as you speak Dutch?" she teased him.

"I have a French mother and I speak it perfectly," he said, and then began to laugh. "But not at the French court. There I do not know a word of the language. I stammer and stutter, fall over my feet, tread on the hems of the ladies' dresses. They think I am a feeble-minded oaf."

"Why do you behave so?"

"To delay my wooing of La Grande Mademoiselle. You have heard of her? She is large and rich. You will be surprised how difficult it is to make love to a woman when you cannot speak her language." His arms tightened about her. "Though if you knew no English there would be no difficulty at all." Her joy was so great that she did not know if she was laughing or crying. "But I do know one Welsh phrase," he went on.

444

"You spoke it in the great bed at Roch and I memorized it. What does it mean?"

"It means, dear God this happiness is too great for me to bear," said Lucy.

"Is it as great now as it was at Roch?" he asked.

"It is greater," said Lucy. "It will never grow less." And she believed that, so great was the peace.

Five

The month of May had seen the people of London rejoicing in the streets over the birth of their Prince, and Lucy opening her eyes for the first time in the great bedchamber at Roch Castle, but April was the month when their son also became aware of the fact of light. It showed him sparkling water, and a sailing ship passing somewhere just beyond his ken. He stretched out his hand and made a grab for it, as later in life he was to stretch out his hand for so much, and brought the hand back empty. He placed it over his button nose, minute fingers spread wide, and gazed up at the reflection of light upon the ceiling. His eyes were blue and the feathery down on top of his head was pale gold. He was a perky baby, very forward considering he had been in the world for three weeks only, knowing what he wanted and screaming for it in fury, but a vision of angelic peace the moment he was satisfied. He was satisfied now for he had just been fed to capacity, his digestion was excellent and for the first time he had become possessed of light. The fingers that had been questing in extraordinary astonishment over his nose contracted sleepily into a fist not much bigger than a large walnut. This he placed in its habitual resting-place beneath his chin, withdrew his gaze from the ceiling and fixed it upon his mother's face.

She gazed back, searching for family likenesses, the constant preoccupation of all convalescent mothers, and once again, as so often when she looked at him, she thought of the little prince whom she had seen holding the hand of his older brother on that day of the Guildhall banquet, and she hoped that Charles would agree that he should be called James. At present he was called Jackie because Peter Gosfright, confronted with him for the first time, had ejaculated, "The jackanapes!" Of another likeness there was no doubt. In the

446

breadth of the tiny face across the cheekbones she saw
Charles, and when the fingers uncurled they were abnormally
long, like his father's.

She placed the tip of her own finger against the fist and the
tendrils uncurled, and curled themselves again about her
finger reminding her as always of the claws of the little bird at
Roch. He smiled at her. They told her that babies did not
smile until four months old and that the appealing quiver of
his mouth was only wind. But he had already brought up his
wind very satisfactorily when she had held him against her
shoulder after his feed. This, she maintained, was his smile,
kept for her alone. She returned the smile and kissed the top of
his head. He turned his cheek inward to her breast and
slept.

Suddenly she felt dreadfully tired and lay back against the
pillows of her bed with her sleeping baby in her arms. To feel
tired and at times to be in black depression was usual after
childbirth, they told her, and strong though she was she had
had a hard time giving birth to this baby. "Too much riding,"
Aunt Margaret said. "For a woman to ride with a baby on the
way is asking for trouble, and so I told you at the time but you
paid no attention, headstrong girl that you are." But Lucy no
longer minded Aunt Margaret's sharp tongue; she was too
thankful to her for her gift of family loyalty. And the tiredness and sorrow that accompanied her joy in Jackie had
another and deeper origin than giving birth to a baby. She
lived still under the shadow of all that had happened to
Charles, and to her through him, between the conception and
birth of their child, and it was a deep shadow.

2

The invasion upon which Charles had built such high
hopes had been a failure. The landing on the coast had
been abortive, and an attempt to bring the Parliamentary fleet
to battle had failed also. In sight of each other, and ready to
fight, the two fleets had been separated by a great storm.
There had been nothing for it but retreat to Holland for

refitting, but the half-starved crews were demoralized and could not be rallied again. A magnificent reception at The Hague and the offer of generous financial support for one week only had been for Charles only final humiliations. That at sea he had proved himself as a man of courage, and a commander able to rally to himself the support even of starving men, had made it all the harder to come back to the life of political intrigue he hated. If he was to save his father and his own future he must learn the arts of beguilement and deception but how could a prince live on borrowed money and keep his dignity? How could he learn the ways of cunning and keep his integrity?

He had asked Lucy these questions one night of despair at Scheveningen, and it was then that she told him they were to have a child. "Between us," she said, "between ourselves in our hidden life, there need be no deceptions. Together in our marriage, and with our child, we can always have truth."

"What did you say?" he demanded. "A child? Lucy? Did you say a child?"

In the moonlight she saw his illumined face. She had been afraid he would be dismayed but instead he was transfigured with delight. A son! He had no doubt it would be a son. Of course it would be a son. All remembrance of failure vanished in the realization that he had fathered a son. There was no dismay because taken by surprise he had forgotten who he was, and also forgotten that there had ever been other fathers. In the stillness of the night he and the girl and the unborn child were alone in the world.

But after Lucy was asleep dismay came. He remembered his failure again and the cupboard bed that had been a refuge for the simplicity of human love became a sort of trap. He drifted into a sleep and the trap became a sticky mesh like a fishing net. Entangled in it he was aware of some black obscene crouching shape at the edge of it. Striving to escape, sweating with terror in the manner of his childhood nightmares, he awakened both himself and Lucy.

"It was just a dream," he gasped out to her.

"It has passed," she said, soothing him. "And do not

struggle so. You will hurt the baby." And she drifted again into her peaceful sleep.

The next day they went back to The Hague, he to the palace and she to the Vingboons, and a few days later Robert Sidney came to her there to tell her Charles was very ill with small-pox.

"I must go to him at once," she said.

"Are you mad, Lucy?" Robert demanded, and he grabbed her arm as she was rushing away to get ready.

"But he may die!" she gasped.

"He may," agreed Robert. "But royal mistresses do not attend royal deathbeds. The code does not allow it and Charles will not want you there."

He had not meant to be cruel but though he had not lost his sensitiveness he was more downright in his manners than he had been. Seeing how he had hurt her he was sorry and took her in his arms to comfort her, for he thought she must be near to tears, but he found her dry-eyed, stiff and hard with anguish. He let go of her again, feeling as though his genuine compassion had been flung back in his face. Lucy was very changed from the little girl who had jumped into his arms like a bird in the garden at St. Giles. "Are we nothing to each other now, sweetheart?" he asked her.

"I do not know," she said dully. "I cannot think. Please will you go away?"

But Charles was a strong young man. He recovered and went away to Breda to live there quietly, to save money. He found a lodging for Lucy not far from his own and she was there for some months, hardly anyone knowing where she was.

It was a strange time, for Charles was absorbed in the struggle to help his father, a struggle that became agonizing just after Christmas when the news came that the King was to be tried for high treason. All his time was spent in reading his father's long letters and writing appeals for help to the Dutch Parliament, to the Scots, to the English Parliament itself, to anyone at all who might be able to help the King. There were many days when Lucy did not see him, and when he did come to her lodging he was tired and anxious and only wanted to sit with her in front of the fire and be comforted; how he was too miserable to specify. But she was clever at knowing how. Sometimes she sang Welsh songs to him, or they played chess. At other times they had a meal together in front of the fire and afterwards she spread her mother's cloak on the floor and he lay on it and they talked of the baby, and he laughed at the ridiculous contrast of the shirts she was making, one for him and one for his son. Over the fireplace they hung her little mirror and her father's picture and it was part of the ritual that he should listen to the sea-shell before he went away.

On other days they went for strolls together through the streets of Breda, beside the canals that at first were red and yellow with fallen leaves and then when December came were sometimes still and frozen under snow. And sometimes they went to the great mediaeval church to whose walls the little houses clung like chickens to their mother, and sat there in peace.

January came and Charles was nearly beside himself, for no answer came to his appeal to Parliament. Coming in one afternoon at dusk from a walk beside the canal close to her lodging, where she went almost daily to feed the gulls, Lucy found Charles in her little sitting room writing at the table. He often came to her lodging to work for it was quieter than his own and her presence, or even the atmosphere of her presence, when she was out, gave him peace. He had lit the candles on the table and the movement of their flames in the slight draught of the opened door, and the flicker of firelight, sent queer shadows leaping in the room. Lucy never spoke if Charles was working. Passing him with no more greeting than a touch of her fingertips against his cheek she took off her cloak and sat down beside the fire. She was tired, for the child was heavy now and she was glad to sit still. Beyond the uncurtained windows the dusk was blue for it was a cloudless evening, warm for January and very still. It was utterly peaceful and yet Lucy found that her heart was beating fast. Presently Charles sighed, straightened his shoulders and began sanding his papers.

"You have finished?" she asked.

"Yes," he said.

She came and stood behind him, placing her linked hands beneath his chin that she might lift his head up and kiss the lines of worry from his forehead. It was one of the ways she had with him; she had many such little ways and he loved them all. Then she saw his papers and her hands dropped from his face and gripped the lace that fell from his neckband, for she saw that lying beside the letter that he had been standing there were three blank papers signed with his name.

"What are you going to write on those papers, Charles?" she asked sharply.

"Nothing," he replied, and lifting one of them he quickly folded it within his letter; but not before she saw that the letter was yet another appeal to Parliament.

"Why do you send Parliament a blank, signed sheet of paper?" she demanded, her hands twisting in his lace. "And what are you doing with the other two?"

"They are only copies."

"To be sent to whom?"

"To other persons in England. Dear heart, you are throttling me, and the matter is of no importance. Forget it. We will play chess now."

Lucy's mind was working like lightning. "They can write what they like over your signature on that piece of paper," she said, "and hold you to it."

"Take your hands away," said Charles with a spurt of anger. "I tell you the matter is of no importance."

"You have said in that letter that you are offering any terms they like in exchange for your father's life." The words were screaming in her mind but they only came out in a breathless gasp of fury. "You are a fool, Charles! They can ask for your life instead of his."

Charles dragged her hands away and got up. His more than six feet of height seemed to tower to the ceiling and his usually sombre eyes were bright with anger. To offer his life in exchange for his father's was exactly what he had intended. He had signed his carte blanche in a mood of dedication and exaltation and was in no state of mind to be called a fool by this little nobody of a girl whom he had been idiot enough to marry. She presumed. She was always presuming. She never seemed to realize either the honour he had done her or the increasing embarrassment she was likely to be to him. Glaring down at her he saw that she was as angry as he was, her cheeks scarlet. How dare she be angry? He took her by the arms and shook her. It was the first time that he had touched her in any way but the ways of love and the moment he had done it they were both horrified. She set her teeth in her lower lip to stop its trembling and looked up at him, the colour draining from her face, and in a moment she was in his arms and they were both sobbing in reaction from their shock and fear. They were eighteen years old. That there was nothing whatever that Parliament could write on that piece of paper was something they did not understand.

Lucy recovered first. She pulled herself out of his arms and straightened herself.

"I understand," she said. "It is something you must do and that you ought to do. I love you more than ever. Seal up your letter and I will get our supper and then we will play chess."

The carved chessmen belonged to Charles and he had taught Lucy to play. He was not a man who either expected or asked for intellect in a woman, only for beauty and vivacity to delight his senses and make him laugh, but her quickness and skill as a pupil had charmed and surprised him. She was not of the stuff of which scholars are made but her lively mind and eager pleasure in new places and new skills made her a delightful companion when her heart was at ease. But tonight though she did her gallant best she could not concentrate and the game promised nothing except a victory too easy for his pleasure, and suddenly he impatiently swept up the pieces and put them back in their box.

"I am sorry," said Lucy humbly.

"I must go back to The Hague early tomorrow," he said. "I do not know what will happen from one day to the other and I must be where my advisers are and with my sister and brother-in-law."

"I will go to the Vingboons so that I can be near you," said Lucy. "Or would you prefer me to go to the farm?"

"To neither," said Charles. "I want you to go to your aunt at Rotterdam and to stay there until the boy is born."

"But I cannot do that. I am too far from you there!"

"Listen, Lucy," he said urgently, "there is nothing we can either be to each other or do with each other just now. I cannot be or do anything that is unconnected with my father and my future as his son. I want an undistracted mind and a man can't have that if he is worrying about a woman. Women make one anxious, the way they have babies, and other things they do that can be a trial when a man must keep his attention on serious things. I love you very much, you know I do, but I would rather you were safely with your aunt until things are easier for both of us."

He slipped one finger inside his collar and eased it, and drops of perspiration stood on his forehead. It had had to be said and he only hoped he had said it as tactfully as possible. She knew quite well that the status she must keep for the moment was that of mistress and not wife, yet she was slow to understand her duty. Then suddenly his dark troubled face cleared. "Be a good girl, Lucy, and when these troubles are over I will take you to Paris!"

Lucy was speechless. He had changed since the days in Wales when they had been equals, taking the centre of the stage together. Now he was pushing her into the wings. But then that stage had been the small one of her world and now they were in his large world and it was different. It was the setting that was changing, she told herself, and not his way of thinking; yet in her heart she knew it was his way of thinking.

"Can you not say something?" he demanded impatiently. "Do you not want to go to Paris?"

"One day," she said. "But now? What am I to do now?"

"I have told you. Go to your aunt at Rotterdam."

"May I go first to Wilhelmientje to collect some clothes I have there? I will not try to see you while I am at The Hague."

"You may, dear heart. Sidney shall take you there

tomorrow. I am going now. I want a good sleep tonight."

"Will you not have it here with me?"

"No. All that is ahead seems rushing towards me. Do you know that feeling? This quiet time here with you at Breda has been dear and peaceful but darkness has washed over it now."

That she could understand and there was no lack of love and no bitterness in their parting. But she hardly slept all night for he was right about the darkness. She was so lonely that night that it frightened her.

3

Robert Sidney found her a girl he hardly knew when they rode back to the Hague together, so quiet and saddened was she. But yet he did know her for he remembered the sad little girl with whom he had driven to London when she was missing her father, and whom he had comforted with the thought of the green star. Would she remember? "You and Charles are on the same green star, Lucy," he said.

She turned her head quickly with a sudden smile of remembrance and the hood she was wearing fell back from her hair. It was the same hair, springy and untidy, and in a moment or two wet with the fine misty rain. Was Charles expecting to turn her into a Court lady, Robert wondered? If so he would find her intransigent material.

"The green star!" she said. "That was the day I took you to visit Old Sage. He is dead now and I shall never know where he came from or who he was."

"I can tell you, for I found out about him. Are you too grown up now for storytelling?"

She was almost herself again, her eyes alight with curiosity. "I shall never be too old for storytelling," she said. "And I loved Old Sage. Tell me."

So he told her the story of the night when the mob was surging outside the palace at Whitehall and he and her father had gone to find Old Sage, and the three of them had rescued Father Ignatius and Old Sage had been put in the pillory. And he told her of his visit to Father Ignatius and the story the old man had told him. Lucy listened with concentration and asked many questions, for her intuition told her that she was connected with this story by more than her love for Old Sage.

"Patrick's ship was wrecked on the coast of Pembrokeshire?" she asked for the second time.

"That was the rumour," said Robert.

"What year would that have been?"

Robert made some calculations. "Probably in the year sixteen hundred and six or sixteen hundred and seven," he said. "Later perhaps."

"My father was a boy then," said Lucy thoughtfully. "He was a boy when Old Parson came."

"Since this is a storytelling day tell me about Old Parson," commanded Robert.

So Lucy told him about the old priest with a wound on his head and lost memory. "But he is better now," she said. "I think he is nearly well because when I left Roch he was remembering things."

"What sort of things?"

"He remembered a dumb friend he had loved. He told me he thought he had been the cause of his friend's dumbness though he could not remember how. He felt sure his friend had died but he was not unhappy because he knew his friend had forgiven him."

"Say that again," said Robert and Lucy said it again, her wondering eyes on his face. "Can you remember anything else?"

"No. Except that his dead friend told him that it is quite true that a person for love's sake can choose to suffer for the guilt of another and take it away."

"I can hear Old Sage saying that," said Robert.

They looked at each other and Lucy's lips parted in surprise. Robert's eyes were very bright and illumination seemed coming to her mind from his eyes. Then for a moment fear came, putting out the light. Something in the story she had just heard threatened her but she did not know what it was because the fear paralysed her thinking.

"There is The Hague," said Robert quickly, for her fear was invading his own sensitive mind, and though he did not know why they must escape instantly from Old Parson he knew that for Lucy's sake escape they must. "Seen from a distance these Dutch cities never look corporeal. They belong to dreams."

They had been riding through a belt of woodland and the bare stretched arms of the motionless winter trees had gathered the mist like cobwebs about their sad skeletons, their presence adding to Lucy's sense of dread, but as they rode out from the shadows she saw that a shaft of pale sunlight was lighting the steeples and the high-pitched roofs. "We shall see the storks soon," she said.

"You like storks?" enquired Robert. Storks seemed to him a safe subject.

"A stork is our family crest," said Lucy. "Only we call him a heron because there are almost as many herons in Pembrokeshire as there are storks at The Hague. A little stone figure of our stork-heron was not destroyed with the castle. It is there now, in the kitchen where Old Parson and I talked about—about—"

She broke off in confusion. So storks were not a safe subject after all, thought Robert. No subject is safe when the mind has been refused some knowledge that must not be allowed entry; created to search out knowledge it hates to be denied. "Forget the story I told you," he commanded Lucy. "Forget Patrick. It was too sad a story for you to remember. Forget it."

A week later, when she was back in Rotterdam with Aunt Margaret, she did forget it. The small skeleton in her cupboard was swept away, cupboard and all, by the overwhelming horror of what happened next.

4

It was a cold February day darkened by low motionless clouds that seemed unable to shed their burden of snow. A few flakes drifted down to the dull grey water of the canal, but that was all. Lucy, sitting in the window to catch the last light on her sewing, found herself unable to look out. She had a feeling that if she did she would see some sorrowful sight; some beggar dragging his misshapen body along on crutches, an idiot child or a woman weeping. Then she pulled herself together. One had queer fancies when one was expecting a baby but one must not yield to them. She dropped her sewing in her lap, sat upright and looked steadily out of the window. At first there was nothing to be seen; only the deserted cobbled way beside the water. Then a man wrapped in a heavy black cloak suddenly appeared and strode past the window. With his hat pulled down over his forehead, his head bent against the eastern cold that met him as he walked, she could not see his face but he seemed a figure of doom that made her shrink back. Then he vanished from sight and the slam of the front door seemed a dreadful thing as it shattered the heavy quietness of the grey day.

Aunt Margaret, who had been dozing by the fire, woke up with a start. "What is that?" she asked. Lucy was standing upright, her face white, watching the parlour door. Her lips moved but she said nothing when Peter Gosfright came in. "You silly girl, Lucy, it is only your uncle," said Aunt Margaret with relief, and then turning to her husband in outrage, "Peter! Do you know you are still wearing your hat and cloak?"

Then he told them, and he was too shocked and angry to choose his words carefully. On January the thirtieth the King of England had been beheaded outside his Palace of Whitehall. The Hague had been stunned by the news. Kings had been murdered often, or deposed, or killed in battle, but never before executed by their own subjects on a public scaffold, their last agony lifted up and exposed to the full view of their people. And this king had been a good man, Peter stormed on, doing the best that he knew for his people, and a religious man who had put his trust in God. Was this the lot of good men in this evil world? Did God sleep? He stopped speaking, removed his hat and dropped his heavy cloak to the floor.

There was silence. To Lucy it seemed that the room was full of whirling darkness and that something had come out of it and hit her a blow in the middle of her forehead. She put one hand to the place and groped for the door with the other. "Stay here, Lucy!" commanded Aunt Margaret, but Peter said, "Let her alone." After that she did not know what she did but when she came to herself again she was kneeling on the floor in her bedchamber packing her saddlebags to go to Charles.

She was at all times a quick recoverer and her mind started working again, bringing her to her feet under the impact of another blow. Charles was now King of England. He wished her to be known only as his mistress and so she could not go to him. "I am only his mistress." She spoke the words aloud and sat down on the edge of her bed. It was the smallpox over again only worse. She could not go to him. The holding together in the disasters of life that could bring such unity to husband and wife would never be for them. A queer little vision came to her, her father and mother clinging to each other after the wheel had come off the coach on the journey to Golden Grove, and the unborn baby's life had been threatened ... And the baby had died ... As the vision faded her own child moved in her womb, Charles's son that he must have to comfort him. Nothing must happen to Charles's son.

She lay down on her bed for a while and with all the resolution she could summon drove her frantic mind away from the scaffold to the bridge above the stream where her parents had clung together, and from there along the way to Golden Grove and up the steps to the terrace where the damask rose grew. She looked for it in vain among the green leaves, but just as her thoughts grew frantic once more the leaves murmured to her of the cave where she had found it within herself.

"Go in. Go down the stony passage that leads to the cave at the heart of the world that is also your own heart. He is there, as well as at the heart of all earth's flowers, and he is the peace of the world, and the joy of the world, and all that is. The love of lovers is one of the reflections, and there are many trembling in the troubled waters of our living, trembling for a moment and then broken and lost. But he is not lost. And what he is, no man knows."

She opened her eyes. The murmur of leaves had become

another voice. There had been no words that her physical ears could hear yet she knew what had been said to her. Was Old Sage rewarded for his long silence by a new and heavenly power of speech? She got up and washed her face and brushed her hair and went downstairs, and talked so calmly to Margaret and Peter that they marvelled at her.

"She is all emotion on the surface but underneath she is cold," Margaret said to her husband in bed that night. The solid, kindly burgomaster cleared his throat to disagree but found as always that the words that would express his thoughts were not to be found. Nor were his thoughts themselves easy to catch hold of unless they concerned his weaving business and the price of wool. He had many thoughts but they swam like small fishes in the dark water of the tank of his mind, coming up so suddenly and briefly that no sooner did he dive for a shining tail than it had vanished. He did however wonder how Lucy was getting on in the darkness of her own curtained bed. Was she asleep? But he had no time to wonder more. That was another of his difficulties, wonder always plunged him into instant slumber.

Lucy was discovering that those who are allowed the one must have the other also and the turnover from light to darkness can be immediate and inexorable. She lay in her bed longing for the comfort of the voice again but there was only thick dark silence. She longed for sleep but when it came at last it brought no release, only fear as she waited for the moment when she must step out upon the scaffold. The fear was not so much of the death but of stumbling and losing the dignity of her courage. It was difficult to see where her feet must be placed in this darkness. There was a vast crowd out there, quite silent. Yet it was not night for them, it was broad daylight, and they all had eyes, and in a moment the eyes would devour her blinded face. Yet she must step forward with confidence, out and forward as though to the arms of a lover and she must not stumble.

Then suddenly it was all different for she was climbing a ladder. She was on the wrong scaffold. The eyes were waiting just the same but it was the wrong scaffold. Whose scaffold was this? The question was so insistent, and the fear that came upon her so appalling, that her feet could not find the next rung of the ladder. She stumbled and fell and the darkness from past and future came roaring over her head as she fell into the abyss. It was empty. Darkness and nothingness. Darkness that fell like a curtain.

Then she was awake and aware of her body again, drenched with sweat, and she could see the outline of two wooden posts and the small patch of light that lay upon wooden planks. Whose scaffold was this, and where was her son? Had they torn him out of her womb and was that why her body was so cold and trembling? Yet when she searched for him he was still with her in her heavy body and she could feel his life under her shaking hands. And there was that light that lay upon the boards of the scaffold. What was it doing there? There should be blood upon the floor of a scaffold, not silver moonlight. She stretched out a hand and felt the velvet of the bed curtains and saw again the two posts at the foot of the bed.

The nightmare was over and she quieted herself. It was her mind she must take care of now. She must not remember that what had been done to one king could be done to another, or to his son. She fixed her eyes on the moonlight for light was what she must think of in the weeks that were coming. Light and peace. The peace of the voice. The peace that she and Charles had agreed was so important on the evening when they had sat on the sand-dunes in the sunset. She said the word aloud to herself as the best talisman she knew against nightmare. Peace.

In the weeks that followed she broke down only once and that was when she heard how Charles had received the news of his father's death. He had burst into agonized sobbing, gone to his room and stayed there alone for hours, remaining afterwards bewildered and dazed with grief. Then he had put on the purple of royal mourning and in apartments hung with black had set himself to the burden of correspondence. That was how Lucy had to picture him through the weeks while she waited for her baby; in that stuffy black room, his clenched hand holding the long quill pen, while obsequious courtiers were thick as crows about him and messengers came and went.

For this thing that had been done had horrified not only The Hague but the whole of Europe and letters of condolence poured in upon the new King. The Czar of Russia did more than condole, he banished every Englishman from his dominions instantly, for if this was the way that Englishmen treated their rulers such barbarians could no longer be tolerated upon the sacred soil of Russia.

Lying awake one night Lucy wondered what Charles thought about when he lay awake. Did he have nightmares? Did he remember that blank sheet of paper signed with his name? Nothing, it would seem, had been written on it. That act of courage had been in vain. Nevertheless he had sent the paper. He had done it.

And did he think of the great Earl of Strafford, the scapegoat who had not saved his king after all? He had laid down his life for him but it had been in vain. All in the end had been failure. Nevertheless he had laid down his life. He had done it.

"The words 'in vain' are not known to us here. Nor is failure, nor success. But the life laid down is known to us. And love in its true profundity is known. And the maintaining of faith is known. These are for us the sun and moon and stars."

It was the voice again with its peace. Lucy smiled, turned her pillow over and lying down again tried to imagine how it would be when among all the important messengers to the palace there would come a humble servant with a letter from Rotterdam sealed with the crest of a master weaver. Charles would lift his head suddenly and break the seal with eagerness, and then his dark face would light up with a delighted boyish grin before he folded the letter and slipped it inside his doublet, and said not a word to a soul. And then perhaps he would come and see her.

He did not come but he sent Lord Wilmot with a letter of love and congratulation and a diamond star in a silver box.

Kneeling on one knee beside the bed where Lucy was enthroned with her baby Lord Wilmot had pinned the star on Jackie's robe. "His Majesty bade me tell you, Mrs. Barlow, that one day when this child is grown he will himself place the Star of the Garter on his son's breast. This trinket, which is for you to wear now, is in earnest of that."

His mission accomplished Lord Wilmot had stayed for a while laughing and chatting with Lucy, had drunk the glass of wine Margaret Gosfright brought him, then had bowed and gone away. Lucy had wished he could have stayed longer for he was merry and gentle and she knew that of all his courtiers he was the one whom Charles liked best. After he had gone away the longing for Charles became and remained almost intolerable.

5

"For we are two and should be three," she said to her son, as the remembering brought her round full circle to the now of this April afternoon, with the bells of Rotterdam tolling out five o'clock over the roofs of the city and the sun so far declined to the west that the shadows of the houses fell across the canal outside her window, dimming the brightness of the water to the glimmer of moonstone.

Charles was King of England. How would this affect herself and Jackie? To get back the throne of England it was possible that he might stick at nothing. If this marriage got in his way would he repudiate it? She did not believe he would but she had faced the possibility and taken her decision. Jackie must know the truth about himself. She would tell him as soon as he was of an age to understand that he was his father's legal son, and he would have his secret sense of integrity even as she had hers.

There was a knocking at the front door below her window and then the sounds of arrival. Aunt Margaret and her husband were hospitable and liked to entertain their friends, of whom many belonged to the community of Scottish weavers who had settled at Rotterdam and who did business with Peter

Gosfright. Lucy, as friendly and hospitable as her aunt, enjoyed these sounds of arrival and upstairs with her baby would tune in to the tremors of welcome, kindness and pleasure that would thrill through the old house on these occasions. It had a large heart and liked to entertain and was well able to communicate its pleasure in what was happening downstairs to Lucy upstairs.

Who had just come in? Lucy listened and the first thing she knew was that the house itself was so thrilling with excitement that it almost sang out the news. Magi, it said, magi. Three men from afar come to worship. No, not Scots weavers! These men talked like kings. Could she not hear how the voices rang out with the authority of trumpets? Yes, that was Aunt Margaret twittering. How she twittered! Yes, that was Uncle Peter gratified but excessively anxious. Had he enough wine? The horses? What state was his stable in? The door of the bed-chamber burst open and the intimations of the house were drowned by the twittering of a thousand sparrows as Aunt Margaret flew in. Stout though she was her feet hardly touched the floor.

"Lucy! The King! And two others with him. Lord Wilmot who was here before and Colonel Robert Sidney. Three of them. And you in that shabby wrapper and your hair like a bird's nest. Get up at once and put your gown on. Give me the child. Give me the child, I say. Be quick, Lucy!"

Lucy was sitting up very calmly with her baby in her arms. "It does not matter what I look like," she said serenely to her distracted aunt. "Jackie is looking like a king's son."

Margaret calmed down and looked. Yes, Lucy was right. Jackie was at all times impervious to the noise and disturbance of the world. It did not concern him yet. It was still only the perimeter of the magic circle of warmth and love that contained only himself and his mother. His flushed cheek was on her breast, the golden fluff of hair was like a small flame burning on his forehead and he had placed his hand over his nose again as though to ward off intrusion.

A man came leaping up the stairs two at a time and stood in the doorway. Lucy looked up and smiled at him. She had

463

forgotten how tall he was. But then so much had happened to them both since they had last been together that it was no wonder if there was a little forgetfulness. The purple of royal mourning suited his new, tragic dignity. She saw at once that it was as she had feared and he was changed. He was not the old Charles but a king, a man sanctified and set apart. And there was no light in his eyes. And then suddenly as she looked at him the light came and he smiled like an urchin boy. Then he bowed to Aunt Margaret and held the door open for her exit, closing it behind her so quickly that it caught the tail of her gown and he had to open it again to free her.

But at last they were alone and he was kneeling by the bed, astonished beyond measure. "A son," he said. Jackie opened his eyes and considered the newcomer. Then he removed his hand from his nose and curled its minute tendrils about his father's long finger. Jackie's magic circle had enlarged itself. Now they were three.

Six

Charles was not able to leave her that night. The other wise men, having paid their respects, went away but Charles remained. Who could have believed having a baby was such a miracle! Other people had them, indeed having babies was such a constant preoccupation of the human race that the world was cluttered with them, and their cries of joy or demand intermingled with the chirps of sparrows under the eaves to make the background music of almost every home in the world. Yet it seemed a miracle that had not happened before.

"Such a small home," Charles murmured as night turned towards dawn. He was thinking of the interior of the four-poster; for the pale light was not strong enough yet to show him the lineaments of the room. For the twentieth time that night he turned over to look through the parted curtains at the cradle beside the bed where his son was sleeping. He could see the top of the baby's head and the outstretched fingers of the hand that Jackie had placed over his nose. They were ridiculous. How could fingers be so small and yet be fingers? And who could have believed that being a father was like this? This awe and sense of fulfilment. This awareness of the extension of one's own being, reaching forward and back through time. And the extraordinary deepening of the love that bound one to the woman, so that they and their love seemed fused into one Godlike unity. Like God? Yes, for they had created a world. What was a baby but a new world? It was all there in that scrap in the cradle; a whole complex universe of beauty and delight, thought, will and action. Did other men feel like this, all the millions of men who had begotten children? Had his father felt as he did now at his own birth? His father! Suddenly, with that stab of now familiar pain somewhere at the back of his head it was all sweeping over him again, and he turned over into Lucy's arms in a storm of sobbing.

She took it with quiet and strong compassion, for the long strange night together had seemed to hold the whole range of human experience. The few hours of sleeping and waking, of ecstasy, joy and now sorrow, had lasted for a hundred years and yet flown like a few moments. What was this queer thing, time? No one knew. Just as no one knew the meaning of human life or love or death.

Charles's grief spent itself and she made no comment upon it. He did not need that she should. Presently he said, "I must go back to The Hague today. There is so much to do. The worry and the business are endless. You will come with Jackie to the farm as soon as you can?" And she replied, "We will come."

2

The days at the farm were happy days. The sea air and the peaceful rhythm of life made Lucy feel stronger, though she was never again to get back the health and vigour she had known before her baby's birth. Jackie, lying in his cradle beside his mother in the sunny garden, grew and flourished amazingly and Lucy, in the painstaking letters that she wrote regularly to her mother and grandmother, did her best to communicate something of the wonder of him, but she was not good with her pen and the very vastness of her happiness made it impossible to describe.

She wrote too to Betje, who had now married her Frenchman Louis Fragonard and gone to Paris with him; for he had tired of cooking for the insensitive palates of the Dutch and was now in the kitchen of no less a person than Cardinal Mazarin himself. This great prelate, the virtual ruler of France, had a stomach sensitivized by the strain of his responsibility and Betje in consequence was something of a grass-widow and had opened a little milliner's shop in a street not far from the Cardinal's palace. "If Jackie and I ever come to Paris," Lucy wrote to her, "it is with you that we shall lodge."

Charles came out to Scheveningen whenever he could and he and Lucy carried Jackie out to the sand-dunes or down to the edge of the sea, taking it in turn to hold the baby. And at night in the cupboard-bed the cradle was in their dreams, and to be awakened at first dawn by Jackie's imperious cries was no hardship but a continual miracle.

Charles spoke little to Lucy about the worries that beset him for with her he wanted to forget them, but she did know that he was torn in pieces by the divisions within his Council. The older men, led by the faithful Hyde, believed that he could only be restored to his throne by the Marquis of Montrose and the Scottish Royalists, the Duke of Ormonde, and the Irish Catholics, but the Duke of Buckingham and the other young men in the Council pressed him to close at once with the powerful party of the Scottish Covenanters, whose emissaries had been for some while at The Hague. They demanded that he should sign the Covenant but the great marquis, before leaving The Hague for Denmark to raise troops for Charles, had implored him to do no such thing. And to make confusion worse the English Parliament had sent as their ambassador to The Hague one of the lawyers who had drawn up the charges against the late King, and a party of Royalists had quietly entered his house, murdered him and gone quietly away again. Charles had had no hand in the murder but the Dutch States General were too enraged to give him further financial help and he was not made for the corrosions of poverty.

Lucy loved her husband too much to be unaware of the change in him, for he was altering almost as fast as his son. The deepening dignity and resolution she loved but there was something that disturbed her, and that was his own opinion of himself. He was wearing his sacred kingship like a halo about his head and her intuition told her that no man is in more danger than when he is self-haloed. That His Sacred Majesty must be restored to his throne was already an *idée fixe* and what if restoration were long delayed? What effect would that have upon him? But at that point a shadow would come over Lucy's mind and she would turn quickly away to the joy of the moment. It was sufficient. Each hour together was a brimming cup of gold.

A note from him was delivered to her early one morning by a servant. "Dress in your prettiest gown, dear heart," he wrote, "and put Jackie into his best lace cap and both of you meet me in the woods in an hour's time."

She did as she was told. Though he had no money he had bought her some lovely dresses on credit; one of them was made of cornflower blue silk that matched her eyes and she chose it because it was his favourite. It was a fine day but the wind from the sea was keen and she wore her mother's cloak and carried Jackie tucked into its warm folds. With her head held high, because she knew this must be something of an occasion, she walked over the dunes to the woods. When Charles came to see her at the farm it was always on foot as Tomos Barlow, but when she reached the woods she found a coach there, with a coachman and groom in attendance upon the two black horses, and beside it stood the King of England. He laughed and bowed to her and handed her in with some ceremony.

"Where are we going?" she asked, when they were sitting together on the cushioned seat, Jackie in the crook of his father's arms, and lurching along the uneven track beneath the trees.

"To visit a lady I wish you to know and love," he answered. "In fact two ladies. And why are you not wearing the diamonds I gave you? You never wear them."

She flushed. "I did not know it would be your wish," she answered, "But I have the brooch in its case in my pocket."

"Of course it is my wish," he answered imperiously. She did not like it when he was imperious for the hard tone of his voice brought back that slight shadow to her mind. She took the brooch from its case and fastened it in the lace of her gown with slow dignity.

"You do not like it," he said sharply. "Why is that?"

She answered quite truthfully, "Because decked in diamonds I feel more like your mistress than your wife."

"Under promise of their secrecy I have shown these ladies my copy of our marriage lines," he said.

"Why did you do that?" gasped Lucy.

"Because those who are closest to me must know that Jackie is no bastard. My son and I will always face the world together and care nothing for its opinion, but the inner circle must give him the respect that is his right."

Why did the shadow touch her mind again? Because his concern seemed more for Jackie than herself? But she loved Jackie more than herself. Because of his possessiveness over the child? Then Charles broke into a sunburst of laughter and the shadow vanished. He had pulled off the baby's lace cap and found that Jackie's first golden fluff of hair had now entirely vanished and he was bald as an egg.

"When I come back again I may find his hair as black as mine," he said.

Instantly the sun went in and the shadow returned. "Come back again?" asked Lucy. "Are you leaving The Hague?"

"The States are still so infuriated over the murder of the Parliamentary Ambassador that they have asked me to leave Holland, so for a time I shall go. Do you not want to know whom we are visiting?"

Lucy was trembling; angry that he had not told her this before, desperately anxious to know where he was going, hurt by his sudden change of conversation, but she choked it all down and asked shakily. "Who are these ladies whom you love?"

"One of them you have told me you admire already," he answered.

"Not the Queen of Bohemia?" she whispered.

"Yes. The two are my aunt Elizabeth and my sister Mary."

She was silent for a while, trying to control her trembling. That other family who had always meant so much to her but whom she had seen only distantly, passing by, were coming nearer now. In a short time she would be curtseying to the Winter Queen and the Princess of Orange. Knowing what they did would they greet her as niece and sister? If so the nimbus about the moon would perhaps become a band of comfort about her. Yet it seemed impossible of belief.

"Do not be frightened, dear heart," Charles encouraged her. "You are more beautiful than any of my aunt's daughters. I once told my cousin Sophie she was handsomer than you but it was a deliberate fib. I tell lies to all the royal ladies to whom they try to marry me and I tell them so boorishly that they soon want no more of this perfidious fellow. Sophie wants no more of me."

"Shall we see her today?" asked Lucy anxiously.

"We may do so but I think not, for her daughters bore my aunt. We should see them if we stayed to dinner but from dining with the Queen of Bohemia may God preserve me."

"Why is it so dreadful?" asked Lucy nervously.

"She is the most trusting, loyal and hospitable woman in the world but she is also the world's worst housekeeper. All the tradesmen cheat her, and no servant who has ever served her moderately well is ever dismissed whatever his subsequent state of degeneracy. Anyone with the least claim upon her can invite himself to dine whenever he wishes. Sitting at her table you may find yourself with the impeccable Marquis of Montrose upon your left and some old dotard in a greasy doublet spluttering his food upon your right. The meat will either be bloody or burnt. But my aunt reigns over it all in dignity and serenity. She is so generous with the very little money that she possesses that her daughters are portionless and her house is starting to fall to pieces over her head, but the sufferings of her life have left her, I think, not much disturbed by material misfortune. She is a great and noble woman."

"Yet you do not, like the Marquis, dine with her."

"I am her nephew," Charles explained, "and nobility of character can press very hard upon a person's relatives. Willynilly they are involved in his or her sacrifical deeds while not themselves having a taste for sacrifice. You see what I mean? But do not look so worried, dear heart. I shall never be a noble character."

"I was feeling sorry for the portionless princesses," said Lucy. "And why is their mother bored with them?"

"One of those family things," said Charles airily. "She is a man's woman and idolizes her sons. We are here. For God's sake take Jackie from me. Why do you not get a nurse for him? Do you not know that kings cannot be seen carrying their own brats?"

Lucy did not know, but what she did know was that he was as nervous about the coming interview as she was. She took Jackie from him as the coach passed through the gateway of the Wassenaer Hof, swept round the courtyard and drew up at the foot of the steps. Charles handed her ceremoniously from the coach, the halberdier on guard saluted and the great doors opened from within.

They were in a large hall panelled in dark oak and hung with tapestries. One bowing servant took her cloak from her and another led them towards the wide dark staircase. Lucy found she had become two different girls. One was trembling behind the brave façade that she had unfolded from her fear as a peacock opens its tail, and the other stood back in the shadow of the hall and watched with amazement as the regal figure in the blue silk dress walked across the hall beside the King of England, diamonds sparkling on her breast and her marvellous baby held proudly in her arms. Was that radiant vision her? Or was this her, this observer in the shadows? Or was the fear that had put forth the peacock's tail her? But that would make three; the fear, the façade and the observer. She was conscious of flushed cheeks and dry lips that she moistened with the tip of her tongue, and the discomfort seemed to bring her divided being back into unity again. She was just fear. That was all. That is what a human being is; a hot frightened animal.

The major-domo was announcing the King of England and Mrs. Barlow in a high room that seemed full of rainbows, dogs and monkeys. The sun shone through windows that were mosaics of coats-of-arms in coloured glass, and the pinks and blues and greens splashed their colours on the pale silk that covered the walls, on the polished floor and the white dress of the tall woman who stood to receive them. Why, thought Lucy confusedly, these rainbows are the nimbus about the moon. Here I am with the other family.

The tall woman was bidding them welcome in a deep beautiful voice. Lucy could not hear what she said above the chattering of the monkeys and the barking of the dogs, but her deep curtsey came easily to her in spite of her shaking knees, for it seemed natural to sink down before that tall whiteness; especially as someone had had the forethought to take Jackie from her. She might have stayed where she was at the Queen's feet had not his roar of protest brought her up again, to find that the person who had removed Jackie was the Queen herself.

"A boy, thank God," she said, looking with appreciation at the furious countenance of her great-nephew. "How I love a baby boy. Be quiet, child, that I may look at you."

Jackie was not a baby who protested long, he was too healthy and too interested in the world about him. He was still and silent instantly, gazing fascinated at the large pendant pearl earrings that swayed above him. The tears that hung on his lashes incommoded him a little in his scrutiny of this new phenomenon, and the Queen wiped them away with her handkerchief. "Why, he is like my godson James!" she ejaculated. "Look, Mary, is he not like James?"

There was a soft rustling as the Princess of Orange in her mourning dress of violet satin drew nearer to inspect her nephew, and Lucy sank into another curtsey. "These small infants always look alike to me," she said with cold hostility.

She was very changed from the little princess Lucy remembered. Her hair was curly and pretty as ever and she had a delicate porcelain look about her, but her mouth was sullen and obstinate now and her eyes had a wary expression. Lucy remembered the Hague gossip about the many love affairs of the Prince of Orange, and of the baby whom the little Princess had lost when she was only fifteen, and was full of pity. She smiled at the Princess and wanted to love her but Mary turned away pointedly and began talking to her brother. Lucy flushed with sudden shame, as though the image of herself that she must present to the world were the truth; and also with a spurt of anger, for the princess's behaviour seemed to her an insult to her husband as well as herself. But Charles appeared not to have noticed anything amiss. He was fond of his sister and laughing with her seemed to have forgotten his wife.

"I have lost my heart to your son, Lucy," said the Queen. "Now let me have a look at *you*."

They sat down together by a large window and Lucy found that she was able to meet the appraisal of a pair of eyes as piercingly blue as her own. She was not afraid of this tall gaunt woman with her thin, strong, slightly aquiline face, though she could understand how others were sometimes intimidated. The Queen was startlingly direct, and there was about her appearance and manners the simplicity of real greatness that passes unconscious judgment on the trivial. Except that she dressed always in black or white there was nothing in her appearance to show she was a king's widow, for she saw no reason why the tragedies of her life should condemn her to the hideous elaboration of royal weeds. She dressed in the way that suited her, in simple flowing dresses cut low to show her still lovely neck and shoulders, her only jewels her moony pearls. The sober ladies of The Hague were slightly outraged by her dresses but she never minded what people thought.

Her gaze softened as she inspected Lucy. "You are not what I expected," she said. "I commend my nephew's taste though I am very sorry indeed that he has married you. But you were both so young and caught in the storms of love; coming as they do from the deeps that are beyond control, one does not consider the fabricated wisdom of the world."

Lucy wondered if the Queen had forgotten her. She was looking at a portrait that hung on the wall opposite. A picture of the dark, sad King of Bohemia hung over the mantelpiece but the man she was looking at was not the Queen's greatly loved husband but a much younger man, with a broad forehead and large firm mouth, and eyes so keen and living under the peaked eyebrows that they seemed to be looking straight out of the picture into the mind of the beholder. As abruptly as she had forgotten Lucy the Queen returned to her.

"What am I saying to you, child? Oh yes. The deeps. In another world than this, Lucy, and I do not speak of an imagined heaven but of the world of the spirit that is present with us here and now, you will not regret Charles, but in what we are accustomed to call this world I would like to know what you are expecting?"

Lucy answered instantly, "Your Majesty, that I shall find living a lie more and more difficult. I did not know that a month ago, but I know it now."

"But you must do it," said the Queen sternly. "Just now, with his hope of winning his throne hanging in the balance, Charles must have every chance. And he must make the right choices." Again the Queen's eyes had gone to the portrait opposite her. "If you have any influence with your husband, Lucy, do not let him commit himself too deeply to these gentlemen of the kirk who are now at The Hague. They betrayed his father and they will betray him. His greatest servant, as he was his father's before him, is the Marquis of Montrose. But kings, Lucy, do not always recognize to whom they should give their trust and loyalty. It would seem that kingship brings with it a tragic myopia."

"My husband does not often speak to me of his affairs, Your Majesty. Playing the part I do how could I expect his confidence in such matters?"

"A pity," said the Queen abruptly. "You have sense."

The current of sympathy was flowing warmly between them. To Lucy at nineteen the middle-aged queen seemed an old woman and she marvelled that she remembered one's helplessness when the deeps overflow. For the King of Bohemia had died many years ago. But women do not love only once, she remembered. The deeps can open again. And perhaps yet again, once more, one last time. But surely the Marquis was betrothed to the Queen's daughter Louise? Suddenly she was ashamed, as though her flash of intuition were an insult to the woman beside her. Yet she could not take her eyes from the eyes in the picture that were looking into her mind.

"That portrait was painted by Honthorst," said the Queen calmly. "He gets a good likeness. Do you want Apollo on your lap? If not, smack him and put him on the floor."

A strange little golden-haired monkey had settled himself on Lucy's knees and was gazing in amazement at the baby in the Queen's arms. He was not jealous, only utterly amazed. But not so amazed as Jackie. He considered the golden vision for a moment or two and then reached out a microscopic fist, five tendrils uncurling from it, groping and closing and uncurling again with the immensity of his unsatisfied desire. He whimpered a little. He wanted the thing, he gripped, yet he never had it.

"From the very beginning," said the Queen sadly, "our longings are very ill-matched with our powers of attainment. It is the human condition." Then she noted Lucy's brown fingers moving caressingly in the golden fur and smiled. "I see you like monkeys. Moving as I do always at the centre of a zoological radiation it amuses me to watch the reactions of my guests. Some wade towards me as though through some fungoid growth, others advance as happily as though my periphery were a border of daisies. You were one of the latter, and I noted the fact with pleasure. Do you like my French greyhounds? My sister-in-law the Dowager of England prefers spaniels. A taste for monkeys we share. The sister-in-law relationship is not an easy one and I thank the maker of us all for that point of contact with her."

Charles, now standing beside them, burst into a shout of laughter, then sobered on a memory. "When Lucy was a child she had a marmoset called—now what was he called? Well, she gave him to me."

"And you do not even remember his name," chided the Queen. "She gave you her world, you were unaware of the fact and later no doubt tired of the creature and allowed others to care for it. Probably it soon died. Now do not contradict me for I know small boys. When do you leave for Paris? I look forward to coming part of the way with you."

"Would the last week of this month suit Your Majesty? Mary is coming a short way with me as well as yourself. Also, of course, my suite and her servants and yours."

So he is going to Paris, thought Lucy, and remembering Charles's promise to her at Breda her heart beat fast. Would he remember? Charles wanted to discuss his plans with his aunt and presently she found herself in another window with the Princess. The Queen had somehow inveigled her there without her knowing it and she found she was happy where she was. This, she knew, is the mark of a perfect hostess; the ability to move her guest from station to station on the chessboard of her salon in such a manner that where she wants them to be is also where they are glad to be. Lucy wondered what the Queen had murmured in her niece's ear for the Princess was in a better humour. She was smiling a little and even regarding the baby in Lucy's arms with a dull sad interest. "Yes, he is a Stuart," she said in relief.

"He has my mother's fair hair, Your Highness," said Lucy gently, for knowing now what it meant to bear a baby her thoughts were very often with the mother who had borne her, and the grandmother who had borne her mother. "At least," she amended, "he had before it came off."

They were silent, for neither girl knew what to say to the other. A greyhound pushed affectionately against Lucy's knees and another monkey, a grey one this time, jumped on Mary's shoulder. She pushed it off pettishly.

"My aunt has too many creatures," she ejaculated. "She cannot afford them but she says they are all presents from her friends and if people give her gifts that eat what can she do? But I heard her actually ask the Marquis of Montrose to give her the golden marmoset, and he did."

"Was that the one that sat on my lap?"

"Yes."

"Then no wonder my son liked him," said Lucy. "Would Your Highness like to hold Jackie?" She spoke without thinking, wanting to give joy, but when she saw the childless girl holding the baby so stiffly, a queer mixture of yearning and loathing on her thin face, she reproached herself for a blundering fool. She put out her hand impulsively and touched Mary's cheek. "Your Highness will have a son soon," she whispered. "I know you will. I will pray that you will."

The ice was broken between them and they sat on the windowseat together and presently Mary was talking eagerly of the coming journey. She was going, she said, because she did not like The Hague. It disagreed with her and a holiday might make her feel stronger and then perhaps she might bear a child.

"Of course it is easier to travel to France by sea," she said, "but Charles is taking the land journey so that he can show himself as King in the Spanish Netherlands. That will be good for his cause."

The door opened and there was sudden movement among the rainbows, dogs and monkeys chattering and barking, laughter and voices and a sea-sound of silken skirts in motion. Four princesses had entered the room with some precipitation, unannounced and uninvited by their mother. The Queen drew herself up, a little angry, but seeing that the invasion was led by the little Princess Henrietta who loved babies, and that her eldest daughter Elizabeth, coming last and closing the door carefully, sent her a glance of dignified apology, she relented. They all did what Henrietta wished though she was the youngest but one. Smiling, the Queen presented her daughters and Lucy had a quick impression of the four. Elizabeth tall and dark, her face grave with a scholar's gravity, Louise the artist, betrothed to the Marquis of Montrose, her face full of humour and intelligence, the adorable Henrietta, blue-eyed, fair-haired and fragile, and the dark pretty Sophie whom the Queen had hoped would marry Charles.

Mary had handed Jackie back to his mother and Lucy stood holding him proudly, the feel of him in her arms giving her courage in the centre of this rustling, exclaiming, perfumed and inquisitive group of female royalty. But for him she would have been afraid for Charles had deserted her and was on the other side of the room. Even he could have too much of women, especially when they were related to him.

The Queen too stood a little aloof, her face as still as though carved out of stone. Statuesque too were the long folds of her white dress. Though she was so much stronger now waves of tiredness and depression could still quite suddenly break over Lucy, the shock of them making her sensitive to the realities of the lives whose outward appearance was a weaving of colour and light before her eyes. Through the mist of sunshine and rainbows she saw two stark figures of dark and light. Her young husband in his deep purple mourning, his black hair tumbled about his dark face, was playing with the greyhounds and the monkeys in the oriel window. With the sun shining upon them they seemed fabulous creatures of silver and gold and they leaped and fawned upon him, and his face was full of tenderness for them, for like all his family he loved animals. The scene was primeval; man moving through the sun and rainbows of the garden when he was alone, at home with the creatures and adored by them, his mind without knowledge of human love or hate, his memory a calm peaceful pool to mirror only the stars and sunshine and the bright eyes of the trusting beasts. He was alone but not conscious of loneliness for his garment was made of the purple shadows of evening, when he walked beneath the trees and was companioned by the stillness and quietness of God.

It was the Winter Queen's figure of grief that was a dazzle of whiteness like frozen snow. If the woman had brought human love to Adam she had brought grief too; tears and partings and forsakenness. Perhaps he had been better off without her; playing with the creatures or alone with that quietness under the trees.

The two tall figures seemed to tower suddenly to the carved roof above, then receded from Lucy, leaving her conscious only of the laughing girls who had formed themselves into a circle about her. She could not know that of them all only the plump Sophie would live long and cheerfully and be a mother of kings. Of the others two would die young and two would escape to convents from a world they could no longer endure. Just for a moment it seemed that they were pressing her in and in to some central point of grief, yet when she reached the centre grief broke into miraculous joy, for Jackie was in her arms. At this central point of creation there was joy. She laughed and was back upon the surfaces of life, with the Queen pressing them to dine with her and Charles remembering an important engagement.

Driving back to Scheveningen Lucy felt herself still held in that rainbow light. Her husband's family had been kind to her. The nimbus about the moon had indeed been a circle of comfort and she dared to ask Charles, "Am I coming to Paris too?"

He smiled at her. "Why yes, dear heart. I promised you Paris. I do not break promises."

Lucy smiled back. "It will be wonderful to be with you. And wonderful to travel with the Queen."

"But you cannot do that! You cannot take part in a royal progress. You must follow me a little later. Wilmot will bring you. He will take care of you on the journey and in Paris. You had better go by sea from Brill. By land the journey is long and troublesome and I take it only for reasons of State. You must have some woman to attend you. Get yourself a reliable maid. You should have done that long ago."

Lucy was ashamed that this news of a separate journey should upset her so much, for what else could she expect? The King of England would not go on a royal progress visibly accompanied by his mistress and her baby. But how could she bear to be parted from Charles now that they had Jackie? They were an indissoluble trinity. She swallowed her tears and asked equably, "Where am I to live in Paris?"

"Wilmot will find you a lodging somewhere," said Charles airily. To her horror she heard an edge of anger in her voice as she said, "I will lodge with my dear Betje and her husband. Then when you want me to ride with you she can look after Jackie. I would not trust Jackie with some strange landlady found by Lord Wilmot who knows nothing whatever about babies."

"Marry come up, you cannot bring Jackie!" ejaculated Charles. "You must leave him at Rotterdam with your aunt."

As they drove under the green shade of the trees it seemed as though darkness had fallen. Lucy did not think she could have heard right. Leave Jackie behind? But it was impossible. Charles must be mad. Then she remembered that a parting between her and Jackie was indeed impossible.

"I am feeding Jackie," she reminded her husband.

"Get him a wet-nurse."

"Indeed I will not. I do not want my son suckled by a Dutch-woman. Babies absorb characteristics with their milk. Yes they do. My grandmother said so. Do you want a dull, solid Dutch baby? Do not laugh, Charles. Please do not laugh. I have told you that my grandmother said so."

Charles blew his nose to hide his laughter. "Would you consider Scottish milk?" he asked from behind the folds of his handkerchief. "There are all those Scottish weavers at Rotterdam. Your uncle must employ a number of them. The Scottish are loyal on the whole and an honest and brave people. I have no doubt their milk is the best in the world."

"Welsh milk is the best in the world," said Lucy, "and my son shall have no other." She was not amused by the conversation and she was hurt that Charles was amused. "Charles, Charles!" she burst out. "How can you bear to go away and leave Jackie behind you?"

He sobered instantly. "Because my son is too dear to me and too important a personage to be exposed to the dangers of travel at so tender an age. And Paris behind her fine façade is a stinking hell where fevers breed from filth. And the barricades have only just come down after the war of the Fronde and who knows when they will go up again? So if you do not want to part from Jackie, Lucy, you had better not come with me."

He was angry now and in spite of his love for Jackie vaguely jealous. Whom did she love best, himself or the boy?

"If I feed Jackie he will catch no fever," said Lucy obstinately. "And if the barricades go up again he and I will be safe with Betje and her husband."

"I have made my wishes known to you," said Charles. The fingers of one hand were drumming on his knee and when she glanced at him his bearing was that of His Most Sacred Majesty.

"I will leave Jackie at Rotterdam and I will follow you to Paris," she said.

Instantly he turned back to her, a boy again, his set face breaking up into charm and laughter. He took her and her baby into his arms together and unity was once more restored. Jackie, squeezed too tight and very hungry, burst into roars of fury and his parents into laughter. Nevertheless this first quarrel over their child had left its mark.

Seven

I

Lucy sat at the high western window of her lodging, and watched the stormy sunset light streaming over the towers and roofs of Paris. It had been a day of stifling summer heat with a thunderstorm in the late afternoon, but now the thunder was no more than an angry mutter in the distance and behind the towers of Notre-Dame the sun had torn the clouds apart and made of them savage banners of red and purple.

She was not at ease in Paris. The surface of her life was gay, and her heart beat high with hope because in this new reunion Charles seemed more in love with her than ever, but this unease, united with the longing for Jackie, left behind at Rotterdam, and the fact that she did not quite trust Anne Hill, the girl who had come with her from Holland as her maid, kept a shadow of anxiety always at the back of her mind. And hidden below her surface vivacity there was always her tiredness.

She looked out again over the city and wondered why it made her afraid. It was beautiful now, its steep roofs washed to a silver cleanliness by the storm, and she tried to think that a faint flower scent came to her, carried on a wandering air from some great man's garden, perhaps from the garden where Cardinal Mazarin's strange monkeys and tropical birds chattered and fluted. She could see it in her mind's eye as Betje's husband had described it to her, with its roses and lilies and tinkling fountains; and looking down on it from the window of the room where he spun his webs of power she saw for a moment the olive-skinned enigmatic face of the man who was the virtual ruler of France. The King and his brother were still children and he held their mother in the hollow of his hand.

How men hated him! That was what was the matter with Paris, Lucy thought suddenly. Hate. In the stinking alleys and filthy tumble-down hovels lived human beings so degraded by poverty that even she, who had so loved the sin-eater, turned her head aside when she saw them gaping at her from their shadows as she jolted over the cobbles in Lord Wilmot's coach. Between these travesties of human creatures and the silken beings who danced at the Louvre there were contrasts so great that only hate could be begotten of them; and from hate fear was born. It was the poor who hated and the rich who were afraid, and when trouble broke out the Cardinal, the archetypal figure of power, was somehow always the enemy.

The sun sank behind the fiery clouds and Lucy got up and lit the candles, for Charles was coming tonight and supper was laid on the table. With her back turned upon the window, and its view of a city that made her afraid, she looked at the room that was now another of her homes. Stone-walled and strongbeamed, it looked safe, and suddenly she was happy as she rustled round the room, and into her adjoining bedchamber and out again, making all ready for Charles, and letting her fancy rove through the little kingdom of the old house beneath her.

It was tall and narrow. On the floor below Betje and her husband lived and Anne had her room. The millinery shop was below again, and on the ground floor was a bakery. The smell of fresh bread, bringing memories of Roch, was one of the joys of this home. A narrow staircase wound about its newel-post from top to bottom of the house and when Charles came to see her the first Lucy knew of his arrival was the creak of every third stair as he strode upwards.

He always came to see her as Tomos, wearing a big shabby hat, riding perhaps from his mother's apartments at the Louvre, or from Saint-Germain, the country palace where she also had a suite of rooms and where she often stayed with Minette. At other times he came from the house of the English ambassador or the lodgings of one of his friends, for he had no settled home except these attic rooms. She had hardly trimmed the candles when she heard his step and a moment later she was clinging to him as though they had met after an absence of years instead of days; for their life was full of uncertainty and the tense atmosphere of Paris heightened it.

As they ate their supper and drank their wine Charles laughed often, telling Lucy of his mock courtship of Mademoiselle, which he had begun again to keep his mother quiet, and the eccentricities of Sir Edward Hyde his chancellor, and the comic feud that existed between him and the Dowager Queen. Lucy laughed too and then cajoled him gently to speak of more serious things. To her delight, because she knew it would please the Queen of Bohemia, he was turning now less to the Covenanters for support and more to the Marquis of Montrose in Scotland and the Marquis of Ormonde, who was rallying the wild Irish to the Royalist cause.

"You write often to the Marquis of Montrose?" she asked.

"Often. He is a great man. I tell him in every letter I write that he has my loyalty and support. But it is to Ireland I hope to go soon. If we can win Ireland the tougher nut of Scotland will be easier to crack."

"Very soon?"

"As soon as possible."

She sighed but she made no comment. Then she asked him to describe these three men to her; the Chancellor, Montrose and Ormonde, and she said their names over to herself. These were the King's greatest servants. These he should trust and these only. Shyly she told him so and he laughed and pulled her curls.

"There is a fourth," he said. "A man whom my mother detests almost as much as she does old Hyde. Dr. Cosin. He was once Dean of Peterborough and now he is our Protestant chaplain at Paris, with rooms at the Louvre and at the English embassy, where he preaches to us all on Sunday. Wilmot should take you to hear him one day. He is a fierce, difficult man but he has great loyalty. My mother will capture the souls of her Protestant children only over his dead body and I believe he would die for the Church of England and for me should his duty demand the sacrifice. What is the matter, Lucy?"

She was white. Dr. Cosin who had given her the silver piece, Dr. Cosin her grandmother's friend, and she must presently appear before him as the King's mistress. "It is nothing," she said. "It is the weather. It was hot till the storm came."

Anne Hill had come into the room once or twice, bringing a dish of strawberries for them and a fresh bottle of wine, but they had hardly noticed when she came and went for she had the silence of a cat in movement. She was slender with regular features and smooth corn-coloured hair under her cap, and she would have been beautiful had not a bad burn ravaged one side of her face. Her father had been one of the Rotterdam Scottish weavers and she was well-mannered and discreet. Aunt Margaret, who had chosen her, had been pleased with her choice. Anne's calmness, she had hoped, would check Lucy's impetuosity and her tidiness not be without effect upon Lucy's hair and wardrobe. And the two girls were so different that they should surely get on well together.

Up to a point they did. But Lucy, unable to be happy unless she had the affection of those about her, was aware that she had not won Anne's, and in the girl's demureness she felt a hint of mockery. Well, what could she expect? Anne would probably not have entered the service of the King's mistress had she not been well paid. That her father had died in her childhood, and that she and her mother had lived in great poverty until her mother had died too, Lucy knew not from Anne herself but from Aunt Margaret. Anne did not confide in her. She confided in Anne sometimes, hoping to win confidence in return, but she did not. That was partly why she was faintly afraid, for it is dangerous to tell too much to someone who does not return your trust. There was another reason. Sometimes there seemed to come from Anne a queer breath of evil. And yet once or twice she had seen in Anne's face a gleam of light that softened her disfigurement like the reflection of light on water, gone in a moment but mysterious and lovely. Could a person both be evil and yet reflect light? She did not know but though she feared her maid she could not dislike her.

The door closed finally behind Anne and Charles, who had been appreciative of her graceful exit, said, "It is a pity about her face for that girl of yours has the smallest waist I ever saw. Though yours was nearly as small, dear heart, before you had

Jackie. Not that having a baby spoilt your beauty for you are lovelier than you ever were and it is time my mother saw you. I have arranged it. Wilmot will bring you to Saint-Germain tomorrow."

"Charles!" gasped Lucy in terror. "Go to Saint-Germain to see your mother! I cannot do it. I cannot!"

"Why are you afraid?" asked Charles. "You have confronted my aunt of Bohemia and her livestock, daughters and monkeys and all. And since we have been here you have ridden in the forest with me or Wilmot, and come for picnics on the river and faced Buckingham and the rest and queened it over them, and now you quail at thought of meeting one poor old widow woman."

"She is your mother."

"Yours too. And she knows it. She has seen my copy of our marriage certificate. And you will see old friends, Lady Dalkeith whom you met in Exeter, who is now Lady Morton, and Minette. She is five years old now and a fairy child."

"Then I will come," said Lucy with sudden courage. "But I hope it is only your family and not one of your mother's levees."

"It is one of her levees, but Wilmot shall get you there in good time that you may have a little while with my mother alone. Now do not be afraid. Keep your head up and be bold. Shall we play chess before we go to bed?"

2

It was Betje who helped Lucy dress for the levee, for Anne was having her day off, and Lucy was thankful for it, for Betje with her broad homely Dutch face, her goodness and honesty, was like firm ground beneath her feet. " 'Those who bring forth fruit out of an honest and good heart,' " she quoted. "That is you, Betje. You make me think of golden corn ripening under the sun, the good bread that feeds the world."

"There is a strong smell from the bakery today," said the practical Betje. "A sunny day too. Will you wear your golden gown?"

"Yes, and the diamonds the King gave to Jackie and me. Where do you think Anne goes on her days off? It makes me anxious. She should not go out alone in this dreadful Paris."

"Do not fret yourself over Anne. She is older than she looks and knows how to take care of herself. And she does not go out alone. She goes out with Mr. Edward Prodgers, one of His Majesty's gentlemen. He came one morning with a note for you from His Majesty and when he had delivered it to me he idled for a while in the shop. You know Anne helps me sometimes, with your permission, and she was there that day. Her eyes seem so grey and cold, then she looks up and they are full of fire. He bought her a pretty blue hood. It is hot again today and you will need your fan. Where do you keep it?"

"It is with my gloves," said Lucy distractedly. "And where they are I do not know. Anne thinks me untidy and so she keeps my things in order for me. It is kind of her but I can never find what I want and I wish that His Majesty had not insisted that I have a maid. He was born to shout for his gloves and have a servant bring them, but I was born to find my own gloves underneath my own chaos and that is the way I like it. And I am afraid of Anne." Absurdly she was near tears and Betje's arms were round her. But in a moment she had recovered and was ashamed of herself. "It is because I am not myself yet after the baby," she apologized to Betje.

"It takes a long time to be well again," comforted Betje as she fastened the golden dress. But silently she wondered why Lucy took so long to recover. Had she suffered some injury? And was Lucy's dislike of Anne an unreasonable or instinctive one? "You do not let Anne look after your private treasures do you?" she asked.

"No, no!" said Lucy. "I always wear my ring and if the diamonds are not on me they are in the secret drawer of the little writing desk that His Majesty gave me. He bought it especially because of the drawer. He told me to keep my papers and my letters from him there because it is so wonderfully secret."

Betje searched for and found the fan and gloves, her silence so pregnant with her contempt for secret drawers that Lucy went on talking in an effort to lighten the sense of strain between them. "Anne tells me so little," she said. "I do not even know what her life was like before she came here."

"Bitterness and grief," said Betje. "One day she told me of it. Then she regretted she had spoken and asked me to respect her confidence."

"Then I will not ask you what it was that she told you," said Lucy. "Poor Anne! Now I will not find it hard to love her. How can one not love someone who has suffered?"

"Everyone has," said Betje drily.

"Oh, they have, they do," cried Lucy with a warm gust of compassion. "One should love and never be afraid. One should love everyone, everything."

"Nevertheless," said Betje as she left the room to see if the coach had come, "prudence is a virtue."

Lucy had understood Betje's silence and she went to the desk that stood on the table beside her bed and opened the hidden drawer. The packet of Charles's letters was by this time too bulky to be carried about with her but she took out her marriage certificate and pushed it down inside the bodice of her dress. It must never leave her now. If it were found the finder might talk of what he or she had read, Charles's secret would become known and he might think that she herself had proclaimed it. Then he would think she had betrayed not only him, but the King of England and he would not love her any more.

3

Sitting in the coach beside Lord Wilmot Lucy straightened her shoulders and held her head up, as Charles had told her to do, and turned and smiled at her companion.

"You look very regal in your golden gown, Lucy," he said. "Charles is a lucky fellow."

And he meant what he said. When Charles had commanded him to assume responsibility for the welfare and safety of the beautiful Mrs. Barlow he had bowed and expressed himself as conscious of the honour done him, but his inward being had reverberated with profanity. But on the journey from The Hague he had found Lucy plucky and uncomplaining, friendly and amusing. And she had found him a kind and sensible young man as well as a charming one and was at ease with him.

"We are commanded to call at the embassy and pick up two more of the Queen's guests," he said. "One is Mr. John Evelyn who is on a visit to his father-in-law the Ambassador. He is one of these learned bookish fellows."

"Who is the other?"

"Another bookish fellow. His Majesty's chaplain in Paris, Dr. Cosin."

She was glad Charles had already prepared her yet she could not speak. In ten minutes now. In fifteen minutes.

"What's the matter, little love?" asked Lord Wilmot. "These scholars are nothing to be frightened of. Apart from astronomy or theology, or whatever useless subject they are learned about, they know nothing. Ask them to bake a loaf of bread when you are starving or apply a tourniquet when you are bleeding to death, they might as well not have been born. Here we are at the embassy. Lucy, you bold bad woman, see how good an actress you can be."

She would have accepted the challenge with hidden laughter if it had not been for Dr. Cosin. As it was, though she did accept it, the little girl within her to whom he had given the silver piece was crying bitterly. Lord Wilmot had left the coach and was exchanging courtesies with the two gentlemen who had joined them. Mr. Evelyn, grave and gentle in a snuff-coloured coat, looked as though he would have been happy inside Mr. Gwinne's rampart of books, and Lucy would have smiled at him if her face had not felt so stiff and frozen. Dr. Cosin, tall and gaunt, had changed. His black beard was streaked with grey and his face deeply lined.

Lord Wilmot turned round and held the coach door wide. "Gentlemen, will you enter the coach? May I have the honour of presenting you to Mrs. Barlow? She is also, by command, attending the Queen Dowager's levee."

He winked at Lucy and stood back. The two gentlemen had

heard of Mrs. Barlow for the King's infatuation for her and
her son was the talk of the English community. They looked
with alarm at the golden girl who sat facing the horses. It was
a fine day and she seemed to focus the light upon herself. She
was sunburnt from the picnics on the river and her blue eyes
blazed in her brown face. Her diamonds caught the sunlight
and a ruby burned on her thin brown hand. She inclined her
head with hauteur but she did not smile; she could not lest she
burst into tears. Nor could she stretch out a hand to Dr. Cosin
in greeting for her hands were trembling and she had locked
them tightly in her lap.

"Will you get in, gentlemen?" encouraged Lord Wilmot.
"Dr. Cosin, will you sit by Mrs. Barlow?"

But Dr. Cosin, embarrassed, preferred to sit beside an
equally embarrassed Mr. Evelyn with his back to the horses; a
position which did not agree with him at all. Lord Wilmot
stepped gaily into the coach and sat beside Lucy and the horses
moved forward. The conversation was at first between the
gentlemen only for Lucy felt as though she had a tight band
round her throat and she could not speak. But presently courage demanded of her that she should not sit with downcast
eyes and she looked attentively from one face to the other. Mr.
Evelyn, the contempt in his eyes perfectly plain to her, made
some courteous remark about the weather and she acknowledged with a smile that there was indeed a great improvement
on yesterday.

Then she looked steadily at Dr. Cosin who sat exactly opposite her. Would he remember her? But how could he? The
change in his face told her how much he had endured since
she had last seen him. That chasm of trouble would have extinguished all trivial memories. Yet if his eyes were sunken
now they were as piercing as ever and when he looked at her
there was no contempt in his glance, only sadness and puzzlement. Then he too took refuge in the weather. The storm had
cleared the air, he said, and it was cooler today. She agreed and
suddenly the iron band round her throat was loosed. She
always spoke with the Welsh lilt but when she was deeply
moved she would forget herself and speak almost as Nan-Nan

would have done. "Like a breath of sea air it is. Yet it is far enough away we are from that."

"You come from the sea, madam?"

"I have lately taken a sea voyage from The Hague to France."

"Madam, I was speaking of your home."

"I am from the sea, sir. The coast of Pembrokeshire."

His mind groped back across that chasm to the woman of whom Lucy's voice had instantly reminded him. His old friend Mrs. Gwinne. She had come from Pembrokeshire. Mr. Evelyn was now in animated conversation with Lord Wilmot. It was as though he were alone with this girl.

"Mrs. Barlow, what was your maiden name?"

"Lucy Walter. I am Mrs. Gwinne's granddaughter. And once at her home at St. Giles you gave me a silver piece. But it is not possible that you can remember that now."

"I remember," he said gravely. "I thought of you then as a child from the sea."

"And you gave me your blessing."

"Yes."

He leaned back in his corner and was silent in settled sadness. After a while tall green trees stepped past the windows of the jolting coach and the air was sweetened by them. But Lucy was in misery. She had already caused grief to her father, her grandmother and Justus and now this man who had been so kind to her as a child was in sorrow too because of what he believed she had become. Unaware of what she was doing but driven by a subconscious longing to be comforted by Charles or Jackie, or by both of them, she put her hands over the diamonds that sparkled on her low-cut golden gown. They were Charles's gift and they were Jackie's diamonds as well as hers. Underneath them, between her breasts, she could feel her folded marriage certificate and a glow of reassurance went through her. She had her hidden integrity that later Jackie would share with her. If only Dr. Cosin could share it too then he would not be so grieved. She pulled the bit of paper half out of her gown then pushed it back again. If only she could tell him! But she had promised

Charles. Only her family and his must know. She had promised.

The great trees continued to step past and there were deer beneath them. Then they stepped back and there were flowers and lawns. The coach swept round the curve of a fountain and drew up at the foot of a flight of marble steps. They were at the Palace of Saint-Germain, and so suddenly that Lucy was taken by surprise. The mask of the bold, experienced Mrs. Barlow dropped and she could not find it. Nor could she find her fan and gloves. She jumped up like a frightened child, her face flushed and her lips trembling, and she did not know where they were. Mr. Evelyn and Lord Wilmot, nearest to the steps, got out of the coach and stood waiting to hand her out. Dr. Cosin, seeing her childish distress, was still with her to help her.

"You have lost something, Mrs. Barlow?" he enquired.

"My fan," she whispered. "My fan and my gloves." And she bent over distractedly to look under the seat.

"They could hardly be under the seat," he told her gently. "Look, they are here, pushed down between the window and the cushions."

"Oh thank you!" she cried, looking up at him gratefully and with the same little girl's face that he remembered from Mrs. Gwinne's parlour. "I have to meet the Queen, you see. It is the first time."

"Keep your courage up, child," he rallied her. "Look, have you lost something else? A letter I think." He picked up her marriage certificate from the floor and held it out to her. It had dropped from her dress when she bent over. She looked him steadily in the eyes. "Will you please read this in privacy," she said. "And afterwards return it to me."

He bowed and stepped back that Lord Wilmot might hand her from the coach. It was as they went up the steps that darkness fell upon her. "The maintaining of truth is so hard." This was the first time she had broken faith with Charles. Yet what she had done she had not meant to do.

"Your Majesty, I have the honour to present my wife to you. Mam, this is Lucy."

Charles's tone had dropped suddenly from that of high ceremony to one of slightly belligerent family intimacy. Let Mam be nasty to his girl and he would have her blood. His tone deepened Lucy's misery. She had just broken her promise to him and now here he was at her side in utmost loyalty. With his hand under her elbow to help her she rose from her deep curtsey and for the first time dared to look at her mother-in-law.

Dressed in black, a black lace veil over her head, her small face ravaged by illness and grief, the Queen had aged out of all recognition, but her dark eyes were bright, and her manner when she spoke and the movements of her small hands were vivacious as ever. Sitting in a throne-like high-backed chair she looked at Lucy, and she tried to smile but she could not. There were no rainbows in this room and only one small dog yapping angrily at the stranger from his mistress's knee, for the penurious Queen could no longer afford the monkeys and dwarfs that had once formed her retinue. The sun shone but compared with the Queen of Bohemia's friendly room this one felt like a chamber of ice, and Lucy trembled with the cold.

"Charles," commanded the Queen, "find Lord Jermyn and see that all is in readiness for my levee. Mrs. Barlow, please be seated. Morton, stay with me please."

There was a note of pleading in the last sentence that steadied Lucy, for it showed that the Queen was nervous too. A little warmth crept into the room.

"Sit here, my dear," said a kindly Scottish voice and Lucy looked up briefly into the face of the woman she had last seen weeding the flowers in the garden at Exeter. She had aged too but her face had gained in nobility. She smiled at Lucy and moved to stand beside the Queen.

"Mrs. Barlow, we can speak openly before Lady Morton," said the Queen. "She is so close a friend that all my griefs and distresses are known to her."

"I am afraid that I am one of them, Your Majesty," said Lucy. Courage had returned to her and she sat composedly on the low stool where she had been placed, her eyes meeting the Queen's with compassion. The Queen, startled, hardly knew whether to be vexed or touched.

"Mrs. Barlow, you are indeed," she confessed with a sigh.

"Your Majesty, I beg you not to call me Mrs. Barlow. It is the name of the woman I must pretend to be and not the woman I am, and I would be grateful if I might be excused from acting a part when I am with Your Majesty. I am your son's wife and the mother of your first grandchild. Will you not call me Lucy?"

For a moment or two the Queen was deprived of the power of speech. Then she said with some severity, "My dear, you appear to have a very high opinion of yourself."

"No, not of myself, Your Majesty. Of myself I think nothing. But I am proud of the blood of the Welsh princes that runs in my veins. And I am proud that my husband chose me to be his wife, and I am proud of our beautiful son."

The Scottish Lady Morton, to whom the blood of Welsh princes seemed no particular matter for congratulation, nearly fainted where she stood. She had been attracted by Lucy both at Exeter and again today when the trembling girl had sunk into her graceful curtsey, but a speech as bold as this was an outrage. Yet the Queen, astonishingly, was not angry. Leaning forward she asked eagerly, "Is he like his father? Charles, you know, favours my family. Is he a Medici?"

"No, Your Majesty," said Lucy, "he is a Stuart. He is fair in complexion with blue-grey eyes and so we have called him James."

"I wish I could see him," said the Queen. Then suddenly she recollected herself and severity came back to her face. "But that cannot be at present. The fact of this marriage must not be disclosed. That I know has been impressed upon you. Lucy, you should never have allowed yourself to love my son and even less should you have allowed him to fall in love with you. In what has occurred you are entirely to blame."

"Madame Mère, could we help it?" Lucy cried out, heart-broken. Then the door opened and Lord Jermyn stood bowing on the threshold.

"Your Majesty's guests await you," he said.

"Stay here, my dear," Lady Morton whispered to Lucy as she prepared to attend the Queen. "I will send Lord Wilmot to fetch you in a few minutes."

Lucy went to the open window that looked out over the palace garden to the roofs and towers of Paris in the distance and tried to fight down her fear. For she had remembered something, Herman Vingboon talking of the probable marriage of Charles to La Grande Mademoiselle and the pressure put upon him by his mother. Yet even then the Queen had known of his marriage. There would be no mercy for her, Lucy knew now. The Queen of Bohemia had spoken about the storms of love with understanding, but then Charles was not her son. His mother is a tiger for him, Lucy thought. Are all mothers tigers for their sons? Shall I be like that one day for Jackie?

The door opened again and she heard the hum of talk and laughter and the sound of music. "Ready, Lucy?" Lord Wilmot asked gaily.

She remained for a moment with her back to him. The darkness of her broken promise still filled her mind and the fear of the tiger was cold in her heart. She had a forlorn feeling of lost identity. She did not know who she was. Then the hum of distant gaiety told her who she was at this moment, Mrs. Barlow the King's mistress, and who one is at the moment is always the determining factor in what one must do. She turned round to Lord Wilmot with a brilliant smile, warm and glowing in her golden dress. "I like you, Lucy," he said as they left the room together. "You are an excellent trouper."

They found the long salon already vibrating with that high-pitched ear-battering noise that is the human sound, as each individual member of the herd endeavours to assert his individuality in the face of all the others doing the same thing. What would other animals think of this noise? Lucy wondered, and she remembered the sound of horses neighing and stamping and the great roar of the lion in the Tower of London. Both sounds had been noble. I do not like the human sound, she thought, it is selfish and it could become cruel very quickly.

This fashionable throng was peaceable and kindly enough at the moment. Apart from the English exiles it consisted of French nobility who had come to pay their respects to the Queen Dowager of England and the young King. At present it was as well to keep on good terms with them for it was too early yet to know which way the wind would blow. The King might regain his throne or he might not. When it became apparent that he was unlikely to do so then there would be no further point in being agreeable. Meanwhile he and his brother were attractive young men, and the perfumed French ladies and their fantastically elegant husbands circled round the two tall brothers like high-stepping obsequious peacocks about two royal stags, and the high voices almost drowned the lovely sound the musicians made playing on the terrace outside the open windows. I cannot be with Charles, Lucy thought. I cannot even come near him to share his triumph.

But presently she was having a little triumph of her own as the young men who had ridden with her and Charles in the woods and shared their picnics gathered about her; among them Buckingham, Lord Wilmot, Robert Sidney and Lord Taaffe.

The latter stood grimly planted at the edge of the group. He disliked social occasions; but he liked Lucy, and vouchsafed her the suspicion of a wink. He was a tall red-headed Irishman with a lean weathered face that looked as though it had been exposed to wind and rain from the cradle. When he smiled it folded into creases of tolerant amusement that were more expressive of his kindness and goodwill than his speech, for his manners were brusque and he had a hot temper. He looked well on horseback but off his horse he hardly knew what to do with his ungainly arms and legs. Most women found him unattractive but he gave Lucy a sense of security, and because he was there she began to feel happy in the midst of the fun and banter. Almost it seemed as though this was going to turn into a rainbow day after all.

But not for long. The young Duke of York, attracted by the laughter coming from the group round Lucy, managed to disengage himself from the peacocks and edge his way towards it.

Lucy found him standing in front of her, smiling shyly. Rising from her curtsey she looked up at his face and saw it young and smooth, the blue-grey eyes as innocent as Jackie's, and pity for his vulnerability, and longing for Jackie and fear for him swept over her so sharply that tears came into her eyes. "Why are you crying, Mrs. Barlow?" he asked her gently.

The Duke of Buckingham had an uncanny talent for spotting the truth and placing a fingertip painfully upon it. "She is crying for her little bastard," he said loudly and cruelly.

Instantly the others laughed and rallied round her and Lord Wilmot dried a few tears that had spilled over with his lace handkerchief; yet dimly through her shame she was aware that Lord Taaffe had lost his fiery temper and that only Robert Sidney's grip upon his wrist had prevented him from striking Buckingham. As quickly as he had lost his temper he regained it, bowed to the Duke, came to Lucy and took her to a windowseat where she could sit down and recover herself. For a few moments he stood in front of her to shield her from the curious glances of the room, yet it seemed that no one had taken much notice of the little incident and he sat down beside her, disposed of his long limbs as best he could and then was silent, rubbing his large nose with his forefinger as was his habit when he could not think what to say to a woman.

Lucy spoke first. "Thank you, my lord," she said gratefully.

Her simplicity put him at his ease and to his great surprise he found himself uttering aloud his considered opinion of her. "You are a fine girl," he said. "Pity you are Welsh. When I first set eyes on you I said to myself, 'that colleen is Irish'. Then I heard you speak and there was no doubt of the land that bred you. A pity. You sit a horse well but you do not hold the reins as you should."

"I hold them in the way my Welsh father taught me," said Lucy indignantly. "And no Irishman shall make me change it"

"Madam, I do not intend to try. I know the obstinacy of the Welsh. Come now, we will not quarrel. You are a fine girl and

I take you to be a good one at heart. How you came to the King is none of my business but see to it that you make it yours to be loyal to the poor fellow. If they marry him to that battle-axe Mademoiselle he will need a girl like you to give him a bit of comfort. Have you seen La Grande Mademoiselle?"

Lucy shook her head. She was uneasy and he cursed himself for a blind fool. There was something here that he did not understand and he too was silent.

They both looked up at the same time and saw the same thing. Charles, now also free of the peacocks, was coming slowly towards them with a woman beside him. "Is that Mademoiselle?" whispered Lucy, and all the colour drained out of her face.

"My God no!" ejaculated Lord Taaffe as though the mere suggestion were an outrage. "That is the Duchesse de Châtillon."

He spoke her name with tenderness, as all men did, and Lucy remembered it from Herman Vingboon's gossip, and her body turned cold. Charles and the Duchesse were drifting along so deep in talk that they were oblivious of the people near them. They might have been quite alone in some empty garden, or in some cool and lovely country of the mind. His hand was in the crook of her arm and though they moved so slowly they reminded Lucy instantly of herself and Charles, blown by the wind. They had moved so fast and these two drifted with slow grace, yet it was the same wind and the beauty of the Duchesse was very great. She was tall and fragile, older than Charles. They came so near that Lucy heard the whisper of her silks and saw the absorption of her delicate listening face. Charles was talking to her in easy fluent French. They drifted past, and Lucy did not know what one did with pain like this or shock like this. She longed only for night to come and to be alone.

Lord Taaffe, for all his brusqueness, was a sensitive man and hardly knowing what he was doing he put his large red hand over Lucy's that were clasped together in her lap. He was shocked to find them made of ice. Poor girl. He must turn her thoughts. Make her laugh. Say the first thing that came into his head.

"Look, lass," he said, "you see that gargoyle there? That is the Chancellor Sir Edward Hyde. The Queen Dowager hates him like hell, and he drives the King mad with his hectoring, yet Charles is fond of the old fellow and there is no doubt Hyde has a good headpiece on him."

Lucy responded as well as she was able and studied the Chancellor, a smile of tenderness coming slowly to her face because she knew he was one of the faithful ones. The effects of shock were passing now, she was in control of herself again and preternaturally observant. Stout and red-faced he was no beauty, yet she loved him.

"And that old scarecrow with a beard like Elijah, talking to him, is Dr. Cosin the King's chaplain," continued Lord Taaffe.

"I know," said Lucy softly. "I came here in Lord Wilmot's coach with him and Mr. John Evelyn." Lord Taaffe could scarcely refrain from slapping his thigh and roaring with laughter as he wondered what Dr. Cosin and Mr. Evelyn had found to say to the lovely Mrs. Barlow. Then he suddenly got to his feet, pulling Lucy with him, for there had been a stir at the end of the room, the stir that comes when a personality of some notoriety is making an entry. "It is! Yes, by cock it is!" he ejaculated. "The battle-axe herself. There she is. Stand on this stool, Lucy. Her entrances are not to be missed." He was laughing for he found La Grande Mademoiselle of France a comic figure.

"I can see her now," said Lucy soberly.

A splendid young woman had entered and the company in the salon fell back that her way might be clear to the chair where the Queen Dowager sat enthroned. Anne-Marie-Louise de Montpensier, the greatest heiress in Europe, was the daughter of the Duc d'Orléans, younger brother of Louis the Thirteenth. Tall, fair and blue-eyed, and holding herself magnificently, she came down the way prepared for her like a ship in full sail, giving at first sight a powerful impression of brilliance and beauty. But at second sight Mademoiselle was not quite so beautiful as her many flatterers told her she was, and as she herself most firmly believed. Her tall figure was too robust, her nose large, her blue eyes slightly protuberant. She wore too many sparkling jewels and her hair was arranged in too many brassy ringlets. Highly emotional, voluble as a cataract and heroically generous, everything about her was on a scale so large that a throne seemed the only suitable place for her, and she herself believed she was born to be a queen.

But whose queen? The King of Spain had been considered and the young Louis the Fourteenth was a possibility, even though he was many years her junior. At the moment his mother was trying to persuade her that the King of England was the only king for her. They were certainly a well matched couple, she considered, both so tall, he so dark and she so fair, and would look magnificent enthroned together. But would the throne materialize? No one knew yet and like everyone else she did not wish to commit herself until she was sure. And she was not sure of Charles himself either. His mother declared he was in love with her but it was difficult to make any real contact with him, he was so gauche and awkward. She herself could speak no English and he seemed incapable of learning French. Did he really love her? Out of the corner of her eye as she came in she had seen him talking to the Duchesse de Châtillon with great fluency. What language did they talk?

She was feeling troubled and uncertain as she made her way to the Queen and even, though no one would have guessed it, in need of encouragement. She found it in another pair of blue eyes meeting her own. They belonged to a girl in a golden dress, with a sweet and friendly face, who appeared almost stunned by admiration. Mademoiselle smiled at her condescendingly, lapped up the admiration and passed on.

Lucy was stunned indeed but not by admiration. What she felt was compassion for poor gaudy Mademoiselle walking along in her dream of glory. Had she ever looked with seeing eyes at the exquisite woman to whom Charles was still talking? You will never have the throne of England, my dear, she thought; indeed I do not think you will ever have any throne. You will be rejected and so shall I. I am nearer to you at this moment than to any other woman in the room. She stepped down from her stool saddened with her knowledge but in a moment she was laughing and joking with Lord Taaffe. Why should he be bored because she was downhearted?

But things mended and the day took a happier turn. She could even smile at the little comedy of Charles and Mademoiselle that she and Lord Taaffe now watched from the windowseat to which they had returned. The crowd was thinning as people went out into the garden and the machinations of the Queen Mother were clearly discernible. She despatched an emissary to Charles, outside on the terrace, and presently, though not at once, he returned to the salon alone, grimly humorous.

As he lumbered slowly up the room his expression changed, his lower lip dropped and his face took on a hangdog expression. But a vacant smile appeared as he approached Mademoiselle and he accelerated speed with every appearance of eagerness to be with her, only to stumble over a footstool and land at her feet. He was up in a moment, apologizing and kissing her hand. They stood together exchanging their courtesies, and the talk in the salon died down to a murmur and every pair of eyes turned towards them. They were as well matched as the king and queen in a pack of cards, but like the card king and queen there was a pasteboard rigidity about them, and when they started to walk down the room together Mademoiselle no longer moved like a ship in full sail. For how can a woman sail beside a man who jerks?

They circled the room and returning towards the Queen passed within earshot of Lucy and Lord Taaffe. Charles was stumbling over his French, his fingers clutching for the words he wanted as though they were elusive moths hovering in the air. Pursuing the word *ravissante* with desperation, as though he must catch it before it escaped out of the window, he beheld that same window filled with a most comforting glow; a man's red head and a girl's golden dress. The notion that His Majesty's fine eyes had a hardly discernible squint had occasionally occurred to his loyal subjects. It was more than discernible now. One eye implored Lord Taaffe's aid, while the other told Lucy she was the only girl in the world. He paused. "My Lord

Taaffe," he said severely, "my mother has been complaining that you have not yet paid your respects to her. I beg you will follow me now and repair the omission." And he passed on with Mademoiselle.

Lord Taaffe bowed and followed slowly and Lucy, having risen from her curtsey, stayed standing where she was in case Charles should want her. She waited for some while quite still, her head held as though she listened to music that she alone was hearing, her eyes bright with the vision of what she alone could see. It struck Charles, when he came to find her, that he had never seen her look bored and that full of vitality as she was she never minded waiting. After the waves of Mademoiselle's ebullience her quietness was like that of a pool lying still among the rocks beside the sea, and her eyes when she looked at him brought back a memory of a blue sky he had seen with her in Pembrokeshire.

"Waiting near a crowd of people what do you hear and see?" he asked her in a low voice.

Her answer surprised him. "I try to hear the echo of a song they have brought from far and sing within themselves all the while they chatter nonsense, and to catch on their faces a glimpse of what they will be at their journey's end. Sometimes on first waking I have found myself with a singing rising up all round me but before I have understood the words the thread has broken and it has vanished. And that glimpse, it comes like light on a face and then is gone, but if you have once seen it I do not think you could ever dislike the face it visited; not even if that face afterwards became evil. I think that evil is not immortal but that the light is."

As she spoke he remembered when he had seen that blue sky. It had arched over the Valley of Roses when they had run to each other in the innocent beginning of their love. They must get out of this hot room thick with chattering voices and stale perfumes. Not caring whether they were seen or not, his hand gripping her arm, he took her quickly to where a door opened on to the terrace, ran with her down the steps and down the sloping lawn beyond to where he knew there was a pool and a tiny fountain hidden among ilex trees.

The Queen and Mademoiselle saw them go and Mademoiselle's painted face was suddenly dignified by a passing shadow of wistfulness. The Queen, surprised by it, wondered if she could warm up Mademoiselle's cold caution about that problematical throne with a little flame of jealousy.

"My son is in love with that pretty girl," she said.

"As well as with the Duchesse?" asked Mademoiselle acidly.

The Queen sighed. She perceived more and more that her eldest son was not taking after his sainted father in anything except obstinacy. Her husband had had the Scottish loyalty in matters of the heart but Charles had the Spanish passion. But it was waste of time trying to explain one's children to oneself. They were as they were and must be endured. She sighed again and found Lord Taaffe bowing and paying his respects to her for the second time that day. Was the man mad?

Charles and Lucy came under the shade of the trees and it was quiet, and the grass that on the lawns above had been parched by summer heat was here fresh and green because in the centre of the coolness there was a small pool in a marble basin, and the jet of a tiny fountain sprayed from the hand of a satyr no larger than a thrush.

There was a seat by the fountain and a little girl was sitting on it. She wore a white dress with a blue sash and her hair, so pale in colour as to be almost silver, was tied up with a blue ribbon. She was delicate and small and she sat very still watching the falling water. The ceiling of dark leaves gave shade but it allowed sunbeams to come through here and there, touching the little girl's hair, scattering coins of gold like flowers on the grass. Lucy's heart contracted with sudden happy pain. She had felt the thorns of cruelty in the palace she had just left but here, as in the Queen of Bohemia's high-ceilinged room, love was waiting for her.

"It is Minette!" Charles whispered to Lucy. And he called her softly with a music in his voice that Lucy had never heard before, not even when he spoke to Jackie. "Minette! Minette!" So doves coo, she thought, when the sun is warm and their hearts are at peace.

The little girl looked round and saw them and for a moment or two her joy seemed to fill the dell. Then she jumped up and darted over the grass, quick as a dragonfly, and Charles caught her and carried her back to the seat and sat down with her on his knee, so absorbed in her that Lucy was left standing by the fountain. But delighting in the two she watched she was not conscious of forsakenness. Minette had laid her hand against her brother's cheek and he was untying her hair-ribbon and tumbling her silvery curls with his large hand. Intuitively Lucy knew that Charles loved his little sister with the best that was in him and in her gladness she was not jealous, not for herself and not even for Jackie, for this was a love that would never become tainted for him; not even by that satyr.

She loathed the little creature. What was he doing in this cool fresh place? He reminded her of her broken promise to Charles, and he threatened the little princess with some evil fate. Yet it was he who held up the delicate spray of water. She abandoned the puzzle and turned her eyes to Charles. Had he the strength to defend her and Minette?

"Have you run away again, you mischief?" he was asking his sister. "Poor old Morton!"

"Morton is with Mam," she told him in a small piping voice. "I ran from Marie. She is fat and cannot catch me. I knew if I hid here she would not find me."

"Why should she not find you?" he asked her.

"She does not like dark trees and she does not like the fountain man. He frightens her."

"He frightens me too," said Lucy.

Charles looked up and saw her standing on the other side of the fountain, her golden dress shining through the misty spray. "A leaden toy no more than a foot high," he mocked her. "Forget it. Come here and make my sister's acquaintance all over again. You loved her in her cradle and set her gold balls swinging. Do you remember?"

"I remember," said Lucy, and she rustled round the fountain and sat down beside him and smiled at Minette. To her surprise and delight two arms were flung instantly round her neck and Minette's butterfly kiss alighted on her cheek. Then the child was in her lap and they were hugging each other and laughing. Minette loved her. She loved Minette. The fountain man was forgotten in the joy of it.

5

Lord Wilmot's coach that had brought Lucy, Dr. Cosin and Mr. Evelyn to Saint-Germain took them back to Paris again but Lord Wilmot was not with them, for after the heat and irritations of his mother's levee Charles had wanted to go riding in the woods and had commanded his closest friends to go with him, and so the two elderly gentlemen found themselves alone with Lucy.

Mr. Evelyn sighed. He had not an eye for a pretty woman; that is to say he could recognize the mere face of female beauty there before him but it brought no kindling to his eyes and no lift to his spirit. His intellect was too highly developed. He would have enjoyed the use of the latter in conversation with Dr. Cosin but this could hardly take place in the presence of the King's mistress. He considered the problem for a moment, found it too much for him, closed his eyes and slept so deeply that Dr. Cosin and Lucy found themselves virtually alone facing each other across the coach. He took her folded marriage certificate from his pocket and gave it back to her.

"Lucy," he said, "your grandmother told me long ago that you were a happy-go-lucky little girl. It seems that you are still careless with your property. You must not keep your most precious possession so loosely tucked in your gown that it falls out. I agree with you that you must keep it with you, lest it be stolen, but in some safer way than the one you are employing now."

"I will make a bag for it and hang it round my neck," said Lucy. Then for the first time she dared to look at him. His former aloofness had gone and he smiled with such kindness that her shame was comforted; so much so that she could even speak of it. "When I gave you that paper to read I broke a promise to my husband. I almost think I broke my heart too."

"Your action was not premeditated. Sin lies in the intention, Lucy, and the intention in your heart towards your husband is love. I shall of course respect your confidence. Your secret is safe with me and I am glad I know it. I have daughters of my own and I shall now count you as one of them."

At this she cried a little and he waited patiently while she found her handkerchief.

"How this marriage came about you will perhaps tell me one day," he went on. "Now there is no time. But there is one thing I should like to speak of before Mr. Evelyn awakes. Your loyalty to the King demands that you should act a part, and that in your case puts you in some danger. To a certain extent we are all actors, and we must be. We must wear the mask of courage however afraid we are and we must perform the actions of love however loveless we feel, but here we are in a hopeful case for it may be that the mask will bite deep, the actions shape and probe like the hands of a sculptor on clay, and we shall actually become braver and more loving. But you with the help of God must not and will not allow your mask to bite deep. You understand me?"

"Yes," said Lucy. "I have already felt afraid of the corroding."

"Continue in your fear, but continue even more in your trust in God and your practice of the Protestant faith of the Church of England. Why have I never seen you in the Embassy chapel?"

The last question shot out with such fierceness that Lucy jumped, and looking at him she saw his eyes blazing with the fierce passion of the prophet Elijah confronting the priests of Baal. She remembered how he had said, "The Church of England is my firstborn." He had spoken gently then but now the words resounded in her memory as though the roll of drums was behind them. Here was a man upon the warpath and she thought she understood the nature of his thoughts.

Here they were, a little band of exiles set down in this wicked city of Paris, a stronghold of Rome, its ruler a corrupt and worldly Cardinal, and their only defender under God was himself. But let the enemy look to his defences for he had looked to his. From the King down to the smallest scullion running around the Embassy kitchen, not a single Protestant soul of them should be plucked from his hand while the breath of life was in him. He drew in a draught of that same breath and exhaled it like a warhorse, demanding of Lucy on the outflowing draught, "Why have you not answered my question?"

Lucy was seldom flustered but she was now. "It was because I was afraid," she murmured.

"Of what?"

"All the good religious people looking at me, nudging each other and whispering about me. 'That little hypocrite kneeling with her eyes downcast as though she were a nun, she is the King's mistress.' "

"Those who whisper or nudge during divine service are neither good nor religious," thundered Dr. Cosin. "And those who dare call others hypocrites are invariably hypocrites themselves. Can you not face such littleness with the courage of your own integrity? I am ashamed of you, Lucy."

"I will ask Lord Wilmot to bring me next Sunday," said Lucy humbly, her cheeks scarlet. "My husband said that he might do so."

Dr. Cosin's rage fell from him and he said gently, endeavouring to rivet her armour piece by piece, "There is another service that you may care to attend, Lucy. After the death of the late King I compiled a service of intercession to be held every Tuesday, that being the day of His Majesty's murder, both in Paris and at The Hague. As this service contains intercession for your husband you may be glad to attend it, both here and at The Hague. It is attended only by the few and may be less of an ordeal for you than the other. Though you must attend the other," he added sternly.

"I will come always to the Tuesday service," Lucy said humbly. "Is it held at the Embassy chapel?"

"At The Hague it is. Here it is held in the little chapel at the Louvre. You know perhaps that his late Majesty appointed me as chaplain to the Protestant members of the royal household. I have been given three rooms at the Louvre close to Her

Majesty's own quarters, to serve as bedroom, study, and a chapel for the recitation of the daily offices." He smiled grimly. "The arrangement is a matter of chagrin to her Catholic majesty but as it was her husband's wish and command she has acquiesced in the arrangement. I hope, Lucy, that you say your prayers at home?"

"I have by heart some prayers of yours that my grandmother taught me, and Dr. Jeremy Taylor whom I met at my cousins' home of Golden Grove taught me a prayer."

"Dr. Taylor is a good man and writes well but you should approach the Almighty in your own words as well as his and mine."

"My own words have no lustre," said Lucy. "The prayers of great and good men are shaped and polished with their skill and use."

"Nevertheless the Almighty would prefer yours. He can provide the lustre. His touch as he receives our poor offerings is that of the alchemist."

Mr. Evelyn woke up abruptly as the coach jolted over a stone. Lucy was so grateful to him for his long sleep that presently, childishly, she rubbed her eyes and feigned sleep herself. But a few moments later, as a totally incomprehensible conversation washed over her head, the soothing noise of it carried her away into a dream of the stream running through the Valley of Roses.

Eight

I

Charles's companions found him delightful company in the woods. He was always happy out of doors, on horseback or at sea, happy with his dogs, with children or with his friends, and when he was happy his gaiety and charm were entrancing. He was a good raconteur and men were glad to sit up all night listening to his stories. All his friends loved him and Lord Taaffe left his own devotion on record in a letter he wrote. "May I never drink wine if I had not rather live at six sous a day with him than have all the pleasures of this world without him." And Lord Taaffe liked his drink.

Yet when they had returned from the woods, and had had supper and settled down for a jovial evening, the King's mood changed. He grew silent and melancholy and said he would go to bed. Moodiness was not in his nature but since his father's death these fits of sadness would come upon him suddenly and he would want one thing or another thing and not know what he wanted because the one thing he did want, to put the clock back and be to his father the son he would have been had he known what was going to happen, was denied him.

"Time!" he muttered as he led the way upstairs to his bed-room, accompanied by Robert Sidney, Lord Wilmot, Edward Prodgers and Lord Taaffe. "Time is the devil's work. The devil shrouds the future in his own darkness. If men could see what is to come there would be no sin in the world."

Lord Wilmot and Prodgers loyally agreed with His Majesty but Robert murmured something to the effect that men were men, and even if they could see the road ahead would still run off it since to run crooked is of the nature of men. Lord Taaffe said nothing. He was bringing up the rear with a bottle of wine, it being his opinion that whatever a man knew or did not know he could still drink.

In his bedchamber, as his patient friends had expected, Charles no longer wanted to go to bed. He went to the window and stood looking out over the garden. The four, who could not sit down unless he did, eased themselves into the perpendicular position most comfortable to them and endeavoured to admire the view with him. In the vault of the sky stars were thick in a pall of black velvet, and there were fireflies in the garden. The scene had great beauty but it was not a familiar loveliness and the smell of the night was somehow alien. When would they go home? Already their clothes were getting shabby and their pockets empty.

"They no longer dance at Whitehall," Charles said. "On our dancing nights people would row up the river to listen to the music. What is London like now? Shrunken and waspish like a woman whose beauty has deserted her?"

"No, Your Majesty," said Lord Wilmot. "While your throne remains empty she is a widow woman with a veiled face but under the veil she is eternally young."

"Garlanded with her wild flowers," said Robert. "They will still be growing in all the odd corners and crannies."

But the King remained melancholic and standing. There seemed something more wrong with him tonight than one of his usual fits of sorrow. Prodgers, who had an old wound that hurt when he stood, plumped up the cushions in the royal chair with a meaningful sound but the King remained standing. Lord Taaffe poured the wine and clinked the glasses.

"I did not tell you to pour the wine," said Charles coldly.

"Sire, you do not need to put yourself to the trouble," said Lord Taaffe. "Have you ever found me backward in this service to Your Majesty?"

Charles laughed, turned round and flung himself into his chair, holding out his hand for his glass. For a moment it seemed that his black mood had lifted, then it was back again. "I cannot go to Ireland," he burst out suddenly. "Hyde told me so today. Ormonde has had a bad defeat and will not have me now. I am King yet I am as bound hand and foot by the prohibitions of politicians and commanders as though I were a babe in arms. If I cannot go to Ireland then where the devil can I go? I cannot stay idling here."

They tried to console him. Lord Taaffe said that he would go to Ireland all in good time. Once they had had their fill of murdering each other in the old country it would be safe as houses. Just let them have their fill. Charles swore that he did not want safety. Robert Sidney clinched the matter by saying grimly, "Sir, having just lost one king it would not be for the good of our cause that we should so soon lose another. Your Majesty's advisers have a case."

There was a long silence. Then Charles said like a child, "Ireland would have been that much nearer England."

"Your Majesty has not touched your wine," Lord Taaffe pointed out.

Charles pulled himself together. He felt as miserable as before but he would not provoke them any longer. He waved them to their seats and groped back over the stilted conversation to something that should start the talk flowing easily again. "London's wild flowers," he said. "Now that is something I know nothing about since I have never visited the crannies where they grow. How little I know of my own capital city; only the great houses and the churches, the river and the cheering crowds in the streets. Tell me about the corners and crannies that I have never seen."

This was still a hobby-horse with Robert Sidney and he was away on it in a moment, telling Charles of small deserted gardens where the roses had grown to the tops of the trees, of hidden courts with fountains in them, of broken steps in dark corners that led to locked doors, and music that could not be reached sounding within. And he told of the strange characters he had found in such places, saints and sinners and fantastics of all kinds, people who brought a new dimension to life and gave back to tired minds the lost sense of mystery. Finally he spoke of the one he had loved the best.

"Not far from Your Majesty's Palace of Whitehall I once met Socrates. In a hidden corner of Covent Garden, close to the portico of the church, I found him selling herbs under a dark tree. There within sounds of the bells of Westminster time turned back on itself and I watched Apollo's swans flying into the sunset."

He paused and drained his glass and Lord Taaffe refilled it. Not long before his lordship had left the room and fetched more wine, for since the royal house of France was still paying for their drinks there was no need as yet to stint themselves. But for the generosity of the Bourbons what happened next might never have happened at all, for Robert's habitual caution would not have deserted him.

"How did you find the place?" asked Charles and Robert replied, "A child took me there. A little girl by the name of Lucy Walter."

Charles had been politely attentive before but now his interest was captured, for throughout this black evening he had kept somewhere at the back of his mind the picture of his golden girl standing by the fountain in the garden. That hidden fountain under the dark trees was just such a place as Robert had been describing, a place where time turns back upon itself. Nothing would satisfy him now but to hear the whole story of Old Sage as told to Robert by Father Ignatius. "Lucy never told me of this old man," he said when the story was finished. "She has forgotten him now, perhaps."

"She has not forgotten," said Robert. "We talked of him together not long ago, riding from Breda to The Hague, and I told her the story I have just told you. It interested her because at her home at Roch their old parson, also a figure of fantasy, had told her of a dumb friend of his youth and his description reminded her of Old Sage."

"In what way was this old Welsh parson a figure of fantasy?" asked Edward Prodgers. He had drunk very little for he was a man of great caution and his keen analytical mind was always entirely under his control. He was a strange man, possessing unusual powers of intuition and discernment.

"He arrived at Roch Castle in the true fairytale manner, found in the snow by Mrs. Barlow's father," explained Robert. "He was a victim of a shipwreck, apparently, but too bewildered to give a coherent account of himself."

Lord Wilmot and Lord Taaffe, bored with this childish and

to them meaningless conversation, now found themselves
stifling the yawns which were not permissible in the royal presence. Mr. Prodgers also pressed two fingertips to his lips
before asking with sleepy politeness, "At what date was this
arrival?"

Sleepiness is catching and Robert had to pause a moment
before he replied, "Mrs. Barlow was a child at the time."

"Did the poor gentleman recover his wits?" murmured Mr.
Prodgers. "I gather that he did, since he subsequently became
the parson of Roch."

"Gentlemen, you are half asleep and talking nonsense,"
Charles interrupted. "I am going to bed."

He got up yawning, but Mr. Prodgers had not missed the
little snap of haste with which he had ended the conversation
and when later he reached his own bedchamber he was in no
hurry to go to bed. The story that had caused him to wonder
whether the young Catholic Irishman who had only fancied
himself a priest had become the Protestant vicar of Roch had
sounded entirely fantastic in the telling, but Mr. Prodgers was
well aware that truth is invariably more extraordinary than
anything a man's imagination can conceive, since a man's
mind is limited and truth is not.

He knew this and knew too how man, galled by his sense of
inferiority, likes to twist truth if he can. He had already received his orders from Lord Jermyn and the Chancellor; he
was to slip away to Pembrokeshire and if the facts he found
there proved stubborn he was to do a little of this same twisting. Obviously now his first contact must be the parson of
Roch. If the shock of the shipwreck had slightly disordered his
wits it was possible that he had now recovered them; such
things happened in old age. Slipping away was something he
often did and his disappearance would not surprise Charles
who knew perfectly well that many of the men about him
were spies; some for his cause and some against it. Mr. Prodgers would always be for the King, whom he loved, but he
had no sense of disloyalty in his present assignment. A mor-
ganatic marriage would not benefit Charles. And he did not
like Lucy. At first he had admired her grace and liveliness but

when he had attempted to express his admiration she had
turned into a little mountain wild-cat and he was smarting
still.

2

On the Sunday following the visit to Saint-Germain Lucy
bravely attended the service at the Embassy. Lord Wilmot
bestowed her between himself and Robert Sidney with Lord
Taaffe sitting behind her, so that if there should be any
breathings of gossip they should not go directly down the back
of her neck. She was scared at first but her courage returned
with the sense of stalwart protection about her, and the
glimpse she had now and then of Charles in his chair of state
some way in front of her, with the Chancellor and Ambassador on each side of him. When he sat she could only see
the top of his dark head above the carving of the highbacked
chair, but when he stood he was so tall that he was visible to
the whole room. There was no stiffness in his dignity for his
grace always gave life to his performance of his duties. Her
heart beat high with pride and she told herself that her husband had power. He could be a great king. But if worse misfortune came what would it do to the incipient greatness?
Foster or destroy it?

The question was in her mind when Dr. Cosin stood up to
preach his sermon, and she realized that he already was what
her husband had it in him to become. The hammering out of a
man's worth is never over, he is caught between hammer and
anvil until his perfection is achieved, or perhaps until of deliberate choice, in one world or another, he chooses extinction
rather than the love of God; but perhaps there can come the
time, thought Lucy, when he has advanced so much towards
selflessness that he can almost be said to be safe; not entirely so
while one drop of self remains in him and he retains his free
will to indulge it, but almost. "You are nearly safe," her spirit
said to the spirit of the old man in front of her, "and so to us
who are in dreadful danger give your strength."

Dr. Cosin was very well aware of their danger and he

preached upon the subject of endurance. Most of his little
congregation, the King included, had already suffered much
but they had been continually on the move, in battle or on the
march, defending their houses or fleeing from them. Now
they faced the test of exile, with nothing to do, hope deferred,
poverty increasing, humiliation mounting. For this he endeavoured to prepare them, choosing his words with care, for sometimes a chance phrase, if it is well made to hold the truth, will
sink to the deeps of a mind and find lodging there, floating to
the surface again in time of need on the buoyancy of its own
shapeliness.

"It has been the lot of many a saint before us," he cried out,
"and of far more worth and dignity than any we are, to be in
adversity, to be persecuted, afflicted, tormented, to be robbed
of goods, and lands and lives and all. Let not this make us
stumble either in our religion or our loyalty, and that we may
be firm in our trials and constant to our profession."

Lucy was one of the very few who heard every word of the
sermon. Lord Taaffe heard a sentence here and there, and
might have heard more but for the distraction of Lucy's power
of concentration, which destroyed his. Very few pretty girls
can forget their prettiness and even fewer can sit still, he told
himself. Lucy could do both. Never once did her hand go to
her hair or her eyes round the room comparing her beauty to
that of other women, never once did she fidget or sigh. Only
the King could match her for stillness, and he found himself
looking from one to the other as though they were the only
two in the room. The King had already claimed his loyalty
and love and Lucy was fast claiming his admiration.

Sitting just behind her he marvelled at the fine texture of
her skin and its colour, the colour of the darker petals on the
honeysuckle. His eyes went to the well-shaped dark head held
proudly on a long neck. She was not an arrogant girl yet she
had her proper pride. She turned her head a little and he sat
enchanted by her profile, a short straight nose, sweet lips and
obstinate chin. Lord Taaffe got on well enough with the wife
in Ireland to whom he had been married but he was not a man
who doted on women, whom he considered on the whole to be

515

more productive of trouble than pleasure, and the flood of emotion that suddenly swept over him was sufficiently unfamiliar to shock him profoundly.

"Damnation!" he ejaculated under his breath. "Fall in love with the King's girl? My God no!" Dismay took the place of delight and he dragged his eyes from the tendrils of dark hair that lay in the nape of Lucy's neck and fixed them on the chair of state in front of him, and the little he could see of his sovereign's head above it. His love and loyalty were engaged there, with the King, not here with this nuisance of a girl. "You damn fool," he told himself.

He did not again look at Lucy and when the service ended he left abruptly, for he must come to terms with this at once. Women! Why had he been such an ass as to leap to Lucy's defence that day at Saint-Germain? It was always coming to a woman's aid that was the undoing of a man. Had he not learnt that by this time? He strode from the Embassy out into the street vowing to keep out of the way of the King's girl from now on.

3

The knowledge that Anne had suffered never left Lucy's mind and she saw her maid glorified by the light of her own compassion. Her fear of Anne had almost vanished; she felt it only occasionally and then as a momentary stab of warning, soon forgotten. She loved Anne now and sweetly tried to win her love in return, and Anne, despite herself, so softened towards her mistress that sometimes they laughed and talked together as though they had always known each other. And then Lucy would realize how little she understood Anne, and Anne would refuse to try and understand herself, and there would be a troubled constraint between them; troubled upon Lucy's side because the longed-for love seemed to be receding again, troubled upon Anne's because she did not wish to be troubled.

Anne Hill had long ago forged her own image of herself as the heroine of her own misfortune. Life had from the beginning been embattled against her and she was embattled against life. She was without fear and her weapon was a quiet, cold anger. She never lost her temper or raised her voice. She never cringed to anyone or asked for mercy for she did not want mercy only to be revenged on life.

Her first memories were of her mother's sufferings rather than her own and they had bitten deep because she had loved her mother; and she was capable of love as deep as her anger.

Her mother had been a native of Rotterdam, a fragile girl who had fallen easily to the tempestuous wooing of Angus Hill, a handsome Scottish émigré who had been driven overseas by the restless discontent of an ambitious, passionate man who could never bring his circumstances into line with his demands upon them. A fine weaver, rooted in the Presbyterian faith of the Covenant, he had had integrity both in work and faith but no power of looking at either from any standpoint but his own. If a man did not work as he did or believe as he did that man was damned. If a woman could not measure up to the demands of his passion, or find herself in complete agreement with him upon every point, or run her Dutch household in the Scottish manner of his mother, then she had failed him.

Vrouw Hill, though physically fragile, had been a woman of strong character and extremely obstinate. She had chosen to break rather than bend. And Angus had chosen to break her rather than let her go to hell in her own way. And the same with Anne. Secretly he had adored his little daughter and if she had obeyed him and shown him affection his love for her might have been their salvation, but from the beginning she had been heart and soul with her mother. Even so he had continued to love her and to be convinced that she too he must break in order that he might save her soul.

The culmination of their three-fold tragedy had come when Anne was eight years old. They had been poor for a long time for Angus, unpopular both with employers and fellow weavers, had not been able to keep in steady employment, and there had been the further complication of the terrible headaches from which he had suffered. Since he had possessed great courage in the bearing of pain the extent of his suffering had not been perceived by a wife who no longer loved him and a child who had been antagonistic from the beginning. In his religion he had always been fanatical and as his illness increased he had become increasingly unbalanced. Convinced that Anne was already in the grip of the devil, and would be lost if he could not rouse her to a knowledge of her danger, he had preached to her ceaselessly upon the subject of damnation and hell fire; but to her it had seemed that there could be no hell worse than his religion and no devil worse than her father, and she had fought against them both with all her power. She had struggled alone, for her delicate mother had succumbed to the tuberculosis that was the scourge of the Low Countries and had become too ill to leave her bed.

The crisis had come one winter evening when her father's warnings had goaded Anne past endurance. "I would like to be in hell," she had shouted at him. "I am not afraid of hell fire."

Her father had been poking the fire and had left the poker in it while he strove with her, and the horror of what she said had made the pain flame up in his head so appallingly that he had not known what he was doing; he had only known that he must save this adored child. At whatever cost he must make her understand. "And so you are not afraid of hell fire?" he had asked quietly. "I must make you know what it feels like." And he had taken the poker from the fire and laid it against her left cheek.

What happened afterwards lived now in Anne's memory in nightmare confusion. She remembered the pain, and hearing a child screaming and not knowing it was herself, and seeing her mother standing in her nightgown in the doorway, wild-eyed and screaming too. And then the crash as her father collapsed and fell, and then the neighbours rushing in.

Angus had been unconscious all night and in the morning he had died and the apothecary who had been called did not tell Anne and her mother, because he did not know himself, that Angus had died of a tumour on the brain. And in any case he had been more concerned with the injured child and her frantic mother than the monster who had so ill-used them.

And so they never knew that Angus had lived out his whole life under a shadow and in his darkness had done the best that he knew. Neighbours had been good to them and as soon as she was old enough Anne had worked as a child weaver to earn money for her mother. She had loved her mother with extraordinary passion and Vrouw Hill, supported by that love, had managed to stay alive longer than her apothecary had believed possible. Then she had died and Anne's heart had turned to stone.

With her home gone she had turned from weaving to the work of maidservant in rich houses and her exquisite sewing, her neatness and discretion, made her invaluable and she earned good wages. She never fell in love since in regard to men her desire was for vengeance, not love, but at the same time it was a source of bitterness to her that though her mysteriousness attracted them her disfigurement repelled. She could tease and torment them only up to a point and then they escaped, leaving her with a pride so wounded that she loathed beautiful girls.

And so she came to Lucy and wished her harm. And yet she was also attracted by her. For the first time since her mother's death she was aware of the warmth of love, of compassion and consideration, and was constantly reminded of her mother. Yet she could not yield to Lucy's love since her jealousy of this girl who had everything, even a child and the love of a king, was eating her up. In the love-hate that she felt for her there was great danger for them both.

4

Anne would not go with Lucy to the Embassy Sunday services since she was without religious faith. For hell one needed to look no further than this world, she told Lucy, and if a creator of it existed she hated him. But she did consent to go one day to the chapel at the Louvre, for she had a lively curiosity and was fascinated by Paris. Until she became Lucy's maid she had never left Rotterdam but on the voyage from Brill she had discovered that she was adventurous, and now she found that seeing a new country and a new city was giving her the only real pleasure she had ever known. She made up her mind to stay with Lucy, whose life showed every likelihood of being a wandering one. "I would like to see the Palace of the Louvre," she said. "I hate these kings and queens and noblemen and cardinals, and their wealth that is an insult to poor and suffering people, but I like to see where they live."

Lucy smiled. "You need not hate my king," she said. "He is poor as a church mouse."

"I do not hate him," said Anne. "And I would like to come with you today. You are going to the Louvre to give thanks, are you not? I will come with you."

Lucy gave her a glance of delighted surprise and impulsively held out her hand and Anne took it. Yesterday they had heard that Charles had escaped assassination. Edward Prodgers, who had come to say goodbye to Anne before starting upon some journey, had told her of it and she had told Lucy while she was dressing her hair, making the most of it with intent to hurt. But the intensity of Lucy's reaction of shock and terror had taken her by surprise and before she had known what she was doing she had put her arms round the shaking girl, and later had fetched her a glass of wine to restore her. And she had been nearly as shaken as Lucy, not because of the threat to Charles but because this was the first time since her mother's death that she had put her arms round another human being.

They were silent as they drove through the hot streets, each looking out of the window beside her. Anne watched the pageant of Paris with cool interest. She had no real compassion for the poor and suffering of whom she had spoken to Lucy but she regarded them as potential allies. She was of the stuff of which agitators are made. Any attack upon privilege would have her adherence, for all such attacks had about them the sweetness of revenge. Lucy watched the people today not with her usual compassion but with fear, since every depraved or hungry person seemed a threat to Charles. These were the men with the sharp knives who hated kings and princes. Charles had escaped this time but she remembered his grandfather Henry of Navarre, his coach halted for a moment in the traffic, turning to get a better light on the letter he was reading and receiving in his breast the knife of a man who had just leaped upon the wheel of the coach. She was trembling by the time they reached the Louvre.

"Were you afraid on the drive?" asked Anne in surprise.

"Not for myself," Lucy replied.

Anne clicked her tongue solicitously. "You have your faith to support you, madam," she said. "Otherwise you would not come here to pray."

Lucy's happy spirit was in the shadow that day. "We pray for the safety of those we love," she said, "we pour out our heart and soul for them. But still they suffer and die."

"That, madam," said Anne icily, "is why I now no longer pray."

Lucy knew in her heart that Anne was wrong, and herself too in her momentary despair, yet she knew of no arguments to bring against that horse sense that on the face of it is always right; only the old argument that the face of things is seldom the true face, and the point of view of Old Sage when he had shown her at Rotterdam that the failures of true love are blessed of God.

"Look, Anne," she said, "we are here. This is the Palace of the Louvre where the Queen Dowager was born and where she has a suite of rooms. Is it not grand?"

Anne regarded the magnificence with cold curiosity, her eyes narrowed, yet when she turned round to Lucy the lids were raised and her eyes blazed with such passion that Lucy, alarmed, wondered that fire did not descend from heaven to burn the splendour to a cinder. They drove round to the back of the palace and through a humble courtyard reached a humble door, for it was through a rabbit warren of domestic offices that the Protestant chaplain and the Protestant faith were reached. They were admitted and Lucy, who knew her way now, led Anne down a long passage and up a twisting stair, and then down another passage.

She pushed a half-open door and they were in a small chapel, where the congregation was already kneeling. They made their way to the back of the chapel and knelt too, members of a small gathering of the older and sadder among the Paris émigrés, for the young and gay considered the Sunday service at the Embassy sufficient duty and did not wish to burden their spirits further with the ancient shadows and smells that hung about the back regions of the Louvre. But Lucy today, enveloped in her own shadow, felt at home in this small room and was almost at once aware of peace somewhere beyond her darkness, as the sun is beyond a thick mist, and was able to greet the invisible light as she murmured the prayer that Jeremy Taylor had taught her. "Keep us O Lord for we are thine by creation; guide us for we are thine by purchase." She never now used the first person singular when she prayed for she was no longer herself alone, she was Charles and Jackie too. And Anne. For the first time she found she was Anne too. "Let thy mercy pardon our sins and thy care watch over us."

Dr. Cosin entered in his black gown. Lucy looked up for a moment and saw his tall figure outlined against the light that came through the window behind the simple table with its cross and candles. Even on a fine day the light was dim in the stonewalled room and the distant murmur of the world faint as the sound of a distant sea heard within a cave. Then his deep voice lifted above the murmur as though a wave had surged into the cave and she was carried away into absorbed prayer for her husband.

She knew some of the prayers by heart now for she had asked Dr. Cosin to write them out for her and he had done so. When he was old enough she would teach them to Jackie. The first they repeated as a litany.

"O Lord, guard the person of thy servant, Charles our King. Who putteth his trust in thee.
Send him, and all that are loyal to him, help from thy holy place.
And evermore mightily defend them.

Confound the designs of all that rise up or conspire against
him.
And let no wicked hand come near to hurt.
O Lord hear our prayer. And let our cry come unto
thee."

The next prayer was usually her favourite because when they
came to the angels it was in Jackie's voice, that she had not
heard yet, that she seemed to hear the words spoken and with
Jackie's eyes that she saw the silver tents like upturned lilies.

"Almighty Lord God, ruler of princes when they are on
their throne and protector when they are in peril; look
down mercifully from heaven, we most humbly beseech
thee, upon the many and great troubles of our gracious sovereign. Defend his person from all dangers, both by sea and
land. Bless his counsels. Prosper his enterprises. And command thy angels so to pitch their tents round about him,
that he may be preserved from the hands of all that seek his
hurt, and may be speedily established in the just right of his
throne, through Jesus Christ our Lord. Amen."

But today it was the third that seemed most relevant.

"Put the spirit of counsel, of courage, and of unity, upon
them that are loyal to him. And to those that either openly
oppose him, or those strange children that dissemble with
him, that thou wouldst infatuate their counsels and blast
their endeavours, turning their hearts close to thee their
God and to the King; which we beseech thee to grant for
Jesus Christ his sake, our Lord and only Saviour."

Infatuate their counsels and blast their endeavours. Had it
been because this small colony of sad and shabby people
prayed week by week in this place that Charles had not been
murdered? She did not know, she could not know, so inscru-
table is the will of the God who never answers questions, but
the mere possibility made her heart leap up like a bird.
She was happy driving home but Anne could not respond to

her mood, thankful though she was to be back in the streets again. What had induced her to let Lucy beguile her to that place? Though hell fire had not been mentioned by the spectral man who had groaned out the prayers it had seemed not far off, and the old terror had once more opened like a pit in her mind; the terror she had felt for so long before her father actually threw her into hell. No one knew what it was like to hang on the edge of a black pit waiting for something vile to happen. And then when it was over and you were expecting to be happy you found yourself left with memories too dreadful to admit happiness among them. You knew you would never, now, be happy.

She turned her head to reply to some remark of Lucy's and met the glance of the other girl's clear eyes, and saw her serene face. Behind that peaceful façade of beauty she must have a few bad memories, for who had not in this appalling world, but no memories of hell. She had a father who loved her and whom she adored. Anne knew that for she had seen Lucy standing before her father's picture and had seen the love in her face. And because of that father's love Lucy did not hate men. And so she had a lover and a son. The confused miseries in Anne's mind suddenly unified into hatred of Lucy. It was all she could do not to strike her face.

Sitting in front of her mirror at bedtime, with Anne brushing her hair, Lucy found herself talking of Jackie. "You have not seen my baby yet," she said. "When we get back to Rotterdam I will show him to you. You will love my baby, Anne." She raised her head to smile at her maid in the mirror and saw the reflection of Anne's face, white and set, and remorse seized her. How could she have spoken in that insensitive way? Anne had no baby. In a tempest of Welsh emotion she jumped up, put her arms round Anne and kissed her disfigured cheek.

To Anne this seemed an outrage of condescending pity. Who did they think they were, these painted dolls who had never known a moment of discomfort in all their pampered lives? Did they think that pity was all that was required of them by a suffering world? Pity never filled an empty stomach or staunched a wound. Yet though she did not respond she withdrew herself from Lucy's arms quite gently and as the routine of going to bed continued, and she was examining her mistress's dress for possible damage, she herself began to talk of Jackie. Was he like his father? Was his father devoted to him? Yes, Lucy said, the King adored his little son. "I am glad, madam," said Anne. "That you are the mother of his son gives you the pre-eminence."

Lucy was puzzled. "The pre-eminence?" she whispered.

"His Majesty is young and of an affectionate disposition, but you are the prettiest, madam, I am told. Lovelier than Lady Shannon or the Duchess. There is the girl in the Channel Islands, but maybe she is forgotten now. It's a long time since His Majesty was in Jersey and she did not follow him."

Though the room seemed full of mist Lucy knew she must keep control of herself. Charles would not like her to lose her dignity in front of her maid. She sat very erect on the edge of the bed. "How did you know this?" she asked gently.

"I overheard Betje and her husband talking. There is much gossip about your king, madam, even in the palace of Cardinal Mazarin. Of course any gossip I hear I keep to myself."

"That is right, Anne," said Lucy. "All royal persons are at the mercy of gossip and most of it untrue. I have all I need. Blow out the candles please. I enjoyed our outing together but I am tired and I shall sleep at once. Goodnight, Anne."

"Goodnight, madam," said Anne. She extinguished the candles and left the room. For some time she stood listening at the head of the stairs but she did not hear the creak of Lucy's bed. With her uncanny power of silent movement she drifted back along the passage, opened the door a few inches and looked in. There was enough light to show her Lucy still sitting on the side of her bed. She closed the door without sound and floated down the stairs to her own room. She lay awake for a little while, the memories that had tormented her buried now beneath the sweetness of revenge. Then she slept deeply and dreamlessly. Yet, unaccountably, when she awoke she was crying. She had not cried since her mother had died.

5

The days passed and Charles did not come and he sent no message. Lucy longed for him and yet she was glad to have a breathing space in which to face the two new facts of her existence; Charles was not a faithful lover and it had been cruel of Anne to tell her so. Anne was cruel. She spent two miserable days and then Betje, coming into her room when she knew Anne was out on an errand, asked her what the matter was? Lucy shook her head and was silent for she had pledged her faith to Charles with the gift of herself to him, to Anne with the gift of her kiss, and what was the pledge of faith but the promise never to hurt this human being if one could help it, either by word or deed, and above all not by the disclosure of their failings to another.

But Betje was so sure that she knew what the trouble was that she dared to put it into words. "That cat Anne Hill has told you of the gossip she overheard," she declared indignantly, her large hand gripping Lucy's shoulder. She shook the shoulder a little. "My dear, you should not take on so. You live too much in your Welsh fairy tales. Do you not yet know the world you live in? Gentlemen are gentlemen the world over, especially if they are royal gentlemen. That the King loves you there is no doubt, and you had better see to it that you do not put yourself in the way of losing his love with reproachful glances and moping ways. That is a sure way to lose a gentleman's regard, especially a royal gentleman who can pick and choose where he likes."

Her bracing common sense was salutary, and Lucy acknowledged its truth. She lived too much in fairy tales. Had she expected that those lovers in the Valley of Roses would never grow older, never become battered by the storms of the sea to which the silver stream ran down? I am not such a fool, she said to herself, and one must trim one's sails to the storms as they come. But the stream and the crowned swan are real as the sea and we shall find them again.

"My love, there is another thing," said Betje, breaking in on

526

her thoughts. "Anne was deliberately cruel to you and I think you should dismiss her from your service."

"I cannot do that," said Lucy.

"I think you should do it," persisted Betje.

But Lucy only shook her head. She had pledged her love to Anne as she had to Charles and she must forgive. One day they might both have much to forgive her. How could she tell? She had broken her promise to Charles. Life, truly lived, is not an exercise in safety and no one is secure in a storm at sea.

When a few days later Charles came to see her she had never loved him so much. Each of them was bound to fail the other again and again and because they were one must bear the burden of the other's failures as well as their own. Scape-goats: We all are, she thought in astonishment. Not only the great ones but all of us. And to be so is a great exercise of love.

They were sitting on the windowseat looking out over Paris and once more the sun was setting, not this time with banners of stormy light but vanishing beyond a veiling of pale colours that lay along the sky like the horizontal waves of a gently breaking sea. Charles was in a gentle and tender mood and Lucy was suddenly overwhelmed all over again by remorse at the thought of her broken promise, and it seemed to her a fearful thing that she was deceiving him and that he should not know what she had done. Why not tell him of it and begin the mutual burden-bearing now? He would not be angry. He would understand. And so, her hand in his, she told him.

The result was not what she had expected. For a moment he seemed unbelieving, and then he was on his feet, angry, hurt, absurdly upset by such a small fault. He had a fanatical fear of betrayal. He had trusted her and she had broken her promise. Too late she saw her mistake. There are circumstances in which confession can be a selfish thing. "I did not mean to tell Dr. Cosin," she pleaded with him. "Can you not forgive me?"

"I can trust no one," he burst out. "There are spies round me all the time. Even the men I call my friends may be plotting my life for all I know. I thought I could trust you but I can trust no one. Not even you."

She began to cry bitterly. It was said of Charles in later life that he could never bear to see a woman cry, and in a moment Lucy had him with his arms round her. But for the first time his arms felt slack about her. "Stop crying, dear heart," he said impatiently. "If you had to blab like that it is God's mercy it was only to Cosin. He is trustworthy. Now stop crying for I have much to tell you."

"You are not going away again?" asked Lucy.

"Yes, to Jersey with James."

Jersey, where the girl was who had not followed him but had remained on her island within sound of the sea. Was Jersey like Pembrokeshire? Did the flowers grow on the cliffs in the same way and the gulls cry? All she said to Charles was, "Not to Ireland?"

"No. Things are too bad there."

"But why must you go to Jersey?"

"Because I am no longer welcome in France," he said bitterly. "Mazarin has been watching the tide and now, with Cromwell settling well into the saddle in England, my cause lost in Ireland and Scotland divided, it has turned against me. I am a liability and he will pay me to leave France. I was asked to leave The Hague and now I am bribed to leave France. Jersey is still loyal."

There was despair in his voice. So much had happened in the past week of which she had known nothing. His failure of faith, and hers, seemed for the moment almost small things, and her tears and his anger equally small. She clung to him and whispered, "I will come to Jersey with you."

"It is far too dangerous. We are likely to be attacked at sea."

"I like danger."

"And what about Jackie? Is he to lose both parents? You must go back to Rotterdam and look after him. I have arranged it. I cannot spare Wilmot but there is a French lady whom he knows travelling overland to The Hague and she will look after you. It is a long journey but it is September now and beautiful weather. Cheer up, dear heart. I hope their ill humour will not last at The Hague and that they will have me back. Let us have a gay supper, and music to give us peaceful dreams, and then a happy goodbye in the morning."

He slept that night but Lucy lay awake and was too exhausted in the morning even to pretend to be happy. Also there was something she had to say, something unpleasant that had been better said last night, only she had lacked the courage. "Charles," she whispered as they stood together in the window in the autumn sunshine, "I have no money."

"No what?" asked Charles. He had heard her the first time but the state of his finances was such a skeleton in the cupboard that whenever the door opened a little, and the bony face looked out, he kicked the door shut again, and the kick had become a reflex habit.

"No money," repeated Lucy.

"Money is a detestable subject," groaned Charles. "Are we to discuss it during our last moments together? I loath the thought of money."

"So do I when I have not got it," said Lucy. "Charles, I have not yet paid Betje all I owe for my lodgings. I cannot leave without paying her. And Anne has not had her wages. And my aunt at Rotterdam. She and her husband have been good to me but I cannot impose on them for ever. Yet if I go to the farm I must pay for my keep. Charles, what am I to do? Could you not give me something out of the Cardinal's bribe? Jackie and I can live on very little but we must have something."

"There will be little left of that when I have paid my debts. I am over head and ears in debt."

"Shall I sell the diamonds you gave to Jackie and to me?"

"No!" thundered Charles. He pulled his purse out of his pocket and a ring off his finger and gave them to her. "There is little in the purse but the ring will fetch something. When that is spent apply to my family at The Hague."

It was so sordid, such a shadow on their love, that turning away from him and looking out over the city dreaming in

September light Lucy cried out, "I hate Paris! I hope I shall never see it again."

"You will," said Charles bitterly. "Paris is the city of sorrows and we shall both come back."

Nine

Lucy left Paris under the shadow of its sorrows, grieving over the lovelessness of her parting with Charles, and once more afraid of Anne. But her travelling companion was kindly, the fair land of France lay under the enchantment of autumn sunshine, and Anne, stimulated and delighted by travel, was again her smiling friend.

The memories of Paris became unreal, slipping away as dreams do when the sun rises, and then one night as she lay in bed praying for Charles she was conscious of a strange click, heard and yet not heard, as though a shutter had folded back, and saw a little picture of him standing at a window in moonlight, listening intently as though to the sound of the sea, and knew he was safely in his castle at Jersey and that he thought of her with love. The little flash of clairvoyance was the turning point of her journey. After that she journeyed into light because with every mile she was closer to Jackie, who was a part of Charles.

When they reached Holland the sun poured its light from a great sky upon the flat green land that was now almost as much home to Lucy as the mountains of Wales, yet when she saw the steep red roofs of Rotterdam she felt a sudden pang of longing for the grey rock of Roch Castle, discovering that through all our lives every homecoming brings a pang of longing for the spot of earth that is for us pre-eminently home.

But she had forgotten Roch by the time she reached the tall house by the canal; though she was hardly aware of it, nor of greeting her uncle and aunt, though she did so with charm and politeness. She was aware of nothing until she found herself with her son in her arms; in which room and in what circumstances she did not afterwards remember. He had come to her arms instantly, grown and changed though he was, and she a stranger to him. At first she could not see him at all, only feel his warmth and smell the fragrance of a clean and healthy baby. Then her sight cleared and she saw his rosiness and the depth of his eyes, and from their depth, as she had expected, her husband spoke to her.

2

Once again Lucy and Charles were together in the happy town of Breda. The States General that had desired the young King of England to leave Holland had suffered a slight softening of the heart, and it had been indicated to him that he might return for a while if he wished. In February he and James left Jersey and after a meeting with his mother he went to Ghent, where Lucy joined him, and from there they travelled together to Breda, where she was established in her old lodgings.

That first afternoon in the familiar sitting room they wrote to her aunt in Rotterdam, in whose care Anne and Jackie had been left, asking that Anne should bring the King's son to him as quickly as possible. Mr. Prodgers, whose quiet disappearance in Paris had now terminated in an equally quiet reappearance at The Hague, was already with them, having brought Charles his favourite embroidered coat to wear at Breda. When the letter was finished Charles summoned him from below with his silver bell and Lucy gave it to him. He was to ride with it to Rotterdam and Anne and Jackie would travel to Breda under his protection.

"We will come as fast as possible, madam," he said to Lucy, and his lean controlled face relaxed into a kindly smile as he took the letter. She returned the smile, for it seemed that he had forgiven the anger with which she had once repulsed him. She was glad for he was the King's faithful servant, and those who formed a chain of loyal protection about Charles must keep the links between them strong.

Prodgers bowed and left the room and Lucy and Charles sat for a while on the windowseat, looking out at happy Breda.

Charles was wearing his old coat that he had had before his father's death. It was a holiday garment and shabby though it was he liked to wear it when his mood was relaxed. It was dark green with scarlet and gold embroidery. Wearing it he looked like Prince Kilhwch in unwarlike mood, and Lucy smiled. "When Jackie comes we will hire a coach to match your coat and go driving with him every day."

Charles laughed, his mind leaping forward to the thought of Jackie. He was almost ashamed of the fact that a longing to see a scrap of a baby could almost overshadow the business that had brought him to Breda, business of which Lucy as yet knew nothing. Presently she would have to know but he did not look forward to telling her. She was not one of those wives who automatically think that whatever their husband does is right. It would have been pleasant to have an automatic wife but that was not the sort of wife he had. But if she had her failings as a wife she was a good mother.

"How soon shall we see that scrap?" he asked her when they were at supper, the candles lighted and the stars thick in the sky.

She laughed. "I do not know. In a few days' time we shall hear the coach wheels in the street. But Jackie is no longer a scrap. He is a big boy of eleven months. If he were not so lazy he would be walking by himself."

"He will walk by himself for me," said Charles.

Lucy doubted it. Jackie was a charming but wilful child and had as yet done no one's bidding. Supper finished Charles said he had a letter to write and Lucy cleared the table and trimmed the candles for him. Then she sat on the windowseat watching him and time rolled back upon itself for he was sitting at the same table where he had signed his carte blanche, offering his life for his father. He had been at his greatest then. What was he doing now? She felt anxious and was hard put to it to remain motionless and silent until the letter was finished. Then she asked, "To whom were you writing?"

"To the Marquis of Montrose."

"You are still his friend?"

"Of course. He is working for my cause in Scotland with all

his power. He is in the Orkney's now. When he reaches the mainland he says the whole country will rise to him for me."

Lucy came and stood behind him as she had done before, and looking down over his shoulder at the sanded page a sentence leapt up at her. "As I wrote to you before, I will never do anything contrary to that power and authority I have given you. I will never fail in friendship." The words might have been written in letters of gold, they gave her so much joy. She slipped her arms round his neck and whispered, "O Dduw, y mae yr hapusrwydd yma yn ormod yw ddal."

"That phrase again!" ejaculated Charles. "Surely an extravagant one with which to comment on the commonplace fact that a man is loyal to his friends?"

"No," said Lucy.

Three days later, in the early afternoon, they were together again and heard the sound of wheels in the street outside. They stopped at the door. Lucy flew downstairs and was a little surprised to find that Charles was not with her. He was, of course, the King. To have run down the stairs as she had done would have been undignified, but it always chilled her a little to discover afresh how perpetually present in his mind was the kingly image. Then she forgot everything for Mr. Prodgers had dismounted from his horse and opened the coach door, and a smiling Anne was stepping out of it with Jackie in her arms. Anne had taken a great fancy to Master Jackie and had constituted herself his nurse as well as Lucy's maid. It was a joy to Lucy, for their shared love of the child was a bond between them. With Jackie in her own arms she kissed Anne, thanked Mr. Prodgers charmingly for his care of her and carried Jackie upstairs.

The King of England stood with his back to the fire, outwardly composed and even stern, so stern that Lucy was afraid Jackie might be frightened of him, but with his unseen heart beating like a bellows. Setting her son on his feet just inside the door with her hands under his armpits she said to Charles, "He can walk a few steps if I hold him up, but I must hold him."

Father and son regarded each other. Jackie was a sturdy

child, dressed as was considered suitable at that time for males of tender years in a full blue silk dress that fell to the ground in long folds, his short fair hair hidden under a tight embroidered linen cap. In one hand he carried his coral, for he was cutting a troublesome tooth, and the thumb of the other was in his mouth. His eyes grew round as saucers as they travelled up and down the astonishing length of his father, but he lacked words to express his astonishment and Charles had to express it for him in a shrill whistle. Jackie had heard that whistle before, out in the garden. The birds made it, the black ones, but he had not known that a man could make it. This was a wonderful man, a green and scarlet man. He took his thumb out of his mouth with a tiny pop and his wicked grin spread from ear to ear. Charles slowly compressed himself downwards, to the tune of an expiring whistle, balanced carefully and held out his arms. Jackie held out his, balancing himself with equal care, the coral in his right hand and the fingers of his left hand spread like a starfish.

"Let go of him, dear heart," whispered Lucy's loving husband.

"He will fall," Lucy warned.

"Let go of him I tell you!" commanded the King, and Lucy let go. Alone Jackie staggered a few drunken steps and fell into his father's arms. Crowing with ecstasy he was lifted higher and higher as the red and green man rose slowly towards the ceiling. Then the journey was over and the small boy looked into his father's face, liked it and once more grinned his wicked grin. "You rascal!" ejaculated Charles. "You jackanapes!" But he was annihilated. In later years it was to be said of him that he loved his son as his own eyes.

The next few days had about them something of the old Pembrokeshire idyl. It was not the same, for the boy and girl were now a man and woman who had experienced the world as it is and not as they had hoped it would be, yet the same light was on those days, the light of spring and of sun on water, they still loved each other and above all they had the child. He was an idyl in himself and the miracle of his making still astounded them.

They lived very privately, for themselves alone, with the presence and service of Mr. Prodgers and Anne a mere background of kindness that was hardly noticed. They hired a coach lined with red velvet, with a golden fringe, and drove with Jackie through the old streets of the city, and sometimes out into the country where the sails of the windmills flashed in the sun and the grass was greening beside the blue canals. The weather was idyllic, so warm that in the evenings when Anne was putting Jackie to bed they went out and strolled together and heard the thrushes singing in the hidden garden, coming home at twilight to supper and music and a game of chess.

Then abruptly the bliss ended. "Dear heart, I will not see you for the next few days," said Charles one evening. "I shall be busy with affairs of state."

He spoke with finality, endeavouring to shut a door, but as always Lucy was too quick for him. "What affairs?" she asked sharply, her foot in the figurative door. "Why will you never tell me anything?"

"Affairs of state are nothing to do with you."

"That is not true."

"I have told you many times that they are not."

"Telling me a thing many times does not make it true. I am your wife and what concerns you concerns me. Are you receiving messengers from the Marquis of Montrose?"

His dark face flushed, for he was very angry with her. Once more, who did this chit of a girl think she was? But because he had managed to keep his voice even she did not realize his anger and she thought he was ashamed. Why? Her quick mind pounced on the reason. "Are you receiving messengers from the Scots Covenanters?" They were sitting one on each side of a small table and Lucy had her elbows on it, a position which Charles considered the most belligerent his wife could take up. Her determined chin was in her hands and her blue eyes bored through to the back of his head. "That awful blue stare." Groaning within himself Lucy's husband was unconsciously echoing the words of her grandmother. "Are you? Answer me Charles."

"I am your sovereign. You have no right to question me and if I answer it will only be because I choose to do so."

There was a smouldering light in his eyes but Lucy refused to be warned. She merely waited. She had her anger in better control than he had and her will was stronger. When he spoke again he made each word sound like an insult flung at her.

"Argyll's Covenanters came to me in Jersey. Hyde was just leaving for Spain but Buckingham was with me. I committed myself to them. I am to go to them in Scotland and they will crown me there. Then with their help I will invade England and recover my throne. Tomorrow I receive them here in Breda to discuss plans and make the final arrangements. That is why I am in Breda."

Lucy's quick mind had digested every fact. "If Sir Edward Hyde had been with you in Jersey you would not have committed yourself to them. The Earl of Buckingham is an atheist and an opportunist. He has no sense of honour. Why do you let him guide you? Why are you so weak? You signed the Covenant in Jersey."

"I did not," said Charles. "I merely implied that I would do so."

"Then you will sign it here in Breda."

"I have not said so."

"And what of the Marquis of Montrose? If in Scotland you join yourselves with his enemies you might just as well stab him in the back with your own hand. It would be a quicker end for him than the one he will have at their hands."

Charles suddenly lost control of himself. "Do not be a fool, Lucy! He said in his letter to me that he had only to land on the mainland and Scotland will rise to him. To *him*, mind you not to me. He is an arrogant man."

"You are jealous of him."

"No!" thundered Charles. "But I believe him to have as much power behind him as the other party. He can look after himself. The balance is even, like this," and he held out his cupped hands side by side. "Until the time comes when I can reconcile the two parties I must stand between, ready to move either way as the balance falls."

"You mean you must be two-faced as Janus."

"I must recover the throne. That is paramount. That is the work my father left me to do."

"At the cost of treachery?"

"There will be no treachery. From the throne I can protect my friends."

Neither could comprehend the point of view of the other. Lucy could not see that a great end makes all means legitimate. Charles could not see that if an end can only be gained by a two-faced opportunism it is not worth gaining. They were too young even to try to bridge the gulf and look at the problem with each other's eyes. Into the bitterness of their silence there came a loud screaming. Anne had gone out for the evening with Prodgers and Jackie was being murdered in his bed.

His parents were with him in a flash without knowing how they had got there. No one was murdering him but he had had a little nightmare and had wished to draw attention to the fact. Plucked from his bed by his mother, snatched from her arms by his father and carried into the sitting room to sit by the fire on his father's knees he had what he wanted; to be in the sitting room of an evening when the fire was lit, not to be banished to his bed all lonely by himself where he could not see the pretty fire or hear his mother singing. Yet he continued, with intent, to howl, for he could not talk yet and it was necessary that his parents should be told about his nightmares and the fear that came with loneliness.

It was only outwardly that Jackie was an entirely normal child. His mother's nightmares before his birth had not been without their effect on him. When his grandfather's death had sent out its eddies into every corner of Europe how could the mind of his grandson remain unaffected? His parents only dimly understood this but they were both aware of a shared remorse, the remorse that is inseparable from the joy of bringing a child into the world. For what of the world? It drew them together and their quarrel was forgotten. Indeed the Covenanters, Montrose, the sacred throne of England and the divine right of His Majesty King Charles the Second all fell through the floor as Jackie's parents tried to staunch his grief. Lucy tried a little warm milk, Charles tried walking the floor with his son, but though Jackie's roars sank to sobs he refused to be entirely comforted; he was not sure yet that his parents had learnt their lesson.

"Try singing to him," said Charles. "He likes you to sing that Welsh hymn. He likes the tune."

"Grufford Gryg's hymn," said Lucy and she sang it in Welsh, very softly and slowly.

> "Who's the Man commands the crown?
> Fair God, pierced is His bosom,
> Christ, worthy king of heaven ...
> It's He our flowing language
> Should name as both One and Three;
> Father and Son offered up
> And faithful Holy Spirit;
> You're our Lord above all lords,
> Our bulwark, and our Father ...
>
> "Because His hands knew torment,
> Because He rose from the grave,
> Let us ask our God on high,
> There, where He bought us heaven,
> Ask the Father, dear Saviour,
> Jesus is called full of grace,
> Watch over us, bring all men,
> Our refuge, home to heaven."

When she had sung the last note she could not for a moment look up for the words seemed to her at this time so full of sorrow. When she did look up she saw her husband smiling at her over his shoulder in triumph. Jackie had put his thumb in his mouth and gone to sleep. Charles carried him to his bed, then gently kissed Lucy and went away to his own lodgings.

The next few days Lucy did not see Charles and knew only what Prodgers told Anne and Anne told her that the King had been closeted for hours in his bedroom with the Scottish gentlemen, no one knowing what had passed between them. But Lucy was not a girl to remain idle when she was in deadly terror and she had already written a letter to the Queen of Bohemia. Her landlady's son, who could ride fast and well, had taken it to the Wassenaer Hof. A few days later there was the sound of coach wheels, then a swish of silks on the stairs and her door opened precipitately. A tall veiled woman entered and Lucy, with Jackie in her arms, stood up and curtseyed. When she rose from her curtsey and looked up she saw that the Queen had removed her veil and that her face was disfigured with weeping. She seated her visitor in her own low chair and said. "I hope Your Majesty does not blame me for what I did."

"You did right," said the Queen. "When a good man turns to wrong-doing one must do all in one's power to bring him to his senses, but since in this fallen world evil has terrible power your action was as useless as the hour I have just spent arguing with your husband. And weeping before him. I do not recollect that I have ever wept before a man before. Lucy, to put a crown on a man's head addles his wits. An *idée fixe* in the mind of a king must automatically be right because he has it. The mere possibility that he may be mistaken cannot be entertained." She was in great bitterness and despair. "Charles my brother is dead," she said harshly, "and if Charles, my nephew, goes to Scotland and trusts himself to the Covenanters he will die as his father did. And that death will be merciful compared to the one that will be suffered by the Marquis of Montrose."

Her voice grated to a stop. Lucy stooped and put Jackie into her arms as the best comfort she could think of.

"When does His Majesty leave for Scotland?" she asked and her voice was as harsh as the Queen's.

"Soon, for his new Council is mostly made up of the young men and they will have their way. You will scarcely see him again, and nor shall I. Since we disagree with him we are pushed aside. In these circumstances women turn to their children. Your boy has grown, Lucy, and he is a fine boy."

For a little while the two women concentrated upon Jackie,

taking resolute delight in him. Then the Queen went away. She had travelled to Breda with her nephew-in-law, who had come to act as arbitrator and intermediary between Charles and the Covenanters, but she was to drive back to The Hague alone with her servants. Lucy herself awake that night, lay thinking of her and of her last words as she said goodbye. "Do not reproach him or plead with him again, Lucy. You will only increase his obstinacy and harden him against yourself. If he cannot take your wisdom to Scotland with him let him take your love."

So she was loving when next she saw her husband, and he looked so harassed that it was easy to be loving, and she tried to divert him. He on his side showed her affection and was careful to tell her nothing. Breda hummed with business, for the Scots had their advisers and secretaries with them, the Prince of Orange had his servants and Charles had his Council, and gossip was rife. But Lucy would not now listen to the bits of news Anne brought her from Prodgers. If Charles would not tell her anything then no one should. Then the Scots went away and he prepared for departure. He was to sail in a ship lent by his brother-in-law and it comforted Lucy a little that if Buckingham was one of his retinue so was Lord Wilmot. She would miss her friend but she was glad Charles would have the companionship of his unfailing kindness through whatever lay ahead.

On their last evening together Charles briefly told Lucy the main terms of the Treaty of Breda. As soon as he reached Scotland he would be crowned. In return he would promise that Presbyterianism should be established throughout his dominions and would sign the Covenant. The Scots promised him invasion of England by their armies and restoration to his father's throne. This seemed to Lucy a programme of such danger that she was speechless. Charles, secretly agreeing with her, could find nothing to say either. He stayed with her that last night in Breda but they lay in their bed like strangers, numbed by sorrow, longing for the morning that the parting might be over. When it came they might have been a man and a woman who had no love for each other, so tame was it.

Charles kissed his son and put him back in his bed, and then kissed Lucy, his arms limply about her. But suddenly he tightened them. "You will be faithful," he said, stating a fact.

"You are right," she said. "I will."

She heard the door slam and heard him ride away and merely felt exhausted, dry and dull. It took Jackie shouting for his breakfast to restore her body to movement again.

3

Charles sailed for Scotland at the beginning of June, leaving behind him in Paris and at The Hague two communities of dismayed followers who knew they would have to tighten their belts before he came again. He also left behind him a weeping mother and a young wife and son quite unprovided for. To this latter problem he had meant to pay some attention before he left but in the event it had slipped his memory. It had not slipped Lucy's but she had been too proud to ask again. As soon as Charles had left Breda she took Jackie and Anne to the farm, where they could live cheaply. When she had returned to Rotterdam from Paris, with nothing left in the purse that Charles had given her, she had realized that her aunt's hospitality was not what it had been, but she knew that the Flincks in their comparative poverty would never grow tired of her and she sold the ring that Charles had given her in Paris and decided to stay with them while the money lasted.

She was at the farm when she heard the news that had been broken to Charles just before he sailed. At the beginning of May the Marquis of Montrose had been captured at Grange Castle near Dundee and taken to Edinburgh, where he was driven to the prison of the Tolbooth in the hangman's cart. On May the twenty-first he was taken to the thirty-foot gallows by the Mercat Cross, called the Maiden, to be hanged, drawn and quartered, and it was said of him that he went to it with majesty and composure. In his last speech he said of his King, "It is spoken of me that I should blame the King. God forbid! His commandments to me were most just and I obeyed them." And so once more a hero escaped through fiery torture from a world of men not able to endure the challenge and the reproach of greatness while it immediately confronts them; only worship it once they have done away with it.

After Lucy had been told the news she went out on the sand-dunes with Jackie and sat there with the sleeping child across her knees, and wondered in a daze of misery how this could be. Few men were entirely evil and few were entirely senseless. Why could they not learn? Charles had felt remorse for the death of the Earl of Strafford yet he in his turn had committed the same stupid crime as his father, and for the sake of immediate advantage failed in loyalty to the best friend he had. Is that the crime, the stupidity, wondered Lucy? This greedy clutching at the immediate advantage? The saints and heroes do not do that, since their large vision takes no account of self.

Two more sentences from Montrose's speech came to Lucy's mind. "God be glorified in my end. God have mercy on this afflicted land." And then a third. "I had not any intention in my heart but what did aim at a joint and individual prosperity of the King and his people." But no, Lucy told herself, it was the Earl of Strafford who had said that. They had been alike, their eyes set upon horizons far beyond themselves. Christ had been the same, she remembered, wanting only the salvation of men and the glory of God. Even her old friend the sin-eater had been like that, living only to carry away other men's sins, and perhaps he too, though with dim understanding, had died his lonely death as well as he could to the glory of God.

With her problem still unsolved she yet felt a little comforted. What consoled her, she found, were two facts; that these men came into the world at all, and that after they had left it they were revered as though they were not dead but living. The facts seemed to imply that they had come from somewhere and had gone somewhere, and the implication opened up a horizon so great that there seemed room in it for the forgiveness and perfecting of every sinner who had ever existed under a sun so tiny that it was no more than a spark in the vastness of creation.

That summer passed for Lucy in a continued state of

numbed exhaustion. At first no news came, or could come, from Charles. He had sailed away into the northern mists with his load of guilt and remorse and she could not visualize him as ever arriving anywhere. She hardly wanted him to arrive, for people said that when he rode into Edinburgh he would see the severed head of Montrose looking down upon him from the Tolbooth. And after that, what would happen?

But gradually she grew happier. The sea and the sun and the life at the farm were good. Jackie, sitting in the high chair where she had seen him in vision before he was born, was enchanting. He was getting noisy now, beating with his wooden spoon on his chair, shouting at the top of his voice, crawling, and finally staggering, about the farmhouse. The noise did not disturb Lucy for it came upon her gradually, and like all mothers she was more aware of the glory of her son than the disturbance; others in Jackie's vicinity were sometimes more aware of the disturbance than the glory, especially after Anne left, for she had been a better disciplinarian than Lucy. She had to leave because Lucy could no longer pay her wages, but kindly Vrouw Flinck, who was never forgotten at the British Embassy at The Hague, got her a post there and Lucy saw her when she went to the Embassy for the intercession for the King, and they promised each other that when it was possible they would be together again. The band of exiles at the weekly service were few, poor and shabby, and would have been hungry but for the Queen of Bohemia's dinners; her doors were always flung open to them at midday and in the mêlée of disorderly servants, monkeys, dogs, noise and scuffle one could always come by a little nourishment. Lucy, well fed at the farm, did not attend these dinners and Elizabeth of Bohemia did not attend the intercession service, for like most royal persons she had a deep-rooted hatred of being stared at while she prayed. On state occasions there was no avoiding the ordeal and she strengthened her spine and folded her hands like a queen on a tomb, but praying in private she could let her spine look after itself, put her head on her arms and cry.

But if Lucy did not see the Queen at the Embassy she did

sometimes see one or other of the exiled noblemen whom Charles had not chosen to take with him to Scotland. These gentlemen, lingering for a while at the Dutch court before drifting back to Paris, felt one solitary appearance to be a duty. Sitting in her accustomed place one Thursday, her eyes fixed listlessly on her hands folded in her lap, she was conscious of a faint movement within her as though deep in her numbed spirit water stirred beneath the ice. She looked up and saw that Lord Taaffe had just come in and was gazing at her with dismay. It was only long afterwards that she remembered that look, for it vanished in a moment as he bowed to her and took his seat beside her.

How could a man be dismayed when a girl smiled at him like that? Her joy had seemed to break from within and her tired, blanched face was at once young again. He had been shocked to see the vital Lucy looking so depleted and now and then he would look at her to see if his presence was still keeping her young, and each time she would know that he was looking and turn her head and smile at him, still young. She was thinking that here was another who loved Charles, one more link in the chain that surrounded and protected him, here beside her, praying with her. But why was he not *with* Charles? That was where he should have been. Tactlessly this was the first question she asked him when the service was over and they were out in the sunny street together. "Why are you not with the King, my lord?"

His face darkened with anger. "Those goddam Covenanters limited His Majesty's retinue," he said shortly. "He took Wilmot. He did not take me. Wilmot gets on with Buckingham."

Lucy remembered how he had nearly struck Buckingham at the Queen's levee. "And you do not," she stated.

"Could any man who loves the King like Buckingham? God help us, he is as arrogant a man as his father was, and as dangerous. Once let a man think he knows all and the devil has got him, and once let him persuade his King of the same thing and we are all damned." He swallowed, failed to choke down his anger and became purple in the face. "In God's mercy the assassin's knife rid our late King of Buckingham's father, and if his son follows Montrose up the ladder to the top of the Maiden it will be no more than he deserves."

"Will you please hold your tongue, my lord!" said Lucy, suddenly as enraged as he was. "And if you mix up the mercy of God with your terrible notions you do not deserve to receive it. And all this because you are jealous of my Lord Wilmot."

Lord Taaffe's anger broke up in mirth, he flung back his head and roared with laughter. "You are quite right. Wilmot's protective powers are not to be compared with mine and I go berserk at the thought of him in Scotland with the King."

"I do not wish you to have a seizure, my lord," said Lucy, "so will you stroll down the street with me and talk quietly of horses and the providence of God? The King rides well, and a good horseman can usually escape from his enemies. And if we did not both believe that God's providence watches over him would we have been praying together?"

"Lucy," said Lord Taaffe, "I can pay you no greater compliment than to say the King deserves you."

They walked on, deep in talk, and other worshippers, coming out into the street, stopped and regarded their retreating backs with concentrated interest. Something to gossip about was always a mercy in the boredom of a life of exile. Anne, who had leaned out of an upstairs window in order to wave to Lucy, that being a friendly custom they had established together, was hurt that Lucy, talking to Lord Taaffe, had forgotten her. She too watched the couple as they went away, and saw how at the end of the street they did not part but stood together under a linden tree. The incident, she decided, was worth noting in the record she had promised to keep for Mr. Prodgers, who had sailed with the King to Scotland. He had asked her to write down any little happening that might be harmful to Lucy's reputation should it be necessary later, for reasons of state, to attack it. Anne had been reluctant to give him her promise, for she and Lucy had been happy together at Breda, but the bitter jealousy of Lucy remained, her intimacy with Prodgers was now deep and he had her more in his power than she realized, and she had given it.

Lucy and Lord Taaffe were happy under the linden tree, he asked where she was living and she told him. "You will stay there with those kind people?" he asked.

"I hope so," she said soberly. She could not tell him that she had hardly any money left, that she would not ask charity of the Flincks or of her aunt and she did not know what she would do. He would think Charles had been careless about her and that he must never think. "And you?" she asked. "What will you do?"

"I am going back to Paris," he said. "I see it this way. The King will be victorious, we hope and believe, but if it goes the other way and he has to flee again it will be to his mother in Paris that he will go. Then I shall be there, at his service in his desolation."

"I should be there too," said Lucy in a low voice.

"No, because we do not envisage defeat but victory and restoration. Stay here, Lucy, where you have friends. Do not cut yourself off from them."

For her sake he spoke hopefully but she knew perfectly well that in his heart he did not expect victory and restoration. His judgment was that of Sir Edward Hyde and the Queen of Bohemia, not of the younger men.

"I will remember what you have said," Lucy told him. Then she curtseyed and they parted. Anne, still looking out of the window, hoped that Lucy would remember her and come back down the street to wave. But Lucy did not remember. She crossed the road and turned the corner of the street.

"I hate her now more than I like her," said Anne to herself as she closed the window. "She does not really love me. She only pretends she does."

Lucy had hoped that Lord Taaffe might have come out to the farm to see her, but he did not come. What did come, to her joy, was a command from the Queen that she should bring Jackie to visit her. She dressed him in his best and hired a coach and they drove to the Wassenaer Hof. She was taken up the familiar staircase and found her hostess alone in the

547

high-ceiling room with her dogs and monkeys. Grief for the
Marquis of Montrose, for her daughter Louise in her sorrow
and for Charles in his danger, had greatly aged the Queen.
How much she grieved for herself Lucy could not know. Her
concern for others was as deep as ever, her charm unchanged.

For a little while they sat in the deep window, the colours of
the rainbow falling upon them, and watched Jackie playing
with Apollo the golden monkey, and then the Queen asked,
"Lucy, did you know that my niece Mary of Orange is expecting a child in January?"

Lucy's heart sang with joy. Daily she had prayed for her
sister-in-law, as she had promised she would, but she took no
credit to herself since without doubt half Holland and all the
Princess's family had been doing the same. She had thought a
little more deeply about the mystery of prayer since that drive
with Anne through the streets of Paris, and now she knew that
to think one's prayer had value destroyed its value, since religion seemed always a thing of paradox. The poetry of John
Milton had not penetrated to Lucy yet or she might have murmured to herself,

> *God doth not need*
> *Either man's work or his own gifts ...*
> *... his State is kingly.*

And then there would have been a second paradox. God
chooses to make up the ocean of his love with innumerable
minute drops of human love. The ocean is all-human yet since
each infinitesimal drop is his own gift of himself it is also
entirely divine. Lucy's singing joy was in the goodness of God.
"I am glad," she said to the Queen.

They talked for a little longer about nothing, for the death
of the Marquis of Montrose and Charles's danger in Scotland
were subjects that neither could bring herself to speak of, and
Lucy wondered why the Queen had sent for her until Her
Majesty said, "Lucy, how do you live? Are you distressed for
money?"

Lucy had woken up that morning in a state of despair, wondering what to do next, but never, unless Jackie was in want, would she take money from Charles's family. She smiled cheerfully at the Queen. "Your Majesty, I am in no distress. Charles has been very good to me."

Elizabeth of Bohemia, feeding the daily hordes as she did, was herself so deeply in debt that she was relieved to hear it; yet knowing her nephew, and knowing Lucy to be possessed of a pride not unlike her own, she was not quite sure that the girl was telling the truth, and she put her hand in her pocket and brought out a small leather box. "It is a little trinket that I had as a girl. No, do not look at it now. Wear it sometimes for love of me. I am, you know, very fond of you."

Lucy was dismissed. She got up and curtseyed, kissed the Queen's hand and murmured her thanks. Then she held Jackie up in her arms to kiss his great-aunt. To her surprise she felt the Queen's arms come round herself and Jackie together and the Queen's kiss on her cheek. Half-blinded by tears she got herself and Jackie out of the room and down the stairs. "I shall not see her again," said a voice in her mind.

Left alone the Queen sat down at her escritoire and took a long letter from her sister-in-law out of its wrapping of folded silk. Her favourite dog flopped down on her feet and Apollo leapt on her shoulder, for they knew she needed comfort. Her Majesty the Queen Dowager of England wrote an atrocious hand and her spelling was wild in the extreme. Her Majesty the Queen Dowager of Bohemia had never been in sympathy with her sister-in-law, was not now and never would be, and her extreme irritation with the woman was not eased by the difficulty she had in reading her letters. She had read this particular letter ten times, and had more or less mastered it, but had disliked the tone of it more violently with each reading; though she supposed that the news it brought, from a dynastic and worldly point of view, was good news.

The marriage of Charles and Lucy was invalid. Queen Henrietta Maria's dear Lord Jermyn (I have always loathed the man, thought Queen Elizabeth) had had his doubts and after consultation with the Chancellor and the Queen a trusted secret agent had been sent to Wales to search out the details of it. Guided by the marriage register in Roch church he had found the lawyer who had been present at the wedding and through him had discovered the priest who had performed the ceremony.

With this old man he had made careful acquaintance, gaining his confidence with gentleness. He had been suffering from loss of memory for some years but was now having fitful returns of it, and when these fits came upon him he would remember his name, that he had lived in London as a young man and had friends there. He had talked about them to the Royalist agent. The marriage itself had never been mentioned between them and the agent had not made contact with Lucy's father. He had however seen him at a distance and found him a boorish farmer and the castle itself a derelict ruin.

He had returned to London and with the help of the old man's information made various contacts there, the most valuable being with a Spanish priest who for years had been living in sanctuary at the Spanish Embassy. He was of a great age too, but his memory was good, he was excessively garrulous and had not objected to signing his name on a piece of paper containing his statement that Patrick O'Donovan, now residing in Pembrokeshire as a Catholic priest, had in fact never been one. Charles Stuart and Lucy Walter had been married in a Protestant church by a Roman Catholic layman.

Queen Henrietta Maria then went on to say that dear Lord Jermyn and the Chancellor had thought it best to say nothing to Charles at present. If he died in Scotland, which God forbid, or if he won back his throne, then the truth must be disclosed at once for Jackie was a bastard and could not succeed his father. But if Charles returned to Paris defeated, and that too might God forbid, then in dear Lord Jermyn's words, "The time to tell him is when he tires of the girl."

The Queen of Bohemia folded up the letter, put her face in her hands, and cried.

4

That evening, with Jackie asleep in his cot in Lucy's room and the men out fishing, Vrouw Flinck and Lucy sat together just inside the open door of the farmhouse. The summer night had brought no chill with it and the flowers in the garden exhaled a breath of scent that was still warm with sunshine. There was a faint leap of flame in the hearth and it was reflected in the polished wood of the furniture. The glow shone out and then dimmed, shone and dimmed, and the rise and fall of the distant waves was steady as the ticking of a clock. Even the cool welling of the stars, as the huge arc of the sky darkened and they awakened into pulsing light, seemed rhythmic. All things were united in peace; only Lucy in her loneliness felt forsaken and cast out from the oneness of creation.

"What ails you, love?" asked Vrouw Flinck.

"I must leave you and this place where I have always been so happy."

"Where will you go?"

"That is what I do not know."

"You are no longer happy with your aunt. Much love is needed if one woman is to be dependent upon another in a home that is not her own, and though a contented baby can give great pleasure in a childless house a growing boy gives less. Now here there is deep love between us and with Jackie it is as though one of my own boys was small again. If your money is spent I will share with you all that I have, and my husband would say the same."

Joy that there could be so much love in the world, joy that poor people are so much more generous than the rich, destroyed all Lucy's sense of isolation. "Yet I cannot do it," she said. "I will not be dependent. I could work at The Hague. I could work at the Embassy with Anne as a maidservant, but would the King like that?"

"He would not," said Vrouw Flinck decidedly. "You are too well known at The Hague. Yet in Paris, Lucy, you could earn your bread and no one would know it. Would you like to live with Betje and work for her as her assistant? She needs your

help and can afford to pay you well. This plan is Betje's own.
She wrote it in a letter and sent it to me after you left her.
Knowing the King's poverty she was afraid for your future.
But you are a great lady now and though you have no arrogance
you have your pride. Betje is only a fisherman's daughter."

"She is a greater woman than I am," murmured Lucy.
"It will be an honour to work for her. I will go to bed now
Vrouw Flinck, and think about it. I will tell you in the morn-
ing."

In the bare clean room that had been home to her and
Charles and was home to her and her son, Lucy stood at the
window and remembered that Paris was the city of sorrows
and that she had hoped never to go back. But she also remembered that Lord Taaffe had said, "It is to Paris he will come. I
shall be there at his service in his desolation." And she had
replied, "I should be there too."

Her decision was made and by the light of the moon and
stars she counted up her resources. Of coins she had only
enough left to pay Vrouw Flinck for one more week, but she
had her ruby ring and the diamond brooch that belonged to
her and Jackie. And the Queen of Bohemia's little trinket. She
had still not looked at it for Jackie had been in a demanding
mood when they got home and she had kept it for a quiet
moment. She took the box from her pocket and opened it.

Inside was no trinket but a necklace and earrings of pearls
and emeralds. The stones were not large and the necklace and
earrings of delicate workmanship, suitable for the slender
neck and small ears of a young girl, but Lucy knew enough
about jewels now to realize they were valuable. She cried
and she knew she could never part with them, save only to
keep Jackie from starvation. With the ruby ring Charles had
given her it was the same. That left only the diamonds.
Charles would be very angry when he found out but what else
could she do? It was the only way to pay for the journey to
Paris.

A few weeks later history repeated itself for Lucy was once
more boarding a ship that was sailing for France. Mijnheer
Flinck had heard about it and arranged her passage for her.

She was not such a great ship as the last but she was nevertheless a lovely thing and she had a familiar look about her. Nor was Lucy's embarking so grand. Then she had gone aboard in the fine new clothes that Charles had given her, in the care of the elegant Lord Wilmot, both of them attended by their servants. Now, because she had wanted it that way, she had said goodbye to the Flincks at the farmhouse and came up the gangway alone, in a shabby dress, carrying Jackie clutched in one arm and a bundle in the other and followed by a seaman carrying more bundles.

Two men were pacing the deck, one was short and stocky and the other tall and lean, with a red head. They turned and Lord Taaffe saw Lucy. For a moment his dismay seemed to attach his feet to the deck. He could not move. Could he not escape this girl? Then his manners returned and he came to her with his usual cheerful grin. "You are travelling to Paris too, Mrs. Barlow? That is good news. Give me the boy. He is too heavy for you." He relieved her of Jackie and her bundle and smiled down at her again. "Now I shall be able to look after you as Wilmot used to do. Come and meet Captain Axel, the commander of the *Sea-Horse*. She is a lovely ship."

Ten

Lucy had been outwardly smiling but inwardly anxious as she went up the gangway of the *Sea-Horse*. Her journey to France wás assured but how was she to get to Paris? How could an unprotected girl with a small child travel in safety? The answer was that she could not. All she could do was to pray that she would find other travellers to Paris on board with whom she could seek protection. And her prayer had been answered by Lord Taaffe.

It was a good voyage. They did not have very good weather, but she did not mind rough seas, and Captain Axel and Lord Taaffe vied with each other to pet and spoil her and Jackie and make them happy. Once more Captain Axel reminded her of Justus, and when they reached France and she and Lord Taaffe had to leave the *Sea-Horse* she found it almost as hard to say goodbye as he did.

He gave her a parting present, two rolls of fine cloth, one deep crimson and one green, to make warm garments for herself and Jackie for the winter. His father, he told her, was a cloth merchant who did business in several of the Netherlands towns. "Our home is at Brussels," he said, and then he paused. They were standing in his cabin and he was holding her hand. "You will always be welcome there," he added suddenly and then, as Justus would have done, he crimsoned to the roots of his hair, dropped her hand and turned away. He was a little in love with her, she realized, and she was sorry but glad it was only a little.

And also glad that Lord Taaffe was not; that had been made quite clear to her by his look of dismay when he had seen her coming aboard the *Sea-Horse*. That had hurt a little at the time but the hurt had vanished as their friendship grew. Lord Wilmot had been an amusing, cool and kind protector, but

Lord Taaffe was much more, and though occasionally their
Celtic tempers flared they suited each other like well-matched
hand and glove. They came from much the same kind of background; from an old castle in a western land where the prevailing wind was from the sea and if there was much wild
weather there was also greenness and freshness, with rainbows
over the mountains and warm fires and singing in the castle
hall at night. They both loved a country life, horses and dogs
and children, so that Lord Taaffe found Jackie no infliction.
Though even if he had not loved children, he asked himself,
how could he have resented the small son of the two human
beings whom he loved best on earth?

For by the time the voyage ended he had had to admit it to
himself. Lucy, if the fates had dealt more kindly with them
both, would have been the woman for him. But the fates had
not dealt kindly; excepting only that they had given him a
strong will, loyalty, and complete confidence in both. He had
done his best to avoid the girl but it had not been possible.
Very well then, let them enjoy the journey to Paris together.
He had control of himself and Lucy was still deeply in love
with Charles, and more than in love with her child. He knew
the signs of maternal passion in a woman. Lucy was above all a
mother. He considered that they had nothing to fear from the
journey to Paris and in the event he was right, for Jackie came
out in spots.

What the ailment could be Lucy and Lord Taaffe did not
know and there was no medical knowledge available to enlighten them. In the inn where the indisposition first made
itself felt Jackie emptied his bowl of food upon the floor and
howled, while spots came up all over him one after the other in
a very terrifying manner. A modern physician would probably
have diagnosed a mild attack of chicken-pox, but the innkeeper said it was smallpox and the guests said it was the
plague. A wild babel of excited French voices arose and it was
made abundantly clear that once more there was no room for
the child in the inn. Lucy wrapped her son in her cloak and
went back to the hired coach, and with all the bundles piled on
the opposite seat and Lord Taaffe riding beside them they

drove on. He was exceedingly anxious. He would not be able to face the King if Jackie died on the journey.

But Jackie was not the dying kind of child. At the end of that day's drive he was peacefully asleep and the day after, apart from his disfigurement, well but fractious. But those spots, occurring as they did in such a precious and valuable child, had left no room for thoughts of passionate love. Lucy remained unaware that it existed. Lord Taaffe poured his anxieties on top of the flames like a bucketful of wet earth and stamped them down.

Yet he was glad indeed when he had carried Lucy's son and Lucy's bundles up to the rooms at the top of the tall house in Paris and handed the lot, including Lucy, over to the smiling Betje. "I will not see the girl again," he said to himself with absolute finality. But he had reckoned without Lucy herself. When it came to the parting she suddenly could not bear to say goodbye to this man whose companionship throughout the journey had been like a stone wall shutting out a storm. She had always addressed him as "my lord" but now for the first time she used Charles's shortening of his Christian name, "Theo, don't leave us!" she cried and clung to his hand. She was without knowing it utterly exhausted and her first reaction to Paris had been the old fear.

"God help us, you are not afraid, are you?" he rallied her. "That is not like you. What have you done with your pluck?"

"Come and see us," was all she could say. "Promise."

"I will come," he said, and roughly pulling away his hand he turned his back on her and ran down the stairs. Even then, though his roughness had startled her, she was obtuse as a blind mole and in a few moments, as she talked to Betje and hugged her, thoughts of Charles came rushing over her; Charles running up the stairs three at a time, having supper with her in this room, singing with her; and all the evening she talked about him to Betje.

That night in bed she was overwhelmed by her physical exhaustion. She was in Paris again, the city of sorrows where men fought in the streets and kings were murdered, and

Charles was not here to look after her and Jackie, and with
Lord Wilmot in Scotland and Robert Sidney back in England
she had few friends to protect her. Then she remembered
Lord Taaffe and was no longer afraid. How long would it be
before he came? The thought of his promise was so warm and
comforting that she fell asleep.

2

Dr. Cosin laid down his pen and rubbed his chilled hands
together. Warm autumn sunshine had been ended by a spell
of cold weather but he could not afford a fire in his damp
study at the Louvre. Nor could he afford much food for a body
which was now much tormented by the stone and by rheumatism. But the body, he had decided, should not be left. It was
possible with discipline and training to keep the mind burning
clearly at the top of the tower, as in a lighthouse, unaffected by
the gnawing of rats in the structure below. Nevertheless the
various dyspeptic discomforts consequent upon semi-starvation and the stone appeared to be responsible for a certain
depression of spirits. Faith and depression were not mutually
destructive for faith could be carried, and carried well, in a
dark lantern, but one missed the glow.

"I am not alone in this," said Dr. Cosin to himself, and he
thought of the communities of exiles at Brussels, Antwerp,
The Hague and Paris. Many had given up in despair and gone
back to England to make their peace with the Commonwealth. The best remained, vowed to stick it out till the
end with the King, but they were growing miserable and pov-
erty-stricken as church mice; indeed more so for the mice in
his study did not look too distressed and he suspected that
they had access by secret tunnel to the kitchens of the
Louvre.

Yet the mice were in better case than himself and the Queen
Dowager, who was now nothing but a bag of bones in her
shabby widow's-weeds, for her allowance from the royal
family of France did not stretch to cover the needs of all her
dependants and in her own way she was as generous as the

Queen of Bohemia. And she was just now stricken with grief. Her daughter the Princess Elizabeth, whom she had not seen since she had left England, had died a prisoner in Carisbrooke Castle, but the young Prince of Gloucester was still there in the hands of his enemies. And the news from Scotland was bad. The Scots had as yet made no attempt to crown their King and were playing with him like a company of cats with a tormented mouse in their midst. Mice, thought Dr. Cosin, how my mind does run on mice. Poor unfortunate lady.

His pity did him credit for the Queen had made no attempt to hide her dislike of him. He was no longer paid for his services to the Protestant community and the Anglican chapel at the Louvre had been taken from him by the order of the Queen Regent of France. And the soul of the little Princess Henrietta Anne had been stolen from him by her mother. The Queen's promise to her husband, that their children should be brought up in the Protestant faith, she had set aside now that he was dead, and the little princess had become converted to her mother's faith. And other adult Anglican exiles had also been grabbed from him by the Queen Dowager. She still had great influence and in Paris this autumn there was more hope of a full stomach if you were a Roman Catholic than if you were a Protestant, and he believed that she did not hesitate to point it out.

Suddenly Dr. Cosin's pity deserted him and he ground his teeth in rage. That abominable woman! She should not get the Duke of York nor, if he ever got out of Carisbrooke, the Duke of Gloucester. Nor should she tempt away from him any more of his own. "No, God help me!" he ejaculated, and gripped his pen again. He was writing a book on the canon of holy scripture and treatises for the building up of faith to be circulated among his flock. His own tongue having been silenced in his own chapel his pen was now the best weapon that he had.

For a long time there was no sound in his room except the scratching of his pen and of the mice behind the wainscot. The light grew dim but he dared not light his candle yet for candles were expensive. Then came that alarming pain in his eyes and he had to lay down his pen, take off his spectacles and

put his hands over his eyes to rest them. He was very much
afraid that he was going blind and if he did how could he
finish his book? "It is only the hunger," he said to reassure
himself. "They say hunger affects the sight. The body should
not be felt and pain and weakness I can control, but not sight.
Not blind, my God, not blind. In mercy grant me light."

There was no answer and darkness invaded not only his
room but his mind. The scratching of the mice grew intolerable, and then he heard the chiming voice of a small child
and was back in the days when the Princess Henrietta Anne,
then still a Protestant, had been brought by her governess to
visit him. His own children were growing up now and dearly
though he loved them he missed their youth. He had bought
special lollipops for Minette and kept them in his cupboard,
but she was not allowed to come now and he could hardly buy
food for himself, let alone sweets for children. For a moment,
in his darkness and confusion, he thought it was Minette on
the stone steps that led to his study but then the child
stumbled and let out a yell and he heard a girl laughing. A
much younger child than Minette and a younger woman than
Minette's governess.

There was a tap on his door and he said, "Enter," but
though he did much visiting among his flock he could not
imagine who was about to enter and he peered like a startled
owl as the door opened and shut again. A gust of perfume
assailed his affronted nose and his weak eyes blinked at the
glow of a crimson skirt in the shadows, and the vivid frog-
green of some small creature hopping near the floor. Who
were these bedizened persons? He groped for his spectacles
and could not find them. Much to his annoyance they were
found for him and placed upon his nose.

"Dr. Cosin, we have come for the service in the chapel but it
is empty. I asked the way to your study and a servant showed
me. Dr. Cosin, you do not look at all well and it is dark and
cold in here. Dear sir, you do not remember me."

He remembered the pretty Welsh voice but for the moment,
in his confusion, could not put a name to it, and not realizing
that his hands were shaking he was momentarily annoyed

that this unknown female had put his spectacles on for him, and even more annoyed that she should pick up his tinderbox and most extravagantly light not one candle but two. He adjusted his spectacles and got her focused. She was a pretty girl with a tangle of dark hair under her scarlet hood. "I am Lucy Walter," she said. "And this is His Majesty's son Prince James. We call him Jackie. Make your bow to Dr. Cosin, Jackie."

Jackie fell headlong over a book that his host had left on the floor and screamed blue murder. His unconcerned mother picked him up and dusted him down, and transferring more books from a stool to Dr. Cosin's table sat on the stool and set her son upon her knee. Jackie, still yelling, caught sight of the gaunt greybearded old man behind the table, was astonished and instantly silent. He put his thumb in his mouth and gazed.

"I am sorry for his noise, sir," said Lucy. "He is a noisy child."

"Children heard or unheard always have been and always will be my delight," said Dr. Cosin. "I used at one time to be visited by the little Princess Minette, and I kept lollipops for her in that cupboard. She is not allowed to come now."

Lucy was deeply sorry for him. "Is it because she is no longer a Protestant? Is the Queen Dowager no longer kind to Protestants? Is that why we no longer pray for the King on Thursdays?"

"The Queen Regent of France has now forbidden us to hold services at the Louvre," said Dr. Cosin grimly. "Sir Edward Hyde pleaded for us but in vain. We shall however be continuing our weekly intercessions for His Majesty at the lodgings of one of the exiles in Paris. Next week we shall be there and I will give you the address."

"And this week?" asked Lucy.

He smiled at her. "Before you leave, Lucy, you and I and Jackie will hold the intercession service together. My dear, that is a very beautiful gown you are wearing."

There was a note of anxiety in his voice. His guests were very gay and very beautiful. Lucy's deep crimson gown was like a tulip and Jackie's was green as spring. They were bright-eyed and well fed, the only well fed exiles he had seen for a long time. Who was supporting them? Lucy read his anxious thoughts, looked him straight in the eye and smiled reassuringly.

"Jackie and I are living in my old lodgings with my Dutch friend Betje, who is married to Cardinal Mazarin's chief cook. She keeps a milliner's shop and I am her assistant. She is a clever needlewoman and she helped me make my gown and Jackie's. I wanted to be in Paris so that if things do not go well in Scotland, and my husband comes back here, I shall be waiting for him."

"You did right, Lucy," said Dr. Cosin, and sneezed, thereafter blowing his large nose with the blast of a trumpet. Jackie was fascinated but Lucy was not. "You have no fire," she said, "and it is cold as the grave in here and there is a dreadful smell of mice. Why have you no fire?"

"I have no fuel," said Dr. Cosin.

Lucy jumped up and put Jackie on his lap. She took a little box of comfits from her pocket and laid it on top of the large bible on the table. "Give him one if he yells," she said and was gone before Dr. Cosin could stop her.

Jackie found himself deserted. His fat cheeks crimsoned, he screwed his eyes shut, opened his mouth and roared. Dr. Cosin reached for a comfit and there was instant silence as Jackie sucked. A few last tears still clung to his long eyelashes but an expression of bliss came over his face as he moved the comfit from here to there in his mouth, to wherever he had a tooth. He had few teeth as yet but he knew how to use those he had. Presently he opened his eyes and was fascinated by Dr. Cosin's long beard. He pulled it but it did not come off. Dr. Cosin rescued his beard, placed it inside his gown for safety and contemplated this child upon his knee who might one day be King of England. Why not? He had been born in lawful wedlock, the true son of the present King's true wife.

He was a fine child, only eighteen months old but big and strong. He was a Stuart but he had a beauty denied to the Stuarts, his mother's beauty. It was in his smile as he played with the buttons on Dr Cosin's gown, and in the lovely curve of his cheeks, and when he repeated for Dr. Cosin's benefit a few strange words that he could now say, Mam, Shir Da, Pisherbouten, Ollypol and Gome, his voice had the true Welsh lilt. "Your Royal Highness is a dangerous young man," Dr. Cosin told him. "You have too much charm."

"Ollypol," said Jackie and pointed his forefinger at the bag of comfits. "Lollipop," Dr. Cosin corrected him, for as a scholar he was a stickler for correct language, and was giving him just one more when Lucy returned with a rustle of tulip skirts and another whiff of that perfume (surely the Dutch Betje would not have given her perfume?) and followed by a handsome young serving man dressed in the royal livery of France and carrying a big basket of sea-coal. With a smile and a bow to Dr. Cosin he knelt before the fire.

Dr. Cosin was not pleased with Lucy. "Madam, I ordered no fire," he thundered.

"No, sir, but I did," said Lucy politely. "I went down to the kitchen, following my nose, and this very kind young man understood my wishes perfectly although I do not as yet speak very good French."

The young man hid his amusement as he lit the fire. Her French was indeed atrocious, but very voluble, and he was her servant for ever. "Madam has but to command," he told her before he left the room. "My name is Pierre Latour."

"I will remember," Lucy assured him.

"You are making yourself very much at home, Lucy," Dr. Cosin told her with a touch of sarcasm. Sitting now before the fire with Jackie on her lap again Lucy considered this. "Yes," she said. "I know how to make homes. If Jackie and I can come to live here I shall hang my father's miniature on the wall and then it will be home."

"You love your father?"

"He is my firstborn," she said, quite forgetting that the phrase had originally been given her by Dr. Cosin himself. "By that I mean that he was the first person I truly loved. He came even before Nan-Nan and my brother Justus."

"You write to your family?"

"I do not write letters easily, and after I have written to my husband, though it is a joy to write to him, I do not wish to see a pen again. But I do write occasionally to my family, my father and mother, my grandmother and my brother Justus. My father writes to me and for him to have to get his pen to paper is a worse agony even than it is for me. He tells me only of the weather and the crops but at least I know he lives."

She smiled, and Dr. Cosin realized that for her to know that her father was still with her in the world meant more than perhaps she knew herself. He was slightly ashamed of his questioning but in spite of the evident well-being of herself and Jackie he was aware of unexplainable anxiety for them. He wanted to know that Lucy was not separated from her family. "The King writes to you?" he went on.

Lucy's smile became radiant. "Yes, His Majesty writes to me. He is easy with his pen. You should see him at it! The quill flies over the paper as though it was still on the wing of a bird." The radiance died. "He tells me that he loves me and Jackie but he does not tell me how it goes with him in Scotland, and I do not think it goes well."

Dr. Cosin was no longer listening. He had heard some sound outside the room. Lucy listened and heard the running of very light feet on the stairs. Only a fearless child, running from authority with wickedness and joy, would pelt downstairs in that headlong manner. She tucked Jackie under her arm, seized his lollipops from the table and hid them quickly in the empty cupboard. He opened his mouth to roar but the sudden astonishing entry of a little girl silenced him. Taking no notice of Lucy and Jackie Minette ran across the room to Dr. Cosin. She would be all her life very faithful in friendship and she had not forgotten him.

"My governess is out," she said. "She has a ruby ring and she has gone to sell it because my brother James needs a new shirt. I am with Mam but while she talked to my Lord Jermyn I ran. Is there anything in the cupboard?"

"Princess, there will always be something in my cupboard for you," said Dr. Cosin rashly, and she ran to find it, but it was only when Jackie recovered from his astonishment and gave utterance to his outraged feelings (for were they not his lollipops?) that she realized there was another child in the room. "A little boy!" she ejaculated and held one out to him. He grabbed it and they sat together in front of the fire with the box between them. Lucy looked at Dr. Cosin in dismay. "The Princess's dress is patched and she needs new shoes."

"She will not get them from the Queen Regent of France," said Dr. Cosin. "When the tide is going out poor relations are best forgotten. When the last jewels are gone I do not know what our royal family will either eat or wear."

"I will make a new frock for the Princess," said Lucy instantly, and Minette looked up and smiled. "I know you," she said to Lucy.

"Princess, I was with you and the King in the little dell by the fountain at Saint-Germain. You kissed me then. Will you kiss me now?"

Minette came and kissed her gladly, and she had not forgotten because she had already the royal gift of a good memory. "My governess told me that your name is Mrs. Barlow," she said, and then, searching round in her mind for the right thing for a princess to say next she enquired politely, "Is Mr. Barlow well?"

"He is well and in Scotland with the King," said Lucy.

Jackie knew who the King was and Lucy had been trying to teach him to say, Sir, my father. "Shir Da," he said, and then glancing round and finding nothing more to eat he looked at his mother and suggested hopefully, "Gome?"

"Jackie, we do not go home until we have prayed for the King on Thursday," said Lucy decidedly. "We came to do that and we will do it."

Dr. Cosin got up slowly, for the rheumatism in his knees was agonizing, and they knelt down together. Jackie knew how to kneel and was proud of the accomplishment. Presently he fell over but after lying on his back for a few moments he then took up the cross-legged yogi position. On the whole he found it the most comfortable for prayer. Dr. Cosin was repeating the petitions for the King when he realized that there was another guest on the stairs. The descent was that of an ailing woman who must come slowly with one hand on the wall. He knew who it was but he did not pause in his prayer, or look round when his guest entered, and following his example neither did Lucy. Nor did Minette for she hoped to remain unseen behind Lucy's skirts.

And nor did Jackie for he was listening intently for that word he liked. Sound was at present his favourite mystery. Words, his mother singing, birds chirping, people playing harps and lutes, china clinking, dogs barking and coach wheels rattling on cobbles made up for him a marvellous symphony of joy of which he lacked words to tell. Though he loved to roar and scream he liked also to listen and look. What came in through the holes at the sides of his head and the windows each side of his nose was astonishing at times, and so he listened now to the sound booming over his head. It was one of the big sounds, like thunder or wind, but it was saying the same things that his mother said in her voice like a lute. "Defend his person from all danger, both by sea and land," boomed the wind. "Bless his counsels. Prosper his enterprises. And command thy angels so to pitch their tents about him …"

There it was, that glorious word like a flower bell turned upside down. "Pisherbouten!" he shouted, so loudly that the prayers came to an abrupt stop. "Pisherbouton!" And once again, even from the steady yogi position, he overbalanced and his cheek came against Dr. Cosin's hard shoe. He did not roar this time but he sobbed. It had been a long day and suddenly he was tired. Lucy picked him up, set him on his feet and commanded and threatened her Maker with silent intensity. "Make him go to his grandmother. God, you can do everything, so make him run to his grandmother. If you do not take him to his grandmother I shall never pray again."

In a brief glance Lucy had seen his grandmother in her shabby black gown, ill and embittered, every trace of her beauty gone. She was no figure to attract a child but Lucy had taken the kingdom of heaven by storm and Jackie staggered towards her with his arms stretched out; actually to preserve the equilibrium but with every appearance of affection. The

Queen's face changed. She smiled and the charm that was never quite lost all her life long lightened her ravaged face. She bent down and held out her arms to the baby. He lurched into them, leaned against her in his great tiredness and was comforted. The poor Queen too was comforted and loved Jackie and never ceased to love him while she lived.

She had come in anger to reprimand Minette and to tell Dr. Cosin once for all exactly what she thought of him, but what could she do now but let Lucy help her to her feet and sit her by the fire with her grandson on her lap, while she searched his face for likenesses and found him a true Stuart and kept what she had to say to Minette until later. She even, to her own subsequent horror and astonishment, found herself incapable of protest when Dr. Cosin boomed forth into one of his heretical speeches.

"Your Majesty will excuse us if we now bring to a conclusion the Protestant prayers for his King's majesty which the honour of your entry has momentarily interrupted ...'That he may be preserved from the hands of all that seek his hurt, and may be speedily established in the just rights of his throne, through Jesus Christ our Lord. Amen.'"

From this prayer he passed to the litany for the King, and then he gave the congregation his blessing and the Thursday intercession service for His Majesty was at an end.

Charles, shivering with cold and fatigue, had just hidden himself in a hayloft in the Highlands. Only Prodgers was with him, for it had been against the advice of Buckingham and Wilmot that he had escaped from Argyll and the Covenanters and ridden to join a promised rising of Royalist Highlanders. But the clans had failed him. Now he lay in the hay hoping the pursuit would pass him by yet knowing in his heart that it would not do so. Strangely, for no apparent reason, a little warmth came to him, as though from the glow of a fire. He thought of Lucy, and of his comic son, and of Minette, the three whom he loved best in the world, and he even smiled a little. He constantly thought of them. Children are not treacherous, and Lucy, he knew with absolute certainty, would be loyal to him to the day of her death and beyond. He hid his head in his arms and tried to conjure up the picture of her glowing face.

3

Lucy and Jackie were happy living with Betje. For one thing Lucy was leading a useful and orderly life. Betje needed her help and she gave it with a will, serving in the shop and stitching in the evenings under Betje's tuition at all the pretty things they sold to the ladies of Paris. Lucy loved Betje more and more, and she liked Betje's husband, and he liked her and was grateful for the help she gave his wife. Betje and her husband were still childless but they had not given up hope of a child of their own; Jackie awoke no jealousy in them and their nerves were strong.

On Thursdays Lucy went to the intercession service and there she met other exiles. Since Dr. Cosin accepted the King's mistress as part of his little congregation so did they, and when she brought Jackie with her they were enraptured over the King's lovely son. But Lucy could not always take Jackie because he was too heavy to carry and to hire a coach was expensive. But what she did take always, heavy though it was to carry, was a basket of food that she and Betje had cooked. It was scrupulously divided among the hungry; though Dr. Cosin resolutely refused to take his share. Occasionally, to punish him, Lucy did what he did not approve of and visited him at the Louvre, with Jackie on one arm and a basket on the other. Then a servant was sent to tell Her Majesty the Queen Dowager of England that her grandson was at the Palace and a lady-in-waiting came down to Dr. Cosin's study to fetch Jackie, and he was borne away to visit his doting grandmother. Dr. Cosin noticed that, herself excluded, Lucy showed no jealousy and spoke of the Queen Dowager always with compassion. He was proud of her.

Lord Taaffe, having paid his respects once to the Queen, did not visit the Louvre again and never came to the intercession service, but he did keep his promise to visit Lucy and Jackie, though it grieved Lucy that he came so seldom and stayed so briefly. The first time he came he brought her some expensive perfume. His money was running short and he had to go short of food to buy it, but the longing to give her just one gift was overwhelming. Why he had to choose something so apparently useless and frivolous as perfume he did not know; unless it was that it has a strange power of giving confidence. Why, who can say? The hope of the eternal spring? He lacked confidence in Lucy's happiness and he had not the right or power to fight for it himself.

With his own happiness he was not concerned. What did it matter? It was the King who mattered, and Lucy. He was an extrovert and did not examine his own feelings very closely; if he had it might have surprised him to find that the King meant more to him than any other human being, more even than Lucy. It was torture not to be with him in Scotland. There was little warmth and no comfort in his cheap lodging and sometimes he would go out at night and tramp the streets of Paris, cold with November mists, wrestling with his jealousy of Buckingham and Wilmot who had been preferred before him, and with his passion for Lucy. Both were destroying things, corrosive things, eating into the mind and soul as hunger eats into the body.

He was nearly at the end of his resources now and was too proud to ask anyone for help. Semi-starvation bred strange fancies and sometimes it seemed to him that there was some evil presence with him in the streets, an adversary with a dark net creeping up behind him, ready to throw its folds over him to strangle him. And not him only. All round him were those who had already been destroyed. He saw wrecks of bodies huddled under archways, dreadful faces peering from doorways, remnants of human beings who had once been capable of beauty and goodness. But the adversary had come and now the stars looked down upon the mess with glittering indifference, an indifference almost as terrible as that of the men and women who passed by in their painted coaches on their way to some banquet in a palace warm and scented as a flower.

He felt strangely lost as he watched them go by. By birth he was one of them but by misfortune he was linked to the lurkers under doorways. So where did he belong? Where was his home? Where is any man's home? In his young and pious days in Ireland Lord Taaffe would have said it was the heart of God, but he could not now equate that heart either with the indifference of the stars or with the wreckage of human life about him, and so it was not in his power to answer his own question.

Yet it was the asking of it, he thought later, and he had asked with a compelling desperation, that in some unexplainable way precipitated one of the strangest happenings of his life. One night an old man with a stick bumped into him. Whether he had lurched, or the old man had lurched, he did not know, for they were both suffering from hunger and fatigue. He steadied the old fellow but for a moment neither looked at the face of the other, each fearing what dreadful thing he might see. Then just at the same moment each took courage and under the flaming light of a tavern they looked and were astonished, for each looked into the face of a friend and each at the same moment asked the same question, "Are you in need?"

The old man replied first and his reply was startling. "I have a great hunger. For food perhaps, for warmth a little, but my true hunger is for God alone."

He spoke the most exquisite French in a high comical voice and his eyes under the domed forehead were bright with intelligence. It was impossible to tell how his small face, puckered and wrinkled with age where it was not thickly bearded, could express so luminously the greatness of his compassion. Yet it did so. His next remark was as startling as his first. "My lord," he said, "I will come home with you."

The "my lord" startled Lord Taaffe. "Do you know me?" he asked.

"Whether you are a lord in the worldly sense I do not know. I honoured in you, and greeted in you, that divinity which reigns in the hearts of all men." He paused and the penetration of his bright eyes as he looked at Lord Taaffe's was extraordinary. "Have you a bottle of wine and a loaf of bread at home?" he asked.

"Sir, I have not," said Lord Taaffe. "I eat only every other day and this is my hungry day. And I have no home, only a lodging so vile that I trust it is temporary."

"Kindness such as I see in your face would make a home out of any odd corner where you might choose to entertain a guest," said the old man, and fumbling under his threadbare coat he brought out a gold ring that hung round his neck by a piece of string. He untied the knot and handed the ring to Lord Taaffe. "Go into the tavern behind you and purchase a bottle of wine and a loaf of bread," he commanded.

But Lord Taaffe, looking at the beautiful chased ring, protested. "Do you not know, sir, that this is a valuable ring? You cannot give this in exchange for a mere bottle of wine and a loaf of bread."

The old man did not actually laugh but his tender amusement took charge of his face in much the same way as his compassion had done a few moments before. The beholder was no longer aware of the face at all but only of the grace it mediated. "Young man, you are thinking that ring might buy me a warm cloak tomorrow when what I want is to eat and drink with you tonight. Only worldly men think of tomorrow. The ring has value, yes, for it speaks to me of the union between us and of my desire to prolong it. The tavern is behind you."

He was still amused but his authority was so great that Lord Taaffe, himself accustomed to command, was inside the tavern before he knew what he was doing. He felt a twist of anger when he saw the greed with which the tavern keeper snatched the ring, yet more vivid than the anger was the memory of the old man's penetrating eyes, and he thought to himself, "He knew I was hungry as the devil."

Carrying the bread and wine hidden under his cloak he went back to his friend and they walked on together towards his lodging. It was as well it was not far for the old man was lame and could only walk slowly. Away from the tavern light, and looking down from his superior height, Lord Taaffe could hardly see him but was very much aware of him, since he radiated now a cheerful courage that was almost visible. Possibly it was painful for him to walk. If so the effect of his painfulness upon Lord Taaffe was the disappearance of the despair he had felt as he walked the streets alone. It could not live with the grace that now possessed him.

They groped their way up the stairs to his attic room and he lit the candle he had hoped not to light and kindled the fire he had meant to do without. But he did both things with extraordinary joy and when he could once again see the old man's face he knew where it had come from.

"My lord," said the old man with delight, "we have a banquet."

Looking at the bread and wine he carried, and remembering the banquets to which he had watched the rich men driving, Lord Taaffe flung back his head and roared with laughter. Then he set to work to make his guest as comfortable as he could. There were two battered chairs in his room, one rickety table, his bed in the corner and a cupboard in the wall that held the few things he needed. He pulled the table and chairs to the fire and cushioned the old man's chair with his folded cloak, sat him in it and tucked the blanket from his bed about his guest's shaking knees; for the old man's joy had not altered the fact that he was cold and that the climb up the stairs had been long and steep. Then he took two cups for the wine and a wooden trencher for the bread from the cupboard and put them on the table. Never had the hospitable preparations of a host taken such a short time and never had he felt such delight in their performance; so much delight that he laughed again.

"You call this lodging vile?" chuckled the old man. "You keep it clean as paradise and the view from the window could not be bettered in the heavenly mansions."

It was true. From the attic room they could look over the roofs and lights of Paris, with the great sky of stars arched over them, and in the old man's company the stars no longer looked indifferent. From this height the misery and evil of the streets was hidden beneath a web of light, and trying to recall it to his memory Lord Taaffe found that he could do so only as a distant dream.

"It cannot be right to be so forgetful of it," he said aloud.

"In the days of your prosperity you were not aware of the depth of other men's evil and pain," said his guest. "Now through the gift of hardship it has been revealed to you that you may succour them. But thank God for a temporary amnesty, for it is his will. He desires that you should mount into his heart when the day is over and see evil drowned in his prophetic light. My son, will you sit down and sup with me?" A few words spoken in a high comical voice, weak with age, but strength and wisdom filled the room and Lord Taaffe sat down with humility, as though in the presence of the King, and he had such a sense of being now no longer host but guest that he had to be reminded of his duties. "My lord, will you break the bread and pour the wine?"

It seemed at first that he could not lift his hands to the task, for they lay heavy on his knees, then with awe he did so. The moment of meeting with the old man had been like the opening of a door; through it he had moved into a new dimension of life, where the world itself and all experience and action within it had sacramental value. It gave to each thing, a ring, a bottle of wine, a view from a window, an extraordinary preciousness and yet brought a sense of dream. For the value of these things was in their signification. They passed away as shadows do but reality remained. The ring had gone but this man was for ever his friend.

For ever? He wondered about the eternal life of the soul and abruptly, jerkily, he tried to put into words the misery that had come upon him in the street. To no other man could he have spoken of it. "The lurkers under doorways, the criminals, the utterly depraved. How can one reconcile them with the love of God? They are lost souls."

The old man smiled and the room was full of his tender amusement. "There are no lost souls."

"But our religion teaches us to believe in hell."

"Correctly. Have you not yet been in hell? It is a common human experience but mercifully, like all experiences of sinful men, temporary."

"Those men in the streets," said Lord Taaffe, patiently bringing his friend back to the point that was sticking in his soul. "If they die in their sins will not their hell continue?"

"My son, the whole creation rests in God and is purged in the flame of his being. Can any sane man picture a continuing hell within the being of God?"

"Many men do," persisted Lord Taaffe, "and retain their sanity."

"Hardly in the eyes of God," said the old man drily. "But no doubt God's idea of sanity and man's differs at times. Evil, even the evil in the soul of the worst man you know, dies in God. Not the soul but the evil. How long the dying may take, how it may come about, God alone knows. But evil dies and the death of evil is the only death. There is no other. That is why the adversary is busy in the streets. His time is short."

But Lord Taaffe was not satisfied. "What if a soul in the last resort should prefer evil to the love of God? May a soul choose to share the death of evil?"

Great grief filled the room. "I cannot conceive such a thing," murmured the old man. "I cannot conceive how a soul who has caught only the faintest echo of God's voice, calling to his child, could still reject his love. Absorption into God or absorption into nothingness, there may be that choice, I do not know. But what I have told you I know. But no man can convince another of his own truth, only tell it."

"I have distressed you," said Lord Taaffe and he was grieved at what he had done. He and his small attic room had been host to one after the other of the great graces; compassion, courage, joy, strength and wisdom; the attributes of God. But now there was this grief. Yet grief too was an attribute of God, for Christ had wept.

"No, my son," said the old man cheerfully. "I merely for one moment uncovered a perpetual grief to share it with you, for such sharing brings comfort. The hardening of men's hearts against the love of God in man, their failure to listen or to look either in compassion when men suffer or in worship when spring comes again, these things wound me as though blood flowed from the heart. The spirit can bleed as well as the body." He looked thoughtfully at the wine in his cup and smiled as though he were already entirely comforted, and something that was not grief began to grow in the room with enormous power. "This wine, this symbol of God's life poured out for us, what is it but grief transmuted into love? Or love into grief. Love and grief are not divisible while sin and its suffering are with us still. When evil is destroyed then who can say what love will be like? The glory is not yet revealed."

"So little is revealed," said Lord Taaffe.

"That you must accept," said the old man with a touch of sternness. "If it seems to you that revelation tarries you must remember that man, and not God, made time."

Had he for a moment felt rebellion, wondered Lord Taaffe? The sensation had passed quickly as the power grew. For one piercing moment love possessed him utterly, love of a quality which he had never known. It had the purity of flame but also a great homeliness. He felt such an extraordinary unity with his guest that each might have been within the heart of the other. Earlier in the evening he had felt alienated from the heart of God and the old man had said that his chief hunger was for God. While the moment lasted he knew that man's home is in the heart of every other man and that home and God are also indivisible. The piercing experience passed but the knowledge remained. "My alienation is ended and your hunger satisfied," he said to his guest.

The old man nodded and smiled and began to struggle to his feet. Lord Taaffe felt a pang of dismay that his guest should wish to leave him but he realized that he was right. The greatest moments in life are, and should be, brief. Man in his earthly weakness, like a seedling plant, cannot stand too much light. He helped his guest to his feet and taking his warm cloak from the chair put it about the old man's shoulders. To his joy and relief but a little to his surprise, the gift was accepted with humble gratitude. "Thank you, my lord," was all he said.

They went down the stairs together and Lord Taaffe opened the door. "I will see you to your lodging," he said.

"My son, it is not necessary. Our shared meal has put new life in me. I shall think of you often and always to bless you. In some future time, with increased knowledge, we shall again speak together. Peace be with you, my lord."

He had gone and the door was shut. Lord Taaffe, looking at it with bewilderment, did not feel that it had been shut in his face. He had not heard it shut and in the darkness at the foot of the stairs he had not seen his guest leave him. It was as though he had vanished. But he felt no sorrow for peace was taking possession of him.

He went back to his room and began setting it to rights and preparing for bed. Just once he asked himself a question, "Who was he?" And he remembered that night at Saint-Germain when the King had been in sorrow and Robert Sidney, to divert him, had spoken about the odd corners of London and the strange fantastic creatures to be found there. He had described meeting with an old man whom he had called Socrates. Did one in truth, when walking the streets, sometimes meet the Great Ones?

4

The winter clamped down upon Paris with iron cruelty. The rich grumbled, pulled their cloaks about them and drank more wine, the poor said nothing but by day drew upon their reserves of courage and by night huddled together for warmth. The poor, thought Lord Taaffe, are in the human family what the wrens are in the family of birds; they cock up their cheeky tails like a flag, and when they can no longer bear the cold they flock together into a hidden corner and cling so close that they become indistinguishable; just a pile of skeleton leaves blown into a heap by the winds of adversity. I am glad I am now one of them, he thought as he tramped to his work in the early morning. For he had found a job of work to do. He cared for the horses at the tavern where he had bought the bread and wine, sharing the labour with an ostler who was too old to work alone any longer.

It had not been his intention that Lord Taaffe should become a common labourer but passing the tavern one day, his mind full of the old man, he had found himself inside enjoying a drink he could not afford, and discovering the tavern keeper's need had been astonished to hear himself offering his help. Going outside again, astonished at what he had done, he had found himself filled with an amusement that was not his own, and had laughed aloud.

The tavern was a poor place and he was paid a mere pittance, but it helped him to continue in his attic room. He would have had sufficient food to keep body and soul together had he not helped the poor in the streets and spent money on the battered horses who came into his care for a short while in the tavern stable. There was so little he could do for the horses; only salves for their sores and a good bran mash, and a few moments of loving horse talk in the waste of their lives. It broke his heart to part with them. And it broke his heart that look as he might in the streets he never once caught a glimpse of the old man.

Nevertheless his friend was continually with him in the renewal of his mind. His lodging no longer seemed to him vile and he returned to it at night with a sense of homecoming. The room was full of peace and the nights being for the most part clear and frosty the great sky of stars seemed to grow continually more beautiful.

When he walked through the streets it was no longer as an aristocratic observer but as yet another poor man tramping to his work. He made friends among those he had helped, and when he stopped to speak to them he would beat his arms across his chest for warmth because like them he had no cloak. Being now one of them he was less aware of evil in the streets; when some whiff of darkness came to him from a passer-by he looked at him as a man looks at a lump of coal, knowing it has a life-giving flame at the heart. "The heart" was a phrase very much in his mind these days. It came to mean to him the innermost core of a man where God is patiently at work making the place into a home; for himself and for other men. "The creator of the universe tunnels in us like a blind mole," was his irreverent comment.

Sensitive with his new awareness, every human creature smiting at his heart, he went to see Lucy. The effect on him was catastrophic. Never had she seemed more beautiful or more desirable, and her affection and concern woke up in him a corresponding longing to be loved and cared for. He wanted her to take him in her arms and comfort him for the poverty, hunger and cold. He was a man of strength and independence. What had become of these qualities? He had never supposed for one moment that either could ever fail him and he was suddenly angry both with Lucy and the old man; and also with the King who had gone to Scotland without him and left him at the mercy of this girl. Like everyone else he was hard at work blaming those he loved best for the weakness of his own nature, and his rapped out answers to her anxious enquiries stung Lucy to a corresponding annoyance.

"I tell you I have mislaid my cloak," he said.

"How can you mislay a thing like a cloak?" she asked, persevering with a sore subject in the maddening way of women. "You cannot mislay a cloak."

"Surely I know what I have done with my own cloak."

"But that is just what you do *not* know. Theo, you have always told me you have plenty of money, but have you?"

"Do you suppose I would lie to you?"

"But Theo, you are getting so thin."

"I am a lean man. I always have been."

"Being lean is one thing and being thin is another, and I know the difference."

"Women know everything," said Lord Taaffe.

Betje, her suspicions as much aroused as Lucy's but wiser and more practical in her ways of expressing them, entered with a silent tongue and a pleasant little meal upon a tray. The Celtic tempers died down again and Jackie, who had been in bed and asleep behind the half-open door in the next room, immediately awoke. He liked food and could smell it even in the depths of slumber. "Gum," he called. The exact meaning of this word was not clear but it appeared to express grace before meat. His elders turned and saw his Highness, clothed in the royal nightgown, peeping round the door, his round face rosy with sleep but his eyes bright as diamonds. "Gum," he repeated joyfully.

He should have been put back to bed instantly but who could refuse such a child? He ran to his mother and was enthroned upon her lap. From this eminence he commanded her attention and she did not notice the exaggerated slowness with which Lord Taaffe ate his meal. When they said goodbye all was harmony between them but out in the street going home he cursed himself for his unkindness. How could he have been so cruel to his darling girl?

For the next few days he was tormented by the thought of his cruelty. Physical weakness and exhaustion were things he was not accustomed to; he was unaware that they expand failings into gigantic sins and worries into griefs too heavy to be borne. The longing to go back and comfort Lucy for his unkindness was at war with a warning voice that ejaculated Fool, fool, inside his head. The voice was as maddening as the sound of someone hammering a nail in crooked, the longing was a great rush of warm water trying to sweep him off his feet, and succeeding on the third day.

Betje through the window of her little shop above the bakery saw him coming and abandoning her customers came out to the landing to meet him. Through the open door he could see that she had Jackie with her and wondered if Lucy was out on an errand. Then Betje broke into urgent speech. "Oh, my lord, I am glad you have come! I do not know what to do with Lucy. I do not know how to comfort her."

"Did I wound her so deeply? The damn' fool!"

"Nothing to do with you, my lord. It is her father. He has died. I have never seen anyone take on so and yet she has not seen the old man for years. She did not sleep at night and she has not eaten all day. Now she is crying and it might be her firstborn child that she has lost. Do go up, my lord, and see if you can comfort her. She will do herself an injury."

"The Welsh are a very emotional people," Lord Taaffe explained, but his own Irish tears were springing and his heart turned over. He knew a little how Lucy loved her father and he went up the remaining flight of stairs three at a time.

For one mad moment Lucy thought it was Charles coming to her, but Charles who did all things with grace would have touched her with gentleness. Lord Taaffe's large hands turned her over as though she were a sack of coal and sat her up on the bed with a bump. The shock checked the tearing sobbing that had gone on for so long and frightened Betje. He sat beside her with his arms about her and she leaned against him and began to cry more naturally. Presently she did not cry at all and in her exhaustion was conscious of very little except the strength of this man. To come from her grief to his arms was like coming in from a storm to the shelter of some fortress. Presently, when she was entirely quieted, he dropped her on her pillows and went to fetch some food for her. Betje, her timing in regard to food always reliable, was already half-way up the stairs with a bowl of gruel. He took it back to Lucy and fed her with the same practical ability with which he nourished ailing horses.

It was not possible to withstand his determination and Lucy was too weak to try. She was not only physically exhausted with hunger and weeping but also with the misery of fore-sakenness. Charles had not written to her lately; he seemed lost in the darkness and snows of the north and reach out as she might in her prayers, and her midnight thoughts of him, she could feel no sense of union, only sorrow and confusion. It had been a relief to turn to thoughts of her father working with his beasts and his land, content before the kitchen fire at night within the shell of the beloved castle. She had thought that they were still upon the same green star together and had dreamed that one happy day she would go home to Wales and take his grandson to visit him. Now her father too was gone. His body was laid in the churchyard at Roch but where was he himself? Where was her father?

"Where *is* he?" she whispered to Lord Taaffe, and with the gruel not quite finished she pushed away the bowl. He put it down and took her in his arms again, but silently, for like her he found it impossible to visualize such a man as he believed her father to have been in the kind of conventional heaven of which they had been taught as children. Nor could he picture himself there. Nor her. "He is one with all he loves," were the words given to him. "And with whom he loves also. Love lives on, you know, and when the soul is not imprisoned in the body it is free as a bird to be where it will."

They were the right words for Lucy. They took her to Roch
and for a moment she seemed to see a bird flying over the
beloved fields, floating around the castle tower and sailing out
to sea on the wind. Only a symbolic picture but it seemed to
hold a truth to which she would presently cling. But for the
moment it was Lord Taaffe to whom she clung. "Do not go
yet," she implored him. "Not yet." He held her until suddenly
like a child she fell asleep, then put her back on her pillows.
For a moment she half waked and realized that he was leaving
her. "Come back soon," she whispered.

"I will," he said, and stood by her until she was asleep again.
Then with reluctance heavy as lead he left her.

Outside in the street going home he wondered where the
words had come from that had seemed to comfort her. Before
he had met the old man he would not have known what to say.
His poor Lucy, he thought, she was so loving that she had
great power of grief. "Love and grief are not divisible," the old
man said. He must be back again to comfort her as quickly
as he could manage it.

But he did not manage it for more than a week for even his
strong constitution could not hold out for ever against the
combination of not enough food, no cloak and bitter weather.
He caught a chill and for a few days was shivering with fever
under the blanket in his attic. Then, too soon, he went back to
the horses and had no spare time because the old ostler in turn
became ill.

But at last he was free to set off in the cold winter dusk to
the house that was now home to him. He had kept himself
going through the days of illness thinking of that house; the
warm smell of the bakery that was his first greeting as he
opened the door, the busy shop on the first floor full of colour
and laughter and the frivolous pretty things that made women
contented, and above that Lucy's room where he could sit and
talk with her and play with her son and know blessed ease to
his spirit.

Whatever the difficulties deep below them he had this ease
with her, the ease of home. As he turned the corner of each
new street he mentally set up the tall house at the end of it,

light shining from the windows, and so held himself upon his feet. "There it is, only a few more yards," he kept repeating. He had employed this ruse as a boy in Ireland, when he had ridden too far and got caught in a storm and could hardly get home. He would set up the old castle with light in the windows always just ahead of him and think of the fire in the hall, the dogs lying before it, and his mother's welcome.

But the way was longer than he had remembered, the wind was rising and it was beginning to snow, the first snow of the year. He had had the sense to borrow a tattered horse rug from the stables and wore it over his shoulders. He would leave it in the bakery and Lucy would not see it. This, he thought with confusion, had been a bright idea and he was proud of it. But where was the castle? He pulled himself up, and taking a grip upon his scattered wits leaned back against the wall of the house beside him. The cobbled lane was almost empty and seen through the whirl of snowflakes it looked unfamiliar. "You fool, you've taken a wrong turn," he said to himself.

He staggered away from the wall and turned to go back the way he had come, but now he met the full blast of the wind and realized to his dismay that he was facing a blizzard. The snow was driving in his face so that he could not see if home was at the end of the lane, but a beam of light shone through it and he remembered that the castle had always reminded him of a lighthouse. He put his head down and began to struggle towards it, dragging his feet through the snow, repeating to himself, "The lighthouse."

And now he thought he was fighting his way out into the sea to save people from a wreck of some kind. The white spray of the waves was breaking over his head and the water was cold as ice. Some boyhood memory was with him and he muttered, "Very cold for a summer's night." He fought his way through a couple more waves, head down against them, and then some sense of an approaching presence made him jerk his head up again and he saw one of the ship's survivors coming towards him, borne along by the greatest wave of all. He could see the figure quite clearly because for some peculiar reason a ship's lantern was swinging beside him, a little above his head, and it looked a frail figure. He lurched forward to the rescue and a great wave carried her straight into his outstretched arms.

"I have got you," he gasped in a voice that was rough and hoarse from his recent chill, and he gripped her with all his strength, holding her above the waves. "Got you," he reiterated, his triumph so gruff and great that it sounded savage. "Got you."

For a moment Lucy was so terrified that she could not even scream. Then her courage returned, and she cried out, wrenched her right arm free and struck out blindly at the faint blur of a face that she thought she could see above her. The Paris streets were not safe for women and she had been told that when a man attacks you the right thing to do is immediately to place your thumbs on his eyeballs and press hard, but she could not get her left hand free and neither could she see the man's eyes. But her right fist, more by luck than skill, landed full upon his forehead and he lurched back against the wall. A sensible girl would now have picked up her skirts and run for home but Lucy was immediately seized with anxiety and remorse. Had she hurt the poor man? The swinging lantern shone upon his face and she peered up anxiously. "Theo!" she gasped in horror.

He peered down at her. The blow had lacked the force that Lucy could have used had she not been numbed with fright and cold, but even so it took him a moment or two to get her face in focus, and a few more moments to return from Ireland to Paris.

Then a sudden rush of joy, coming up from the depths of the spirit, seized both of them at the same moment, bringing with it a strength and clarity that although not physical yet transformed both body and mind. For a few illumined moments they were well and whole. It was a moment of recognition and they clung together as though they had been parted for a hundred years. Time seemed to sweep back upon itself, carrying them to where forgotten memories waited beyond time, then with a gust of wind and snow they were swept forward again, the memories uncaptured, and they knew where they were. All the more they clung together because it was not where they wanted to be.

But it was where they had to be and the man demanded, "What are you doing out here alone in this storm? It is not safe."

"I only ran round to the apothecary to get some cough mixture for Jackie. He has a little cold. Theo, where are you going?"

"To find you. To comfort you."

"But you were going the wrong way."

With strength and clearness dying away Lord Taaffe's mind was now given over to the obstinacy of the sick. "No, I was not going the wrong way. I saw the castle at the end of the street. Do not dawdle, Lucy, we must make haste." And he tried to pull her round to face the storm.

She locked her arm in his and said firmly, "Home is with the wind behind us. The wind will take us there." Then as he resisted her she said sharply, "Theo, you are to come with me. Do as I tell you."

He capitulated and was aware of little except the relief of doing so. Resistance and struggle were all very well up to a point but beyond that point abandonment could seem the final good. He longed to sink down into the whiteness of the snow but was aware of Lucy and her determination that he should not do so. Lucy. She was a very determined girl. Abandonment to Lucy. It was she who was the final good. To be lost in her was what he wanted.

Lucy was intent upon getting him home, putting him to bed and looking after him. The light of the swinging lantern had been fitful but it had shown her two horrifying facts; a ragged horse blanket instead of a cloak and the haggard face of a sick man. And he had told her he had money and she had been fool enough to believe him. She thought with a sort of rage he was a typical exile and that many of Charles's friends were in much the same state. And she was Charles's wife. For most of them she could do nothing but for this man she would do all that she could. She reached the door and pushed it open. "Betje!" she called. "Betje! Come at once."

Eleven

For the Royalist exiles that New Year was one of alternate sorrow and hope. The first sorrow was the death of William of Orange ten days before Princess Mary give birth to a son. Lucy was not the only one to weep for her, sad that the arrival of the longed-for baby should be overshadowed by such grief. Yet she had a boy, Lucy said to herself, and babies are the supreme joy of the world. She should know who had a son. Spring ran them very close, and so did God, but then spring was the birth of joy and God had once been a baby, so the three could hardly be divided.

And then came another joy, the news that at the beginning of January Charles had been crowned King of Scotland at the ancient Palace of Scone. The fact that the coronation had been a humiliating farce, imposed upon a king who was virtually a prisoner and had already been tormented past endurance, did not penetrate to the minds of his friends in France. He was a crowned king now, and all Europe realized the fact, and waited for news of the triumphant invasion of England that would surely follow. But the spring months went by and no news came.

Lucy was now receiving occasional short letters from Charles; before his coronation, he said, he had been too busy to write. They were light and amusing letters, giving descriptions of the hours-long sermons he must sit through. "All the Stuarts," he told her, "have reduced sleeping through sermons to a fine art." Yet if the letters kept upon the surface of his life his love for her and Jackie shone through very clearly in the little sentences that kept breaking in out of context. "Dear heart, I dreamed of you last night ... Just at sunset I wondered if you were putting Jackie to bed ... My love, do not forget me."

Parts of these letters she read aloud to Lord Taaffe, when he came to see her, but these little sentences she could not share with him and though she read without hesitation he always knew when she missed them out and shared her heartbreak. Indeed he more than shared it since of the two of them it was he who suffered most.

Their contemporaries at the courts of France and Holland would have been consumed with amusement had they known that the tough Irishman and the King's mistress, of all people, were in anguish because for one night only they had been lovers. What of it? Were homeless exiles not to seek the comfort of a little loving to alleviate their lot? Anyone who thought otherwise was a fool. They would not have understood, if they could have seen it made visible, the quality of the integrity that despite their failures gave such distinction to Lucy and her lover. Both had the gift of a dedicated loyalty. They were not faithful when it suited them, they were faithful to the core.

"All true glory, while it remains true, holds it. It is the maintaining of truth that is so hard." In her girlhood Lucy had accepted what Old Sage had said of peace in the narrow sense, love being merely the love of man and woman and truth the troth they plighted to each other when they were married. Now she saw this troth as a symbol. The glory was a much greater thing than the love of man and woman, the troth something that must be maintained with love itself. In this realization she knew that she might one day find comfort, though she could not find it now, for the breaking of the symbolic troth seemed to have broken her heart, too.

Lord Taaffe, less reflective than Lucy, was in a worse case. All he knew was that he had never felt more wretched.

Neither could understand how it had come about. Lord Taaffe had prided himself upon his control in every department of life; even when it came to his drink he knew when to stop, he thought. Lucy, though she had told herself in Paris that one day Charles might have much to forgive her, would never have dreamed that it would be for disloyalty to him.

After the exhaustion and cold of the snowstorm Lord Taaffe had been for a few days extremely ill, but Lucy's and Betje's nursing and his own strong constitution had quickly put him on his feet again with no apparent signs of weakness. Lucy had her grief for her father in control and allowed no signs of it to appear to sadden other people. Both had actually been tremulous with the blows that had struck them and abnormally sensitive to every gust of emotion.

On the day that Lord Taaffe had said he was going back to his attic the next morning their tempers had flared. Lucy had said he was not fit to go. He had said he was. They had argued hotly and made it up again, Lord Taaffe winning, and to take away the sting of battle Betje had served them a delicious supper in Lucy's sitting room. Later, entirely reconciled, they had stood before the fire to say goodnight and suddenly tomorrow's parting had seemed impossible. They had shared so much, the journey from Holland, Lucy's grief for her father, the strange encounter in the snowstorm, Lord Taaffe's illness, and hard things shared unite those whose response to them is made of the same sort of courage. Yet the unity did not seem new. It was old. And suddenly the deeps had opened again, as in the storm, and they had been helpless.

He left the next day, as he had said he would, but he had come to visit her in the old way and patiently they had tried to understand their dilemma. They did not reproach each other and they did not argue, since sorrow had carried them down to the ancient roots where they were one. When Charles came home should they tell him? Both in their honesty wanted to tell him but put his happiness before their own comfort. Why should his faith in Lucy be taken from him simply to make them feel more comfortable? They considered that they did not deserve to be comfortable, but the thought of discomfort made Lucy put into words Lord Taaffe's worst fear. "I may have a child," she said calmly, "and in that case he cannot help knowing."

"If the child were born before he comes home it could perhaps be adopted and he need not know," he said.

There was a silence and it tingled. "Do you suppose," enquired Lucy in a voice like silk, "that I would allow any child of yours and mine to be *adopted*?"

He looked round quickly and saw the danger sparks in her eyes and the angry colour in her cheeks and for the first time in weeks his old grin flashed into his face. "No," he said and flung back his head and once more roared with laughter. And Lucy laughed too, with sudden delight, and he remembered the storm at sea when they had been on deck together and a wave had come over the side and broken over their heads. She had been more like a man than a girl and he realized that she was now, and had been all through this time of trouble. And he realized too that he had not the slightest desire to make love to her again. At the roots their love went deeper than love-making.

But there was nothing masculine about Lucy when she realized that the child was coming. She was instantly all mother, her first reaction one of joy. But afterwards came sadness as she wondered what Nan-Nan would have said. She had promised Nan-Nan that she would never bring a little bastard into the world and now she had broken faith with Nan-Nan as well as with Charles. Nevertheless there was to be a baby; a new spring. And no child of hers should ever suffer as the little Betsi who had been taken away from Nan-Nan and had died. No child of hers should ever be taken from her, not even by its own father, since fathers who must be about in the world cannot take proper care of small children. Neither Jackie nor the child who was coming should ever be taken from her. Never.

Her resolve passed through her being as though it were one of those strong stakes that gardeners strike into the ground to give backbone to some fragile flowering thing. She would cling and twine about it now as though it were salvation. She was not a weak woman but her broken promise had destroyed her confidence in herself. She took Jackie into her arms and spoke her vow aloud to him. "I will not let anyone part us, Jackie." He submitted to her clinging arms for a moment or two, since he was a loving child, then wriggled free, for breakfast was on the table. "Gum," he said.

The delight that had sprung up between Lucy and Lord Taaffe at the thought of a child was something they nourished carefully now that the child was a fact. His anxiety and remorse he hid from her. The fact that the carrying of this child was not so easy as it had been with Jackie was, she hoped, her own secret. Betje, who took things as they came, clucked her tongue at the frailty of human nature but was secretly delighted that a baby was to be born under her roof; she had a strange passion for delivering babies and much talent for it. The thought of Betje's talent was a marvellous comfort to Lucy as she sat by the open window of her sitting room making clothes for her baby, for as time went on her exhaustion became greater and she was sometimes frightened. She had vowed she would never let her children be taken from her but what if she were to be taken from her children? "I will not die of this baby," she resolved. "I will *not*."

Another resolve was that she must go to the Louvre to visit Dr. Cosin, for he must know about the baby from herself and no one else. Lord Taaffe went too. Never in his life had he felt more embarrassed but he would not let Lucy go alone.

Dr. Cosin took the news very badly indeed. They were the last couple in the world of whom he would have expected such a thing and he told them so with both grief and anger, his hands shaking so much that he upset his inkpot all over the manuscript of the book he was writing, utterly destroying the very purest gem of all his thinking, whose true lustre he was not able subsequently to recover. He loved Lucy, and of all the young men about the King the one he had most respected had been Lord Taaffe, and he told them that too as they mopped up the ink. And what of the King? That this should happen in his absence was something His Majesty surely did not deserve. He said that too, out of the bitterness and grief of his spirit, and then abruptly pulled himself up.

Was this the way to talk to sinners? Was he not himself a sinner? And was he not to blame for this? These were two members of his own flock and he as their shepherd should have protected them with more constant prayer. And the Queen too was to blame. She should have taken better care of a girl whom she knew to be her daughter-in-law. Lucy had been living all this time with some poor little milliner in a back street when she and her son should have been at the Louvre under the care of himself and the Queen. *Mea culpa,* he said to himself, *mea culpa,* and he fell silent, looking down at his clasped hands, composing himself to listen patiently to the culprits' excuses.

But none came. Surely they were not brazen? He looked up in sharp anxiety, but they were not brazen. There were tears on Lucy's cheeks and Lord Taaffe's weather-beaten face had the dignity of his selfless regret. But they were making no excuses and Dr. Cosin suddenly felt humbled by their silence. He himself had always had a particular aversion to the sins of the flesh and in his own youth had been protected from them by the depth of his pride and self-respect, but the founder of his faith had handled such matters gently, reserving the divine wrath for pride, hypocrisy or oppression of the weak. Dr. Cosin had not oppressed the weak as far as he knew, he hoped he was not a hypocrite, but a proud man he undoubtedly was.

When he spoke again it was to say, "I have always been deficient in the abandonment of love, that utmost self-giving that does not count the cost. I have much to learn from you both." They looked at him in astonishment and he sighed deeply. "But the adversary likes to trip us up with the best that is in us, and that is the human predicament."

"One cannot go back," said Lucy sadly.

"No," said Dr. Cosin. "But we can learn nothing in this world until we have learnt our own weakness." Suddenly his unwonted gentleness fell from him and he swung back to his usual mood of fierce command. "Lucy, you will now take up residence at the Louvre. It is where you should have been from the beginning."

Lucy's mood changed too and she lifted her head to do battle. "No, sir. The Queen would not have me here in my present-circumstances."

"I see no reason why she should be told of them. I insist that you come to the Louvre."

"Sir, I cannot leave Betje."

"It is not fitting that Prince James and his mother should be living over a shop in a back street."

"Sir, I will not leave Betje. She is the best friend I have and she is an excellent midwife."

"In this very room, Lucy, you wondered if the Louvre would one day be your home."

"Sir, must all my foolish remarks be remembered against me?"

Lord Taaffe, recovering now from the embarrassment and strain of the last half hour, could no longer restrain laughter like the neighing of trumpets. Dr. Cosin looked at him reproachfully. "I should be obliged, my lord, if instead of laughing at my predicament you would come to my assistance."

"Sir, you do not know Lucy as well as I do," said Lord Taaffe. "Argument is useless. But I can assure you she is living in a comfortable house with good friends. She is happy there and should stay where she is."

"I bow to your superior wisdom," said Dr. Cosin drily.

2

Yet Lucy went to live at the Louvre. The early summer brought not only renewed fighting to the streets but also a spell of intensely hot weather and Paris was not salubrious. "A damnable foul stench," was Lord Taaffe's description of what his nose encountered when he turned into the street where Lucy lived. The Parisians took the turmoil, heat and smells of their city more or less in their stride but the country-bred Lucy was weighed down with lassitude and her face had an alarming pallor.

Lord Taaffe was now suddenly in a state of temporary solvency for one of the Royalist agents, coming from Ireland, had brought him a gift from his family, a valuable heirloom diamond ring. He sold it and hired a coach and on a day when the streets were quiet took Lucy and Jackie for a drive to one of the fresher parts of Paris. The jolting of the coach was perhaps more tiring than the better air was reviving, but Lucy was so cheered by the sight of green trees, by Lord Taaffe's presence and Jackie's joy, that she enjoyed her outing and forgot her anxiety over Betje's husband. He had not gone to work that morning, feeling very ill, and though the placid Betje described his disease as just a summer indisposition Lucy, though she had not seen him, had felt alarmed.

She remembered her alarm as they turned into the familiar street, and when they drew up at the door and a white-faced Betje came out to meet them she turned cold. "Do not come in!" said Betje.

Taking no notice of her warning Lucy moved impulsively to go to her but Lord Taaffe was too quick. He got out himself and stood in front of the coach door. "What is it, Betje?" he asked.

"My husband," said Betje. "He has smallpox. I have had it but Lucy has not."

"I must help Betje," said Lucy. "I never catch things. Theo, get out of my way." With her hands on his shoulders she shook him hard but he was an immovable column of obstinacy.

"I will take her somewhere safe," he said to Betje, "and then come back and collect the things she and Jackie will need until she can come back to you again."

"I do not catch things and I must help Betje," cried Lucy, beside herself, and she dug her fingers into Lord Taaffe's shoulders.

He swung round angrily. "Do not be a fool, Lucy. What of Jackie, the King's son? what of *my* child? What effect will a mother with smallpox have on *her*? If you do not think of the children I do. Let go of me and sit down."

"He is right, Lucy my love," Betje called to her. "It is the children you must think of."

Lucy went limp and sat down. Lord Taaffe jumped in beside her and they drove away. Jackie, affected by the atmosphere, screamed not blue but purple murder. When he had yelled himself silent Lucy said, "Theo, you said 'her'. Do you want a girl?"

"Yes," he said, and grinned down at her, his anger gone.

She smiled back at him. "Do you know, for a moment or two I quite forgot the children. Can you imagine such a thing as a mother forgetting her children?"

"Confronted with poor Betje's face I am not surprised. But he will recover, Lucy. These Frenchmen are very tough."

"Where are we going?"

"To the Louvre to ask Dr. Cosin's advice."

Dr. Cosin gave it with decision. "I said before and I say again that Lucy and her son should be at the Louvre. Had I been attended to upon the previous occasion much distress of mind would have been avoided." He reached for a sheet of paper and dipped his pen in the ink.

"Sir, I cannot come here without the Queen Dowager's knowledge," said Lucy firmly.

"Certainly not," said Dr. Cosin, his head already bent over his squeaking pen. "I am writing a short note explaining the circumstances and requesting the honour of Her Majesty's permission for your move."

"And I cannot be parted from Jackie. He must not live in the royal apartments and I in another part of the palace. He has never been away from me and he would scream and be ill."

"That I am at this moment pointing out to Her Majesty."

"And the Queen must know about my condition. I will not deceive her."

Dr. Cosin looked at Lord Taaffe over the top of his spectacles. "My lord, will you be so good as to ask one of the Palace servants to take this note to Her Majesty. My lord will kindly command the servant to wait for a reply." Lord Taaffe left the room and Dr. Cosin turned to Lucy. "Say nothing to the Queen at present. Recent regrettable circumstances do not cancel out the fact that you are the King's wife and that your place is here fulfilling your primary duty, the care of the King's son."

Jackie had been for some while sitting on the floor happily employed in tearing out the pages of one of Dr. Cosin's books, also on the floor. He had been not so much tearing as coaxing them out very softly, for he had surprising patience with such employment, but now with a crow of delight he ripped out a page and waved it aloft.

"Jackie, oh Jackie!" cried poor Lucy.

"The matter is of no consequence," said Dr. Cosin with great and noble gentleness. "Do not chastise the child for the blame is mine that I allow my books to overflow upon the floor." He peered over his spectacles. "Which book is it?"

Lucy handed it to him. "No matter, a trifling book," he murmured. But his heart was heavy. A precious page of manuscript destroyed and now this especially valuable book. Service to the Stuarts always had been, and always would be, costly to their loyal servants. There was something about the family, some element of waywardness and unreliability, that could cause great damage to those who served them. He looked at the beautiful child on the floor, gazing up at him, his stifled sob infinitely pathetic. Jackie had been expecting punishment but now he sensed an absence of anger, an aura of tenderness, and judged the moment right for propitiation. He smiled tremulously and extended the royal hand. He was a typical Stuart. Nothing could be refused to the exquisite grace of their pleading.

"There are no lollipops but there is an orange in the cupboard," Dr. Cosin said brokenly to Lucy. "One of my congregation most kindly gave it to me. I try to keep something there in case the Princess should escape again."

Lucy took the one orange from the empty cupboard and gave it to Jackie. It was a fine orange and looked in the sunlight as though it were pure gold. She did not know why it was she felt so deeply moved as she placed the orb in the hands of His Royal Highness.

Lord Taaffe came back and it seemed that they waited a long while for the return of the servant with Her Majesty's reply. Lucy guessed that she had been discussing it with Lord Jermyn and perhaps with Minette's governess, since the answer had been written by her at the Queen's dictation. Lady Morton had gone home to see to the estates of her husband, who had died fighting for Montrose, but perhaps some of her kindness had descended to her successor, and Lord Jermyn was an easy-going man. The answer was favourable. It was the Queen's command that the King's son and his mother should be accommodated at the Louvre.

Lucy never went back to the rooms over the bakery because Betje's husband died, and Betje, who had always appeared so reasonable and calm, took a neurotic hatred to the house. Her husband's illness had exhausted her, her loss had broken her heart, and the fisherman's daughter suddenly felt an alien in the hot crowded city. But she would not go back to The Hague, she said, until Lucy had no further need of her, and she moved her innumerable bandboxes to the Louvre and was established there as Lucy's maid.

No permission was asked for this removal and the Palace took it for granted that the beautiful Mrs. Barlow should have her maid with her. Betje however even in grief had her head screwed on the right way. Knowing that the proceeds from the sale of Lucy's diamond brooch must be dwindling fast, and Lucy be quite unable to pay her a salary, she opened a miniature millinery establishment in an empty room near her bedchamber. The convenience for the hierarchy of the Palace servants was very great. Neither of the two queens ever knew it was there.

Lucy found it hard to keep hold of that serenity of mind which is considered necessary in a pregnant mother. "I must not have another nervous child," she kept repeating to herself. "Not another screamer like Jackie. I must not have nightmares like I did before Jackie. It is not fair on my child. I must be calm."

It was not easy for they were in great anxiety for Charles. They heard that the invasion of England was to take place at last and then there was no more news.

3

Charles had been assured that as soon as he crossed the border every Royalist in England would rise for him. The Government, he was told, would be overthrown even before he reached London.

Early in August he marched to Carlisle with his army of ten thousand men, and though the Cromwellian army was dangerously near he was received with joy. Then, as the Queen of Bohemia had warned him, he found that his most dangerous enemies were the ones behind his back. The Covenanting ministers who had followed him from Scotland publicized the fact that he had promised to enforce the Presbyterian faith on all his subjects, with the result that the expected Royalist rising did not take place. The disappointed Scottish troops began to desert. Charles marched bravely on but Cromwell and his army outstripped him and were encamped outside Worcester before he arrived there. On September the third, early in the morning, he and his staff met high up on the cathedral tower to hold their last desperate council of war. They decided to divide the army and attack from two different points. As soon as the King and his cavalry had broken through the Parliamentary lines General Leslie, commanding his Scottish cavalry, would follow on with a second attack.

The charge of the Royalist horse with the King at the head of them was splendid. They broke through the enemy lines and the Parliamentary troops gave way, but the following struggle became desperate and presently Charles knew why. Leslie and his cavalry were not there. The General was sitting motionless at the head of motionless troops. Charles fought his way back to him and cried out, "In the name of God, charge!" But the General and his men remained like carved statues. Charles rallied his men and charged again but his outnumbered and exhausted troops were pushed back against the walls of the city. He would have appealed to Leslie again but an old cavalier stopped him, crying out, "He has betrayed you. You must shift for yourself or you will be delivered up as your father was."

The battle raged now both within and without the city walls and Charles rode back into the city to a scene of horror. The autumn sunshine shone upon streets piled with dead and wounded men and horses, and blood was running in the gutters. They fought on, the King riding from one broken regiment to another, ceaselessly rallying them, calm with the greatness of his despair. But at last it was over and Cromwell's army poured into the city. The King was still on horseback, still unhurt, and Wilmot and Buckingham were alive and beside him. A group gathered round to protect him but he refused to fly. They fought their way to a bridge, at the south of the city, and defended themselves there till evening.

It grew dark and still Charles would not fly. "Shoot me," he said to his friends. "I will not live." Buckingham and Wilmot pleaded with him. If he was taken prisoner and executed the Royalist cause was lost for ever. Would that be his father's wish? At last, hardly knowing what he did, he yielded and rode out of the city with his friends to become just one more among the pitiful little groups who were struggling away over the darkening fields towards the refuge of the woods. He did not know when he rode away that two thousand men had died for him that day and that three thousand more, many of them badly wounded and less fortunate than the dead, faced the tortures and miseries of imprisonment.

4

Before the news of that disastrous battle could reach France Lucy's baby had been born. Jackie's birth had been hard but this was long-drawn-out and agonizing and Betje did not think that Lucy would survive either the birth itself or, when that was over, the collapse that followed. At first she was too tired to want to survive, and she had strange illusions. Sometimes she was floating down the Thames; she could feel the motion of the water and it brought her exquisite peace; she had only to let go and it would take her to the sea from which she had come. Then she would remember that she must not leave her children and she would hold Lord Taaffe's hard hand and his grip kept her back.

Once she floated apart from her body and looked down upon it from above, seeing it as a tattered garment to which she had no wish to return. But she saw also the minute round red head of her daughter lying beside the body in the bed and in a flash she was back in her body; to feel once more the pressure of the hard little head in the hollow of her shoulder seemed worth the seven heavens. She must not leave the children and after that return to the red-headed baby she did not want to. Her glowing baby had risen in her life like a new spring breaking through the weeping of winter, and was the glory of the world.

In actual fact Mary was not a pretty child. She was small as yet, though healthy and compact. Her face was red, the hard grip of her small hand extraordinary. The difficulties of her birth did not seem to have affected her in any way. She was contented and she cried only when she was hungry; and then with passion. Her likeness to her father was ludicrous. In spite of his anxiety he had laughed at sight of her; and so did everyone else, although they hardly knew why. Just a wrinkled red-faced brat with a little round head as hard as a bullet, but she had something about her, some exquisite promise. "She will always be happy," said her mother. "And funny and good." She had not felt that way about Jackie. Mixed with her adoration of her son there was always somewhere at the back of her mind an aching anxiety. But for Mary she had no fears and her love for her was one of pure joy.

Reports of this comic baby reached the Queen Dowager and she paid her a visit. Lucy could hardly believe her eyes when she opened them one afternoon and saw the Queen standing beside her bed, for when she had told her of the coming baby Her Majesty had understandably not received the news with anything but anger and contempt. The girl had not for long maintained the faithfulness expected even of the King's mistress, and yet she believed herself to be his wife. The Queen had dismissed the little jade from her presence with such curtness that Lucy had expected she would be turned out of the Palace, and wondered why she was allowed to stay. The reason was one she could not possibly have guessed; upon consideration the Queen found she was grateful to Lucy for now, when the right moment came, there would be no need to feel compunction in telling her the facts of her supposed marriage. The girl now deserved what was coming to her.

Yet when she heard how greatly Lucy had suffered her heart, rendered kinder by secret gratitude, softened. She had herself suffered much in childbirth and she was sorry for the poor girl, and one day when she was playing with Jackie in her boudoir she said upon impulse, "Jackie, we will go down and see your mama." They went along the passage together and down the stairs, the Queen gliding along with no more sound than the autumn rustling of her skirts, Jackie stumping thunderously, for he was now so sure of his balance that he could concentrate upon the noises a boy can make with his feet when going about the world; and they were many.

"Be quiet Jackie," said the Queen when they reached Lucy's door. "Your mama is ill."

"Shister," said Jackie. "Not want."

"You must not be jealous, Jackie," said his grandmother, and receiving no reply to her gentle knock she opened the door and went in. The room was peaceful and full of sunshine that seemed concentrated on the miniature which hung on the wall beside the bed. The Queen saw the man in the picture very clearly. His head was turned to the right and he was looking down. Following his glance she saw that Lucy, the babe in the cradle beside her, was asleep.

The Queen stood and looked down at her daughter-in-law in her defencelessness and she was sorry. No doubt there had been extenuating circumstances. She turned to the cradle expecting to have her heart further wrung. Mary however was not asleep. Nor was she pathetic. Her round red head and her red face glowed cheerfully under the hood of the cradle, and her brilliant blue eyes seemed to the astonished Queen to be regarding her visitor with a very royal condescension. Suddenly, a spasm of wind attacking the baby, her face wrinkled into an expression of distaste and she waved a minute hand with what appeared to be a gesture of dismissal. Shaken, the Queen turned back to Lucy, who had awakened.

"What a very remarkable baby," she said with awe.

"Shister," said Jackie. "Not like."

"Will Your Majesty be so good as to put him near me on my

bed," said Lucy. "I do not want him to be jealous. Will Your Majesty please be seated?"

The Queen placed her grandson beside his mother and sitting on the chair beside the bed talked for a few interesting moments about her own confinements, Lucy's confinements, her babies, Lucy's babies, their feeding and habits. Then she asked, "You have called her Mary, I believe? Is that your mother's name?"

"No, Your Majesty. My baby is called after my great-grandmother Mary Rhys, who herself was great-granddaughter to Rhys ap Thomas, one of the noblest Welshmen who ever lived."

Lucy spoke with pride and her blue eyes, looking up into the Queen's, were as brilliant as her daughter's. Her Majesty found herself humbly murmuring something about the aristocratic purity of Welsh blood, and then rising to her feet again she smiled kindly upon Lucy and went her delicate, rustling, autumnal way. Lucy lay in her bed astonished and happy. What had come over the Queen? Then she smiled. Mary had come over her. Throughout the interview Mary must have been in control of the circumstances. Happy in the thought that neither circumstance nor emotion would ever make havoc of her daughter's life Lucy fell asleep again.

Into this nursery warmth and comfort came the news of the tragedy of the Battle of Worcester. All Europe thrilled to the stories of the young King's gallantry, but that was small comfort to those who loved him, for where was he? Once more, as after her father's death, Lucy was asking Lord Taaffe desparingly, "Where *is* he?"

"Safe in the woods," he said cheerfully. "And Wilmot and Buckingham will be with him. They will travel by night and lie up by day and get safely to the coast."

It was hard for Lord Taaffe to speak cheerfully for he was nearly out of his mind with rage. That he was not beside the King now was the bitterest thing that had ever happened to him. He did not doubt that the friends who were with His Majesty would give their lives to protect him but Buckingham was a dandy and Wilmot was not physically strong, and neither of them had the country lore that he possessed, who was cunning as a fox in the wilds.

He dreamed at night that he was with the King, the two of them winning through as men do who have trust in God and each other and bodies strong and sinewy as the bodies of beasts. Red fox and royal panther. The undergrowth closed behind them and they were neither seen nor heard; only smelt perhaps at farmsteads where food was taken; a slight aroma of fox.

But the dream turned to nightmare and he would be standing before a tall man with lightless eyes and a sagging mouth that had forgotten how to laugh, and saying, "Sir, I have seduced your girl." Then he would wake up suddenly to the half-light of dawn and the sound of the vegetable carts rattling over the Paris cobbles, knowing where he was but still conscious of the black figure. It would grow like a wave and fall upon him, drowning him in ridiculous and useless despair. And all this because he could not endure Buckingham. If he had only taken the trouble to keep a cool head and get on with that pestiferous fellow he would have gone with the King to Scotland instead of the delicate Wilmot. It was the devil's own work that one man's hot temper could plunge many lives in sorrow.

Lucy was in better case for she had the children to look after. She must play with Jackie and sing to Mary and continue to comfort Betje in her grief. And she could pray, not as she would have liked to pray for Charles in his danger but sufficiently to be able to experience in some measure the eternal safety beyond time and place of those who are greatly loved.

Twelve

The weeks of anxiety dragged on. It was the end of October and golden weather. Frost at night was loosening the leaves on the trees and in the garden of the Louvre the gardeners swept them into heaps of treasure but always more came drifting down through misty sunshine on the stairways of the air. Jackie, taking his walks with his mother up and down the garden paths, laughed to see them and while they were in the air he thought they were red-yellow birds, but when he picked them up and looked at them he found that the big flat ones were painted pictures that showed a river with tributaries running through the fields of a strange country, and the fields, his mother told him, were full of poppies and corn.

But when with shouts of glee he was picking up handfuls of leaves from the heaps and letting them shower down again through his fingers, then he was a magician making gold to buy a new gown for his mother and a coach for Shir Da when he should come home. He was two years old now and could chatter to his mother of these things and she marvelled at the alchemy of his mind, for the leaves were whatever he liked to make of them.

Mary also took the air, carried in Betje's arms, for her mother was not strong enough yet to carry her. She was nearly two months old, small for her age but preternaturally observant. Held up in her cocoon of wrappings to survey the world she did not seem unduly astonished at what she saw but gazed out at it with serenity, ready for anything.

But Lucy was not ready, for her tired mind had reflected the dreamlike quietness of the autumn weather and mediated it to an exhausted body. The visions of the night seemed a dreaming within a dream, and waking was not yet to reality but to a larger dream peopled indeed with dear images that came and went through veils of beauty, but images not completely possessed, for she was hardly alive again yet. But the news that Lord Taaffe brought on a day at the end of October stabbed her into sudden and agonized life. "The King is in France," he said. "At Rouen. The Queen has just had a letter from him. He is safe at Rouen."

She had been alone in her room when he entered like a sunburst with his news, too beside himself with joy to be careful with the sword he carried. For Lucy it was a two-edged sword, sharp with joy and a great shock of terror. She was standing at the edge of an abyss; yet all around her head the birds were singing and her mind was numbed by their tumultuous joy. She could not speak and Lord Taaffe could not speak either as he crossed the room in two strides, sat upon the couch with such suddenness that it shot back against the wall, and took her in his arms. Lucy gasped, caught at her breath and used the strength of his arms as a shield to ward off that shaming terror. He was ashamed too. In his joy that Charles was safe he had entirely forgotten the danger she was in. Was that how he loved the King? Yes, it was. He knew it now.

He took her hands, looking down at them, afraid to meet her eyes. "Tomorrow the Queen and the Duke of York and a company of his friends ride out to meet him. I go too but I have asked the Queen if I may ride on ahead today, and perhaps reach him at Fleury. Only Wilmot is with him and I can be an added protection on the road to Paris. She gave me leave."

"I am glad," said Lucy.

"Lucy, I will tell him. It is best that I should do it."

"But you will take all the blame on yourself when the blame is equal."

"*I* will tell him."

She did not argue for she found she was thankful that she need not say the words. Putting a bad thing into words was always so hard; though afterwards there was relief because the sounds had been made, or the words set upon paper. There was a sort of catharsis in utterance. But she could not speak. She bent her head silently and in a hurry to be off he gripped her hands tightly for a moment and then left her.

2

Though the departure of a small company of people could make little difference to the life of the Palace yet the Louvre seemed to Lucy strangely quiet after they had gone. Waiting times are always quiet, she thought. Autumn is quiet with summer dying and winter not yet here. One is quiet, waiting for death. Am I waiting for death? She asked the question peacefully for her sharp joy that Charles was safe had turned to a quiet thankfulness that had banished fear. Charles was still on the same green star with her. The death, if there was to be a death, could not alter that fact, and for the moment it was enough.

She was sitting on a seat in the garden in the morning sunshine, watching Jackie at his game with the leaves, when she saw Lord Taaffe coming towards her at the end of the lime avenue where she was sitting. He was walking quickly and the sun shone down on his copper-coloured head and the tawny riding-coat he wore. He seemed all warmth and strength and she realized afresh how much she loved him and yet she was peacefully held in her deep thankfulness that Charles was with her still.

How was it that her love for the boy of her idyl had not passed away with the coming of this other union? Perhaps because there was nothing of an idyl about this later love. It had never seemed romantic; simply old and strong. Lord Taaffe passed out of the sunlight into the shade of the trees and his figure darkened; the warmth and glow were fading and it seemed for a moment that he was not coming towards her but going away, back again into the shadows of the past from which he had come. But she had no time to puzzle about it for the striding figure quickly became neither a young sun god nor a wraith, but simply a tired, worried, dusty man in a hurry, a living embodiment of life's confusion. At sight of him her own peacefulness began to fade. He sat down beside her and dropped his clasped hands between his knees. It was the first time she had ever seen him look defeated. She saw he did not know where to begin and she had to help him.

"Where is Charles now?" she asked.

"He is with the Queen and the Duke of York and their company. They met in the woods just outside Paris. They will be here by afternoon. I did not wait for the greetings. With the King's permission I rode straight on to you."

"How did you find the King?"

"I hardly recognized him. His youth has gone. But he is I think in good health. That is not the case with poor Wilmot. I met them on the road between Rouen and Fleury. Buckingham was not with them for he went to Rotterdam. Last night, at the inn at Fleury, Wilmot had a room to himself to get some sleep and I kept guard over the King in his bedchamber. He did not want to sleep. We talked through the hours. He asked after you and Jackie."

"Did you tell him?"

"Towards morning I told him." He paused. "And it went the wrong way."

He could not explain but Lucy understood. "You took the blame, trying to save me from his displeasure by bringing it upon yourself, but you did not succeed. He understood you but he did not understand me. That is natural since I do not understand myself. Is he angry with me? I want to hear what he said for I must know where I stand. I must know his exact words. Is he angry?"

"He did not seem so and for a while he was silent. He lay on his bed and he neither moved nor spoke, then he said, 'What of it? I have more to think of now than the infidelity of a woman. Wilmot is finished. Will you take his place with me? I must have someone close to me whom I can trust.' It was so extraordinary that at first I could not speak. Then I asked him how he could trust me after what I had just told him and he said, 'She's a pretty jade. One can trust no women and few men. I have always known you are one of the few.' That was all he said."

"And you said you would take Lord Wilmot's place?"

"I said I would never leave him as long as he had need of me."

"I am glad."

"Do you realize what you are saying?" he asked.

"I know what I am saying," she replied. "You are the King's man now and so can no longer be my man in any sense that the world can recognize. And I am the King's woman as long as my life lasts. He may not want me any longer but I shall be as much his as you are. He went away from us, as the sun goes down in the west, and in our night we found each other. Now he is back and I have no more to give to you or you to me."

"That is not true," he said.

She thought a moment and then replied, "No, it is not. Before our birth to this present life it is all darkness, we remember nothing, and beyond our death it is darkness again for we do now know where we go. It was in winter darkness that we loved each other and there is a thread that links the three darknesses together. I think that I shall go through what is left of my feeling my way by that thread, knowing that somehow, somewhere, it will bring me back to you again. If you know about that thread too then that is what we give to each other, our knowledge that our hands are on the thread."

"I know about it too," he replied. "The link is very old and very strong."

"And yet in the idyl I belong to Charles," she insisted. "But it is a young love, as the idyl is young, young as Eden."

"Eden is both old and young," he told her. "And the idyl too. And the love of a man for his king is as old as either."

She was silent, then she murmured, "It is cold and I must take Jackie indoors." The sun was still shining warmly but she was shivering. She might speak bravely but in her physical weakness she was afraid. Would Charles forgive her? If he meant to forgive her and have her with him still would he have asked Lord Taaffe to take Lord Wilmot's place? But he would forgive her for the idyl's sake, and was she not his wife and Jackie's mother?

They walked back along the lime avenue to the Palace,

Jackie trotting after them kicking up his leaves, and Lucy asked about Lord Wilmot. Had he been with the King all through that dreadful journey?

"They could not always keep together," said Lord Taaffe. "At one time Buckingham had to go one way and Wilmot another while loyal Royalists who knew the country had to guide and keep His Majesty. But Wilmot told me how at one point he and the King met again at Moseley Hall. I think he will never forget it. The King came in out of the darkness limping and leaning on a stick, an old greasy hat pulled down over his face that was lined and haggard as that of an old man. When Wilmot got him to his bedchamber he found him in a dreadful state. His feet blistered and bleeding, his shirt soaked with rain. He was so bewildered with exhaustion that he could not be persuaded to let go of the thorn stick that had been his best friend for so long. Yet when Wilmot knelt at his feet to help him he knew who he was and bent down and kissed his cheek." He paused and burst out, "Would to God I had been with the King on that journey. Did no man of all the fools with him even know how to look after his feet?"

Lucy was crying silently, her Eden love welling up in her as she pictured the scene. She wanted to have her husband in her arms again to love him and look after him and heal his wounds of mind and soul and body. But would he want that? The Valley of Roses was a long time ago.

She spent the rest of that morning making her two rooms, her bedchamber and her little sitting room, gay and pretty, and rehearsing Jackie in his bow and his greeting to his father. Betje tactfully suggested that it might be as well to remove Mary, secreting her for the moment in Betje's bedchamber, but this kind offer Lucy indignantly refused. Mary was her beloved daughter and must remain. So Mary remained, looking out wisely from her pink lined cradle, her coral in one hand and three bells on a ribbon in the other. It was she who first seemed to hear the sounds of arrival. Her blue eye widened and the hand that had been jingling the bells was suddenly still.

But Charles did not come that day or the next. When he die

come, on the evening of the third day, Lucy had just put the children to bed. She heard the door of her sitting room open and shut and thought it was Betje with her supper, but when she reached the further room she saw Charles.

She went into his arms quite naturally, as she had always done, and he put his arms round her and kissed her lightly on the cheek, then held her away from him, looking at her. "Mrs. Barlow," he said. "Do you know, on that devilish journey we would often talk to each other under assumed names. Barlow was one. Sometimes Wilmot was Mr. Barlow and sometimes I was. I travelled very safely as Mr. Barlow. I got the feeling that you protected me."

He spoke lightly but his huge black eyes gazed straight down into hers in a way that exerted an almost intolerable pressure upon her; as though he were trying to get the truth out of her by physical force. It was all she could do to keep her own eyes upon his, but she did, and her voice was as steady as her eyes. "I prayed for Your Majesty's safety by day and by night, knowing as I do that sincere and penitent prayers are accepted of God. I am Your Majesty's humble and contrite servant and your loving wife. Do not put me from you by calling me Mrs. Barlow. I am Lucy. I am sorry, and I will never fail you again. I am Lucy."

Her voice died away and her eyes devoured his face. She could understand now what Lord Taaffe had meant when he said he had hardly recognized the King, for this man was not the Charles she knew. He had become thin as a scarecrow and his skin, darkened and roughened by exposure, was scored with new lines. This was the face of a man who would never become young again, nor trust anyone again; except the very few. It was a guarded face and the mouth was hard. Suddenly he smiled and the charm was still there.

"Lucy, I am sorry you have been ill but your pallor becomes you." He took her chin between finger and thumb and turned her face to the light. "The bones of your face are good and you will always be beautiful. I shall always love your face."

He pinched her chin affectionately and dropped his hand. He had never before treated her in quite this way; as though she were a woman for his amusement only. She knew now that there had been a sort of death; she had dealt him a blow from which he would not recover.

But he was struggling to forgive her, trying not to remember that when he had been hiding in that damnable loft, staying himself upon the thought of her loyalty, her heart had probably already strayed from him. For he was a fair man. "I cannot blame you for unfaithfulness to the marriage vow, dear heart," he told her lightly. "I have not the right. Now that's enough of our sins and failings. We have a son to keep us in good humour with each other. Where is Jackie?"

"It is after his bedtime and he is asleep now. I am sorry you have come so late for I had trained him to make his bow and say, Sir, my father. Only he pronounces it Shir Da."

"I trust I still have some rights," he said drily, "and one of them is surely the right to look at my son in his sleep."

Lucy led the way silently to her bedchamber where Jackie in his cot and Mary in her cradle lay sleeping side by side. A nightlight was burning to comfort Jackie should he have one of his nightmares, but she lit the candle and shading the flame with her hand that it might not waken the children, she held it so that the King could look at his sleeping son. Jackie in sleep was almost unbelievably beautiful, and his innocence and vulnerability caught at the heart. He lay defenceless on his back, one hand hidden under the counterpane, the other flung up on the pillow as though to ward off the night terrors.

His father looked at him long and speechlessly, great vows forming in his heart. This boy should never suffer as he had suffered. He should have everything it was in his father's power to give him, yes, even the throne. This was his true son and he would yet win back the throne of England for Jackie. If his mother was a jade she had at least given the child her beauty and the boy himself would never fail him. That he knew, looking at the perfect face. That was not the face of a son who would ever forsake his father. His spirit, that had been wrung out day by day by ceaseless betrayals and hypocrisies, by an evil smiling deviousness that he had had to emulate himself in order to survive, was suddenly refreshed. His wife had failed him, but he had Jackie.

Charles dragged his eyes from his son's face and turned politely towards the cradle. Lucy, suddenly cold, lowered the candle and Mary was illumined in her rosy nest. Red-faced, red-headed, buttoned up in determination, she was so comical a baby that neither heartbreak nor tension, nor heightened emotion of the sort that Jackie caused, could survive in her presence. Charles took two strides into the next room and exploded with laughter on the hearth.

"The little brat is the spit image of Taaffe," he said. "'Sdeath, but I'll twit him about her! When it comes to producing children, Lucy, you go from the sublime to the ridiculous."

It was harsh laughter but it was good to hear him laugh at all. Lucy laughed too. Once more Mary had been the emolument in a difficult situation.

3

Settled again at the Louvre Charles flung himself with a forced cheerfulness into whatever action was possible. He consulted with his friends and advisers and he vanquished his mother and the Queen Regent in the affair of Dr. Cosin's chapel; on the first Sunday after his return it was in use again and he and his household gave thanks there for his safety. That over he could find nothing else for which to give thanks and fell into something like despair.

Winter came down upon Paris and the perennial revolution was still muttering in the streets. The French royal family and the peacock aristocrats, having welcomed Charles and listened with polite interest to his tales of his adventures, then dropped him. He seemed only able to talk about his troubles and people in trouble are so dull. They are also a reproach with their lean faces and shabby garments, and the look in the eyes as though they expected to have something done for them. And what more could be done for these boring exiles? The Queen Dowager and her family had free house room at the

Louvre and if there was occasionally delay in the payment of their minute pensions they must remember that there was a civil war on. The rumours that the English Queen was short of fuel, that the Princess Minette had to go to bed when her one chemise was being washed, and that the King was wearing Lord Jermyn's shirt were not verified in case they should be true.

The exiles smiled grimly and huddled closer together, and Lord Taaffe was once more reminded of wrens in winter time. The great old man with whom he had spent that unforgettable evening had told him he would serve the poor, but he had not expected that those who needed him most would be the King and the King's family. He now held the distinguished post of chamberlain, equerry and cupbearer to His Majesty, which in practice meant that he was the King's dog's-body. He shaved Charles, polished his shabby boots, groomed his horse, borrowed money for him and saw to it that whatever else ran short the drink did not. He managed to appear always good-humoured and confident, his great laugh rang out often and his red head was a cheerful sight to the depressed royal family on their fireless days.

Lord Taaffe found his own comfort downstairs with Dr. Cosin and Lucy and the children, where there was almost always warmth and laughter. They were on the whole a little better served than the royal family for Pierre Latour, the servant who had fetched the coals for Dr. Cosin on the day of Lucy's first visit, saw to it that they were never without at least a small fire in his study.

Lucy frequently had none in her sitting room but Dr. Cosin did not know this, and the pleasure which she and the children took in his company he accepted with humility as a personal compliment. It was also a source of slight irritation to him, for his writing suffered sadly. His powers of concentration were great but with Jackie playing and chatting on the floor, Lucy murmuring to her baby, Betje in and out, Lord Taaffe in and out, the continual stream of visitors in trouble that he had always had continuing as before, his pen was more often idle than active and the idleness was more painful to him than his increasing physical weakness and infirmity. When he wished to pray and meditate he had to take refuge in his cold little cell of a bedchamber, and here he was occasionally visited by his old friend Sir Harry Verney.

The two elderly gentlemen would sit side by side on the bed, the chairs having been removed to the study for visitors, Sir Harry wrapped in the tattered ruins of a fur coat, Dr. Cosin in his blanket, and talk together of the matters near their hearts. Almost always they spoke of selfless matters such as the welfare of their families and the plight of their King, but occasionally they could not help looking back to the comforts and grandeurs of the past, and Dr. Cosin would recall the way of life of those vanished personages, the Master of Peterhouse and the Dean of Salisbury, shake his head and murmur sadly, "So unlike my present existence, much beset by mice and nursing mothers." Then Sir Harry, a jolly man when not actually hungry, would take a look at the two shabby figures sitting on the edge of the hard bed and burst into laughter. And Dr. Cosin would cheer up and say, "But this is pastoral work. This is a care of souls. And one of the souls in my care is that of my King."

Charles was often with him in the evening when they could be alone and they would talk late into the night, and sometimes he would come with Lord Taaffe to visit Lucy and the children in Dr. Cosin's room. This situation of the two fathers and the two children he had accepted with grim humour, since his utter dependance upon Lord Taaffe and his ever growing love for him made anything else impossible, and he always greeted Lucy with affectionate courtesy and never failed to admire her baby before turning to his own son, but that he was turning from her was obvious to them all; Lucy herself knew it, with death in her heart. He would stay for a while and then picking Jackie up in his arms he would carry him away upstairs to play with Minette, and it was a long time before he was returned. That he was trying to wean their child away from Lucy was as obvious as the fact that he had tired of her.

"But she is your wife, sir," Dr. Cosin said to him one

THE CHILD FROM THE SEA

December evening. "I may speak openly of your marriage for
Lucy has told me that you know she once inadvertently revealed it to me. And she is a good wife. Will you listen while I
plead for her?"

Charles listened courteously but Dr. Cosin thought he had
done no good. There was a sort of death in the young man
against which he could make little headway. Yet a few days
later he tried again; to be instantly silenced.

"Do not speak of her," said Charles curtly. "She is not my
wife. I have just been told that our marriage was illegal. I shall
always do my duty by her, for I once loved her and she is the
mother of my son, but more than that is not now required of
me."

The room was growing dark and neither could see clearly
the face of the other, but Charles was sensitive enough to feel
how great was the shock that kept Dr. Cosin silent for so long.
When he spoke it was with anger and bitterness, and with
none of the ceremonious respect he usually showed when
speaking to his King. "Sir, I have myself seen the marriage
certificate. Who is now endeavouring to separate you from
this girl who is your loyal wife? The fact that you are once
more seeking the favours of Mademoiselle de Montpensier
makes me suspect your mother. Now that she herself has
failed to convert her sons to her own faith she is determined to
marry them to women who will."

Dr. Cosin's outraged sovereign was silent for a moment and
then laughed loudly. "Dr. Cosin, it is true that I am again
courting my cousin, and now for the first time I am doing it in
deadly earnest for my situation is deadly. If I am ever to make
another attempt to gain my throne I must have money."

"I understand the necessity, Sir," said Dr. Cosin grimly, "but
I grieve that the happiness of two women must be sacrificed to
it. I refer to Lucy and to Mademoiselle herself. Is it possible for
Your Majesty to enlighten me as to why you are not legally
married to your wife?"

Charles considered Dr. Cosin to be almost as tiresome and
prosy as his Chancellor but he could be tolerant with them
both for they were among the few whom he could trust, and

patiently he told Dr. Cosin the facts of his supposed marriage to Lucy. "My mother told me the truth of it herself," he said, "and of how she had come by the knowledge. She gave me a few days to get over the shock and then she once more began to discourse upon the charms of Mademoiselle. For years it has been her favourite topic of conversation. It may be that when I am married to the woman her tongue will be silent."

He had ended on a note of bitterness and in the darkening room despair hung heavily. Dr. Cosin was filled with compassion yet he inexorably brought the conversation back to where it had started. "Lucy Walter," he reminded Charles. "Does she know that she can now expect nothing from you except that duty which a king owes to a discarded mistress?"

"She knows nothing yet," said Charles heavily. "After Christmas, I thought. Let her have a happy Christmas with the children."

"And who is to tell her?" asked Dr. Cosin. "Yourself?"

There was a long silence. "I cannot tell her," Charles burst out. "I cannot do it. My mother must tell her."

Dr. Cosin pondered this. "No," he said at last, with great dignity. "I fear that I do not trust Her Majesty to do it as it should be done. I have daughters of my own, as Your Majesty knows. They were much with me after their mother died. I should understand how to speak to heartbroken young girls of the fact of death. For to Lucy this will be a sort of death. When Christmas is over I will tell her myself."

Thirteen

I

Christmas came and they tried to be gay. Sir Edward Hyde the Chancellor came from Antwerp, very gouty and irritable but able to hobble into the chapel at the Louvre to watch the King and the Duke of York go up to the altar to make their communion together. They knelt alone, clearly seen, and sitting at the back of the chapel with Jackie enthroned upon her knee Lucy watched too, gazing at her husband as though she had never seen him before. His figure dazzled in sunlight and became more kingly as she gazed, and her love rose in a great tide, she herself lost and dissolved within her love, and carried by it to be intimately with him. Then the tide ebbed and seemed to carry her further and further away, so that his figure became something seen very far off; still infinitely dear, but no longer hers. Her sense of loss was so grievous that when the rest of the congregation went up to the altar she could not join them; she was too far away now even to kneel where he had knelt.

Yet she watched them filing up and kneeling before the altar in line after line. Lord Wilmot was there, a little recovered from his illness, and Lord Taaffe and many others whom she knew, for the celebration was a public one for all the English exiles. Dr. Cosin, who was the celebrant, looked absorbed and happy as he moved through the rituals of his priestly duty, and his voice was strong as he spoke the great words that he adored. Lucy looked often at his consoling face, and back in her own rooms again she regained her self-control and turned to the happy business of making Mary's first Christmas, and Jackie's second a thing of joy.

She tried to do the things they used to do at Roch at Christmas. She had coaxed a wonderful yuletide log out of Pierre Latour and had it blazing in her sitting room, and she and

Betje had made garlands of evergreens from the garden of the Louvre and hung them round the walls. She had collected all the candles she could find and from the central beam hung a kissing-ring, gay with painted nuts and oranges.

Betje's little millinery establishment had provided the gifts for the children, tiny animals and birds and flowers made out of scraps of velvet, satin and feathers. They were hidden in a basket, waiting for the hour before the children's bedtime when Lord Taaffe had promised he would try and be with them, if His Majesty could spare him. When the hour struck it appeared that His Majesty had been gracious for the door opened and his lordship came in, carrying his flaming head as though it were a torch of obstinate delight. Lucy had noticed before that he carried his head in this way when times were bad, as though he said, "I will enjoy myself or be damned. And damnation to the man who stops me."

Laughing he seized his daughter in his great hands and held her up till her own red head touched the rafter beside the kissing-ring. She was so small and young a baby but she was not afraid as another would have been. From her eminence she bestowed upon the world far down below her the little flickering smile that Lucy declared was not wind but genuine pleasure. But the world was a long way away and suddenly her face puckered. Her father lowered her into his arms and held her firmly and she was happy again, her cheek against his chest.

"Christmas," shouted Jackie. "Somethin' for me? Somethin'? For me?" Standing up on tiptoe he explored one of Lord Taaffe's capacious pockets, and finding nothing there but a rag that had been used for polishing His Majesty's shoes he ignored his mother's shocked remonstrance and went round to the other pocket, where he found a little horseshoe.

"It is for him," said Lord Taaffe. "Cast by the pony of the King of France. I begged it from the stables." He felt in a third pocket. "And this for my daughter." It was a tiny charm of a shamrock leaf. "Such a useless gift but I had it as a boy," he explained apologetically.

Lucy was touched nearly to tears. "When Mary is older I

will put it on a chain, and each day when she puts it on it will remind her of her father."

"With such a noisy father will she need remembrance of the fellow?" asked Lord Taaffe, and he laughed again, the reverberation in his chest causing his daughter to lift her head from the earthquake beneath her in profound astonishment. What was that? She did not know. Would it do it again? She did not know. Was she afraid? No. Held in the grip of her father's hard and bony strength she was never afraid, though sometimes excessively uncomfortable. She laid her minute shell of an ear back on the earthquake and it rumbled away into a loud rhythmical thumping. Now here was another new thing. What was that? She did not know, but felt it to be a safe thing, and fell asleep on top of the safety.

So, thought Lucy, Theo was not expecting that life would separate him from his daughter. She felt a glow of comfort and tried to feel as gay as she should be feeling at her children's first Christmas party. Betje was here, helping her, and presently Dr. Cosin came in, his face softening at the sight of the lighted candles and the children. And a little later the door flew open and the King himself strode in with Minette upon his back.

"We have run away!" cried the little Princess as she scrambled down and ran to Dr. Cosin. "We have run away from them all and we are not going to care what they say."

"Only for a few moments," said Charles, "to bring you these." He took two boxes of chocolates from his deep coat pocket and laid them on the table beneath the kissing-ring. "And more where these came from, for the King of Spain in his pity for my poverty has sent me thirty boxes for my private consumption. There is generosity for you!" And he laughed harshly, put his arm round Lucy and kissed her and then dropping into a chair took his son upon his knee.

"Shir Da," murmured Jackie. Charles took his son's face into his hands and the two looked at each other. Jackie's hair was soft as silk against his father's fingers and his cheeks were warm. He liked the feel of his father's hands, and the loving darkness of his father's eyes, and he smiled. The King caught his breath, as the ice that had hardened over his mind and heart suddenly cracked, and found himself laughing again, not now with harshness but with hope. His laughter was infectious and quite suddenly everyone was happy, for it was Christmas day and the yule log burned in the hearth to remind them of the feast that long before the birth of Christ had been kept in celebration of light, the feast when the bonfires had been lit and worship had been offered to the sun god who so soon now would bring the lengthening days and the hope of renewal. And then, beyond hope, the spring itself, cold and sweet and pure as living water, light sparkling on wet leaves, and birds singing.

Ah, dear God, the vernal freshness of the earthly spring! Deep in his soul Dr. Cosin could hear it ringing and singing of the greatest hope of all, the hope beyond all hope, the great end, the dying of the self into God and of death into life. Only he had the power to formulate the source of the joy that was swinging the thoughts of the others from one fair memory to the other, for only the spiritually advanced move instantly out beyond time under the sudden stress of joy; the rest of us turn again to cling to the symbols. Lucy, sitting a little apart, remembered the love of William Walter that had been her first experience of the divine. Memory after memory of his fatherly love flooded into her mind, filling it with light. Possibly the world had despised him as a failure and a weakling but she and God knew that he had been no such thing.

And so a few days later, when Dr. Cosin came by appointment to Lucy's sitting room to talk to her, it was the thought of renewal that was uppermost in his mind. It was as an April child that he greeted Jackie before sending him off to find Betje, and when Lucy apologized for the lack of a fire in her room he replied, "No matter, it is warm as spring today."

Lucy herself was shivering, the more so since this was the first time Dr. Cosin had ever come to her room, and had done so now because, he said, the interruptions in his own were constant and he wished to speak with her in privacy. What had he to say to her? Was he grieved that she had not been able to come to the altar on Christmas day?

"Spring," he said, "it always returns Lucy. I want you to remember that however terrible life may seem at a given moment darkness always passes. Spring is the smile of God and his joy is entwined in the roots of our existence and cannot be destroyed. No night is without its hour of total darkness and no human soul escapes moments of total despair, but spring comes back and the God-centred soul is tough enough to cling to the knowledge and utterly refuse to let it go."

"Sir, what are you trying to tell me?" Lucy broke in abruptly. She had gone white and her face had a look of hard obstinacy that he had never seen there before. He feared she had not heard a word of what he had tried to say to her, the rumble of speech had done no more than bring some premonitory fear of her own to the surface of her mind. "If my husband is sending me away from him I will not go without Jackie."

He could only serve her by coming to the point quickly. "It is worse than you think, Lucy. Steel yourself, please. His Majesty had discovered that his marriage to you was illegal."

He did not look at her for in such a moment she needed privacy. After a long pause he heard her say, as though from miles away. "That is not true. I have my marriage lines here inside my dress."

His eyes still on the fireless grate he said, "Keep them there. Invalid though they are they may yet be of service to you. Do you wish to hear the facts at once, or would you prefer me to leave you now and tell you tomorrow"

"Tell me everything at once, please."

He told her the truth as plainly and clearly as possible. He had talked the matter over with the King again, with Sir Edward Hyde and Lord Jermyn, he had seen the various documents and read the deposition of Prodgers. He had no doubts of the truth of what he was telling her and he allowed her to have none. "Do you understand what I have told you?" he asked.

"I understand."

He looked at her now and realized that she was standing up; that she had herself in excellent control. She looked as before except that her eyes, always so soft and bright, had turned to lumps of coal in her face. "My child, do not think that the King is going to send you away. He has not said so. Your position now is the same as it has always been. It was only His Majesty and ourselves who knew the truth. I am convinced that he will always care tenderly for you and your son."

She gave her first sign of a slipping control. "Jackie!" she gasped. "Is Jackie a bastard too?" Dr. Cosin, speechless, could only nod his head. "A bastard," she replied, "and so the King has no right to him and cannot take him from me."

Dr. Cosin got up, thinking he had better call Betje, but Lucy was suddenly at the door of her bedchamber. "Lucy!" he said, "one moment. Remember that you still have your integrity. You married in good faith and are in God's eyes what your faith has made you. The judgment of men is worthless. Truth is only to be found in God, where you and your children also have your home."

She turned to the door as though she had not heard, then turned back again. "You think I have not listened to your comforting. I have heard every word and it means nothing to me."

She had gone, closing the door silently behind her. Dr. Cosin could only go too, groping his way back to his study and his prayer. Few things of late had hit him as hard as this.

The King also was much beset at this time. In deciding that now it was absolutely necessary that he should marry Mademoiselle de Montpensier he had reckoned without La Grande Mademoiselle. This latter lady had her dignity and she also had the wit to put two and two together. Charles had left her for Scotland speaking abominable French, but he had returned from that country speaking it perfectly. If his adventures had been in truth as he had reported them he had had neither leisure nor opportunity to study the language; therefore his first wooing of her had been a mockery to keep his mother quiet.

Yet she considered him improved and sometimes she encouraged him. Then she held aloof again for now that she had it in her power to marry him or not, just as she pleased, she hardly knew what she wanted. His prospects were at present worse than ever but her wealth might improve them, and she still felt herself born to be a queen. And no other king, indeed no other man, seemed to want her. She had a disfiguring skin trouble now and could find no cure for it. Yet she could not forget how he had treated her and she complained to his mother that she still had much to complain of. How, she asked the poor Queen, could she be expected to take Charles seriously when his infatuation for the Duchesse de Châtillon had flared up again? And while he still had that Mrs. Barlow and her children under the same roof with him?

The Queen saw that they must get rid of Lucy and told Charles to send her away at once. But the King was becoming less and less amenable to maternal interference. "In this weather?" he asked curtly. "A girl who for years has believed herself to be my wife? And where does she go? And who has Jackie? Be reasonable, mam. There are many things to be considered and discussed between Lucy and myself before I can let her go."

"*Let* her go? Does she wish to leave you?" asked the astonished Queen.

Her son looked at her with sombre, miserable eyes. "As to her wishes, Mam, I do not know them, but I suspect them to be much the same as mine, or yours, or of any one of us. If only it were possible to go back and begin life again, taking with us the knowledge of ourselves and the world that we had gained through our suffering. If only with that knowlege we could start afresh, our betrayals, as well as our mistakes, would be effaced." He broke off abruptly at sight of his mother's face and suddenly she was in his arms. "I am sorry, Mam," he whispered. "I am sorry."

2

As the days went on Lucy longed for Holland, the one place in Europe that felt like home. She longed for the windy, clean country as once the Israelites had longed for the promised land, but Charles like Pharaoh of old would not let her go, and neither would Dr. Cosin or Lord Taaffe. They wanted her to leave the Louvre but to stay in Paris with friends of Dr. Cosin, so that they could look after her, and they could not understand how this once so loving girl could want to cut herself adrift from those who cared for her so much.

"You do not get on well now with your aunt at Rotterdam," pleaded Charles, "and there is no one else in Holland to look after you and Jackie."

"Betje and her mother," said Lucy obstinately. "I am going back to Holland with Betje. She hates Paris as much as I do now that her husband has died. People are murdered here and they fight in the streets and there is blood as well as filth in the gutters. There is disease and starvation here and dreadful wickedness. I am taking my children away from Paris."

As she spoke this last sentence she looked at Charles, her face set and obstinate, for the fight for Jackie had already begun. Charles wanted his adored little son to live at the Louvre in the care of the Queen, so that he could see him often; Lucy was sure Jackie would be safe and happy only with his mother. Charles felt he could not force her; as she had already seen he had not the right. Nor just now had he the heart.

Lord Taaffe was also concerned for his child and just once, very tentatively, he told Lucy that if she should ever think it best his Irish home was always there to receive his daughter. The result of this remark was shattering. "Send Mary to Ireland to your *wife*?" she asked incredulously.

"I am so poor, Lucy," he pleaded. "I will send you all I can for the child but it will be so little."

"I would die rather than send Mary to your family," said Lucy bitterly, and she was too upset to tell him about her mother, and Betsi who had died. Instead she left him with a very sore place in his heart because of her bitterness. Could this be the girl who had said she would go through the rest of her life with her hand upon the cord that bound them together? "You know I would have married you if I could," he pleaded, searching for the old Lucy. "You know I would come with you and the children to Holland if I could. But I cannot leave the King."

"There is no further need to discuss the matter," she said coldly, and he went away heartbroken and uncomprehending. Dr. Cosin understood her best for he had seen how she had taken the news he had told her; the shock had come at her like a death blow. He had seen such a thing happen before. In time her loving nature would re-establish itself but for the moment she was almost without feeling, and without the power of reasonable thought. The only thing she had in the way of thinking was this obstinate conviction that whatever happened her children must remain with her, and that she must take them away from Paris.

"For the time being she must have her way," he told the two young men at last. "If she does not her reason may be affected."

"But she is not well," said Lord Taaffe. "She is still a sick girl."

"All the more reason for going back to Holland to the sea. You must remember that she comes from the sea, and the sea-born do not breathe the air of cities with ease. I hope she will return to us later, but meanwhile Betje is a sensible woman and will take care of her."

And so Lucy went, and her farewells had a strange charm and dignity, for in them something of her old loving self returned; but only as in a dream and as though she moved through the figures of a dance. She curtseyed gracefully to the Queen and thanked her for her kindness, and with Mary in her arms she knelt with equal grace, Jackie beside her, to receive Dr. Cosin's blessing. Alone for a few moments with Lord Taaffe she did not say no when he put a little old signet ring on her finger and whispered, "The thread is tied to it." Indeed she smiled and nodded and then kissed him gently. Alone with the King she knelt and kissed his hand and wished His Majesty health and prosperity. "For God's sake, Lucy, do not make it sound as though we shall never see each other again!" he said irritably. "You know that whenever I can I will come to see you and Jackie."

"I shall not see my husband again," she said, and then asked with a fear and anxiety that nearly broke his heart, "Do you wish me to return the wedding ring to you, the ruby that your father gave you?"

"No. Wear it still but do not sell it, Lucy. If things get financially worse with us all sell the diamond brooch but not my father's ruby. That must be for Jackie one day."

"But I have already sold the diamond brooch," she confessed.

He was suddenly angry. "You sold the diamond brooch without my permission! But you had no right. It was given in the first place to my son."

"Your son had to eat," Lucy reminded him. "Sir, do not let us wrangle in our last moments together. The thing is done. Your Majesty can rest assured that your son's welfare will always be my first consideration."

Then she curtseyed and left him and she had no tears on her cheeks. It was he who had to fight tears. He had so entirely believed in her. He would have staked his very soul that she would have been faithful, yet Prodgers, who had just returned to his service, informed him that he had it upon reliable information that soon after they had left for Scotland she had already begun to make a fool of Taaffe. She was just a jade like all the rest and he had been a fool to let her keep his father's ring. And whatever her rights, worse than a fool to let her take Jackie. He had thought to come back to them both and keep them for ever and now they were gone. For the first time since an hour of dreadful grief after the Battle of Worcester he broke down and wept bitterly.

Fourteen

When Charles let Lucy go it was to years of wandering in the wilderness, for she could find no abiding place in a world that no longer had the feel of home. And she was restless with exhaustion; so tired that at times everything about her looked misty; there were no clear outlines. A modern physician would have treated her for continuing shock and extreme anaemia, but the apothecary at Rotterdam whom she consulted, driven to him by the fear that she might get too ill to look after her children, thought she needed cupping. It did not seem to do her any good.

When she and Betje reached Holland Lucy went first to Aunt Margaret at Rotterdam, for she thought that Betje needed to be alone with her mother for a while. The visit was hardly a success. Peter Gosfright was kind as ever but her aunt, though she did her duty by her niece, made it clear that though a royal bastard could be forgiven a love child of lesser birth was something of an outrage. "I would not have believed it of you, Lucy," she said. "Have you told your mother?"

"No," said Lucy sadly.

"Better not at present," decided Aunt Margaret. "Both she and your grandmother are in bad health just now. How sad it is. And such a shockingly plain child. She has none of dear Jackie's beauty."

But Aunt Margaret soon ceased to think that Jackie was dear, for his behaviour was deplorable. The moment the coach had driven away from the Louvre he had begun to scream, and he had screamed on and off ever since. The Louvre had become home to him, his first true home, and he missed his grandmother, Minette and Dr. Cosin, and above all he missed his father. He was not well at Rotterdam, and ceaselessly he wept for Shir Da and demanded to go home. In despair Lucy packed her boxes and went to the farm at Scheveningen.

There her welcome was warm and she had a period of peace. Vrouw Flinck had no reproaches for her, only love and compassion, and Mary was made as welcome as Jackie and was equally loved. Both children flourished in the good air and Jackie grew happy again; though still he missed Shir Da. But it was too good to last. Mijnheer Flinck fell seriously ill and needed quiet, and Lucy removed herself and her children to lodgings at The Hague that Anne found for her.

Anne had heard of Lucy's arrival at Scheveningen and had visited her there. Betje, never quite trusting Anne, had been sorry, but Lucy had been touched by Anne's pleasure at seeing her again and had turned moth-like to her flame of kindness. Anne that day had been very kind, and she was kind in helping Lucy to move into the lodgings with the children and sorry to see her exhaustion. "You are not well, madam," she said.

"I have not recovered yet from my baby," said Lucy.

"You said that after Jackie," Anne reminded her. "Madam, you are not able to look after yourself and your children alone. I am tired of working at the Embassy. I will come and be with you again."

"But Anne, I cannot afford to pay you proper wages. His Majesty is now so very poor. And he wanted me to stay in Paris. I came here against his wishes and I cannot ask him for too much."

"I will come for half the wages that I had before," said Anne. "Just for the pleasure of being with you and my dear Jackie."

Betje, when she heard this, said quickly, "Do not employ her."

"I have already said I will have her back," said Lucy. "It seems that I cannot manage alone until I am stronger and she must be truly fond of me to come for so little money. And I have always felt that we must love each other."

Betje clucked her tongue in annoyance but she said no more. All this talk about love. She was a loving woman herself but she kept her affections well leashed to her reason, like good dogs, but Lucy's were all over the place like spilled wine. And what good did it do? Lord Taaffe had done her no good, though Mary was a nice little thing, and Anne would do her no good. But it was useless to argue with sentimentalists of Lucy's type. They spilled themselves out and there it was.

But Anne was no sentimentalist and she was fond of money, as Betje had discovered in Paris when she had seen the girl beguiling the customers and pocketing the tips, so what was she after? Betje worried for a while and then became absorbed in nursing her father and comforting her mother. She was not by nature a worrier and if she worried it was about one thing at a time.

Lucy soon found that Mary was a touchstone for friends. Because of Mary she found that acquaintances she had made in the days when she was received by the Queen of Bohemia were cold to her now. Herman Vingboon could take Mary with a twinkle in the eye but his wife could not. Lucy drew in upon herself, absorbed in her children and her friendship with Anne, and in the letters she received from Dr. Cosin and Lord Taaffe.

Dr. Cosin wrote short formal letters in exquisite handwriting, enquiring into the progress of her prayers and studies, requesting that she keep her life blameless and her courage high. Each letter ended with the request that she would always endeavour to keep him informed of her welfare and tell him if he could ever be of service to her.

Lord Taaffe's letters accompanied the sum of money he sent regularly for Mary. Though it was small it never failed to come, but she often wondered what sacrifices he had to make to send it at all. Only once did he send her a sum on the King's behalf, with apologies from Charles that it could be no more, but it was all he could lay his hands on at present. This was the only time that Lord Taaffe, to excuse the King, mentioned their poverty in a letter. It was increasing. The winter was very cold and the King's clothes were practically in rags.

Then he went on to tell her the gossip of Paris. Mademoiselle had made it finally clear that she was not going to share her wealth with a pauper king, and His Majesty was divided between joy at the loss of the woman and acute anxiety at the loss of the money. The Marquis of Ormonde, Lord Lieutenant of Ireland and Lord Taaffe's idol, was now sharing cheap lodgings with the Chancellor. It was a sight, he said, to see the two friends walking the streets of Paris together, the short red-faced Chancellor hobbling along with the help of a stick and the tall fair Marquis striding with ease; their feet were the only means of conveyance that they could afford but the feet of the Marquis were in better case. The King kept wonderfully cheerful, he was developing a most excellent wit and hiring himself out to be entertaining at parties.

Lord Taaffe had thought this last bit of information would make Lucy laugh, but actually it brought on a fit of weeping. How low could one fall for want of money? What might she herself do or become if the time came when she would not get enough food for the children?

It was soon after this that the rumours about her began to circulate. She herself was not aware of them at first, even though she found herself increasingly shunned. Then she had a letter from Aunt Margaret that stunned her. "Niece," wrote Aunt Margaret, "your uncle and I are increasingly distressed by the stories of your reckless behaviour which our neighbours are not slow to impart to us. We know how great are the difficulties of your position but we do implore you to be more circumspect in your manner of life. You will know to what we refer. Your uncle thinks it advisable that you and your children should return to Rotterdam and make your home with us."

Lucy replied that she did not know to what her aunt referred, that as far as she knew her quiet life with her maid and her children had been all that her uncle and aunt would approve of. She thanked them for the invitation but reminded them that Jackie had not been well at Rotterdam. She thought the proximity of the canal had not been good for his health and that the King would wish him to remain at The Hague. To this letter there was no reply from Aunt Margaret, but

THE CHILD FROM THE SEA

Peter sent her a generous sum of money with the request that she should not tell her aunt what he had done, and with loving humiliation she accepted it for the children's sake.

She tried hard not to be miserable about the rumours, since they were not true, but one day she was too unhappy to keep her trouble to herself and she spoke of it to her maid. Anne was sympathetic and after a little thought she said to Lucy, "Madam, since you have lost your old friends turn to those who do smile upon you. It may be that they need your friendship." That seemed to Lucy a right and loving suggestion and she followed it. She befriended several poor souls who were down on their luck and she learned much from their courage and patience; and Mr. Prodgers, to whom Anne wrote regularly, learned much about the sort of company now frequented by Mrs. Barlow.

His motive in endeavouring to destroy Lucy's reputation was simple. He wished to serve the King, the only person in the world whom he truly loved. He had always suspected that Lucy might prove an embarrassment to His Majesty and now she had done more than embarrass him, she had separated him from his son. Charles, having proved in Scotland that Prodgers was a loyal servant, had talked to him openly of his longing for Jackie. To Taaffe he could not speak of it since by mutual consent the subject of Lucy and her children was not mentioned between them; and speak of it to someone he must, it pained him so.

"Your Majesty should simply take possession of your son," Prodgers had said. "The problem is perfectly simple. You are the King."

"As he is not my legal son I have not the right," Charles had replied. "If Mrs. Barlow were a woman of dissolute character, if she were doing my son definite harm, then rights or no rights it would be my duty to remove him. But such is not the case. She is a good mother and I cannot break her heart by taking her son away from her."

After that conversation Prodgers's course was perfectly clear to him. Anne's course was equally clear, since in spreading damaging lies about Lucy, and repeating the results of

them to Prodgers, she was acting under his instructions; and
he rewarded her well, being himself well paid as a Royalist
agent. But her motives were less simple than his. She was
nearer to loving Prodgers than any man she had ever met. A
clever man himself he respected her powers. He could have
made a very good secret agent out of her, he considered, for
she had coolness, quick wits and courage. He thought that he
might yet do so and he took the trouble to attach her to him
and to let her see the genuine admiration he felt for her and
the reliance he placed upon her. This was something new to
her and she responded from some deep place of unsatisfied
longing within herself that nothing had touched as yet except
her affection for Lucy.

And it was here that she became more than confused. She
was pulled in two by her bondage to Prodgers and her love-
hate for Lucy. Service to Lucy satisfied her as service to her
mother had once done but her jealousy of Lucy's beauty and
the pain of her bitterness because Lucy had had so much and
she so little were eased by the harm she was doing to her
through Prodgers. And then she did not want to leave the children; in some vicarious way they seemed hers. The confusions
were many but could not prevail against the possessive presence of Prodgers. He had immense power. He did not need to
be physically present with Anne to be in command of her
mind and will.

Quite suddenly Lucy found she wanted to leave The Hague.
She had had a sad letter from her mother telling her that Mrs.
Gwinne had died and that Elizabeth herself was feeling exceedingly unwell. The latter piece of news did not disturb her
too much, since her mother was always feeling unwell, but she
had many bouts of crying over her grandmother's death.
Then came a letter from Dr. Cosin and it too contained bad
news. The King had had a serious illness. He was now recovered but it had left him in great depression. A treaty had been
signed between France and the English Commonwealth. He
was banished from France and was going to Germany.

"I begged that I might accompany His Majesty, as my Lord
Taaffe and his other friends are of course doing," wrote Dr.

Cosin, "but he wishes me to remain in Paris to care for the exiles here and I must obey. And now I come to the matter that concerns yourself. My child, are there persons at The Hague who do not wish you well? I ask because rumours of compromising behaviour on your part have reached the community here; I regret to say that they have reached the King. I do not believe them, and I have told His Majesty that I do not, but it may be that your open and affectionate nature has led you to some indiscretions which have been misconstrued, and I beg you to be on your guard and to remember the conversation you and I had together during our drive from Saint-Germain to Paris. My child, your situation is extremely difficult and causes me much anxiety. I am always your friend and father in God and I wish you and your children would return to Paris and remain under my care."

Just for a moment Lucy wished it too, believing she could almost face Paris again to be under his wise guidance. But the Queen Dowager was there and the Queen would try to take Jackie from her and so she could not go. But she cried bitterly with longing for him, and with sorrow for the King in illness and banishment. But why should she stay on in this place that once had been so kind to her but now was not kind? She would always love The Hague but now it seemed not to love her. The only real friends she had now were Betje and her mother, but Mijnheer Flinck had died and Betje had married again. She still had their love but she did not see them often. And there was another reason for leaving The Hague. Jackie was growing a big boy, beautiful, adorable but naughty, and perhaps because of the rumours he had no suitable friends. But where could she find them? In her dilemma she turned to Anne for advice.

Anne said at once, "Brussels."

"Why Brussels?" asked the astonished Lucy.

"When we sailed in the *Sea-Horse* from Holland to France with my Lord Wilmot I used to talk with one of the seamen, the one who had charge of the captain's cabin and waited upon you there. As a boy he had been in the service of Captain Axel's family in their house at Brussels. He talked much of the city and its beauties and I have a fancy to see the place. You know, madam, how I love to travel and see other countries and other cities: I have a great fancy to see Brussels."

Anne's eyes were shining and Lucy said, "We will go there." And then she remembered that Captain Axel had told her she would always be welcome at his home. Madam Axel would perhaps be kind to her and help her find lodgings and friends for Jackie. With her usual travail with the pen she wrote to her and received a kind but formal letter from Madame saying that she would be pleased to welcome Mrs. Barlow and her children, and help them find suitable lodgings.

Charles had impressed upon Lucy that he must always know where his son was and she must never move from one place to another without writing to tell him. And so again she took up her pen and spent half a night in literary composition and anguish—the anguish because once more she must ask him for money. When her journey was accomplished there would be little left from Peter Gosfright's gift.

2

At first life in Brussels was almost happy. Madame Axel and her husband, who in the first place had agreed to have Lucy only to honour their son's promise, found her different from the girl they had expected. Knowing that Jackie was the King's child they took it for granted that Mary was too and they felt honoured by the presence of two royal children under their roof. They found Lucy lodgings not far from the English Embassy, and gave her an introduction to an English family living at Brussels whose children were of a suitable age to play with Jackie.

Lucy was with them one day when they were visited by Sir Henry de Vic, the elderly bachelor ambassador, and he took a great fancy to pretty Mrs. Barlow and invited her to a party at the Embassy. She went, and very soon there was between them that amused and bantering tenderness that can spring up between an ageing man and a young woman; a battledore and shuttlecock game of love played across the gulf of years that divided them. With Lucy there was something deeper because she was secretly so afraid and exhausted, and Sir Henry with his dignity and assured position gave her a feeling of refuge and strength. And he reminded her of Lord Carbery. They were not the same type of man for Sir Henry was neither a scholar nor a great aristocrat, but a red-faced jolly elderly gentleman who owed his position to a gift for diplomatic kindness, but the two were alike in their tenderness for female youth, and their love of children.

Sir Henry was enchanted by Jackie and Mary. He sat them on his knees and put sugar plums in their mouths, opened expectantly like the yawning caverns of young birds, and he took them round his garden holding a hand of each and discoursing to them in the language he kept for his horses and dogs and for young children, a strange affair of enquiring clicks and explanatory grunts, endearments and soft neighings of amusement that they seemed to understand perfectly. Lucy confided in Sir Henry more than she realized. She even told him about the rumours that had made her so miserable and driven her from The Hague to Brussels. He told her that any pretty young woman who had been a mistress of a king was sure to be bothered by the pestiferous things, pinched her cheek and told her to regard them no more than she would regard gnats on a summer's day.

But what she had to regard were her debts to the Brussels' trades people. But she was not worrying too much. The King would have received her appeal for help by now and as he was soon to be with his sister he would be able to borrow from her if he was out of pocket himself; the Princess would help them for Jackie's sake for she also had a little son. And she was cheered too by a happy thing that happened to her just now; a small thing but somehow so delightful that she was reminded of what Dr. Cosin had said about the perpetual return of spring. It was too small a thing to be called a spring but it was warm and happy.

She received a letter early one morning from Sir Henry asking her to dine with him that day to meet a friend of his, a young Englishman whose home was at Antwerp. He travelled a certain amount for his business and was in Brussels for a few days. His name was Harvey. She remembered the name and though it brought no image to her mind she was thrilling with pleasure as Anne helped her to dress. The dresses that Charles had given her were shabby now but the blue one she had worn when he took her to visit the Queen of Bohemia still matched her eyes, and she wore the Queen's jewels and her ruby ring.

Sir Henry had sent his own coach to rattle her over the cobbles to the party but she hardly noticed the jolting. Indeed it seemed to her to travel smoothly as a boat upon a river borne by the tide, and the Brussels streets washed by a shower of rain shone as silverly as flowing water. There were patches of blue sky between the clouds and she thought suddenly of London and the Thames, and felt a sharp pang of longing for England.

There were a mere half-dozen guests at Sir Henry's party, all known to her except a tall man with a pleasant plain freckled face who bowed before her with a twinkle in his eye. Sir Henry was an accomplished host. "Mr. Harvey," he told Lucy in tones just loud enough to be heard by his other guests, "is the nephew of a man whose name is well known in the cultured and scientific circles of Europe, Dr. William Harvey, physician to his late majesty King Charles the First of England."

There was a murmur of pleasure from the guests; they had never heard of Dr. Harvey but Sir Henry's kindly glance had included them in the cultured and scientific circles and they went happily to dinner. No one minds shining in the reflected glory of a distinguished relative and Mr. Harvey was happy too. Lucy would have been equally happy only the roar of lions was echoing in the caverns of her memory and it scared her a little. She was seated beside Mr. Harvey at dinner and her eyes rested upon his freckles with a puzzled expression.

"Smuts," he said. "Smuts, a Welsh boy. Do your memories stir?"

They not only stirred, they came suddenly flooding over her like the silver water upon which a short while ago the coach had seemed to float. She was a small girl again, taken by Robert Sidney to visit the lions at the Tower of London, and when she had gone home again she had sat before the fire and told her grandmother and Nan-Nan about her day. About this day she could not tell them. Or could she? If tonight she talked to them in her bed would they hear? With her usual directness she startled poor Smuts by suddenly asking, "Do the dead know about the good things that happen to us?"

He was acutely embarrassed and swallowed a fish-bone. When he had succeeded in washing it down with a drink of wine he said, "I cannot tell you, madam. I am a business man and not a necromancer. But you had remembered that day and think it good that we should meet again?"

"I have remembered it all," she said, "and I think it good we should meet again, but not good that you should call me madam. I am Lucy who looked at lions with you. Smuts, before you came to live at Antwerp, did you ever see my brother Justus?"

This extremely fragile girl had a mind like quicksilver, he realized. His own was sound but slow. He did not know how hers had got from the dead to Justus but he moved his after it as well as he could. "I met him once or twice, I think, but I knew your elder brother better." He looked down at his wine-glass. "Perhaps I ought to tell you, Lucy, that I am not a politically-minded man but as far as I have any politics I think like your brother Richard."

"I do not mind," said Lucy. "What can we do, any of us, but go where our thinking takes us? Smuts, if you are not a Royalist perhaps you go sometimes to England?"

"Only occasionally," he said, "and then only on business. I may be going this year."

"If you do," said Lucy, "and if you see Richard, give him my love. I never write to him for I am a bad correspondent. I write occasionally to Justus, and he to me, but he is a bad correspondent too and somehow our letters make little contact. But yet we still love each other so much."

She was suddenly near tears and Smuts was again embarrassed. "If I go to London I will make a point of seeing

Richard," he said, and he meant what he said. He thought Lucy was one of the loveliest girls he had ever seen but she looked delicate and defenceless. Rumour had already told him that the King had tired of her. Richard should come over and look after her, and so he would tell him if he could find him. Justus too, but Justus was a Royalist and might not be granted a permit to leave the country.

It became their duty to talk to their neighbours at the table but later in the evening they found themselves sitting in the window together and Smuts said, "It is an odd thing about one's childhood memories. They either vanish altogether or they are more vivid than yesterday. I remember every detail of that visit to the Tower of London. Do you?"

"It has come back to me," said Lucy. "The Tower frightened me; it seemed to menace me in some way and I think I tried to forget it. I don't want to think of the Tower itself, only the river, and being up on the ramparts and seeing London sparkling in a burst of sunlight. The sun pushed through the mist like a blessing hand with fingers spread out, and everything was made new. You told me something your uncle said about newness, but I don't remember it."

Smuts remembered. "That we are made new with every heart beat, as the world with every spring. New birth is the rhythm of the world."

When they parted that evening he gave her a card with an address on it. "It is my home at Antwerp," he said. "If you come there at any time my wife and I will be glad to see you and help you in any difficulty. And I would like to say that though I am something of a Puritan I honour and admire our King. I would never take part in any action that injured him and if I could serve him in any way I would gladly do it." He bowed to her and she curtseyed and drove away in the coach through streets now lit by moonlight, so that she thought again of London and the silver Thames. What I would give to go back and see it again, she thought. I would like to see London again before I die.

3

After that evening thoughts of London seemed coupled in her mind with thoughts of death, and then came a letter from Richard, including a loving little note from Justus, to tell her that her mother had died. It was not the grief that her father's death had been, for she had never loved her mother as much as her father, but she remembered now the times when her mother had herself been most loving; their times in the bower at Roch, the times when they had clung to each other after Nan-Nan had died, her mother's selfless farewell to her when she left England. "That was my mother," she said to herself over and over again, "that was my true mother," and she was filled with sorrow because their love had lain only in pools and had not spread its living water to refresh their whole life together.

And then she remembered her father and mother standing together after the wheel had come off the coach on the journey to Golden Grove, united in sefless love and fear for their unborn child. She would remember them always so, she told herself, only without the fear that belongs to earth, retaining only the love that is of heaven. She longed for Justus but she knew there was no hope of seeing him because he had told her in his letter that he had applied for a permit to come to her but it had been refused.

Her mother's death made her feel anxious as well as sad. Her life was one long fight against exhaustion, headaches, dizziness and perpetual backaches, a fight that day by day she always won, but nevertheless she began to worry again about the children. All their security was in her. Jackie in particular clung to her like a limpet. He had been moved from place to place so often in his short life. He had been introduced to his father and loved him and then been taken from him. Sometimes he was treated like a prince and sometimes not. He had no settled home or permanent father as other boys had and it worried him. Why was Shir Da not with them? he kept asking his mother, why did they not go back to that big place with the garden and the trees? He had liked that. She promised him

636

that he would see Shir Da again and said that perhaps one day he would go back to the big house, but he was a sensitive child as well as a nervous and emotional one and he picked up her fears and uncertainties and did not rely upon what she said. But upon his mother herself he relied utterly. She was always there, always loving and always the same. Only with her did he feel safe. If she left him too long he started to scream.

Mary was such a contented, courageous little person that her mother hoped she was unharmed by her uncertain existence. She appeared so. She was one of those who knew how to polish the passing moment and was always absorbed in the practical tasks in which she delighted, washing the faces of her dollies and putting them to bed in the wooden cradle, talking to them and singing them to sleep, trotting after her mother and Anne as they went about their tasks and trying to be helpful, for she was a selfless child. But inside herself she was uneasy too when her mother was away from her. She would try to comfort Jackie when he screamed, patting his wet face and kissing him and trying not to mind when he pushed her roughly away and she fell on the floor. She knew how he felt. Life seemed to hold no real certainty that when a person went out she would come in again. Unlike Jackie she had no memory of her father that could be called a memory, though she had a hole in her somewhere from which a strength had been withdrawn, and perhaps because of this her love for Sir Henry de Vic was even greater than Jackie's. Both children loved him and Lucy was aware that his grandfatherly figure was without doubt giving them something they badly needed, and she was deeply grateful to him.

4

And then one morning Anne came to Lucy, her cheeks pink with excitement, and said that a messenger had come from the King. His name was Captain Daniel O'Neil and he requested the honour of an interview with Mrs. Barlow. Lucy could hardly control her voice to say with composure, "Ask him to come up, please, Anne." Daniel O'Neil. She did not know the name. Charles must have a new servant.

A moment later Captain O'Neil was bowing before her. She curtseyed to him, instructed the children to make their bow and curtsey and sent Anne to fetch wine. Then she seated him in her own chair by the window and sat opposite to him, her hands folded in her lap, observing him as carefully as a good hostess can allow herself to do while he laughed and joked with the children, and paid her compliments so carefully balanced between sincerity and fulsomeness that she did not know what to think of them, just as she did not know what to think of the man himself.

He was still young and had lean good looks but his eyes were reckless and his mouth hard. He had charm and knew how to use it but it had become a little tarnished with too much use. He was well dressed and Lucy always slightly distrusted a well-dressed exile, for it costs money to be well dressed and where did he get it from? She remembered Charles without a shirt to his back and Lord Taaffe going hungry to give her a bottle of perfume, and she suddenly did not like this man. As though he read her mind he said, "Of late years I have been principally attached to the Princess of Orange, but His Majesty has now honoured me by appointing me one of the grooms of his bedchamber." That was it, Princess Mary paid her servants well. Lucy was ashamed of herself and asked gently, "Is the King well?"

"Yes, madam, His Majesty is well and he sends you this." Anne had now taken the children away for their walk and they were alone; he leaned towards Lucy with a smile that suddenly won her heart, laid a heavy purse in her lap and looked tactfully out of the window. He was kind and his face had lighted up at the mention of Charles as though he loved him. It was so much easier for Lucy to trust than distrust that her shame increased.

"Did the King write to me?" she whispered, and she made no attempt to keep the longing out of her voice.

"No, madam, he is much pressed for time, but he sent you a message. He is at this moment travelling by water from

Namur to Liège, where he will break his journey before going on to Spa to join the Princess. While he is at Liège he wishes you to bring his son to see him. I have already hired a coach for the conveyance of yourself and the child and I and my servant will ride with you. Can you be ready to leave tomorrow?"

For a few moments Lucy found it difficult to draw breath, she was so painfully and desperately happy. And then so afraid. And then again so happy. But what of Mary?

"My little girl," she said. "I have never left her. May she come too?"

"No, madam," said Captain O'Neil firmly. "One child is enough. Your maid looks a sensible girl, able to care for your daughter, and the little girl herself looks sensible."

"She is," said Lucy, considering the problem. "And she has a serene disposition and she is fond of Anne. I could not have left Jackie but I think I can leave her. I will come, Captain O'Neil."

"There is no question about that, madam," he said with amusement. "The King's orders have to be obeyed." He finished his wine and got up. "May I fetch you and your son at eight o'clock tomorrow morning? May I say how greatly I look forward to the journey in your company?"

But he did not enjoy the journey as much as Lord Taaffe had once enjoyed a similar one, for the spectacle of a mother so wrapped up in her son that all other males about her were degraded to the position of mere servants to one small boy did not appeal to his temperament. He and Jackie took a mutual dislike to each other upon this journey. Jackie was quite aware that the man was trying to steal his mother's attention from him and the man thought the boy a damnably spoilt little brat. And in this opinion he was quite right.

The King was only to be in the town for a short time and Lucy wondered if she would see him at all, for Captain O'Neil took Jackie to the inn where he was staying and she was left behind alone in their lodgings through hours which seemed interminable. Then Captain O'Neil came back. "His Majesty thinks it would be best if you fetched Jackie yourself. The boy is so enamoured of his father that we fear screams if you are not there."

"Has Jackie already screamed?" she asked anxiously, as they went down the stairs.

"Only alone in the coach with me," said Captain O'Neil grimly. "He had stopped by the time I delivered him to his father." He did not tell Lucy that the application of the flat of his hand to the brat's posterior had so astonished Jackie that his roars had ceased on the instant.

It was only a short drive and then Lucy found herself going up a wide staircase. Captain O'Neil opened a door and they went in to a large sunny room where Charles and Jackie were alone together. "Maman! Maman!" cried Jackie, scrambling off his father's knee and racing to meet his mother. He was a bilingual child, chattering in French and English, with Welsh and Dutch words stuck in here and there like currants in a cake, but French predominated. Then he took his mother's hand and pulled her across the room to where the King was now standing silently by the window. Lucy curtseyed and kissed his hand and through the buzzing in her ears and the beating of her heart heard him telling Jackie to go with Captain O'Neil to the next room. "Do as I say, my son. You will see your mother again in a few minutes," he said with firm gentleness. To her astonishment Jackie instantly did as he was told.

She was a little dizzy when she rose from her curtsey and Charles took her arm and put her kindly into a chair, but he continued to stand, looking down at her. "You are still not strong, Lucy," he said. "I am sorry." But when she looked up at him she saw no sorrow. No look of youth had come back to his face and it was already beginning to look as though carved out of dark wood, hard and firm, life in the eyes alone. All the old charm would be there once he laughed and talked, she knew, but she could not win him even to smile at her when she thanked him with all her heart for his gift. "I am in funds at the moment," was all he said. "My sister has been generous. Lucy, I have only a little time and we must talk of the boy."

"Are you not pleased with him?" she asked anxiously.

"He is a beautiful boy and you have done well in your care of him. He is healthy, good-natured and loving. But totally ignorant. I find he can neither read nor write."

"I am trying to teach him," said Lucy. "But I have never been a good scholar, as you know, and so perhaps I am not a good teacher. And, sir, he is still so small."

"Old enough to read and write," said the King. "Lucy, I have a proposition to make to you."

"Will you not sit down, sir?" pleaded Lucy. "Standing you seem so far away from me."

He sat, but it seemed to bring him no nearer. It seemed that Dr. Cosin was right and the rumours had reached him. And I do not know even what they are, she thought, so how can I defend myself? It is better to be silent. Defences and excuses are contemptible. It is better to be silent. Her thoughts could get no further for Charles was speaking again.

"Lucy, it is not possible for you to care for our son as you would wish to do. He needs education and discipline and a settled home and you can give him none of these things. The life you both lead is good for neither of you. Lucy, for his own sake let me have Jackie. Leave him here with me now. I join my sister tomorrow and she will help me to look after him. Then we will send him to my mother in Paris, and I will have him with me always as soon as my prospects improve. That I swear to you. Though why should I need to swear it when you know he is the light of my eyes? And you, Lucy, why do you not go home to England to your mother?"

"She is dead," said Lucy.

There was a silence. "I am sorry," said Charles. "But you have other relatives. If Mary is a difficulty her father's home is open to her."

"Small children should be with their mother," said Lucy, "and I trust neither of mine to anyone but myself. For Jackie to have a tutor and a settled home it is not necessary for him to be taken from me. If you would give me a small but dependable pension I could provide him with both. Sir, I know your poverty, but until we find ourselves actually in the gutter there is always something we can do without; a horse, perhaps, or a dog or a bottle of wine, or even a woman. Women are expensive. Surely you could deny yourself for your son who is, you say, the light of your eyes?"

She was so exhausted that she had lost control of herself and pent-up bitterness that she did not know she had in her was pouring out. Her face was like marble with the bitterness and obstinacy together. He was very angry. What right had she of all people to talk to him in this way? He knew the truth about her now; Prodgers had made it indisputably clear and it had nearly broken his heart. He had to master the anger before he could speak again. "Lucy, until now I thought I had no right to take your child from you, but I now believe that for his sake it is my duty to command you to give me my son. And as his father I do so command you."

Lucy had not yet regained control either of herself, or of the bitterness. "Am I owed nothing?" she asked. "Do you ever think how happy my life might have been if I had not met you? My father could see nothing but disaster in our love, and he warned me, but I would not listen. Now I have lost honour and good repute, and home and health." She paused, and found herself gasping for breath.

Charles was on his feet looking for the silver bell that would stop her tongue and rid him of her presence. Remorse and despair were breaking over him again, the same agony he had felt when he lay sobbing in the woods, reliving the degradation that had brought him to the carnage of Worcester. Was this what it meant to be the King? He felt as helpless in this mess of his own evil as a fly in a spider's web. He found the bell and rang it wildly. "For God's sake keep the child, Lucy," he said. "And go."

She walked down the stairs with Jackie and O'Neil with perfect composure. She would not have believed it possible but composure was necessary for Jackie's peace of mind. A group of men were talking in the hall of the inn when they passed through. One detached himself and came to them and greeted her and Jackie. It was Lord Taaffe. He looked at her face with concern, took her arm and went with her to the door of the coach, while O'Neil went tactfully round to the other side to speak to the coachman.

Out in the clear air and the sun with his strong hand gripping her arm she felt better. He had not written her a real letter for a long time, only brief, kind notes with the money for Mary. He would not have failed to hear the rumours and she could neither look at him nor defend herself. Even as a child she had never known how to do it, and now she could hardly control her trembling sufficiently to speak to him of his child. "I would have brought Mary with me if I could," she said, "but it was not allowed. She is a darling little girl. She has a wonderful character, strong yet loving, and she looks after me."

"Tell her she must always do that," said Lord Taffe, and he helped Lucy into the coach, lifted Jackie in after her and stood back as the coachman came to slam the door. For the first time she looked at him and tried to smile. Their eyes met and his face softened. He smiled back and raised his hand in farewell. Lucy did not know what had been in her own eyes, but looking into his she had looked into the depths of a charity too great and too humble to concern itself with blame or criticism, and she drove away knowing that even if she never saw him again in this world, yet all was well. She leaned back in her corner of the coach and found she was longing for Mary.

5

Back again in Brussels Lucy found that Mary had been longing for her. When she arrived Mary ran to her and buried her face in her mother's cloak. Lucy had to sit down and take the child on her lap before she could lift the small face and look at it. Tears were running down Mary's face but she was making no sound. "Has she been well, Anne?" Lucy asked.

Anne looked round from her boisterous reunion with Jackie to say, "Quite well, and good and sensible, but very quiet. It has been her first parting from you, madam."

Lucy was astonished. She had not known that Mary loved her so much. Then as the days passed, and Mary trotted after her wherever she went about their rooms, she began to understand from her daughter's stumbling conversation that she and Anne had been entertaining a visitor in her absence, a man who had come with the other man in the coach but not gone away in it with maman and Jackie. He had given Mary sugar plums but Mary "not like". It was plain that the little girl was disturbed and had feared this man. Yet unlike the highly-strung Jackie she was never afraid. "And I had a bad dream," she whispered to her mother.

"What was it, my darling?"

But Mary once more hid her face against her mother, clinging like a bur, and she could not tell. Lucy asked Anne, "Who is this man Mary talks about?"

"Mr. Prodgers, madam," said Anne cheerfully. "He came here with Captain O'Neil on some business for His Majesty and came in several times to see me and Mary."

"Why did you not tell me before?"

"I would have told you in good time, madam."

"And if he came with Captain O'Neil why did he not ask to see me before I left?"

"I do not know, madam."

"Is he still in Brussels?"

"I do not know. I have not seen him again."

"Did Captain O'Neil, after he brought me back here, go and see him before returning to the King?"

"Madam, how can I tell you when I do not even know if he stayed in Brussels?"

"Anne, what was this nightmare that frightened Mary?"

"Did she have a nightmare? Poor poppet, I did not know. It may have been because she missed you; that and too many sugar plums from Mr. Prodgers."

Lucy told herself that she was a fool to be suddenly so suspicious of she knew not what. And why torment poor Anne about it? It was nothing to do with her.

Yet as autumn passed into winter Lucy found herself once more shunned by friends whom she had made; and Jackie and Mary were no longer welcome at their houses to play with their children. The rumours had begun again. Her sense of alienation and homelessness, rooted not only in the fact that her husband had repudiated her but perhaps even more in the fact that her husband was not her husband, deepened into a darkness of the mind that not even her children could alleviate.

At last one day she could not bear it and she went to see Sir Henry de Vic and told him about the rumours. He had of course heard them and had been distressed. When Lucy told him they were unfounded he believed her, for he knew her well enough now to trust as well as love her. His faith and affection were more to her that day than just a candleflame of kindness; it was as though from her own outer darkness she looked through a half-open door into a warm firelit home. Before she knew what she was doing she told him all her troubles; though not about her marriage to the King that was not a marriage, for Charles would not wish that. Sir Henry held her hand as they sat before the fire but was silent for a time. "These rumours must be stopped," he said at last. "My dear, I must think. Come again tomorrow." Then he sent her home in his coach and did his thinking.

When she came again he said, "Lucy, will you do me the honour of becoming my wife?"

The room swam round Lucy. A voice hammered in her brain, "Charles, I belong to Charles," and yet at the same time the door that had been half-open swung wide and the warmth that flooded out was hardly to be distinguished from the flood of warm tears that was rising in her. She could not speak and Sir Henry misconstrued her silence.

"I am an old man, I know, but I can protect you and the children whom I also love."

Sir Henry was not a Welshman and was astonished to find Lucy sobbing on the floor at his feet, her head on the arms she had laid across his knees. He could not know it was the position she had taken up years ago in the harness room at Broad Clyst, with William when he had warned her that Charles would bring her only sorrow, but he sensed that she had come to him as a terrified child to its father and his hands were on her hair in the manner of a father. Yet he had no more parted her from Charles than William had done years ago.

"You are good," she said when the tears were over, "and I want to marry you. It will be peace and safety for me and the children and I could make you happy. If I did not believe I could make you happy I could not do it."

"You will make me happy," he assured her.

"But Charles," she said. "It seems as though I am still his property. I cannot do it without his permission."

"It should be easy to come by. The King is my good friend and he has always shown me kindness. It is best, I think, that we should go ourselves to see him. Letters can be misconstrued. He is at Cologne now but you will not get my old bones on the road in this weather. As soon as it improves we will go. Meanwhile you and I and the children will be seen together as much as possible, and that will give you some protection from the rumours."

Actually it only changed their tenor. Sir Henry's kindliness had already won him the reputation of being a good-natured old fool, and the fact that Lucy was now obviously under his protection did not improve her reputation but merely worsened his. He was an old dotard. Could he not see what the girl was? Brussels hummed with gossip that spread to The Hague. The Queen of Bohemia heard it, and through her Princess Mary, and through her the King, who felt a bitter anger. The sadness of his parting with Lucy had made him miserable for days; yet she had gone straight back to de Vic. And de Vic was his friend, he had thought. Who else among his friends was going to grab his girl? The surface of his mind was so busy grappling with his many problems that he failed to notice the running to and fro of the thoughts below. The surface of his mind had repudiated Lucy. The thoughts below made possessive circles about her.

As soon as the weather improved Lucy and Sir Henry set out. Lucy would not leave Mary behind so Anne and both children travelled with them, and when Sir Henry and Lucy went to visit the King they took Jackie with them so that his

father should see him again. It was Sir Henry's kindly thought
and not a very subtle one. When Charles saw his son come in
holding the hands of his mother on one side and Sir Henry on
the other jealousy boiled up in him. Jackie made it worse by
not immediately running to his father. He was going through
a period of shyness. He smiled at Shir Da, then finding that his
mother had withdrawn her support to make her curtsey he
clung with both hands to Sir Henry. It appeared that he had
now found the father figure he had craved.

"Jackie, make your bow to His Majesty," said Lucy, and
Jackie came forward and bowed and then looked at his father
with a face of delight. But the harm was done.

Charles might have been kinder had he been feeling less
wretched, but his own life just now was a very fair imitation of
hell. The young Duke of Gloucester, set free at last and returned to his mother, had been nearly torn in pieces as the
focus of a great war of religion. Who was to have his soul, his
mother or Dr. Cosin? Large forces had been embattled upon
each side, no holds had been barred, and for the exiled King,
only able to express himself upon paper, it had not been
funny. Prince Henry was now safe from his Catholic mother
in the care of his Protestant sister, but the King had other
troubles. All his plans were turning to dust and ashes, all his
hopes withering, and he could never forget day or night that
in England men who worked for him were imprisoned, were
tortured, and died. It was no moment for him to be confronted
with Lucy and Sir Henry and with anger and contempt he
refused their request.

"Why have you left your post in Brussels without my permission?" he demanded of Sir Henry. "I ask that you will
return there immediately."

The terrible little interview lasted only ten minutes, then
the King rang the silver bell and they were dismissed. He
made no attempt to keep Jackie with him. He simply wanted
the three of them out of his sight as quickly as possible.

At the inn, before they started their journey back to
Brussels, Sir Henry was at first almost incoherent with anger.
"What right has he to forbid us to marry?" he kept asking

Lucy. "Is your happiness nothing to him? We will marry. We have a perfect right to do so."

"Your career will be wrecked," Lucy told him. "Charles is King and I discovered long ago that when he thinks of himself as King he deifies himself. In letting me keep Jackie he did not do that. He thought of himself then, I think, simply as a man who had done me wrong. Now he has acted as King."

"We will marry," repeated Sir Henry.

"No," said Lucy, white-faced and obstinate. "I cannot do it."

The door that had opened showing her warmth and light and safety was closing, yet she felt something almost like relief. Her hidden thoughts too, like those of Charles, made rings about him in the deep places of her mind. Down there he was her husband still.

Fifteen

I

After the return from Cologne Lucy found life in Brussels impossible. Sir Henry was perpetually worrying about her and begging her to reconsider her decision. For his sake chiefly she wanted to go, but she found she longed for The Hague again. It was the nearest thing to home and she was gasping for fresher air, Betje and the sight of the sea. The rumours, she was sure, would have died down by this time. Anne too was quite ready to leave Brussels, but she wanted to see Antwerp. "Perhaps one day," said Lucy. "But now I believe I would feel better if I could go back to The Hague."

Betje found them lodgings at the edge of the town, near the woods and not too far from the sea. The wind found them there. On stormy nights it roared through the trees and on still nights, if she leaned out of her window, Lucy could faintly hear the sound of the waves. She revived enough to take the children to visit Betje and Vrouw Flinck at Scheveningen, and to walk with them in the woods. Seeing their delight in sands and sea and trees she thought of herself and Justus and was back again in their childhood at Roch.

She was happy too because Charles had promised her a pension of four hundred pounds a year. She thought she knew why he had done it. He had refused her the security of marriage to Sir Henry de Vic and he wanted to make some reparation. She was touched and deeply grateful and with her thoughts circling back to Roch she relived the days of their idyl. When she could not sleep at night she would turn over the happy memories as though they were the pages of a missal, so often and so imaginatively that the boy Charles seemed to come alive again. "But he has never died," she told herself. "If our life is the whole of our life, then the whole person is the child and the boy, and the young man growing into the old

649

man, who gropes his way through the shadows of the last wood to find the child laughing on the sands."

She was happy, as though spring were in the air, and she hoped that no one except Vrouw Flinck and Betje knew she had returned to The Hague. Anne seemed happy too. She enjoyed shopping at The Hague and visiting her friends there, and Lucy did not want her to be bored and gave her all the freedom she wanted. There was no boredom for Lucy in the quiet days but they were too good to last, for the fact that there are a few people in the world who enjoy being alone is not understood by the majority of the human race.

"Pray heaven that is no one to see me," Lucy said to herself one sunny autumn afternoon. Anne was out and she was sitting at the edge of the woods with her sewing, with the children playing near her. They were seven and five years old now and they played well together. Jackie gave the orders and Mary obeyed with loving care. Jackie was good at giving orders. There was no need to guess which of Lucy's two children was of royal blood.

"No one I know," she decided with deep relief. From where she sat she could see through the trees the house where they lodged, a pleasant house with a pretty garden, and she could see the man who had just fastened his horse to the post beside the garden gate and was walking up the path between the autumn flowers, a tall well-dressed man whose imperious knock she could hear from where she sat. She did not know him and dropped her eyes thankfully to her work. He had probably come to ask for lodgings, which he could not have, for she, Anne and the children and the landlady and her husband filled the little house to capacity; and that also was a matter for satisfaction.

She had always liked men better than women, and she still did, but she did nowadays sometimes wonder whether they were worth the devastation they caused, and, surprised at herself, wonder also if she was about to join that large company of unmarried women who thank heaven fasting for the single state. Yet when she faced the question squarely she realized that the Queen of Bohemia had been right when she told her she

would never regret Charles. He was a part of her and she had
lived, and was living now, far more deeply because of him.
And suffering was a part of deep living; living without
suffering was like paddling in the shallows. Sometimes she
wondered humbly how Charles felt about her now. Was she
simply a little jade who he regretted or was she a part of him
still? She knew how Lord Taaffe felt about her. He had parted
from her but he kept his hand upon the thread.

There was a crunching of dry autumn leaves beneath heavy
boots and looking up she saw the tall man coming towards her
through the trees. For a moment she was filled with dismay.
Dear heaven, not another man! *Not* another! Then she took
heart again. The landlady had perhaps gone out. Simply a
stranger who had had no answer to his knock. Reassured, she
smiled charmingly up at him as he stood before her, smiling
charmingly down at her. It was no good. She *did* like men.

A dark handsome man, wearing a green coat and scarlet
waistcoat, yaffingale colours, and carrying his large feathered
hat in his hand, a man who would soon be too stout and too
florid but was at the moment still keeping a firm hold of the
splendour of his prime. His moustaches had a fine twirl to
them and he wore a small pointed beard. Nothing was familiar about him except his merry dark eyes, his crooked smile
and his bright clothes, but they were familiar and somewhere
larks were singing, as they used to do in Seven Dials meadow
that bordered the village of St. Giles. This man was not an
unwanted intrusion from the future but, like Smuts, a messenger of spring coming to her from the past.

"Tom!" she cried. "Tom Howard."

He sat down beside her and they both began to laugh, since
the memories they shared were those of childhood and
comedy. They remembered the coach in which Nan-Nan and
Lucy and the three boys had driven from Covent Garden to St.
Giles, with the coachman tied up in the boot, Tom on the box
and Justus blowing the horn. They remembered watching
Prince Charles come up the river in the royal barge, and the
unicorn wood and its magic.

"And now here we are," said Tom, "exiled in a foreign land,

in another wood, with a whole waste of years and a fearful war between that wood and this."

"Nevertheless we are still ourselves," said Lucy. "That is what is so lovely about meeting old friends again. They may have put on weight, or lost it, they may have changed, but never out of recognition. They are their eternal selves." She paused. "Do you know, meeting an old friend again makes me feel almost as though I had met God."

Tom Howard had always patiently ignored Lucy's flights of fancy and was himself still. "Yes, I have put on weight damnably," he agreed, "and you will wonder how I have done it. I am now in the service of the Princess of Orange. I am Colonel Howard, her Master of the Horse. Amongst us, Lucy, you can always tell if a man is in the service of the King alone or of the Princess too. It is a matter of girth."

"I have noticed that," said Lucy. "Tom, these are my children."

Jackie and Mary had left their game to look at the gorgeous man in green and scarlet. They made their bow and wobbly curtsey. Tom was not very good with children. He poked Jackie in the chest and chucked Mary under the chin but did not know what else to do with them. They suffered this and then with dignity they withdrew. They knew the man meant well but they did not like being treated that way just because they were smaller than he was. It hurt their dignity. They were, whatever their size, themselves. And so, to keep those selves inviolate, they withdrew.

Presently Lucy and Tom strolled a little way through the woods, though Lucy cleverly directed their steps so that she always had the children in sight. Tom thought it was he who directed their steps. He had Lucy's arm in his and kept it pressed hard against his side. "Do you remember how I used to call you my little wife?" he asked with melting tenderness.

Lucy came to a dead stop. "Now listen, Tom," she said. "You will not, while we are together at The Hague, usurp any of the privileges of a husband."

Tom laughed. His laugh, that once had been high and gay, had now, with growing weight, fallen to a lower register and become a subterranean rumble. "I have an excellent wife, and down in the town here there is a pretty little girl who—"

"Thank you, Tom," Lucy interrupted. "Now that things are clear between us shall we walk on? How did you know I was living here?"

"People talk of you," said Tom carefully. "Why do you live so far out from town?"

Lucy had been aware of his carefulness and she guessed its reason. "To be near the sea, and to avoid gossip. When I was living at The Hague before there was much gossip about me. I thought if I lived out here and was never seen about in the town it would not start up again."

"It has already done so, my dear," said Tom. He was still holding her arm firmly but in a different manner.

"You have enemies. Did you know?"

She did not answer his question but asked, "Did you believe the gossip?"

"I waited to believe or disbelieve until I had seen and talked with you. Now I disbelieve. But who are your enemies?"

"I do not know."

"You must have your suspicions."

She said with a little gasp, "I have wondered lately about a man called Prodgers. And a Captain O'Neil. But both are servants of the King and I cannot think of anything they could have against me."

"Then why do you suspect them?"

She told Tom about Prodgers's visit to Anne at Brussels while she was away, and of Mary's dislike of him and her nightmare. "I know it is ridiculous to trust the instinct of a small child," she said, "and yet I did. Mary is wise. And I felt something was wrong myself, too." She paused. "Some sort of smell of evil. Do you know what I mean?"

Tom did not. He had never smelt either good or evil. He ignored the silly question and asked her instead, 'Can you tell me why the King wanted you to visit him at Liège?"

"Yes, I can tell you. He wanted me to give him Jackie."

"And you refused?"

"Yes. Small children must be with their mothers."

"Could O'Neil have known of your refusal?"

"If he was in the King's confidence he would have known why he was fetching me, and since I took Jackie back to Brussels with me again he would know I had not done what the King wanted."

"And if Prodgers was still at Brussels when O'Neil brought you back he could have told him. Were there rumours about you in Brussels?"

"Yes."

"When did they start?"

"After I came back from Liège."

"Is your maid trustworthy?"

"I used to fear her but we have been together for a long time now. I do not know what I should do without her. What are you thinking, Tom?"

"I was merely asking a few questions. Where are those children? It is getting chilly and you should go in. And I must go back to the Palace."

"Come to the house and drink a cup of wine before you go," said Lucy. It was good to have him with her. He had brought with him some of the sense of security that had belonged to her childhood. Nan-Nan and her grandmother seemed not far away.

Autumn passed quietly into winter and Lucy was happier than she had been for a long time. Tom Howard found a tutor for Jackie, a charming white-haired old man who came daily. Lucy meanwhile tried to teach Mary with the aid of her own old hornbook, which she still possessed, and when they got tired of that she told her the old Welsh stories that her own mother had read to her in the bower at Roch. Tom Howard came to see them often and at Christmas brought them gifts.

Early in the new year Lucy was for a short while exceedingly ill with a fever. She had little recollection of it afterwards; though one memory, of Anne kneeling beside her bed and crying, her face pale against the night, like a cameo on dark velvet, remained with her as a source of wonder. Had Anne been crying for love of her? Fully aware again she found

Jackie being wonderfully loving but very much under foot, and Mary looking after her with so much competence that Anne and the landlady declared admiringly that she could have taken charge of her mother by herself. It seemed that the little girl had a wonderful gift, which she discovered for herself during this time of trouble. She had healing hands. Her small palms, laid upon her mother's forehead, could take away headaches. And when Anne had earache Mary made it "all better".

When Lucy was declared by others to be well, but was actually feeling worse than she would have believed possible, Tom Howard came to see her with troubling news. "Lucy, O'Neil is at The Hague. He has come to fetch a gift of money the Princess is giving the King. He wishes to see you and has asked me to speak to you on his behalf. He has the King's command to take Jackie back with him to Cologne." He paused and then went on again, "I also understand that part of the King's present from the Princess is to be left with you. The first instalment of your pension, with added to it a considerable sum as a Christmas gift from His Majesty."

There was a long silence while Tom looked out of the window, and then Lucy asked him in a strangled voice, "Is the King bribing me to part with Jackie?"

"It appears so, Lucy."

"But how could he think I would do such a vile thing as part with my child for money? What have they been telling him about me?"

"I should like to know, Lucy."

"What am I to say, Tom?" she demanded in anguish.

"Did you not tell me that the King said to you at Liège that you should keep your son?"

"Yes, he said that."

Tom swung round. "Then write a letter to the King that I can give to O'Neil. Say simply that you are ready at all times to obey His Majesty's commands, but nevertheless you hold him to his word that you should keep your son. Accept the pension but refuse the Christmas gift. I will tell O'Neil only the pension money is to be left with you."

Lucy wrote the letter and for a few days could do nothing but sit in her chair by the window in a daze of anxiety, and wait until Captain O'Neil himself came to see her. "Madam, I must leave The Hague and return to the King in a few days. We must get this matter settled. It is the question of his son's education that worries the King."

"Jackie is at this moment downstairs with his tutor," said Lucy. "Now that the King has generously granted me a pension I am able to give my son all that he needs." She wondered if she had spoken, for she had not heard her own voice. She wondered if she would be able to speak again, but she did; she said she was holding the King to his word and keeping her son.

Captain O'Neil was not yet corrupted, he merely shared with Prodgers the conviction that desired ends are never achieved if a man is squeamish about the means, and had not noticed that this is one of the most satisfactory means of entry into human affairs the devil possesses, and he was troubled by this badgering of a sick woman. At the moment he had not the heart to go on with it and presently left Lucy and went downstairs to talk to Jackie and his tutor. It did not take him long to find that Jackie had remained impervious to education. Then he talked to Anne in the garden and found her to his surprise unco-operative. What had happened? Was Prodgers losing his power over her? Well, no matter. The thing was done now and the King's mind left without scruples in the matter of taking Jackie from his mother.

In a few days Captain O'Neil was back to finalize the wretched business, bringing with him a heavy purse. But it was no good. Lucy was less well but more obstinate. She accepted the pension money but handed back the rest. He fought her for a while, and then desisted. Even in a good cause there were depths of cruelty to which he would not sink.

2

But Lucy could not get well and at last was forced by Tom and Anne to see a doctor. It was the air of The Hague, he said. It was detrimental to the health of many and he advised travel and change. Where should she go? She did not want to go anywhere but Tom and Anne were adamant and she remembered Anne's wish to see Antwerp, and she remembered too that Smuts was there. "We will go to Antwerp," she said.

"It is a long way," Tom warned her.

"Anne and I will manage," said Lucy. For some reason Antwerp was drawing her. If she had to leave the little house by the woods it should be for Antwerp. Steadfast to her promise she wrote and told Charles she was taking his son to Antwerp, to the house of a Mr. Harvey, nephew of his father's doctor, and they set off. Tom Howard was grieved not to be going with them, but he held his position as Master of the Horse rather precariously and was afraid to ask for leave. The Princess, as well as the Queen of Bohemia, was much beset by exiles wanting work and food; should she grow discontented with a servant there were plenty of others to choose from.

Lucy, Anne and the children travelled slowly, taking with them Mary's dollies, Jackie's balls and wooden soldiers and the writing desk that Charles had given Lucy. It went everywhere with her, and her letters from him were still in the secret drawer. The journey took all Lucy's courage but she was upheld by the growing conviction that she was journeying into joy.

Smuts and his wife gave them a kind welcome and looked after them for several weeks while Lucy recovered herself. She was even happier with them than she had been with Monsieur and Madame Axel, for they had young children and Jackie and Mary were very contented playing with them. Never had Lucy seen Jackie so happy with any family as he was with the Harveys. He wept when they had to go away to the little house that Smuts had found for them.

It was not lodgings this time but their own wonderfully cheap hired house, built of mellowed red brick with a steep red-gabled roof. When they saw it first it was glowing like a rose and the sun was twinkling in the small windowpanes. It stood high in a row of such houses, in a quiet humble part of the city, and looked down upon the river. The estuary was not too far away and there were gulls on the river. Behind the house was a small hidden garden with a vine growing over an arbour, and many tulips had pushed up their green leaves in the flower borders beside the paved paths.

Inside the house were cool tiled floors and simple furniture. The parlour only was given a touch of luxury by a long golden curtain with a silk fringe, a spinet and a superb map hanging on the wall. Though the house was small it had empty attics in the roof which made a splendid place for the children to play. From the dormer windows of these rooms they could see far down the river with its shipping, and right out over the beautiful city of Antwerp. Lucy, Anne, Jackie, Mary and the dollies settled down instantly like birds in the nest and were happy.

It was lying on the settle in the parlour, looking at her father's miniature that she had hung on the wall beside the golden curtain, that gave Lucy the idea of having a miniature of Jackie painted for his father. She longed to give Charles some gift that should show him her gratitude both for the pension which had made it possible to have this little house, but even more because he was allowing her to keep Jackie. She took it for granted that the silence following O'Neil's return to the King meant that Charles had remembered what he had said to her, and had accepted her refusal as final. She was optimistic these days; the little house was so full of happiness.

She told Smuts of her wish and found he knew of an Englishman who was now at Antwerp, a Mr. Samuel Cooper, who was an excellent miniaturist. And so Mr. Cooper came and painted Jackie looking out of the open window at the river, the ships and the gulls, his head a little to one side as he listened for new notes of music to add to the harmonies that were already in his head. His face was serious and thoughtful, his long curls falling on his shoulders. It was an exquisite miniature. When it was finished and framed Lucy laid it in a velvet case and put it away until she could find some safe way of sending it to the King.

3

It seemed to Lucy that there had never been such a lovely spring. Swallows nested under the roof and thrushes in the vine arbour and the little house rang with birdsong. The river flowed full and shining and the sky was always a glory of changing light. It was sunset when the miracle happened, the hour when Lucy played with her children before Anne put them to bed. "Maman, play the spinet," said Jackie suddenly. "Play and sing." Lucy was startled for though she often sang to the children it was a long time since she had tried to play any instrument. Looking back she thought the last time was at Breda with Charles, when she had played the air of the old Welsh hymn. She tried to play it now. Her fingers were stiff at first but presently she was absorbed in her playing and then she began to sing.

The children sat enthralled and Anne in the nursery began to cry. She had always scorned tears, the bitterness of her early life having frozen them at the source, and the burst of crying that had come on her at The Hague when she had thought Lucy was dying had shamed her. The shame had remained, but slowly changing its character. What sort of a creature was she that she could love a woman enough to weep for her and yet try to destroy her? What sort of power had this man Prodgers had over her? She had always despised women so lacking in respect for their own individuality that they could hand themselves over to a man they loved to do what he liked with. And she had not even this excuse, for she did not think she really loved Prodgers, though she had come very near to doing so. He had, she suspected, most subtly played upon her vanity and crowned her queen of a phantasy world that was more than half evil. With Lucy struggling back to life again she had ignored the instructions in a letter from Prodgers, that O'Neil had brought her, and had taken her first step out of the unreal evil kingdom. But reality was harsh and she could not take the final step, only cry helplessly when some beauty, such as the light of this perfect spring, Jackie looking and listening while Mr. Cooper painted him, and now Lucy's singing touched her changing self so sharply.

The three men who had come quietly up the steps to the door of the rosy house stood there listening, and one was profoundly moved. So often at morning or evening, when the world came freshly from the hand of God or turned again to her rest, there was a single voice heard, perhaps a bird singing or the stirring of wind in a tree, that moved one as a fuller music could not do. "Watch over us, bring all men, our Refuge, home to heaven," Lucy sang. There was silence, and then Lucy playing as though to herself alone.

The three men began to move as though to the slow measure of some preconceived plan. The youngest sat down on the steps as though to wait, the tallest leaned against the wall as though to wait also, but not for long, and the stocky man quietly opened the door and went in and up the stairs. At the half-opened door of the parlour he paused. Lucy let her playing die away and said without looking round, "Who is there?" She was not startled because peace possessed her. And she had been expecting a coming of some sort, for all day she had been remembering the coming of the three men into the house by the canal after Jackie's birth. That too had been in April, and light had been on the water. But she knew it was not Charles at the door. Not yet. "Who is it?" she asked.

"Justus," he replied.

She was in his arms in a moment and they clung together motionless, and the simplicity that had always been in their love for each other came back to Lucy like a cool breath from another world. She held him away from her, as she had done when he had come home from school as a small boy, as though to verify what she already knew. Essentially he was not changed. He was Justus, stocky and strong, reliable, honest, good, and these characteristics had deepened as he grew from boy to man. His shoulders had broadened and he had put on weight, and the physical change seemed an expression of his growth in quality. Then he smiled at her and he was a boy again, his boy's grin a laughable adornment of his man's authority; and to his relief Lucy laughed. For a moment her appearance had startled him. Was this elegant fragile woman, with violet-shadowed eyes and sharply hollowed face, his tomboy sister? But when she laughed she was the old Lucy

There was a gentle knock on the already open door and turning Lucy saw Richard. She went into his arms too, for in him too she could delight, so impressively handsome was he, and so evidently prosperous. There was no doubt now as to where his allegiance lay for in dress and bearing he was a prince among Puritans, his simple clothes perfectly cut and superbly worn, his fair hair cut short, smooth and shining. He had great charm and the riddle of his being was as great as ever. It was he who did the necessary talking for his emotions alone were undisturbed by this meeting. He and Justus had met Smuts Harvey in London and Smuts had told them they must come over. They had been delayed by the difficulty of getting a passport for Justus, but he and Smuts together had got it at last; Justus for reasons of health was travelling to Italy by way of the Low Countries. They had gone straight to Smuts's house at Antwerp and he had told them where Lucy was living.

"We found the way quite easily," said Richard. "We and a servant. Justus travels in style. It was he who could not come without his servant."

"A servant! Where did you leave him?" asked Lucy. It was so unlike Justus to travel with a servant.

Justus grinned. "Sitting on the steps below." He went to the window, thrust his head out and shouted, "Hi, you fellow, come up."

Light feet leapt up the stairs and a merry boy with curly hair and sparkling dark eyes stood in the doorway. He was bareheaded and plainly dressed in grey homespun but Lucy saw him in vivid green with a feather in his cap. "Dewil!" she cried. "Dewil!" It was almost too much.

And if Anne had not appeared at that moment in the doorway with wine for them all it would have been too much, for she was nearly dying with joy.

4

The days passed in a daze of happiness. Lucy and Justus were much alone together for Dewi was much occupied in seeing the sights of a foreign town, and Richard, after he had listened with a sympathy that surprised her to Lucy's story of all the many things she had not been able to put into her letters, and had told her about their mother, was also out a great deal and occasionally away for a few days. "Government business," he said.

"I do not know what he is doing," Justus told Lucy as they sat in the vine arbour one day together. "I never do know and I do not ask, for he is my brother and I do not want to dislike him any more than I do already. Whatever he does he is well paid for it."

It was obvious to Lucy that Justus was not well paid for his work as a poor man's lawyer. He was exceedingly shabby. He had told her a little of what he did, living by choice in a poor part of London and trying to sort out the troubles and tangles of humble people. She took his hand. He worked at repairing old furniture in his odd moments, to augment his meagre income, and his hands were roughened and stained. His face lighted up when he spoke of his furniture and she knew that it was as beautifully and lovingly handled as were the lives of those who came to him in their troubles.

"I like your hands," she said, "and you must not dislike Richard, for disliking anyone does not match your hands. And he has been very kind."

"Yes, he has developed a kindly manner and it oils his way. After we had seen Smuts it was his idea that we should come over at once and bring you what our mother left for you. It would not have been safe to send it."

He had brought a parcel with him into the arbour and laid it beside him on the seat. Lucy had asked no questions, knowing she would be told about it in Justus's own good time. At no period in his life had he liked to be hurried. He unwrapped it now and laid a shabby leather case on her lap. She opened it and saw her mother's wedding pearls. Instantly she was back at Roch, standing on the dais with Nan-Nan and looking down at her father and mother playing and singing with their guests in the hall below, and saw the candlelight gleaming on her mother's pearls. It was Justus's turn to take her hand and hold it while she cried. It distressed him that she now cried so often for he saw her little bursts of weeping as a symptom of her physical weakness. She needed a change and a good holiday. More than that, she needed to come back to England for good and let him look after her.

"Our mother left some money for you too. There is still some legal business to be done and it would be a help to Richard and to me if you would come back to England with us and stay for a while. Will you? You know what London is like in the spring and summer; a jewel girdled by the little villages among their meadows and flowers. Will you come? You and the children and Anne."

She gasped. "I do not think that the King would let Jackie come. It might not be safe for him."

"Richard and I have thought of that. You could come under an assumed name. No one would know whose child he was. If that did not please the King Jackie could stay here with Smuts Harvey and his wife. He loves playing with the Harvey children."

"No, he would not be happy. He cannot bear to be separated from me."

"It is time he learned a little independence, Lucy. He is growing a big boy. It would do him good."

"No! no!" cried Lucy.

Justus smiled at her. "I believe it is you cannot bear to be separated from him," he teased. "I never met such an infatuated mother. But think about it. Keep it in your mind."

He said no more for Dewi came out to join them with the children running at his heels, for he was a Pied Piper to them and they would have followed him anywhere. At nineteen years old he was lithe and gay and walked with a lilting step, whistling like a blackbird. The three of them were playing some game. They circled the garden and went back into the house, the whistling and laughter lingering on the air. Lucy smiled, delighting in them, but Justus groaned comically, for Dewi was something of a problem.

On his father's death he had travelled to London to be with Justus, whom he loved, and since he was good with horses had found employment as a groom at a great house in the Strand. Justus told Lucy that he was courageous, affectionate and honest, but that responsibility for him was no sinecure because of his fiery temper.

"Our father spoilt him and now I cannot teach him to control it. He gets into a fight in a moment. He was dismissed from the first house for knocking a man's teeth out, and now he has just been thrown out of a second for emptying the slop bucket over his mistress's head because she thrashed her dog. In the good old days they sent these tempestuous young men on the Crusades, and as you see I am trying foreign travel for Dewi. Also I thought you might be a good influence."

Lucy laughed, unable in these halcyon days to take Dewi's temper too seriously. He was a wonder of a boy, she thought, and he and she had recaptured all their old love for each other.

A few days later Lucy and Justus went for a stroll by the river, talking of Old Parson, who had died only a short while after their father. His mind had grown steadily clearer, Justus told Lucy, and he had died serene and happy. Lucy managed not to weep, but she walked more slowly. Justus was grieved that she could walk only so short a distance, and so breathlessly, but for her, after her illness at The Hague, it was wonderful to be walking at all. They were facing the sun and at first she did not recognize the two men who were coming towards them, then with a gasp she pulled Justus away from the path into the shadows between two beached boats. The two went by deep in talk, a slender young man of middle height, elegant in spite of shabby clothes, and an older man, tall and fair, who walked with long strides.

"English," said Justus.

Lucy had gone white. "Lord Wilmot and, I think, Lord Ormonde. Justus, the King must be in Antwerp."

She was so shaken that they went straight home and found
Dewi in the garden weeding and tying up the tulips, which
were full-blown now and getting weak at the knee with the
weight of their own glory. He had much of his father in him
and if he could not be with horses he was happiest with his
fingers in the earth. They told him what they suspected and he
leapt to his feet with shining eyes and cheeks flaming with
excitement.

"The King in Antwerp! Shall we see him? 'Sdeath, after he
left Roch I used to cry in the night!" He took a flying leap over
a bed of tulips and fetched a broom to sweep up the mess he
had made on the paved path. Lucy remembered suddenly his
dog-like devotion to Charles at Roch, and also Nan-Nan's prophetic "seeing" that he would serve a king and be beloved by
him.

Two days later a letter was delivered from Lord Ormonde.
It told her His Majesty would call upon her on the morning of
the following day. She was in great anxiety. Had he come to
Antwerp especially to see her, and was it about Jackie? She
was so distressed that it was Justus who had to do the thinking. Richard was away already and he decided that he and
Mary had better go to the Harveys!

"But why?" asked Lucy.

"This is to be a happy visit," said Justus, smiling at her. "I
believe the King will spend the day with you, and he will want
to be alone with you and Jackie. Anne will cook the food and
Dewi shall stay to wait upon His Majesty."

Dewi's face, that had been black as a thundercloud
cleared. He was devoted to Justus, but any suggestion that he
should accompany his brother to the Harveys would have
been met by one of the explosions of his temperament that
Lucy had not yet witnessed. "You need not come back until I
fetch you," he said airily to Justus, when next day he showed
him off the premises. "The King may stay some days with
Lucy and myself. That is what he did at Roch."

Justus grinned and held out his hand to Mary. Lucy, watching from an upstairs window, saw the companionableness of
their departure. Justus and Jackie had made little contact with

each other because Jackie was jealous of Lucy's love for her brother, and Justus privately agreed with Captain O'Neil that Jackie was a damnably spoilt little brat, but with Mary he had made fast friends. They were birds of a feather, Lucy thought, and her heart gave a lift of joy. In her uncle Mary had yet another safeguard for the future.

Lucy waited for Charles in the parlour but Dewi and Jackie, restless with impatience, sat at the foot of the stairs to watch for him, Dewi wearing an orange-tawny doublet and Jackie a little suit of green.

Charles came quietly, dismissing those who had attended him at the door, and the first Lucy knew of his arrival was the sound of voices and steps on the stairs, and then the door was flung open and Dewi announced His Majesty.

Dewi had worshipped Charles. To him the King was more than a hero, he was a god, and from top to toe he was a glowing flame of joy. Even the short, crisp dark curls stood up on his head as though they aspired like flames, and the sunshine blazed upon the orange-tawny doublet. Jackie was not shy today; he had jumped from the stairs to his father's arms and was still there. Lucy curtseyed, then wobbled and found she could not get up. Charles put Jackie down and with one hand helped her up while with the other he gripped Dewi's arm.

"Is this Dewi?" he asked. "The little fellow who lay across the door at Roch Castle to guard me?"

It was a guess on his part, prompted by the knowlege that Lucy had her brothers with her, but he had the royal gift of inspirational guessing; which was one of the reasons why men loved him.

"Sir," said Dewi, struggling with Welsh emotion, "I would die for you."

"Shir Da," said Jackie, "I have a puppy that my uncles gave me."

"Show me your puppy," commanded his father. It was fetched and resembled a tiny white fur muff. Legs could scarcely be found but two glowworm points of light within the fur added their quota of illumination. The room was full of light and love and Charles was painfully confused. After Th

Hague rumours, represented to him as the truth, he had been filled with something like hatred for Lucy and had come to Antwerp himself to get his son away from her. And now he found himself in the midst of an idyl and in the presence of a woman who looked like a dying queen, her face as fragile as a transparent sea-shell, her enormous blue eyes searching his face with love. He was, he found, still holding her arm. "Jackie," he said, "I will see you again. The puppy too. Dewi, I want to talk alone with your sister."

They were alone and that he might not look at her again he looked round the room. It was so simple, and very beautiful, but there was nothing in it to hold the eye and he had to look at her again. She stood with her shoulders straight, her eyes looking into his. "Sir, I know that many ugly things are said about me. I do not know what they are and I do not want to know. Nor do I want to defend myself. Sir, I make mistakes, but in my heart I am your wife and I am always loyal to you."

He stared at her. Could he believe her? He had lately discovered that two more friends whom he had trusted were in Cromwell's pay, reporting his movements to his enemies. And now there was yet another, Tom Howard. His sister had just dismissed him from her service for suspected spying. This had hit him hard. Tom Howard, who had been his companion as a boy. When good men crumbled under the stress of an apparently hopeless exile how could he trust a slip of a girl? Yet how he longed to believe her. He wanted to take her in his arms and be back with her again in the days of Roch.

"Sir, may I show you something?"

In old days she had always treated him as an equal but since the unhappy business of Taaffe, above all since she had known she was not legally his wife, she had like all his servants acknowledged in speech and manner the divinely appointed difference between King and subject. Today of all days, when he had come here to exercise his kingly right and take his son away from an unworthy mother, the change in her manner hurt him. There was something about this house. It exerted a strange influence. Whose house was it? Instead of answering her question he asked abruptly, "Who owns this house?"

"It belongs to some old gentleman, sir," said Lucy. "Mr. Harvey made all arrangements for me and so I did not meet the old man or hear his name. It seems he travels a good deal."

"A business man?"

"Mr. Harvey merely said that he went where he was wanted."

"Very mysterious," said the King drily. "Is there a garden?"

"Yes, sir, there is a charming secluded garden."

"Then could you show me what you want me to see in the garden?"

"Yes, sir. We shall be alone there. Dewi has taken Jackie down by the river. I will ask Anne to bring the wine to the arbour."

Anne was called and instructed while Charles fidgeted. He wanted to get out of the house. He could not say what he had to say within its peace. "Lead on, Lucy," he said impatiently.

She took him out to the vine arbour and they sat in the green shade and looked out to where the tulips burned in the sun. The atmosphere of peace in the garden was the same as the one in the house. Anne brought the wine, curtseyed and left them. Lucy took something from her pocket and slipped to her knees to present it to the King. "Sir, it is a miniature of Jackie. It was painted by Mr. Samuel Cooper and it is my gift to you, in gratitude for your generosity in giving me my pension; and for more, much more than that; for your loving goodness in leaving our son with me."

Charles took the miniature in his hands and was speechless, and she misconstrued his silence. "It did not cost too much," she said anxiously. "I did not have to take too much of my pension money to pay for it. Mr. Cooper charged me very little because he said Jackie was such a beautiful boy that it was a joy to paint him. Sir, is it not a good likeness?" Forgetting herself she had leant one arm across the King's knee and was looking eagerly up into his face.

"It is a wonderful likeness," said Charles slowly "And I thank you for your gift. It will never leave me." Then suddenly his control snapped. "For God's sake get up and sit down, Lucy!" he implored her. "And pour the wine."

She did so and he drank silently, trying to get hold of himself again, one hand in his pocket clutching the miniature in its small case. He struggled for words. "You will be here for long?" he asked.

"I do not know, sir," said Lucy. "My brothers want me to go back to England with them for a little while, just for a rest and holiday, and I do not know what to do. I could not go without my children and I do not know whether you would wish me to take Jackie out of the country."

A sudden light seemed to explode inside Charles's head as a vista of hope opened out before him. He began to think quickly and silently, and to keep Lucy quiet he automatically put out a hand and held hers. He thought he could see what Lucy's brothers had in their minds. They were dismayed to see how frail she was, horrified at her loneliness and the ambiguousness of her position. Once they could get her back to England they would do all they could to keep her there, he had no doubt. And he could surely find some way of insisting that they did so. It was all easy now. There need be no cruelty. She would think she was going back to England only temporarily, and a short parting from Jackie, for Jackie's sake, was something to which she would surely agree.

"No, Lucy," he said gently. "You cannot take Jackie to England. He is my son and it would not be safe for him."

"I would travel under an assumed name," said Lucy. "I would be a Dutch lady and her children visiting her relatives in England. There would be no danger then."

"There might be," said Charles. "Spies are everywhere. There have been several attempts at Royalist risings in England and all is plot and counter plot, a tissue of treachery and lying that leaves me unable to trust even the men who were boys with me."

"Every day," said Lucy, "Jackie and I say together the prayers that Dr. Cosin wrote for your protection. There is one that I say many times a day. 'Send him, and all who are loyal to him, help from thy holy place. And ever more mightily defend them. Confound the designs of all that rise up or conspire against him. And let no wicked thing come near to hurt him.'"

He found he was still holding her hand. Oh God, could she speak so and yet be what men said she was? In this place she seemed his girl still yet how could he tell? How could he know? But there was Jackie. He forced his mind back to Jackie.

"When I came to Antwerp I did not know where to lodge," he told Lucy. "I knew Dr. Harvey's nephew lived here and we went to him for advice. I liked him and his wife and heard how much they loved Jackie. It seems our boy plays happily with their children. Leave him with them, Lucy, while you go to England. It would be good for him."

It was the same advice that Justus had given her. She was a little shaken but she gave the same answer. "Jackie has never left me."

"He must learn to stand on his own feet. How can he grow up to be an independent man if he is always tied to your apron strings? He will have to learn how to accustom himself to short partings from you, and this will be an ideal beginning. You will be back so soon. I do not command you, Lucy, I only ask you to think about it for our son's sake."

She was silent and he knew how much she was suffering as she faced the truth of what he had said about their son. And behind that truth lurked his deception of her, for right back under her spell though he was, almost trusting her again, he still meant to have Jackie. He hated himself. Was he any better than Howard and the rest? Could a man never run straight? "Dear heart, I will stay with you for the rest of this day," he said. "Do not give me your answer until I have to leave you."

But when the evening came, as on that day when he had gone to Rotterdam after Jackie's birth, he could leave neither wife nor son. He had fallen right out of life as it was into life as it had been; or might have been. Dewi was despatched with a letter to assure Lord Ormonde of the safety of the King and then Charles forgot he was a king. He played with Jackie and saw him put to bed. Lucy sang to him in the parlour and when darkness came they sat at the window and watched the stars come out, and saw the riding lights of the ships reflected in the water.

At night it seemed to them that they slept little, but talked dreamily, drifting on a tide of peace. Their talk was never of now but only of then. "Do you remember how we sang to the seals? Do you remember the stream in the Valley of Roses and the wishing well where we dropped the pins?" The bare lovely little house seemed to have built itself around them like a living entity. It took great care of their thoughts and memories. It knew what to exclude. Though just once, between sleeping and waking, Lucy murmured to her husband, "To do what is best for those one loves, that is what one must do. I will go to London for my brothers' sake, to please them, and I will leave Jackie with the Harveys, for his sake and because you wish me to do that." Then she was asleep again.

She woke in the first light of dawn and found Charles, fully dressed, standing beside her. "Lucy, I must go now. I do not want anyone to see me leave your house. Do not move."

But to be with him till the last moment she slipped out of bed and pulled her cloak over her nightshift. Then they opened the door. Dewi in his orange-tawny doublet was lying across the threshold, his drawn sword beside him. He was so deeply asleep that he did not hear the door open, and his face in sleep looked young as the face of the little boy who had lain outside the door at Roch Castle.

"Dewi," whispered Lucy. "Dewi." Charles looked at her. "Do not wake him. But tell him, when he wakes, that I will keep my promise. One day he shall be my servant. Go back to bed, dear heart."

He kissed her, stepped across Dewi and ran down the stairs. Lucy went back to bed and she did not know whether the flood of tears that came to help her were of grief or joy. But as soon as she could she checked them, for she must not let the children see her with a swollen face. She turned her wet pillow over and found a little box lying under it. She opened it and inside was a diamond brooch. What Charles had had in his mind when he brought it she did not know, but she knew what he had been thinking when he left it, for he had written on a torn bit of paper, "Not for both of you this time but for you alone." So she was forgiven for the sale of the first brooch. Forgiveness seemed golden in the air.

Sixteen

I

When Lucy suggested to Jackie that he was now a big boy and that only little boys were always with their mothers, and that perhaps now they could not be together the whole of the time, he gave the matter his consideration and conceded that she might be right. He wished to be a big boy. Building upon this wish she carefully unfolded Shir Da's plan. She would have a holiday with Uncle Justus and he should have a holiday with Uncle Smuts and his children, and when they met again they would have much to tell each other.

He said he would be pleased to be with Uncle Smuts but where was maman going? She said to England, and immediately there were yells. When she had calmed them down and sorted them out they were found to be composed both of fear and anger. It was too far for maman to go. It she went a few miles away then she could come back instantly if he did not like it without her, but it would take her a long time to come back from England. And he wanted to sail with maman on the big ship. And Anne and Mary were going to England too, and why should they go and not he? He yelled again, with sheer rage this time. He had inherited the love of ships and the sea from both parents and was thwarted in his very soul. His mother decided that she must write and tell Charles that she could not go to England

But at this crucial moment Richard came home and with him, to Lucy's great surprise, came Tom Howard. She was delighted to see him but distressed to find that he had left the service of the Princess of Orange. When she asked why he merely laughed, "I was no longer wanted," was all he would say. After that, it appeared, he had had an unexpected meeting with Richard and had accepted an invitation to return with him to Antwerp. "He needs a roof over his head,"

Richard explained to Lucy, and Tom joined Richard and Justus and Dewi in the attics that had once been the children's domain.

None of them would accept Lucy's decision to abandon England. "If you let that little brat dictate to you in this way," Tom warned her, "you will as surely as the night follows the day make a tyrant of him. Who is he to say where his mother is to go or not to go? If you are not careful, Lucy, you will ruin that boy."

It was the phrase "that little brat" that horrified Lucy. Was it possible that her exquisite child could be described in such terms? Had she spoilt him? She was still worrying about it when Jackie came to her and said with royal graciousness, "Maman, you may go to England."

It was Tom Howard and Justus together who had brought him to this frame of mind. They had reminded Jackie that the plan was the wish of Shir Da, and Shir Da was King. Tom further pointed out with some grimness that kingly fathers had been known to thrash disobedient sons, and so had non-kingly uncles. Jackie after deep thought came out with a startling remark. "I may myself be king one day," he said, "and will wish to be obeyed." Then descending gracefully from Tom Howard's knee, where he had been enthroned, he went to Lucy with the royal permission.

"And what, may I ask, has Lucy been saying to the brat?" Tom demanded of Justus.

"She has told him that she is the King's wife and he is the King's son," said Justus. "She wanted him, she told me, to grow up with a sense of his own integrity. What else could she tell him?"

Tom rubbed his nose. "Life is a mess," he remarked. "Poor Lucy. Poor girl. Justus, I am coming to England with you."

Justus looked at him keenly. "As a Royalist you will be in danger," he warned him.

"I will risk it," said Tom. "Richard, as no doubt he has told you, remains here for a while. And so I understand does Dewi."

"Dewi wants to see Holland," said Justus. "What Richard

wants I do not know. He is the most secretive fellow on earth."

"And the one man I know who is never in a mess," said Tom.

2

The ship chosen was the *Seagull*, sailing from Flushing, and if she was not in Lucy's eyes quite as lovely a ship as the *Sea-Horse* she was yet superb. But much tribulation had to be surmounted before they reached the haven of the point of no return.

It was decided that Jackie should say goodbye in the little house, go to the Harveys with his puppy Snowy two days before his mother left and not be at the dock to see the departure. Apart from a flood of emotion in the little house at the moment of parting all seemed well and Jackie departed with Smuts weeping but resigned, and as soon as he arrived settled down well with the children he liked so much.

But to Lucy's horror he and Snowy came with Smuts and his wife and children to see them off. Smuts explained that the previous day Jackie had suddenly decided that he must see the big ship that was to take maman to England. When his will had been thwarted his screams had been terrible. He was anxious to know that the ship was big enough and safe enough to take maman, and it had seemed best that he should see for himself. When he saw the *Seagull* in her pride he could not at first speak for excitement, for he had not known that a ship could be as lovely as this. Then he demanded that he should go on board.

"No," Tom Howard whispered to Lucy, but Smuts said, "Let him see for himself that you will be safe."

So they all went on board together and Jackie was shown the cabin where his mother would sleep. He also saw the captain on the poop and the dark-faced men at the capstan, smelt the salt in the breeze and heard the gulls screaming. Once again he could not speak but his cheeks flamed and his eyes shone.

The captain shouted an order and it was time to go. They

said their farewells and Mrs. Harvey went down the gangway with her children. Jackie had said goodbye to Tom and Justus and Mary and was in his mother's embrace; but with a determined Smuts, Snowy under his arm, standing beside him, ready to grab him at the first slackening of Lucy's arms.

"Be a good boy, my darling. I will soon be back," she whispered. She had been utterly resolved not to cry as she had cried when they had said goodbye at the little house, but the moment was a terrible one for her. There can be a dreadful finality about a ship leaving the shore. She did not cry but her breath came in gasps, and without her knowledge her arms tightened about the child from whom she had never been parted in seven long years. And he, her gasps shivering through his body, knew suddenly that all his safety was leaving him. He began to cry and sob and scream all at once and twined his legs and arms about his mother like a young octopus. They both took leave of their senses at the same moment. Lucy picked up her son and ran for the safety of her cabin. Snowy struggled fiercely from beneath Smuts's arm and bounced after them, a round white ball of determined fluff. When the three reached the cabin Lucy banged the door and shot the bolt. They fell on the floor and crouched there trembling until the ship was well out to sea.

The weather was perfect and the *Seagull*, white wings spread, even lovelier in performance than she had been in promise. Yet the first day of sailing was not a happy one for Lucy, for she was in disgrace with the two men. Tom was furious and Justus, for the first and last time in their lives, could not bring himself even to smile at her. "You know the interpretation the King will put upon this," he said. "He will think that you deliberately deceived him, meaning to take Jackie with you all the time."

"He will never think that," said Lucy. "He will understand. I am sure Smuts will write to him and explain how it happened."

"He may or he may not. The poor fellow had to leap for the gangway in a hurry. He fell on the quay and it looked as though he had hurt his shoulder. A broken collarbone in all probability. A painful thing."

"When we get to England I will write to Charles myself," said Lucy.

Tom, who had just joined them, said grimly, "Do so. And may your letter arrive in time to prevent his suspicions from hardening into conviction. Once let a Stuart have a conviction in his mind and you can never get it out again. I have warned you."

"The thing is done," said Lucy with surprising calmness, "and there is no point in recrimination between us."

Secretly she thought there was now such trust between herself and Charles that he would understand. The men shrugged their shoulders and went to join the captain in his cabin for a drink. It all simmered down and the *Seagull*, the wind behind her, sped joyously over the sea to England. The sea was blue, the sky cloudless, the air like wine and Lucy was so invigorated that she could not think of danger. She had borrowed the name of her beloved Vrouw Flinck and was an unknown Dutch lady travelling with her children. How could there be danger for Jackie? She sat in the sun with Mary and two dollies, Sally and Polly, and watched Jackie's ecstatic delight in the big ship.

The *Seagull* was bound for the Port of London and so to Lucy's joy she returned to England as she had left it, by way of the river that was to her the loveliest in the world. To sail up the great estuary with a favourable wind, to see English gulls circling about the ship and English cormorants sitting on the sandbanks with their absurd wings spread wide in welcome, was bliss. The shores of the estuary were like arms too, held so wide that at first they could hardly be seen, then coming closer with their treasure of green fields, villages and churches. Then the shore birds came out to welcome them, swans and ducks, and all the while the white sails above their heads were no whiter than the clouds of England sailing before the wind.

They came to London and the river was full of shipping, a gleaming thoroughfare of busyness and beauty, the city with its thousand eyes looking out upon all that went up and all

that went down from where it lay like some splendid beast
stretched out beside the water. As they came slowly to their
mooring place they could hear a deep humming purr, an echo
it might be of the roaring of a lion deep beneath the stones.
But the great beast was amiable today in the hot summer sun.
It allowed Lucy and her children to come on shore with joy in
their hearts, and a sense of special safety falling down upon
them from London's special sun.

3

Lucy, Anne and the children settled down happily in a house
in the Strand, their landlady a kindly woman to whom Justus
as a lawyer had been of service and who for his sake could not
do enough for them. Mary's dollies and Jackie's toys were unpacked, and Lucy's little writing desk that went everywhere
with her was set upon the table in her bedchamber. Inside it
were her papers and letters and her jewels. She was careful to
keep it locked and the key hung round her neck.

Justus went back to his home but was with them as much as
possible. Tom Howard came and went but they did not see
much of him and Lucy was concerned for his safety. In leaving Antwerp there had been so many things to think of that it
was not until they were on board the *Seagull* that she had
suddenly realized that Tom, as a Royalist, would be in danger
in England. She had gone to him in great contrition, ashamed
that she had not thought of this before, but he had laughed
at her fears. "I have done this often, Lucy," he had assured
her. "I know how to protect myself." Nevertheless she was
anxious sometimes, but only sometimes, so great was her
happiness.

With her legacy from her mother she now had enough
money for a few luxuries and she hired a coach to take Anne
and the children to see the sights of London. Sometimes Justus
went with them but occasionally, when she felt well enough
she went herself. She took them to see the house in Coven
Garden where she had lived as a little girl, and to St. Paul'
Cathedral and to London Bridge, where she stood with Jacki

on the exact spot where she had first seen his father as a little boy coming up the river in the royal barge.

"Shall I ever be king of this country?" he asked loudly, leaning over the parapet, her hand gripping his little blue doublet, his great wondering eyes gazing at the vista of river and shipping, churches and palaces, clouds and birds. "Will it all be mine?"

"Hush, Jackie," she whispered in panic. "Remember that you are not the King's son here, you are just my son, the son of Vrouw Flinck. You are Jackie Flinck."

She hoped he had not been heard. Two men were leaning over the parapet near them but they seemed deep in their own conversation. Nevertheless she realized how right Charles had been to forbid her to bring Jackie. "Forgive me," she whispered to him. "But you know I did not mean to do it." She was absurd enough to think that he did know, so strong was her belief that after the day and the night in the little house at Antwerp their love was indissolubly strong again.

There was one place to which Lucy allowed no one to take her children and that was the Tower of London. When they were out on the river one day Jackie noticed the pile of stone and asked what it was and she told him, "A zoo. They keep animals there," but to her great relief he did not ask to see the animals. He merely said, "I do not like it," and looked the other way.

Lucy found London very changed from the old days of colour and splendour. The people and their clothes seemed muted. London was beautiful still but she was like a lovely widow who has covered her face with a veil. There were few people now in London whom Lucy knew. She took her children and Anne to see Aunt Anne Byshfield and found her kind and pretty as ever. Aunt Anne was not a critical woman, like Aunt Margaret, and it was not her habit to sit in judgment. Of all Mrs. Gwinne's daughters she was the most like her mother. Lucy was in her arms at once, and then the children, and then Anne because she looked after them so well. It was presently obvious to Lucy that Aunt Anne had taken a fancy to young Anne, and she was delighted because she could see that Anne was pleased; people seldom took a fancy to her and she was touched almost to the point of confusion. And Aunt Anne was fascinated by Mary. She was prepared to love both children because they were Lucy's, but Mary and her dollies took instant possession of her great-aunt's compassionate heart.

Lucy went alone to visit old Mr. Gwinne. To find him now within his ramparts of books was like struggling through a labyrinth, and when she did at last reach the heart of it he did not know who she was. His failing mind now understood what he read but nothing else. The little house seemed utterly dead without the presence of her mother and grandmother and Nan-Nan, and that was the only day when sorrow overwhelmed her.

There were a few pilgrimages that she made alone; to the landing-place where she had gone so often as a child and where the mulberry tree still leaned its arms upon the wall, to the unicorn wood, to the dark yew tree where once Old Sage had had his herb stall, and to the church beyond. To the church she came more than once, sitting on the same seat where she had so often sat by Old Sage. It seemed to her that he was beside her still, and not only in the church, for here in London he was seldom out of her thoughts. "He was one of the Great Ones," she said one day to Justus. "I mean, he *is* one of the Great Ones. They sometimes come back, I believe, and go about the world. I watch for his face in the streets."

It was then, in that moment of vision and dream, that Justus put his arms round her and told her part of his great plan. He and she and the children and Anne would travel, by easy stages that would not tire her, to Roch. They would see again all the places where as children they had been so happy. They would see their father's grave. After that he stood silently, his cheek against hers, and the rest of his plan, that Charles had guessed, he kept in his mind alone. Lucy should not go back to Europe. He and she and the children would live together at Roch and he would practise as a country lawyer. He would be a poor man's lawyer but they would have enough to live on

But he dared not broach this last bit of his plan yet, only hold her closer. No lover, no husband, can love a woman as a brother can, he believed. Brother and sister share such a depth of memories.

Lucy began to tremble in his arms and then she gently freed herself. "No, Justus," she said. "Wales is a far place for me to take the King's son. His Majesty would not wish it."

Justus let his arms fall to his side and his usually gentle thoughts took a savage turn. Damn and blast the King, he thought, damn and blast the whole royal breed. Almost he could be a Parliament man like Richard, or a parti-coloured man like Tom, running with the hare and hunting with the hounds. Who could blame Tom? Loyalty to kings brought men nothing but sorrow. Then with a swing of shame he was himself once more. "We will talk of it again, Lucy," he said, and to please him she smiled and nodded.

4

But they did not talk of it again for the next morning as Lucy and Anne and the children, with Snowy the puppy, left the house to do some shopping, they were arrested. Before they left, looking out from the window above, Lucy had seen three men strolling up and down and a coach drawn up a little way down the street, but she had no sense of alarm, so safe did she feel in homely London. Indeed the three men had made her smile for they seemed figures of comedy. One was tall and thin, a mournful Don Quixote, another jolly and red-faced, a Falstaffian figure, and the third a white-faced man to whom she did not pay much attention until they went downstairs and out into the street, when he put his hand on her shoulder and arrested her in the name of the Lord Protector. Then for a moment the world turned dark, but she straightened herself and said quietly, "I am a Dutch lady, widow of a sea captain, on a visit to England with my children. I have done no harm. With what am I charged?"

"You are to be examined by the Privy Council, madam," said the man politely. "You and your maidservant. You are to bring your son with you. The little girl may remain here with your landlady."

"Under all circumstances my little girl remains with me," said Lucy firmly.

The man yielded, then said with a flicker of a smile, "I have no instructions to arrest the puppy, madam." Before Lucy could reply Jackie said, with an exact imitation of his mother's gentle but utterly obstinate tones, "Under all circumstances my dog remains with me." His head was up and he had Snowy in his arms, and it did not appear that the rotund little bundle of white fluff could be prised out of them with either ease or speed. The man shrugged his shoulders and they got into the coach. Don Quixote and Falstaff got in with them but the white-faced man stayed in the street. Lucy was enormously proud of her son for in this moment of crisis there was not even a hint of screams or tears. He showed a royal courage. Anne was quiet and calm and so was Mary. Lucy's thoughts were quick and clear. Only one thing really mattered. No one must know Jackie was the King's son. Therefore no one must know that Justus was her brother. But Justus must know what had happened.

"One moment; sir," she said to the man in the street who was about to slam the coach door. "I am not a rich woman but I must have a lawyer to advise me. I have heard of a Mr. Justus Walter whose fees are not high. Could you inform him of my desire that he should help me?"

"Mr. Justus Walter has already been arrested, madam. Also Colonel Howard."

He slammed the door and the coach moved off. Lucy and Anne could not speak to each other, since the two men were with them, but their eyes met and Lucy could only hope that Anne understood that Jackie's paternity must not be revealed. Jackie himself was mercifully now awed and silent.

It took them only a short while to reach Westminster. They were taken to a block of government offices and into a small ante-room. Falstaff stayed with them, his bulk separating Jackie and his mother, but he was kind. He told Lucy that Colonel Howard and Mr. Justus Walter were now being examined separately by the Council, and he thought they might have to wait some while for their turn. He was right, for it was an hour before they heard the slamming of a door and then the sound of men's boots tramping down a stone passage. Lucy's hopes that she might see Justus or Tom faded away with the dying footsteps.

"Now is it my turn?" she whispered to Falstaff. "Probably, madam," he answered. But the summons, when the door opened and a man in black with a sword at his side stood there holding it wide, was for Anne Hill. She went with him at once, white-faced but composed, and Lucy was proud of her. "She will be back in a few moments," Lucy said to the startled children. But Anne did not come back and Jackie began to show his first sign of fear. Sliding off the seat he tried to get round the mountain of flesh beside him to where his mother and Mary sat hand in hand. But he was instantly replaced, and his mouth opened. In terror of what might come out of it Lucy asked, "Please may I tell my children a fairy story?" Falstaff smiled. "I have no orders to the contrary, madam."

Raising her voice enough for it to get round Falstaff to Jackie Lucy embarked instantly upon his favourite story of Prince Kilhwch and his wonderful horse, and the white-breasted greyhounds with their collars of rubies. She had told it so well that even Falstaff sat enthralled, a plump hand laid on each knee and his eyes on Lucy's face. A pretty wench, he thought. A pity if they hanged her for a spy. But still Anne did not come back and even while her story ran on, waxing mightier in creations of her own imagining, Lucy was aware that her physical strength was running out. When her own time came to go before the Council would she even be able to stand? Suddenly the door opened and she looked up to greet Anne. But the black man with the sword at his side was alone. "Your turn, madam."

"My maid?" she asked him. "Where is she?"

"Waiting for you in another room, madam. Come at once."

She turned to Falstaff. "My children," she gasped. "They will be terrified without me."

He smiled. "As soon as you are in the Council Chamber, madam, I will take them to your maid. Do not fear for them." He was immensely kind. Even in hell, she thought, one can find kindness, and she felt braver. She kissed her children, told them they would be taken to Anne, that she would join them very soon, and then they would go home. They listened wide-eyed and nodded, but just as the door closed behind her Jackie let out a wild cry of "Maman!" And as she was led down the passage she heard him scream.

After that she was aware of nothing until she found herself standing before a long table facing a line of grave-faced men in sombre garments. The room itself had a richness of dark carved wood and a line of sunlight slanted from a high window. They asked her name and she said that she was Vrouw Flinck, widow of a Dutch sea captain, and that she had come to England on a holiday with her two children. They asked her if the Dutchman had fathered both her children and she said yes. They asked how it was that she was travelling in the company of Colonel Thomas Howard and Mr. Justus Walter and she said with truth that she had met them in Antwerp and they had offered their protection for the journey. They asked her some searching questions about her late husband and she became a little confused, and faint from the long standing. They were kind, and allowed her a chair to sit on and a glass of water.

Then the man sitting in the centre of the table told her she was Mrs. Barlow, alias Lucy Walter, that she had borne a bastard son to Charles Stuart, eldest son of the late king, and that this son was with her, together with a daughter of uncertain paternity but certainly not the child of Captain Flinck aforementioned. She was now, he told her, a spy in the pay of Charles Stuart, who had himself sent her upon this mission to England. What she knew, what she had been sent to find out, they would discover from her later. Meanwhile she would be held in custody by order of the Lord Protector. Had she anything further to say?

Strength had come back to her again. She stood up and denied all that had been said. She was Vrouw Flinck, she had

684

never been mistress to Charles Stuart and her son was the son of her late husband.

"We have your papers, madam," he said coldly. "We have your letters from Charles Stuart and the paper containing his promise of a pension. We have not yet had time to examine them fully, but we have them. Your writing desk was removed from your lodgings immediately after you left the house."

She was despairing and confused but still she tried to protect Jackie. They might send him to Carisbrooke Castle and he might die there like Princess Elizabeth. "Yes," she said, "I did bear a son to the King. But he died. The boy now with me is not the King's son."

There was no more to say and she found that she had to sit down again. They let her rest for a moment and then she was taken away, down the long stone passage that had already echoed to the steps of Tom and Justus, being taken she knew not where. A door was opened and she was in a little room with Anne and the children, and Jackie was clinging to her crying hysterically. Then they were being taken down some steps and out under the blue summer sky. They were in a street. And presently they were going down steps again and being helped into a boat. The waterman pushed off and they were out on the river travelling towards London Bridge. The sun and air, the circling gulls and the happy traffic of the busy river revived them, and Lucy soon had the children laughing and happy. For them now the queer thing that had happened to their shopping expedition had turned into just another of their river trips. "Where are we going, maman?" asked Jackie.

"You will see," replied Lucy gaily.

They were passing under the bridge and she remembered vividly her journey as a child with Robert Sidney. While the children were crying out in delicious terror at the strange echoing noises under the bridge Lucy whispered to the man beside her, "Where are you taking us?"

"To the Tower, madam," he whispered back. "By the order of the Lord Protector."

She realized that she had known the answer before she

asked the question. They were out in the sunshine again and came very soon to the familiar steps and saw the great fortress looming above them, but the darkness that had fallen upon her as a child spared her as they got out of the boat, so engrossed was she with the children. Jackie was clinging to her with one hand and clutching his puppy with the other. She looked down at him and he gazed up at her, wide-eyed and terrified. "It is the zoo," she said. "Where they keep animals. I told you about it. I came here when I was a little girl and I had a happy time. You will too."

She smiled back over her shoulder to Mary and Anne who were following. Mary's answering smile was not very sure of itself but Anne's was serene as a summer's day. Thanking God for her maid's steadiness Lucy mounted the steps with a dignity that even Anne Boleyn and Lady Jane Grey, who had come this way before her, had not been able to equal. Catching the infection of courage from his mother and from Anne Jackie recovered the royal composure he had shown in the street when they had wanted to take away his puppy.

"A beautiful boy," thought the man who was waiting in the shadows of the doorway above them. "And the girl moves like a queen." It had never been the custom for a Lieutenant of the Tower to act the part of welcoming host to any but prisoners of the very highest rank, but Sir John Barkstead had been curious to see this couple and he came forward now and bowed politely to Lucy and her son, as long ago Mr. Cottington had bowed to Robert Sidney and the little Lucy. This repetition was surely a good omen, she told herself. That visit had had a happy ending and by the mercy of God this one would too.

But once inside the Tower the two visits no longer resembled each other. They were taken to no friendly library this time but handed over to a warder who took them upon what seemed an interminable journey through echoing, ascending tunnels of stone, and once they heard the roaring of lions in the deeps below them.

Then they were in their cell, and alone, and it seemed that they were not to be separated for there were two beds in two corners of the cell, with a small truckle-bed pushed under each. And they could see the river from the barred window. And presently food was brought to them and because they were ravenously hungry that was good too. Their apprehensive thoughts clung to these comforting things and found respite. "We are being kindly treated," said Lucy. And indeed it was so. No crime had been proved against them yet. They were simply awaiting in custody the pleasure of the Lord Protector. They were here on a visit, the children were told, and when after their meal they were tucked up on one of the beds with the puppy they were instantly asleep.

Lucy and Anne sat on the hard bench by the window and without the children the respite was suddenly over. "What did you say, Anne?" Lucy asked.

"The truth, madam. They asked me if you were Mrs. Barlow, mistress of Charles Stuart, and if Jackie was his son, and I said yes."

"When they asked me the same thing I said I was Vrouw Flinck and Jackie the son of my dead husband. You knew, Anne, that I travel under an assumed name for Jackie's safety."

"Did you not notice that there were three men in the street when we came out, but only two got into the coach? I looked back as we drove away and saw the third going into the house. I imagined he would quickly find your private papers and so when I stood before the Council it seemed the truth would be best."

"You were right, Anne. But how did he find my papers so soon? My little desk was hidden under my clothes in the big chest, and my letters from the King were in the secret drawer."

Anne smiled a little. "These men know women always hide their treasures under their clothes, and secret drawers are not hard to find."

"Mine was hard to find."

"No, madam. I found it long ago on our first visit to Paris."

The two looked at each other. Anne had been very white all day but now the colour flooded her face, making the scars of the burning stand out clearly. "Did you read my letters from the King?" asked Lucy quietly.

"Yes. I did not love you then as I do now. You are the first person I have loved since my mother died."

Lucy took Anne's hand but she did not look at her since Anne was now crying a little, and she knew her maid was not the type to cry easily or to wish to be looked at while she did it. She did not know that she had more to forgive Anne than the reading of her letters, nor did she know that the effect of this imprisonment upon their outward lives would be negligible but upon their relationship to each other deep and lasting. When she spoke again it was to turn their thoughts back from a forgiven treachery to the dilemma of the moment. "We have told a different story. Will that weigh against us?"

"It may, madam. We are suspected of being spies, I believe. That seemed to me the reason for all the many questions they asked me about yourself and your way of life, and about Mr. Justus Walter. They suspect him too. I imagine all will depend upon how soon Colonel Howard is able to clear himself, and afterwards we hope to clear us."

"Colonel Howard?"

"He is a Parliament spy. Did you not realize it? How else could he have come so openly to England?"

"Tom, Tom," murmured Lucy, and she would hardly believe it. Tom, who was so kind and had been a boy with Charles, a traitor to him. Tom a traitor to Charles. She was too stunned to weep.

"The Colonel would have an easier task if Mr. Richard Walter had come over with us," said Anne.

"Yes," Lucy answered sadly. It would always hurt that Richard was a Parliament man, but she was not so fond of him as she was of Tom. Then with a movement she felt the presence of her marriage certificate sewn inside her corsets. At least that, the most precious to her of all her papers, had not been in the little desk. And her ruby ring was on her finger and her mother's pearls round her neck. But the diamond brooch and the Queen of Bohemia's jewels were in the desk. "My jewels, Anne," she whispered.

"If they do not return those they will be thieves," Anne said. "And they call themselves Godly men, servants of God and all the rest of their clap-trap. We have a hold over them there."

They ate their supper and went to bed, Jackie sleeping beside his mother and Mary beside Anne. But Lucy could not sleep for clouds had covered the sky and exhaustion and darkness were soon busy with their habitual task of turning every molehill of trouble into a mountain of tragedy. Tom spying on his King. Anne reading her letters. She could understand now why Charles's thoughts were always so neurotically occupied with the subject of disloyalty. It was a hideous thing and the fear of it a sickly poison in the blood. Anne she had forgiven already, for to love Anne, she intuitively knew, was one of the reasons why she was still alive, but that did not lessen her grief or her fear lest that one thing had not been the end of Anne's treachery. And she was afraid that in spite of his kindness her affection for Tom had turned to something very like hatred; for it was not against her that he had sinned but Charles. "Oh God," she prayed, "Not hatred. Do not let me hate."

But still she seemed imprisoned in a hatred of Tom that mounted slowly as the moonless darkness deepened the horror of the place where she was. She tried not to think of the things that had happened within these walls, but it was impossible not to think of them for grief and agony were imprisoned in each cell of this evil body of stone in whose grip she lay.

This Tower was not a place, it was a living demonic thing whose dark spirit fell upon her again as when she was a child. The terror then had seemed prophetic. Was it this it had foretold? No, not this. The menace was still in the future. She drifted into a half-dream in which she was wrestling with the thing, trying to keep it held to her own being that it might not fall upon Jackie, but she did not succeed for Jackie suddenly cried out and awoke and came scrambling up into her bed like a terrified nestling. Broad awake now she pulled him under the blanket with her. "It was only a nightmare, my darling," she said as she hugged him. "Tell me about it. What was it?"

But like Mary Jackie only trembled and could not tell her what it was. But the mere fact of their two bodies clinging together, the comforting warmth of human flesh, soon steadied them both and Jackie whispered, "Tell me a story, maman."

For the first time in their lives she found herself telling him a grown-up story, no fairy prince this time but the story of the man who had been in her thoughts ever since she had come back to London. She told him about Old Sage. She described the herb stall under the dark tree beside the white Ionic columns, and told him how she used to sit in the church, and the sweet smell that came from the herbs stored in the roof. Jackie was fascinated and for an hour they whispered together of the marvellous old man, and Old Sage was as much with them as though he had noiselessly unlocked the door of the cell and walked in. "And he is dead," Jackie said at last with sudden sadness. "He is gone."

"Not gone," Lucy answered instantly. "The Great Ones come back."

"What do they do?" asked Jackie.

"They come back," repeated Lucy, "And go about the world. They go where they are wanted."

Jackie murmured something and was asleep, and presently Lucy too was asleep. They slept deeply and peacefully and were awakened in the morning by the sun shining on their faces.

5

For the children the days passed pleasantly. They were allowed to go to the inner garden with Anne and play there, and on the third day they had toys to play with because a wonderful thing happened. The door opened and the warder came in carrying a bundle which he gave to Lucy with a smile. It contained a few garments and kerchiefs, Mary's two dollies Polly and Sally and Jackie's favourite toy, a wooden model of a mounted cavalier. Also, carefully wrapped in a little shawl was Lucy's miniature of her father. "Anne!" she ejaculated with shining eyes, "Colonel Howard is free already!"

"The landlady could have packed the bundle," said Anne.

"The landlady does not know which are the children's favourite toys," said Lucy, "Nor how dearly I love my miniature." She searched everything carefully, even the petticoats on the wooden dollies, but there was no letter.

"They would have searched the bundle before it was given to you, madam," said Anne. But Lucy went on looking and then saw that securing the bonnet on one of the dollies was a pin with a green head. "Look!" she said to Anne. "That pin belongs to Colonel Howard."

Two days later the Lieutenant of the Tower himself took the children to see the lions, and they came back to the cell for their midday meal chattering of what they had seen and done. But Anne, Lucy realized, though she laughed and talked with the children, was more deeply unhappy with each day that passed. "What is it, Anne?" she asked.

"Nothing, madam," replied Anne.

Lucy could have gone to the garden too, if she had wished, but she was not strong enough for the long steep journeys of the Tower and so she spent the days lying on her bed, locked in the cell, alone and glad to be alone, gathering her strength. This lying still at every opportunity to gather strength was now a daily necessity. At first she had rebelled but now she treasured her lonely times. She prayed as well as she could, saying daily Dr. Cosin's prayers for Charles, remembering all Dr. Jeremy Taylor had taught her and praying the prayer he had given her, widening it to include them all. "Keep us, O Lord, for we are thine by creation; guide us for we are thine by purchase. Let thy mercy pardon us and thy care watch over us."

And she turned the pages of the book of memories that she called her Book of Hours, lingering a long time over the ones that had borders of bees and butterflies surrounding people whom she loved stepping through golden sunshine in gay garments, with illuminated capital letters for words like Love and Joy and Peace. These were the pages that held her memories of Roch, Golden Grove and the golden hearted rose, her grandmother and Old Sage, happy hours with Lord Taaffe, and above all memories of the three idyls with Charles; the days together in Wales, the time of happiness after Jackie had been born, the day and night together in the little house at Antwerp.

Sometimes her memories became confused and the people who walked in the sunshine did so in oddly assorted couples. Indeed it seemed to her sometimes that she was looking not backward but forward. Lord Taaffe laughed with Nan-Nan in the garden at Roch, and Charles sat and talked with Old Sage in the church at Covent Garden, and Old Sage was no longer dumb; indeed it was he who talked while Charles listened. And Parson Peregrine walked with Lucy's children holding to his hands. She had thought much of Parson Peregrine since the stones of the Tower had closed about her. His prison, the hulk ship, had been not far away and she did not doubt that he had died there. But she had not thought of him with sadness because in her Book of Hours he always walked in gold, on a path that was bordered by the roses and lilies of a martyr's death.

And since she had been in the little house at Antwerp there had been another who walked that same path. He had appeared mysteriously, the only figure whom she did not know, a lame old man who walked slowly. He had a wrinkled, bearded face, very bright eyes and a domed forehead. He reminded her of Old Sage but he was not Old Sage. He was smaller physically but equally great.

When they had been at the Louvre Dr. Cosin had read her and Jackie a poem about heaven written by Bernard of Cluny, and it reminded her of her Book of Hours, for in it the blessed were walking among flowers.

> *And through the sacred lilies*
> *And flowers on every side,*
> *The happy dear bought people*
> *Are wandering far and wide.*

Could that be a part of heaven, she wondered, watching those one loved, unknown to each other on earth, delightfully united by one's loving? But how great must be the power of love that could make that union, and how selfless, for on the pages of her book she never found herself. But how did one learn to love like that? How did one get to heaven at all? How? Lying on her bed in the Tower she cried out again to God, "Do not let me hate Tom for what he is doing to Charles. Do not let me hate. Do not let me hate Anne." But she did not hate Anne. She had forgiven her for reading her letters. So why did she pray not to hate Anne?

Towards the end of their stay in the Tower a night came when she knew why. In the timelessness to which prayer carries the one who prays she had known how deeply she would soon need the help of God. It was a night of moon and stars, very still, and Jackie, so often disturbed by bad dreams, was sleeping happily and peacefully beside her. But Mary, her mother sensed, was wide awake in the opposite corner of the cell. Yet she dare not call to her for fear of waking Jackie.

Presently Mary came quietly creeping to her. "Have you a pain, my darling?" whispered Lucy. But Mary was seldom concerned with her own troubles, only other people's. "Anne," she whispered to her mother. "She is crying, maman. Anne is crying."

"Get into my bed but do not wake Jackie," whispered Lucy, "and I will go to Anne. Mind you go to sleep."

Mary nodded and did as she was told and Lucy put her mother's cloak round her shoulders and went to Anne. She was sobbing almost soundlessly into her pillow but even so Lucy was appalled that someone she loved, lying only the room's breadth away from her, could be in despair and she not know it. She pushed Mary's truckle-bed under Anne's and knelt down on the floor beside her. She did not insult her by asking her if she was afraid; Anne was fearless and had not for a moment felt scared of the Tower. And this was something much deeper than fear. "You must tell me, Anne," she said. Though Anne had turned her face away from her the movement had told Lucy that she knew she was there. There was no reply until Anne's sobs gradually became manageable. "No," she said.

"You must," said Lucy. "Whom have we in the world just now but each other? And we do not know what we have yet to face. Because we are innocent we are hopeful, but we may deceive ourselves. The innocent frequently suffer for the sins of the guilty."

There was a long silence and Anne's sobs utterly ceased. Then she turned her face to Lucy. Only the light of the moon illumined the room and it may have been that it was a face less ghastly than the one Lucy saw. "You have put it into words," she said. "That is why you are suffering now. Why you have suffered so long. For my sin."

"I do not understand," said Lucy, "but I do know that you must tell me what troubles you. We may die in this place and we must both die in penitence."

To men and women of their generation this was a matter of supreme importance. Priests would labour at the bedside of the dying, almost tormenting them, to see that no stone of sin was left unturned and unrepented of. In no other way, they thought, could a soul pass on in peace, and who knows if they were not quite right. There was no priest with Lucy and Anne but the extraordinary beauty of complete silence seemed to have fallen upon the prison. Anne told it all and it seemed to both her and Lucy to take hours. Actually it was soon told. Just a short story of vile treachery, with cause and motivation so deep and entangled that it was not possible for either girl to understand them.

"And yet," said Anne at last, "I love you. I have never loved anyone except my mother, and you and the children. It was when I thought you were dying at The Hague that I began to get free."

Lucy had listened all the while with her face buried in her arms laid upon the bed, and so Anne could not see her face. She had heard all that Anne said to her, and understood it, and she knew that her life was in ruins because of Anne. The day and night with Charles at Antwerp, that she had hoped had restored trust between them, would remain with him merely as an untrustworthy dream. The reality that would persist was his poisoned mind. Hatred, she found, was not hot but cold. It broke over her in waves so that she shivered. What was the good of truth? What was the use of love? She had given Anne both and was smashed to pieces, and now there was no help anywhere. None at all. Yet a voice deep in her was crying for help, a child's voice saying childishly, "God? God." Just in that way had a child in a cave summoned help. No glow of comfort now, no golden hearted rose, only a sense of tearing and rending and then a voice speaking out loud, "You are utterly forgiven. What you did is washed away by all your tears."

She heard the voice but did not think it was her own. Nor did she know that her head had come up from her arms until she found Anne's terrible ravaged face within a few inches of her own. Their lips met, Anne's burning hot, Lucy's ice-cold from the hatred that was still breaking over her. Anne slipped her hands under the cloak and felt Lucy's body. "My love, my love," she cried, "you are cold as ice. Go back to your bed and let me cover you up warmly. There is room there for you and Mary too."

Lucy gave a gasp of relief. There had been a moment when she had thought that Anne was going to take her into her own bed to warm her. If she had been made to lie beside the woman in the same bed she would have screamed. But Anne put her back in her own bed and said to Mary, who wakened when they came to her, "Lie close to your mother and keep her warm."

Once more there was the ghastly rending within her and the voice that was not her own speaking. "Go back to bed, Anne, and go to sleep. It is over. All is well between us."

"Madam, madam," whispered Anne, and went sobbing back to her bed. Lucy heard her crying softly for some while, but now it was merely the weeping of exhaustion and relief and presently she was asleep.

"Is Anne happy now?" Mary asked from within the curve of her mother's arm about her.

"She is happy now," said Lucy.

"Are you warm now, maman?"

"You are like a little warming-pan, my poppet. Now go to sleep."

So Mary slept and Jackie, dreaming blissfully of lions, had

never waked at all. Lucy lay without movement until morning came and the great Tower with its enclosed burden of misery woke to another day.

It was a warm and sunny day and Anne and Jackie spent it in the garden, for Lucy had a bad headache and Jackie was in a noisy mood. To keep his noise away from his mother was, Anne knew, the best service she could render today; and as for the rest of her days, they belonged now to Lucy and her children. Mary was with them in the garden during the morning but after the midday meal in their cell she would not leave her mother. She sat on the floor beside Lucy's bed and played quietly with her dollies. "Go to sleep, maman," she said. Lucy smiled and shook her head. She did not want even to try to sleep while her headache was so bad. Sleep shot through with pain brought nightmares.

She lay still, holding to something she had heard Anne say last night. "I began to get free." She remembered her childhood's thoughts of two webs, the dark and the light. Had the web of madness and hatred spun about Anne in her youth kept her a prisoner against her own consent and knowledge? If so it was not Anne herself whom she hated now with such horror but simply evil.

She put her hands to her head, wanting to still the pain that she might think. They were gently removed and Mary's small hands took their place. Her daughter was standing beside her. "Maman, I will make you better. Then you will go to sleep and have a lovely dream." It happened. Under the child's hands the headache went slowly away and with astonishment Lucy found herself at peace from pain, and drifted into sleep.

She passed from one happy dream to another, small dreams gay as pages from the Book of Hours; but they were only stepping stones that carried her deeper, right down to the roots of being, to the kitchen at Roch. The fire burned on the great hearth and she was standing looking down into the well of living water. A man was standing beside her wrapped in a cloak and she was talking to him, and the conversation seemed familiar to her. "Is it true that one man can take upon himsel the sin of another?" she asked. "Can he save him that way? Is it really true?"

"Yes," said the man slowly. "If the sinner will accept salvation, it is true."

Lucy remembered now. These words had been spoken before, and the man beside her was Old Parson, who was dead. She had been remembering the sin-eater when she had asked him that question. "Tell me more," she said.

"The man who is the cause of the suffering can be saved by the man who bears it, if the tortured man for love's sake can take the sin upon himself together with the pain. That is the way it is. It is quite simple, if the sinner for love's sake will accept salvation. And she has."

The slow old voice had changed. This man was speaking with the tongue of angels. He was no longer Old Parson. He was Old Sage, who was also dead.

"But I did not know that I suffered for her, I did not know I had taken her sin upon me."

"You pledged yourself to love her when you were in Paris," Old Sage reminded her. "You knew that you must love her. When you accept the burden of love you pledge yourself to know not what. Knowledge of what we are doing is not always given to us even while we fulfil the pledge."

"Treachery is hard to forgive," said Lucy. "I have not forgiven Anne. It was not my voice that spoke the words."

"No," agreed the man beside her. "But you called upon God and Christ within you spoke the words. Will you now betray Christ?"

"It is hard to forgive treachery," Lucy repeated.

"Indeed it is. I found it so," agreed the man. "I found it harder to forgive the treachery of the smiling friend who betrayed me to the stake than to forgive the men who lit the fire. Indeed it was only in the flame that I could do it."

He was no longer speaking with the tongue of angels. He had a high weak old voice and he was no longer Old Sage. His head came out from the shadows of his cloak in much the same sort of comic way that the head of a wise old tortoise appears from its shell, and she saw the bearded face of the old man in her Book of Hours who walked between the lilies and the roses. She looked at him for a long time and could not have told when his face changed from that of a mere man and became the face of forgiveness itself. She woke up, and knew she had slept for long. Her patient little daughter was still with her, sitting on the floor beside the bed dressing and undressing one dolly after the other to make the time pass.

"Mary," she said softly, and there was healing in the mere speaking of the name, since it was one of the loveliest in the world and belonged to her daughter.

Mary looked up and smiled. "Maman," she replied.

6

They all slept well that night but were awakened at first light by the sound of voices and tramping feet in the passage outside the cell. Lucy, waking suddenly, might have been frightened, only the voices were so cheerful and one, almost beyond hope or belief, she recognized.

The door was unlocked and Justus walked in. He sat on the edge of Lucy's bed and hugged her briefly, then said, "You are free. Get up quickly and get dressed. You too, Anne. Get the children dressed. You are free but you cannot stay in England. There is a ship on the Thames sailing for Flanders in an hour, on the ebb tide, and a boat waiting for you at the water steps to take you out to her. You will find food and all you want on board. Be quick. Jackie, do as you are told. Yes, you can take the puppy."

It was still so dark that they had to light candles to see what they were doing. Justus packed their few belongings into bundles as they dressed, Mary directing the bestowal of her dollies with quiet competence, and briefly told Lucy all that had happened as he did so. He had been cleared and set free two days ago but had not been allowed to see her. He and Tom had spent the night packing Lucy's belongings at the lodgings and they were already on board. Her little desk had been returned to her, her papers and letters safely back inside it and her jewels untouched. Tom had cleared Lucy and Justus and convinced Parliament that they were not spies. It had not taken too long, for he was a trusted Parliament agent.

"He is not coming to say goodbye to you," said Justus. "He thought you would not want to see him."

"I hope never to see him again," said Lucy. "I can forgive anything done to myself but how could he behave so to Charles?"

"You will have to forgive him," said Justus grimly. "He has been good to you, and he has got us free, and he will be returning to Europe later. The working of other people's minds is always incomprehensible but one must forgive."

"You are coming with me, Justus?" whispered Lucy.

"I am not allowed to, my dear. I shall not be allowed to leave England again and you will not be allowed to return. This is goodbye. Thank God for those days of paradise together at Antwerp. I wish I could have seen the old man who let you have his house so cheaply, and thanked him for it. If you ever see him, thank him for me. It is goodbye for you and me but do not forget that Richard and Dewi are on the other side of the Channel, and Smuts and his family. You have friends. You are not alone."

He talked on as cheerfully as he could and did not look at Lucy. They were quickly ready and went out into the passage where a warder was waiting for them with a lantern. He took them down to the arched doorway by which they had entered the Tower, where the Lieutenant was standing. He bowed pleasantly to Lucy and Justus and showed them the order for their release, signed by the Lord Protector, that he held in his hand. Then the door was opened and they went out, and a glorious rush of fresh air met them. In a moment it seemed to blow away all the terror and smells of the prison. The sky was now a translucent green and the morning star was shining. London lay sleeping beside the river and the silence was deep. They went down the steps to the boat that was waiting and it seemed that Justus was not allowed to go out to the ship with them. They must say goodbye here on the steps. They did so and it seemed to them both a terrible rending of farewell. Yet all round them was this great cool freshness and silence.

Lucy found they were out on the water, the warder still with them, moving swiftly down the river towards the waiting ship. Jackie was cuddled up against her with his puppy in his arms, and Anne and Mary held together for warmth under Anne's cloak.

"Maman," said Jackie suddenly, "what day is it?"

"It is Thursday, July the sixteenth," said Lucy.

"Thursday July the sixteenth," repeated Jackie thoughtfully. "I will not forget that date."

Seventeen

Charles never saw Lucy again and he did not forgive her for taking Jackie to England. The letter she wrote him from London, trying to explain how it had happened, arrived not long after one in a similar vein from Smuts Harvey; but that letter came only one day after Charles had been told that Mr. Harvey, the nephew of his father's doctor and a member of a loyal Royalist family, to whom he had gone in absolute trust when he arrived in Antwerp, was a Parliament man.

It was only one step from there to think he was a spy like Howard. And only one step further to think that Lucy herself was in the pay of Howard and Harvey and had been used by them to spy upon him. Her marvellous charm during the day and night in the peaceful house at Antwerp had had its purpose and he wished he could remember what he had been fool enough to say to her there. And he wished he knew what she had said about him in London. That it had been useful to Cromwell he did not doubt since she had so soon been set free. When, later, plans for an invasion once more went wrong and good men suffered torture and imprisonment he did not hold her guiltless.

And now it was not only men like Prodgers and O'Neil who implored him at all cost to get his son away from Mrs. Barlow. The Marquis of Ormonde and Sir Edward Hyde were doing the same thing. That the King should have gone to Antwerp with the express purpose of taking Jackie from his mother, and instead had spent the night with her, leaving her house without the boy and minus the diamond brooch which had been supplied for purposes of bribery, had shaken them. They had known their sovereign to be weak where women were concerned but that he could be quite as helpless as this they had

not known. If only to part the King from Mrs. Barlow her son
had better leave her and come to the King.

Charles now agreed with them. Because he believed she had
betrayed him, and because this treachery was the bitterest of
all, his thoughts of Lucy were equally bitter. They were to get
the boy from her, he said, by whatever means they chose so
long as they were not cruel. He took the initial step. He commanded Lucy, Anne and the two children to lodge in Brussels
in the house of Sir Arthur and Lady Slingsby, loyal Royalists
who were, he had been assured, kind as well as loyal, and then
he washed his hands of the whole business.

Lucy obeyed his command. The house was a pleasant one
adjoining the park but she found herself virtually in prison,
and she did not find Sir Arthur and Lady Slingsby kindly
people. The task of getting Jackie from her was their responsibility but they had the help of Edward Prodgers and Captain O'Neil. The royal command of no cruelty they
interpreted as meaning that physical force must not be used.
Lucy must consent to part with the boy. The winning of this
consent by mental cruelty did not, to their way of thinking,
come under the heading of cruelty at all, and Lucy was subjected to the whole range of its pressure.

She retained her courage but not her common sense. Her
mind had become confused under the pressure of illness and
anxiety and she could not see that Jackie's only hope lay now,
and not at some future date, with his father. She could only see
that she must not give him into the hands of these evil men
about her. She saw them now as wholly evil and Anne agreed
with her and encouraged her in her refusal to part with her
son.

Anne had broken free from Prodgers and would no longer
speak to him. After a brief, bitter quarrel she had told him
that unknown to Lucy she had written to the King and told
His Majesty how he had been deceived. Prodgers had merely
laughed. "I thought you might do that," he had said. "You
have much courage, my girl, and I admire you for it. His Majesty would not take your word against mine, I believe, but to
be on the safe side I spoke a warning word to his secretary."

Colonel Howard came to Brussels but Lucy refused to see him. Richard, because he worked with Tom, she would not see either. Dewi, who had found work as a groom at a big house in Brussels in order to be near her, she was allowed to see occasionally and his love was a comfort.

But poor Dewi found himself in a cleft stick. His loyalty to Lucy conflicted now with his loyalty to the King and his love for Charles was part of him. He could only live with his dilemma by refusing to think it out. As his intellectual powers were not great this was not too difficult, but the unresolved conflict made him irritable and his temper was in a permanently volcanic state. He had discovered now that Tom was a spy and he hated him for it but cautioned by Richard he kept out of his way. Then, one evening at dusk, they met in a lonely street. They quarrelled and Dewi went berserk and shot Tom, wounding him badly. Poor Tom took the calamity with humour and recovered. Richard, returning to England, forcibly took Dewi with him and handed him back to Justus, declining to accept future responsibility for him.

Lucy took the horrible business very much to heart and it only increased her mental confusion. One night when Sir Arthur lost his temper, and threatened to put her in prison while he took Jackie from her, she started screaming hysterically and ran out into the street with her son, trying to escape. The pitiful scandal of this was the talk of Brussels and she found that many were on her side. One of them was the Spanish Ambassador, Don Alfonso de Cardenas, and he wrote to Charles telling him of the treatment she had received. But the persecution continued. Some of Lucy's papers were stolen from her and Prodgers, losing patience at last, made an abortive but terrifying attempt to kidnap Jackie. And then suddenly the unbelievable persecution came to an end, for Lucy yielded.

She was secretly visited by the Marquis of Ormonde. Dismayed by the revelations of the Spanish Ambassador he came himself to enquire into their truth. He talked first with Sir Arthur Slingsby, and heard what he had to say in the icy silence of instant and total dislike. Then he asked to see Mrs.

Barlow, steeling himself for the interview with resolution but distaste. Cruelty to a woman must be stopped whatever her lack of moral fibre, but he was not himself attracted to women of her type.

He found the woman lying on a sofa, a typically fibreless position, endeavouring to educate her children with the help of an old hornbook, a bible and a ball of string. The last was perhaps for the making of cat's-cradles but a little white dog was playing with it on the floor when he entered the room. Education was perhaps not progressing very fast, but he heard the children's laughter before the door was opened and he was announced. "The Marquis of Ormonde." There was a moment of shocked silence and then Lucy tried to get up. "Please do not rise, madam," he said formally. But Lucy struggled up and stood clinging to the back of a chair, looking up at him with terrified eyes.

He looked at her and was conscious of a sudden sense of vertigo. Was this the notorious Mrs. Barlow? Had some appalling mistake been made? Was he in the right room? He must be for here were the two children. His monarch was less of a fool than he had thought. Taaffe also. For a moment his thoughts whirled as madly as a flock of disturbed birds, then suddenly settled as he took his habitual command of himself, the persons present and the situation. But even with the persons seated and the situation in perspective uneasiness remained. There was somewhere, concealed like a snake in the grass, an appalling mistake.

He talked gently for a few moments, admiring the children and the dog, and Lucy found her terror dying away. For this was Lord Ormonde, one of Charles's greatest servants and Lord Taaffe's hero, and like all the truly great he had a quality of courteous humility that gave ease to the heart. Presently Anne took the children away and they were alone.

"He is a very beautiful boy, madam," said Lord Ormonde gravely.

He was so gentle that Lucy did not find it difficult to ask a direct question. "Has your lordship come to take him away from me?"

He was equally direct. "Not without your permission. I have come primarily because I have heard that too hard a pressure has been put upon you in this matter. It is undoubtedly urgent but no urgency justifies cruelty."

"There has been no physical cruelty," said Lucy, "and for the rest, I would rather not talk of it. But is it not always cruel to separate a child from his mother?"

"Against her wish, yes. With her understanding and cooperation, no."

"You spoke of urgency. Do you think it an urgent matter that Jackie should be taken from me?"

"Yes, I do. The boy is a bundle of nerves. Do you not realize it? His father can give him a good education and a settled home. What can you offer him?"

Lucy evaded the question. "What education? What home?" she asked.

"The King has in mind a little school near Versailles where a group of children of noble rank are taught under the care of the Ecclesiastics of Port Royal. It is a good school and he would be with boys of his own age. And the home would be with his grandmother."

"Would the Queen make him a Catholic?" asked Lucy.

A twinkle was seen in the Marquis's kind eyes. "Not if Dr. Cosin could prevent it, madam. It would be a case of which of the two could move first and fastest."

Lucy smiled and a small glow of happiness came to her, the first for months. It was the mention of Dr. Cosin. He had passed entirely from her life but now she remembered him sitting in his shabby study, with Jackie playing on the floor. And she saw Jackie running in the gardens of the Louvre that he had loved, and remembered how he had cried when they had left Paris. And he had loved his grandmother too, and his little Aunt Minette.

Her clouded mind had begun to clear a little. The struggle for Jackie had been between herself and men whom she thought of as wholly bad. It had seemed a struggle with evil. She had forgotten what might lie behind the evil façade; Dr. Cosin, gold leaves drifting in a garden, a kindly grandmother, a minute but motherly aunt, a good school. Phrases that people had used about her son stabbed her mind. "The little brat. Totally ignorant. A spoilt child. A bundle of nerves." Her mind was clearing. The Marquis realized that change was in the air, one of those changes that shape history. Only a change of mind, a reorientation of a tortured human spirit, but who can tell where such a change will take many lives? He sat in silence and waited.

"Can you take him yourself?" she whispered.

"Hardly, for I must leave tomorrow. The boy needs assurance of the happiness to which he goes. At present he is terrified and it will not be easy to bring him from one frame of mind to another. Only you can do it."

"I cannot hand him over to any of the men here."

"Indeed, you cannot. I will talk to the King. We must send the right man to fetch the boy, someone who will inspire his love and confidence. And for yourself, madam, I can assure you that you will suffer no more persecution." He paused and added grimly, "I shall take pleasure in making that absolutely certain." He got up. "Do you wish to see me again?"

She shook her head and then asked, "Are you trusting me?"

"Absolutely. You have seen what is for the boy's good and are a mother capable of sacrifice. And the boy is worth it. Your little daughter, madam, also commands my admiration. The eyes of a very wise woman look out from her child's face. I congratulate you on your children, and your children on their mother."

He bowed and left her, but not without a raft to cling to in the storm of misery breaking over her. She was trusted to be a good mother.

But the waiting time was hard, especially when news came of the death of Lord Wilmot. She mourned for her kind friend, and remembered the lament for Siôn that Geraint the Harper had sung at Golden Grove:

> *Yesterday at home, proudly,*
> *And today, under the shroud*

Men who are youthful and brave
Go early up to heaven...

That he should die so young, who might have lived had times
been happier, seemed an epitome of the experience of them
all. Their lives had gone awry because the times were twisted.
And the times were twisted because men's thoughts, that
should have been lifting straight upwards to God like larks to
the sun, moved only in evil spirals about themselves. Yet
perhaps Lord Wilmot, set free, was more fortunate than poor
Tom. Somehow because Lord Wilmot had died her heart
began to soften towards Tom.

She prepared Jackie as well and selflessly as she could.
Whether the King intended that she should be totally parted
from him she did not know, but she let him think that they
would see each other again. He could remember the Louvre,
she found, and his grandmother and Minette, and they were
happy memories because they were memories of safety. He
had felt very secure in the big house that kept things out, and
in the gardens where he played in a silence soft as a feather
bed. He seemed to dread school only a little, for he wished to
play with other boys. He was sorry he would see maman only
occasionally but her spoiling had bred selfishness in him and
he was getting fretted by her perpetual headaches, and Anne
scolding him and telling him to be quiet.

He was in fact growing up and becoming conscious of his
superior sex and there were time when females wearied him,
and when a cheerful young man called Thomas Ross, a gentleman of the King's bedchamber, arrived to take him to Shir Da
he took an instant fancy to him. And so did Lucy. Charles and
Lord Ormonde had chosen their man well. He had a kind,
amused, sensible face and there was about him a feeling of
wholesome strength and goodness that was balm after
Prodgers and O'Neil. He stayed with them for a couple of
nights and listened patiently to all Lucy's pathetic instructions
in regard to Jackie's feeding, ailments, nightmares, sensitiveness, tastes and tempers.

The last night came and Lucy took her marriage certificate

that Prodgers had looked for endlessly and never found, from the lining of her corsets and sewed it into the lining of Jackie's new blue doublet, that he would not grow out of for some while because it was too large, and told him he must keep it secret for the present but never part with it.

He listened to her with great round eyes. By some alchemy of grief working upon the clouded mind of a sick woman she had come round in a circle to believe that the certificate recorded a real marriage. Jackie thought so too. He was very certain now of his own importance and it upheld him in the moment of parting from maman. For in spite of having Snowy in his arms and of knowing it was right that the King's son, together with his dog, should enter now into a man's world, and in spite of the fact that maman did not cry at all when she said goodbye, and that the last memory he had of her was her lovely smiling face, the blue eyes full of light, being taken from her was a dreadful moment. As the coach rattled away he gasped, but Thomas Ross's strong arm came round him as he whispered in the boy's ear, "The King said I was to buy you a little sword. Shall we go and choose it?"

Pushing Anne away Lucy went straight upstairs and fell on her bed. She lay there for days in a daze of grief and exhaustion and seemed hardly aware that Mary sat beside her all the time, trying to get the Lord's prayer properly by heart from her hornbook. She was a poor scholar but she thought it would please maman, when she was better again, to find that her daughter could at last say it through correctly. Also she had an idea, never to leave her, that saying one's prayers was the best thing to do in desolation.

At the end of four days Lucy sat up and said she was going to The Hague.

"Think of the journey, madam!" said Anne, aghast.

"If I stay longer in Brussels I shall go mad," said Lucy. "I want the storks. There was a stork at Roch. A little one in the kitchen."

She was unreasonable in her grief and poor Anne packed their belongings, hired a coach and they set forth. Lucy survived the journey with surprising resilience. Actually there was something about a journey that always had a tonic effect upon her. The sense of movement, of road or river passing away behind her yet unrolling its newness like an unfolding map, always gave her a sense of hope. You suffer to the point of agony but you pass on. And still on. The lovely horizon recedes but a day will come when it will not do so. Time and space will be outdistanced and the road pass off the map.

They went to the farm at Scheveningen and it was spring. Lucy revived enough to go out on the dunes, where she would sit for hours watching the sea. They might have stayed all the summer but Vrouw Flinck and Betje still did not like Anne. She was patient under their dislike but she was not happy, and her happiness mattered supremely to Lucy.

They found a tiny house at The Hague beside a canal. It had windows that caught the sunlight and storks walked up and down outside the front door. Mrs. Barlow had been forgotten in a fresh crop of stories about someone else and no one realized Lucy's identity. Anne was happy now with all the work of the house to do, and Lucy sat at the open window of her parlour and watched her daughter playing beside the canal with other children.

Mary loved helping Anne with the housework, and doing lessons with her mother, but she was friendly and she liked to have companions in her play. And she talked to all and sundry in a way that her mother found rather alarming. One day Lucy saw her in conversation with an old man who leaned upon a stick, and then she saw them walking away together hand in hand. In a panic she called Anne, who ran after them. She came back not having caught the truant but with reassuring information about the old man, gathered from neighbours.

"He lodges just round the corner," she told Lucy. "A very old gentleman, a little touched in the head but quite harmless, and the children love him. They go into his courtyard and he tells them stories. No, he is not a native of The Hague. He comes from Antwerp."

"Antwerp," murmured Lucy, and remembered the little house. It was strange to think that she had once been happy.

The days of dull despair in which she lived now seemed to have lasted for ever. Her heart ached for Jackie and her body ached as she drove it through the slow mechanical motions of each day. Her mind was dark, emptied of faith, and it was only when Anne or Mary was with her that she knew she was alive. She still knew that this was Anne whom she must love and her little daughter whom she must protect. The thought of Mary walking away hand in hand with a stranger frightened her, reminding her of Jackie walking away hand in hand with Thomas Ross. She had not seen Jackie again and she would not see Mary again if she did not go after her and fetch her back.

When Anne had gone back to the kitchen she got up and went outside and began walking shakily in the direction taken by Mary and the man. She would have run if she could but she could no longer run. It was not far to the corner, and a few more steps brought her into the lane that turned uphill at right angles to the canal. A door in the wall was ajar, she pushed it and saw inside a small courtyard with a well and a fig tree, and sitting on the low parapet of the well was the man talking to a group of children, of whom Mary was one. She went in and he made room for her beside him but did not stop talking to the children. He did not look at her, he merely made room for her as though she was expected. His whole mind was concentrated on the children as he told them about King Solomon talking to the butterflies.

Lucy sat with her hands folded in her lap and the shadows of the fig leaves flickered over her blue skirt as though wings moved. Butterflies. A boy and girl watched them in the churchyard at Broad Clyst, but the frail things hovered over a dark sea, a wave came up and they were drowned in darkness. She was too. It was dark as night. Then she was conscious of a silence that was filling with light and knew that the dawn of a new day was coming. Patches of blue showed through the leaves that filled the window and it was morning. The shadow of the fig leaves moved on her blue skirt and she knew where she was.

The courtyard was empty now of all the children save Mary

who was playing with her dolls, deep in one of those mysterious dramas that lonely children play out with such absorption and delight. Her murmuring voice was just audible, but not always like itself, for though she was the sole actress she was playing different parts. It seemed to her mother that she moved in light, and that the courtyard was full of it. It came from someone beside her, Lucy thought, but when she turned her head there was no one there except the old man. He looked round and smiled and she had seen him before, in the kitchen at Roch in her dream.

"It has taken me longer than usual to find you," he said.

"Have you found me before?" she asked in surprise. She was feeling strangely alive. The courtyard was full of life and she was breathing it in.

"No, not you in what you feel to be your individual being. I go where I am needed but the many to whom I am sent have become one person to me, my Lord. He says go here and go there, and I go about the world and wait and watch, and he comes. Very often he wants so little, perhaps only a loaf of bread and a glass of wine and a few words clearly spoken. Sometimes more, sometimes less."

"My maid told me you live in Antwerp."

"I have a small house there that a grateful patient left me. I was an apothecary once. I live there when I am not needed elsewhere, and when I am away those who need my house are brought to it. My Lord is very economical. Nothing goes to waste in his hands. People think me a crazy old man. Is that what you think?"

"No," said Lucy, "for I lived for a while in your house. At least I think so. Has it a map upon the parlour wall?"

"Yes, a good map. I consult it before I go upon my journeys."

"There was no craziness in that house. Only sanity and peace. We behaved sanely there. We loved and understood each other. My brother asked me, if I ever met you, to thank you for that house." So much life had come to her that she was talking as easily as though she were no longer a sick woman. "You came to me in a dream," she told him. "How could you do that? For you are a man of flesh and blood, are you not?"

He laughed. "Yes. My name is Jacob. But why should a man of flesh and blood not visit you in dream? In deep sleep mind touches mind. I have no recollection of you but we do not always remember what we do in sleep. Of what did we speak, you and I?"

"Of forgiveness. You said that only in the flame had you forgiven your enemy."

"Now that is strange," said Jacob. "Strange, for I have a memory of death at the stake. I remember how they piled the faggots round me, blocking out the sunlight, and how fear came with that loss of light; and I have never been a man to be afraid."

"So we come back?" asked Lucy. Though her hand was on the thread she wanted reassurance.

"I think it probable. It is a matter of choice, perhaps, but a choice made often, for look at your little girl at her game. There are many heroes and heroines in a child's private play but only the one player. They may know the way it is. I remember, I think, a life of pride and power that crumbled in the flame. Pride of the intellect, the power of wealth and station. Beyond the flames I was without them, almost a nothingness, since even the beliefs for which I died were proved wrong by the great simplicity I found there.'

"Yet you died for them," said Lucy.

"Yes. Perhaps that is why they let me come back, a poor and simple man, my only gift a skill in tending suffering bodies, my only life my Lord, my only faith a belief in the necessity for love. And now, in what do I serve you? Take my hand and tell me, for you and I have only a short while together."

She took his hand and said, "I am in a daze of nothingness. I do not know where to go or what to do."

"Let Mary take you home now. In the morning I will come and talk with you and we will enquire of my Lord what it is that you should do."

He came the next morning, a weak old man who walked slowly, but once again he brought life with him and she found she had strength enough to talk to him. By telling her a little of himself the day before he had made it easy for her to tell him much of herself today, and she was astonished at the intimate things she told him. When she had finished he was silent for a time and she had the feeling that he had gone away and left her. But he was still beside her. He had travelled within himself, she realized, a journey of enquiry into the deeps. What image had he placed within himself? Perhaps none. Perhaps his prayer was imageless. Where he had gone was no golden hearted rose, only the silence.

He came back to her and said she should go to Paris, and her whole soul rose up in passionate denial. "I cannot. Jackie is in Paris and I shall not be allowed to see him as soon as this."

"Certainly not. It would distress the child."

"But how can I live in Paris and not try to see him? I could not bear it."

"All we are asked to bear we can bear. That is a law of the spiritual life. The only hindrance to the working of this law, as of all benign laws, is fear."

"I would never get there. I should die on the journey."

"If you fear you will die on the journey that you will surely do. The choice is yours." He looked at her with very bright eyes and the room was full of laughter. "On a sea journey do you propose to die? A *sea* journey? What a waste."

She laughed and the sound of her laughter was strange to her; she had not heard it for so long. Then she asked, "But why must I go to Paris?"

"To make amends."

"To whom?"

"To someone whom you have wounded. Do you wish to die leaving a wound you could have healed still bleeding?"

"I did not know I had wounded anyone," murmured Lucy. "I did not know I could be so cruel."

"All hell is in each one of us," Jacob told her gently.

"Who is this person?" Lucy asked. "I cannot remember anyone in Paris to whom I have been cruel."

"I do not know who it is. It was not told me."

"Then I am going to Paris on a wild goose chase."

"People of the world frequently describe the ventures of faith in such terms," the old man agreed.

He got up to go and it seemed to Lucy that his going would be the worst thing that could happen. "Stay a little longer," she implored him. But he smilingly shook his head. "I shall see you again?" she asked. He did not answer and she could not interpret the benediction of light that was upon his face. Then he was gone and she missed him so much that the next day she and Mary went round the corner to the fig tree courtyard to take him some of Anne's little cakes in a basket. He was not there. The landlady said he had left The Hague for Antwerp early that morning.

Eighteen

Lucy could give Anne no reasons for wanting to return to a city she had always hated, but Anne was sure it was to be near Jackie. She would not be allowed to see him and the nearness would only increase her grief. Poor Anne could see nothing but misery at the end of this journey but she could only do as she was told and pack the luggage. And once they were out at sea her spirits rose. Like Lucy she loved travel and unlike Lucy she also loved Paris.

They arrived there in serene autumn weather and went straight to the house of some English exiles whom Lucy had known when she was at the Louvre, and were given two rooms on the top floor of their small crooked house. Mrs. Moore, aware of Lucy's reputation, had been at first uncertain if she wanted them, for she was a respectable woman, but she and her husband were poor as well as respectable, and badly in debt, and Mrs. Barlow was able to pay well for her rooms.

And so once more Lucy hung her mirror and her father's miniature on the wall, and put the sea shell that Justus had given her on the table beside her bed, and set to work to make a home. How many homes had she made by this time, she wondered? She seemed to have lost count but she took infinite trouble over this one because she believed it was the last and she wanted Mary to remember it as a pretty home as well as a happy one. It was not difficult because the house was in a quiet street and lime trees grew beside the cobbled way. The windows looked out into the branches and they were bird-haunted and the leaves golden.

There was a small church upon the other side of the street, old and dark, with a deep-toned bell. One went down three steps into it and it was like going down into a cave. An old priest said his mass there and a few people came at the summons of the bell, old and poor persons who wavered with weak footsteps, for this was not a fashionable part of Paris and the ancient church was not attractive to the younger folk.

Lucy never went to mass for she knew Dr. Cosin would not approve, but whenever she felt strong enough she and Mary crossed the street and sat together at the back of the church. At first it seemed pitch-dark inside and then the few votive candles, lit by the poor, began to shine out and illumine the reds and blues and golds of the statues of the saints. They were crude statues but the darkness hid their crudeness while the candles illumined their gold. Mary was fascinated by this little church and Lucy loved it too. It was a holy place and held a silence so deep that when she shut her eyes she thought she was in one of the churches of Cantre'r Gwaelod, the lost land that had sunk below the sea off the coast of Pembrokeshire. Something remotely resembling happiness came to her in that church, and in the rooms that looked out into the gold leaves of the lime trees, a shadow of the happiness she had known in the house at Antwerp.

The owner of that house was always in her thoughts and seemed to be the mediator of happiness, as he had been the mediator of that upsurge of life in her body that had enabled her to come here. Yet she came no nearer to meeting the person, man or woman, whom she had unknowingly wounded and whose hurt she had come to heal. She never crossed the street without looking about her, half expecting to see this person, but she could speak to no one of the purpose of her visit. Both Mrs. Moore and Anne would think her mind had been affected by her illness. Well, perhaps it had. Perhaps the old man's mind had been affected by his great age. Perhaps he and she were both a little mad. If they were not she would meet the one she had hurt, if they were it was no matter. She had found a peaceful haven and she could hardly believe it was Paris that had given it to her, and she was not far from Jackie.

Anne could not understand that she did not seem to be asking to visit Jackie, did not even seem to be fretting for him. She did not see Lucy crying at night because she longed for him so much, what she saw was the outer serenity of Lucy's consummated acceptance of the fact that she would not see her son again. Physically he was so close that when a windless blue sky arched over Paris she could be sure it arched over Versailles too, and when the gold leaves of the lime trees floated past her window on a west wind she pictured other leaves floating down to small boys playing in a garden, and they caught them in their hands and laughed. Once Mary did the same thing. She put her hand out of the open window and caught a floating leaf. It was, she told her mother, a golden bird, and they laughed together.

Lucy was very intent these days on making Mary laugh. Because the little girl was always so good and sensible, and not very pretty, she had been put in the shade by the beautiful tempestuous Jackie, and because she was also selfless she had not minded. Lucy woke up to the fact that her daughter had the serious demeanour of the mother of a family, and a power of accepting responsibility which no six-year-old should have been allowed to develop. She was horrified and the last of her strength was given to loving Mary, devising ways to make her laugh and making new clothes for her dollies. Her mind turned in upon Mary and she almost forgot the purpose for which she had come to Paris.

The time came when she no longer went out. The stairs had defeated her and presently her only movement was from her bed to the sofa by the window. Anne sent for an apothecary who said she was in a decline and there was nothing he could do. A decline was a diagnosis that covered a multitude of diseases then unknown. That Lucy had fought off the inevitable end of pernicious anaemia for so long was either a miracle, or a fulfilling of equally unknown laws concerning the dominance of certain types of mind over certain types of bodies.

One day when Mary was downstairs with Mrs. Moore Lucy told Anne that she was dying, a fact which Anne had realized long ago. In their different ways they were both matter-of-fact women and they set to work instantly to plan for Mary. "I do not want her to go to my Aunt Margaret," said Lucy. "She would not be sufficiently loved and my aunt would not speak well of me to her. It does not matter, but I would like Mary to remember me with love."

"It matters very much," said Anne, "and I have thought of this. I shall never leave Mary while I live but I cannot give her a home and so I shall take both of us to England and we shall live with your Aunt Anne. Mrs. Byshfield loves Mary and she likes me and she will be glad to have us, and Mr. Justus Walter will be near at hand. And when the King goes back to his own Lord Taaffe will go with him and then Mary will live with her father. I shall go with her, of course, as her maid, and when Mary marries I will be her housekeeper."

Lucy laughed and cried together. "You have it all arranged, Anne."

"It is always as well to be prepared for things in advance," said Anne. What she did not say was that weeks ago she had written to Mrs. Byshfield, telling her that Lucy was ill, and had given her this address. Mrs. Byshfield, she had thought, should also be prepared in advance. Like Lucy she was torn between tears and laughter. There was grief because Lucy was leaving her, but joy that there was so much to do; for Lucy herself now and for her child later. She gave no sign of either. She was calmly and quietly competent.

"There is nothing you want?" she asked Lucy. "No one you want to see?" Lucy smiled and shook her head. "Jackie I must not see. Justus I cannot see. I need only you and Mary."

But when Anne had left her she cried because she would not see Dr. Cosin again. Ever since she had come to Paris it had been an unceasing ache to think he was here, so near her, and she could not see him. She knew him well enough to know that he would come at once if she sent for him to help her in her dying; all the more readily because the sinner that she now would believe her to be would be in dire need of help. And that was where the difficulty lay. He would ask her of her sins and he would not be content to leave one stone unturned, and she could tell him nothing without betraying Anne. She knew that anything she told him would never be revealed, but he himself would know and it seemed a part of her love for Anne, and of her suffering accepted for Anne's sake, a part also of her loathing of treachery, that she should never tell anyone what Anne had done to her. So she must die without seeing Dr. Cosin again, and he would, till his own death, think her a depraved woman. It was a hard thing for her to have to accept, even though she knew it did not matter. And she was of course a great sinner. Who was not? One knew it as one came near to death.

2

Mrs. Moore, though gossip was the dearest love of her heart after God and her husband, had at first told no one that the sick lodger in her house was Mrs. Barlow. Her fellow exiles of the devout sort would have been horrified that she had taken such a woman under her roof; they did not know how serious her debts were nor how generous the sum that Lucy paid for her rooms. But when she found that Lucy was dying the situation was changed. For one thing she was a good woman and her heart softened towards a young mother who must leave her child, and also she could now present herself to her friends as a woman of compassion, which indeed she was. Before and after the Sunday services at the Louvre female heads came together, gossip hummed and Mrs. Moore found herself on a pedestal. It had been a wonderful Christian act to open her home to the King's discarded mistress and endeavour to bring her to repentance in her last hour. Someone, she never knew who, told Dr. Cosin what a wonderful woman she was.

Mrs. Moore had always been nervous of Dr. Cosin. It was one of the trials of life in exile that homely people, accustomed in their own country to their own humble parish priest and a congregation of their own sort, could find themselves sharing a chapel with dukes and princes, and ministered to by some eminent divine whose great mind had some difficulty in getting to grips with their simple problems.

That the situation could be equally difficult for the eminent divine was not known to Mrs. Moore when some days later she found herself, after the Sunday service, penned in a corner of the chapel of the Louvre by the black towering figure of Dr.

Cosin. He had grown more alarming with the years, more emaciated, sterner, sadder. He lacked the gentle humility and sweetness of a man like Bishop Ken. He was not that kind of saint. Perhaps, with his temper and the remnants of a stubborn pride still hanging in tatters about him, he was not a saint at all. It is possible to be a hero without being a saint. And it is possible, thought poor Mrs. Moore, for a tall thin holy man to look exactly like a vulture of the desert, Elijah or John the Baptist, dessicated and terrible. Dr. Cosin was doing his best to speak with gentleness but he was extremely angry and boomed above Mrs. Moore's head like doom.

"Madam, I commend your compassion in sheltering this young woman and her child in their hour of need. It was a Christian act and worthy of you. But why was I not informed? Am I not by appointment of God and the King the shepherd in charge of our congregation in Paris? To what am I to attribute your failure in this respect?"

Mrs. Moore was too confused to know. "A woman of her sort, Dr. Cosin," she murmured. "I scarcely thought you would wish to associate with her now."

She could have said nothing worse and she knew it in the awful silence that followed. Dr. Cosin strove to control his temper and she waited with shaking limbs for the earthquake and the fire. But the voice that came at last was quiet. "The fault is mine. I have not visited you lately. I have been ill and my pastoral duty has been sadly neglected. Had I visited you I should have found Mrs. Barlow in your kind care. Later today I will hope to wait upon you both. I think it might be wise if you did not tell her of my intended visit."

He bowed, the dark looming presence was withdrawn, daylight flowed in and Mrs. Moore could breathe again. He came, as he had promised, in the pale lemon sunshine of a November afternoon. He sat for a few moments with Mrs. Moore and her husband and then went upstairs to see Lucy. She was always in bed now and Anne had moved her bed to the window so that she could see the last of the leaves leaving the lime trees, and the reappearing tracery of bare branches against the sky. Birds came and went in the branches and were a delight, and so was

Mary, sitting beside her mother and sewing her sampler; a far more professional affair than her mother's had been at more than her age.

At sight of Dr. Cosin Lucy's face flooded with joy but not surprise. She had been thinking of him so constantly that it was hardly surprising to see him standing beside her bed. At first she thought he was a vision of her own creation, for this was happening to her now. She would think of her father and see him standing at the foot of her bed smiling at her, and hear the rustle of Nan-Nan's skirts across the floor. But when Dr. Cosin sat down beside her and took her hand she felt the rough ageing skin against the smoothness of her own, and when she put out her other hand and felt the fold of his cassock it was harsh between her fingers. She smiled at him and said briefly, turning her head towards her daughter, "This is Mary." The little girl made her curtsey, looked fearlessly at the old man on the other side of her mother's bed and smiled. He smiled back. She curtseyed again and left the room.

Lucy laughed softly. "She approves of you," she said. "She will not now leave me alone with anyone of whom she does not approve."

But Dr. Cosin could not as yet focus his mind upon Mary. "Why did you not send for me?" he asked.

"I did not answer your letters. I cut myself off from you. I did not know what your thoughts of me might be."

"It is never understood," said Dr. Cosin sadly. "The love of a priest for the souls delivered to his care is never understood. As a child you must often have watched the shepherd at his work. Did you never realize the greatness of his love?"

Lucy was silent, remembering John Shepherd at Roch. Dr. Cosin was right. There were so many ways of loving and one could not know them all. "I am sorry," she said. "I ask you to forgive me."

"The forgiveness is granted. And now that we are together again you will let me help you. You wondered what was I thinking? That there had been gross exaggeration. Human beings delight to exaggerate the moral failings of others, since to do so increases their own sense of righteousness. I also

721

reminded myself that if you had in any way fallen to temptation do I not myself know its fearful power? For the rest, I could only pray for you, asking God that if it should be his will you would return to me."

Lucy could only cry and Dr. Cosin reproached himself. "I am distressing you. We will say no more now about the great matters that will presently concern us. But I must tell you, Lucy, how much I admired you for yielding Jackie to his father. He is well and happy at his school."

Lucy's tears ceased as she demanded to be told about Jackie. There was not much he could say for Jackie's stay in Paris had been brief and Dr. Cosin had himself been ill and not allowed to see the boy. But he enquired about him often and all the reports were reassuring. Then there was a silence and he sighed heavily.

"There is one thing, Lucy, which I must tell you that will grieve you. Perhaps it will help you if I say that I have myself suffered the same sorrow that I must now ask you to accept." Lucy looked at him anxiously. Jackie was well and happy. What could it be? Dr. Cosin sighed again and continued. "I may have spoken to you of my beloved eldest son. Some while back, in England and away from my care, he secretly became a Catholic. He is now of course in great danger. I admire his courage but my grief is great."

Lucy held his hand tighter to express her sympathy, and presently she said placidly, "So Jackie is a Catholic now."

"That woman!" exploded Dr. Cosin suddenly. The veins stood out upon his forehead but with a mighty effort he controlled himself. "While I was laid upon my bed, extremely ill, the Queen Dowager without a word to me, and without even applying for permission to his father or to you, captured the child."

Lucy tried to comfort him. "Do not be so distressed, sir. What could you do? And there is a happy side to what has happened. The Queen and Minette will love him all the more because of this. He is theirs now and they will love him." But Dr. Cosin did not seem comforted and she tried again. "When Charles is restored to his throne, and I know that he will be and sends for Jackie to be with him, as I know that he will, then all Jackie has to do is change over again."

Dr. Cosin had a certain grim sense of humour and it came to his rescue. For the first time in many months he laughed. "How do you know these things?" he asked Lucy.

"I do not sleep well and so at night I pray for my husband and children and I find that I know these happy things. I expect God is so good to me because he knows I am dying."

So she knew. "About that, my child, we will talk tomorrow," he said. "Now I am going to leave you for you are tired."

He got up. Now, she thought, she must say it, for tomorrow would come the turning over of the stones of her life. "Dr. Cosin, there is not anything about my past life that I shall be able to tell you. It is secret and belongs to myself alone."

Shocked, he looked at her and saw in her eyes that old obstinacy that he knew only too well. But he also saw her tiredness and all he said was, "I will come back when you are more rested." Then he gave her his blessing and left the room.

At the top of the stairs he nearly fell over Mary sitting there sewing her sampler and waiting to go back to her mother. She got up politely to let him pass. He looked at the child. The face upturned to him was hardly that of a child at all. He had never seen such wisdom in young eyes. But wisdom could lead to happiness. He gave her his blessing too and passed on. The stairs had a twist to them and round the bend he nearly fell over Anne, sitting at the bottom of the flight to intercept him.

She got up. "Sir, I must speak to you, but this house is so small that Mrs. Barlow will hear our voices in the parlour below her and Mrs. Moore will listen at the door. It is only a few steps to the church across the road. It is quiet there. Come with me, please. At once."

It was not a request but a command and she was putting her cloak round her shoulders as she spoke. Her urgency was a wave that lifted and carried them out into the chill autumn evening and across the road. As he went down the steps into the small church, so dark, stony and strong, Dr. Cosin's first impression was of some ancient fortress upon a frontier, a defence against the enemy. Then he became aware of points of light here and there in the darkness, and gleams of colour that came and went in the flicker of candleflames in the draught. Then Anne shut the door and the small flames steadied. Peace filled the place and he knelt to pray.

Anne waited beside him, her hands clenched and her fingernails biting into the palms of her hands. When she had first seen Dr. Cosin, on the day when Lucy took her to the chapel at the Louvre, he had seemed a grim figure, reminding her of her father. She had hated him and been afraid of him and that it should be him of all men to whom she must uncover the horror of herself was hardly to be borne. The sweat ran down her back and her tongue was sticking to the roof of her mouth. If only the man would stop praying and let her get it over. Did he suppose she had brought him here simply to say his tedious prayers?

He supposed nothing of the sort and in a few moments turned to her and asked, "What is your trouble, my daughter?" He could hardly have made a worse beginning, presenting himself to her as a father figure at the very start. She trembled and was speechless. "Is it something to do with Mrs. Barlow?" he encouraged.

She nodded and gasped, "Yes." And then the fear eased and speech came, but in a spirit of bitterness. "I know what you have come to do, sir. You want to torment my mistress about her sins, turning them over and worrying over them and trying to make her repent of things she never did. She never did anything wrong except my Lord Taaffe and that was only nature. It was I who did it all. It is I who am foul as a stinking kennel, and she will not be able to tell you one thing about herself because she cannot without telling you what I did. And that she will never do. I know her. She will never tell you one word of what I did to her. Why must you come here tormenting her? Why can you not let her die in peace?"

"I hope and believe that she will do so," said Dr. Cosin. "When you have told me what I am waiting to hear she will be free to speak to me openly of all that is in her heart, and then she will have peace. Forget my presence. In the silence of this place is divine mercy. You have only to speak quietly to the silence. Words will be given you."

Something dreaded, perhaps a comparatively small thing, can block the whole future like a black mountain set upon the path. It cannot be surmounted, yet it seems there is nowhere to go now except on. Then the first impossible steps are irretrievably taken, the first words spoken past recall, and the thing grinds on its way almost by its own impetus. Then unbelievably it is over. The agony, whatever it was, is over. The dark hill is behind, the sunlit landscape is in front. But at first it is seen only through a mist of exhaustion. Anne heard nothing of the words of forgiveness and counsel spoken to her. But what they represented was in her possession. She had tasted the divine mercy in the cell at the Tower. Now she drank of it as though it were a stream flowing out of the black mountain she had just surmounted.

They went out into the street and Dr. Cosin said to her, "You must tell Mrs. Barlow tonight that you have put into words what she herself could not tell me. Tell her I will be with her tomorrow." Anne heard this and nodded and they parted. There was nothing further to say. Dr. Cosin was overwhelmed by the thought of Lucy the scapegoat lost in a desert of loneliness. Anne was too happy and too tired to have any thoughts at all.

3

When Dr. Cosin came next day to Lucy he said, "When you did not answer my letters, when you withdrew yourself, it was as though I received a wound. I prayed that you might be returned to my care but the answer has been long in coming. Now my prayer has been answered and the wound is healed. For this I thank God."

Lucy smiled. She had slept all night like a child. There was nothing now that she had to hide from Dr. Cosin, nothing that she could not say to him. She had come to the end of the evasions, the half-lies, the uncertainties and confusions of human life. The way before her was short and straight and where she was going, Jacob had told her, there was a great simplicity.

Dr. Cosin turned over the stones gently and carefully. They had a little trouble over Tom. Her heart had softened towards him but she was not sure she had entirely forgiven him for his treachery to Charles. "You make it harder for the King to forgive," said Dr. Cosin. "You hold him back. We are so united to those we love that our every attitude affects them. Forgive for him as well as for yourself. If he returns to his throne his first difficult task will be to forgive his enemies. If he can do it he will be a good king. If he cannot may God help him and England. Help him now to forgive." So she forgave and was so serene that Dr. Cosin was astonished. Were they to get through this without the bitterness of death? Did she not realize that she was leaving her children? In her happiness at being with him had she in fact faced what death really is?

"Your jewels, my love?" Anne said to her next morning. "Who do you want to have them? And your clothes?"

Lucy lifted her hand and looked at the ruby ring which was still on her finger. The blue gown that Charles had given her was hanging on the door. She had worn it so often that it seemed moulded to her figure. But in a few weeks from now her body that had worn jewels and clothes, told stories to her children and played with them in the sunshine, putting arms round them and kissing them, would not exist any more. The instrument of her loving would be lost, for there were no physical bodies where she was going.

The pages of her Book of Hours, her dreams of heaven, had been shown her in terms of earthly imaginings and she was going to a mode of existence that could be neither imagined nor known in such terms. All she knew now, at this moment, was that she would never again hold her children in her arms. Her body that was the ground of her motherhood was ceasing to be and the realization brought terror. Fear, she knew, must be met by action. Anne had not known she could still sit up, she had not known it herself, but she did so now, trying to assert her old dominion over her body that she might be a mother a little longer.

Bring paper and pen and write down what I tell you," she said. She found she could think quite clearly. Jackie must have the ruby ring and the diamond brooch, her writing desk, the sea shell and the book in which she had written down the prayers he and she had prayed together. Dr. Cosin would take charge of them. Her pearls, the Queen of Bohemia's jewels and the signet ring Lord Taaffe had given her were for Mary. Her father's miniature for Justus, her mirror and her clothes for Anne. That was all. She had nothing else.

When Anne had written down her instructions she lay flat on her back and closed her eyes. Anne thought she was asleep but she was not. She was simply hiding her fear. Anne and Mary must not see it lest when their turn came to die they should remember and be afraid too. The fear did not pass and she remained as she was until Dr. Cosin came to see her. Then she opened her eyes and looked at him and he saw in them the bitterness of death. He had had an intuition that it would be today and he had come prepared.

He bent over her saying clearly, "Motherhood is never lost. Remember that death is also a mother. For a little while you must be a child again, go back to the womb and be born to a new life, a new mode of loving and a new spring. Now I am going to give you the sacrament that God himself may make you fearless for your journey." The fear went out of her eyes. He gave her the sacrament and sat by her till she fell asleep.

After that her mind began to wander and she thought she was at Roch. Aunt Anne Byshfield arrived and the unexpected comfort and relief that this gave to Anne, and the bewildered little Mary, must have reached Lucy for though she hardly recognized Aunt Anne she seemed to share the comfort.

Only Dr. Cosin was with her when she died. A little while before she had murmured a few words and he could tell that he was back in her childhood, passing back through it to reach the new birth. Then she was silent for a time and then seemed to come back again for she held up her left hand and said, "My wedding ring!"

She had already given him the ruby ring to keep safely for

Jackie and her hand was bare. "You have already given it to me, my dear," he reassured her.

"A little bird," she murmured with delight. "Holding to my wedding finger. Now I am united to all wild things, I am married to the beauty of the world."

She smiled and her hand dropped. Then she drifted away and a short time later she quietly died.

She was buried in the Protestant cemetery at Paris, followed to her grave by a small group of mourners. She was twenty-eight years old. It was a sad grey day, a wet mist dripping from the trees, and Dr. Cosin saying the last prayers beside the grave was plunged in that desolation that seizes the old when they must face the death of the young. A life that might have been long and happy ending after twenty-eight years in the mud of a foreign cemetery. He had stood by many such graves as this during the last grievous years; young men and women overwhelmed by war and grief, by loss of hope, by their own moral degradation under the pressure of exile and hardship. Perhaps Lucy, if she was remembered at all, would go down to history as one of the latter. He himself knew better.

There was a sudden burst of song. A robin, apparently unaware that autumn had already passed into the dank misery of early December, was singing his autumn song in the wet dripping bush at the head of Lucy's grave. He sang his song, spread his wings and flew away. Dr. Cosin found that his mood had changed. "I am married to the beauty of the world."

Nineteen

I

There are days in the lives of nations, as in the lives of individuals, that do not seem to belong to this world. They pass like a pageant of sunlight clouds across the sky, lifted above the sorrows of the mundane world beneath. For a short while the brightness of the passing falls upon the things below, ugliness is blotted out and possessed by joy men do not merely exist but live. Centuries after they have passed into history they are still alive in a nation's memory. John Evelyn wrote on one such day, "I beheld it and blessed God." It was the day when the King came home to London.

Oliver Cromwell had died, and through the dark confusion of the days that followed his death the desire of the people had begun to push up like green shoots through the earth. Across the water the exiles had waited, shivering and hungry through the coldest and most poverty stricken winter of all. Then the miracle happened and spring burst through. The majority of Englishmen and women were weary of the iron power that had held them captive for so long. They had never forgotten the young Prince of Wales who had been so much loved years ago. He was a man now and their King. They asked him to come home.

All the way from Dover to London, through Canterbury and Rochester, along the lanes that wound between flower-decked hedges, under the arching green trees and through the villages where the bells pealed in the church towers, the progress was one of mounting joy and triumph. May the twenty-ninth, the King's thirtieth birthday, was the day when London unveiled her face and was a widow woman no longer. It was a fine day and from dawn the people were astir. The walls were hung with tapestries, flags flew from every tower and spire and the streets were strewn with spring flowers.

729

Everyone was dressed in their gay best and the girls wore white. The bells started ringing early and all through the morning the tension mounted. The procession of the King and the princes, leaving Blackheath in the early afternoon, would pass over London Bridge to the city.

Midday drew near, every window was crowded with faces and the streets were lined with excited people, good-natured foot soldiers ready with their pikes to hold them back should their enthusiasm pass all bounds. The army would be much in evidence in today's procession for it had been General Monk, marching from Scotland through the snow of the previous winter, who had been largely responsible for translating the longing of the people into action; and with no blood spilt. That was one of the joys of this great occasion. The revolution that had brought back the King had been a bloodless one.

All the clocks of London struck twelve. Officers came and went with shining swords, notables passed by and were cheered, dogs crossed the streets and were also cheered. Cats likewise. The fountains began to run with wine and then at last, far off, came the roar of cheering. They were coming. Bells were pealing and trumpets sounding and the roar grew until it drowned even the bells in its deep thunder. Golden coaches appeared as though from a fairy tale. Cavalry in silver doublets trotted by followed by infantry tramping joyously and waving their swords. Sheriffs, heralds, trumpeters all streamed by in gorgeous garments and were greeted with cheers. Then a pause and more flowers began to fall from the windows.

Then, riding alone, a curious little lonely space before them and behind them, came three fine young men riding three magnificent horses. People were crying and laughing together, the cheers choked in their throats when they actually saw his face, so that just where he was he seemed to carry an aura of quietness with him, a small circle of peace at the centre of the thunder of rejoicing. He rode a little ahead of his brothers plainly dressed in a dark suit, the only points of colour the blue ribbon of the Garter and the scarlet feather in the hat he carried. He rode slowly, looking up to the windows, raising th great plumed hat in greeting, looking straight into the eyes of his people when he could and smiling at them with a grave tenderness. The hard bitter lines that had so aged his face through the worst years of the exile were scarcely visible today and he looked what he was, a young man in the prime of life, tall, straight and strong, possessed of great dignity and elegance and extraordinary charm. And something more, a hint of power. They had not got a weak king, they realized with relief, and the power was not the bigoted sort that had recently enslaved them. There was tolerance in the strong face.

The King rode on through the cheering crowds and came at last to his Palace of Whitehall, and what his thoughts were as he rode past the spot where his father had died, and was brought into the banqueting hall where the last hours of the late King's life had been passed, no one knew. They only knew he was not able to finish the speech he had prepared or to fulfil quite to the end the programme planned for his first evening He said he was weary.

2

Some while later, tired but no longer exhausted, the King found himself alone at evening in the great bedchamber whose windows looked out on the Thames and its shipping The discreet and invaluable Chiffinch, his servant, had just helped him to dress for a supper party he was giving, a small and intimate affair of great importance to him. Chiffinch had suggested, with great respect, that the royal watch was fast, but had been so snapped at, hurried and chivied, that the King was arrayed for conquest thirty minutes too soon. The clocks of Westminster said so, striking the hour, and could not be gainsaid. He had laughed, apologized to Chiffinch and told him to fetch him when she came. She was twenty years old and incomparably beautiful. He had met her first in Holland and now they were reunited in England. She was Buckingham's cousin. He had never been so greatly in love. Except perhaps that first time.

The bedchamber was vast and a little lonely and he went up

a flight of steps to the King's closet, which he planned to make his private sanctum of which only himself and Chiffinch should possess a key. He intended to hang a few exquisite pictures on the walls and to keep here the collection of clocks and watches he was planning. Timepieces fascinated him. They were like living creatures, busy as bees and as full of talk and song as birds in spring.

He shut the door behind him, went to the window, opened it and leaned out. It had been a hot day but the wind had changed and a cool air was coming off the water. The sun had just disappeared behind a bank of cloud to the west but overhead the sky was still deep and clear and a few white gulls circled there. Looking to right and left he could see the amazing jumble of buildings that was Whitehall and here and there light shone from a tall window and was reflected, broken and trembling, in the water. Just below his own window floated one perfect white swan. There was peace in his mind and he thought of his sisters, Mary and Minette, and of his mother and Jackie. Especially he thought of Jackie and longed for him. Presently they would come over, his mother and sisters to visit him, Jackie to be always with him, and there would once more be dancing and music at Whitehall and the citizens of London would row up the river at evening to listen to the music of the King's fiddlers floating over the water.

But first must come hard work and difficult adjustment. He had to learn to be a king. He knew very well that behind the façade of the rapturous welcome he had many enemies. He must win them over. He must get to know his people and they must get to know him. What sort of king did he want to be? He thought he had expressed it in one of the speeches he had been endlessly making. "My whole wish is to make you as happy as I am myself." He had meant that. After all the years of exile he wanted to be happy. He wanted to be the cheerful King of a happy people. He did not want for England an unsmiling greatness. A people and their King could, he believed, be both great and gay. His old idealism had not been quite destroyed by the exile, it had surged up again in this new spring and he had made his plans. There was to be an Act of Indemnity and Oblivion and the words of it were already forming in his mind. He wanted forgiveness, not vengeance. He knew he would be forced to bring some of the regicides to justice but it should be as few as possible. He wanted the foundation stone of his reign to be forgiveness.

He stopped thinking and his mind became as still as his body that was leaning against the side of the window, utterly relaxed for the first time in years. London, stretched out along the river, seemed as dreamily quiet as he was himself. Perhaps after their rapturous reunion she was now as glad to rest as he was. The breeze was blessedly cool against his face and he was aware that it was freshening. It was his fancy that it brought him a breath of the sea. Along the western shores of his kingdom the waves were now beginning to sound out their presence, surging over the rocks and into the caves. A gust of wind blew over the river and again came the fancied breath of the sea. There was a sudden sweep of white wings, a rush of air passed his face, an impression of beauty and power as a gull swept past the window.

"O Dduw, y mae yr hapusrwydd yma yn ormod yw ddal."

He straightened up and for a moment his whole body trembled, though not with fear; more as though a lute, tuned to the same pitch as another, vibrated to its song. Where had the voice come from? From the wind and the sea or from within himself? A trick of his own memory, something triggered off because she had loved gulls so much? Yet he was held in a moment of serene, profound happiness. It held him, and still held, and might have held for ever had not some sudden harsh sound in the Palace broken the spell. He moved from the window and a past memory came with disturbance to his mind, dragging him back into the web of human machinations. What if that letter had told the truth? Sorting through a mass of papers before he came to England he had found a letter written to him by Anne Hill, a letter which a secretary had not given him yet through some extraordinary negligence had not destroyed. The letter had been confused, badly written and badly expressed. He had read it through quickly, thought the girl mad, destroyed and forgotten it. Now he remembered it perfectly.

For a few moments he fought against belief, since it is the nature of man to fight against truth, and because he was deeply in love with another woman. But the little closet was filled with the freshness of the sea and the echo of that happiness sounded on, and presently he believed. The acceptance of belief made Jackie doubly precious and suddenly everything else was lost in longing for his son. But Jackie would come. One day they would lean out of this window together and look at London lying along the Thames.

He became aware of a discreet coughing and an anxious shuffling movement below. It was Chiffinch. How long had he been down there in the bedchamber and what was it that he was supposed to do now? He remembered, went to the window of the closet and closed it. Something of her would always be here among his ticking clocks and watches but life had to go on and he was greatly in love.

He went down the steps to the bedchamber. Chiffinch bowed. "Sir, Your Majesty's guests await you and supper is served."

NOTE

A reader who can persevere to the end of this book may like to know what became of some of the characters. The tragedy of Jackie is well-known. It is interesting that the pocket-book found on him when he was captured after Sedgemoor, and which is now in the British Museum, contains prayers written in the manner of Jeremy Taylor, and one wonders if his mother wrote them? His imprisonment in the Tower as a boy must have made a great impression on him because when twenty-nine years later he was there again, under sentence of death, he begged that his execution might be postponed for twenty-four hours, that he might be still alive on Thursday July the sixteenth, the date when he and his mother were set free. Perhaps he hoped that deliverance might come again on that day. His request was not granted and he died on Wednesday July the fifteenth.

Mary was re-united with her father, who after the Restoration became the Earl of Carlingford, and lived with him in Ireland for six years. She then married William Sarsfield of Mayo, who brought her to England, but four years later he died of smallpox. Her second husband was William Fanshawe of St. Martin's-in-the-Fields, Master of the Requests to Charles the Second, and her home became the part of London that Lucy had known so well. She was the mother of children and she appears to have had the gift of healing, for she touched for the king's evil. The Covent Garden apple women, knowing her to be the sister of the Duke of Monmouth, called her Princess Fanshawe. Mary died before her husband and was buried in Barking church, and when William Fanshawe also died he was buried beside "his dearly beloved wife".

Lord George Scott, in his researches, could find no reference to Justus after 1656, but Richard married and had children. We can hope that the Dewi of this book had his wish and became the royal servant of whom Pepys wrote, "being a Welchman will talk very broad of the King's being married to his sister". A David Walter, groom of the bedchamber, is several times mentioned in the *Calendar of Domestic State Papers*.

Dr. Cosin was appointed Prince Bishop of Durham by a grateful King. In his direst poverty he had refused to sell his books and in the Restoration was also restored to his library. He was a well-loved but well-feared Bishop. It has been written of him, "He snuffed battle from afar, sought it out with zest, and laid about him with undisguised relish. He never sank to the vulgarity of abuse but enlivened each encounter with a ready trenchant wit." He continued to suffer much pain and at the end of his life was greatly distressed that he could not kneel. He would say, "Lord, I bow the knees of my heart."